CITADEL

- UNDERVERSE -

Book 5

2ND EDITION

JEZ CAJIAO

TABLE OF CONTENTS

Thanks, and an Explanation

So, I'm sure, if you've read the others in the series by now, you're aware that this is the second edition! That came about because, basically, I learned a lot and wanted to improve on the originals. Simple, right?

It seems it, but believe me, there's at least as much work put into it the second time around, as there is the first!

I do have to thank some people though, because without them this wouldn't have been anywhere near as polished,

First, my Beta and Proofreading team. These guys tear through the manuscript at an amazing speed, sending me errors, grammar, punctuation and the million random things that seem to slip by me no matter how many times I read them, so seriously, thank you guys.

Kristen, Spencer, Scott, Shawn, Neil, Chris, Richard, Ben and Denny, you're legends! Thank you all each and every one.

Secondly, *You.* Seriously, each and every one of you that have taken the time to read my words, my madness, and to have left a review, thank you. Those reviews might only take a few seconds for you, but they make a *massive* difference to me, they mean the difference between Amazon showing my books to others who might like them, or ignoring them, and that in turn allows me to write full time, and to feed my wife and children and keep a roof over their heads.

You are literally feeding my family, so thank you.

Third and by no means least, are my Dad's.

Paul took me on as a child, taught me to be the barely stable monstrosity I am, and how to pour my drinks right, how to stand for what I cared about, and how to shrug off the things that didn't matter. You raised me to be a man and showed me right from wrong, and a lot of who I am, is because of you. You raised another man's son, and never let that be an issue between us. Thank you, Dad, for loving me.

Alan took me into his family as an adult, he gave me his daughter's hand in marriage, and showed me kindness and patience. He dedicated his life to helping others, and raised two beautiful daughters, and was Pops to three, at least partially feral grandchildren. He died on the 3rd of May 2021 and the world is poorer place without him in it.

He took my Brother-in-Law George and I into the clan, always made us feel welcome, and despite us both being a little crazy and stealing away his little girls, we'll always be thankful to him for the love he showed us, and this book is dedicated to him.

UnderVerse Synopsis

Book One:

Jax is working a dead end job, in a semi-stable relationship, and searching for his missing brother, while plagued by dreams of the UnderVerse. This terrible alternate reality is where he, and his brother Tommy, are pulled against their will on occasion. When in the dream they inhabit artificial bodies and fight to protect abandoned villages and more, standing between the inhabitants of the Old Empire and the creatures of the night.

They awaken back on earth once the threat has passed, or they've been killed, with their injuries following them. While they heal at a tremendously accelerated rate, it still requires days to recover, and in that time, they hide their injuries, lest they be locked away for self-mutilation.

After one such session, Jax decides to come clean to his GF and explain everything. Badly injured and bleeding heavily, he arrives at her home, only to find her in bed with another man. He loses control, half beating the man to death, and having his skull shattered in turn by her, using the baseball bat he'd bought her for self-defense.

Jax comes to in the hospital, chained to the bed, and is interviewed by the police and warned he faces a significant jail term. While alone and contemplating this, an unknown doctor slips in and assures him it has all been taken care of, before drugging him.

When Jax wakes up this time, it's to find himself restrained, again, but on an airplane heading to meet 'the Baron Sanguis'. A lawyer assures him that should he carry out the reasonable requests of his new employer, then not only will all legal concerns be a thing of the past, but he will find his brother as well. Jax accepts, warned that refusal means death, and meets the Baron, an inhuman monster who admits to being an interplanar traveler, and a member of the original nobility of the UnderVerse, the Realm that Jax and his brother dream of.

To be free and to find his brother Jax must travel to that shattered Realm, and open a stable portal back to this Realm, as the mana here is simply too low in concentration for the portal to be held open for more than bare seconds. Alternatively, a portal from that side, to here, would be secure and enable the nobility to return with servants and forces intact, ready to reconquer their home.

Over the next several months, as Jax is trained for the 'little task', he discovers more about the past of that Realm, including that the voice of madness that occasionally speaks to him, and that he'd written off as himself being mad to some degree, is actually the voice of the Eternal Emperor Amon, a fragment of His soul being all that's left, clinging to the genetic line.

Amon was murdered, by the Baron, His son, and others of the nobility, with the aid of the God of Death, Nimon. In the process, and as his price for this, the followers of the other nine greater gods were purged and their temples cast down. Leaving the God of Death, who dragged one of the moons down to impact the Realm, with a powerful enough surge of His 'aspect' (death) that He managed to banish the other Greater Gods.

Jax grows to hate the Baron, but has nothing left in his life beyond his missing brother, and so takes the opportunity, training heavily, before facing eleven other nobles' choices in the arena to 'earn' the right to go to the UnderVerse. He wins, barely, and trades the remains of his opponents and their personal items to their sponsors, in exchange for several magical artifacts, before passing through the great portal.

Once on the other side, and having made a deal with an opposing noble 'house' for access, he finds himself in a ruined tower. The Great Towers were bastions of the old Empire, powerfully magical, self-sustaining and intended as entire self-contained cities. At half a mile wide at the base, two to three miles high, and sustained by their own mana collectors they acted as garrisons and secure imperial bastions in places of danger.

The Tower that Jax finds himself in, however, was never inhabited fully. It was finished, intended as a research and security station, but had only a skeleton crew when it was assaulted by a SporeMother. The SporeMother, a multi-limbed monstrosity of legend, flooded the defenders with undead and possessed creatures, birthing DarkSpore creatures, parasitical clouds that could puppet flesh, turning the unprepared defenders into attackers, claiming the Tower. The few remaining survivors, beleaguered on all sides, ordered the Tower's controller Wisps to shut the entire structure down, sealing the Wisps themselves away, and preventing the creature from being able to feed on the mana of the Tower to grow stronger, expecting that the Tower would be assaulted and retaken shortly by the Imperial Legion.

Then, before reinforcements could take the Tower back, the Cataclysm came. Seas and mountains rose, islands vanished and the creatures of the deep and of nightmare were set loose to roam. When Jax arrives at the Tower he finds it dark and silent, populated by the ancient dead, with only occasional more recently killed adventurers scattered here and there. He also encounters Sporelings, immature SporeMothers, hidden in the portal chamber, fighting them and locking himself away in a side room.

Jax uses one of the spells he gained, resurrecting one of the Sporelings he killed to form a companion to fight alongside him. Using his new companion, Bob, and his weapon of choice, a bastardized naginata, Jax proceeds to clear the Tower partially, discovering the 'Hall of Memories' and its sleeping Wisp, Oracle. He is gravely injured, and alone, Bob having perished in the fight to enter the room, and when he awakens the Wisp takes the chance it unthinkingly offers, to use some of the stored knowledge of the Hall of Memories, in the form of spellbooks, to enable him to defeat the undead outside the room.

Unfortunately, all magic he has accessed so far has been through books such as this, impressing outside knowledge across his brain and damaging it each time. This final spellbook is one too many, and results in scarring, internal bleeding and more. Jax is dying and Oracle, the newly awakened Wisp, bonds herself to him in an attempt to save him, gaining access to his manapool and enabling herself to cast the needed healing spells to save his life.

Over time Jax recovers, and with Oracle's guidance, reawakens and names Seneschal, the Wisp that controlled the tower, reactivating the mana collectors and beginning the basic repairs the Tower requires, as well as awakening the Goddess of Fire, Jenae. This awakens the SporeMother, now ancient and decrepit, but still powerful. In the fight that follows between Jax, Oracle, the newly reformed Bob and the SporeMother and her minions, the Eternal Emperor Amon makes contact with Jax, guiding him to use an artifact recovered in the Tower earlier. This Silverbright potion (Dragon's blood) transforms his weapon from a standard construction into a basic magical, but evolving, weapon. Jax kills the SporeMother, but is gravely wounded. Over the next day, as he is healed, the companions clear the remaining sections of the Tower, and find the creature's nest underground, along with the remains of the Golem Construction Cradles or Genesis Chambers.

They also find the Wisp responsible for the golems, name him Hephaestus, and take the time to reclaim the single working Genesis Chamber. This begins the construction of the most basic of stone golems to protect and rebuild the Tower. In the process, HeartStones are uncovered, a magical way to send a memory, as a method of communication. Most are long drained of mana, but the fragments that remain make it clear that Barabarattas, lord of one of the two nearby cities, has been trading slaves to the SporeMother in exchange for Sporelings, hoping to raise a captive army of SporeMothers.

The Wisps sense an intrusion higher in the tower and Jax explores, finding a group of slavers, heavily armed, using their slaves to loot an old armory. Jax attacks when seeing a child beaten, killing the slavers, with Oracle's help, and driving off the two airships that had been docked on the balcony. One is damaged and crashes in the courtyard below, while the other escapes to land at a nearby lake to effect repairs.

The freed slaves pledge allegiance to Jax, and while they rest, he takes one of their number, Oren, the captain of the crashed ship, down to the courtyard. He discovers that they were pressed into service, and had no desire to work with the slavers. The remaining surviving crew swear as well, and inform Jax that there is a third ship. This is the warship that was enforcing the City Lord's will, and it was still incoming, having stopped to raid a village along the way. Jax and the slaves use the weapons they have, the remains of the damaged ship and subterfuge to lure the warship in to land, while Oracle disables their engines.

Jax and Bob, aided by some of the former slaves, fight and kill the soldiers aboard the warship, capturing the crew, freeing a group of slaves taken from the villages and locking the crew in those same cages. Jax formally claims the Tower as his, and through the right of blood, having found that he is an illegitimate son of the Baron Sanguis, and therefore noble in his own right, he begins the right of Imperial Succession.

Barabarratas, like all nobles remaining in the Empire, with no Imperial House to swear to, had been unable to lay claim formally to the Imperial Throne, but once the succession has begun, sees a way to claim the throne. He threatens war against Jax, unless he surrenders. Jax, being short of patience and self-control, as well as occasionally being an asshole, in turn declares war on Barabarratas and his city of Himnel, taunting him before leading his people in a wake. The end of the book comes to Thomas, Jax's brother, languishing and injured in a jail, before being sold as fodder, the lowest caste of soldier, to the Dark Legion of Nimon.

BOOK TWO:

Thomas fights his abusive jailor and draws the eye of a Paladin of Nimon, who grants him a chance to prove himself. Thomas is happy to take that chance and prove his worth in battle to escape the rank of fodder.

Jax awakens with a hangover, the wake having gone well, and proceeds to set about trying to repair the Tower. Two of the new recruits, now citizens of the Great Tower, Oren the Dwarf airship captain, and Cai, a Panthera humanoid with a skill for organization, assist him. Teams are formed for hunting and defense, with a personal squad geared around Jax. This is formed from ex slaves who are determined to never be cowed again. Lydia leads them (mace and shield, heavy armor), with Jian (dual wielding swords), Arrin (mage), Cam (Axeman), Miren (archer), Stephanos (archer) and Bob. Jax and his new team go to try and capture or recruit the escaped second airship, but upon arrival at the lake, find the ship deserted.

They are attacked as they search by small four-armed amphibious creatures known as the 'Mer'. In the course of the fight, Jax realizes they are young, ranging from a young adult, to a child, and they were attacked by goblins prior to Jax's arrival, attacking him in pre-emptive self-defense. The young ones are joined by older, more experienced warriors, who agree to a truce at first, and then request help to deal with the nearby goblin horde.

Jax agrees, and three of the Mer join them, assaulting the goblin camp. In the course of the fight, Jax saves the life of one of the Mer, the oldest of the younglings, and upon clearing the ruin, and rescuing the surviving crew of the airship from them, claims the land as part of the Empire. In the process, the goblin cave is revealed as a buried outpost, complete with basic golems, which are claimed and returned to the Tower.

The Mer village remains neutral, but several of their people join Jax, including the youngling, Bane. The leader of the Mer that join the Tower is Flux, an accomplished adventurer, and he supports Bane's desire to be Jax's bodyguard. Several of the older Mer decide to join the Tower, many of whom are skilled, but crippled. Jax heals them, magic being increasingly rare in the UnderVerse since the fall of the Empire, and his abilities and the knowledge stored at the Tower are revealed as being incredibly valuable. The rescued crew join Jax, bringing their ship and joining the resurgent Empire.

The older banished Gods are awakened, and Jax has a disagreement with one, Tamat, the Lady of Assassins. Using a draconic legacy from Amon, Jax manages to beat Her in Her weakened state, before being forced back by Jenae, who begins the process of spreading the worship of the original Gods again. The Gods are weak, but They have abilities They can grant, and information from the past that is relevant. Nimon is unaware They are back.

Jenae, after an earlier disagreement with Jax, helps him to find that his brother was recently in the city of Himnel. Oren and the others implore Jax to free their families, to bring them to the Tower from Himnel. He agrees, pausing only long enough, to have his body inked with tattoos, guided by Jenae, Ame, a Mer runesmith, and a tattooist named Renna.

While attempting to find a hidden entrance to the city, used by smugglers, Oracle, who has fallen in love with Jax, and he with her, is captured and taken deep underground by the Drow, a race of Dark Elves that are scouting the city for an unknown reason. Jax catches some of them, and in a bout of frantic insanity, imbues his body with sufficient mana that he gains a new ability 'Mana-Overdrive' speeding his movements and strength up, but it is short lived, and results in a 'crash' afterward. Jax uses this ability to kill two of the Drow, and then, driven mad by Oracle's capture, pain and fear allows his darker side to come out as he tortures the Drow for information.

Bane calms him down, hides the body from the others, and guides Jax back to himself. Jax's group, now including Barret, a former soldier and a member of Oren's ship's crew, dives underground, hunting the Drow. Over the underground trip, they meet Ashrag, an ancient Cave Spider, who remembers the Empire, and despite her monstrous appearance, was once an Imperial Citizen. Jax resurrects ancient Oaths, claiming them as his own at Amon's direction, and passes out from the mana drain. This convinces Ashrag and, after fighting a group of her brood, she swears allegiance. She agrees, on the condition that Jax free the tunnels of the Drow who view her kind, and their bodies, as a great delicacy.

Jax eventually leads his team through the various dark places, and finds Oracle, captured by the Drow leader, a Drider. The half woman-half spider, has several smugglers held captive and fights the group. Jax is triumphant, but Cam dies at the hands of the Drow. Oracle is freed and the smugglers are mainly compliant, save their leader, who ends up making a comment that Jax disagrees with pointedly, and dies.

The last few Drow fight a retreat, until they are killed by a new threat coming the other way along the tunnel. The three newcomers slaughter the Drow, then, after a tense standoff, are revealed to be Imperial Legionnaires. The Imperial Legion has been dismissed and derided since the Cataclysm, slowly dwindling in numbers and through several bad apples in leadership, have become outsiders in their own homes. They are disliked and disrespected by the locals, even as they march out to fight the creatures that nobody else can.

The Legion is falling apart, its members lost and despairing, until Jax resurrects the Oaths, and finally a chance at a future is given back to them.

The three scouts, Yen, Tang and Amaat swear to Jax, and reveal that they are even now, below the City of Himnel.

BOOK THREE:

Jax leads the group to the surface, fighting off a group of local thugs who attempt to hunt the Legionnaires, and eventually reach the Arena and Arena Master Mal, one of the local leaders of the Smuggler's Guild. This is the man Oren had recommended as the best choice of an ally in the city. At the same time Jax is in the process of capturing a small group of Djinn, who offer allegiance in exchange for freeing their captured clan mother from the Skyking.

Mal agrees to help, for a fee, and introduces his team; Soween, his right hand, Jay his muscle and Josh his mage and Soween's husband. While Jax is resting, and about to finally get some 'private time' with Oracle, who can assume human form and size at will, Mal receives a message from the local crime lord, the Skyking. He demands Mal turn over the 'Legion' having discovered that it was Legionnaires that killed its people. Mal refuses, and instead, to gain the time they need, arranges a series of arena fights with the 'captured' Legionnaires, including Jax, and betting games.

While Mal makes these arrangements, Jax and his team visit a local healer, intending to get some of the deep seated injuries to his brain that are slowing his ability and level growth addressed. Along the way, Jax is surrounded by the enslaved, seeing the casual cruelty of the people, the way that nobles laugh and stroll, while slaves on the verge of starvation carry their bags. Amon sees this and their twinned rage escapes control, resulting in a temper-tantrum of epic proportions, leveling a section of the city and freeing the slaves, while also releasing Amon to face Jax inside his own mind.

Jax manages to defeat Amon, but in the process, discovers that he's had an unrecognized parasitic inhabitant all this time. He tears it free, gutting himself in the process, and only survives through the intervention of his team getting him to the healer, and the divine help of Jenae.

The Legion, having lost contact with their scouts, and seeing the devastation in the city, send a small, but elite team out to investigate, and with their help, Jax is returned to the Arena. The Legion settles in to protect him.

Jax is drained by the healing, and Centurion Primus Augustus, one of the four Primus of the Legion, fights in his place in the Arena that night, slaughtering all thrown against him.

Jax awakens and meets Mal and the others, works to integrate himself with the Legion and meets the non-human members of the shipyards who've been brushed aside by Barabarattas and his kind as 'sub-human'. They are recruited, and a plan formed. Rather than escaping with everyone through the hidden Smuggler's Path and robbing the city for the Tower's needs, a new more daring plan is concocted.

The airships are built in the shipyards, and Himnel's greatest weapon is under construction, the battleship. Currently it's a bare structure, open to the elements, but under the plan, additional volunteers are brought in, and the battleship is sealed up, and made, minimally, airworthy. The Legion are contacted and given orders, in three days they are to capture the shipyards.

Having little alternative, and no love for the city, as well as a legitimate authority encouraging it, the Legion agree.

Jax fights and recovers that night and trains, dragging Grizz, the Legionnaire into his group, as well as Yen and Tang. The next night, after the fight, he leads his team to raid and rob the Magical Emporium, a golem secured shop. The presence of the golem leads Jax and the others to discover a hidden section below the main shop, unknown by all. They realize that long ago it wasn't a shop, but a golem repair and construction facility. The golems are claimed, the construction facility below ground being ordered to begin repairs and construction, while golems there are used to repair ancient mining golems, which are sent to the Tower, burrowing underground. The rest of the golems are sent to wait in the river for the assault on the shipyards.

The following night the Arena fight is 'fixed', but Jax, with the help of his team, wins, and they launch the assault. Combining the assault on the Skyking with the one on the shipyards, Jax and the small Legion team, along with his own, take the Skyking's tower, killing them all. Halfway through the fight, when confronted with the rarely seen Anubai, a heavily magical species, Jax activates his trump card, his Tattoos. Rather than being decorative, they are in fact magical runes enabling him to channel mana through them, helping him to turn the tables on his foes.

In the fight, they capture the first of the airships circling on 'overwatch' over the city. To capture the others, Jian assumes control of one of the ships and accidentally, being unfamiliar with the controls, fires a giant fireball at the tent city of recruits around the Dark Citadel of Nimon. Jax, as the leader of the group, is blamed and declared Apostate, and a holy war begins.

The ships are brought under Jax's control, and return to the shipyards, to be crewed by his people. In the following confusion, Jax is hit in the head and injured. The ships flee Himnel, having stolen the vast majority of the city's manastone store, which are needed to power the engines of the ships.

Without stones, Barabarattas is unable to give chase, and the ships head out to sea, hoping to leave the impression that they're not from the Tower, and as Jax had ordered. Unfortunately, Nimon is aware of the truth.

The Dark Legion attacks the stragglers leaving the city, and their latest recruit, Thomas assists in killing some of Jax's Legionnaires. Jax awakens when they are far out to sea, close to the Sunken City, a flying city from the old Empire that crashed into a seamount. He confirms the orders to land there, to make the ships secure, and then to make for the Great Tower. He also finally gets some 'private time' with Oracle.

BOOK FOUR:

Jax meets the Legion leadership, Prefect Romanus, and Alistor, his right hand, as well as the crew of the battleship and many of the refugees. While in transit, Jenae informs Jax that knowledge he needs is lost in the Sunken City, and he vows to find it. Jax is still recovering, but by the time the ship lands, along with its much smaller escorts, at the Sunken City, he attempts to meet the two local parties from both Himnel, and its enemy city Narkolt.

Both are found to be led by 'nobles' but Himnel's is using slave labor, as well as being offensive, and suffers an 'accident' involving a sword. Narkolt's group are slightly more respectful and are given 24hrs to come back and discuss their intentions. The remaining guards from the Himnel group are given the same chance. As part of the discussion Jax uses an Imperial Ability, freeing the city of the souls of the unquiet dead that were condemned to roam it eternally, granting them their peace.

Once this is realized by the nobles, they ignore Jax's warning, and lead their people into the city's depths, searching for loot and artifacts. Jax orders the Legion into it as well, then leads his team in. In searching the depths, they are trapped by a landslide and explosions, set off by one of the nobles from Narkolt, and are forced into the depths.

Jian uses one of two books Jax gives him at this point and summons a demon to assist him, although it becomes clear the demon cares little for anything but gaining its own power. In the search, they are attacked by a group of feral Gnomes, explorers trapped long ago by the undead revenants and worse. These Gnomes were forced into a small pocket that, with typical gnomish ingenuity, they made into a livable space. They were then enslaved by a Skinwalker and its controlled Leviathans, forced to give their water and more to it, leaving them a water source heavily contaminated by metal, to drink and to raise crops from. The result is that the Gnomes essentially are driven feral, regressing and attacking each other. A small group is preserved as best as they can, while the greater population succumbs to madness.

These mad Gnomes attack Jax and, in the process, he and Oracle heal one of them, at least partially restoring his mind. Giint is broken by the things he's seen and done, and joins Jax, not knowing what else to do. The remaining feral Gnomes attack, and are driven back, as Jax and the team attack the Skinwalker and its pets. Jax wins the fight, but the Skinwalker, unbeknownst to them, is inside the creature they just killed, and escapes.

Back with the Dark Legion, Thomas, wounded from long ago injuries, is offered up to the Dark God, allowing His blood to mingle with Thomas' and regaining his magic, as well as sparking to life a dark seed, as he begins to fall in love with Belladonna, his squad leader.

Jax uses an Essence Core and gains the ability of flight and increased mana regeneration through meditation. Jenae reaches out, informing them that a hidden force is incoming, led by the Drow, with captive SporeMothers. Jax orders Oracle to go to the fleet resting overhead. They are to leave immediately and fly at full speed to the Tower to defend it. Jenae makes it clear that the Gnome's original ship, while hidden, is still usable, but the DarkSpore the SporeMothers could release would result in massive casualties if the fleet doesn't leave.

A small number of the Gnomes have been swayed by Giint and wish to join Jax, agreeing to lead him to the hidden ship. He leaves them to prepare, attacking the nearby camp of the undead, led by a necromancer from Earth, a previously sent through 'volunteer'. Bartholomew the Lich, or 'Barry' as Jax refers to him, appears and traps the team, only to have Lydia, in a burst of desperation, seize the hidden power of the Valkyrie, turning the tide of the battle and beginning her own ascension. Barry is killed in the fight, and Jax, when he recovers the rest of the loot from the vault, also awakens a slumbering Wisp. Jax, his team, and the Gnomes race to reach the ship, receiving injuries along the way, but reach it just as the enemy arrives overhead.

The ship is powered up, and the Wisp is permitted to bind itself to the Gnome's ship, gaining control. They use explosives from the Gnomes to free the ship of its hidden location, and then fight their way out of the Sunken City.

One of the enemy ships crashes in the fight, releasing the SporeMother and leaving it behind, while the others follow. In the fights that come, Jax and his team are badly injured, and Stephanos dies, killed by a Drow. Just as all seems lost, Mal appears, flying his own ship and driving the Drow back, having left the fleet to come and help.

Jax and the others start to recover, only to have Jenae reach out, informing them that Nimon has dispatched His Dark Legion, an advanced force, to make a portal close to the Great Tower, and plans to assault it. With that, Jax orders Tenandra, the name the gnomish ship's Wisp has chosen for herself, to get them to the fleet with all haste.

JIAN

PROLOGUE

"**G**od, I hate this damn forest!" Thomas grunted, staggering to the left as he slammed into, then bounced off, a broken section of tree that had been hidden behind a low-hanging broken branch.

The Trailmasters were good—they really were—but when they led the way and destroyed the trees in their path with magic, there were always sections of the underbrush left jutting out.

"Yeah, well, shit happens!" Coran yelled, grabbing Thomas and righting him, making sure he wasn't trampled by the nearly three hundred men and women of the Dark Legion advance that were running behind him.

"Seriously, man, what the hell!" Thomas huffed, rubbing his side. He'd been running with the others, five abreast at the front, charged with the responsibility of shoving the remains of the ferns and branches aside. He'd heaved a particularly wide palm frond-like branch out of the way and had slammed straight into an up-jutting chunk of tree. Running at barely below a sprint, he'd had no time to change direction. He'd bounced into Turk, then rebounded off Coran on his opposite side. The entire front had been disrupted as the second file behind him shifted and slowed slightly to avoid hitting them or impaling themselves on the fragment of tree.

"Pay attention, boy!" Turk shoved Thomas forward again, the massive half-orc's powerful blow making Thomas stagger as he tried to catch himself.

"What the hell's going on!" Belladonna shouted, glancing over from the far side of the second file.

Thomas bit his cheek in fury at his sergeant catching him fucking up. Worse, this was his first time in the first file, and he'd been determined not to be the one who showed the squad up.

"Thomas." Turk's irritated answer promised pain later. "The halfwit child wasn't watching his path."

"I damn well was! I…" Thomas snapped back, only to be shoulder-checked by Coran, who glared at him and shook his head.

"What was that, *boy*?" Turk snarled, and Thomas bit down on his response.

"Nothing, sir."

"Sir! *Sir*?!" Turk bellowed, his voice rising in anger at being addressed like an *officer*, when Belladonna cut him off by calling Turk to her side.

"Oh, thank God," Thomas muttered. Turk glared at him but obediently swapped places along the line, taking up the front right instead of front left position.

"You got off lightly!" Coran grunted, jumping over a small half-buried log and landing in a puddle of muddy water, filth spraying in all directions. "Belladonna doesn't interrupt Turk for me!"

"Yeah, well, you're a fugly bastard," Thomas called back, grinning and swinging his kukri-like blade at the hanging vine before him.

At the speed he and the line were running, they couldn't hack down all the obstructing foliage that survived the Trailmaster's destructive spells, but each cut weakened the underbrush, ensuring that, by the time another dozen or more had slashed at it, the trail would be clear for those farther back.

Each squad of ten took their turn at the front, as his was doing now, for a ten-minute stretch that had them drenched in sweat and panting by the time they fell back to the rear of the column, allowing the next squad to take their place.

Each squad was separated into first and second file, and each took their time in the lead, hacking and slashing, trampling the underbrush down. Occasionally, oh so rarely, they got lucky and crossed a section that had been perfectly cleared already.

Most of the time, however, it was a case of frantically stomping, staggering, and trying to damage the obstructing plant life around them without falling and being trampled, as three others had so far…thankfully, none of their squad.

By the time the corpses had passed under Thomas' sabatons, as far back in the line as he'd been, there was no hope for the two men and one woman in the crushed armor. He'd swallowed hard, refusing to dwell on the horrible experience of your fellow soldiers trampling you to death, rather than slowing down.

The Dark Legion advance was charged with creating a new road to the Great Tower of Dravith. They were apparently ignoring the original one, despite the easier route, because it would be days longer. If the only cost were paid by the men and women of the Dark Legion?

"Challenges just make us stronger," Thomas muttered, glaring at a vine that swung down, its other end burned loose by the Trailmaster floating leisurely ahead on a disk of compressed air.

Thomas swung his blade, timing it perfectly and hacking through the vine as it flew past, making him grin at a flash from his notifications.

"Ding," he whispered, having been watching for it for days. "That's level thirty in small blades." He resisted the temptation to open the notification, knowing that there'd be an evolution of his skill, and Gods knew he'd been waiting long enough.

Any minute, and they'd….

A horn sang out from the middle of the column, and Thomas sighed with relief as his file split, peeling off to either side from the lead position and slowing as they dropped back down the ranks to catch their breath. In barely a few minutes, they'd be running at the back of the pack instead, with a nice, smooth, trampled path to follow.

The heavily armored force, clad in black, with bronze or gold ornamentation signifying higher ranks, ran past. Thomas grinned inside his closed helm, his labored breath rasping and echoing in his ears.

It was intoxicating, this feeling of power, of being one of the greatest forces in the known realms, and that was without the bonuses.

As a Dark Legionnaire of Nimon, not only was he now beyond the laws of *all* others, responsible only to the Dark Church, but he no longer cared about any minor details of life.

He was fed, given everything he needed, and more. He was challenged every day to become the best. The camp provided everything to a Dark Legionnaire–training, food, whores–and it was all paid for by the Church, so he would never have to worry about anything ever again.

All he had to do was run, fight, and kill.

Thomas ignored the tiny voice shrieking in the back of his mind that something was wrong, that there was more out there, that he shouldn't be satisfied with just this. However, the wretch who'd survived the dungeon and everything else that had been thrown at him knew better.

He had finally found where he was supposed to be all his life, after being dragged this way and that by dreams, wounded and hunted, tortured, and abandoned. The only one he'd ever been able to rely on since his childhood, when they'd lost their mother, was his twin, Jack. Since he'd lost him, the world had grown darker and grimmer every day.

Friends had stabbed him in the back in this new world. He'd been tortured, beaten, starved, and sleep deprived. Tommy had lost everything, and through the constant abuse, had learned that what a man truly needed was a purpose.

Well, he'd found his.

Some fucking dickbag had captured the Great Tower, a feat that the Dark Legion had been training and preparing for, apparently. Then he'd claimed overlordship of the continent through some stupid ancient law of Imperial Right.

Then the fucker had *raided* the city of Himnel. Yes, it was a shithole, to be fair, and Thomas would have cheered at the thought of that wanker Barabarattas being robbed at any other time. But the cowardly fucktards had used an airship's main cannon, the realm equivalent of a WMD, on the sleeping Dark Legion's camp.

Hundreds were killed, possibly thousands injured, and the kind of people who would do something like that needed to be curb-stomped into the next hemisphere.

Worst of all, though? The asshat who'd done it had laid claim to his brother's gamer tag: Jax. He'd actually managed to get the dark God, Nimon, the only real God there was, to hate him personally. This asshole made the God of Gods sit up and declare him an enemy of the Church.

Thomas knew he'd never see his brother again, not in reality, not beyond his dreams and wishes. But, if there was even the slightest, miniscule chance that Jack would find his way here, Thomas couldn't risk the Dark God hating him by proxy because of the things this asshole did.

No, Thomas would kill this fucker himself, and he'd expend every effort on making it as fast, yet painful, as possible, so Nimon would forget that name as quickly as he'd become aware of it.

CHAPTER ONE

"Jax! Wake up!" Oracle cried.

I rolled to my feet, displacing her and searching the room frantically, trying to spot the threat.

"Jax!" Oracle shouted again.

I spun on her, my mind filled with a mix of fear, aggression, and a need to fight.

"What?" I shouted, then I felt it. A sensation of terrible warning, and it emanated from the northeast. I grabbed my naginata and sprinted for the door. Tang threw it open and got out of the way barely a second before I'd have taken it off its hinges.

I bolted for the ladder to the upper decks, leaping and triggering my Soaring Majesty ability and flew out the hatch.

I spun in the air, dropping onto the lower deck and staring into the distance, my eyes locked on something that was still beyond the horizon, a structure literally hundreds of miles away. Oracle focused on the feeling, receiving a message from Seneschal even as Jenae spoke it to me, Her voice grim as it rang in my mind.

"Beware, Eternal, the Dark Legion of Nimon has begun to march on the Great Tower of Dravith. The War of the Gods has begun."

"Tenandra!" I bellowed, spinning around. "Get us caught up to the fleet. Fast!" I turned to the others as they raced up on deck behind me, ready for a fight. "The Dark Legion is heading for the Tower. We need to get there now!" I only hoped we wouldn't be too late.

"What happened?" Tang asked.

I shook my head, adrenaline making my heart thud. Gesturing for the others to come with me, I strode to the Wheelhouse.

Grizz hurried to the door and opened it, glancing inside then leading the way, his legion training dictating that I should never enter a room first whenever possible.

I hurried inside, the clomp and clank of the others filing in causing the room to seem over-filled. Composing myself, I sat on a desk, thinking while I waited for the others to get settled.

"Okay, everyone," I began, when a knock sounded at the door. Soween ducked her head inside, earning a grunt and wave from me to come in and close the door.

"Right," I started again. "The shit's hit the fan. The Dark Legion has set off from Himnel, and they're headed straight for the Tower. I don't know how many, how long, or how they're traveling, but Jenae managed to give us a warning almost the same time Seneschal sent one. Oracle, what did he have to say?"

"It was Decin who found out about the Dark Legion." Oracle took up the narrative as she flew into the middle of the room and slowly turned to face us all.

"He saw the trail of destruction and skirted it at a distance before heading at full speed to the Tower.

"We've got a week or so, most likely; maybe two, at the very most. That's the best-case scenario. Worst case, although it's the least likely, is four days, which is only possible if they have a hell of a lot of mages and mana potions. It also depends on the force's mana, as they're using it to smash a path through the forest."

"Trailmasters," Yen grunted, shaking her head in disgust. "The Dark Legion like to boast that they're far faster than the true Legion and have taken to hunting monsters in the areas around Himnel; the ones that are worth gold either as alchemy ingredients or bounties, anyway. They use a group of specialist mages to lead the way, destroying everything in their path with magic, while the soldiers follow along behind and other mages use spells to increase their speed."

"Sounds well-thought-out," I admitted.

She nodded. "It's a tactic from the Imperial records, except that there should be a full legion at the front, right behind the mages, to protect the builders who followed behind, laying the roads. We've not had mages in the legion capable of that for hundreds of years, and no need to make new roads anywhere, so…" She shrugged.

"Well, it looks like they're using that tactic against us." I frowned, thinking quickly. "Oracle, what else can you tell us?"

"There are several hundred Dark Legionnaires. Decin didn't want to get close enough for an accurate count, but they're going as fast as they can, and they have at least a few wagons behind them. They're making the aggressive time, heading straight for the Tower. Seneschal and Heph are changing the Tower to a War footing; all indoor repairs are being halted as they work to shore up and seal the Tower from the bottom. Decin intends to go back out on patrol as soon as his crew have restocked the ship. Oren is working on the *Agamemnon's Wrath*, but she's nearly done, and they're going over the plans now."

"Good. Tenandra, how fast can you catch us up to the fleet?" I asked. Jian and the diminutive Wisp exchanged a long look.

"Lord Jax…" Tenandra started, wincing. "The *Interesting Endeavor* is badly damaged, and the Gnomes are all aboard the *Falcon*, but even if they were here, working around the clock, we couldn't increase our speed by much."

"How long?" I demanded.

"A day to catch up, if we go as fast as we can"

I shook my head. "That's too long. If they're using magic to travel at high speeds, I need to return to the Tower as fast as possible. How long for the fleet to get from here to the Tower?"

She grimaced. "Judging on no more than a ten percent increase in speed over their current, and that is dependent on guesswork at this stage…" Tenandra calculated slowly. "Fifty hours, at a minimum."

"Are you shitting me?" I stared at her. "The worst-case estimate is a few days; that puts us arriving at the same goddamn time! They're on foot, trailblazing through a forest!"

"They also have specialized magic to assist them, and we're flying decrepit and half-built ships that are well over a hundred miles farther out than they are," Oracle said, redirecting my ire from the little Wisp and diffusing it.

I glared at her as well, then forced myself to take a deep breath, relaxing my shoulders and sitting back upright from where I'd hunched.

"You're right," I grudgingly admitted, nodding to Tenandra. "I'm sorry for snapping at you. Right, I need options, people!"

"Take Mal's ship," Lydia suggested, causing Soween to glare at her. "Not permanently, don't worry!" Lydia patted the air between them reassuringly. "We change over to tha other ship, kick tha Gnomes back over 'ere and tell 'em to fix it as best they can. Then we 'ead back to tha fleet at full speed, load up tha fastest ships with as many legionnaires as we can, an' leave tha rest to follow along behind..."

"No, that black ship is still out there somewhere." I shook my head gravely. "If they see us all essentially abandoning the fleet, you can bet they'll attack again. We can't take all of them, but we could take...maybe two? Cram as many of the legion elites onto the two fastest ships we have, head straight for the Tower, the rest protect the fleet," I mused. "I wonder how far I could get using my flight ability..."

"A dozen minutes, at best," Oracle stated calmly, gesturing at the rest of the room to calm down as they all objected at being left behind.

"Dammit," I grunted, then shrugged. "Fine. I get to go tell Mal the good news then, I guess. Bet he's gonna be pissed."

"Considering the Gnomes?" Soween said with a wry grin. "Yeah, I'm thinking that's likely."

"Shit."

"Yeah, shame, boss. It was hilarious at the time." Grizz somehow managed to look mournful. "Any chance we could do a swap, you think? Give him this ship, and we take his?"

"Never!" Jian said, gaping in horror at Grizz before turning to me. "You...you wouldn't, right?" he asked. For a second, I considered it–just a second–but I shook my head quickly.

"No; even if it wasn't for the fact that the ship probably has all sorts of cool little weird things in it, knowing the Gnomes. It's Tenandra's body now, and as such, she'll always have a home with us."

"Uh, point?" Tang leaned forward to interject. "So, just so we know for the future, is she a member of the ship's crew or the captain of this ship? You know, seeing as it's her body?"

"Why, thank you for adding just one more feather to my load, Tang." I growled at him and looked back to Tenandra. "Okay, not a good time to bring this up."

Tang had the good grace to look embarrassed by his question and its timing.

"But you do need a full crew and a captain. They will look after you and maintain your...body. The captain's purpose will be to give you advice and to run the crew. You will be equal to the captain, until you prove yourself to me, but above all others aboard the ship. We'll figure out a way to integrate the fleet and the legion soon, I guess."

Tenandra gave a small yet elegant curtsy and smiled when she rose, nodding her acceptance. For the first time since I'd met her, I saw happiness in her.

"All my existence, I was a slave, although in a gilded cage. To know that, once I prove myself, I will be free, in the service of the Empire, yes, but still free? It is a balm to my soul," she whispered.

"You will be, Tenandra; at least as free as any of us truly are, anyway. After all, would you step aside and let some of these scumbags live?" I asked, arching one eyebrow. "If that wanker back there, the one who was trying to get into the vault, was a member of the noble families, like he claimed, you could have just let him have what he wanted, right?"

"Well, yes, but…" Tenandra said slowly.

"But you knew he was an asshole, and you weren't going to let him get away with it all?" I persisted, and she nodded. "Good."

"If he'd known the right commands to give, though, I would have been unable to refuse him," Tenandra added, uncertainty in her voice.

"And if he was strong enough, and we weren't, he'd have been able to take anything he wanted from us. There are always ways that they, and we, can do things. It's all about choice," I said firmly. "You chose not to allow him access once you saw his true nature, and because of that, you're free now."

I left her mulling that thought over as I stood and looked around the room.

"Okay, people, get your gear together. I'll go see Mal and set things in motion over there. Bane, get the Alchemy gear, will you?" I got a nod from him. "Thanks; everyone else, you've got about ten minutes. Get your gear and be ready. I'll get Mal to prepare to cushion your fall onto his deck, so be ready to jump. Tenandra, you'll need to fly us over their deck as soon as everyone's ready. I'm sorry that we have to leave you already, but I'll get Mal to leave his crew aboard in case you need them." I headed to the door, Oracle and Jian remaining behind with Tenandra while the rest of the group followed me out, splitting up to gather up whatever belongings they had.

I climbed up to the upper deck above the wheelhouse and surveyed the burned, broken decking, the warped metal, and the obvious reasons that rain had been able to get into the wheelhouse. I groaned, remembering the Fireball that had started it, then the devastation caused by my own heavy landing.

"What are you going to do, then?" asked a voice from behind. I turned to see that Soween had followed me.

"I'm going to go see Mal, explain what's happened and that I need him. Again." I shrugged. "No doubt he'll gloat over it and use the excuse to gouge another concession out of me."

"He might, if a deal hasn't already been struck," Soween said innocently.

"A deal?" I asked, arching one eyebrow. "He won't like that."

"Mal likes you, sir." She smiled. "We all do. We hated the shitty world we lived in; that was why we all banded together in the first place. It's harder to take advantage of a group. Mal just wants what you're selling."

"What I'm selling?" I frowned in confusion.

"You know, the whole Empire thing," Soween retorted, waving her hand around. "He…*we* want in, but we've been burned before, and that's why he doesn't want to swear. We don't want to be the outsiders forever, but that doesn't mean we're going to give it all up for free, you understand?" She gave me a pointed stare.

"You want me to make it worth your while?" I asked, wanting to make sure I understood.

"Yeah, and we want a limited Oath, one with a get-out clause, so that, if you don't keep to your end of the bargain, we can leave. We keep our ship. Any others that we capture will be offered to you for sale first, but if you don't take them, then we're free to sell them wherever we want."

"Right, and what's this going to cost me?" I eyed her cautiously.

"That's for you and Mal to sort out," she admitted. "I'm just giving you a quiet bit of advice, start the ball rolling, if you will."

"And the deal you mentioned?" I persisted. "For getting me to the fleet and aiding in the assault?"

"Never mentioned that. I said there might be a deal we could work out to get you to the fleet, sir, one that may be revolved around that fancy alchemy set you have below decks." Soween casually gazed out over the side of the ship at the waves far below, then glanced at Mal on the deck of his ship.

Predictably, he was screaming at someone. As I squinted, I was fairly sure it was Giint, actually…

"I need the alchemy set," I admitted after a few seconds of silence while we both watched Mal. His face had gone from white to red to blue, and his choice invectives pierced the air in the distance.

"Well, we need potions, so maybe we could do a deal on the potion side of things. After all, you did agree to hand over some of the potions you made with our ingredients." She broke off and squinted hard at the rear of Mal's ship as it drew ahead slightly. "Is that Jay? Is he…is he *nailed to the stern?!*"

"Yeah, that looks like Jay…and yeah, although it looks like he's just tied to it," I agreed, trying to keep the worry out of my voice as I forced a grin and waved to him. He was evidently secured spread-eagle by dozens of small straps to the rear of the ship, as well as being gagged.

"You know he's scared of heights, right?" Soween asked me carefully.

"I know he's a fucking idiot; that's about all I know about him, actually." I smiled evilly.

"Okay, well, he's going to be absolutely useless after that." Soween rubbed the bridge of her nose. "Look, we need potions, you need to get to the fleet quick. We all win if you win, so how about a nice, straightforward deal, and you give me a lift over there before Jay has a heart attack?" Soween offered, sighing. "You give us, say, thirty healing, fifteen stamina, and fifteen mana potions, all 'average' or better in strength, and we call it even?"

"Five of each of health and stamina, two mana," I countered.

"Twenty health, ten stamina and mana," she responded.

"Ten of each."

"Twenty of each, and we provide the ingredients."

What she was asking for was heavily in my favor. Had she asked for those things in normal circumstances, I'd have just given them to her as thanks for all the help they'd given us so far…if I had them.

"I'll agree in principle." I raised a forestalling hand at her attempt to protest. "But you'll have to wait, as I've not got that many potions made up, and you traded me all the ingredients you had already."

"Oh, we can get more," Soween said easily.

"What am I missing here?" I wondered aloud.

"Let's just say that we know of places to get some herbs, that's all." She grinned smugly. "We get you to the fleet, then you go with a couple of cruisers straight for the Tower. We'll follow along, take a little detour on the way, get a few herbs and whatnot, then we catch up to you at the Tower. You make our potions, maybe you and Mal come to a deal for the future, maybe not. My concern is Mal's company, keeping them all alive, fed, and flying. I can give you advice, but you have to make the decisions."

"Are you harvesting the herbs yourself?" I asked. She shook her head. "Fine; how much will they cost you?"

"That's none of your business, sir," she said coolly.

"Fine. I've no time for this. I agree to the deal on the condition that whatever price you're paying for the herbs, you buy everything they have for me, and I'll reimburse you when you get to the Tower."

"Some of those ingredients are expensive," Soween warned me, watching my expression carefully.

"Over or under a platinum piece for the lot?" I asked, pulling one out of the pouch.

"Under…at least, it damn well better be." Soween swallowed hard and stared at the coin.

"Then I expect change." I handed her the coin as Oracle came out of the wheelhouse and flew up to me. "Are you ready?" I asked Oracle, and she nodded. "And you?" I turned back to Soween, who nodded slowly, still staring at the coin in shock.

"Okay, how are we going to…"

Soween broke off with a grunt as I wrapped my left arm around her shoulders, crouching and lifting her under her knees into a princess carry.

"Like this!" I said, squatting slightly and shoving off hard, like a normal jump, but activating Soaring Majesty at the same time.

The result was epic, even as I tried to ignore the pain of the Ability's drain on my health and mana pools.

I flew off the deck, Oracle having to push hard to keep up as I jetted across the few hundred meters of distance that separated the ships in flight.

I grinned at the sight of Mal's open-mouthed stare as he watched us flying over so spectacularly, followed by the grimace as he clamped his mouth shut and glared at me.

We landed seconds later, and I staggered, unfortunately, being new to the whole "flying like Superman" thing, nearly dropping Soween.

I skidded along the deck, recently wetted by one of the fast and frequent rain squalls that kept washing over us. Steadying myself, I set her safely on her feet. She scowled at me, straightening her jacket and holding up one finger in rebuke.

I regarded her finger then felt the prick of the dagger that she'd drawn unseen and tapped to the inside of my right thigh.

"Next time you think of doing something like that without warning a girl, you think twice, understand?"

"You asked me to fly us over," I ground out.

"Why, yes." She pasted a sunny smile on her face. "Yes, I did sir, and you might want to consider then, if I *asked* you to do it and was *expecting* you to do it, what could possibly have pissed me off that much about what you did…hmmm?" Soween maintained her sweet smile, nodding across to the ship we'd just left. Her husband, Josh, looked over forlornly at us.

"But Josh…" I sputtered.

She cut me off, her dagger flashing in the sunlight as she slipped it back into a sheath. "But Josh didn't know we were going; all he knew was that I was going to talk to you. Next time, Lord Jax, if you could think about a married man's feelings before you cart his wife off, that'd be appreciated, okay?" She smiled again and stepped back, stalking over to where Mal stood glaring at me like a scalded cat.

They exchanged a handful of words, and Mal glowered before striding forward.

"What the hell did I do?" I asked Oracle under my breath.

"Nothing, honestly." She glanced back at Josh. "I think you just surprised her, and she used the first excuse she could think of as to why she didn't warn him first herself. Just go along with it. If it becomes a problem, I'll step in later."

I rubbed my head, confused, then shrugged and regarded Mal as he came to a halt nearby, practically quivering with rage.

"You set those little…" he snarled at me.

"Ah, nope. You asked me to send them over, if you remember?" I shot back at him. "Anyway, sorry, Mal, but I've no time to fuck about right now. Soween told you about the deal, and what's happened?" I asked.

"She told me that she made a deal with you to give us potions, and in return, we get you to the fleet, fast," he said through gritted teeth.

"The Dark Legion is marching on the Tower," I informed him. "The *Interesting Endeavor* is going to cross your deck in a few minutes. My team will jump over, and I need you to cushion their landing as best you can, then it's full speed to catch up to the fleet."

Mal stood obviously ready for an argument, but he saw that now clearly wasn't the time, as he instead spun around and started bellowing orders.

"Mal!" I called to him as he walked away.

"What, goddammit!" Mal spun around, fists shaking with suppressed rage, before taking a deep breath and trying again. "What?"

"How long to catch the fleet?"

"About three hours," he replied grudgingly.

"Then I need a room. Some of the Gnomes have…issues. I need somewhere private to work on healing them."

"Issues?" Mal spat on the deck. "You're goddamn right, they do! That fucking Giint is the worst of them! And Jay's missing; I know that little bastard had something to do with it, and he won't…"

"He's strapped to the stern below the big windows."

"What?" Mal blanched, freezing in shock.

"Jay; he's strapped to the stern," I repeated, allowing a little grin to surface despite the stress. "No idea what happened, but I'm betting he tried to pick on Giint."

"God dammit!" Mal swore, storming off and shouting more orders.

I glimpsed a Gnome racing past, a huge grin on his face, and I caught his arm, spinning him around.

"Find Frederikk for me, quickly…and Giint!" I ordered.

He nodded, tearing off and cannon-ball diving down a hatch and out of sight.

"This is going to be a long day," I muttered as a Gnome shouted something. Two more fell from the rigging onto the upper deck, fighting, barely an arm's reach away.

CHAPTER TWO

I t didn't take Mal long to get the matting sorted, and a few minutes later, the rest of the squad was leaping down to land on the deck, Jian coming last of all.

I could see his reluctance as he looked up, watching the heavily battered and corroded hull of the *Interesting Endeavor* curving away from us. For a split second, I almost asked if he wanted to remain with the ship, but I shook my head and buried the consideration. He had a role in the team, and he needed to do his duty.

I liked Jian, and I understood his reluctance. He'd grown used to his position as the pilot or helmsman or whatever, and he liked working with Tenandra. But I had to make decisions based on what was best for the Empire, and for me.

Tenandra would be fine, and she also should be constrained by her Oath of service to follow along. If she wasn't, and she ran for it, or if something went wrong, and she crashed…well, I had to take that risk.

I checked the team over, only finding one injury, and that was Grizz, weirdly enough. For the first time in seemingly forever, his luck had abandoned him, and he'd sprained his ankle on landing.

Oracle healed him quickly and examined the nearest Gnomes. As soon as I was sure everyone was aboard, and Tenandra had curved aside enough to clear the air before us, I turned and gestured to Mal, who stood on the upper deck, talking to Soween.

He responded…well, he responded with a rude hand gesture, actually. That said, it was still an acknowledgement, and the ship picked up speed.

"You sent for me, my lord?" a voice spoke from behind me. I turned around to find Frederikk standing there, absolutely dripping with black gunk.

"What the hell happened to you?"

"The ship's bilges," he said calmly.

"This is a brand-new damn ship," I objected with a frown.

"It is, and the bilges were spotless."

"Were?"

Frederikk smiled through the thick, viscous coating. "We sealed the chamber above the bilges and needed to be sure it was tight."

"And?" I warily eyed the ooze that was rapidly pooling around his feet. "And what the hell is that?"

"And there was a hole after all!" he replied happily. "I knew there would be, but to be sure, we mixed up something that would run slowly, so we could find it and fix it."

"What exactly did you mix?" I grimaced at the trail of black footprints across the deck, and the practically apoplectic Mal, who'd just seen the state of his beautiful ship.

"Black treacle and cooking oil," the sodden Gnome said proudly. "Mixed it right up, and it's perfect. Makes it really easy to see where the hull isn't secure."

"And you got those ingredients from…?" I pressed, not sure if I should be laughing or shouting at him.

"The ship's stores," Frederikk said, still smiling proudly. "There wasn't much, so we used it all. Can you tell the captain to get us some more?" He paused, cocking his head to the side. "In the meantime, I think I saw some honey down there as well; I'll mix it in and see how far we can stretch it out…"

"WHAT THE HELL…" Mal screamed, leaping down the last few steps from the upper deck and striding in our direction. Behind him, Soween and two others were hauling a pale, shaking Jay back up onto the deck with a rope.

"Frederikk," I said slowly, trying to keep the grin off my face, "I'm going to let you explain this to the Captain, but for now, it's time I started healing your people. Can you send them to me, one at a time?" Frederikk nodded his assent, clearly relieved, and wiped some of the gunk from his face so he could see better.

His moustache and short beard were left angled in the direction he'd wiped, like it'd been Something about Mary'd. I couldn't help but close my eyes and stamp down that horrific mental image.

"Okay, send the first one to me in…" I realized I still needed a room for the process and began hunting around, just as an enraged Mal reached us. "Perfect timing, Mal!" I greeted him, my concern with the situation warring with my inbuilt need to fuck with him.

"What…you! He…!" Mal gasped out, gesturing wildly from Frederikk to me to the sticky black footprints to the area where a sweating, trembling Jay had collapsed to the deck and was holding on for dear life, while Soween tried to get him upright. The traumatized man frantically clung to the nearest stanchion. "You!" Mal practically screamed at me.

I smiled, long and slow.

"Hey, buddy! So, was having all the Gnomes working on your ship all you hoped it would be? Bet you're glad about that promise to do whatever favor I asked with a big smile on your face, eh? And even more so, now that this is a separate deal?"

"You…*you*…!" he grated out.

"No, no, Mal." I shook my head magnanimously. "There's no need to thank me, don't worry."

He lunged for my throat, only to be shoulder-checked by Soween, who'd just moved over to join us. I was still chuckling as I dodged.

"I'm gonna kill 'im!" Mal swore, trying to get past Soween, who was frantically shoving him back.

"Perhaps you could go somewhere else, please, sir?" she grunted.

"Yeah, about that…if you can sort me out a room to work in, I can get started on fixing the Gnomes'…problems?" I offered.

Mal slowed slightly, albeit with his arms still outstretched and fingers twitching.

"Their 'problems'?" Mal whispered slowly. "Whadda ya mean, 'their problems'?!"

"They were locked up in a hidden cavern and fed upon, while only being able to drink from contaminated water sources for almost a hundred years. You might not have noticed, buuuut…"

"They're fucking mental!" Mal screamed, lunging at me again. "You set mental fucking Gnomes loose on my ship and gave them drugs!"

"You asked for them," I countered.

He went from red to blue again as Soween called two other crew over to help her in restraining the captain.

"Perhaps you could go below now, sir?" she grunted, shooting a warning scowl at me. "Second door on the right from that hatch there." She indicated a hatch in the deck. "You'll find one of the guest quarters."

I nodded and smiled my thanks at her, then turned to Frederikk.

"Send the first of the Gnomes there; the most unbalanced first, I think. Once we heal them, they'll take a while to recover, so don't expect them back to work for the day, at least," I warned him, receiving a satisfied nod in return. Confident that he would comply, I returned my focus back to Mal and Soween.

"Mal, I'm sorry. This was another opportunity to wind you up, and we both know you'd have done the same if our positions were reversed," I conceded. "But in all seriousness, I need to reach the fleet and fast. Please, get me there as fast as possible." Mal scowled, subsiding slightly and visibly calming himself before shoving the restraining hands loose and storming towards the upper deck.

"Fine!" he snapped. "But you get that fucker fixed first!" He pointed at Giint, who was happily trotting across the deck to greet us.

"Ah…bad news there," I called after him, moving quickly to the open hatch. "Giint's the only one who's been healed already!" I jumped down out of sight as Mal exploded again.

I could hear him ranting somewhere overhead as I counted along and moved into the room Soween had indicated, finding it completely bare of any creature comforts and filled with crates of what smelled like dried food.

I shrugged and shifted some things, clearing enough space to give me half the room to work in. At the sound of a grunt from behind, I turned to find Giint standing there.

"Giint, right. Good man, Gnome…whatever." I fumbled for the correct label, finally just shrugging. "You and I haven't spoken much; what are your skills?" I asked curiously as I waited for the first of the Gnomes to be sent down to be healed. Idly, I wondered what Oracle was doing. Last I'd seen, she'd given up on examining the Gnomes and had flown off the side of the ship, diving down out of sight.

"Skiiiills?" Giint echoed, scratching his grimy beard and considering his equally filthy hand, as though unsure whose it was. "Giiiint good at baaangs…good with crossbow…gooood at buillllding!"

"Anything else?" I asked, and he frowned at me.

"Gooood at lotsss," he grumbled sullenly.

"Any weapons other than crossbows?" I persisted, and he nodded, dipping his hands into the bags on his belt to yank out a kill-stick and an axe. He flourished them halfheartedly and then slipped them back out of sight.

"Okay…that kill-stick, what do you call those?" I pulled my own out of my bag, showing it to him.

It was a club, about as long as my forearm, composed of a rough grip, a lever that could be flicked up or down with a thumb to activate it, and three sets of discs set in it that revved up like a chainsaw and essentially chewed through anything.

"Buzzzzer," Giint said, shrugging.

"Can you fix mine?" I asked him, handing it over.

Giint took it and briefly inspected it before spitting on the floor. He glanced up at me and realized I was glaring at his spit. He casually stepped on the wet glob, grinning in what he probably though was a charming way as he brandished the buzzer at me.

Bane and Grizz, who'd just entered the room, grabbed him. In less than two seconds, he had dagger tips pressed against his throat, his right kidney, and his balls, forcing him to freeze in place.

"Now, now." I shook my head and snorted. "It's okay, guys; he's sworn the Oath, remember?" They grudgingly released Giint, who rubbed himself, checking for injuries.

"Fuck's sake, Giint, sod off somewhere else if you're going to keep doing that," I snapped several seconds later as he was still rubbing. The deranged Gnome jumped as though he'd totally forgotten we were there, and he grinned impishly, making his way toward the door. "Giint!" I called. "The buzzer?" I held out my hand expectantly, and he looked at my buzzer still in his grasp, holding it up in acknowledgement.

"Giint fiiix!" he assured me. "Make betteeeer!" He winked mischievously, sidling off. A few seconds later, a growl and a fight started up in the corridor. Grizz reappeared seconds later, dragging a female Gnome by the hand.

For her part, she had gripped Giint's ear firmly and looked like she was determined to batter him senseless. I had my work cut out for me with these nutcases.

"Oracle?" I asked into our bond. *"Where are you? I'm going to try to heal one of the Gnomes…"*

"I'll be right there!"

"Okay, who are you?" I asked the female Gnome, then raised placating hands as she turned her irate gaze to me. I recognized her from the Gnomes who had sworn to me…vaguely. She was one of those who'd looked the most unbalanced, and also one of the first to actually start swearing, so I was confused to all hell and had no time to consider what was happening.

"I…I…I am!" she eventually spat out, releasing Giint and smiling at me suddenly, her face split by the huge grin.

"You have gift for me? You want something?" she purred, smiling in what was clearly supposed to be a seductive manner. In reality it made her look crazed in a way a honey badger with rabies would have run from. I shuddered involuntarily, then relaxed as Oracle flew into the room, sharply focused on the little Gnome.

"Let's sort this right out," Oracle said in a low growl as Giint backed away quickly from her.

The unfortunate Gnome was about two and half feet tall, with black hair that stood up and shot out in all directions. She was filthy, covered in grime, dried blood, and what seemed to be snot from her constantly running nose, wearing an extremely faded and patched red dress that fared little better. The ragged garment appeared to have once belonged to someone much taller, which she had crudely hacked down to fit her shorter stature.

Despite her slovenly, petite exterior, her shape hinted at what appeared to be a fantastic figure, for another species, anyway. She glared, grinned, and shot

31

suspicious glances around the room constantly, then tried to show her figure off more, smoothing her dress down, until Oracle grew to her full size and froze her in place with a stern look.

The two women were silent for long moments until the Gnome growled something and looked away. Oracle nodded in satisfaction.

"Okay, now that...*whatever* that was...is done, come in, please. Lie down on the floor, and we'll see what we can do to heal you, okay?" I gestured to the cleared space, and she edged forward hesitantly, entering the room and lying down, but continuing to glare defensively at us all.

I felt Oracle building the spell, and I settled down, getting as comfortable as I could in full armor and beginning to meditate.

Minutes became hours as she worked tirelessly, and my mana bottomed out more times than I could count, the surge of pain from the mana migraine raising its ugly head then dying away again as I remained deep in the trance. Eventually, Bane's hand on my shoulder, gently shook me from my trance.

As my eyes opened, I caught a glimpse of the glowing box around me fading. I blinked, once again slightly weirded out that it occasionally became visible.

"Tingles..." was all Bane said as he shook his hand out absently. "We're about ten minutes from the fleet." He gestured toward the bow of the ship, and I nodded silently, smiling my thanks. I couldn't keep from groaning as I shifted, my legs feeling both fantastically healed and weirdly achy from remaining so long in the same position.

The first Gnome who had entered the room, though, was gone. In her place lay an unconscious, tiny woman. Oracle had clearly taken the time at some point between working our magic to clean the small creature's face and hands, and the diminutive woman was almost unrecognizable as the filthy creature who'd entered the room earlier.

While the previous person and this one lay in the same location, it seemed that was all they shared. The woman lay comfortably on the floor, breathing easily in a deep sleep. Occasionally, she twitched as her levels were unlocked and her physiology improved, and I was startled to realize that she had none of the same defining features as she had first presented with.

The twitches, the fervent glances, and the seemingly permanent glare of mistrust and fear were totally gone. In their place was a Gnome woman who looked like she'd been dragged through a hedge backwards by her hair and really needed a bath, but beyond that, should be fine.

"How bad?" I asked Oracle, climbing to my feet and looking from the small, hovering Wisp to the woman on the deck.

"Not as bad as Giint, not by a long shot, but not good," Oracle admitted. "I've learned a lot from that, and I think we can help Giint some more as well. But really, the thing that will help her the most now is good food, a safe place to live, and patience. And a cause, actually, now that I think about it.

"When Giint first came around, before we healed him further and unlocked his leveling, he was far worse than any of these Gnomes. The corruption and poisoning he endured made him into a Badunka rider, which meant he'd lost all access to the 'special water' unless he brought in metal or bodies for the master; you remember?" She spoke softly, looking sorrowfully at me.

I regarded the small form resting peacefully at our feet. "I do." I turned to Grizz. "Can we get someone to watch over her while I go up onto the deck?"

He saluted, stepping out and returning quickly with Miren, Jian, and Lydia, the rest of the squad filtering in as well, or as near as they could with the size of the room.

"Thank you," I said. "I don't want to leave her on her own, but I need to fly to the battleship as soon as we're in range." I felt the squad's dismay at the thought of me going on my own, until Lydia spoke up.

"Then I'll be comin' with ya." She stood straight, flexing her golden wings slightly.

They were huge, even when they were furled. On a whim, I fired a Greater Examination at her, having meant to do it for ages. What I saw made me freeze in awe.

Lydia Artun

Lydia was born in the village of Cornut, daughter to an abusive father who regularly beat her and her mother. She was married at a young age to a man many years her senior. When she was unable to bear any living children, she was sold by her husband to the slavers of Menneheim, spending the next twelve years between hard labor and the slave pens until she was rescued by the Lord of Dravith.

In her desperation and determination to protect her Lord, Lydia called out to a legend she was taught as a child, one that she dreamed of all her life. Years of frantic belief and wishing channeled her as-yet-unformed mana into this desire, and the unlocking of her magic provided her with the knowledge of a forgotten class. When combined with the terrible stress and fear of losing the one she most loves, this resulted in a unique opportunity.

Lydia is the first Valkyrie to walk the realm in seven hundred years, and while she is untaught, untrained, and has no mistress to lead her into unlocking her powers, her long-dead sisters are watching her through the veil.

Weaknesses: Death and Earth magics are 25% more effective against a Valkyrie.
Resistances: Light and Air magics used against a Valkyrie are 50% less effective.
Critical Weaknesses: Direct attacks against her wings by death magic can sever her connection to her sisters.
Level: 19
Health: 750/750
Stamina: 460/460
Mana: 230/230 (100 reserved for wings)

Jez Cajiao

"Holy fuck, Lydia," I muttered, my eyes wide as I absorbed her information. "You're a Valkyrie?"

Lydia smiled slowly. Her face, all harsh angles and bone, transformed as her expression brightened into pure joy.

"Ah...aye, ah don't know how it happened. Ah just...ah just called out to 'em, ah guess, an' they heard me. They spoke to me; ah couldna understand most o' it, but...yeah...they changed me."

"The other Valkyries?" I asked, rereading the information again.

"Aye. They said somethin' 'bout needin' a master, but as I 'ave one, all I needed was a push?" She shrugged, and I could see she was embarrassed, yet proud at the same time. She shifted her wings, as though unsure of them, and swallowed hard. "They said...they said that my powers would come, and that, when I was fully grown, my wings wouldn't be like this...they'd be real." She reached up, lightly touching one of the shimmering golden wings. Her fingers seemed to press against something, then they were through, the feathers having the texture of mist at her touch.

"Can you fly?" I asked, half curiously and half in awe.

"Sort of," she admitted, shrugging awkwardly again. "At least, I think so? I know if I be pushin' my mana into 'em, they become solid for a bit, but I don't know how long for, or what to do...?"

"Okay, well, we can try and figure this out later. Maybe this time, you can wait here," I suggested, but she shook her head.

"One o' us should be wi' you always," she insisted firmly, Bane and Grizz nodding in grim agreement, echoed a second later by Arrin, who'd been silent since wandering over to join us.

"I'm going to a battleship that's staffed entirely by people who are sworn to me, and the majority of the legion are there. I don't think there's anywhere safer," I objected, and Bane facepalmed.

"And that's why it'd be the perfect place to assassinate me," I finished in tandem with Bane.

"Regardless, wherever you go from now on, one of us should always be with you," Grizz said calmly. "We are your personal squad, and until you recruit specific bodyguards, we do that, too." He grinned at me mischievously. "Besides, I have bets to collect on!"

"Do I even want to know?" I groaned, and he laughed at my discomfort.

"There was a pool on if you and Oracle would..." he started, and I held my hand up.

"And that's all I needed to know. I'm fairly sure you're not supposed to talk about the Scion of the Empire's sex life this much, though, you know."

"Really? It be a common thing in most places to discuss tha sex lives of tha powerful," Lydia said dubiously. "The bar I used to work in, before...well, anyway, back then, we all talked about who tha nobles were rumored to be screwin'?"

I recalled the tabloids and entertainment news from back home and acknowledged that in Roman times, it was likely the same, as in medieval times, the servants probably all spoke about it. I realized that such things being said in front of me rather than behind my back just meant that they all either trusted me, or my "hey, call me Jax" informality was starting to bite me in the ass.

"Well, never mind." I sighed in resignation. "Just remember that I'll get you fuckers back for all this." I gestured Lydia to the door. "Right, let's go up on deck. You can test whether your wings can become solid enough to fly, and if they can, you can come with me to the Battleship. If not, I'll take Tang, because…"

"Because I'm his favorite," Tang interrupted.

I grimaced in the direction of the seemingly empty hallway, where his voice had floated in from. "*Because* he's a legionnaire and can give a report to those necessary, he'll be lighter than the man-mountain that is Grizz. Most importantly of all, if he gets too heavy, I can just drop the fucker, and he can try to swim back instead, since nobody will miss him."

"You've got a point there," Grizz agreed with amusement. "We really wouldn't miss him."

"I would," Bane countered, and silence fell as we all paused, looking at him. "I'd have to watch Jax 'round the clock again, and I've already seen enough to have nightmares."

"Yup, I was waiting for that." I grimaced, shaking my head.

"I was getting worried," Grizz replied and we all ignored Tang's grumbles as we exited the room, leaving Miren and Jian to watch over the unconscious Gnome as she continued to level.

We clanked and banged up the stairs, still as fully armored as we could be. Apart from Grizz, we were all missing sections, with cracks, chips, stains, and dents where our plates were still intact.

We moved up onto the raised deck and joined Mal, Soween, and the helmsman before I allowed myself to look forward and let out a sigh of relief upon seeing how close the fleet was.

The ten ships bobbed and dipped ahead of us on the air currents, the battleship occasionally losing a random plank or piece of detritus as it went. For the first time, I could see the awe-inspiring monstrosity in the air.

The battleship was the size of a World War Two aircraft carrier, which meant it wasn't far off the dimensions of a small tower block that had been turned on its side.

The other ships, the fast scouts especially, were tiny by comparison, looking more like seal pups around an orca.

I frowned, wondering if orcas and seals got along, then shrugged and decided that I really didn't care. They could be banging each other on the discovery channel, for all the interest they'd get from me.

I shoved the distracting thought aside and contemplated the distance between us and the battleship, noting that one of the cruisers had dropped back and was flying close to us. A dozen legionnaires with heavy bows at the railing checked us out as we passed them steadily.

When the legionnaires recognized us, they relaxed and saluted raggedly, but the grins on their faces made it feel heartfelt.

I saluted them in return, and Mal must have pushed a bit more from the engines, as we pulled ahead again, steadily gaining on the battleship.

I glanced back, spotting the *Interesting Endeavor* far to the rear, and I was relieved that she was keeping up I resolved to send her a crew to help Tenandra and some manastones, just in case.

"What do you think?" I asked Lydia, who wore an expression of nervous delight.

"I think I can do it," she said, straightening her shoulders determinedly.

"How long to get us ahead of the battleship?" I asked Mal. He grunted, while the helmsman responded for him.

"About twenty minutes to get ahead of them, my lord," the old man said, ducking his head, and I nodded my thanks.

"How the hell are we going to get everyone over there," I wondered aloud, rubbing my chin, and the old helmsman spoke up deferentially.

"Well, my lord, only way to do it, really, is by rope ladder. Keep both ships slow and steady, and when it gets close enough, you just…jump."

"You just, what? Hang off the side until they're close and then jump?"

He nodded.

"That's crazy," I muttered.

Mal snorted, rolling his eyes. "I thought you could fly?" he asked, one eyebrow raised.

"I can, but the others can't…well, Oracle and Lydia can, but still…" I grimaced.

"Wait, what?" Mal asked, his gaze shooting to Lydia. "You can fly now as well?"

"You see the wings?" she responded dryly, flexing and opening them wide. The movements made me think of the Protheans, in the way they had looked so much like Earth's angels of myth.

"I thought it was an effect, like from the armor or somethin'…" Mal grunted.

"Nah, rare class ability," she said easily.

"Seven hundred years since anyone managed to unlock it; I'd say rare is an understatement," I argued with a snort. "Legendary, maybe?"

"Anyway…" Mal interrupted, scowling at me. "Regardless of who can fly, and who, like *normal* goddamn folk, can't…we'll get you in front of the battleship in about fifteen minutes at this speed. They'll need to keep her steady, or you'll end up with your team squashed when she gets lifted by an air current…if only there were some way to, oh, I don't know…send someone over there. You know, like an insufferable smart ass who kept harpin' on about how they could fly?"

"I hate you, Mal," I said calmly.

"You're just jealous." He grinned, looking ahead.

"Jealous?" I asked incredulously.

"Yup," Mal confirmed. "I happen to be a free man; one word can turn this ship around, and we're off. No stress, no responsibilities, nothin'…but you? Well, you started a war with practically every single noble family out there. They won't be satisfied until they catch you, give you a show trial, and sentence you to death. I bet you'll even be hung."

"He's already hung!" Oracle called up from the deck below without missing a beat. I grinned at the look of consternation on Mal's face and walked to the edge of the railing, peering down to where Oracle smiled up at me, having paused her examination of Giint.

"Well, Mal, I'm gonna have to leave you, as I need to high five my girl for that one!" I said, the huge grin threatening to split my face.

It might have been shit talking, and about as juvenile as it was possible to get, but it was also awesome when it paid off, and that line was one I'd remember for years to come. I reveled in the glower on Mal's face and couldn't help it. He'd spend days replaying that comment in his head and trying to find a good counter.

"Yeah…well…" he sputtered, clearly searching.

"Don't," Soween advised him quietly. "It's not worth it, and you already look about as foolish as it's possible to look."

"God dammit!" Mal snarled, stomping off to look out over the sea.

I turned and caught Oracle's eye, grinning again before I shifted my attention to Lydia, who was rolling her eyes at my argument with Mal.

"You two are as bad as Bane an' Tang," she said, sighing. "They're always tryin' to beat tha other at everythin' as well."

"Meh." I shrugged. "Right; we're close enough that I could fly over from here," I said, all joking aside as I judged the distance. "Tell me about your flight?"

"I…errr…" Lydia hung her head. "I don't know," she admitted softly. "I don't know if I can fly properly, or if they be only for show, or if I be meant to glide with them at this point." Lydia went on quietly enough for my ears only, obviously embarrassed. "Without havin' a trainer or a guide, all I know is that one day I'll be able to fly, and properly, and that a hundred o' my mana be reserved for my wings now. I can make 'em solid, but only for a short amount o' time, an' then they'll go back to…this. I can hide 'em as well, but that's literally it. That's all I know."

"What about the way you were fighting before?" I asked. "You were awesome!"

"I can speed meself up; it's called 'Judgement of the Unworthy,' and it's my main class Ability. I can burn through my health and manapool to speed up me body, makin' me much faster and stronger, but only for a short time."

"Is it leveled?" I asked. "I mean, does the ability evolve in the same way that my Mana Overdrive does? The first, I don't know, thirty or so times I used it, it drained me really fast and slowed my mana regeneration, but now I'm past level ten on it, so it's much slower to drain. Is your ability like that?"

"I don't think so," Lydia replied dubiously. "I know that it's not meant to be used a lot. It be kind of a last-ditch thing, as it'll drain me. It cuts out at ten health and mana from now on, but the first time, it doesn't, for some reason. You know, back in the Prax…there should have been a trainer for me, I think? To stop me from goin' too far? I don't know, really…"

"Well, it's an amazing ability, either way, and we'll help you as best we can to learn. Who knows, right? Maybe Oracle can find some information on it, or we can ask the Gods. After all, you have serious resistances to Air and Light magic; maybe one of those Gods can help us?" I offered, and Lydia smiled as she contemplated it.

"That would be…"

Congratulations!

You have discovered a new Quest: A Pillar of Strength.

Your bondswoman, Lydia, commander of your personal squad and close friend, has begun to evolve into a Valkyrie. To complete her evolution, and to become all she could be, she requires four things.

Resolution of the Past: 0/1
Completion of the Quest of the Last Valkyrie: 0/1
Find a Class Trainer: 0/1
Discover/Create/Recover Suitable Armor: 0/1
Reward: A full Valkyrie under your command, possibly more, 50,000xp

Accept: *Yes/No*

"Okay…" I muttered, blinking as the quest leaped up before me. I read it over and clicked accept, immediately looking to Lydia. She was clearly reading her own notifications, then blinked, nodded to herself, and smiled as she saw I'd accepted it.

"Thank you." She looked away so that I wouldn't see the tears in her eyes.

"Anytime," I replied, squeezing her shoulder. "We can talk more about this tonight. I'm sorry, but we have to move, now that we're in range. Are you sure you want to try this now?" I stood straighter and gestured toward the ship looming ahead of us. People were streaming out to stand on the deck and wave at us, clearly knowing who we were.

"Aye," Lydia said grimly. "Ah need ta learn, ain't no better time than tha present."

"Okay, then, I'll be with you, side by side, but only you know what you need to do." I nodded to her wings. She drew in a deep breath, saluted me, then closed her eyes and did…*something.*

Lydia's wings flared with light. Before, they'd been comprised of golden light, each feather indistinct and ephemeral. But suddenly, they were present in reality. The pinions were huge, white, and glowing with an inner light, making the world around us almost seem drab by comparison with these glorious white feathers.

"Fuck me, it's like a bleach commercial," I said without realizing it.

"What…?" Lydia asked distractedly.

"Nothing." I shook myself. "Okay, I doubt you can do this for long; you ready?" She grinned her confirmation.

"To be clear, I know precisely dick about flying with wings, so I hope it's an instinctual thing on your part." I raised one questioning eyebrow.

"Only one way to find out." She took three quick steps to the side of the railing and leaped off, diving over the side of the ship and into the open air.

"Fuuuuuck!" I ground out, rushing after her and jumping over the side as well.

Lydia had leapt gracefully, even dressed in battered armor that was missing the breastplate and helm. She looked amazing in her new form. I reverted to an equally instinctual response to diving over the side of anything and lifted my legs, wrapping my arms around my knees and shouting as I went.

"Cannonball!"

CHAPTER THREE

I plunged through the clouds after Lydia, who beat her wings roughly and irregularly, flying in random directions.

I grunted and straightened myself out, diving after her and holding on as long as I dared before activating Soaring Majesty.

As soon as it took effect, the feeling of being terrified and plunging to my death lessened somewhat, and I smoothed out my flight, curving around and closing on a frantically thrashing Lydia.

I spun and dove, coming up from under her and flipping around to face her, reaching out to catch her arms and fighting against the pull of the wind as I straightened her out.

"Stop!" I shouted over the sound of her terrified and irregular wingbeats. "Lydia, just stop!" She grabbed on tight to me, frantically staring into my eyes.

"I can't do it!" she screamed.

"You're wrong! You *can* do this, and you goddamn will!" I grasped her arms firmly and stared into her eyes. "You made it this far, you're the leader of the squad charged with the Lord of Dravith's personal security, you're a fucking badass, and you're a goddamn Valkyrie!" I shouted into her stunned face. "Now act like it, Optio!"

"I...I..." she cried, still trying to make sense of it all.

"I've got enough magic left for thirty seconds of flight, Lydia!" I screamed. "If you don't learn to fly in the next ten seconds, we'll both die!" With that, I spun around, wrapping her arms around my chest from behind and starting to lift her upwards while she frantically beat her wings.

"At the same damn time!" I shouted.

She nodded frantically, took a deep breath, straightening her wings out fully, then beat them once, hard.

We lifted like a rocket had been rammed up my ass, lunging upwards, before sagging back down when she stopped beating them.

"Again, you daft sod! Don't bloody stop halfway!" I shouted. She growled in my ear before beating them again, and again, faster and faster, to send the pair of us blasting upwards.

"We're going to be alongside the ship soon, but they can't see you yet," I called to her, gesturing upwards. "So you fly for them, Lydia! Show them who you are!" She met my gaze, worry in her eyes for a handful of seconds, before her resolve firmed. She shot her focus skyward, eyeing the low, dark clouds the fleet was flying over and that we'd plunged through.

The Valkyrie released me and beat her wings, shooting upwards, a slight wobble all that betrayed her inexperience. Lydia flew straight for the battleship, the clouds seeming to part magically for her as her speed increased. I struggled to keep up, having to bite down and push harder, increasing the drain of both health and mana to increase my speed.

I hurtled after her, barely making it up in time for her to erupt from the cloud cover to fly higher and higher, before flipping over and gliding around, lining herself up with the battleship.

I closed the distance and pulled in alongside her. Tears of pure joy flowed down her cheeks as she zeroed in on the deck.

We covered the last few hundred meters in seconds, and she flared her wings, the action seemingly a reflex now that she was no longer terrified. She swung her legs forward, causing people to scatter from the section of deck below her as she dropped, and I landed next to her.

While she landed on her feet and ran a few short steps to kill her momentum, I, of course, came in like a damn boss. Landing hard, my right fist and right knee slammed against the deck, left leg bent and out to the left, left arm thrown behind me.

"Holysufferingfuck!!" I ground out between clenched teeth as the deck below me, thick planks of oak or something similar, creaked under the force of my landing, and I heard the crunch of my kneecap.

I stayed like that for a long second before Oracle, who'd been following us, hit me with a heal, and I let out a long, grateful sigh.

I straightened up, coming to my feet as Lydia's wings faded back to translucent. Oracle swept in to land nearby in her full-sized, rather than treat-sized form.

"Next time you do that, I'm going to leave you looking like an idiot with a broken knee," Oracle whispered to me furiously through teeth gritted in a wide smile for everyone else.

I swallowed and nodded in sheepish thanks as I caught the looks on the faces of those around us as they cheered.

I smiled and held up a hand, waving to people, then reached out, grasping Lydia's right hand in my left and lifting it as well, getting more cheers.

I glimpsed her eyes and saw the stunned amazement. As many of the cheers were for her as they were for me, and plenty of those cheering were hard-bitten legionnaires.

Whatever else had happened in her life, she'd grown up poor, she'd been made to feel as though she had no value, then the asshole she'd married, who should have been the one to worship and raise her up, had sold her into slavery when she didn't give him sons.

She'd spent her entire existence being beaten and tortured, mentally and physically, made to believe that she was useless and that the world would always take from her. In the space of a few short weeks, all that had changed.

To me, Lydia showed all that was wrong with this realm, yet she also showed all the amazing potential. I was damn well determined to help her into the best possible version of herself.

"Lord Jax, Lady Wisp, Lydia," Romanus greeted from my right as he strode through the crowd. Gawking people were being systematically moved aside gently but firmly by Restun, the Legion's Centurion Primus, to let him pass.

"Romanus, Restun!" I called, having to raise my voice above the din of the people all around us. "Good to see you, my friends, but we need to talk." I fixed them with an intent look that let them know I was deadly serious.

"Legion!" Restun bellowed into the air, his trained voice cutting through the clamor like a hot knife through butter. "An escort for the Imperial Lord!"

It took bare seconds as the legionnaires around us moved like the gears of a well-oiled machine, splitting the crowd and forming up to give us a corridor to the bridge. They smoothly maintained the space by moving with us, making sure that nobody got in the way.

The crowds parted, understanding that something had happened. While they were still clearly overjoyed, and the morale boost of seeing our flight was fresh in their hearts, they stepped aside quickly.

"It's a hell of a relief to have you back, Lord Jax," Romanus said quietly as soon as we reached the first hatch, stepping in ahead of me and leading me through the rabbit warren of passages and stairwells to the quarters I'd been given next to the bridge.

"It's a relief to be back," I said, indulging in a quick smile before setting my lips in a grim line. "I just wish it were with better news. Can someone get Athena and Augustus as well, please?" I asked the accompanying legionnaires as we stepped into my quarters.

"Aye, sir!" one of the legionnaires barked, clapping fist to chest in salute before peeling off and jogging down the hall and vanishing from sight as Lydia closed the door to the corridor, leaving her, Oracle, Romanus, Restun, and myself inside.

I took stock of the room, observing far more conveniences than had been present before, including three rough chairs, a table, and a long, low cot.

Someone, or several someones, had been working their arses off to make these items in the little time they'd had. "Thank you." I said.

"It was the pleasure of those with a little woodworking skill to make these for you, Jax," Restun said gruffly. "There will be more, and better, soon."

"Now, I don't think that's what you wanted to discuss?" Romanus cut in grimly.

"No, but we need…ah." I broke off at a knock on the door, and a familiar legionnaire opened it quickly, ducking his head in.

"Captain Athena and Chief Engineer Elise, my lord?" he announced hesitantly.

I waved for him to let them both in.

He stepped aside, and they rushed in, quickly standing to attention.

"Athena, I need you to maintain this course and this speed, as well as ensuring that any nets or blankets or bedding and such that you can provide are piled up on the foredeck. Mal is going to pull across the ship's bow, and my squad will be dropping from ropes to join us here," I stated. She nodded, slipping back out of the door to relay the orders before returning quickly.

"Wha' happened?" Elise asked gruffly. The short, broad dwarven woman spoke with a rough Scottish accent, and it always made me smile. Or at least, it usually did. Even the incongruous differences between the grim dwarven chief engineer and the tall, willowy, gaudily dressed elven captain, Athena, failed to elicit more than a momentary smile from me.

"The shit hit the fan," I replied tersely, before sighing at the looks on their faces due to the unfamiliar phrase. "It's an idiom from my home…land." I sat in one of the nearest chairs and gestured for the others to make themselves as comfortable as they could. "It means something has gone very wrong, and in this case, it's the Dark Legion." As soon as I mentioned the Dark Legion, Romanus and Restun stiffened, dark intent in their eyes.

"There was an…incident…when we were leaving the city, you'll remember?" I asked, and everyone nodded. "Well, as Nimon has personally named me an apostate and declared me an Enemy of the Church, it seems those fuckers are on their way to the Tower. I don't know how many there are in total, but there's a force of around three or four hundred, and they're using a lot of magic to race toward our fortress."

"Trailmasters?" Romanus asked.

"Apparently so," I said regretfully. "They're headed for the Tower," I repeated, "and we're all here. There's a basic, and very weak, force of hunters and volunteers to protect it, as well as a few golems, but they're all construction variants, so they won't be a great deal of use."

"What are your orders?" Romanus persisted.

"I want to split the fleet and the Legion. We can't take too many, in case there's another stealth attack on the fleet. So I'll take two cruisers, and of the, what, hundred plus legionnaires we have? I'll take sixty and two of the War Golems. The others will remain here, protecting the fleet and continuing to make repairs to the battleship."

"We could take more," Romanus countered, but I shook my head.

"I don't think so." I leaned forward, resting my elbows on my knees, and clasped my hands together. "We were attacked by a small fleet of ships that were hidden with magic. They used catapults to fire dozens of DarkSpore at us. They also had tame juvenile SporeMothers on the decks, as well as appearing to be commanded by a group of Drow. With all that, do you really think it's a good idea to leave the ships defenseless?"

"Most definitely not; however, the primary task of the Legion is to protect the Empire." He frowned with concern. "The heart of the Empire is you. I assume you won't be staying here and sending the Legion ahead to protect the Tower?"

I shook my head.

"In that case, I recommend taking more of the Legion and at least two fast scouts or another Cruiser."

"Athena, how many ships do you think you need to protect this battleship and these people against what I just described?" I addressed her.

"At least six more than we have." She swallowed hard. "I'd want a cordon of ships out a half-mile at each of the compass points, not to mention two on high-altitude overwatch."

"See?" I asked Romanus.

"Of course." He inclined his head in acknowledgement. "However, how many are in the enemy fleet?"

"Well, there were eight," I said, shrugging. "The last we saw of it, there was only one ship left, and it was damaged…"

"Ah!" Romanus perked up.

"But! As far as we knew, the cities of Himnel and Narkolt were at war, and all the information we have still says that's the case. That's not even taking into account the SporeMothers and Drow, yet a mixed fleet from both factions was used, and it was hidden with magic. Another ship could be hiding off our starboard bow, right now, and we'd never know it."

"Or you could have destroyed them all, and the damaged one has crashed."

"Could be, but I doubt it. I'm not that fucking lucky," I retorted grimly, making Restun smile.

"Luck is what you make of it," Romanus said.

A knock rocked the door again, followed by the same legionnaire sticking his head in and speaking quickly. "My lord, Tribune Alistor is here…"

I gestured to let him in. Romanus quickly brought a stern-faced Alistor up to date while I weighed the details.

"What do you think?" I asked the room in general. "Give me some options, please."

"I take half the Legion on one of the cruisers, we perform a rear-guard action, alternating a stand-up fight with small forces of the Dark Legion and ambushes, after the Cruiser rakes the column by air, firing the ships' cannons," Restun suggested after a nod from Romanus.

"Not what I'm looking for, although it's a possibility. Thank you, Restun," I said after a few seconds' consideration. I needed the delay, yes, but I couldn't afford the losses.

"We send a small cadre of the Legion's elite ahead, along with the support personnel, specifically Denny and his group of combat engineers. They can lay traps at the halfway mark, then fall back and fortify the Tower, while the rest of the Legion sets up for a fight at a halfway point. We hit them again when they've been injured but have grown lax in their watch. Use the ships to provide covering fire and take out the column with ranged and cannon fire, then the Legion mops up," Romanus suggested.

"Leave the Tower and head to sea," Alistor stated bluntly.

"What?" I blinked, not sure if I'd heard right.

"You suspect that the Dark Legion force is an advance party; a scout, correct?" he asked, and I frowned but gestured for him to continue. "Then, I recommend you leave the Tower. It would be a mighty fortress if it were intact, but you stated previously that it is damaged and weak. Therefore, there is no point in making a last stand there. Leave the Dark Legion to take it. It will tie them down as they try to hold it, and our ships can take us to a new, hidden location to build a new force," Alistor said as though it was a stroke of genius. When he glanced at the others and saw no support for his plan, he sighed and went on.

"The Dark Legion is our equal, as galling as that is to admit, and that is in terms of training alone. Add in their numbers, better equipment, and the fact that they are supported by a God? Realistically, if we were to defeat the advance force, we would likely be greatly weakened. Add their main force, one that we can assume will be dispatched either shortly after to follow along, or once their advance force is destroyed, and we would be compelled to retreat.

"I simply suggest we don't waste the lives of the Legion in an unlikely scenario. Instead, we leave, head to another continent. We have supplies for the ships, after all. Food stores may be low, but we could stop off and purchase more from several villages and forage, not to mention fishing. Water can be summoned by magic. Once we reach the nearest continent, we search for remnants of the Legions, we take command of them, and build a new army, then return and defeat the Dark Legion at a later date. This is simple logistics."

"And what about the Tower itself?" I asked through gritted teeth. "What about the goddamn people there?"

"They have airships, do they not?" He waved his hand dismissively.

"They have two ships. That's not enough to get everyone out safely, let alone considering the stupidity of abandoning the Tower!" I snapped, fighting to keep my anger in check. "Not an option I want to hear again."

"That's understandable, Lord Jax," Romanus said smoothly, lifting his hands in supplication. "Alistor was giving an option, as you requested, that's all."

"A cowardly one," I heard Lydia mutter under her breath. Alistor stood straighter, stepping away from the wall he had been leaning against and glaring at her.

"You have something to say to me...*Legion-Aspirant?*" he snarled with thinly veiled derision. Before I could remind everyone that, even though Lydia was unofficially accepted as Optio of my personal Guard, she wasn't yet a full legionnaire, Romanus was there, stepping between Lydia and Alistor.

"Tribune Alistor was offering options, that is all," he repeated firmly, shooting Lydia and myself a warning look before turning back to level a similar glare at Alistor. "Despite suggesting actions that are inimical to everything the Legion stands for *in abandoning the innocent*,"—Romanus's tone was scathing—"they are still a valid, if despicable, option."

"Alternatively, if the Tower was surrendered, it would tie up the Dark Legion," Restun added coldly, scowling at Alistor. "Then our ships could retreat to a staging point and be sent for lightning raids on the main force, using the primary cannons to devastating effect, while they would be compelled to leave a holding force at the Tower."

Restun looked at me in question, and I gestured for him to continue. "Rather than leaving the continent, we could use our newfound mobility to our advantage and harry and ambush the Dark Legion instead of facing them in open battle."

"A coward's way," Alistor retorted scathingly.

"Really, dude? *That*, coming from *you?*" I pointedly ignored the reddening of his neck and his furiously clenched jaw.

"Do we have any reason to believe the fleet that attacked us at the Sunken City is working with the Dark Legion?" Romanus asked calmly, interrupting the building tension between Alistor and me.

"No, but we can't discount it," I replied. "Did you get all of your legionnaires out of the Prax?" I glanced from Restun to Romanus. "I'm sorry; I should have asked when I first arrived." Another knock interrupted to announce that Augustus had finally arrived, filling me with relief, considering what I had planned. As he stepped inside, the tell-tale wisp of mist hung in the corridor, and I suppressed a laugh, more than a little amused at the pair of them.

"You can come in as well, Hellenica," I called out. And a few seconds later, she slipped in as I reached out and gripped Augustus's wrist in greeting. He pumped my arm once, jovially, then leaned against a wall, watching over us all in an identical pose to Restun's, simply on the opposite side of the room.

"Three died underground, two more in storming the Himnel camp," Romanus relayed, his face set. "The Himnel ship was captured. The Narkolt vessel was permitted to leave when it became obvious that those aboard were free, not slaves, and word reached the Legion team that you had ordered us to leave." He looked directly at me then, a question in his eyes.

"You did well. I'm only sorry we lost those legionnaires." I drew in a deep breath. "I'm also thankful that you listened to Oracle, as that couldn't have been an easy call to make. I've had the time, both in the Sunken City and when we were catching up to you, to have a good think about things. As such, until such a time as someone more suited comes along, I need an heir." I couldn't help smiling at the shocked faces that watched me, especially Augustus'.

"There are some incredibly good reasons for this, but first and foremost, this is a tactical decision. I've taken the time to consider what you said, Romanus, about my role and my place in all this. I might not like some of it, but I'm sure as shit not standing down. As such, I've had it beaten into me that, if something happens to me, the Empire returns to what it was: a leaderless mess that's slowly falling apart."

I stood up and crossed to stand in the middle of the room, facing Augustus.

"I need to have an heir, Augustus, and I know, given your personal situation…" I winked at Hellenica before looking back to him. "…there will be some who will disagree with my choice. However, as I am the Scion of the Empire, and the highest authority within it, I also decided that I don't give a fuck." I drew in a deep breath, and I felt Oracle reaching out and sinking my mana into the proclamation.

Attention, Citizens of the Territory of Dravith!

Jax, High Lord of Dravith, Scion of the Empire, has named an Imperial Heir!

All Hail Augustus Vertais Asen Amon, Heir to the Imperial Throne and Imperial Duke of Himnel!

As always, the proclamation opened in everyone's vision, overriding their wishes and remaining until they had read it, the fancy letters formed of golden smoke on an ornate backdrop of black surrounded by scrollwork.

I dismissed it, and scanned the room, trying not to chuckle as I thought about the asshole, Barabarattas. I'd stripped him of his title, and not only had I just replaced him in the peerage, but since the fall of the Empire, no noble could lay claim to a title beyond Lord, as they had to be ratified by a member of the Imperial family.

By assigning myself to the role of High Lord and Augustus to the title of Duke, I'd practically pissed on all of their titles while making it clear that there was still hope for them if they behaved themselves.

The new Duke Augustus gaped at the screen before him in utter shock and a tangible degree of horror as he tried to comprehend what had just happened.

"Well, let me be the first to congratulate you…Duke!" I laughed, stepping forward and gripping his shoulders as he dismissed the screen. "I'm sorry I had to do this without consulting you first, but you'd have tried to talk me out of it."

"Jax…I…"

I grinned, then returned to sit down. Romanus and Restun stepped forward, each going to one knee before Augustus, and he froze in astonishment. I noted the scowl on Alistor's face, but just as I was about to say something, he finally took a knee, as did the others in the room.

"Please, no, there's no need. Stand!" Augustus said, his voice weak with surprise and horror but growing stronger as he went on. "This is a temporary ascension. Please, tell me that's so?" he turned pleading eyes to me.

"Until you're dead, or I find someone better," I said, quoting an old movie I'd loved.

"Oh, Gods no," Augustus whispered, reaching for Hellenica, who looked stricken, as she took his hand in hers.

"There are no rules regarding your relationships, either," I interjected forcefully. "You are my heir because I need to ensure the continuity of the Empire, Augustus, and I know of nobody else who is as suitable. You're a good man, you have the utter devotion of your legionnaires, and hell, assassins wouldn't last seconds against you.

"You know my wishes regarding the Empire; Gods know we've spoken of it enough. No slavery, a safe place for the innocent, justice for those who need it, punishment for the guilty, and a future for my...*our* people. I needed to make sure that was protected.

"I approve of your relationship with Hellenica, so let anyone that has a problem bring it to *me* directly." I scanned the faces present and found no open dissent, although Alistor gave me an obviously forced smile. "After all, my lover and partner is Oracle, and let me assure you, if I hear a single disparaging word about that relationship, I'll be *very*...blunt...in my response.

"Now, moving on...Augustus, I'll bring you up to date soon, but right now, we need to start moving. As the saying goes in my lands, a good plan executed now beats an excellent plan executed later. I've listened to your advice, and as it's my place, I've made a decision.

"Romanus, I want sixty legionnaires, fully armed and provisioned, along with two-thirds of the manastones prepped. We will find a clear spot to land when we reach the coast, and they, I, and my team will transfer over and take two cruisers and a fast scout. I'll need someone to lead the legionnaires with me, as Augustus will be here." I caught the brief frown that crossed his face, and I grinned.

"Get used to it, Augustus. Now that you're a member of the Imperial family and in the line of succession, you and I can't both be placed at risk!" I ignored his indignant sputtering as I continued outlining my plan. "I'll take two of the War Golems, a Complex and a standard; you pick which," I directed to Augustus before turning back to Romanus. "I'll need the rest of you all, not to mention the ships, at the Tower as soon as possible, but I can't wait for everyone. Athena, how long would it take the fleet, heading at the maximum safe speed, to reach the Great Tower?"

"Jax, we are already traveling faster than I believe we should, but if we were to reduce to a safe speed, fifty-two to sixty hours, depending on the winds." She frowned. "My estimate is due to the condition of the battleship, the damage from that storm..."

"And how long for the fastest two cruisers and a fast scout?" I interrupted.

"Maybe eighteen; at most twenty-four, providing they push the engines to the limit and the winds are favorable," Athena confirmed. I looked questioningly at Romanus, who sighed in acquiescence.

"I understand the necessity, and I am pleased by your forethought, Jax," he admitted. "Bearing that in mind, and as Duke Augustus..."

"Please, Prefect!" Augustus begged, gawking in horror at the man who'd led him for his entire adult life.

"Very well, as *Augustus* will be remaining here, I will lead the Legion with you, personally," Romanus amended, sharing a look with Restun, who nodded once. "And it seems the mighty Centurion Primus will join me."

I experienced an immediate rush of both relief and terror. There would be no better men to have by my side, if it couldn't be Augustus or Tommy. My asshole also involuntarily clenched at the knowledge that I'd be unable to escape Restun and his evil training plans.

"Then let's get a damn move on." I scratched the back of my neck. "Alistor, I'd like you to get things moving now, please, and make sure to include Thorn in the teams that come with me, as we all need some repairs and new armor." I dismissed him with a gesture, and he rose, striding from the room with the bare minimum of a salute. I bit down on my irritation; I'd torn his world apart, and his attitude was understandable, but I relaxed the instant he was out of the room.

"Lord Jax, I appreciate your patience..." Romanus said, sighing at his subordinate's brusque departure.

"I know I'm not what you all hoped for. I came in and dragged you from your homes and upended centuries of tradition. That's why I'm being patient. *However*, I'll be honest, I'm pretty shit at being patient, and if his attitude doesn't improve, and very damn soon, I'll be giving him a sharply pointed lesson in respect." I sent a controlled flare of magic into my casually retrieved naginata.

The entire room understood my thinly veiled warning as glowing flames licked along its length. I hoped this would be the end of it. I regarded Restun, who practically vibrated with outrage at the disrespect shown to me, and I had another, if slightly evil, idea.

"In fact, who deals with disciplinary issues in the Legion currently?" I asked Romanus.

"As Prefect, it is my responsibility, but since the loss of the Legion-General, I have had my hands full with much of his role, not to mention the logistics required by recent events. I apologize, Lord Jax," he said, bowing his head and making as though to sink to one knee.

"Ah! No," I said, holding one hand up. "I told you, Romanus, you don't need to kneel to me. Once was enough. Moving on, however, I'd like to discuss a slight restructuring. As things stand, I obviously can't continue to have my squad outside of the chain of command."

Romanus looked relieved and returned to his chair, while Lydia stiffened, fearing she was about to lose command of her squad.

"Of course, Jax. It's your right and privilege to order the Legion as you will," Romanus said calmly, but I detected the changes in their postures, all tensely watching me.

"I don't want to change much, don't worry." I held my hands up reassuringly. "Your own role as Prefect is to manage the Legion itself, while the Legion General would consider and plan things from an overall tactical position, while you, as Prefect, would take those aims and develop the strategies to make them...well, to make them happen?"

"Yes, that is a simplified description, but it is accurate," Romanus confirmed, smiling.

"Good, and I understand the Tribune is essentially what in my home would be called a staff officer, someone who would be responsible for carrying out the orders of those higher, dealing with pay issues, paperwork, and so on?"

Romanus nodded, but frowned, likely expecting me to remove Alistor from the position.

"Excellent," I muttered, thinking back to the general thoughts I'd had over the last few days. "Don't worry, I'm not going to be changing anything like that. I'm the outsider here, and while, yes, I'm the Scion, I'm a brawler at heart. I want to learn; I *need* to learn, and to have you help me. The last thing I want to do is screw up the Legion. So, we will leave things the same there, with me essentially picking up some of the Legion General's role for the time being." I took a deep breath and continued outlining my carefully crafted thoughts.

"I want to fold my squad into the Legion, with Lydia remaining in command of them. You've made comments before about my team not being up to scratch, Restun, and I can't believe I'm saying this, but I'm not either. We need your help. I'd like the Centurion Primus to take over the full training of my squad and myself, personally. I know you'd already agreed to train us, but I think it needs to be formally acknowledged and permanent..." I said, even as my asshole clenched even tighter.

"He seemed happy to do it when we talked about it before, but he would have a specific role, and it would be to turn my squad—should they choose to stay with me—into full legionnaires, worthy of the rank of Praetorian Guards."

I felt as much as heard the indrawn breaths around the room.

"We are none of us fit for that yet, not even close, but these are the people I trust most. Due to such a high-profile role, I'll offer them a choice. Some might want to take a step back, and that's fine. I want a team of ten or so; it seems to work, after all. I'd like the Centurion Primus to put forward some suggestions to replace any who may choose to leave. He will become the first member of the Praetorian Guard and have the responsibility of training the rest of us to reach that same height. Lydia will be formally accepted as Optio of the Praetorian Guard when she reaches the rank of full legionnaire, if, and only if, she passes the Primus' tests.

"I would have chosen Augustus to lead the Praetorian Guard if it were based simply on my own comfort, as I know how damn skilled you are, my friend." I shot a look at him and smiled. "Not to mention that I think Restun will probably make me want to die in the process of training me, and I'll wish for easy days like those in the arena, but I have to be realistic."

Augustus winced as he pondered the hell I was setting myself up for.

"Restun, do you accept the rank of Centurion Primus of the Praetorian Guard?" I asked him, standing and crossing to stand before him. He straightened, flooded by the first sign of emotion beyond anger and determination I'd seen. Pride rose on his face, and relief as he nodded brusquely.

The return of the Praetorian Guard was the ultimate dream for the Legion, and making him, a staff sergeant who terrified other staff sergeants, into its gatekeeper would ensure that only the best of the best were permitted.

"Thank you." I held my hand out to him and took his wrist in my own. "Congratulations, Centurion Primus Praetoria." I felt Oracle adding our mana into my words, and a second proclamation was created.

Hear this and rejoice, Legionnaires!

**Restun Ath Noria, Centurion Primus of the Legion of Himnel,
is now Centurion Primus Praetoria,
the first member of the Praetorian Guard of Imperial Scion Jax Amon.**

I pulled up my character sheet and verified that, yeah, my name had been changed. I was no longer Jax, but now Jax Amon, and I grinned, deciding that if I had to have a surname again, one that identified me as part of the Emperor's family wasn't too bad.

I returned my attention to Restun, who was practically vibrating with a suppressed need to be moving, and no doubt training, new members of the Praetorian Guard.

"Right, before we're dragged off to begin training, and remember, I need time to plan and to give orders as well, Restun..." I interjected, staring insistently at him. "I guess it's time to bring you up to date."

It took half an hour to fill everyone in on the events back at the Sunken City, and another two hours to go over my plans for now, embryonic as they were.

Once that was done, and Athena had confirmed we were at least seven hours at top speed from the coast and the nearest safe place we could land to manage the transfer, I shooed everyone out of my room.

I smiled at the sound of Lydia asking Restun for details of his training plan as they walked away. Then I sighed, knowing I was in for a world of pain after basically giving Restun permission to kick my ass for the foreseeable future.

I sat back in the chair, lost in thoughts of the pain that was coming, until Oracle leaned in and kissed me deeply. Then she gently but firmly disengaged my arms from around her neck before ordering Bane from the room.

I hadn't even realized he was on the ship, much less into the room, I'd been so distracted by the planning. Clearly, the Legion had accepted his role, as they had not even consulted me about admitting him into the room after my squad had jumped on board. Once Oracle chased him out, she turned back around, leaning with her back against the door, grinning at me.

I smiled back, standing and tugging off my armor, as she lifted her arms above her head, sending a glittering red dust showering from her hands.

As it flowed down her body, her clothes dissolved, leaving behind the little red outfit she'd teased me with before, and I immediately sprang to attention.

Or at least part of me did. I almost fell over in my haste to remove my armored pants, but as quickly as we could both manage it, I was naked, and she was in my arms.

The next several hours were spent, not in rest we both knew I needed, but in a different kind of relief, one that was very welcome indeed.

CHAPTER FOUR

A knock on the door stirred me from deep sleep, and I snorted, shaking my head and looking around the room.

"Mrpgh?" I grunted, trying to focus my sleep-addled mind. Blinking repeatedly, I couldn't help grinning as the sight before me came into focus. Oracle and I had been damn thankful for the cot that had been provided for us. It was low, but wide enough for the two of us to share it comfortably, even if there wasn't a blanket that was large enough.

I'd solved that minor issue by falling asleep half across Oracle's naked body, and the fantastic "pillows" came into focus for me as I blinked one last time, stirring fully to life.

"Oh yes, *please*," I whispered, leaning my head to one side and kissing the skin there, feeling it tighten in reaction to my lips as I moved up, flicking my tongue out and grinning naughtily into Oracle's eyes.

The knock sounded again, and I sagged into that most wonderful pillow, letting out a regretful sigh.

"Yes?" I called, lifting my head, and a second later came a muffled response.

"Ah, sorry to disturb you, Lord Jax," an unfamiliar legionnaire's voice replied, the gruffness from years of barking orders half-hidden by embarrassment and respect, "but Prefect Romanus ordered that you be made aware, we're two hours from landfall."

"Dammit," I muttered. "Okay, thank you!" I called back loudly enough to be heard, resting my face back down on warm skin.

"Two hours," Oracle whispered, reaching down to pull my face out of the valley of her perfect chest and guide my lips inexorably back to the nipple I'd been kissing. I grinned as I felt her other hand questing downwards. I crawled up the bed, reaching out for her as she did the same, and the next hour passed far, far too fast.

We sprawled on the floor, panting, sweaty, and definitely in need of a shower, when another knock sounded out.

"Jax, is it safe to come in?" Bane's voice filtered through the wooden barrier. I swore, trying to catch my breath.

Oracle lifted into the air, her figure shimmering into a clean and decently dressed state in an instant, before she landed delicately and threw the blanket over my nakedness.

"More or less!" I called out, laughing ruefully at her and shaking my head with chagrin. I might have finally gained the ability to fly, but getting clean like that was a hell of a trick I still had to learn. "Then again, showers *are* a hell of a lot of fun as well" I muttered, climbing up and sitting on the bed while keeping my body covered with the blanket.

Bane stepped in, tugged the door closed behind him, and looked from one of us to the other.

"Really?" he scoffed, shaking his head. "We're out there being assessed by the evilest legionnaire in history, his tongue alone beating us senseless, and you're in here...how did you put it...banging like an outhouse door in plague country?"

"You're only jealous." I snorted, shrugging dismissively.

"Jealous? No, more considering murdering you because of that trick with the Praetorian Guard!" Bane growled. "You know you didn't ask any of us if we wanted to stay on the team before setting him loose on us, right?"

"Shit." My heart dropped. "I meant to do that today; I got distracted," I admitted, rubbing my face.

"Distracted...right." Bane angled his face toward Oracle, who looked a little sheepish as she swallowed what she'd been about to say.

"Do you want to leave my team? To return to your village or to do another job in the Tower?" I asked Bane respectfully.

He froze before letting out a subsonic 'thrummm' that was his equivalent of laughter. "Damn, no! I've not had so much fun in...well...ever!" the Mer admitted. "But it's not about how much fun I'm having, anyway. I swore to follow you and keep you safe, remember? I'm not going anywhere, but I can't say the same for the others."

"Who?" I asked, relieved that Bane, at least, was staying.

"You need to speak to them all," he insisted, crossing his upper pair of arms. "They might be happy to stay, but they deserve the option, and to hear it from you that you put Restun over them."

"Shit," I repeated as I stood, discarding the blanket to get dressed, unconcerned with my unclothed state. Bane had seen it all before.

"Good Gods, warn me first," Bane grunted, turning away. "The last thing I want to see is *that...*"

"You're just jealous," I retorted.

"Of that shriveled prawn? Honestly, all I feel is pity for you and for any females foolish enough to bed you. How do you deal with the disappointment they must feel?" he quipped blithely. The next few minutes while I dressed were spent in a friendly barrage of insults, ranging from each other's sexual capacity to the predilection for farmyard animals and small, furry mammals.

As I settled the last section of my severely damaged armor in place, Bane tilted his head curiously.

"Why are you wearing that?" he asked. "You've always refused to suspect the legionnaires of being a threat."

"Because I want Thorn to see what her armor did for me." I gestured at the irreparably damaged equipment. "I want her to see that, without it, I'd have died a dozen times over."

"It also looks like it was poorly made. It's practically falling apart," Bane pointed out, making me miss a step as I opened the door. I cursed internally, hoping I hadn't just made another tremendous fuckup.

We headed to the bridge, and I couldn't help looking around upon entering the large, semicircular room. I was amazed by the changes that had been wrought in such a short period of time.

Entire banks of dead controls had been left open, and hatches into systems glowed and crackled, with windows boarded over and the wind of our passage whistling through the room as we flew, now there was an efficient and bustling room in its place.

The four main banks of controls were all lit and manned, men and women of different races seated at the controls and communicating in terse but confident voices as they watched through the wide glass windows.

Athena sat in a large chair at the center of the bridge, one leg thrown over the arm of the huge wooden monstrosity as she fiddled with a cushion and argued good-naturedly with Elise.

The tall elven Captain and the short dwarven chief engineer broke off, the first leaping to her feet, while the other simply grunted and nodded deferentially to me.

"Attention!" Athena barked, and the bridge crew leaped up, clapping fists to chests as I walked through.

"Thank you, but please relax," I said, privately amused at the fear on the helmsman's face as he eyed the controls, followed by relief as he grabbed them again.

"My Lord Jax," Athena greeted, gesturing to her chair. "We're closing in on the coast; do you wish to sit?"

"No," I said, shaking my head. "You're the captain here, Athena. I came to get an estimate, that's all."

"Until we land?" she asked. I nodded. "Fifteen, maybe twenty minutes, my lord." She strode to the window and pointed ahead. "You see the meadows to the right?"

Directly below and ahead of the fleet were huge grey cliffs that stretched from north to south, surrounded by hundreds of seabirds that wheeled and dipped into the water, scooping up fish.

Behind the cliffs, the land split, with a heavily forested region to the left, right, and far side. In the middle, a large lake reflected the late afternoon sun.

I drank in the view, amazed at how easily I'd lost track of days and nights, further clarified by my grumbling stomach. On the right side of the lake stood a meadow that gently sloped toward the water, the space she was referencing.

"We'll land there. It'll give us the space we need to unload the battleship and redistribute items to the fast scout and the cruisers. Romanus ordered the cruisers *Ragnarök* and *Sigmar's Fist* to be prepared with the *Summer's Promise* as the fastest scout to accompany them. The crews have been getting everything ready. It shouldn't take long to transfer everything, maybe two hours, then you can be on your way."

"Your estimate of eighteen to twenty-four hours; that didn't include this time, did it?" I asked.

"No, Jax." She shook her head. "That was if the cruisers set off at full speed from that immediate moment. From here? Maybe sixteen to twenty hours, considering that the westerly wind is dropping, so it's actually not too bad."

"True." I acknowledged begrudgingly. "Thank you, Athena. I need to get out there. I know I asked you for suggestions for the ships' names earlier; do you have any for me?"

"Three, actually," she said, smiling. "The *Orion*, *Imperial Justice*, and lastly…" She paused, and I nodded for her to go on. "*Dreadnought*."

"I like them." I tapped my chin thoughtfully. "What's your preference?"

"*Dreadnought*," she replied promptly. "After all, once she's finished, I don't think there will be much she'll dread."

"Good point." I smiled. "Very well, she will be christened *Dreadnought* upon completion. Are you happy with that?"

"Very! It was the name I personally chose, and I just won a bottle of rotgut from Elise on that." She winked at me, eliciting another smile, despite my worry over the team.

"Glad to hear it, though I'd be wary of her choice of drinks. She seemed to go for the roughest, judging from the stuff she was drinking when we first met."

"Hah! I'll have you know, I can drink her under the table!" Athena declared, a twinkle in her eye. "Everyone always thinks Elves are all into wee drinks with paper umbrellas and shit in them. Believe me, we can outdrink a wee Dwarf any day!"

"I don't give a shit about how strong it is; I meant that it was cheap-ass crap, according to Mal," I warned her. She frowned, then shrugged in apathetic dismissal.

"Whut? Tha' absolute bastard were givin' in tha cheap shit?" Elise gasped, before chuckling despite her own indignance. "Ach, well, it be tasty at least!"

"Fuck it, it all goes down." Athena heaved a little sigh. "You spend time in the slave pits, and you stop caring about little details!"

"Fair enough." I left them to their debate over who would be drinking who under the table, glancing out onto the deck, as I'd just caught a glimpse of the reflected golden light of Lydia's wings at the far end. "I'm going to go see my team, then get my shit together. I'll see you at the Tower, Athena, Elise; good luck." With that, I clasped their wrists, pumped them once each and released, heading down the stairs onto the deck. Pausing for a moment, I closed my eyes, taking a deep breath of the crisp, cold air that rushed past.

Invigorated, I strode across the deck, watching as the behemoth airship lowered itself in preparation. The bow dipped towards the waves which slammed against the huge cliffs below, and a bunch of lunatics leaned against a low railing that had been attached to the front of the ship. One lifted his arms and screamed, "Whoooo-hoo!" at the top of his voice.

"Those idiots are our idiots, aren't they?" I asked the seemingly empty air nearby.

Bane responded calmly...from my other side.

"They are. More importantly, though, why are you talking to the air? Do you need to go sit down somewhere? Want me to go get you a blanket and a cuttlefish?" That last bit was said in the kind of voice people used when talking to small children when they bruised their knee, and I gritted my teeth.

"No, you dick, I was talking to you...and why the hell would I want a cuttlefish?!"

"They have a large, solid bone in the middle, good to suck on. We save it and give it to our younglings when their teeth come in, since it eases the pain," Bane explained, unperturbed by my outburst.

"Well, fuck you, too," I told him, shaking my head and walking on. I ended up having to take a roundabout route, due to sections of the upper deck being unfinished and entirely missing in many places.

Gleaming tubes and dull metal piping, bracings, and entire mechanical sections were visible through the gaps in the deck, some of which looked like they would take months, if not years, to complete properly. I grimaced as I looked down, until I remembered the shield rune that we'd taken from the Magical Emporium.

If I could get that working and fixed around the ship at strategic intervals, that could be a terminal surprise for someone when their shots burst apart...

I shook my head as I dismissed the thought, drawing a deep breath as I worried about the possibilities to come.

I skirted around another gap in the decking, spotting a Golem, standing seemingly frozen. The massive construct appeared to be holding a wall up as three engineers worked to bolt it into place. I nearly missed a step as I noticed another hulking figure hiding in the corridor behind the engineers. It must have stood at least nine feet in height and would have to be hunched over in the corridors when upright. It had a weird-shaped head, like someone had decided the look they were going for was a split-jawed hammerhead shark and had simply grabbed a troll's head and...pulled the eyes out to the sides on protrusions, leaving the jaw in the middle.

It had a thick hide, akin to that of a troll or an ogre, but despite its huge, muscular frame and its claws, it crouched there docilely, seeming content with watching the engineers.

I fired off a Greater Examination spell, reading it over as I absently fingered the haft of my naginata.

Durg Guntersson, Amilith Laborer

Durg is a Mountain Amilith, a species distantly related to trolls, but usually found at lower elevations. While they do not share the regenerative properties of the Trolls, they exhibit the same thick skin and unconcern with weather.

Note: Durg has received massively traumatic damage to his skull, resulting in a highly diminished mental capacity.

Weaknesses: 25% weakness to Fire, 50% to Death and Light spells.
Resistances: Both Earth and Water magics used against an Amilith are 50% less effective.
Level: 4
Health: 520/520
Stamina: 1060/1060
Mana: 50/50

"What the hell?" I muttered in confusion. I needed to speak to the team; then I'd find out who this Durg was and why he was lurking in the corridors, watching the engineers.

At least he wouldn't be a threat with the Golems present; I remembered Oracle telling me about a subroutine that was inbuilt to defend the citizens of the Empire, and despite the size of the Golems, they were fast.

I turned my back on the gap and covered the last dozen meters to the rest of my team, finding the usual suspects clinging to the railing, along with Barrett, Joya, and, much to my surprise, Giint.

I moved into a gap and took hold of the railing, looking down from the front of the ship as we picked up speed again. The entire ship tilted slowly to one side as it curved toward the meadow, and my stomach dropped as the dive flattened out, grass and small trees suddenly flashing by underneath, instead of the sea. Scanning the horizon, I noticed Mal on his *Falcon* in the distance, heading off toward a small hut at the far end of the valley, on the shores of the lake.

"Sneaky bastard. That must be where he's getting his alchemy ingredients." I shielded my eyes and stared at the hut in the distance. It was tiny, as far away as it was, but it appeared to have fields of crops surrounding it, and I nodded in satisfaction. "He must have been gutted when we chose to land here to do the transfer…" I muttered.

"What?" Barrett called over the sound of the rushing wind.

"Nothing!" I shouted back, then shook my head. It was going to be impossible to talk in this wind until we slowed or landed, and I'd hardly make them happier with me if I made them come inside right now.

I smiled at him and Joya and simply relaxed for a few minutes, waiting as the ship slowly altered course. The vessel leveled out, coming to a halt above a clear section of the meadow and slowly lowering. The flat bottom of the hull crushed dozens, if not hundreds of small trees and plants.

Once the crunching and occasional squeals–emitting from small, furry, unfortunate creatures that had received a terminal surprise upon our landing–had ceased, I turned to the team and spoke quickly, wanting to get it over with.

"Okay, guys, can I have a word?" I asked, seeing the group glancing at me curiously. I looked around again, double-checking, and sighed. We were missing Tang and Yen, but we had everyone else, and I resolved to make do with that for now, figuring I'd find the other two straight after and ask them directly as well.

"This was supposed to be a simple trip to the city…well, a raid, I know, but still. It became a lot more, and now I need to give you all a choice, essentially." I met their gazes solemnly. "Looking to the future, there's going to be a lot more fighting. Hell, it's going to practically become our lives, for the short term, at least, but it seems like a good time to start planning for the future as well." I sighed, noting the way Joya hung back, but Barrett held onto her hand firmly to stop her from leaving, and I smiled at that.

"Some of you joined me from the Tower, others along the way. I know you chose the best we had, Barrett, and you really live up to that, and I'm enormously proud of you all. What I need to know is if you want this, if you want to be part of my team, or Lydia's–as I think you, at least, want to stay?" I asked her directly, and she nodded quickly.

"Okay, then." I smiled with relief. "Lydia's team will essentially become the nucleus of the new Praetorian Guard. A small but highly elite force, trained and outfitted with the best we can buy, make, steal, or loot. The Praetorian Guard are both bodyguards and a fighting force, the best of the best; men and women who would go toe-to-toe with the Dark Legion's champions and kick their ass every time.

"To do this, to make a force this elite, is going to be hard. Hell, it'll take literal years, and I'm thinking that, when small teams are needed, like this little trip, then some of the team would come with me, while others would stay behind. I guess what I'm saying is that I know none of you asked for this. Miren, you wanted to be a hunter; Jian, you're becoming an awesome pilot; Giint…well." I paused and looked at the crazy little bastard, who grinned at me and peered around as though inviting the others to admire his general amazingness.

"Anyway…I want to give you all the chance to think about this, to decide if you want to stay with me or if you want to take a step back and do something else in the Tower." I finished and clasped my hands behind my back, waiting.

There was a long minute or so of silence, before Barrett, Grizz, and Lydia all spoke at once, breaking the tension as we all started to smile.

"What are you planning?" Barrett asked.

"I've asked Restun to be the Centurion Primus of the Praetorian Guard. He will essentially decide the level that we should all be striving for, and kick our arses until we surpass it." I made no attempts to disguise the truth, since they needed to know exactly what I was asking of them. "I want a force that can deal with anything, which means developing a well-rounded team that will grow over time: some ranged, some melee, some stealth and magic, much as we have been, but…" I took a deep breath.

"We've spent the last few weeks running from fire to fire, metaphorically. We've been reacting as much as anything else, and we've let our skill growth go by the wayside. That needs to change. Restun will train us all physically, and to complement that training, all members of the team will get a basic magical education. I'm telling you right now, I can't sodding wait to get Bob back," I told them, unable to keep the excitement from my voice.

"Bob…the skeleton?" Grizz asked Miren in a whisper that could probably be heard on the bridge.

"Shush!" she snapped. Grizz stepped back, abashed, making me grin. The sight of the huge, hulking legionnaire, a man who would have intimidated a professional bodybuilder in battle and could single-handedly take down dozens in a fight, being shushed was amusing enough in its own right. The fact that he had been corrected by a girl in her late teens, who barely came up to his shoulder and looked like she needed a good burger to fuel her slender frame, was priceless.

"Yes, Grizz, he's my minion, but he's also…more. He's evolving, albeit slowly, but he was evolving when we left, and he's an awesome tank. We just couldn't risk taking him into the city, or so I thought at the time. At any rate, take some time to think about it. You can stay with me, but you'll have Restun kicking your arse, and as soon as we have a Tower mage instructor, they'll be running you ragged as well.

"It'll basically be more of what we've been through during the last few weeks together. But you'll get the best gear, training, and supplies that we can provide. You'll also be paid once we figure that all out. Alternatively, you can step back and take another role; no hard feelings, and I'm damn thankful for your help so far," I said. Silence reigned while everyone waited to see who would speak first, when Lydia piped up.

"I was sold into slavery by my own husband," she stated grimly. "Yer rescued, fed, armed, an' taught me, an' helped me to become…to become a Valkyrie. I'm with yer for life and beyond, Lord Jax." She folded her arms across her chest, as much a self-comforting gesture as a defiant one.

"Yeah, this is way too much fun to stop now…but you know, this physical training; any chance of a pass that says I don't have to do it?" Arrin asked hopefully.

"Nope, you'll be trained to the point that you could kick Grizz's arse as he stands now, but I'll make sure you get more magic and get to blow shit up. How's that?" I countered.

Arrin glanced at Grizz, who must have outweighed him by twice at the least, then at himself, and back at Grizz, before he shrugged in acquiescence.

"It'll be worth it, but I'll probably curse you all day. You know that, right?" he asked.

"I'm with you, obviously, but you know you're going to regret this, don't you?" Grizz said, raising one eyebrow. "Primus Restun is...he's like a force of nature. If he's determined to make us fly by forcing us to beat our arms really hard, we'll either all be able to outpace the airships by the end of the week, or we'll be dead. Those are the only possible two outcomes he'll accept."

"I know, and believe me, I'm regretting it as well. But when the options are to rebuild the Empire or die trying, well, I'm in favor of the other guys dying, not us." I shrugged, unapologetic.

"Sounds like fun." Grizz grinned enthusiastically. "So, I'll be a member of the Praetorian Guard? Sweet."

"You will be, if you pass Restun's tests." I smirked at the sudden doubt that crossed Grizz's face.

"You know he's really serious, don't you? As in, no sense of humor at all, right?" Grizz questioned.

I nodded slowly. "Yeah, but who better?"

"Point." He sighed in resignation. I turned my attention to the others, realizing that Jian looked uncomfortable, as did Miren.

"Look, I understand if..."

"Will I still get to fly?" Jian asked, and I nodded, smiling reassuringly.

"I'm hoping so. After all, there's never going to be enough pilots, but we all have different skills. That's part of what makes this work so well. I want the entire team to be able to do a load of different things. You being a kick-ass warlock, swordsman, and pilot? It just works, man."

"I...I'm not sure," Miren admitted, glancing around hesitantly, as if afraid of how we'd react. "I'm sorry, but...all this..." She gestured at the ships that were coming in to land, and the legionnaires disembarking the Battleship under Romanus' and Restun's directions. "With Stephanos's death, with losing Cam..." She drew in a deep, shuddering breath, then clenched her eyes shut. "I don't think...I'm sorry, but I don't think I can..."

"It's okay, Miren," I stepped forward and gently rested my right hand on her shoulder. I looked into her glistening eyes and went on softly. "It's been a shitty few weeks, and nobody blames you for this. Don't worry. I understand," I told her, and I meant it. Hell, she was a tiny blonde waif, not even out of her teens, and two of her closest friends had died recently. She'd been taken as a slave, and now she was fighting in a war. This was exactly why I'd asked them, as I needed to know where I stood and to give them the chance to back out.

I smiled at her, despite feeling a bit hurt and betrayed, making sure none of it showed. I patted her on the shoulder again before stepping back.

"Okay, then, it's just the eight of us." I looked back to the gap in the decking which led down to the space where I had spotted that huge creature, when Giint spoke up.

"Niiine," he said flatly, crossing his arms and glaring at me.

"What?" I blinked in surprise.

"Niiine of usss," he clarified. "Giint go, toooo."

I gaped in amazement. The crazy little bastard was useful, I had to admit that. He could build things like nobody's business, was into alchemy…well…"smelly plants," and was both a good shot with a crossbow and able to make explosives…but…

"But you're batshit!" Grizz blurted, staring down at the Gnome, who glared up at him and reached for a pouch. "Whoa, sorry, Giint, but seriously, you're fucking mad, most of the time…"

"D'yer want to join tha Legion?" Lydia asked him, her voice cutting through the growing tension between the seething Gnome and the towering legionnaire.

"Don'ttt care," Giint said simply, then pointed at me. "You save, you free, and you heal. Giint go with you now."

That was it. Seemingly, that was all the discussion needed on the matter. After a moment's consideration, I nodded my agreement. He was damn useful, after all, even if he was mental.

"Okay, Giint, but you still have to pass the tests, the same as the rest of us, if you want to do this. You have to train, to learn, *and you have to stop with the fucking drugs unless we're safe and don't have to do anything for a while!*" That last bit was delivered in a rush as he pulled out a stick of the Gnomes' super-catnip. He paused, regarding it longingly before putting it away.

"Giint is stronnng, can do thisss," he muttered, shaking his head as he subconsciously patted the bag his drugs had gone into.

I observed the group's widely varied mix of reactions, from amused, to irritated, to weirdly pleased, and that was just Lydia…I shrugged and turned back to the Gnome. "Well, we'll see, Giint. We will see. Go with the others to the cruisers; we'll get set up. Then I guess we all start training with Restun. Before we go, I need to find Yen and Tang, and I need to speak to some engineers, but it shouldn't take long. I'll see you over there."

"I…can I stay on this ship?" Miren asked quietly, then took a deep breath and started to pull her bow out of her bag. "I know I can't keep this," she whispered, offering it to me. Stunned, I paused, thinking, before shaking my head.

"No, that's your bow, Miren. You earned it, as you did the rest of the equipment you got while you were with us. The armor; well, it's no good to a hunter anyway, so you'll need new gear regardless. I take it you want to go back to being a hunter?"

She nodded mutely.

"Then keep the bow and the rest of the equipment, bar the Legion armor. That needs to be returned to Thorn and her armorers. When we get back, you can join the hunters, and you'll be doing a damn important job. We're going to need a lot of meat to feed everyone, not to mention exploring the area."

"Thank you." Her voice never broke above a whisper, and she stood trembling and clutching her bow. Lydia stepped in to hug her, as did the others.

I hugged her as well, then moved away, leaving her and Oracle to talk. The way that Miren and Jian looked at each other, but quickly moved apart, did not go unnoticed, either.

CHAPTER FIVE

I stepped up to the edge of the missing deck plates, peeking down into the empty rooms below. Unsurprisingly, they'd gone.

I judged the distance to the floor to be about fifteen feet, and I took a deep breath then stepped out into the empty air.

As I fell, I spun and grabbed at the edge of the deck. My hands slammed into it hard, but my insane Agility and Dexterity made it easy for me to arrest my motion with a solid grip, then drop to land on the balls of my feet before straightening up and grinning.

"Olympics, baby, I'd be the fucking king," I muttered under my breath as Oracle flew down next to me, and I felt as much as saw the shadow that was Bane landing nearby, then blending in with the corridor.

"What was that?" Oracle asked, and I shook my head, unwilling to go into the explanations that it would take.

"Shame about Miren," I said instead, and she sighed.

"It is. I like her, but after Stephanos, and Cam…"

"I know," I agreed regretfully as we moved from room to room, following the sound of hammering.

"I don't blame her," came a whisper from Bane. "It's hard to lose your friends, and while the rest of us are older, she is still a child."

"Wait, how old are you, Bane?" I asked, and he went silent. "Seriously, dude, how old are you?"

"Sixteen summers," he admitted finally.

"Dude, you're younger than she is!" I thought back to when we'd first met Bane. He'd been exploring Decin's ship with a group of younger friends after the Goblins had captured the crew. Bane had lost a few of them to the Goblins, which had sent him crazy, and he'd attempted to attack them.

"Years are only one way to measure someone's age," he replied sagely.

"Yeah, but it's the right one." I looked in the direction his voice had come from. "I mean, for fuck's sake, Bane, how many years have passed from birth is literally what you're asking when you ask how old someone is. You can't say that then expect me to just leave it. It's like saying that height isn't the only way to measure how tall you are!"

"It's not," Bane said from behind me, becoming visible long enough to gesture into a room two doors further down the corridor. "They're in here, and how tall I am is different, depending…"

"Depending on what?" I asked, moving down the corridor and poking my head into the room to see the same four engineers I'd seen before, the Golem that held a section of piping overhead, and Durg, the Amilith, crouching in the shadows on the far side of the room.

"Depending on if I'm standing up or lying down and if I'm alone with a pretty female," Bane's voice whispered in my ear, then he was gone. I glared into the darkness.

"That's bullshit, and you know it!" I called after him, making the engineers jump as they realized who I was. "Dickhead," I muttered, knowing damn well that he'd heard me as I turned back to the engineers and put a smile on my face.

"Hi, guys…" I said casually, walking into the cavernous room and looking about. The Golem stayed absolutely still, holding a massive, clearly prefabricated section of wall in place as the team, a mixed group of Dwarves, humans, and a hairy creature reminiscent of a werewolf, or at least a woman with *serious* body-hair issues crossed with a turtle, hammered the wall into place.

I nodded to them, and the hairy woman came forward to speak to me while telling the others to get on with the job.

"Lord Jath," she lisped, and I held my hand out, gripping her wrist. "I'm Deira, third mate, thecond thling." I ran it through my mind and smiled in polite confusion.

"Third mate, second sling?" I asked. "What's that?"

"It meanth I wath the third mate on the thecond thling team on the battlethip conthtruction," she said. "Tho, what can I do for you?"

"I'm curious about your watcher." I nodded to the shadows where Durg had vanished, stumbling away down the corridor while looking back over his shoulder in fear. I'd been tempted to go after him and try to calm him down, but considering his obvious fear and his size, I'd decided against it, as I didn't want someone crushed.

"Durg?" she asked, blinking and turning in time to glimpse his retreating back. "Dammit, Toni, go get him back…" She sighed. "Durg ith thort of a good luck charm; we all look out for him, make thure he's fed and hath thomewhere to thleep, that kinda thing."

One of the Dwarves sighed and dropped the wrench he had been using, running off down the corridor as he called out to Durg to "Calm doon, ya big galoot."

"He's lucky?" I asked.

"He ith if you're thleeping near a looth wall. He caught it before it could thquath anyone." She nodded at a nearby panel, and I ran that sentence through my mind, untangling the words before nodding in understanding.

"A loose wall fell, and he caught it. Yeah, damn lucky."

"No offenth, my lord, but what do you need? We have a quota to meet." She gestured to the two remaining engineers, who were working flat-out trying to get the wall up.

"No, sorry," I said, shaking my head. "I don't need anything. I just saw Durg and wanted to speak to him, see if he was okay, and why he was just watching you all."

"He doethn't thpeak, not really. Thomething ith wrong up here…" She rapped her knuckles on the side of her head. "But he'th friendly, nearly as thtrong ath the golemth, and jutht wantth to be left alone. Thome of the kidth were teathing him, tho we took him with uth. We feed him, make thure he'th thafe, and thatth all you can do, really."

"Damn." I winced empathetically. "I'll have a word with my healer, see if there's anything she can do for him," I muttered.

Deira smiled briefly, before the expression bled from her face as she went pale. "I appreciate the thought, my lord, but healerth are expenthive, and…"

"No, they aren't. The Tower's healers will always be free for citizens. I doubt he's sworn, as I don't feel a connection to him, but he will be healed if there's anything we can do. If not, he can either stay with us, and we'll look out for him, or we'll help him however we can."

"Thank you, my lord." She bobbed her head in respectful gratitude.

I glanced down both ends of the corridor leading out of the room and coughed. "I…uh, don't suppose you know the best way out to the ground?" I asked, feeling embarrassed, then annoyed, as I felt Bane's subsonic chuckle.

"Left," Deira said quickly. "Left, then two rightth at the end of the hall."

I nodded my thanks and headed off, leaving her to get back to her team as I jogged down the corridor. "I take it you knew the way out?" I asked Bane, and he chuckled again in response. "Dick."

It only took a few minutes to get to the nearest hatch and from there to the gangplank leading down. As I emerged outside, first stepping back to let an overburdened member of the crew pass with their bags of supplies, I was amazed at the ships coming in to land.

There were three ships grounded already, counting the battleship. Nearby rested a long, low cruiser with a wide deck and a sweeping design that looked almost organic, as well as a plain narrow ship that I just *knew* was a fast scout. The damn thing practically screamed speed in every line. As its sails shook in the gentle breeze coming off the lake, I smiled unconsciously.

The other ships were coming in for a landing as well, clearly intent on redistributing people and equipment as quickly as possible, but I couldn't help but be amazed by the sheer variety of their designs.

Each ship was unique. The cruisers had heavier armor, but where one appeared to be partially coated in iron, the other was clearly wood. One–the *Ragnarök*, I realized, spotting the stylized name across the side of the ship–had flourishes everywhere, intricate details carved lovingly into the ship. As I walked down the battleship's gangplank, the *Ragnarök*'s sculpted railings, copper fittings, and brass embellishing the deck gleamed. The *Sigmar's Fist* was all unadorned iron, and unlike the *Ragnarök*, had both a raised fore and aft deck.

The only thing that was similar, beyond the overall size and general lethality the two ships exuded, were the cannons. They were both clearly designed as machines of war.

Sigmar's Fist boasted four cannons: two on the front, built into the deck and forward facing, and one on either side, ready to be fired to the left and right, with three heavy mortars mounted on the forward raised deck.

The *Ragnarök*, alternatively, had only one raised deck, but appeared to have a cannon positioned on either side and four fixed into place on the front, making me think that she was designed for running down prey quickly. I walked across the meadow toward the *Ragnarök*, having spotted Restun on her deck, gaping at the sheer size of the ships.

The battleship Dwarfed them all, true, but she was practically a tower block laid on her side, and as such, she was mind-blowing in any sense. The cruisers, though…they just looked awesome, and seemed far, far larger than anything that should be in the air.

I remembered having the same feeling the first time I'd seen a jumbo jet, but that, at least, was scientifically created, while this…?

From what I'd seen of the airships so far, they were all bastardized versions of the Gnome ships. Having finally met Gnomes, my ass felt as though it was attempting to form solid neutronium nuggets whenever I considered flying in something they'd built.

As I passed through the meadow and was about to climb onto the gangplank, I passed numerous legionnaires rushing back and forth, carrying equipment and crates. As I prepared to board, something caught the corner of my eye.

I turned, blinking and squinting down the meadow, frowning as I tried to make out what had distracted me. Absent-mindedly, I stepped aside, moving further from the ship due to not wanting to be in anyone's way.

At first, I couldn't see anything unusual. There was a gentle slope to the land leading down to the lake, with a few clear game trails, a bunch of small trees and bushes, some long grass and wildflowers…and…and I froze.

As I looked more carefully, having recognized a ginseng plant, the meadow changed in my vision as one of my earliest abilities kicked in, outlining all the plants before me with a subtle blue glow.

I gasped as I scanned the field, seeing dozens and dozens of glowing plants as my ability kicked in. An involuntary curse escaped my lips as I took it all in, spinning around and looking up the meadow to where the house sat at the other end of the lake.

I suddenly realized what we'd done.

The house was surrounded by what appeared to be cultivated fields, and Mal was coming in to a slow landing alongside it. The meadows had clearly either been seeded deliberately, or were naturally occurring herb gardens.

Not only had we landed and crushed a hell of a lot of the meadow, but more was being trampled by the second, as the legionnaires and other people strode from ship to ship, moving stores.

I winced, turning full circle, and saw Mistress Nerin as she stomped towards me, looking exasperated.

"You realize what…"

"We're in an herb garden, aren't we?" I said, and she seemed to deflate. "I just realized…"

"So did I," she said ruefully. "I never thought to see growing on such a scale…mind you, I never expected to see something like this, either." She gestured towards the battleship, which towered over us, casting a shadow that could hide hundreds.

"I sent Mal to buy all the herbs they have," I explained, and she smiled faintly.

"Well, at least we'll get a good deal. Or someone will," she added after a second. "You didn't agree a price to buy them off him already, did you? I can at least tell you what they're worth."

"I gave him a platinum piece to buy everything they had," I admitted. She gaped at me. "What?"

"A *platinum*?" she groaned. "Boy, someone needs to teach you about wealth. This entire meadow, hell, that valley would only cost two, if that! Most villages are sold for less!"

"Shit." I rubbed my temples. "I earned a load of platinum gambling on the fights and looting the Skyking, so I thought…"

"You cleaned out the entire vaults of multiple gangs, boy!" she hissed, throwing her hands up. "They'd been terrorizing and bribing the city in equal measure for years to gain that, and knowing that damn fool Mal, he probably cleaned out every noble in the city through gambling as well. No wonder they were all getting out of there so fast…"

"Who?" I asked, confused, and she scowled in annoyance.

"The nobles! Damn, boy, you didn't even see them, did you?"

I shook my head, shrugging.

Her tone softened into one of stunned amazement. "There were dozens at each fight, always new ones. He must have been drawing them in and cleaning them out, making them believe they had a chance to get it all back.

"Once they all start comparing notes? They'll soon realize what happened, and that the city must be damn near bankrupt by now. Add to that whatever you got, and I'll promise you Mal got three times that. He can probably buy a continent right now!" She scoffed, rolling her eyes. "You know, for someone who's so sneaky with fighting, you're pretty useless at economy management!"

"Tell me about it," I growled, then sighed, wearily scrubbing my face with my hand. "Look, Nerin, I'm trying, okay?" I drew her aside, walking out to the nearest plant that glowed to my augmented vision.

I crouched, stroking the gently glowing leaves and examining everything from the berries to the stems, tracing them down to the soft soil beneath. Gently, I dug my fingers in, separating the plant from the surrounding ground while keeping the roots intact.

"I really don't know much about this realm," I said quietly. "Where I came from, the world is vastly different. Think of the airships, but made with science, not magic. There's no magic there, or at least I didn't think so while I was growing up. There's a lot of war, though, a lot of nasty shit.

"My brother, Tommy, and I used to fight against that. Not in an army or anything usually, although we both served for a while. Instead, we did what we thought was right, and we fought a lot of small fights against the same kind of people that are in power here. People who'd happily stab you in the back, steal from you, and smile while doing it. In my…realm…it was once considered bad to deal with things yourself.

"We had a force like the city guard, called the police. They were responsible for stopping crimes and ensuring the punishment for the guilty." I carefully put the plant into the bag of holding that she offered to me.

"Go on, boy; this is an herbalist's pouch; the plant won't die in here," she reassured me quietly, watching me with an unreadable expression.

"Thanks," I said. "Just another example of how little I know, eh? Anyway. The plan for the police was good. They caught the criminals, and the courts decided what the punishment should be. The prisons got so overrun that they started just giving warnings and other mild punishments, as there wasn't room to detain them all. Criminals got away with more and more.

"As time went on, people got so intimidated by criminals they stopped telling the police about things, because if the criminals found out who'd reported them, and they only got a warning…well, the criminals would hurt those people. Things continued to spiral out of control.

"When we grew up, well…the police were respected but generally pitied. They couldn't do much, and there weren't enough of them. Add to that, like everywhere, some of them were corrupt or downright evil. It was only a rare few, but they tarnished the reputation of the rest. Where we lived, the criminals were in charge. The only real rule was that respect was *everything*. Some people thought fear was the same thing. It's not."

I pulled up a second and third plant, gingerly transferring them into the bag. Nerin remained silent, working alongside me with quick, efficient motions as she did the same.

"Where Tommy and I grew up, there were gangs; not as downright evil as here, I'll admit, but they bullied, they stole, and they occasionally killed. Drugs were the big thing where we lived–selling them, I mean. They were illegal, so of course, they were everywhere, and selling them meant you made a lot of money.

"We were already outsiders, even then, with the Dreams…well, that's not important, but where most kids and young people played and laughed, we'd learned early on to kill and fight in our Dreams, in bodies that were perfect. Then we'd wake up, and find that we were weak, small, and slow again. So we learned to do things in our real bodies, to intimidate those who did wrong.

"We started to get a reputation. "The Brothers," "The Twins," we got a lot of names. Some gangs tried to run us off, until one dealer tried to kill us. That was the first time we killed. Beat him to death and buried him in Jesmond Dene," I whispered, looking back at the memory, reliving the frantic race to hide the body, the fear over the following weeks and months that we'd be caught and sent to prison. Then, when enough time had passed, being hit with the stark realization that nobody cared.

"He was just another dealer, it turned out," I muttered darkly. "A few days after we killed him, another one turned up and replaced him, selling the same shit. We waited, stayed calm and quiet, and nothing happened, so we spent the money we'd scavenged from his corpse, and we started to work. We carve out our own territory. Handed out beatings to those who misbehaved. We became as bad, if not worse, than the scum that surrounded us. We beat, robbed, and occasionally killed, but we had a code."

"What kind of code?" Nerin asked.

"A stupid one, but it was all we had." I shrugged dismissively. "Our ma was dying. We needed to feed her, and us; we needed to pay the bills, since she couldn't. She was off her head on pain medication all the time. Our code was complicated, but basically, it came down to 'us first.' We decided that the old rules, things like never beating a woman or a child, standing up to the evil strong, and protecting the weak was what we should be doing.

"We agreed there was no point in robbing those who had nothing, but the scum always rises to the top, so we hunted drug dealers, especially the ones who were hurting others. We robbed the robbers and thieves, and we made damn sure they understood to behave themselves in our territory." I snorted, looking back across the years and seeing us as we had been all over again.

"We didn't give a shit about the rest of the world; we looked after our own first. Five streets, that was all we claimed, but fuck, we were busy. Time passed, and we had an understanding with the police. We were too young to go to prison, and we were careful enough that they couldn't prove anything, but they knew what we did and who to.

"After a while, police started drinking in the bars next to our house. We'd be sitting in there as well, drinking, despite the laws about being too young. We'd hear the police complaining loudly about things that happened. Dealers who were selling shit that was cut badly, drugs that were hurting people, then they'd go back to work. After they left, so would we. We'd go check it out, and where the police couldn't deal with things, we would."

We moved further into the meadow, and Nerin listened, letting me get it all off my chest, even as we periodically checked to make sure the legionnaires were still working, and we weren't holding things up. We grabbed two of every plant we could gather, hoping we could replant them in the Tower and cultivate them there.

"Then it all changed. Our ma died, and we were too young to live alone, according to the state, so we were sent to live with people who looked after kids for money. It was shit. Most were just greedy assholes; wanted the money, not us. Some wanted to help us, and looking back now, I realize that.

"But the first house we went to, well, the guy there tried to abuse us…sexually. He regretted it, believe me. That put us on the watch list, though, and once others beyond the local police, who thought we were useful, started to look…well, things got bad, even when that asshole was sent to prison."

Nerin grunted, passing me a small knife as I tried to free a bush from some interwoven roots. I nodded my thanks, cutting it free and continuing.

"Long story short, we ended up out of control, started to go bad, probably would have ended up in prison ourselves, until we were given a choice by a judge who thought we were worth saving for some reason. We joined the army, and we found a home. We were taught, and we learned rules from people who could kick our asses but who looked out for us as well. Life was actually good for a while, until Tommy got thrown out. His Dreams…anyway." I shook my head, forcing myself to go on.

"He was out, and I was sent abroad to fight for my country. I got back, and he was missing. He'd been taken, forced to come here, although it took me another five years to find that out. Then I was taken as well, and I was forced to make a choice. Those five years alone changed everything. I stopped being an asshole, learned to get along with people, even made friends. I found things I liked and things I didn't, like having to work for a living. I became just another guy, if one with a bad temper and a fuck-ton of scars.

"When I was taken, they trained me, teaching me to use weapons, instead of just my feet and fists. Taught me to survive here. The thing is, as much as we were shits back there, we had that code I mentioned. We tried to help people. Hell, we used the money we beat out of the drug dealers to feed people, and yeah, to have fun. That meant I had another choice to make when I ended up here."

Nerin was watching me, her hands moving smoothly as she worked.

"I found a load of people being kept as slaves. They were going to be fed to the fucking SporeMother, and I couldn't have that. I stepped in, I saved them, then I tried to make my new home secure and find my brother. That's all I've been trying to do since I got here: look after *my* people and find Tommy.

"I didn't expect to be a fucking Emperor. I thought the voice in my head was just me, a sign I was crazy, not the remnants of the fucking Eternal Emperor. I literally run from fire to fire, trying to keep everyone safe, and maybe, just maybe, find my brother, fix up my home, and get some lovin'.

"That's literally it. In order to do all that, I need to be the Imperial Scion, it seems. Fine. I need to win a war, also fine, but everyone expects me to know what to do, Nerin. I'm making it the fuck up as I go along, okay?" My narrative ground to a halt as I finally heard the ragged edge to my voice, and I realized I was on the verge of shouting...or crying.

"Whoo, boy..." I muttered awkwardly, standing up and looking into the distance, my face turned away from the others. I forced myself to draw in a deep breath, trying to get my emotions under control.

"I take it that's the first time you've admitted this? Even to yourself?" Nerin asked.

I nodded, suddenly wondering why the hell I'd said all that, and to a woman I barely knew.

"I thought so," she said contemplatively, digging at another plant. "Come on, get down here and help. I'm not doing it all myself." She pointed at a nearby stalk, and I snorted and moved to the next plant. "Do you know what I do, boy?"

I frowned at her in confusion. "You're a healer; specifically, the Tower's healer, or at least I hope so. If you're the fucking cleaner, and I've gotten confused somewhere, this could be a problem."

She shot me a warning glare before replying. "I *am* a healer, boy. As such, I know there's a hell of a lot that goes wrong in the heart and the head that magic can't fix. Sometimes a healer's job is as much to listen as it is to heal. Sometimes, it's all about listening at the right time, and others, it's about kicking you up the arse and making sure you keep your promises!"

"I keep my promises," I grumbled, tugging a short, wide bush with bright red leaves out of the soil and brushing the loose dirt away carefully.

"Good," she said calmly. "Well, considering that you clearly needed to talk, and all of this came out because I asked you about the plants being crushed, I think we need to put some time aside to talk regularly, don't you?"

"I don't know..." I hesitated.

"Boy, the list of things you don't know is huge. That's not the point. What *is* the point is that you *need* to talk. You can talk to me or to that pretty little Wisp who has you wrapped around her little finger, or to that damn Mer who keeps insisting on pretending to be a bush behind you.

"But I'm telling you now, as your healer, you need to make time for it. We're not meant to be in combat all our lives, and it takes a toll. Making time for a drink, a chat, or chasing your little friend around the bedroom is vital, if you don't want to come apart at the seams. So, from now on, regardless of what's happening, and until *I* decide otherwise, you and I will meet once a week to have dinner and talk. It can be about anything, but you will do it, as you remember you told me you keep your promises, didn't you?"

"Yes," I said carefully, wincing as she went on.

"Well, you also agreed to listen when I speak, and to abide by my recommendations as the healer, didn't you?" she crowed triumphantly.

"Did I?" I asked, trying to remember, only to have Bane call out from behind me. "You did."

"Fuck." I hated the idea, yet it was probably a good one. I couldn't afford to have verbal diarrhea in public, after all.

"Good," Nerin said, straightening up. "Now, it looks like most of the legionnaires are aboard. Are we making them wait, or…?" I shook my head, putting one last plant into her bag and handing it back to her. "Keep it; I have another."

"No, we need to get moving, and thank you. For the bag, I mean." I coughed, willing myself not to flush with embarrassment. "And…thank you…for…" I stuttered, trying not to grit my teeth. "Whoooo, boy…that was, well…I needed it, and I didn't realize I needed it until now." I looked back over the last few weeks and realized how close I'd come to boiling over at things.

I'd been growing increasingly unstable and trying to be everything to everyone wasn't helping. I hated the idea of talking to a shrink, even if she wasn't really one, but if it helped? I shrugged and did what I always did when I encountered something I didn't like but couldn't change.

I forgot about it, and I moved on.

CHAPTER SIX

The three of us headed across the meadow back to the ship and were among the last to board. Two more legionnaires, carrying sacks as they trudged up behind us, turned out to be the last. The gangplank was pulled up quickly, and the engines began to purr with power as I scanned the deck.

The gangplanks on the battleship led to access hatches in its sides, as the deck rose so high above ground. Here, we'd literally tramped up on to the deck, finding ourselves surrounded by legionnaires who were stuffing crates and sacks into every available space.

I made my way through the group, sensing Oracle leaving the battleship. Wasting no time, I hurried across the main deck to join Restun, who I'd spotted standing on the upper deck talking to two crew members I assumed were the helmsman and the captain.

I clambered up the short ladder, lifting myself onto the deck, and got an immediate glare from the Alkyon pair who stood with Restun. It took only a moment before I was recognized, resulting in them both lifting their heads and offering their throats in some sort of ritual submission.

"Thank you," I said, coming to a halt nearby, then looking out over the lower deck, which boiled with activity like a kicked anthill.

"Lord Jax, this is Feirin, captain of the *Ragnarök*, and his mate, Eryn," Restun informed me calmly, and I nodded to them, smiling as Eryn steered the ship into a climb, making us all feel heavier as we went. I peered back over the side, finding Oracle as she closed the distance. My pixie-sized companion landed on the rear railing and smiled, then gazed back at the battleship sadly. I stood with her and looked down as we passed it, watching the lone figure at the front of the deck.

Miren lifted her hand hesitantly to wave, then dropped it to her side and turned away, clearly not seeing my wave in return.

"Why did she do it, Oracle? Is she okay?" I asked quietly.

Oracle shook her head. "No, she's really not. I think everyone forgets how young she is."

"Bane's younger," I said abruptly, and she laughed in spite of the somber topic.

"Yes, but he's also a stealth-obsessed murdering lunatic."

"Thank you," whispered Bane.

Oracle winked in his direction then shifted back to her serious tone. "But did you know Miren hates killing? Even in hunting? She wanted to be a hunter because she wanted to be out in the forests alone, not because she wanted to kill anything. She just accepted that it was a required aspect of the job."

"Crap," I muttered. "Poor kid. Restun?" I called over my shoulder, looking for him, and he stepped over to join me, saluting in respect.

"What can I do for you, Lord Jax?" he asked.

"I need to find some more members for my team," I said regretfully.

"Of course. Do you have any specific needs?" He focused on my face, clearly prepared to take mental notes, and I paused for a moment to consider the details.

"Well, I have Lydia and Grizz as front-line fighters. I know Grizz isn't supposed to be–he's a goddamn scout sniper, I heard–but he's damn good at it." Restun flexed his jaw briefly before nodding for me to continue.

"Besides them, I have Jian; he's a dual-wielding swordsman...and warlock, I guess. Arrin is physically sodding useless, but he's damn good as a mage, and Bane is my bodyguard and stealth fighter. Tang and Yen are both good all-rounders; Tang is usually floating between ranged and stealth, and Yen floats between ranged and magic, but I've not heard from them yet if they want to stay, and..."

"We do," a familiar voice confirmed from behind.

I turned around to see Tang grinning at me. "You sure? You know what it means, right?"

Undeterred, he nodded. "Yen and I already spoke to Grizz and Lydia. We want to stay in the team, and we're happy to be under Lydia." He winked suggestively.

I chuckled, grasping his forearm in gratitude. "Well, thank you, mate, and I won't tell Lydia how you meant that!"

"Probably safer that way!" he agreed, laughing and moving to the other side of the raised deck before slipping into stealth and crouching against the railing. I'd watched him do it, yet still, even knowing exactly where he was, I had to concentrate to see him.

There was something about his skills and abilities that, like Bane, made my eyes just skate across the top of him, as though there were things far more important to look at everywhere else.

I shook my head and turned to face Restun again.

"Okay then, I have Tang and Yen still, so that means I need two more; preferably a damage-dealer and a ranged, I guess? That should give us the most versatility..." Then I held up my hand and snorted. "Scratch that. Giint laid claim to the ranged slot."

"The Gnome?" Restun asked, and I got to enjoy the first instance of shock I'd seen on his face.

"Yeah, he thinks he'll be the perfect fit. I told him he could train with us, and we'd evaluate him. By which I mean, you get to evaluate him, as we all think he's fucking crazy."

"Do you wish me to refuse him?" Restun asked.

"No, if I wanted him elsewhere, I'd just tell him no. I want him evaluated to see if you think he could be good as a legionnaire. Every current member of my team will either end up as members of the Praetorian Guard or moved into other roles, eventually. Considering the future, as I said earlier, it's time to stop fucking around. We've survived on a combination of balls, sheer aggression, and blind luck, so far. I need to temper that with skill."

"A Gnome legionnaire..." Restun wondered, rubbing his chin.

"Crazier things have happened," I said with amusement.

Tang's voice floated over to us. "Name two!"

Restun glared sharply at the lax discipline, but I stopped him, putting my hand on his shoulder before he could walk over to discuss it with the nearly invisible legionnaire.

"It's alright, I'm informal most of the time. Tang knows that's how I like to work," I assured him.

He stepped back, visibly relaxing. By a hair.

"Be that as it may, *Lord* Jax," he said pointedly, "there is a place for informality, and I'll be sure to discuss it with him later…along with a disturbing rumor of a banned and blacklisted potion that was used during your excursion into the Sunken City."

I winced involuntarily, remembering the Strength of the Ogg potion that Tang had given me. He'd done it to save my life, despite knowing he'd get into trouble. But he was also a legionnaire, and he'd been carrying a potion that was banned for its side effects.

I resolved to leave it alone. I'd made it clear I wanted him in my team, so Restun couldn't kill him or boot him out. Beyond that…well.

"Any ideas about the new team member?" I asked.

"Three come to mind straight away: Denny, a legionnaire of thirty years, good with a sword, better with an axe. He's a specialist in field construction, repairs, and logistics. Second would be Luthor; he's grim and slower than most, dwarven, but he's as solid a fighter as they come. His secondary specializations are in cooking and leatherworking. Third and final off the top of my head would be Lars; he's a human axeman, but he's fast, and his secondary skills are as a monster hunter, tracker, and climber."

"Damn, they all sound good. I could've killed for something besides the goddamn jerky or trail biscuits we were living on when we were on the Smuggler's Path, and when we were exploring the Sunken City, so a cook actually sounds better than it really should," I said as my stomach rumbled.

"There are others, lots of others, who would gladly join your advance team. Frankly, I expect the entire Legion would volunteer, if they knew there was a chance, and amongst the others, there are several I have my eye on."

"What do you mean?" I asked, having to raise my voice over the wind. He nodded back to the battleship, now vanishing in the distance as we picked up speed.

"The others you accepted as citizens. There are members of dozens of races, some with pasts that make them ideal as recruits for the Legion. Several are ex-soldiers, dozens are fighters. The Trigara, Nigret, for example…" He paused, shifting around to block some of the wind as we continued to pick up speed. "He claims he wouldn't fit in with the Legion, yet he spends all his time with our people, helps wherever he can, and has skills that would be useful, not to mention he's a damn good fighter!"

"I'll think about it, then! Okay, this wind is getting stupid, is there room below?" I asked, and he looked to the captain, Feirin, who shook his head.

"Almost every room is filled to the brim with crates, foodstuffs, and manastones. The stones we have in place now should last us six months or more, but I doubt they'd last us a week at this speed, as heavily laden as we are," Feirin called over the rising sound of the rushing wind.

"Dammit," I grunted, then forced a smile. "Well, we're in your way here, Captain. Apologies, I'll let you get on with it." He nodded respectfully as I led the way down from the upper deck to the main, threading my way through until I found Lydia and the others. The entire group sat talking quietly, leaning against bags of grain and hunching down out of the wind.

"I didn't realize we had so much food," I exclaimed, taking the space Lydia made for me and noting the numerous packages piled around.

"Mal brought it!" she called, grinning. "I swear, that thieving sod took everything he could find that wasn't nailed down! While everyone else was getting loaded aboard the ships, Mal diverted the refugees through a storehouse on the way, told them each to grab a bag, and they did. I think we've got a few months' worth of food, at least!"

"Damn," I whispered, impressed by the stacks of supplies, relief warring with the irritation that it was always bloody Mal who saved the day and made things better. I forced a smile and looked around, pleased to see that Oracle had landed to my right and was staring between two piles of boxes, and was using our newly upgraded healing spell.

I started to get up, then sat back and closed my eyes instead, reaching out to her. Relaxing, I felt her open up to me, enfolding my consciousness into her own and letting me see out of her eyes.

As before, it was peculiar, not least because of her extra senses that I had no analogue for. But stepping in halfway through the spell meant I'd missed a great deal of it, and I could only watch helplessly as she worked.

The intended recipient was Giint, and through the Greater Examination and the new Surgeon's Scalpel variant of our healing spell, I saw into Giint as I never had before. His body was twisted in so many places. The bones that had been broken over decades of fighting, crashing, and generally living like a feral animal had harmed him in ways living beings were never meant to endure.

Our first healings had resolved some of these issues, but not all. Even now, we couldn't fix everything, not realistically, but as Oracle focused on Giint's right arm, I found it to be a microcosm of his overall state.

It had been broken at least a dozen times; each break had warped the bone slightly, as it'd never been protected long enough to properly heal before, instead simply left to heal on its own. The effect was that his right arm was shorter than his left and curved inwards slightly. When we'd healed this and other wounds, we'd removed all the existing injuries, but the effects on the muscles which had twisted and grown tight weren't fixed by the first spell, at least not fully.

I had healed similar injuries in the past, but in Giint's case, we'd simply not had the time to pour the magic in and keep going. This time, Oracle was doing it section by section, and we started to work together smoothly as we went.

The twisted bones and muscles were straightened out and re-aligned, emitting ominous cracking noises that made me glad he was still unconscious. I checked the wrist, finding a buildup of crystals in the joints and removed them before moving on to the hand and fingers.

I shook my head in amazement at the fact he was missing a finger on that hand, and I'd never realized. As I went, I concentrated, using what we'd learned in regrowing my arm and in observing Mistress Nerin's work.

71

Like it was a talisman, thinking of her seemed to draw the healer near, and she slipped down next to us, reaching out to touch him with her magic.

"You missed a bit," was all she said to me as I worked on rebuilding his little finger from scratch.

I grumbled, muttering under my breath as I went on, finally moving back a bit and rebuilding the second joint of the finger, telling myself I would have seen the missing appendage and repaired it before I was finished.

The next few minutes were painful. I hit my limit, running out of mana and feeling the spike of a mana-migraine that blew through my unprepared mind, forcing out a pained grunt. I sat back, disengaging myself from Oracle and starting to meditate as Giint jumped up, screaming wildly into the air while whipping out a kill-stick and a glowing axe. The grunt of pain on my part had been enough to wake him to a possible threat while regrowing fingers and rebuilding his damn arm hadn't gotten so much as a twitch.

I heard the others reassuring him before Restun drew him aside. Breathing deeply, I did my best to ignore them all, clearing my mind of all extraneous thoughts and forcing my body to relax as I built the construct around me to increase my regeneration. As soon as I had the required mana, I activated Peace and sighed at the twin drain and recovery of my mana and health filling me and radiating outwards.

A few minutes turned into an hour as I sensed others settling nearby to enjoy the feeling. I kept working on my meditation until Lydia gently shook me.

I released the feeling of peace and the meditative state, blinking at the shimmering field of panels hovering around me. I stared at them in awe, watching as they faded away.

"Are they always like that?" I asked, feeling a little dazed.

Lydia shook her head. "Nah, it depends how deep into it yer go. Yer managed three boxes this time; each time ye make one, they're like a haze in the air until you get it right, then they become solid an' give off light."

"Solid?"

"More or less." Lydia shrugged. "I pushed my hand through it to wake yer, but I could feel somethin', at least. Not like Arrin's attempts."

I glanced over at Arrin, who lay snoring against a large bag of grain. He was holding it, both arms wrapped around it, and occasionally mumbling to himself or whoever he was dreaming about.

"Man, we really need to find him a girlfriend," I muttered, and Lydia snorted in agreement. "So, he's been meditating?"

"I think he learned a lesson in tha Prax. When he realized he nearly cost Bane an' Tang their lives by not doin' it, he's been tryin' constantly. Every time we stop for five minutes, he's at it. But his be softer than yours, duller, and you can't feel 'em."

"Might be the Peace ability," I wondered, then dismissed the idle thought. "What's up, then?" I asked her, and she drew in a deep breath.

"Well, I thought yer'd better get some sleep. Think tha next few days are gonna be hard, but...well...I wanted to say, 'thank yer' as well." She shuffled awkwardly. "Ain't nobody thought I was worth nothin' my whole life, then this." She choked up, gesturing around and reaching up to tap on the front of her armor.

I studied it, taking stock of the filthy, damaged steel, the scrapes, scratches, and gouges, not to mention the dried viscera that encrusted sections and filled creases, no matter how hard she'd tried to get it out. Still, she didn't see it the same as I did.

I was thankful to her for risking her life and standing with me. I'd given her armor to keep her safe, but it was due to my habit of putting her in situations where she damn well needed it. In her eyes, though? I'd given her all she'd ever dared to dream of and more.

I beamed, reaching out and gripping her shoulder. My smile grew all the wider at feeling Oracle's love for this woman shining through.

"I'm damn lucky to have you," I said as I held her abashed gaze. "I'll make sure you get some armor that's more appropriate, as well," I promised, noting that she'd had to fully dismiss her wings to equip the damaged breastplate.

"Oh no, I'm fine, I mean…I don't…" she stammered.

I held up my other hand to still her objections. "Don't worry," I said. "I know."

She smiled and nodded, relieved, as I released her and laid back. My back popped as I stretched, and I shifted a bag of what felt like goddamn turnips aside, sighing as I got more comfortable and stared into the darkening sky.

"It's going to rain, isn't it?" I said eventually, and a groan rose from nearby.

"Don't you know talking about bad weather makes it come true?" Grizz muttered. At some point, Yen had joined us, and he was reclining with his head propped comfortably on her abdomen, glaring at me in reproach.

"You know that's bullshit, right?" I asked him incredulously, and he snorted.

"Maybe; still true, though. When it rains now, it's your fault," he insisted. I flicked a confused frown at Yen, who blushed slightly then pretended to ignore being caught with Grizz cuddled up to her.

"We have tents," Tang grumbled from the other side of the group, getting scattered agreement from the dozens of legionnaires that were camped all around us.

I peered around carefully, trying not to make too much noise. While I'd been meditating, the entire complement of legionnaires on the ship had found their way to where I was laying, and they had arranged themselves in concentric circles radiating outwards. Every third legionnaire was awake and on watch, scanning practically every direction, as though they expected trouble to float up through the deck to attack at any second.

I laid back again, shifting until I was as comfortable as I could be, and closed my eyes to focus on reaching out with senses I rarely used. Dozens of strands stretched out, glimmering brightly from me to each of the legionnaires and to the ship's crew. Beyond that, hundreds of strands reached back to the remaining fleet as well as the others who fled ahead of us toward the Great Tower.

Those who led to the Tower were slowly growing brighter, while the others, leading back to the fleet, dimmed. Somewhere off to the left and far below, more strands reached up to me. I smiled, shivering slightly as I thought about the enormous spider-queen Ashrag and her minions.

I'd done the right thing there; I honestly believed that, and they'd make great allies. But seriously, fucking spiders the size of houses and horses, with scouts the size of Great Danes, who thought they were puppies? What kind of a twisted God came up with this shit?

I shuddered involuntarily and pulled my awareness back a bit, feeling the threads of golden light flowing out from myself to touch those laying close all around me, and the absolute safety it engendered in my soul.

I was surrounded by nearly thirty legionnaires on this ship, with another two ships on either side, and we were traveling at full speed, rushing to get back home.

I smiled unconsciously as I realized that I essentially had hundreds of brothers and sisters now, of all races, and probably tens of thousands spread across the realm. They'd stand with, and for me.

They'd have my back, and I'd have theirs, and all I had to do was find them; find them and welcome them home.

I had a *home*, a family, and I had to admit, as much as I wished openly for an end to all the conflict and for some sort of peace, I was fucking loving it. I'd never felt so alive as when I was fighting, and that was why our lives as kids, even before coming here, had been so terrible.

In our dreams, we fought and saved lives. We were openly respected and loved, and beyond a bit of pain...okay, a lot of pain...we never had to worry about shit.

We were important, and we had a real effect on the world around us. As kids, we were outsiders with an average education, if that. With the way our world was, we were nothing again as soon as we woke up. We grew to love the dreams as much as hate them for the pain and inability to understand what they were.

Now I knew, and I assumed Tommy did as well. Here, we could achieve something great. We could save lives, and I'd never been so invigorated as when I was surrounded by enemies and fighting for my life.

I finally admitted that to myself, as the hours passed, and we closed in on the Tower.

I'd never return to Earth. Just about the only things I'd really miss were Five Guys burgers and junk food.

I smiled again, opening my eyes at a rustle, just in time to observe a handful of legionnaires attaching waterproof sections of cloth they each carried to make a shelter on the deck for us all.

They worked quietly and efficiently; this was clearly a normal process for them, and I shook my head in amazement. These people were elite in every way, except one.

They had so little magic, it was unreal. Admittedly, they had offensive spells, at least, or a handful of them did, but healing or buffs were almost unheard of. They had no luxuries, maintaining an existence that would have made the Spartans proud.

Yet despite all this, they were cheerful, and the way they lived, joked, and loved? Yeah, they were in for a surprise, because the damn least I could do was give them the home and magic they deserved, even if it wore Oracle and me out.

I laid there silently for another hour or so, staring up at the canvas, listening to the gentle sounds of the drumming rain, the occasional muffled creak of the lines and sails, and the steady humming of the mana-engines, until at last, I fell asleep.

THOMAS

"Seriously?" Thomas asked, leaning back against the rock and twisting to crack his aching back. He forcibly ignored the steadily flashing notifications in the corner of his vision. Every night of the march was the same: collapse, eat, drink their daily ale ration, then fall into an exhausted sleep until they were kicked from their bedrolls to start the next day's sprint.

He'd given up on the notifications now, as they were always stupid ones, like a level in jumping or trail running. Not a single damn point had increased in their physical stats as the goddamn Trailmasters somehow siphoned it off to aid their spells.

"What, you'd rather be running with the others?" Coran scoffed, shoving him roughly from where he sat a few feet away. "Shut it, you damn fool."

"No! Hell, no. I'm up for that!" Thomas quickly clarified, holding his hands up, one still holding his cup half-full of ale, as Belladonna and Turk glared at him. "Seriously, I'm happy to come!"

"You think you get a choice?" Turk growled around a mouthful of the crap excuse for beef and beans. The little tin plate constantly made noises as Turk scraped at it, trying to get every last morsel.

"No, I was just surprised, that's all!" Thomas said again. "I thought they belonged to the villagers…"

"They've gone, so fuck it. Nobody around to request permission for a harvest, so nobody to say no, either. I made a deal with the evening Trailmaster; says we've got six hours to make it back, but after that, we're deserters. I'm betting we can cull the goddamn lot of them in two, then we sprint as hard as we can. *IF* we can make it back into range of the spells, it'll get a lot easier to catch up. If not, well, they probably won't hang us all."

"Seems risky for a handful of pelts, though," Coran opined, and Turk snorted as Belladonna grinned at him.

"They're not just pelts, lad. They're *horned rabbit pelts*…softest fur you'll ever feel. We get half of them, and the Trailmaster gets the other half. When we get back to Himnel, I know a seamstress who'll make us each a cloak or a bedroll of the stuff. She takes twenty percent and asks no questions. Believe me, once you've had one, you'll never pass up an opportunity like this," the squad sergeant assured us, shaking out her fur-lined cloak so we could all see it.

"I got this three winters ago, and I'd sell any of you in an instant for a damn bedroll made of the stuff, so remember that." She grinned, only half joking.

"So, when do we leave?" Thomas asked.

"First thing in the morning, two hours before first light. The village being abandoned is the best goddamn thing that could have happened to us, lad; you'll see." She tossed her ale back and pulled out her own bedroll. "Now get to sleep. I traded our watch for dog watch, so as soon as it's done, we're off. If you expect to sleep at all tonight, it's now."

With that, the rest of the ten-man squad moved hurriedly, and Thomas quaffed his ale, dumping the cup and plate into his bag before setting his own bedroll out. He stripped to his underclothes and clambered in, ignoring the sensation of spiders crawling across his hairy legs. He'd checked too many goddamn times, and it wasn't real. It was just the awful, cheap material the bedrolls were made of...

Thomas was asleep almost before his head hit the pillow, his last thoughts of Belladonna naked in a silky-soft, horned rabbit bedroll.

It seemed like seconds later when he was roughly shaken, the distant clanging of the watch bell signaling the ten-minute warning before the watch changed. He groaned, cursing the timing.

He struggled out of the bedroll, only to spy Belladonna rolling out of hers, her underwear gleaming in the darkness as she pulled clothes out of her bag and started to dress. The sergeant was clearly unconcerned by her own near-nakedness, this being the norm for them all now.

Thomas paused, drinking in the sight of her, until Turk stepped between them, blocking his view and glaring at him. Thomas jumped, having been totally distracted by the memory of the dream, the recollection of her nakedness in the healing and pledging ceremony, and the reality of her here before him.

"Fuck," he muttered, blanching at his mistake in ogling his sergeant, and he hoped, his friend. Embarrassment flooded him, and he looked away as he finished climbing out and grabbed at his clothes.

Turk, fortunately, was an Orc of few words, and he simply stared at Thomas again before shouldering past roughly and nearly knocking him over.

"What the hell, man?" Coran snarled at Thomas under his breath, leaning over from where he was already packing his own gear away. "Seriously, you need to have a long think right now, or you're gonna get gutted!"

"I know!" Thomas snapped back. "I just...got distracted, that's all."

"Yeah, and you fucking stared at her like she was a woman. She's not; she's the fucking sergeant. She'll rip your head off and shit down your neck, and that's if you're fucking lucky!" Coran hissed warningly.

Thomas glared back at him, anger almost perpetually rising steadily, looking for a vent.

"I said I know," Thomas growled at his friend, who bristled in turn.

Finally, Shen pushed between them and looked down at Thomas's half-naked state and the gear that was still strewn about. "Well, brother, you're going to be murdered twice if you don't get ready quick," the massive, dark-skinned man said calmly, patting Thomas on the shoulder as he stared down at him with those weird bright purple eyes. "Do you need help?"

Thomas opened his mouth to snap back at him before getting himself under control and shaking his head.

"No, but thank you, Shen. Coran, sorry for being a dick," he muttered, and Coran grunted something noncommittal back at him. Shen patted him on the shoulder again, dropping his voice to a whisper before he stepped away.

"We have all been there, Thomas. Dream your dreams, then move on. It is not meant to be."

Thomas glanced up at the enormous man and sighed, getting back to dressing. He'd barely finished before having to grab the neatly bundled bedroll Coran chucked to him, slipping it into his bag with a grunt of thanks to his friend.

They made their way through the slumbering Dark Legion, taking up their posts on the outer ring. Each of them presented fully armored, with weapons drawn and grounded, standing ten paces apart in silence, as Nimon had supposedly ordered when he laid down the rules for the legion.

Thomas shook his head absently, just managing to not call the dark God a dumbass, even if only in his head. Not only was it bloody stupid to expose your weapon like this, making damn sure the firelight could show you off to any potential attacker for miles around, but standing at attention for two hours was tiring enough after an entire damn day of running in full armor. Add on the weather? Thomas had heard of people being struck by lightning in storms, because to do otherwise was to be executed by your own brothers and sisters for disobeying the dark God.

Damn stupid set of rules, but hey, at least they were all in it together. Even the commanders had to stand their watch, which was a nice change from the officers who used their rank to sidestep mundane responsibilities, which Thomas had learned to expect over the years.

The two hours passed slowly, the occasional snuffling of creatures in the brush out of sight being the only excitement, besides the memory of Belladonna in her underwear…

Thomas had allowed himself to be distracted, gazing sightlessly out of the slit in his helm at the forest. He had been fantasizing about banging that ass when the ten-minute warning bell for the changing of the watch rang out, making him jump slightly.

The jingle of his chainmail bouncing against his steel armor sounded out. He sighed, knowing damn well that he was going to get grief over that at some point.

The relief squad moved up and out, all on time, which, again, was a nice change in comparison to his army days back on Earth. Thomas nodded to the woman who stepped up to take her turn in the same damn spot, shifting herself to get comfortable in her armor as she let out an audible yawn.

"Anything out there?" the woman whispered before Thomas could move away, and he shook his head.

"A few rats or something; think there's a nest under that fallen log to the left, about a hundred yards out, just at the edge of the firelight. Beyond that, nothing," Thomas replied.

"Well, enjoy yourself, lucky bastard." She grimaced good-naturedly, and Thomas grinned. It was Minette from the fourth squad.

"Hey, you got a longer sleep," he countered, realizing that it was her squad that Belladonna had swapped the watch with, and she snorted softly as he started away.

"Thomas," she called quietly, not turning around.

"Yeah?" He stepped back to her side.

"If there's a few rabbits going spare…?" she whispered. "Might be that I'd be grateful."

"Might be there'll be spares; don't hold your breath, though," Thomas whispered back, tapping her lightly on the shoulder and striding away.

Minette was a good one, as they went. Not much of a looker, but she was fun to talk to, gave as good as she got, and looked after her people. She had ten years left on her stint in the Dark Legion, having sold herself to get out of a situation she'd not talk about. Twenty years, she'd signed up for.

When he'd first been admitted as a Slave-Aspirant, unlike many, she'd granted him some dignity when she was responsible for his training and had spoken for him to be given the chance to become a Soldier-Aspirant. It might not have seemed like much to many, but in that single step up, he'd gone from a slave with no hope of ever regaining rights to his own life, to being a man again. He had dignity, he had worth, and a single naysaying by those who had watched over him in those first days would have prevented his rise in a heartbeat.

He owed her.

Thomas sighed under his breath as he walked away, knowing damn well that, if there wasn't enough for a bedroll in whatever spares he harvested, he'd be giving his up to even the score between them.

If she'd demanded it, or even hinted that she expected it, he'd have told her to go fuck herself. He was a single rank from her now and had the right to do what he wanted, within reason.

It was specifically because she'd never ask for it. Or expect it. He shook his head again as he hurried to catch up to the others, where they gathered beyond the firelight. Once he'd joined them, as the last of their party, Belladonna showed a pass to the watcher.

The mage was responsible for watching over the camp and raising an alert if there was a mutiny or desertion. It was still possible, even as indoctrinated and sworn as they were. That said, it'd be damn stupid, as the result would be both horrifically painful and the perpetrator would show up to any watchman, guard, or Dark Legionnaire as a deserter after that, gaining them both gold and a stat point if they killed you.

He looked over the pass, grunted something, and waved the squad off. Turk gestured for them to go, with Belladonna leading the way. Thomas brought up the rear as he hurried after them, the big orc waiting until he passed to take up his place at the back of the small column.

They ran for nearly an hour straight before angling to the left and picking up the pace as they abandoned the tree line, emerging onto the meadow they'd been told to watch for.

From there, it didn't take long; a sprint up one side of the hill at the far end, then a slow, loud jog down the opposite side, as their noise announced their presence to the colony.

"What is it with these fuckers?" Thomas asked Turk as they jogged side by side, watching the horned heads popping out of the burrows all around to glare at them.

"Whadda yer mean?" the orc growled, glaring up at the sides of the hill as the earth rose around them, his grip on his massive two-handed broadsword making the leather creak as he shifted it.

"I mean, they're fucking *rabbits*!" Thomas said grimly. "Seriously, yeah, they've got a horn, but what's with the aggression? I keep expecting to meet Tim the Enchanter."

"Who?" Turk asked distractedly.

"The enchanter known...as Tim!" Thomas said, grinning, only regretting that he couldn't make the hand gestures as he went on. "'Death awaits us all, with nasty, big, pointy teeth!'"

"What are you goin' on about, yer damn fool?" the hulking legionnaire demanded as Thomas sighed, shaking his head.

"Clearly, dude, you're not a fan of the classics," Thomas said sadly.

"If it's another of your damn fool stories, like the one about the space wizards with the magical swords of light that can cut anything, then shut it!" Turk growled. "We won't have long before..."

A screech of fury interrupted the orc as more and more horned rabbits appeared all around them, and Thomas snorted in disgust at the beasts.

He set himself behind his shield, leaned into it and called out to the nearest one. The creature stood about three feet high at its tallest, including a good six inches of horn, glaring at them with red-rimmed eyes as it panted in fury.

"Come on! I've a recipe for soup made out of you, ya ugly fucker!" Thomas called, and Turk hissed in anger as Thomas instantly became the center of attention.

"Thomas..." Belladonna called warningly to him.

"Uh, yeah?" he asked, confused by the barely constrained anger and the hint of fear in her voice.

"If we live through this, you'll regret that."

"If?" Thomas started to ask, when the first rabbit charged.

It wasn't the one he'd been shouting at. It wasn't one that any of them had been looking at, in fact. One of the reasons the species was so valuable, and feared, was their rudimentary hive consciousness, which allowed them to coordinate the defense of their homes.

Belladonna had intended for them to take up a position in the center, shields overlapping, which would have allowed them to stab out when the rabbits hit them, stunning themselves and providing a considerably easier time of slaughtering them...Thomas had managed to draw not only the entire herd's aggro, he'd done it before his team had been in position.

"Shieldwall!" Belladonna screamed, and the squad fell in on her command, taking a knee, burying the pointed tip of the shield into the dark loam and angling the shield to the side slightly, where the next shield slotted into place.

All except Thomas, who grunted in surprise as the first rabbit appeared seemingly from nowhere. He barely managed to shift his shield in time to stop it from taking him in the thigh with the horn.

Thomas cried out in pain as the shield, not set correctly to take the blow, nearly broke his arm, but true to his years of experience, he lashed out, the flanged head of his mace smashing the side of the rabbit's skull in, killing it instantly.

Before he could recover, he saw them, pouring out of their burrows like a furry wave, the light of the false dawn glinting off the dozens of horns, all flashing towards him.

The second one, he managed to deflect, sending it aside into another that was charging from his right, and he jumped left, aiming for the space the rabbit had just passed through, slamming his mace out behind him blindly on instinct. The rest of his squad watched silently, squinting between the edges of their shields.

Thomas landed, crouched, and was immediately hit in the right knee, then his shield, then a furry blur resolved into a rabbit that had seemingly launched itself off another's back, flying for his face.

His eyes widened when it hit a glancing blow, the horn leaving a long scratch on the side of his helm and sending him staggering back. Another slammed into the back of his left knee, making it buckle as the steel barely held against the force of the blow and the sharp horn.

He fell, another hitting him from the left, somehow managing to get behind his shield and tearing it free as Thomas hit the ground, lashing out with his mace.

A furry form lay crushed beneath him as he landed on his back, bones breaking, the pop of ligaments and cartilage, and a final, wet squeak.

Thomas had a second of clarity, and he heard his own voice echoing in his helmet as he spoke the thought aloud.

"I'm gonna be fucking murdered by rabbits, and no holy hand-grenade..." There was a last split second of peace as he felt the earth shudder around him, and he saw rabbits that had already committed to the leap, flying overhead. A trail of droppings fell from a wiggling pom-pom of a tail...and he snarled in fury.

He wasn't dying; not here, not to fucking *rabbits*!

Thomas slammed his mace to the right, the steel crunching into a furry form, while his left hand snaked out and grabbed the nearest enemy on his left. His fingers closed around the neck, and he yanked it down, using its body to cover his own as he throttled it.

Thomas kicked out, punched, crushed, and yanked, rolling and deliberately diving atop a rabbit that shot under him, missing its aim as he moved.

He used his own weight to crush it, rolling free again and slamming both hands outwards, fingers twisting, mace wedged somewhere furry as he fired ten Magic Missiles at once, one from each finger, taking nine rabbits out in a single wave of gory explosions.

All Thomas could hear was screeches of rage and hatred, the squeal of horns against his armor, and the echoing sound of his heavy breathing and furious cursing.

As Thomas struggled to his feet, the others crouched behind their shields, watching him silently. His anger rose further, wrath filling him.

They'd told him the Shieldwall was the plan during the run. He understood damn well that, if they did come out then were swamped, others could and probably would die. It'd all be his fault, and that knowledge made him roar unintelligibly as the world tinted into redness, as his anger at his own distracted stupidity tore through him.

He'd not been paying attention. Worse, he'd dismissed the threat, thinking he knew what was happening, and now he was about to be murdered by fucking rabbits, in front of Belladonna! Not only would he never have a damn chance with her, but she'd remember him forever as "that asshole who got killed by the fucking rabbits."

Thomas's breath hissed out between gritted teeth, even as more and more rabbits appeared, his gauntlets creaking as shoulders heaved against the confines of the armor.

His health and stamina bars in the corner of his vision flashed and grew by half again, the world seeming to narrow in his vision, and he released a bestial scream.

His armor grew suddenly tighter as his muscles expanded, and even that spurred him to new heights. He slammed one fist down, smashing a rabbit behind its head with a vicious crack as its spine shattered.

He caught one that was hurtling through the air at his face, stopping the creature like it had hit a wall, then whipping it around, using the screeching fluffy bludgeon to clear the nearest enemies from him, when the horned rabbit king made its appearance known, bursting upwards out of the loamy earth and screaming a challenge at Thomas.

It was a rare monster, Belladonna had told them all; only one in a dozen or more herds would have the beast at any one time, as it traveled back and forth, moving from herd to herd, fucking its way to exhaustion until its heart gave out, at which point, there would be a mass feeding. The rabbit that ate the king's heart would grow in strength, taking the old king's place.

Not only was it powerful, rare, and valuable, but the effects of the heart weren't species-specific. While it would have a much lesser effect on a human, lesser wasn't none.

Thomas spun around, locking eyes on the beast and screaming back at it, a roar of absolute fury that transcended species and language barriers, carrying a short message that was clearly understood: *Buckle up buttercup*, that scream said. *Because it's fucking on!*

Thomas threw aside the bloody, broken corpse of the rabbit he held clenched in one hand, and ran at the rabbit on the hill. Instinctually, he back-handed a rabbit that tried to take him down from the side, ignoring the breaking of its bones, much less the spasmodic flopping of its body as it hit the ground.

Other rabbits between him and the king broke and ran as Thomas roared up at the rabbit that stood almost as tall as he was. The king bellowed back, bunching its legs and leaping.

In Thomas' berserker state, he couldn't dodge, and wouldn't have understood the concept even if he'd had the time, but what he did understand was momentum.

As the rabbit flew toward him, he raised both hands overhead and slammed them across and down, clenched together in a hammer-fist that drove aside the horn destined to impale him. Even so, the massive beast's shoulder slammed into his stomach, driving him back, leaving furrows over a meter in length torn into the damp loam.

Thomas twisted at the hip, grabbing the creature's flanks and gripping with all his might as he threw the rabbit aside, sending it flopping and twisting through the air to skid across the ground, screaming, several dozen feet away.

It rolled to its feet, bunched its legs again, and ran at him, leaping upwards and angling itself back, reminiscent of a kangaroo. The powerful legs kicked out, hitting Thomas in the chest and sending him rocketing backwards.

He slammed down, air knocked from him, breastplate dented in painfully by the kick. He grunted then rolled, barely avoiding the rabbit's enormous feet as they slammed down where he'd just been.

Thomas's hand whipped out, yanking one leg back and dragging the rabbit down as he grunted and jumped back up, still unable to get a full breath. Somehow, white-hot wrath compensated where little things like oxygen deprivation and pain tried to slow him.

He punched the rabbit in the face, driving it back and making it squeal. It lashed out, razor-sharp claws carving three furrows across his breastplate with a scream of tortured metal.

Thomas sucked in a massive breath as his diaphragm finally recovered from the involuntary spasm, and he slapped aside another slash with his left hand as he spat out the words that were so familiar after frequent use, his right fingers curling and popping into arcane symbols.

As the horned rabbit king lunged, trying to bite him, Thomas punched it again in the face, left-handed, and he felt the give of bones under his massively swollen fist. His right foot flashed up as he punted the enormous rabbit that stood tall on its back feet…right in the balls.

The creature let out a sudden high-pitched wail of pain, and Thomas slammed his right hand forward, all five digits unleashing the smaller variant of the Magic Missile he'd spent so many years adjusting. The darts slammed home, deep into the mewling creature's skull, before detonating.

There was silence for a few long seconds, broken only by Thomas's harsh, frantic panting as he glared at his enemy until it toppled slowly backwards, slamming into the ground. The rabbits around the collection of burrows let loose a savage scream, nature's impetus forcibly overriding their fear and sending them hurtling towards the king's corpse.

"Thomas!" Belladonna screamed in panic. "Get it into your bag, *fast!*" Thomas glared at her then at the little creatures that raced towards his prize, before sweeping it up and depositing it into the bag of holding. The incoming rabbits faltered, as the biological need remained, but their target had vanished from their reality.

Thomas roared and leaped, landing on a nearby rabbit that had slowed in uncertainty as it cast about for the king's corpse. It squealed as its back crumpled under Thomas's weight, and he went on the rampage, kicking, punching, and throwing them. Out of the corner of his eye, he saw the others emerge from behind their pathetic little shieldwall.

Minutes passed in a blur, fists flashing and bones breaking, the rest of the squad being careful to keep their distance from Thomas as he rampaged back and forth, screaming at the rabbits, occasionally going so far as to pull the king's corpse out to stop them from running away.

An hour had passed from the time the squad arrived at the site, when Thomas finally began to fully regain his mind, and he found himself seated atop a pile of bodies, gathered on a small hill. Blood dripped from his fingers, arms, and hell, even his beard.

At some point, he'd lost his helmet, and he sat panting, staring at a patch of bloody fur stuck between the fingers of his left hand.

He dragged his index fingernail down the crevice, rooting the fur out as the sticky blood began to dry, then sat up, drawing in a deep lungful of air. Instinct and thirst had him flicking his tongue over his lips unconsciously, tasting blood and more fur.

He coughed and spat, reaching for his bag, and pulled out a flask of water. He carefully began rinsing his mouth out and spitting again before trusting himself enough to drink.

"So…" a voice rose from his right.

He flicked his gaze over, exhaustion draining him to the point that he could feel the shakes coming. "Berserker, eh?" Belladonna asked.

He started to shake his head before stopping and shrugging instead. "I…what happened?" Thomas asked wearily, and Belladonna grinned.

"You don't remember?" she asked with amusement, and he shook his head again. "It happens, or so I'm told. Check your notifications, soldier."

"Soldier?" Thomas asked slowly, frowning at her, and she nodded.

"An Aspirant-Soldier is raised to full soldier after three conditions are met: training is completed, he makes his first kill before three witnesses, and he kills his tenth enemy before his direct commander's eyes. You passed the training, and *damn*, you certainly passed the kills. You'll be formally acknowledged as a dark legionnaire after this mission. Until then, you're a soldier," she said, wonder and an edge of concern in her voice. "You'll need practice with the ability you've been gifted, but…damn. I'm glad I traded for you, I'll admit it."

"That's just because of my stunning good looks," Thomas quipped quietly, too tired to be subtle.

"You're not entirely painful to look at, I suppose." Belladonna snorted, a wry smile lifting her lips.

"Everyone wants a moustache ride…even the sarge," Thomas muttered, forcing a grin through the rapidly drying blood. He still tasted the fur and filth on his lips and blinked down at his blood-covered form. "But I need a bath, and soon…fancy helping?" he asked, scratching the blood off the back of a vambrace.

"Are you flirting with me, soldier?!" Belladonna asked in a low, intense voice as she stiffened.

"Depends, is it working?" Thomas replied wearily, finally looking up again and grinning, before the expression slipped from his face at the sight of her white lips pressed together.

"Get your ass down there and get to work!" she snarled.

He winced; he'd gone too far.

The next twenty minutes was spent in an orgy of viscera, as everyone fell to with a will, gutting, stripping, and dumping the corpses into storage as they frantically tried to strip and store all the bodies before they were forced to set off.

"Turk!" Belladonna shouted as Thomas reached for his sixth corpse, his hands shaking with the adrenaline crash. "Thomas is butchering my furs, and he's clearly going to be so slow as to be fucking useless after that, so set off with him. Kick his ass back to the column, and we'll catch up."

"Yes, Belladonna," Turk acknowledged, straightening up and striding over to Thomas, who blinked bleary-eyed at him.

"Up, maggot!" he barked. Thomas staggered upright. Turk chivvied and kicked, yelled, and berated him into a run, half-screaming, half-guiding him along.

Three hours later, the rest of the squad caught up, all bloody, but with high spirits as they bunched up around Thomas. They took turns helping him run as they caught up to the column.

The day passed in a painful blur for Thomas, his muscles torn and strained. His entire body felt like a single bruise, but his mind was too foggy to make sense of it.

That night, as he collapsed on his bedroll, finally clean again, after his comrades had literally thrown him into the cold, crisp waters of a river alongside their camp, he brought up the relevant notification, discarding the rest.

Your Patron has assigned you the Class Dark Berserker!

You have been gifted a new class by your Patron. This rare Class is born of your inherent rage, your desire to tear and rend, to destroy, and through Nimon's gift of Dark Blood, it has been transformed. No longer will you hear the ramblings of a spirit long dead; instead, you will hear the call of your master.

Each time you indulge your dark gift, you will grow stronger and faster, but beware: power is a two-edged gift. When the Gods give, they also take.

Dark Berserkers grow in strength, depending on their rage, with the following levels having the corresponding effects:

Anger: 10-15% increase in muscle mass; momentum-based attacks do 25% more damage
Unhinged Fury: 20-35% increase in muscle mass; momentum-based attacks for 40-50% more damage
Uncontrolled Wrath: 40-65% increase in muscle mass; momentum-based attacks for 55-75% more damage
Insanity: 100% increase in muscle mass; momentum-based attacks for 200% more damage

"Great…I'm a fucking animal," Thomas groaned, closing his eyes and trying to understand why the hell he'd done this to himself. He'd have to spend the rest of his goddamn life trying to keep this beast constrained.

He played the fight through his head again and again, and then, with mounting horror, he remembered the conversation with Belladonna afterwards. He felt his nuts try to reach his chin internally, before a final thought came to him, just as he slipped into troubled, nightmare-plagued dreams.

"Wait, she didn't actually say no…" he mumbled before the world slipped away.

As his breathing deepened and the camp grew silent again, Belladonna rolled onto her back nearby, her bedroll twisted around one leg. She straightened it out in annoyance before lying back, as she contemplated Thomas and his actions today, as she found herself doing far too frequently of late.

"No…I didn't…" she admitted to herself in a whisper so low that nobody without elven hearing would ever catch. She stared up at the stars through the canopy of trees overhead, as she wondered about the insanity of that and what the future would bring.

CHAPTER SEVEN

"Jax," Oracle whispered in my ear, and I blinked, forcing my eyes open and stifling a groan at the gentle, rain-diffused sunlight that painfully forced its way in.

"What is it, Oracle?" I mumbled, feeling exhausted, until she said the magical words.

"We're nearly home!"

I let a small smile escape as I rolled out of the crevice I'd gradually slid into, wedged between a bag of turnips and a bag of grain. Grunting as my back popped, I resolved to either take my armor off in the future, find a bed, or both, for at least the fifteenth time.

I carefully picked my way past legionnaires who still slept, easing over bundles of gear and rolled-up cloaks that covered other slumbering forms until I could step out from under our makeshift tent.

I looked out across the bow. A sense of immense relief flooded through me as I spotted the Tower in the distance. The Great Tower of Dravith was somewhere between two and three miles high; Oracle could tell me exactly, but in that moment, I didn't care. It was pitted and worn with age; sections of it were basically ruins. Interior walls had collapsed, windows plastered over by literal sporeling shit, and fruit and pleasure gardens that had filled balconies for the residents had grown wild over the seven-hundred-plus years that the Tower had languished in the hands—or claws, I supposed—of the SporeMother.

Even here, a good hour or two from landing, I could make out the vast gardens, the trees that dangled precipitously from crumbling railings and balconies, and the empty, gaping sections that marked collapsed floors.

Despite all of that, though, I was coming home.

I could see, in the far distance, a ship launching from the Tower, followed by a second. They were on an intercept course for us, making me smile.

The warship, *Agamemnon's Pride*, was clearly fixed up now, judging from the shape of it, as Oren and Decin came to defend the Tower from any threat.

"Do you think they know it's us?" I asked Oracle, and she smiled and nodded.

"They should; I can feel Seneschal and Hephaestus, after all, so they ought to have told them it was us."

"Fancy flying over to surprise them when they get close?" I asked, and she smiled mischievously.

"I think you might give Oren a heart attack," she warned, before nodding. "But we should definitely do it, anyway!"

I grinned and leaned on the railing, watching as the oncoming ships and the Tower grew in detail. The steady drizzle that marked this morning was fuzzing the edges of things in the distance, but not enough to hide anything.

Soon, some of the others joined me. Yen leaned against a nearby mast, squinting out at the Tower more than the oncoming ships.

"What do you think?" I asked her quietly.

"I don't know," she admitted. "You told us it was a ruin, but it's huge, and, well…I don't know. Whatever spell normally cloaks it from view isn't working on us. I don't know why that is, but if we'd ever been able to find this place, we'd have cleared it out centuries ago."

"It's to hide the Tower from unfriendly eyes," I explained, eyeing the structure proudly. "I guess once you've sworn to me, you're excluded from its effects. Besides, I'm glad you weren't able to, as you'd have, what, turned it over to the city to use?"

"Probably." She sighed heavily. "We'd have hated giving it up, but unless it was recent, like the last few years recent, we'd have handed it over and returned to the Enclave. Now, we'd have marched the Legion out and moved in, then told the city to go fuck itself, even though that'd probably have resulted in them coming after us. Weird the way it's worked out, I guess, as they're coming for us, anyway." She stood straighter, adjusting her hood in an effort to keep the drizzle out.

"Are you sure you still want to be on the team?" I pressed, watching her expression. "Considering what's coming and the changes I'm making?"

"The war, you mean? Or Primus Restun getting to retrain us all to the standards he thinks we should be held to? You know he's broken full legionnaires, right? Left them in heaps, begging for mercy."

"Both. The war wasn't planned, but it's coming regardless, so we have to be ready. Honestly, I can believe he'll be a nightmare, but the more you sweat, the less you bleed."

"I like that saying," Restun said quietly from behind me, practically making me shit myself before I swallowed the curse I'd been about to yell at Bane.

"Uh…it's from my home." I muttered.

"I think it's appropriate." Restun replied blandly. "Now, I am aware that you have a particularly busy day ahead of you in the Tower, what with it being the first day back and a war to plan, so I assume you won't want to start with the full training until tomorrow?"

I sagged in relief and smiled. "No, no, that's for the best. We can start tomorrow, thanks." I said, then I froze at the look of resignation on Yen's face…as well as the conspicuous lack of Grizz, as an empty blanket marked where he'd been slumbering a few seconds before.

"I…uh…" I started to mumble a retraction before Restun, clapped me on the shoulder and smiled cheerfully at me.

"Good! In that case, the captain has said we have perhaps thirty minutes before those ships arrive. While not long, it's enough for a warm-up, at least," Restun announced. Behind him, legionnaires dashed for cover as quickly and silently as they could.

"Yeah…" I sighed, sagging further. I was cornered. As much as I wanted to figure a way to slope out of the workout, I needed it.

Restun had cornered both Yen and me, and Bane and Tang were close enough that he gestured to both of them to join in. To my great surprise, Arrin, Jian, and Giint joined us without being threatened or coerced, followed swiftly by Lydia when she realized what was going on.

Restun spread us all out on the deck and led us through a series of easy calisthenics, starting with a stretch that was right out of a yoga playbook, then pushups, sit-ups, star jumps, followed by running on the spot.

It was a really basic series of exercises, but when I did a hundred of each, then moved straight to the next without a break, it still exhausted me, despite how many points I had in Endurance and Strength.

Restun wasn't the kind of trainer who stood and stared while we exercised, either. No, he was the worst kind; he did it alongside us all and made us look weak and slow in comparison.

He started out just that little bit faster than me, so naturally I tried to catch up and fell into his evil trap. Each time I closed on him, he went slightly faster, until at the end of the half hour, I had collapsed in a puddle of sweat, panting to get my breath back. If I'd had the air to do it, I'd have been groaning and swearing as well.

"A good start to the day," Restun declared.

I stared at him, observing a slight redness to his cheeks...and that was it. The bastard wasn't even sweating! "Tomorrow, we can start to work on things properly. I heard that you have a Tia'Almer-atic leading your training in the Tower; this is good. Once they overcome their debilitating weakness upon first leaving the water, they become formidable allies."

"Flux..." I wheezed. "His name...is Flux...and he works...with Barrett...to train the...Tower's forces," I managed to grind out, groaning as Restun reached down and hauled me to my feet.

"Walk while you talk; you'll recover faster," he instructed.

I stared at him in disbelief. My legs shook so badly I could barely stand. "With your permission, upon arrival, I will examine the Tower and its facilities and provide an estimate on the best positions and roles for the Legion to occupy, as well as determine possible choke points and areas we can fortify to secure the Tower as quickly as possible."

"Yeah...sure, go for it..." I muttered, staggering on wobbly legs around the deck. I privately reflected that, right then, I'd have agreed to his request to chop my head off and mount it on his wall if it meant I never had to exercise with him again.

I made it to the railing and leaned against it, wheezing as the others joined me. I nodded in understanding at Arrin, grinning at the especially broken-looking man.

While the rest of us had at least put some exercise in daily, and were mainly front-line fighters, or legionnaires, he'd gone for a mage's build and had invested all his points in Intelligence and Wisdom, meaning that he was paying especially hard for this training session.

I reached out and slapped him on the back, being too knackered to speak, and he gawked at me with wide eyes, shaking.

"Why...why did...he...do that?" he mumbled fearfully.

I managed to pull my aching shoulders into a shrug.

"He's an evil, evil man," insisted a voice from behind some boxes nearby. I forced myself upright, staggering a few steps until I could see Grizz seated there, safely out of Restun's line of sight.

"You utter bastard," I said, and he grinned up at me.

"You're only jealous you didn't manage to hide in time," he said unrepentantly. I growled under my breath, acknowledging that it was true.

"Jax!" Oracle called from the bow of the ship, and I glowered at Grizz one last time before limping along to see what she wanted.

When I reached her, she stepped in close and put her arm around my waist, hugging into me. I leaned down, kissing the top of her head as I gazed ahead, seeing the ships closing the last few hundred meters. Wincing, I waved weakly at Oren as he passed by on the port side, with Decin standing and watching over us from the starboard side, his ridiculous purple robes standing out clearly.

I waved to them both, and they waved back. Oracle looked up inquisitively at me, and I took a deep breath and climbed onto the railing of the ship.

I caught the look of shock on Oren's face just before I grinned and dove straight off the side.

He twisted the helm instinctively, clearly planning on diving in an attempt to catch me and save me, when I spread my arms wide and flipped over, jetting upwards toward him.

He jerked the ship back on course, gaping at me in a mixture of shock and awe as I circled his ship, then swooped in and landed on his top deck. Jory, the old helmsman, stared at me in slack-jawed amazement as I landed.

The landing would have been much more impressive, I had to admit, if I hadn't nearly collapsed as soon as I put weight on my legs, but a quick healing from Oracle fixed that. I stepped forward, getting a hug and a back slapping from Oren that felt like I'd nearly broken a rib.

"It be good te have yer back, laddie!" Oren beamed as he released me, his hands on his hips as he looked me over. His surreptitiously eyeing Oracle did not go unnoticed, as she was looking particularly stunning today. "An' you an' all, lass," he amended, grinning at her as she…bounced…to a stop next to me, wearing tight skinny jeans, knee-length black velvet boots, and a red bandeau top.

"Behave yourself, you little sod!" I growled at the short, wide Dwarf in mock anger, and he put his palms to his cheeks in fake horror.

"Oh no, what ever will I do? Tha great an' mighty Lord Jax is pissed wit' me? Ah, well…fuck it, I'll get over it." He snorted, gesturing as though slapping a hand away, and grinned at me, looking back at the ship I'd just left so spectacularly. "So, since when can ye fly like ye got a wee fairy stuffed up yer arse?" He snorted, and I casually inspected my gauntlet.

"All humans can fly. Why, are you saying that Dwarves can't? Fuck, that must be depressing. Not only are you short enough to make a Goblin laugh and fugly as a donkey's arse, you can't even fly? Man, it really sucks to be you," I quipped, and he punched me in the thigh, laughing.

"Good te see ye, laddie!" He chuckled heartily, slapping a nearby railing. "So, what be goin' on, then? Heph said ye'd be on tha first ships, but that big bastard back there…" He trailed off as he gestured to the battleship, looming huge even in the far distance.

"That's our new battleship," I said, grinning at the look of undisguised avarice on his face.

"The battleship, ye say?" he murmured greedily, then smoothed the front of his tunic and coughed, trying to look casual. "Sooo, this here battleship, does she no have a name yet? No true captain could leave her without a name, ye know, so I'm thinkin'…"

"She's the '*Dreadnought*'" I interrupted, grinning. "And not only does she have a captain already, she's not going to be officially named until she gets finished. She was literally a framework when we got to the city, so I'm not surprised you don't recognize her."

"Wait. Tha's *the* battleship? Himnel's battleship? Barabarattas–*may he grow a boil on tha end o' his dick*–the Lord of Himnel's favorite project? The one he kept harpin' on about tha' would win tha war fer 'im?"

"Yup," I confirmed, delighting in his incredulity. "We stole it out from under him and filled it with the crew's families, as well as the entire Legion of Himnel. Others are being transported on the three fast ships here."

"Me family?" he said, all joking thrown aside. I realized that his not asking immediately had been because he was too afraid to hear the response. "Ye really got me family, ye swear?" He grabbed my wrists, searching my face for an answer.

I smiled and reassured him that I did, and he let out a long sigh of relief as he released me and shielded his eyes from the drizzle to squint back at the battleship in the distance.

"Whadda yer think, Jory? A day?" He queried his helmsman, and Jory frowned, staring over his shoulder as we came about to fly alongside the cruisers.

"Maybe...more'n likely a day an' a half...two, at most," Jory calculated.

"Not a bad guess there." I grunted. "Athena, the captain of the battleship, said it'd be about a day to a day and a half after we arrived at the Tower before they would catch up."

"Athena? Git tall Elf lassie?" Oren asked suspiciously. I nodded as he cursed.

"What's wrong?" I asked, concerned.

"She's a damn menace, tha' lassie! Thinks she's tha damn best captain in tha sky! I tell ye, she were locked up, slave brand an' all, 'cause she were caught smugglin' shit from tha city aboard a ship that were carryin' tha customs inspector hisself! She's got balls like a cannon's and brains o' mince!" Oren groused, then sighed at the look on my face. "*But*...she do be damn good. She just be crazy an' all," he added.

"Thank God; I thought you were going to say something bad! Uh, question...we already chose the name for the ship, but she seemed to want us to wait before officially naming it. In my world, that was because it was considered unlucky to name a ship before she was finished and launched, so we'd call her the battleship until then, rather than '*Dreadnought*'...is that...?"

"Aye, same custom here, laddie; yer be all right." Oren confirmed with a grin.

"Thank fuck," I muttered. "Okay, how are things back at the Tower?"

He laughed, then regarded me intently. "'Afore I get into that...all the crew's families, ye got 'em all?" he persisted, hunger in his eyes and in Jory's.

"Everyone who was on the list. Literally everyone, plus a few hundred extras," I reassured him. "I think there were a couple of people who refused–didn't want to come–but Barrett said he'd take care of those things. We were kinda busy at the time, so I trusted him to deal with it." I crossed my arms and leaned against the railing.

"I thank ye, Goddess!" he muttered, lifting a small talisman from around his neck and kissing the symbol on it. When he caught me looking, he grinned and lifted it up where I could see it.

It was a simple leather thong, twisted and knotted, with a tiny symbol on it that looked like a stylized flame. When I asked him about it, he cradled it reverently in his palm.

"One o' tha lassies from the village made it. Got tha blacksmith te stoke up the flames, an' then tha Goddess herself blessed 'em, through that damn loony priest!"

"A blacksmith?" I blinked in stunned confusion. "Wait, what priest?!"

"Ah crap, ye been and missed a lot, laddie. We been busy here, no like you, swannin' about at parties an' shite. Bet you did nowt, really, while all ma family nicked tha ships fer ye! Or do it be Mal? Did ye talk to 'im?" He laughed at the glower on my face. "Ah, laddie! Tha' be the face of a man who do be spendin' too much time with Mal, all right!"

"Aye, well, he was useful, but…" I hesitated.

"But he be a man who could annoy a three-day dead corpse into gettin' up and walkin' away," Oren agreed, nodding to himself in satisfaction.

"Well…yeah! Yeah, he's really fucking annoying!" I gestured back at the distant fleet. "You could have warned me!"

"What would ah have said, laddie?" Oren snorted as his ship sped up, guiding the cruisers in.

I glanced ahead, recognizing the hexagonal outline of the wall that surrounded the base of the great Tower. The barrier stood a good mile and a half across with a huge section already cleared and ready.

As the ship angled for descent, the nose dipping towards the ground, I resisted the urge to lift my hands into the air like I was on a rollercoaster and instead focused on the myriad changes that had been made.

The outer walls, which had been overgrown by encroaching trees for centuries, and were reduced to rubble in most places that had not been significantly obscured by bushes and undergrowth, were now clearly marked out.

It must have taken dozens of people working around the clock to strip the plant life back. Even now, a single huge Golem worked to clear a collapsed building, stacking piles of broken stone against the side of the Tower itself.

It was magnificent and strangely terrifying, as I realized just how large everything was, now that I was expected to somehow fix it all up. The concealing layers of trees and shrubs, along with the piled rubble of collapsed buildings, walls, and general debris everywhere had combined to hide the actual size of the area, but as more and more of it was cleared back…I stared in speechless awe, before remembering my conversation with Oren.

"You could have said something like, 'Hey, watch out for that Mal, he'll make your fists itch just by breathing," I muttered, and he bellowed a laugh.

"He may be a shitbag, laddie, but he be a good man, fer all tha'." He seemed to reconsider his words and amended the assessment quickly. "Well, fer a *smuggler* an' all tha', anyway!"

"Weren't you a smuggler?" I pointed out, and he glared at me. "Okay, let's move on from a clearly touchy subject." I grinned at him. "How's it been here?"

"No all bad; me an' Decin have been recruitin' fer the Tower. Stripped that village…Dannick?" he asked Jory, who nodded wordlessly as he leveled us out and started to lift back up. The cruisers behind us took the hint and continued toward the base of the Tower. "Aye, Dannick; we stripped it down to termites an' bedbugs! Barely left the base o' some of tha houses, even stripped away logs an' shit in places. Everythin' else, it be here." He rubbed his beard thoughtfully. "Best one to tell ye all about tha', though'd, be tha' damn cat. Iffin ye can pull him away from Isabella, anyway." He finished with a wink.

I laughed, remembering the beautiful young woman that had been interested in our Panthera friend. "I'll ask him; for now, though, I know you'd rather be heading for the battleship, but I'll ask you to land and find me down there. We need to arrange a council of War." I sighed, thinking that as much as I'd enjoyed the normality of shooting the shit with Oren, it couldn't go on. Not when we'd be under siege in a few days, if not more.

"Aye; I take it tha' Seneschal got in touch, after all? He said he would, but I wasna sure he managed it."

"It was Jenae as well," I confirmed as I moved across to the railing of the ship and admired the huge trees that surrounded the base of the Tower. "She contacted us and spread the word around the same time that Seneschal managed to contact Oracle.

"Look, I need to be down there, so, get your arse landed, and we'll talk soon." I commanded him grimly, the relief of the homecoming washed away by the knowledge of the Dark Legion's encroachment.

He nodded, and I forced a smile before turning my back to the drop, closing my eyes and basking in the warm sun as the rain suddenly stopped...then leaning backwards and kicking off to plummet over the side. I heard him choke off a cry as I fell away from the ship, activating Soaring Majesty as I plummeted to the ground.

As I flew, I inspected the Tower, taking advantage of the opportunity to examine it from the outside in a way I'd never been able to before. The Great Tower of Dravith had been grown in place, from a Seed, as Oracle had told me, albeit along with a metric fuckton of magic.

The Tower had originally been as smooth as marble on the outside, but when the SporeMother had stormed it, killing all the living inhabitants, the three Wisps who maintained the huge edifice had been ordered to go into hibernation. They'd locked down the mana collectors over seven centuries ago.

The entropy of weathering seven centuries and more of storms, not to mention the Great Cataclysm–which the Tower had only survived because the previous master had ordered the mana batteries be drained into the shield to prevent the SporeMother from feeding on them–combined with general wear and tear had resulted in the decrepit wreckage I'd found instead.

The Great Tower was more ruin than functional now, and despite its magical nature and inherent design to withstand sieges and entropy alike, no structure could last forever. Add to that, the SporeMother had been a creature practically of legend, and she'd stormed the Tower with her minions, destroying entire floors and tearing through walls as she went.

When I'd arrived, I'd fought her, but she'd been trapped inside for centuries, starving and growing steadily weaker. If not for the turd sandwich, Barabarattas, actually *feeding* her, it probably would have been a case of me being able to kick her to death when I discovered her presence.

Instead of facing a nightmare on the level where Earth would probably have called for deploying a MOAB and wrote off the country it was in, I'd fought the equivalent of an aged grandmother who'd been hopped up on bath salts. The next option up would have been a nuke, if she'd been at full strength.

I marveled at the sheer scope of the landscape as I descended, passing the tops of enormous trees, the like of which I'd seen on shows set in the US, where twenty men could encircle the trunk and still not reach all the way around it.

Despite all the forces working to degrade it, the Tower itself was as much magical as mundane, containing tens of thousands of rooms, ranging from closets to gathering halls and cathedrals that were hundreds of meters across. There were walls that were thicker than houses I'd lived in, and, as it had once been built to be the bastion and operational base that the surrounding area could be conquered from, it had even been self-sufficient.

It had housed everything from blacksmiths and forges to decorative and functional gardens, wells, bathing facilities, and more. To my surprise, it even had a training labyrinth, although ninety nine percent of it, like everything else, was a ruin.

Regardless of all the decomposition, all of it could be fixed, given time…and that time could be massively reduced, thanks to the haul of manastones we'd managed to raid from Himnel.

CHAPTER EIGHT

I twisted in the air, spiraling around and passing *Ragnarök* as she came in for a landing, *Sigmar's Fist* close behind and *Summer's Promise* bringing up the rear. I waved to the legionnaires who covered the decks and cheered as I flew past, and I flipped over, gliding to a landing on the now-clear grassy courtyard of the Great Tower. Running a handful of steps as I came to a stop, I grinned, unable to help myself as I turned and gazed upwards.

Easily a dozen people were peering out of windows on the lower floors, while a single Golem came clumping out of the Tower to greet me, with more people moving to the balconies, railings, and windows by the second. High overhead, I could just make out the sight of tiny heads poking over the railings to look down, and I nodded in satisfaction before taking a deep breath and reaching out.

I could feel Bob maybe a mile away. He was underground but returning already, the steady, dependable presence growing stronger and stronger by the second.

The first ship drifted down, the huge planks and metal banding creaking and groaning. Several of the stones of the courtyard cracked and shifted as the full weight of the airship settled onto the ground.

I turned back from marveling at the monstrosity of the Tower; the damn thing was big enough that, from this angle, it looked more like an artificial mountain or a cliff than anything else, despite the shattered doors, leaky windows, and collapsed walls that surrounded the courtyard.

I shifted my focus to the ships as the first gangplank was lowered. Lydia jogged down first, followed by the surviving members of my team, and the Legion came after her.

Dozens of them, equipped in full armor, jogged down the planks and spread out into orderly ranks. Their spare gear had been left on the ships as they moved unencumbered, falling into a defensive ring around the landing area, watching and waiting.

I smiled despite myself as I felt the gentle touch on my mind, and I acknowledged it, speaking loud enough that the surrounding people could hear me.

"It's okay, everyone, this is your new home!" I called out. "I know it doesn't look like much right now, but give it time. Believe me, there's going to be a massive improvement very soon!" With that proclamation, I turned back to the Tower and looked up at the colossal golem that had stomped its way out to me, then noticed what it held in its hands.

It was a small silver tray, bearing a single cup half-filled with crystal clear water and a bunch of red and green grapes, undeniably freshly picked.

"Hi, guys, did you miss us?" I asked, reaching out to greet their presences, and sensing their satisfaction at the bond being reestablished fully.

"Lord Jax, it is good to have you home," Seneschal intoned, at the same time as Heph spoke up.

"Aye, laddie, welcome back! I sense you've brought me a wee gift; where is it?"

"Thanks, and it's good to be back," I said, feeling Oracle and Seneschal's joint eye rolling at Heph's blatant attempt to claim the golems. *"And you might have sensed MY golems, but they're war golems and will be put to use damn soon. I've brought two aboard the ships here, with another seven incoming on foot, as well as more being built in the production facilities I claimed in the city..."*

"Ye found intact Genesis Chambers?" Heph barely contained his awe and excitement. *"Where? Do they be in tha ships that be incomin' still?"* he asked, his voice almost frantic with need.

"No, the facility was buried under the city, so I sealed it up again and left a golem to run the production. Look, there's a lot to discuss, so get ready. I'll be bringing a few new people up; is the command center still in the same place?"

"Yes, but we had discussed the need to secure the Creation Table, and that you would most likely require a meeting area, at some point. With that in mind, I had my helpers, plus the Construction and Servitor Golems that were available..." There was an audible pause, during which Heph was conspicuously silent, before Seneschal went on.

"I had them repair the third floor in the south section as best I could, including setting up a simple Council Chamber and providing some basic tables and chairs. If you wish, I will arrange refreshments. There are currently eight chairs inside; how many will be attending?"

"Uh...me, Romanus, Bane, Lydia, Nerin and Restun from here, and get Oren, Cai, Isabella, Flux and Ame down as well," I said, thinking through the upcoming topics and those necessary to the discussions.

"Very well. Do you wish me to include Decin, Hanau, and Riana as well? They have formed the rest of the council that has looked after the Tower in your absence, even if unofficially."

"Joy..." I said grimly. I'd deliberately appointed only Flux, Ame, Cai, and Oren before leaving, along with Seneschal and Heph, to ensure I didn't end up with too many people. I'd added in Isabella upon my return because I'd been talked into it over several conversations with Oracle in the weeks since we'd left the Tower.

I sighed and resigned myself to a goddamn council that was only going to get bigger over time, and just hoped that I could carve it down later...somehow.

"Yeah, okay, invite them all, and obviously, Oracle will be there as well, so make sure we have enough refreshments and chairs, according to what is readily available. This is going to be a long discussion. Also, I need a map, one that we can all see, is it possible to rip the map out of Oren's ship without damaging it?" I tried not to dwell on what would happen once Ashrag arrived, as the size of her alone meant that we'd need to relocate the council to a much, much larger room...although, the sight of her would probably keep most others from attending.

I looked around for everyone else, finding my personal squad pointing things out to the legionnaires around them.

"Unfortunately not, but the Creation Table can provide that, once it is fully repaired."

"Damn. Okay, get everyone together in the council chamber then; we can go over the majority without a map for now."

"It will be done. Many of those you wish to attend are already on their way to the ground floor, having expected you to land on the flight deck."

"I would have, except there wouldn't have been room for everyone to disembark, and the ships would have had to relocate down here to make room for others..." I sighed again, attempting to explain my reasoning. *"It would have made the crews feel that they weren't as valued as the legionnaires, and I'm trying to make this a home for everyone."*

"Very wise. I will inform them, and the Command Center will be ready for everyone by the time you arrive."

"Thanks, Seneschal. Heph, I know you, and how damn addicted to golems you are, so I assume you've been plotting out where the other waystations are; have you found any?"

"Ah, aye. Well, mebbe...ah..."

"Great," I said, dismissing the conversation and turning to the legionnaires milling around behind me. "Welcome home, legionnaires!"

I got a weak cheer in response. "Aw, don't be like that!" I shouted back at them, sparking a few grins. "I know it doesn't look like much, but I promise, it'll soon feel like home. For now, set up tents over there, if you want, or rest on the ships. Feel free to explore, but don't get too attached to the Tower as it is. It'll be changing very soon, then, you'll be able to move in!" I got another halfhearted cheer, and I resigned myself to accept the lack of enthusiasm for now, walking through the group to where Restun and Romanus stood waiting.

"Very inspirational speech," Romanus congratulated me.

I laughed; I couldn't help it. "Bollocks. I'm shit at speeches, but I had to say something. For now, let them relax here. I've got the Tower's council coming down, and we're going up. We can sit in the new council chambers and get some details figured out, then we can start the next phase."

"What will that be?" Romanus wondered aloud, and I cocked an eyebrow at him.

"Oh, I think you'll like it, mate. After all, until now, we've been pushed around and chased. I think it's time we turned around and tore some dicks off, don't you?"

"And the Dark Legion?" Restun asked.

"They get to be the first to enjoy our attentions. The legion is going to be undergoing a rebirth, along with the Great Tower and the rest of the Empire. I think the dickbags who took everything you stand for and pissed on it should get the foremost opportunity to learn a valuable lesson, don't you?"

Restun smiled slowly, and despite knowing he was on my side, I felt a little quiver of fear. He was just evil on a whole different level.

"Right; there's a fuck-ton of stuff to get done, so let's get a move on to these council chambers." I led them across the grassy courtyard and up the dozen cracked and crumbling steps towards the main entrance into the Tower. On the way, I called Lydia and Nerin over to join me, instructing the others to stay with the legion and watch out for any surprises, as well as handle introductions and any other rudimentary needs.

Our small group climbed the steps, and I examined the outside of the lower floors as we went, taking note of the windows and doorways that were choked with rubble and remnants of sporeling excrement. I wasn't sure yet what we'd need to repair first, but those needed to be added to the list.

As we reached the top of the staircase, we came to the enormous new doors, solid stone that I recognized as part of the Tower's structure. The panels had clearly been grown in place by Seneschal, with hinges that looked like they could take a direct hit from a challenger tank without budging.

"Bane…" I said, trusting him to be close by and smiling when a voice a few steps to my right replied.

"Jax?"

"Do me a favor and run back into the nearest ship, grab a bag of manastones, and meet us on the third floor," I ordered, receiving a grunt in acknowledgement before he vanished again.

"Thanks!" I called after him.

Upon striding into the Tower, I felt the sudden drop in temperature that came from leaving the sun-dappled courtyard and moving into an impregnable stone edifice, especially one as huge and imposing as the Tower.

My eyes adjusted rapidly, since it was too light in the chamber for my DarkVision to be worth using, and I scanned the space, impressed by the huge differences that had been made since I had last walked this floor.

When I had left, it had been choked with vines and encroaching trees. Just beyond the areas that sunlight could reach through the cracks and crevices in the outer walls, the entire first section had been filled with fungus growths, mold, and pools of stagnant water, while collapsed inner walls had dotted the area.

The Tower's internal structure was divided by floors with various-sized rooms. Some, like this one, were genuinely huge, as befitted a structure more than two miles high. The ground floor alone covered an area that must have been almost a half-mile wide, and it was also almost entirely ruined. The inner structure was intact in the load bearing areas, as the Tower had reinforced those so heavily in its original designs, and the outside walls, twenty meters and more thick, were intact…mostly.

The devastation was restrained to the interior walls, the floors, and the ceilings…entire sections had collapsed into each other, spilling across the floor to create ramps up and down. Some stairwells were obstructed with piles of rubble, while others had been partially cleared to allow people to travel up and down more easily. I took in the sight in amazement, for the first time able to fully comprehend the huge scale of the Tower, where before I'd simply rushed through it.

"I…" Romanus whispered beside me. "I don't know what to say…" He gazed around in wonder.

It was obvious where sections had been cleared, trees and bushes torn out, and a clear walkway made from the central stairwell to the front door. Enormous mounds of shattered stone had been shoved bodily, by the golems, I assumed, across the floor to be piled on either side of the door, ready to be toppled into place, sealing off the Tower in case of attack.

"She's huge, I know," I replied quietly. "And ruined, as I said before, but that's where the manastones come in. We needed tons of them, and we got them. I don't think it'll be anywhere near enough to restore the entire Tower, but it'll make a hell of a difference…"

"Can it be restored?" Romanus kept his voice low. "In truth, I mean? I don't mean to cast doubt on you, Jax, but a structure that is so large…"

"I know." I rubbed the back of my neck awkwardly. "Considering you can't even see the far side of the building from here, and this is simply the first floor…But you see how high the ceilings are?" He looked up at the soaring, vaulted ceiling supported by thousands of pillars. "That's common on several of the floors." I pointed out a few details as I explained. "There are some where the ceilings are a hundred meters high, and others where they're just…well…normal.

"Entire levels are designed to be used as quarters, multiple doors lining a single corridor that runs from one stairwell to the other. Others appear to be structured as barracks, with armories, drill halls…hell, the entire structure could house tens, if not hundreds of thousands of legionnaires, as well as their support staff, not to mention thousands of civilians."

I led the way across the ground floor. Restun, Lydia, and Romanus produced magelights to brighten the passage, as the few dozen dotted around did little to brighten the inner chambers.

Once we reached the main stairs, we stuck to the cleared section on the far left and marched up them. Romanus was by my side, and for the first time since I had arrived in the Tower, I had the luxury of taking a minute to drink in the sight.

The stairway was huge, like insanely huge; the entire Legion could have marched up it at once, but most of it was covered by a landslide from a higher floor. The golems had evidently been following the path I'd used in the past, as there was now a good three meters of clearance in width. With the ancient banister rising alongside us, despite its age and the deep layers of filth and dust that coated most surfaces, it looked…grand.

Everything was built to a scale that was mind-blowing, yet the attention to detail…I reached out and ran my hand down one of the spindles that supported the banister as we climbed the stairs. The funk of centuries came away roughly, clearly mired in place over countless ages, but beneath it, I could see the outline of carvings, and I remembered that the Great Towers weren't just bastions of war.

They'd been the homes of the noble houses until the surrounding areas could be pacified enough for manors to be built.

I continued upwards in silence, the others talking quietly around me as I pondered the implications.

If the Tower had been constructed, as I'd been told, to serve as a first line of defense, and it'd fallen not long after it'd been completed, due to the majority of the structure being uninhabited, and if the cities had been built already to the south…

"Wait…what was this built to hold against?" I muttered.

Oracle looked at me sharply from her perch on my shoulder. "What do you mean?" she asked cautiously.

I frowned, unsure, feeling the edge of an idea and knowing that it was important.

"Well, the Empire already had the cities to the south. You said they were lesser cities, and that there were others in the area, most of which were lost in the Cataclysm, right?"

She nodded slowly.

"You also said these Towers were rare, like the old way of doing things," I continued, and she gasped indignantly. "Whoa, I'm not trying to piss you off, just go with me on this: if the Tower is the old way of doing things, and the Prax was the new, or current way, and there are cities to the south, it's already a reasonably secure place, right? So why build the Tower?"

"Because the Emperor needed to pacify the area," Oracle said, before trailing off.

"Exactly. You said before that the legion had been clearing out the area, making it safe for travelers, but why here?" I wondered, recalling the map and pulling it up in my vision as I walked slowly up the stairs.

The continent was as I remembered it, over five hundred miles wide, and well over a thousand long, with a huge mountain range running north to south. I navigated the map quickly, zooming in and out with mental commands. I stumbled as I saw what I'd clearly missed before, as new details were filled in, thanks to the conversations I'd had over the last few weeks.

At the far southern tip lay a series of low foothills that rolled into a forest that was easily a hundred miles wide, and two, maybe three hundred from north to south, with a few scattered remnants of villages and ruined cities skirting the edges. Beyond that, a good eight hundred miles from our location, there was only one pass through the mountains that didn't seem to go so high that it'd become impassible in unfavorable conditions.

"It's right here," I muttered, tapping the pass mentally and zooming in.

The map had been populated by a combination of the maps I'd found, the Scroll of the Eagle I'd used weeks ago to get a good view of the surrounding area, and by Jenae when She'd searched for Thomas for me. With such comprehensive updates, Oren and the others who'd seen it had been in awe of the detail.

"What happens to ships that try to sail over the mountains?" I asked, and Romanus, still walking next to me, grew solemn.

"They never return. I was ordered by Barabarattas to take the legion and find out why shortly after the Legion General's death. I refused on the grounds that he had no authority to send us there, but in all honesty, I knew it was a death sentence. Most ships that attempt to fly over the mountains don't make it halfway. The storms and unpredictable weather take them out. Those that have been seen cresting the valleys before disappearing from sight? Never seen again. We don't know why; it could be as simple as the weather on the far side being worse…but…"

"But you know it isn't," I chimed in, nodding my head in understanding. "According to my map, there's at least one city, Chenak, and what look to be either castles or fortifications," I muttered, half to myself, as I peered closer at them.

"You have a map of the other side?" Romanus asked in surprise, and I nodded distractedly.

"Yeah. When I get the chance, I'll get it sorted so you can see it." I dismissed the map from my vision. "For now, though, thinking about it logically, this Tower must have been built to guard the Pass, right?" I asked the group, who had gradually gone silent as we walked, listening to me process aloud.

"I think it was…but there was also talk about the armies of the Night King," Oracle said eventually. "I don't know why; it was never something that was discussed with us Wisps. We were just the caretakers, but I remember snippets, bits of conversations where the tower magus would talk about defensive plans…but not who or what he meant them against. It was just something they all knew."

"Do you remember?" I asked, calling deep into my mind to Amon, but to my surprise, he growled at me mentally. Somehow, he seemed to turn away from me, as though angry. I felt him blocking me off, and I pulled back, surprised.

"Oracle, why did he do that?" I asked her privately, and she frowned, reaching out and putting one hand flat against my temple. Her fingers were cool and soft as she closed her eyes and inspected the strange bond between Amon and myself.

"I don't know. I think He's confused, but I really can't tell. He seems…angry? Afraid, maybe?"

"Yeah," I mused, *"Okay, so let's get this straight, the Night King, who was he?"*

"Truthfully, I don't know, not fully. He was a necromancer, one who summoned enormous armies. He was the only survivor of the three that attacked the Amir Basin; he fled and was never seen again, but…"

"But?"

"There was a buildup of necromantic forces here, on the far side of the mountain, and the Drow were known to have settlements somewhere here…plus…" Oracle broke off as if confused, and before I could ask her anything further, I heard a shout from up ahead.

"Jax!"

I blinked, bringing the real world back into focus, and I realized I'd been lost in the funk of my own mind for several minutes. Cai hurried down the stairs towards me with a huge grin on his face.

"Cai!" I greeted my friend enthusiastically, when a hand grabbed me by the throat, only to be ripped free a half second later as a figure was kicked back, flying through the air to land on the floor with a crash.

He rolled, hands flashing down and slapping against the floor, flipping himself upright as Restun dove past me. The Primus' hands flicked out, seeking to restrain the figure.

The combination of the magelights and the way that Restun moved, fast and direct, no wasted motions as he drove his opponent back and kicked his feet from under him, made it hard for me to see who, or what, he faced.

All I could make out was a blur, a blur that looked camouflaged…

"Stop!" I ordered, stepping forward and grabbing Restun's arm as he drew his sword. It was about as effective as grabbing onto the side of an excavator. Restun inexorably raised his blade, about to stab, when Romanus barked an order.

"Legionnaire, halt!" he cried, and Restun seemed to flinch. He straightened and, still holding his sword, glanced back to me, clearly noticing my hand on his arm for the first time.

"Flux?" I called out, and in the darkness on the other side of the doorway which Restun filled, I heard a pained chuckle.

"Welcome back…my lord." Flux groaned. I tugged on Restun's arm, making him step back. He sheathed his sword and returned to watching everything, seemingly unconcerned, as I stepped into the room and helped Flux to his feet.

He was a Mer, taller than Bane, but older and more lightly built. Judging from the blood that dribbled out of his mouth as he wheezed a greeting to me, Restun had broken him easily.

I shook my head, feeling Oracle casting already, and I pinched the bridge of my nose as she slipped the healing spell into him. The collapsed Mer gasped as his three broken ribs were healed, and a sprained wrist and ankle were each returned to full mobility.

"What the hell were you playing at?" I growled to him, and he let loose with a subsonic thrum that was his race's equivalent of rueful laughter.

"I saw you coming, clearly without Bane, who's supposed to be your damn bodyguard. I decided to demonstrate just how easily an assassin could get to you, even here, in the center of your home…clearly, I was the one who got the surprise, though!"

"Yeah, clearly." I rolled my eyes. "Okay, everyone, this absolute muppet is Flux. He's the leader of the Mer, and he's the one who insisted on my acceptance of Bane as a bodyguard. While this attack wasn't his brightest idea, he's usually pretty smart, so let's all forget about this, okay?" I shot a pointed glance at Restun, who nodded once then went back to watching the hallway.

Flux stepped up to Romanus and Restun, holding his hands out to either side and bowing low, speaking in a quieter, yet clearly well-considered, tone.

"My apologies, legionnaires. I didn't intend to cause a scene; I simply wished to make sure Lord Jax understood the risk he poses to himself when he travels without a bodyguard, even here." Flux slowly straightened, nodding respectfully to both Restun and Romanus.

"We understand, Flux. I am Romanus, Prefect of the Legion, and this is Restun, First Primus of the Praetorian Guard."

"That title is not yet deserved," Restun objected, and I scoffed at him.

"Really? Because, from where I'm standing, it looked like you kicked Flux's ass without pause. I didn't even see him, yet…"

"He should not have reached you at all," Restun interrupted grimly, and Flux nodded in hearty agreement.

"Exactly!" the limber Mer said quickly. "I have been trying to make him understand this, yet he is like a child at times!"

"Oh, well, fuck you very much, mate," I grumbled, rolling my eyes as I turned to face Cai, who'd come down the hall and had paused, standing well back to quietly watch as events unfurled.

"How about you, Cai?" I asked, one eyebrow raised in question. "Are you gonna attack and insult me as well?"

"Probably the latter…" he answered with a nervous grin, his pointed canines gleaming in the glow of the magelights. "After seeing what our friend Flux received for attacking you, I have no desire to receive the same…"

"Yeah, well, it's good to see you too, you old bastard," I grumped, reaching out to clasp his wrist as he laughed and stepped in, slapping me on the back while hugging me.

I hugged him back and laughed despite myself as he moved back and smiled at me.

Cai was "of the line of Panthera," as he put it, and was essentially a feline humanoid, tall and wiry, without a wasted ounce on him. Short, coarse black fur covered his face and hands, and I assumed, his body. His ears flicked idly, constantly listening out for trouble, and he had to be the most patient and relaxed person I knew.

When I'd first freed him from the slavers, it had been his actions that had set me on the road to being a lord. He'd begged me for my protection, and for him and his people to be permitted to live in the Tower.

"The others are on their way. I wished to come and see you before we entered the Council chambers, and to apologize. I know you said no to Isabella being a member of the council, and she is aware that she holds no official rank. She has simply aided me, as do the others. There is much to do each day, and the few of us you placed in charge were forced to delegate further, lest we spend the days in discussion and achieve nothing. I..." He bowed his head and closed his eyes, clearly conditioned to expect a blow, if not worse, for disobeying.

"Meh," I said, walking past him and tugging him along.

"Meh...?" Cai questioned, confused.

"I told you no before because I had a lot less of an idea what it was like to lead people, Cai. Simply put, I trust you. I hear that, in addition to yourself, Isabella, Flux, Ame, and Oren, you have included Decin, Hanau, and Riana; is that right?" I glanced sideways at him, and he nodded slowly.

"Okay, well, if I'm being honest, I think that's a bit unbalanced, as it's essentially four fliers and only one of the villagers, but that's fine. As I said, I trust you. I'll look at the way things go, and I might confirm them, I might not, but I'll give it a try." A smile tugged at the corners of my lips as we walked. The long spiral staircase, ringing the floor as it led upwards, echoed with our footfalls as we went.

It took only a few minutes of climbing before we reached the final handful of steps, and we emerged onto the third floor, heading in the direction where the previous Command Center had been located. We wove through a few rooms filled with debris and random clutter, collapsed seats so old even the termites had avoided them, and more, as we followed a clear, swept path.

As I stepped around the final turn, I found the way clearly lit with a magelight secured to the wall beside a carved wooden door that was obviously new.

I blinked in surprise at that, realizing that it was the room two doors down from the one I'd originally designated as the Command Center. I had to assume the doors were recently made to allow for some privacy in the two rooms. I headed to the first door, pausing as I heard movement coming from inside.

I pushed the door open and got my second shock of the day.

CHAPTER NINE

The room beyond was furnished, if only lightly, and filled with warm light. A half dozen candles burned around the room, with a single magelight mounted above the large circular table in the center, and even the walls had been scrubbed to give an aura of calm cleanliness. There were even flowers and damn sprigs of lavender and mint arranged in tidy bundles around the room.

The table had a dozen seats placed around it already, with the chairs being shifted to accommodate the last two seats that were being hurriedly put into place by two people I didn't recognize.

I frowned at them unthinkingly, before quickly clearing it away and forcing a smile as they blanched in fear. I turned to Cai, questioning him silently as I walked around the table.

He clearly understood what I was asking, as he spoke up, putting his hand on first one of the girls' shoulders, then the other.

"Lord Jax, these lovely ladies are Ootomai and Anesthet, sisters from Dannick who accepted your offer of protection. They worked in their family tavern before coming here, so I took the liberty of employing them to maintain certain locations, such as the council chambers and your own, as well as to help out with the food hall."

"In that case, welcome, ladies." I greeted them warmly, smiling reassuringly. They both dipped into a low bow before rushing away, and I sighed, looking from Cai to Romanus as we took seats.

"Do I really…" I started to ask, and both of them spoke up at once.

"It is appropriate…"

"A gesture of respect is all…"

The pair broke off and eyed each other, waiting, as I grinned at their hesitancy.

"Okay, I can see that I'm going to be outnumbered on this, but how about we keep that kind of thing to a minimum? No bowing as standard practice?" I requested, and they inclined their heads in unison, sharing a smile.

"Jax, showing respect is customary and no great hardship," Romanus said calmly. "As we've discussed before, letting that slip is likely to cause issues in the future. That being said, the bowing that many nobles demand as their due, well…" he shrugged dismissively.

"Okay, so we can at least get rid of that?" I asked, then firmed my voice and straightened in my chair, making the decision, rather than asking for advice. "Make it clear please, Cai, that the Eternal Emperor Amon only required someone to bow when they meet for the first time, when they are being honored, or when they are being formally addressed at court. I have no need nor right to ask for more deference than he demanded."

Cai straightened and nodded in approval.

"Now…" I started as the last few people filed in, amongst them a huffing Decin and Oren, both clearly out of breath. Hanau, who seemed to have merely been on a light stroll, and Riana, who was groaning as much as the Dwarves, followed behind. Bringing up the rear, her hands full with a large tray, was Isabella.

Cai jumped to his feet and helped her, setting out a large pitcher of what turned out to be fruit juice, a bottle of rough whisky, and a handful of cups. Most of us reached into our various bags of holding without thought and pulled out our own cups. I smiled, noticing that habit for the first time.

Almost everyone around the table had at least a lesser bag of holding; they had gotten into the habit of always having their own things with them. It was basically a pouch, after all, but inside? They could store insane amounts of gear.

I was carrying over two tons of weight on me at the moment, yet it felt like I was carrying around forty-five pounds. That was basically a holiday suitcase. When I added on the fact that it was on a strap designed for it, and attached to my admittedly damaged, but still fantastically weight-distributing armor, and that I was at least as strong as, what, three normal men? I'd literally forgotten I was even wearing it.

Inside the bags, along with the various loot I'd not yet unloaded–the copious amount of gold, silver, copper, and goddamn platinum, the pounds and pounds of precious gems, as well as random magical crap we'd simply not yet managed to identify–I also had my usual everyday gear.

I had a bedroll, changes of clothes, a pair of plates, two cups, cutlery; I even had soap, a towel, and something I'd picked up at one point that was supposed to make my hair and fast-growing lush beard extra smooth. And I still carried all the random crap from Earth.

My toiletries bag hadn't been so much as looked at in what seemed an age, and I really, really needed to make time to actually trim my hair and beard.

I dismissed the thought, but I did grin that carrying personal drinkware had become so commonplace and accepted, that while drinks were provided by hosts, only a few cups were offered, as it was simply expected that everyone would have their own to hand.

"Welcome back, my lord," Hanau said, smiling and stepping around the table to greet me. I smiled back and stood, getting a hug from the exuberant Elf. Some of the people who'd not met him before looked on in surprise as he stepped back and sat down, taking his husband, Decin's, hand in his own and beaming at the newcomers.

"It's good to be back, my friends," I said, sitting back and letting a sigh of relief escape at the comfort of the cushions. Even in damn armor, it felt good.

"As much as I'd hoped that today would be a celebration, and we could all drink and relax, it's not going to be. I'll bring you all up to date on my recent adventures, you can fill me in on what's happened here, and then I'll go over my intentions regarding the Dark Legion and the Tower. As always, if you think there's a better way to do something, I'm happy to listen, but I want to hear constructive ideas. If something won't work, offer an alternative, okay?" I received several nods of agreement, and continued once I was satisfied that we were all on the same page.

"Good! Right, before I get started, you're all here for a reason, and that's that you have different skills or knowledge that is appropriate. Heph, Seneschal, can you show yourselves as well, please?" A handful of seconds later, the pair of Wisps appeared in the room.

Seneschal was first, a smoky black cloud that slowly grew, making those of us who had faced the DarkSpore tense at first, before the form of the Wisp who held responsibility for the structure of the Tower appeared to grow from within the cloud. He lifted up from within the misty substance, floating until he stood atop it, then stepped from the cloud onto the table before us. Six inches high, he stood, clearly humanoid yet clad in silvery scale mail that covered every inch. A black, hooded cloak swirled in an invisible breeze, and a polished, silvery mask that reflected the world covered his face. True to form, he kept himself hidden while in full view.

Heph was as different as possible. A rip appeared in the table, seemingly leading to the depths of the world, with a blast of illusory heat, glowing lava, and the sound of hammers ringing on metal in the distance.

Hephaestus clambered out of the rip, making a show of pulling himself into our reality, then stood tall, stomping his right foot once. The rip slammed shut with an audible crash and a blast of floating sparks and gently falling, glowing ash.

Where Seneschal was tall, slim, androgynous, and hidden from view behind silvery armor, Heph had taken the form of a Dwarf, short and broad, with a barrel chest crossed by arms that were bigger than most men's thighs. Aside from a thick leather apron over heavy pants, he was bare-chested, with a shaven head and a thick beard that was plaited into a single braid that hung halfway to his waist.

He was covered by a thin sheen of sweat and had sooty smudges all over. His apron was scuffed, and his clothes boasted that level of dirt that came from a long day in a hard job, yet beneath the grime, they were well-maintained and well-made. I couldn't help but smile at the effort they'd both put into their avatars, as well as their arrival.

Heph looked around at us all before nodding in satisfaction, then he and Seneschal both turned to face me and went down on one knee. Oracle lifted into the air and flew across to join them, landing between them and kneeling as they did.

"Thank you all," I said, smiling gratefully at them. "I'm glad the Tower finally has enough mana for you to be able to manifest like this."

"Aye, me too, laddie!" Heph beamed, straightening up along with the others. "I can get up to all sorts of mischief now!" He winked at Hanau, who'd been regarding the squat muscular figure with unabashed admiration.

"Humph!" Decin grunted, glaring at Heph, who immediately burst out laughing and winked at the Dwarf as well.

"Well, as you've already seen, Heph tends to like to wind people up, so you'll get used to his brand of…humor…" I trailed off, shaking my head at his antics.

"I've asked for you all to be here, as you will form my new council. This might change; some people might join us, and others will no doubt leave or be unavailable at times, but you are who I've chosen so far." I stood and started on my right, introducing people and covering who they were, and what they would be responsible for.

"This is Lydia. You all should at least know her by now, but what you might not know is that she has been accepted by the Legion. She is, as always, the commander of my personal squad. She also has evolved."

Lydia stood up. She'd already unbuckled her armor, but as she set her breastplate aside, revealing her simple padded jerkin underneath, she activated her gift and let out a little grunt of relief as her mana dipped, but her wings became visible again, even if they were only as substantial as golden light for the moment.

She stood proudly, smiling as people gasped and looked on in wonder. Seneschal glided forward, crossing the table with graceful steps, and bowed to her in reverence.

"Lady Valkyrie, it is an honor to see your kind restored to the realm," he intoned formally, and people stared in amazement.

"Lydia is now a Valkyrie, the first of her kind in many hundreds of years, and she has my complete and total trust." I paused, letting that sink in as she sat back down.

"Next is Romanus…"

The big legionnaire stood, smiling slightly as he inclined his head to the rest of the room. "He is the leader of the legion. His title is Prefect, and he is responsible for over a hundred legionnaires and their companions and families who, at his word, left the City of Himnel and joined us, swearing fealty to me." Romanus clapped a fist to his chest in salute, then smiled again and sat back down.

"Restun, Primus of the Praetorian Guard," I introduced next.

He stood, staring around the room as though evaluating everyone, before inclining his head as well. "Restun is responsible for the Praetorian Guard, the absolute elite warriors of the Empire. No legionnaire has reached the Praetorian Guard in over seven hundred years; without an Emperor, they could not be confirmed. As Scion of the Empire, however, I now have that authority. Restun will be essentially beating me and those in my personal squad, as well as those who want to be in the Praetorian Guard, into shape. Expect to see him screaming at me and the others…*a lot*," I finished ruefully as he sat down.

"Bane, I know you're floating around in here somewhere," I said, and he appeared, crouching next to the wall behind me, then straightened up and raised a hand to greet the room.

"Bane is my chief bodyguard and my friend. In time, when we have more to help him, he will lead my bodyguards. Until then, it's just him and Tang, an elven member of the Legion." Bane nodded wordlessly, fading away again.

"Nerin agreed to come from the city of Himnel and join us as the Tower's official Healer." I gestured to her, and she stood, glaring briefly at me before gracing everyone else with a smile then sitting back down. She was of average height, maybe early to mid-forties, and wore two bandoliers of pouches, one over each shoulder, crossing to the opposite sides of her waist. While she may have been the smallest person in the room who wasn't a Dwarf, she was also the one who had generated the most fear in my party over the last few weeks, besides Restun, anyway.

"Oren here…"

The little Dwarf stood quickly and grinned around the room, getting a few laughs in response. "In addition to being an absolute bottomless pit for alcohol, is in charge of the fleet. Or at least he will be once the fleet arrives. Oren, there's a battleship, as we discussed, that's basically a tower block in size, and it'll be here in a day or two. One of your main focuses will be in organizing the engineers to get her finished, as she's literally only half built.

"You'll also need to clear additional space outside of the walls for her to land, so I think that needs to be your first job after this meeting. I imagine it's going to be tight out there, even with the space you've already cleared."

Oren nodded, sitting back and looking serious. He was no longer dressed in his armor, but wore the Himnel airship captain set, which had thankfully been retailored to fit him. When he'd put it on previously, it'd been sized for a human, which had been ludicrous to see, despite that fact it bestowed enough buffs that the laughing was worth it.

I shuddered at the memory of him trying to get his much wider dwarven ass into the pants while shouting "I'm nearly there," and "jus' get in there," as well as "Ach, me meat an' two veg be reet on display here, ya see what I mean?" It had been a terrible, mentally scarring sight to behold.

"Next is Cai; Cai is my left hand when it comes to the Tower. He runs everything in conjunction with Seneschal and makes damn sure everyone's fed and has a roof over their heads. He's about to become terribly busy in the next few days." I smiled sheepishly at him as he stood up and bowed smoothly to the room, while smiling around. "Cai, Barrett used to help with the military side of things, but he asked to step back, as he had little experience, and Romanus has far more. As such, I've told him to work with you moving forward; he's already taken charge of the refugees who are coming." Cai acknowledged his new assistant and sat back down, making a note in the small notebook he always carried with him.

"Next to Cai, we have the lovely Isabella," I said, and she stood quickly, blushing as she lifted one hand and gave everyone a quick little shy wave, swiftly sitting back down and grabbing Cai's hand again. She was a tall half-elven maiden, slim as seemingly all Elves were, but she had one of the sunniest dispositions I'd ever met. Since being freed from slavery and meeting Cai, she walked around with the biggest smile permanently on her face.

"Isabella has taken over as a middle manager, aiding Cai and Seneschal to organize everyone, and that includes making sure details such as this room were prepared, and food and drink made available. We're all incredibly lucky to have her," I commended her indirectly. A silent conversation with Seneschal had informed me how useful Isabella was these days.

"Flux…" I said, and he stood, inclining his head. "Flux is the leader of the Mer in the Tower…" I began, and Ame, who was seated next to him, huffed.

"Of *SOME* of the Mer…" she interjected quietly, and a laugh rose at the way Flux turned to face her with his hands on his hips.

"Of SOME of the Mer; thank you, Ame," I corrected myself, smiling. "Flux has been helping to train people as a militia, as well as teaching people to hunt. Moving forward, I'd like you to work with Romanus and Restun, Flux. Your specific focus, judging from the amazing job you did with Bane." I gestured over my shoulder to where Bane had disappeared…and he coughed, drawing attention to the opposite side of the room, where he leaned against the wall.

"Well, with this pillock, I'd like you to officially move over to the stealth side of things. I need bodyguards; I accept that now. I also need people who are trained as stealth types, spies, thieves, rogues…you know what I'm asking."

He nodded crisply, sitting back down.

Flux, Bane, Ame, and the other Mer who were spread about the Tower were particularly gifted when it came to stealth because of their natural gifts. The Mer, being an amphibious race and spending most of their time in deep water, far from the sun, had no discernable eyes. Instead, their heads were domed and smooth, with wide, hinged jaws and solid bone that curved upwards from where a human would have an upper lip. The solid plate ran back to what would be the back of the head, but on a Mer, instead of hair, a thick nest of tendrils erupted from beneath a short frill of bone.

These tendrils, along with a subsonic pulse that the Mer emitted as easily and regularly as breathing, allowed them to see the world around them with a form of sonar they called worldsense. They were humanoid, with two legs and a central torso, but had two sets of arms. The upper pair was larger, heavily muscled, and terminated in three-fingered hands, while the lower pair was slighter, better for delicate work, with three fingers and a thumb. The Mer also had a gift of natural camouflage which, when mixed with the right training, made them naturally excel at rogue classes.

"Ame, who is notably not a follower of Flux," I said dryly.

She stood, inclined her head, and sat back down, letting out a thrummm of laughter as the rest of the table chuckled. "She is both our resident runecrafter and the leader of the crafters, for the purposes of this council. She is also highly interested in healing, so I'd like you to work closely with Mistress Nerin, please, Ame." I allowed myself an internal sigh of relief as both Nerin and Ame nodded in agreement.

"Decin has been aiding Oren with scouting, keeping the ships in the air and working with the crews to keep them in good spirits, I understand. He has also acted in Oren's stead when Oren was not available. I'll leave it to you, Oren and Decin, to work with the engineers, captains, and ship's crews and sort out your own structure. Frankly, I haven't got the time to fuck about with it, so deal with it between yourselves and come to me once it's done. If I have to step in and enforce roles, or smack someone down, I'll be very annoyed. You know you don't want that, agreed?" Decin and Oren shared a look and both nodded quickly.

"Next is Hanau…"

The slender elven man rose smoothly and waved to everyone. "Hi everyone, I'm Hanau, as Lord Jax says…I've basically been keeping the peace as much as I can, helping to smooth ruffled feathers here and there and keep things moving. Decin and I have been together for a long time, and as you can imagine, I'm generally terribly busy keeping people from lynching him." Hanau said cheekily, clearly enjoying the round of chuckles and nodding heads he'd elicited.

Seneschal had told me, along with Oracle, the basics regarding what Hanau had been doing, and along with Isabella, it was more middle management than anything. Where I would have ordered, Hanau and Isabella asked, sweet talked, and encouraged.

"Thank you, Hanau." I shook my head at the cheerful elven man as he sat back down. "As you can see, he's really shy and retiring," I quipped, getting a round of laughter. "Hanau works much as Isabella does, though he'll primarily be concentrating on the fleet, helping to make sure everyone is fed and watered, and handling the logistics of that role." I shot him a look, and he bowed his head in assent.

"It's basically what I've done forever; that, and navigator, just on a larger scale," he responded placidly.

"Riana," I said, and she started as though she'd forgotten she was next.

"Yes?" she asked, awkwardly jumping to her feet and blushing at the smiles. "I mean, yes, Lord Jax, sorry." She stammered and twisted her hands in her skirt, and I smiled reassuringly at her.

"It's alright, Riana. I know you're fascinated by the Empire's technology, and you're an engineer. With such a skillset, I'd like you to work with Ame, Heph, and Seneschal, primarily. We have a few new golems coming in, and we will be looking to reactivate ancient sites that were used to house golems in the area.

"We will also be improving the Tower, repairing the facilities, and adding new–as well as old–technology into it. You will be involved in the fleet as well, but I want you to focus on recruiting a small cadre of engineers. You'll be responsible for working on things like the Genesis Chambers, integrating runes into our ships and the Tower, and your first order of business will be making those Gods damn cannons safe to actually use. In light of these responsibilities, you'll be receiving skillbooks and memory crystals."

"I...I...really?!" she squeaked, collapsing back into her seat and staring into the distance as her eyes glazed over, daydreaming of the possibilities. Silence filled the room for a long minute before Hanau sighed and prodded her with a finger.

"Ouch! Hanau, why..." she scolded, before realizing we were all watching her, and she coughed. Blushing furiously, she straightened up and fixed me with a professional smile. "I mean, yes, of course, Lord Jax; I can help you with that."

The round of laughter this time was louder, and she went even redder.

"Okay, then, that leaves Seneschal, Hephaestus, and Oracle." I gestured toward the center of the table, where the three Wisps stood.

"Seneschal is in charge of the Tower's structure; he maintains it, freaks out over any damage, and controls the individual aspects of it." Seneschal bowed with a flourish to the small group that didn't know him.

"This is Hephaestus, or Heph for short; he's the artist in charge of the Golems. While the only Genesis Chamber we have here right now is severely damaged, it's..."

"Fixed," Heph interrupted me.

"What?" I asked, startled out of my train of thought.

"It be fixed, laddie," Heph repeated slowly. "Do ye be goin' deaf?"

"I heard you, Heph," I replied through gritted teeth as I fantasized about kicking the little bastard out of the window. "I simply asked what you meant by that. Is it fixed well enough to produce higher-level golems? Is it fixed so we simply know it won't break down right now? Is it fucking redneck stitches and prayers that's holding it together? Give me a clue, you little..."

"It be fixed, in tha' it be no' about to break down. Beyond tha', it can produce class-two simple golems."

"Well...that's something, at least," I muttered. "How many cores do we have?"

"Seven," Heph pronounced proudly. "Caron, the wee boy wonder tha' he be, managed tae find *seven* intact cores!"

"Well, that's damn impressive!" I said, grinning, then reached into my bag of holding, pulling another out and showing it to Heph.

"That means that with the twenty I have, we can really get started!"

"*Twenty*!?" Heph practically squealed, his voice climbing to the pitch a schoolgirl excited about a puppy would emit before he slammed his hands over his mouth. "Aye…well, tha' be acceptable," he muttered, refusing to look at me as he deliberately made his voice low and gravelly.

"Glad to hear it!" I chuckled. "Last of all, and certainly not least, you all know Oracle. Oracle held, and still holds, responsibility for the Tower and now the Empire's magic repositories, including all things magical—be that spells, scrolls, books, crystals, all of it. If it's knowledge, she is the point of contact." I smiled affectionately at her as she dipped into a graceful curtsy.

"Those who have been with me the longest will also be relieved to know she's also now my lover, as well as my companion," I admitted dryly, looking pointedly at Oren and Cai and raising an eyebrow at their exaggerated relieved sighs.

"Oh, thank the Gods!" Oren cried, then went on in a loud stage whisper to Romanus, "It were so damn embarrasin', seein' them makin' wee puppy dog eyes at each other all tha damn time!"

"You know, Oren, that's a hell of a skill; how do you manage to make a whisper heard on the fortieth floor in ways a scream couldn't?" I glowered.

"It be a skill, laddie!" he admitted proudly. "Ye should hear ma wife; she'd be able to reach Himnel from here, iffin she tried!"

"I'll soon find out no doubt, then, as she's arriving on the battleship, I believe," I informed him.

"Seriously though, laddie, thank ye fer tha'. A Dwarf might be solid as a castle in a fight, but yer only as good as tha rock you be built on; mine be ma family. I missed 'em somethin' fierce…" he said, settling comfortably in his chair and smiling contentedly.

"Anytime, my friend. Feel free to spread the word to the crew and everyone else; we gathered those we could, and more joined us besides. That being said, though, there were a few who chose not to join us, from what Barrett said, and they're…well, we won't be going back to Himnel now, unless it's to conquer it, I'm afraid."

I sighed heavily. "As to the City and our trip there, the trip underground through the Smuggler's Path was hard, and in the process, we lost Cam. He was a brave man, and he died protecting us all. He will be remembered."

"He will be remembered," others around the table echoed in unison. I paused, wondering if I'd stumbled upon some kind of ritual phrase of remembrance. I shook away the thought and moved on, deciding that this wasn't the time to derail the conversation any further than it already had been.

"In the course of the trip, we did, however, find some new allies. Although they might not be to everyone's taste, they are Imperial Citizens, and will be damn well protected and respected as such; am I clear?" I made sure that everyone made eye contact and nodded in confirmation before I went on.

"Ashrag is their leader–their queen, actually–and she's old. She remembers the Empire at its height, and she was a citizen then. She was failed by the Legion and her fellow citizens when the cataclysm came, because of her race. Her sisters were murdered, stripped for alchemical parts, and the rest of the hive was hunted. She barely escaped with her life, and that was only after her mother sacrificed her life to buy them all time."

"Her…hive?" Cai asked carefully, and I nodded.

"Ashrag is a spider. An ancient Cave Spider, to be specific, and she's bigger than most inns. She swore to me on the condition that I kill off a group of Drow that were plaguing her. They were also what was causing the issues under the city on the Smuggler's Path, by the way…" I said as an aside to Oren.

"A spider? Are ye serious, laddie? Ye know I've a wee phobia of them…right? Who was it? Was it Oren who put ye up ta this?" Decin growled, glaring at Oren.

I held my hands up, waiting for silence.

"No," I said flatly once I had everyone's attention. "This is not a joke. This is not something that will be acceptable to fuck about with, either. Ashrag was failed by the Empire once, and while she is constrained by Oaths to protect her fellow citizens, just as all of you are, I'll remind you that she has had millennia for the memories of her ill treatment to fester.

"She will be respected and given her due as a vassal queen in the Empire. If it helps at all, the reason she and her kind were hunted at the first opportunity was for Cave Spider Silk. We will have access to it as part of the deal. How much, and at what cost, was never confirmed, so I'll expect it to be a give-and-take relationship, but that's fine." I paused, shifting uncomfortably as my armor pinched, and I went on.

"Ashrag and her brood are traveling here now, using underground passages, and will arrive in about a week or two, I'd guess. That may change drastically, depending on how bad the paths are, but I'd imagine when something her size travels, smaller creatures get the hell out of the way." I shrugged, as I knew little about their speed and travel capabilities, then went on.

"Either way, when she gets here, we will provide food and somewhere safe to rest, and she will send out her brood to find a suitable nest site. They will behave, and so will we." With that, I glared around again, getting a chorus of "Aye," "Yes, my lord," and more.

"Lastly, regarding the spiders, she sent one of her sapient daughters to aid us: Horkesh. She and her guard captured one of the airships and freed the slaves aboard her. They are all on their way here, along with the other ships, so there will be a small contingent present soon for people to adjust to before the main brood arrives. Looking back to the Smuggler's Path…" I paused, snagging a drink and leaning back in my chair, getting more comfortable.

"Once we'd killed the majority of the Drow, the last few fled, only to be killed in the tunnels by a third party. Their opponents turned out to be three of the Legion's Speculatores, a specialist branch of the Legion that is essentially a mix of justicars and scouts. They are damn fine legionnaires, and they readily joined us, aiding us in the quest.

"Once we'd cleaned up the area, looted the shit out of it, and burned Cam's funeral pyre, we entered the city. Turns out that Mal wasn't just a smuggler anymore; he'd taken over the Cloudring District Arena. We dropped your name, and that got us a meeting with him, so thank you for that, Oren." Oren beamed and looking proud, so I hid a grin as I went on.

"That also got us a fight straight away; something about you being a shit-useless smuggler? Anyway..."

Oren's face dropped, and a few of those around the table laughed.

"Once we got things sorted out, it turned out that the City Lord, Barabarattas, had managed to put the Legion under house arrest, and was basically trying to get an excuse together to attack them. All the gangs were also hunting legionnaires, for some reason. Not sure if that was the same reason or not, but we ended up in a fight with the Harpies and their leader, the Skyking. Long story short, it ended badly for them, right after we ended up becoming the Arena Champions, or close enough. We also looted the Magical Emporium while we were there, which turned out to be an old golem maintenance facility. We took nine of the ten golems we found intact: one complex servitor, six simple war golems, and a complex war golem, for your information, Heph and Seneschal." I addressed the pair of Wisps, who were practically salivating with excitement.

"The remaining complex servitor was left to carry out repairs on two of the three mining golems that were found there. They were badly damaged and needed a lot of repairs. Once the two are fixed, they are to be sent here, mining as they come. The servitor is to repair the genesis chamber there then begin standard production of the golems, sending them here as each is completed in small batches. I have no way to communicate with them, so I set them orders to come here, then we'll give them further commands."

"Ach, if only we had all the waystations up an' runnin', laddie," Heph groused. "With them and a few wee modifications, like a Control Tower, we could'a done so much more..."

"Well, that's going to be part of the discussion after this," I clarified, nodding to him. "But first, back to the city. While we looted and killed what we needed to, Mal arranged for the people to be gathered and housed in a few warehouses he knew, and we recruited the engineers from the Shipyards, or most of them, anyway. It helped that we collected Mistress Nerin here, as she healed a great many of them, gaining us a lot of good will and trust." I nodded to Nerin, who smiled back in satisfaction.

"Then, when the time was right, we looted the shipyards, grabbed the best ships that we could control, and we ran for it. Straight out to sea, with the contents of the stockpile and the cream of the Himnel fleet in our grasp. Romanus led his legionnaires out, and they did most of the fighting at the shipyards, also running things after I was injured. It took a few days, but we made it to the Sunken City..." At that revelation, both Hanau and Riana sat up, listening more intently.

"...which turned out to be an ancient Prax, or War-City, essentially like the Tower, but capable of flight. It was badly ruined, full of assholes, and inhabited by the Specters of the crew. I managed to free the crew–unintentionally, I'll admit, when I freed the slaves we'd rescued from Himnel of their collars. Again, long story short, we raided the shit out of the place, and got some extra spells, but more importantly, we rescued two more additions to the Tower.

"The first is the Wisp that guided and aided the crew of the Prax. She has chosen the name Tenandra and has bonded with an airship while swearing fealty. Her new body requires a lot of repairs, and probably a lot of upgrades, considering the age of the ship, at around a hundred years. The second addition is a small group. The descendants and a few surviving crew members of that particular airship…sixteen Gnomes." The room exploded with questions from the older members of the council, as well as a few from the newer ones.

"With everyone talking, I can't understand a damn word, so quiet down," I ordered. "Yes, she's a Wisp, and she's bonded to the ship, at her request. Yes, there are Gnomes; that's the good side. The bad is that they were trapped in a small space and forced to eat and drink heavily contaminated fungus and water while being attacked endlessly by undead, naga, and fuck knows what else, as well as being oppressed by a Skin-Walker, whatever *that* was. In that environment, they reverted to a feral state. With healing, they will be fine, but as drug-addled as they apparently always are, and as unstable as this group in particular is, don't expect great things, at least not straight away." I sighed and went on, telling the last of the story quickly.

"Finally, we were attacked by a small fleet of heavily armed ships from both Himnel and Narkolt. The crew had disguised Drow amongst them, and they carried juvenile SporeMothers, using the DarkSpore as weapons by firing the damn things out of catapults. It wasn't a pleasant fight, and in the process, Stephanos lost his life as well. He will be remembered."

"He will be remembered," The others chorused once again, and I filed that phrase away for later, wanting to ask Oracle about it and hoping I wouldn't have to use it often. "We won the fight, so I transferred to the fastest ships we had and brought half the Legion ahead, to get ready for the upcoming attack. Jenae told us about the Dark Legion, and we need to plan for that. That will be the next conversation, one we'll have after you all bring me up to date on what's happened here," I said grimly.

There was a long pause as everyone looked at each other and digested what I'd said. Finally, Cai spoke, rising to his feet and getting a drink as he did so.

"Well, after Decin dropped you off, Jax, he traveled to the village of Dannick, as you ordered. Once there, after they got over their shock at the arrival of a second airship, and after their fear of another attack was soothed, Isabella basically swept the place clean."

"You're too kind…" Isabella murmured, blushing as she looked down at her hands in embarrassment.

"It's true, though," Hanau insisted, taking up the narrative as Cai took a drink. "Isabella explained what had happened, what the Reeve had tried to do, and that he admitted it and was heading back now. Then she offered your protection and the chance at a new life as full citizens, without the fear of slavery or being at the whims of assholes like the nobility…" Hanau paused, coloring as he changed what he'd been about to say, ducking his head quickly and adding "…apart from those present, of course!"

I snorted and gestured for him to go on, amused by the whole affair.

"Anyway, there was a village meeting, and it was unanimous. Nobody wanted to stay after the others had been taken, and they didn't want to return to the city, so it wasn't a hard choice, not with Isabella telling them how wonderful it was here." Hanau finished.

"Wow, bet that was a shock when they arrived, then." I grimaced in embarrassment, and a few around the table laughed.

"Not really," Isabella replied earnestly. "We were at the mercy of the bandits, the monsters, and most recently, the cities' airships. Yes, it's late summer now, but soon, it'll be winter. The wooden houses we'd made were strong enough to protect us, but they would get damn cold. Living in the Great Tower, a place only spoken of in the bards' tales? One of the ancient wonders? True, lots of the tales were dark horror stories regarding the creatures that infested it, but every tale speaks of the day when a hero will cleanse it and make it the center of the world, a new age of heroes and wonders."

"We all know that bards lie through their teeth," Hanau said. "Their only aim is to get your money, your ass, or both, but still, these stories have been around for hundreds of years. Nobody knew where the Tower was, thanks to the magic, but enough survivors and legends reported it as existing and that it had once been a wonderful, safe place.

"Over time, the bards have tacked on extras about heroes and so on, like the thieving bastards always do, but in this case, it's turning out true. You literally saved all these people; you cleared out the monsters, you're feeding and clothing them, giving them luxuries and safety. What more could they ask for?" Hanau interjected, smiling.

"What clothes? What food?" I retorted, shaking my head. "I've done none of that!"

"Most of it was things they brought from their homes and the stores in the warship, but still, when you've got nothing, anything is a step up."

"Shit," I muttered softly, realizing how bad their lives must have been for them to be so happy to clear out for a ruin that was a horror story in their tales.

"Quite," Cai agreed, picking up the narrative. "Anyway, the entire village wanted to come, so Decin made three trips, not because there were so many people, but because it made no sense to leave anything behind. As things stand now, with the help of the golems, we stripped most of the houses down to the bedrock, bringing the very logs. If the Reeve and his pets ever get there, they'll be in for an unpleasant surprise."

"Oh, now, that's such a shame," I said, grinning with satisfaction.

"Isn't it just?" Cai replied, his eyes twinkling. "After that success, Decin visited a few smaller settlements that hadn't been marked on the map, mainly because they were literally single families or small homesteads..."

"We found them by searching for smoke," Hanau explained. "We found another seventeen people that way. A family of peat miners; they won't say who they were selling to but judging from how happy they were to be brought in and how tight-lipped they are, I'm guessing bandits were blackmailing them.

"There's a trio of hunters, but from their clothes–and the state of the pelts and how hungry they were–I think they were runaways from a village. We also collected two families, one of six and one of three; they'd moved out to set up in an old ruin, thinking it'd be, and I quote, a grand adventure.'

"There had been thirty people originally, and they were trying to set up a new village. Ten survived the trip there, though they lost another one shortly after settling in. They were especially glad to see us, practically mobbing us when we landed."

"So how many people are we up to now?" I asked the room in general, and Seneschal flowed forward, smiling as he answered.

"Well, Jax, we have one hundred and thirty-seven citizens now, although many have not yet sworn the Oath. How many did you bring with you?"

I checked my notifications quickly, unsure how to calculate the numbers, then smiled upon seeing the Citizens tab. I couldn't help letting out a relieved sigh as I saw the total.

"Across the fleet, the refugees, the freed slaves, and the Legion, I have nine hundred and fifty-eight, so that's, what, one thousand and ninety-five citizens, once we've administered the Oath?" I rubbed my chin in consideration, then grinned at the looks of shock around the table, save Oracle.

I suddenly realized that, while I'd seen the notifications, and I'd basically kept myself up to date with things, there'd never been a need to discuss it with the others before. Realistically, the only person besides myself and Oracle who probably knew how many there were in the incoming fleet was Mal. And Soween, of course.

"Well, at least we'll have a lot of people to bring to Jenae and the others," I said, sitting up straight and regarding my council seriously. "That's a discussion for a different day, however. Now that we know what's happened, we can plan for the future."

CHAPTER TEN

"There are three hundred or so professional killers, the Dark Legion, who–thanks to a miscalculation in our escape–have declared me an apostate. They are being driven by their Dark...*Prick*...er, Lord," I explained, "to come here and raze the Tower to the ground. I'm obviously not going to allow that." I took a deep breath and stood up, moving around my seat and starting to pace.

"They're headed directly for the Tower, seemingly unwilling to deviate from a straight line from there to here; is that still the case?" I asked, and Decin nodded soberly.

"It were yesterday, anyhow," he confirmed.

"Fantastic. Clearly, they're fucking idiots, then." I smiled grimly at the group. "Which ship is the fastest we have?" I asked, and Decin straightened up.

"Tha'd be mine, Jax," he said proudly.

"That *was* yours," I corrected. "Is it still the fastest, taking into account the new ships, like the fast scout we have outside, or the two cruisers?"

Decin paused and grimaced.

"Sorry, mate," I said, winking. "Oren, your next job when we finish here and you've arranged for a space for the battleship to land, is to find out which is the fastest ship we have in our newly acquired fleet. You will take Restun with you." I looked over at the Primus.

"You will do as he asks and scout the Dark Legion, then you'll get your arses back here as fast as you can. Restun, I want you to consider plans for a guerilla fight, including a series of ambushes and traps. They can only move so fast because of the Trailmasters. If we remove them, the entire column grinds to a halt, gaining us more time to prepare. I want those fuckers dead."

Restun allowed himself a small smile as he replied with a simple "Yes, Lord Jax."

"Riana, as I said earlier, you are to search out a few others to help you. I need to know that the cannons on the cruisers are safe to use, or, failing that, what the risks are and how likely failures are, from the cannon breaking to a miniature sun appearing on the deck. I need to know *fast*." My tone left no room for discussion, and Riana blinked at me for a second before nodding and sitting up straighter.

"Thank you." I turned my attention to the Prefect. "Romanus, you know far more about the art of war than I ever will, I'm sure. Therefore, I want you to take whoever you need and scout the lower floors and the outer walls. Tell me what state they're in and what you need to make the place into a kill zone; when the transformation is done, I mean.

"Seneschal, we managed to steal, buy, or barter for a grand total of three hundred and seventy-four manastones. Of those, I want to keep the seventy-four for the ships. We're going to need to keep them in the air, after all, and I honestly have no damn clue how many they'll need. So, what can you do with three hundred manastones?"

"Three hundred," Seneschal muttered, tapping his fingers together. "Might I ask as to the size and grade?""

"Here," said Bane, setting a bag down on the table and emptying a dozen out. "These are pretty much the average. There are some bigger and a few smaller, but most are like this."

"Hmmm, reasonable size, good density…with these dedicated exclusively to the Tower, I could bring the overall condition up from the current sixty-nine percent to ninety-four percent, over a period of approximately three weeks. That is the maximum effective speed at which I can use the stones, to prevent excess wastage. Or, I could use stones more sparingly. If we were to use them to repair specific areas, I feel we would gain more."

"Go on…but bear in mind, it needs to be completed before the Dark Legion arrive, as I expect they'll have something to say about us repairing the structure." I waved for him to carry on as I sat back down.

"I would recommend we use the majority to repair the gaping holes and outer walls, then. That will seal up the worst of the damage and bring the Tower up to eighty-two percent, due to the unavoidable losses from using too many stones at once. This will enable us to repair the inner walls as well; to some degree, at least. The lower floors will be entirely repaired, structurally. However, they will not be restored; I must stress this. The non-essential sections, rooms for housing and so on, will be left as they are, although I could possibly look into reusing the remnants of the stone itself to reduce the need for entirely mana-based construction. What I can guarantee will be done are the structural requirements. Walls will be repaired where they affect the strength of the Tower, windows that cannot be replaced will be filled in, the floors that have collapsed will be cannibalized for building materials, and the basement levels shored up and cleared."

"What about the areas we need for living?" I hesitated. "And how will the outer walls be repaired?"

"The outer walls will be regrown to the best height we can rapidly manage, and the courtyard will be repaired, as that qualifies as structural, due to the way the Tower distributes its weight. The outer walls will be capped at twenty feet, with everything inside being stripped back–trees and foliage, I mean. Beyond that, we could repair one of the facilities to standard working order, or possibly create two within a more basic functionality."

"What facilities?" I asked, curious, and he paused, as though unsure if he should comment in front of the others. I nodded and he went on slowly, as though waiting to see if he'd be ordered to stop.

"The Great Tower is both a bastion and a city at its peak condition, Lord Jax. To that end, it was designed to be upgraded and to facilitate the construction of whatever facilities would be needed. This Tower once boasted, amongst others, a training labyrinth, a magma forge, an auction house, though it was never completed, stables, alchemical gardens, and farms." He paused again, and I discreetly gestured for him to continue.

"The only one of these facilities that is capable of being repaired is the labyrinth, as that was not entirely destroyed. The others could be rebuilt but only as the most basic versions of their design."

"So, the magma forge couldn't be rebuilt, but a standard forge could?"

"Correct," he answered.

"Fuck. Thorn is gonna be pissed about that." I pondered my options for a minute then shook my head. I wanted a forge; hell, Jenae had said it would be possible to build a forge that could be upgraded. Maybe She'd meant this, maybe She meant something else, but either way, we had tens of thousands of rooms intact for now. Building outside was just an excess risk I didn't need to take.

"We need food," I said decisively. "We're currently okay for it; we raided the city, after all, and we have hunters out there and can send more out as soon as the ships arrive, but we need to gather more, not simply use up everything we have. Give me options with this," I said, reaching into my Bag of Spatial Folding and retrieving the rare blueprint I'd been given by Jenae when I'd selected Enhanced Construction from the Constellation of Secrets.

I passed it to Seneschal, and he opened it, examining it carefully. Heph stepped in close to read it with him. A few minutes of silence passed, in which the others fidgeted or spoke quietly, while Heph and Seneschal muttered and pointed out details to each other.

"This blueprint could either be incorporated into the Tower grounds or built on one or more of the larger balconies...which..." Seneschal pointed out, but I cut him off, leaning forward.

"Plan for a balcony; several, if that works better, or hell, an entire floor."

"On the sixteenth floor, there is a ruined balcony." He considered for a moment. "It was originally used as a garden for the residents, but part of it collapsed through the roof of the lower floor in a storm sixty-three years ago. If I were to include the section of the floor below, which has been exposed, into the design, it could be done for a lesser cost, enabling either a second smaller facility to be constructed, or an additional glasshouse."

"As part of the repairs, are you including quarters for my people?" I asked, conscious of the startling number of citizens that would be descending on the Tower soon.

"No," Seneschal replied with a shake of his head. "There are thousands of rooms that are at least minimally habitable, as they are secure and simply need to be cleaned and have doors or windows repaired, and furnishings added. I will use some of the mana to break down the rubble that fills the tower, as that can be used to rebuild. The effort is worth it, but the cost to outfit and repair the rooms would exceed the stones you have by a noticeable order of magnitude."

"Okay, what about the living areas we already discussed, such as the food areas and the airship bays on the twentieth and twenty-sixth floors?" I asked.

"The food preparation areas are being restored by the residents; due to their hard work, I have simply repaired the basic structures and have otherwise left them alone. The twenty-sixth floor requires considerably more work, but I have included that in the estimated plans."

"Okay, let's assume that, say, ten percent of the people that are incoming could be put to work on the Tower's needs; how would that alter things?"

"Without being rude, Jax, not appreciably," Seneschal confided with a wry smile. "The Tower is a magical construct, and the golems can do things far more efficiently than any living being."

"Well, fuck you very much," I retorted, smiling at him tiredly.

"As I say, Jax, and to all of you," Seneschal said, rotating to regard the other people seated around that table, "I mean no offense, but unskilled raw labor at this stage is…not helpful. It has taken me over two weeks to train the existing small cadre of helpers to be minimally useful.

"Taking the time to train dozens or hundreds more people would be…painful. It would take a considerable amount of time and effort, and that would divert my attention away from the things that I should be doing to give the Tower its best chance."

"Okay, then, we'll have a separate meeting in a few days, once everyone else arrives, and we'll give out the books and memories that we can. Until then, is there anything else pressing before we go ahead and start to repair the Tower?"

"I have one minor disciplinary issue to raise with you, Jax, but that is all," Cai said, making eye contact to ensure that I knew he wanted to do it in private, and I nodded to him.

"In that case, this meeting is over. Seneschal, how long will it take to make this place safe?"

"Four hours is the fastest we can do it, Jax. The building should be unoccupied, as it may be dangerous to living creatures when the walls and floors move, plus there will be a considerable loss of mana…"

"Do it," I ordered. "Everyone else, bar the Wisps, Cai, and I guess Bane– because he's a fucking cockroach and no matter how hard I try, I can't get rid of him–I'll let you all go. Please get everyone out of the Tower and into the Courtyard. We begin the repair in one hour, and I expect this to be a sight to see." I waved for them to disperse and everyone got up, several bowing, while others made the fist-to-heart salute, before moving on.

Once the room was empty, I stood, and the six of us made our way down the hall to the Command Center instead.

This room was vastly different from the last time I'd used it. The floor-to-ceiling window on one wall was now marvelously spotless and let in the sun. There were still three seats, but they were clearly better quality and had cushions, while a tray laden with food and drinks had been left for us on a small side table.

Once the door was closed, Cai, Bane, and I took up the three seats, the Wisps took up stations around the Creation Table, and there was an air of palpable relaxation.

"I take it there's nobody in the corners?" I asked around, getting smiles from Seneschal and a powerful *thrum* from Bane, who nodded as well, after a slight pause.

"We're alone now, Jax," Bane confirmed.

"Good. Cai, what's this issue?" I asked directly.

"We have a minor problem, Jax. You remember Caron?" Cai asked bluntly.

"The little lad, the one who was finding the Cores after he stood up to me to protect his friend; what was her name?"

"Kayt," the Panthera said with a slight smile. "Her name is Kayt, and she's helping the herbalists now. She apparently has a gift for growing things and loves working with plants."

"That's great! So what's the problem?" I asked, confused.

"Caron is, simply put." Cai sighed, rubbing his forehead. "The boy has an absolute talent for getting into places he shouldn't, including the rooms that are still sealed higher in the Tower. Kayt's mother came to me with this." He held out a hand. I reached out and accepted the small item, letting out a low whistle at the necklace I now held.

Necklace of the Estranged Lover		Further Description *Yes*/No	
Details:		This is part of a matched pair that grants the ability to feel the other's presence once per day. This keepsake, and others like it, were developed to allow married partners far from each other to consummate their love in their dreams.	
Rarity:	Magical:	Durability:	Charge:
Highly Rare	Yes	67/100	82/100

"Where the hell did he get this?" I asked in astonishment, and Cai shrugged.

"Caron has denied anything. He is seemingly terrified that he will be thrown out of the Tower if he's caught. I can't determine who, but it seems that someone has been guiding the boy in several larcenous skills. He's now a novice in Pickpocketing, Lockpicking, and Burglary, with an impressive stealth skill, and his Agility is rocketing, as is his Dexterity.

"I believe a direct order from you will compel him to reveal his trainer, but that might cause issues. Added to that, I know of nobody in the Tower at this point who would have skills sufficient enough to teach him, and it raises certain concerns. As does the fact that Kayt has been sharing dreams with someone; apparently, she's been dreaming of a woman, one who has been questioning her closely on the events here.

"Being a child, faced with what seems to have been a noblewoman in her dreams, she has told them much, both about the location and the current state of the Tower. We managed to cut off the contact several days ago, so there is no information regarding the fleet or the Legion, thankfully."

"Damn. Okay, keep an eye on that, please." I hefted the necklace in my hand. "I might have a look at this myself later and find out what this noblewoman thinks of me appearing in the dream, rather than a child she can bully," I muttered, pocketing the jewelry. "Do you think it was intentional; Caron giving this specific item to Kayt, I mean?"

"No," Cai said promptly, shaking his head. "I think whoever is guiding him simply missed that he'd pocketed it for his friend, and in that regard, we have an opportunity."

"Is Kayt aware that we know?" I asked, rubbing my chin thoughtfully.

"No, her mother simply said it was too pretty for everyday use and that she was going to tuck it away for now. Then she brought it to me. Caron is somewhere in the upper Tower. He disappears for days at a time, 'looking for cores.' At the moment, he has no idea, either."

"Seneschal, Heph?" I questioned them.

They eyed each other silently, before Heph sighed and kicked at the table before him, trying to avoid my eyes.

"Ah, well...tha' be a wee problem..." Heph said quietly.

"Caron is a personable lad," Seneschal said guiltily. "He made friends of us both, and as alone as he often was, and as he was helping us find the cores, we played a game with him…"

"Hide an' go seek," Heph added, sighing again. "The wee laddie be unnaturally good at it."

"You taught him how to hide from you both," I stated flatly, and they both nodded sheepishly. "Wow." I sat back, gently banging my head off the back of the chair.

"I bet I could find him," Oracle offered, and I shook my head.

"No, this is looking more and more like we have a trespasser, and a skilled rogue, at that. I don't want you risking yourself. Bane?" I asked, and he responded by getting to his feet.

"You'll need an extra bodyguard to aid Tang, then," he said.

"I'll have a chat with Flux and ask him to find me a proper team. They can train on the job. This is more important. Take someone else with you, as well."

"I work best alone…"

"Cheena?" I suggested.

Bane hesitated before finally nodding. "I will take her. She taught me much; a good suggestion," he acquiesced.

"I hate to ask you to go now, mate, considering that we know the Tower won't be safe soon, but…"

"But there's a child hiding somewhere in the Tower that has no idea about what's coming, and they have a rogue training them that we need to catch," Bane finished, nodding in understanding. "Don't worry; I'd not want anything to happen to the boy, either. I'll find him, and we'll make sure Seneschal knows where we are. Besides…I want to find out who's skulking around, if it's not me…"

"Well, go have fun, my friend, and remember, the Tower might not be safe soon," I warned. The Mer let out a low *thrum* of amusement.

"Life never is. I'll make Flux aware on my way out."

"Thank you, Bane." I said, turning back to Cai as soon as the door shut. "Is there anything else?" He smiled ruefully.

"A thousand things, and you've brought almost a thousand more, albeit a few days before the majority of the new issues arrive. I think you might be better off with someone else for this, Jax. I was a slave, remember?"

"Ha! You organize things like nobody I've ever met, mate; you don't get out that easy." I snorted, grinning at him.

"Seriously, though, I'm barely keeping up," Cai admitted, popping a raspberry into his mouth and chewing as he rubbed one ear casually. "I have Isabella aiding me, and Hanau has been filling in as well. In truth, I don't know if I can do this. A thousand more people? I'm swamped with the hundred or so we already have."

"We'll be making some changes once everyone's here," I reassured him, smiling slightly. "We're unfortunately at war, and with that in mind, we'll be doing things in a more regimented way. I spoke to Romanus a lot on the way over. As much as his assistant, Alistor, is an arrogant little prick, it seems the ass has a gift for this kind of thing.

"Make use of him. The Tower will have the Legion as its army, and the fleet will keep us safe from the air, but we need to train the citizens as a secondary militia; for now, at least. On top of that, we need to get some structure in the Tower for the citizens. They shouldn't all be coming to you with their every problem, so we should make them into small teams, or hell, large ones. The farmers, they have a leader, yes?" I asked, and he considered their current dynamic.

"They have a more experienced member of the team, but…"

"Then that's the problem, my friend," I persisted, smiling. "In my world, the farmers would have a single person that is responsible for them, their leader. That person would deal with day-to-day issues and would have a meeting with his supervisor if there was an issue he couldn't manage.

"Take some time and think about this, then pick out a leader for each group. Much as the Legion has ranks, the citizens will as well. That will allow you to deal with the bigger issues, and they can handle the lesser ones. Much as I can't deal with everything personally, and I have the council, you should have one as well.

"Right; is there anything else?" I asked my friend, and he sighed, getting to his feet.

"No, Jax. It's just good to have you back," he said.

I smiled, standing up and clapping him on the shoulder. "It's good to be back, man. Thank you for looking after everyone while I was away."

He waved away my thanks and exited the room, leaving me and the Wisps to discuss any miscellaneous details that hadn't been addressed.

"What wasn't said in the meeting?" I asked, and Heph grinned.

"Well, laddie, you be getting' better at this whole 'leadership' thing! Amongst tha other minor details be the fact that there be a strongroom under tha rubble in tha Genesis Chamber. There be a load o' materials buried there, many o' which be valuable. I can either use 'em ta make more Golems, Seneschal can incorporate 'em into tha Tower, or they could be kept ready fer when they be needed most."

"Save them for now," I decided after a moment's thought. "I can't see there being enough material to make a difference in the Tower's construction, right?" Seneschal smiled indulgently.

"No, Jax, they would be more in the nature of luxurious touches; gold lamé on the walls in certain areas, that kind of thing."

"Nah, fuck that," I scoffed, shaking my head. "That's a waste. This is a fortress, and it should look like it. The gold can be saved and used for currency when we have an economy. I've no need for shiny fucking corridors." I growled, remembering the Baron's citadel and all the wealth on unnecessary display.

"Do you wish me to remove the gold and jewels that are already affixed to the walls?" Seneschal asked slowly, clearly hoping I wouldn't ask him to do so.

"No…but don't put any more on, either. Strip anything valuable from the debris and store it in the vault."

"We don't have a vault."

"Do I have to think of everything?" I shot back, remembering a favorite character in a classic parody film, smiling as I recalled his suggestion of putting someone in a rowboat to mark the location of where his hat had sunk.

"Seriously, though…" I murmured after a minute. "There are secure storage rooms in the Genesis Chamber, so make one of those into a vault, please. Put the most valuable materials in there. The rest of the surplus should go into the other storage rooms down there. I've also brought back a fuck-ton of gold, silver, copper, and platinum, as well as a load of gems that need to be stored in the vault once it's secure."

"Very well; most of the rest is as I said in the meeting. However, I felt it best to leave certain details out, restricting them for you only." Seneschal paused to make sure I was watching, then brought up the Tower on the Creation Table, grumbling under his breath about the need to fix the table soon.

It started as a bubble on the seemingly flat, solid surface, then rapidly grew, taking form and spiraling into the air. At first, the diagram was small, enabling us to see the Tower in its entirety, but as he began to explain, specific sections were highlighted.

"First, the mana collectors." Seneschal indicated the spikes that ringed the top of the Tower like the points on a crown. "The stones you brought will enable more than I was willing to admit where others could hear. For ease of reckoning, the extra I did not mention equates to a thousand points of available construction for the Tower. There are several options for these points, including, should you wish it, a greater percentage of the Tower being repaired."

"You would have included the points in that initial estimate if you believed that was the best way to do things, Seneschal. Show me my options, please." I smiled and steepled my fingers as I tried not to cackle maniacally over the hidden extras.

"The mana collectors are still damaged; as part of the repairs, I can return them to full capacity. This will, after maintenance costs and our tithe to Jenae, result in around six hundred points of available capacity per month. These are simply standard mana collectors, however.

"The Prax that were designed after the Great Towers had two systems of mana collectors, one of which was exclusively for everyday maintenance, and the other was a second, heavier-capacity war system. These could, in times of need, drain the mana from the surrounding area, absorbing far more than the usual ambient amount.

"This would result in a sudden leap of around twelve to fifteen thousand points, but it would also cause living things that rely on ambient mana, such as plants and spellcasters, to suffer greatly until ambient mana slowly began to regenerate." As he explained, far larger mana collectors appeared, growing upwards and making the Tower look more like something which an evil eye should be perched above.

"No, I don't see that as a viable option. What else do we have?" I asked, and he dismissed the phantom collectors from the display.

"Understood. There are four more options. First is a Control Facility..."

"Tha' be a damn good investment," Heph said quickly.

"Yes, well..." Seneschal hedged, glaring at his companion, "the Tower had one originally; it was how the golems in the surrounding territories were controlled if there was a need for remote command, and that was how I originally shut down all mana collectors in the area as well. The Control Facility would enable us to build a relay system for controlling the golems in surrounding areas, provided there was a facility for them to link to nearby. This could cost five hundred points to construct from scratch." At his words, a new central pillar grew upwards from the apex of the Tower, adding a good hundred meters onto the height, while a dozen smaller ones extended out from the courtyard horizontally. Lines ran from one to another, creating a net, and it pulsed with power.

"Defensive capabilities are next; *however*…these would take considerable time to prepare and would not be ready for at least a week," the Wisp warned, holding up one hand to stop me as I perked up. "The most basic of facilities include the wall around the courtyard, but the upgrade would add ballistae into the wall and three floors of your choice.

"Each can be configured individually to fire manabolts, solid projectiles, or, through the use of a pressurized reservoir, a limited spray of flammable liquid. In the third configuration, the ballista is obviously a short-range weapon which sprays a fire starter, rather than firing a bolt or load."

"How many could we get?" I asked. "And at what cost?"

"The walls of the courtyard could be covered with overlapping fields of fire, but that would require the trees being cleared back for at least five hundred meters on all sides to be effective. The lumber work alone would take an estimated six weeks, and cost fifteen thousand points.

"We could afford to put two ballistae on the walls, one above each gate, and three each on three separate levels of the Tower, offering a total covering of eleven weapons for nine hundred points. As I said, however, this would take a week."

As he explained, the options appeared, and I examined the demonstrated fields of fire. Unless we somehow managed to get the full fifteen thousand points to use, it was noticeably pitiful, unfortunately. We'd be left praying for them to fly or walk directly into our fields of fire.

"Dammit. What else?" I asked, massaging my temples, getting more and more stressed over all the micromanagement.

"The remaining two are more in the nature of long-term upgrades, but they would be significantly more useful. The first is a mine, although not in the way you are probably thinking. Instead of an underground tunnel where the citizens must labor to collect metals and precious stones, the Tower itself would deploy filaments into the ground. These filaments would sift through the ground, slowly filtering materials back to the Tower. The first and most useful result of this would be in providing building material. They will provide better quality stone for the Tower, enabling us to sheathe the outside in a variety of protective substances, greatly increasing the strength and resilience of the Tower against an attack. This would cost one hundred points per filament."

The entire Tower came back into view, but now, where the Tower sat atop the earth, it began to extrude long, thin lines, not much thicker than wires, which dug and slid through the ground. "It would also provide a small quantity of precious metals and more."

"Lastly…" Seneschal said, glancing at Heph, who grinned excitedly.

"We could map tha continent!" Heph exclaimed, bouncing up and down on the balls of his illusory feet. "It be a way ta search tha land. we'd find out so much more'n we know now. We'd find tha waystations an' more, and as time goes on, laddie, hell, we'd find out all about tha world!" This option resulted in a dozen small rings being set around the Tower over ten floors, each containing hundreds of small glowing points. The final two rings were affixed atop a pillar that sat in a specific position before the Genesis Chamber.

"Cost?" I asked, perhaps a little more tersely than I'd meant to.

"Eight hundred to construct the facility, then a hundred a month."

I sat back, the pair of them watching me with unreadable expressions as Oracle, who'd been conspicuously quiet throughout the entire string of discussions, stood behind me, grown to her full size.

"Take this off," she ordered calmly, hands resting on the joints of my armor. I did as I was told, stripping my breastplate off and shrugging out of the upper arms at her direction. "Don't get your hopes up; you have work to do." She shot me a wry smile in response to the questioning look I gave her.

I groaned involuntarily as she dug her fingers into either side of my neck and began to massage, working my tense muscles as I thought over the plan. Relaxing, I leaned forward, resting my forearms on the edge of the table.

Seneschal had used the Creation Table to show me how each option would look, but there was no perfect choice. Naturally, the one that I both wanted and needed the most, I could neither afford nor trust to work.

"The defensive measures are out," I said after a while. "If they don't go for the gates, those are pointless." I continued to consider for long minutes, before sighing and choosing what I knew I had to.

"Map the continent," I ordered finally. I didn't *want* that anywhere near as much as the others, but damn, I *needed* it more. The control system would be brilliant, but to make it useful, I had to know where the waystations were and where the various ancient facilities had been. Once I had those locations identified, I was going to wish for the control facilities instead, but as I couldn't find the damn places otherwise…

"That leaves us with two hundred points to use," Seneschal mused. "Do you wish to invest them into anything in particular, save them, or add them to the pool?"

I was tempted to crack a joke about making a pool, but instead, I sighed and spoke the words I'd needed to voice for a long time.

"How much to make me a real goddamn shower?" I remained torn between thinking it was a waste and feeling greedy by asking for something for myself, and damn well deciding I deserved it.

"Your quarters are included in the initial repairs, Jax," Seneschal explained gently, smiling at the obvious wave of relief that flooded me. "We already planned for this, as it is…unseemly…for the High Lord of the continent to be scrubbing himself where others can see or passing out drunk in ship's cabins.

"You needed quarters, and while they are not to the standard of quarters higher in the Tower, we have made them as appropriate as possible, given the available resources. We also appointed a series of smaller suites near to your rooms for your advisors, upper members of the Legion, and your personal squad."

"Thanks, guys," I said quietly, humbled by their consideration. I let go of my remaining tension, sitting back and smiling as Oracle finished my brief massage. "Add the points that are left to the mines, or filaments, or whatever."

"Very well; thank you, Jax," Seneschal said. "Now then, the majority of the populace are outside. If you wish to join them, I can begin the restructuring. It would be an unnecessary risk to have you remain inside at this point."

"What about Bane and Cheena?" I asked, standing up.

"They are aware of the risks. I formed an avatar near their last location and stated the situation clearly to them. They have chosen to continue in an attempt to reach Caron."

"Damn; maybe we should stop…" I hesitated, thinking about the risk to the boy.

"Not necessary, Jax. The ships have left the Tower as well, and the vast majority of the risk is confined to the main central and lower floors. The higher ones will simply have the damaged and destroyed items removed and broken down. Each floor has an avatar stating the risk loudly."

"Then I hope this flushes him out," I said as I walked to the door. I felt bad about the risk to the boy, but as Seneschal stated, it was minimal, and there was definitely something going on with him that was a risk to the Tower right now.

"Jax…" Seneschal said suddenly, rethinking his position earlier. "There may be some dirt and other effects at ground level, including dislodged stones possibly causing a risk to the people outside. With your permission, I'll ask them to board ships for their own safety?"

"Of course." Despite the way he was when we first met, Seneschal was really beginning to care about the people of the tower.

I left the room, feeling Seneschal and Heph dismissing their avatars somehow, and I jogged down the stairs with Oracle flying by my side, returned to her diminutive state.

I swore suddenly, realizing that I'd left my armor behind, and turned around before sighing heavily and simply sending a message to Seneschal, as I resumed the run.

"Seneschal, can you not eat my armor when you do this? I think I'm going to need it soon."

"Jax, that's not armor, it's scrap metal," Seneschal responded sardonically. **"Believe me, the armorers will be far happier if I provide them the same weight in metal back in bars than they will in receiving their craftsmanship in the state you brought it back in."**

I grunted, but he was probably right, and I left it at that. Jogging down the last few dozen steps to the next level, I set off across the floor towards the large central stairwell.

I looked over the huge amount of rubble, the mixed stone, metal, and general refuse of nearly a thousand years of decay, and I grinned, loving the reality of a magical building.

It'd take a normal construction crew a hundred years to clean the Tower out to begin repairs, and probably ten times that, if there were managers involved.

I continued down, working my way out of the Tower. Slowing from my jog as I approached the doors, I had to squint until I adjusted to the bright light that glared in from outside, though it made me smile as I looked around at the piles of rubbish, broken wood, shattered stone, and Gods, the remaining filth from the SporeMother and her ilk, which was strewn about the place.

The entire Tower was filled with crap, literal and figurative, and while Seneschal would remove and repurpose all that he could, he was going to leave the sealed rooms, provided they were actually sealed and intact, alone.

Rooms that remained sealed on one side, but–for example–the outer wall had collapsed, then the room would be stripped and everything absorbed. The process was difficult to use precisely, at least to confirm that valuable items would be left behind, so we'd come up with this compromise.

As I walked out into the sunlight, I paused at the top of the steps and gazed around, observing the large group spread across the courtyard while the ships were being shifted. Several ships were already loaded up with people taking off to make room for others to land, collecting the remaining people on the ground

CHAPTER ELEVEN

I took the steps down to the ground quickly, looking up at the nearest cruiser, the *Ragnarök*, as she lifted upwards. People leaned against the railings as they watched the trees slipping past, and kids cried out in joy.

I turned my gaze to the massive trees that ringed the Tower, even the smaller ones had trunks broad enough that a lumberjack would have wet dreams looking at them, and I shook my head slowly as I tried to keep the grin from my face.

This.

This was why I loved the realm so much; it was all so fresh, so new, and so full of wonder and potential. In my world, a structure nearly three miles high would collapse under its own weight. Here, magic compensated for it in part, and other solutions had been found. I had no clue what they were, but Seneschal and Heph had tried to explain them once, and I'd zoned out.

It was enough that the whole place was fucking magical. That was enough for me. A little child, maybe three or four years old at most, being held tightly in a white-faced mother's arm as she clung to the railing for dear life, all the while the child screamed and hollered in joy.

The people around me, a mixture of the Legion and the refugees and villagers who'd already sworn to me, mingled uncertainly. There was a blend of fear and hope on the faces of the people, all watching the Legion, knowing that they were strong and having heard of them in countless tales. Others had seen the Legion before and heard the accusatory tales about them, while on the other side, there were these tall, strong, and proud legionnaires.

They were all, to a person, fit and practically glowing with good health. They were heavily armed, experienced fighters of all races, and the one thing that made them the same–beyond their allegiance to me and the Legion, of course–was the trepidation on their faces.

These massive warriors were scared they'd be rejected by these people. Treated as they'd become accustomed to. Reviled and ignored.

A little girl, a truly little one, maybe a year old, just walking, and unsteadily at that, tottered over to Restun. The most imposing legionnaire of them all. A man every other legionnaire knew would simply reach up and yank the damn sun back down if he decided he wanted it to be night again. He looked down in shock at the little girl who wobbled up to him and lifted her hands, the pudgy fingers clenching and unclenching in an unmistakable command.

Restun shot his gaze up at the mother, who smiled to him and nodded permission. He knelt, reaching out a lightly shaking hand. The man who terrified hard-bitten legionnaires gently lifted the little girl up, wincing as she tugged on his ear, before laughing.

She struggled to climb up his body, and he lifted her higher, turning slowly so she could look out across the people gathered there.

She giggled and waved her arms wildly, and it started. It was hesitant at first, the reaction, but as more and more followed suit, the legionnaires grew more confident and relaxed. They waved back and smiled at the small child, who giggled and cooed at them.

Restun turned her around one last time, showing her to the Legion, before handing her back to her mother, who smiled at him and said something quietly.

He froze and stared at her for a long second before nodding and turning, walking out into the crowd and away from the legionnaires who were mingling more freely and confidently with the people of the Tower now.

"What did she say?" I wondered aloud.

Oracle stepped up next to me, putting her arm around my waist and speaking softly as we watched them all.

"She said, 'welcome home.'"

I sighed, immensely grateful to the woman, a person I didn't even know. What she'd done with those two words and in allowing her child to go to Restun, was more than I could have accomplished with a week's hard labor. She'd shown a level of trust and love for the protectors of the Empire who had been missing from their lives for far too long. As the voices started to rise, as more and more talked and joked, I pulled Oracle close and kissed the top of her head.

"Remind me to ask Cai about her," I whispered to Oracle.

She nodded, hugging me, then let go as we walked down the last step and out to join the others. I strolled through the group, speaking to people and generally letting everyone get used to me being there while I killed time, making my way to the back of the group. As I moved through the milling crowds, I picked up the rest of my team on the way, as well as Prefect Romanus and a handful of legionnaires I'd gotten to know better than others.

"Romanus," I said quietly, and he stepped in closer, angling his head to hear me better. "I need some recommendations from you on the skillbooks, spells, and memory crystals we have. Who would be useful to us right now, and with what?" He smiled, straightening up and looking about.

"Over there. Legionnaire specialist Denny; field fortifications are his passion, and we'll need traps for your plan."

"Denny!" I called out, and the big man stepped up, clapping a fist to his chest.

"Lord Jax," he replied smiling.

"It's good to see you, man. heard you're good at field fortifications; is that right?"

He grinned, looking proud. "I try, sir. It comes naturally to me, and I don't know…there's a certain satisfaction that comes from seeing a job done right, from watching a structure come together under my direction and by my own hands. A field fortification can be simple, but it's still a damn effective way to protect your people."

"How are you with traps?"

He blinked, taking a deep breath. "Ah…well, I kind of experiment with them a little, but there's not usually time to include them in a standard field fortification…" he explained awkwardly.

"Okay, well, I know you like the fortifications side of things. I need someone who can make traps, though. Is that you, or do you know someone better?"

"That's me, too!" he responded quickly, expression eager. "When I say I don't make them often, it's because of the lack of opportunity, not the lack of desire!"

"Glad to hear it." I grinned wickedly at him. "Because there are three hundred Dark Legionnaires headed our way, and I'd like to make sure they understand that this isn't where they want to be, not ever again."

"Jax, we have two skillbooks and a memory," Oracle informed me within the silence of our bond, making me smile at the way our minds worked so closely in sync now.

"Oracle, what level are they?" I asked aloud.

"Journeyman, apprentice, and the memory is from a heliomage." She replied aloud as well.

"A what?" I asked, my train of thought broken.

"A heliomage; a mage that specialized in fire and the use of the sun almost exclusively. They were rare even back when the Empire was at its peak, as they were from a small...well, 'cult' isn't the right word, but, they kinda were, honestly.

"They were an offshoot of the Gnomes, adjusted to live in high places. They worshipped the sun, and the Lady of Fire specifically. For one to have given their memories to the Empire, Jenae must have ordered it or at least given Her permission. They wouldn't give up their worship of Her easily, and for Her to be no longer gaining mana from them...they must be extinct now."

"And the skills the memory has?" I persisted.

She grimaced slightly. "There's no way of knowing, exactly. I just remember the excitement of some of the mages when it was delivered, and the arguments and fantasies some of them expressed about using it and learning their secrets."

I focused back on Denny, who was watching us both with an expression of shock on his face.

"Well, Denny, you want to become a trap specialist?" I offered.

He swallowed hard, gaze flickering from me to Romanus and back. "I...hell yes, sir," he said fervently. "I'd love to."

"What level are you with traps now?"

He sighed heavily. "Level eleven, sir," he admitted, slightly abashed.

"Apprentice grade already?" I asked, impressed.

He nodded, perking up a bit. "I'd spend more time on it, sir, but, well...you know how it is..."

I looked from him to Romanus.

"Cost," Romanus said. "It's one thing to build a trap, but if you leave it, you're possibly setting an innocent up to be hurt after you leave. Along with that, you only gain real experience with traps when they actually work. Legionnaire Denny has a few basic tools, all of which he made himself, but he's had little chance to raise the level, as the traps he makes are typically single-use."

"With better tools and more knowledge, I could build better, but...well, we usually fight monsters, so simple traps, such as spike pits and snares, work the best for our purposes," Denny clarified.

"Okay, Oracle, the heliomage. I take it that's a specialized skill in trapmaking; what would it take for that to be of any use to Denny?" I asked respectfully.

She tapped her chin thoughtfully. "I don't know, in all honesty. I think it's something we need to speak to Jenae about."

"Okay, we need Cai..." I had no sooner spoken his name and he stepped forward, having been walking alongside us, just out of sight. "Damn, Cai, that was fast." I had to laugh at his pleased expression. "Make a note, please, mate;

when we return to the Tower, Denny is to be given the apprentice grade traps skillbook, and I need to speak to Jenae about him, see what we can do with the heliomage skills."

"Speak to the Goddess...about *me,* sir?" Denny grunted, looking half-excited and half-terrified.

"Damn right." I clapped him on the shoulder enthusiastically. "I remember fighting by your side, mate, and I'd be damned if that didn't earn an introduction, especially when you already have the interests." With that, we moved on, and I spoke to numerous people as we went, with Romanus filling me in about their individual skills and interests. I directed Cai to make a handful of notes, planning for more books to be given out, but mainly I just spoke to people as the last few filtered out of the Tower.

Finally, just as a harried-looking young mother chased her little boy down the stairs, apologizing profusely to everyone as she passed about how she'd murder him later for hiding like that...I could no longer contain my excitement.

Shouts rose from a few people nearby, and the Legion moved like a well-oiled machine, interposing themselves between me and my people and whatever risk was coming...before I shouted to them to get the hell out of the way and stand down.

Two hunters and an exhausted-looking Milosh, the leatherworker from the first villagers to join us, staggered out of the trees. Behind them, carrying their catch and covered in blood and flies, with viscera dangling from his filthy, cracked bones, came Bob.

The massive skeletal summon stomped through the trees, emerging into view properly and making the collective Legion tense in anticipation again.

Until Oracle screamed and launched herself into the air, flying right at him.

"Bob!" she squealed, flitting in a loop around his head, then down and around him in fast spirals to inspect his condition and the crap, sometimes literal, that covered him. "Ohmygodit'ssogoodtoseeyou!" she cried breathlessly, stopping right before him and hugging herself, then diving onto his shoulder and embracing his skull.

She'd returned to her six-inch tall form, thankfully, and even then, she flitted back into the air after a second, shuddering and letting all the dirt that had transferred to her fall through her form to the grass below.

I picked my way through the crowd and stopped in front of the massive skeleton minion, looking up at him. I took in the cracked and broken bones, the dirt and all, but mostly, the glow in his eyes.

He stood motionless before me, peering down. The corpses of the hunters' kills for the day had been field dressed and were hanging off him, some strapped to a makeshift harness on his back and across his chest, with others dangling from spikes on his shoulders.

"Hey, big guy," I said quietly, meeting his fiery eyes and smiling. "You remember me?" There was a long pause, then Bob nodded, a single motion, but smooth and clear. I grinned from ear to ear, remembering that it was only just before we'd left the last time that we'd found he could communicate this way.

"You look a little banged up," I noted as I inspected him more closely, wincing at the chips and chunks taken out of the bones, the great cracks that ran across his hulking frame, and the missing sections from the attempt at plate mail I'd shaped from bones last time. "You've been in the wars, buddy."

"He's protected us, Lord," explained a voice from the side and I turned, seeing Milosh.

"Hi, Milosh; glad to hear it," I said, thankful that I'd remembered his name. "Tell me what happened?"

"I go out with him each day, Lord. He takes me with the second group, usually; the first leave incredibly early…" He looked embarrassed but continued when I just grinned at him. "The hunters track some creatures down for us, they hunt them, and I skin them. We bring back what we can use, and we leave the rest out there.

"Bob…I have to thank you, Lord Jax. We were afraid of him at first; nobody really knew what to do with him. When he first started following the hunters out, they usually left him behind because he was too loud, but when they got ambushed by a pair of forest trolls, well…" Milosh shrugged, grinning up at Bob proudly, who reached out and patted him awkwardly on the head, nearly driving him to his knees.

"Forest trolls?" I frowned, and Cai picked up the story.

"There's a cave of them somewhere to the west, and they were making a nuisance of themselves. They're drawn by the smell of blood, so when the hunters started to field dress their kills, they started having problems with the trolls. The time that Milosh is referring to, though, Bob apparently arrived just as the hunters were about to be killed.

"One had already lost his arm, and the other was about to lose more. Bob ran in and stomped one of the trolls into paste and ripped the other's arms off. Trolls regenerate their injuries, so when it ran away, it actually survived, although only just." Cai snorted. "The hunters use it for target practice whenever it shows up, as it's been kicked out of the cave, we think. It basically lurks around and tries to scavenge the remains of the hunters' kills now."

"So long story short, the hunters weren't really interested in Bob until he showed just how useful he could be?" I grinned.

"Exactly; now they love taking him with them, and Bob seems to enjoy it as well."

"What about the guy who was injured?" I asked, and Cai sighed. "More than can be healed unfortunately; he's making the most of still being alive, and he's helping to train the next generation of hunters, but…"

"Nerin!" I called, and a few seconds later, she moved out of the crowd.

"What's up?" She asked quickly, scowling around. "Who's hurt?" Ame was with her, and the pair had apparently been deep in discussion.

"A hunter." I paused, looking to Cai.

"Branden," he supplied, and I nodded.

"Branden the hunter lost a limb to a Forest Troll, so…"

"So you want me to heal him. Honestly, boy, you need to plan better! You spoke of a healing location, somewhere for Ame and me to work from. I take it you haven't planned where it will be yet?"

"I…uh…"

"We will take rooms on the ground floor, and a second area higher in the Tower. The lower location will serve as an emergency station, and Ardbeg will be there, working on leveling his skills on everyone who enters the Tower," she rattled off, barely seeming to pause for breath.

The reluctant Dwarf, who waited behind her, sighed in resignation, quickly forcing a smile as she glared at him. "Because, if he does not reach apprentice grade by the end of the month, he will be no longer be welcome in my team; is this understood?" She pinned him in place with a hard stare, and he swallowed hard and nodded. The prospect of him having to return to putting himself in danger was clearly scaring him into obeying.

"I thought he was going out with the hunters?" I asked Cai quietly, and he shook his head.

"Ame has been, when she's not needed here, but Ardbeg…well…" He raised an eyebrow at me.

"He's still a coward, then?" I asked quietly.

Cai grimaced. "He is, but he's also needed. Any healer, no matter how cowardly, is in high demand, and to be fair to him, he's been roaming the Tower offering free healing to everyone with so much as a scuffed knee. He just doesn't want to leave the safety of its walls, that's all. Ame managed to heal Branden and save his life; she just can't regrow limbs…"

"But I can," Nerin interrupted, sighing and stepping in closer to me. "Jax, I need a proper location, somewhere to teach people, and to have those with injuries that need regeneration to recover. I've been here hours already, and nobody has come to me, because nobody knows about me and what I can do."

"Nerin," I said patiently but firmly. "Speak to Seneschal and Cai; they will provide a space for you to work, but for now, please get ready, because we're about to begin." I politely took my leave of her and turned to Bob.

I looked up into his eye sockets and smiled, seeing so much more there than when I'd left. I reached inside of me, and found him as well. Ever since I'd given him life, I'd been able to feel him, to direct him. Now, though, rather than the emptiness I'd felt at first, and then the sensation of an indefinable *something* that I'd had from him when I left, in its place, there was so much more.

I could feel his focus, his determination, and his protectiveness. He peered around himself, at everyone in sight, and I felt the question, even though I knew he still couldn't put it into words, even if he could have spoken.

"Yes," I answered, looking up at him, and he looked back to me. "Yes, Bob, they're all yours." He seemed to grow larger, almost, taking a deep breath and standing taller, the light in his eyes flaring.

"I take it this is your summoned creature?" Romanus asked as he joined my side and examined Bob.

"Yes and no. He's a permanent summoned minion," I clarified. "He evolves as time goes on, learning and growing in his own right. He started as a simple skeletal minion, but now? After all we've gone through? He's determined to protect the Tower and its citizens." I smiled proudly.

Bob stepped forward and nodded, pointing at Romanus with one enormous, clawed finger. The legionnaires around me gripped their weapons and prepared to defend their Prefect, but before I could do anything, Restun barked out an order to stand down.

He stepped up next to Romanus and scrutinized the huge construct, nodding in approval at the obvious scars of battle that covered Bob.

"Can you learn?" Restun asked Bob, his voice carrying clearly.

Bob watched him for a while before nodding once, slowly.

"Then I'll include you in the lessons I give."

Bob stood there, rock solid and still, clearly not understanding.

"Bob…" I called up, and the minion looked at me. "Restun wants to teach you to be a better fighter." Bob stared at me for a long minute before looking back to Restun and nodding once. Then he stepped around us all and marched toward the Tower, clearly following his usual pattern and intending to take the meat inside.

One of the hunters, a tall Elf who'd been standing to one side, called to Bob and redirected him to an area that was being set up off to one side of the courtyard, and Bob changed direction, clearly used to the preparation area changing location.

"Does that happen a lot?" I asked Cai.

"You mean them moving? Yes, the hunters work outside when it's a nice day; when it's not, they work inside. This morning, it was raining heavily before you arrived; now, it's clear again. No idea why, but while Bob seems to have grasped a lot, he still can't get that if it's sunny, they work outside, and if not, inside." Cai shrugged.

"Weird. Well, I need to repair him, and…"

"Jax, the Tower is empty, beyond Bane's party and their quarry."

"Then let's get started!" I said, taking a deep breath. "Romanus, are the crystals still on the ships, or have they been brought inside the Tower?" I asked, about to smack myself for not thinking of it earlier.

"The Tower Wisp, Seneschal, directed me to have them set inside after our meeting," he confirmed.

I relaxed, turning back to the Tower and gazing at its staggering height. From this close, it resembled a mountain rearing over us more than anything else, and I took in a deep breath, as I felt…something…happening.

It started slowly, a hum of magic filling the air, followed by a slight shudder that seemed to flow from the ground up, washing over the massive structure.

A cascade of dust fell, and somewhere high overhead, we heard the crash of falling stone as the dull grey and mottled stone of the Tower suddenly pulsed with life.

The second ripple that flowed up the Tower was stronger, with visible clouds of dust blown free, carried away on the winds that blew by.

A great boom of falling rock sounded from nearby, and I spun in time to watch a section of the teetering wall that surrounded the courtyard fall inwards, the great blocks smashing down hard. A rumbling boom filled the air as other sections nearby fell, following suit.

"Seneschal…" I called to him in the silence of our bond, concern clear in my voice.

"Don't worry, Jax, I am allowing sections to fall that will be easier to rebuild from scratch. This is all according to the plan."

"Don't worry, people! That was totally supposed to happen!" I called out as the last of the people muttered nervously amongst themselves. A slow but steady stream of people continued to move to the airships, until after another few minutes, only my own small group remained on the ground, with Oren's ship conspicuously waiting for us.

"Ah, Jax? It might be safer if you get on the ship as well..." Seneschal suggested.

I rubbed the bridge of my nose.

"You know, if this was all a movie or a game, this would have been done by now?" I muttered, gesturing to the others to board Oren's ship. "Apparently, Seneschal is having an issue..." A loud rumble of falling stone cut me off, and a sudden blast of air was expelled from the entrance, along with a huge cloud of dust and fragments of stone. "...or, you know, maybe more than one, so let's get the hell out of the way before he kills us all."

"I did recommend everyone take off." Seneschal reminded me in a quick mental burst, then cut off the contact before I could respond.

We quickly boarded the ship. Bob clattered up the ramp last of all, still dripping with blood and filth, much to Oren's disapproval.

As soon as he was aboard, the ship took off, lifting and banking hard to speed away from the Tower. There was a sudden feeling of weight, of pressure pushing down on us, as Jory forced more power from the engines. Then we were rising fast, climbing into the air and passing the huge treetops as the lower balconies of the Tower flew past.

A handful of minutes later, we were spiraling around the Tower, climbing even then, heading for the upper levels.

As we rose, birds erupted from the canopy now far below us, startled as the ground shuddered and the Tower creaked. With a huge groan and a long loud *craaack,* one of the upper balconies fell away entirely.

It was a small section–barely ten meters squared, if I guessed at it–but as it tumbled, it hit the side of the Tower ten or fifteen floors below.

The hurtling multi-ton section of stone slammed into the solid side and tore a hole into the next floor. The wider nature of the floor below each section of the Tower meant that, when the balcony hit, it tore into the open section before taking out another section internally and making the entire structure shudder.

We all waited as long seconds passed, the creaking and booming of falling stone clear even as far back as we were forced to fly, until my brain caught up and screamed in horror.

"Bane!" I shouted into the Ether, horror filling me and making my heart drop to my boots. He'd survived so much, all the battles so far, and for him to die from a miscalculation now...

"He is safe, Jax!" Seneschal assured me. *"The shock of the Tower's damage made him drop his stealth. He and Cheena are at the apex of the Tower, one floor below the Hall of the Eternal. They had tracked Caron and our uninvited guest to one of the elite chambers. Whatever magic is blocking my sight and senses is exceedingly subtle."*

"Oren, get me to the top of the Tower," I ordered grimly.

"Aye, laddie, we're headed up tha' way now…" He snorted, peering down at the damage and completely missing my tone. Jory swallowed hard and altered course, firing more mana to the engines. "Hey! Whut do ye be…oh…" Oren broke off at the look on my face as I yanked my naginata from my bag, bringing the gleaming weapon free and squinting at the balconies as they flew past.

I'd seen one near the top; it had led into one of the rooms I'd already broken into, hadn't it? I searched, planning and estimating the distance. I was well aware that flying cost me both mana and health, so I couldn't afford to waste either with a possible battle to come, but neither could I leave Bane, Cheena, or Caron in the Tower. Seneschal's repairs were supposed to cause little damage; leaving the Tower was a "just in case," so fuck knew how much danger they were truly in.

I breathed deeply, steeling my nerves, then grinning as I reflected on just how goddamn cool it was to be able to fly, even if it was only in this limited fashion.

I crouched and leaped upwards, Soaring Majesty sending me hurtling into the air. The wind blurred past me loud enough to drown out all other sounds as I pushed harder, catching sight of an open door on a balcony ahead, one floor below the Hall of the Eternal.

I angled away from the ship, then turned and aimed at the balcony, no longer approaching from below, but slightly above. I could see movement inside, even though my eyes streamed from the speed I was going.

At the last possible instant, I flipped over, pushing hard in the opposite direction. I threw my hands out, my feet slamming into the floor and carving a furrow in the dust and debris as I skidded to a halt. Caron gaped up at me in awe as Bane and Cheena appeared on either side of me.

The figure lying on the bed in the corner gave a grunt of surprise before sagging back and holding his hands up in surrender as he grinned at us all. "Took you all long enough, didn't it!" he whispered, then collapsed, unconscious.

"Who the hell is he?" I growled to Caron as the boy leapt up and hurriedly grabbed at a series of empty potion vials, scattered atop the sagging desk.

"He's hurt!" Caron called. "He don't mean no harm, Lord! I swear he don't! He's been 'elpin' me!" the lad cried as he searched frantically.

As I straightened, Bane whispered, just loud enough for me to hear as he passed me.

"Oracle's going to be pissed about that landing."

"Only if she hears about it," I growled back. "And it wasn't a superhero landing, anyway!" I rolled my eyes as I stepped in closer, Cheena flanking me.

"Looked like it to me, and I thought you agreed to leave this to us?" Bane asked as he searched the unconscious man, relieving him of several daggers and a short sword before cursing loudly as he reached down and pulled something free.

"Oh Gods no, not one of those cursed creatures!" Cheena growled, fingering her spear as she regarded the unconscious man with a mix of horror and disgust.

"What is it?" I asked, and Caron faced me with tear-stained cheeks as he pulled the dregs of a healing potion free of the pile of rubbish.

"He's a bard…" the boy explained, a nervous smile on his face as Bane held up a lute and Cheena growled.

NARKOLT

"You'll keep your damn mouth shut," Jon snapped at the man before him, rubbing his tired eyes and squinting around his small office, trying to figure out why today, of all days, the Gods had to choose to shit on him from a great height.

"But Tribune…" the legionnaire replied, shock clear on his face.

"But nothing! This is a direct order, Centurion. You are to say nothing about what you learned until you are given specific permission from me to contrary. This is not the time to go spreading this…this…unfounded bullshit. Not until we've had time to consider the relevant facts."

Jon glared at the Centurion standing before him as the man opened his mouth to protest, and he gestured sharply, shaking his head.

"No!" he snapped. "I give you my Oath I will take these details to the General and to the Prefect. But until I say otherwise, this is not the time to spread that kind of talk."

"But he is the *Imperial Scion!*" The Centurion barked out, practically radiating indignation and fury.

"We don't know that!" Jon snapped back. "All we know is that he has claimed the title. For all we know, that damn Himnel Legion saw their position as untenable, and the leadership went rogue, setting up a nobody with a hint of the bloodline to take over.

"No! Honestly? No, I don't believe that…" Jon amended placatingly, holding his hands up and patting the air. "But as Tribune, it is my place to be suspicious, to act as a balance, and to try and see the possible, even when I'd rather not. You know me, Centurion; do you really think so poorly of me that you believe I'd ignore this if I could? Its timing might suck with the war, but still, I'd rather poor timing than no damn Empire!" Jon's irritation leaked through his voice as he tried to suppress it.

Nine months…nine goddamn months he'd been tribune now, ever since Tribune Manella died, and still people looked at him like he was untested and untrustworthy.

"Of course, Tribune," Centurion Hennen said eventually, looking away. "I didn't mean to imply…"

"I know, man, I know." Jon rubbed his face, leaning back in his creaky, shitty chair. "Seriously, if it's true, I'll be leading the charge to his side, but I have to look at all the angles. It's my duty to advise the general and the prefect on possibilities and risks; if I didn't, I'd be neglecting my role and Manella's memory."

There were a few final pleasantries exchanged, a few general "oh of course nots" and declarations of trust. But when the door closed and Jon slumped back, he still sighed and looked out of the window, reflecting on the shitty luck that brought him into this position years ahead of anything he could have wished for.

There'd been an "accident" nine months ago, one that resulted in the deaths of the entire Legion leadership. The General, Prefect, Tribune, and three of the Centurion Primuses had been gathered, at a noble's request, to look into the disappearance of his daughter.

They'd been summoned to the Great Cradle, where the ships were being constructed, and they'd followed the noble and his guards inside. Jon had been with seven others as part of the honor guard.

He'd been called in and given some orders from the legion general, sent back outside, then a goddamn airship exploded.

The entire side of the building had been destroyed in what was either a fantastically unlucky explosion or a deliberate assassination attempt. It didn't help that, of all the honor guard, he alone survived, and the orders he'd been given by the Legion General were naming his successors, including promoting Jon to the position of Tribune.

It was a role he'd never aspired to, and one he'd nearly not reached, when a second "accident" two weeks later nearly killed him and succeeded in making him paranoid to an insane degree.

The next few months were spent in an orgy of investigation. His only redeeming quality, which even his most fervent detractors had to admit reflected badly on the "dead man's shoes" attempt at promotion the rumors credited him with, was that once he got his teeth into something, he never let go.

He knew there was something suspicious going on, especially with the two named to replace the general and prefect, virtually unknown retired legionnaires from outside the city. They'd left to farm as old but sensible men, cousins who'd served their time together. Though they returned looking the same, they exhibited strange habits, and little things constantly triggered Jon's paranoia.

Twice now, he'd been sent on "investigations" by one or the other, and they'd been blatant assassination attempts. Once, he'd even been poisoned in the Legion Enclave, yet the alchemist hadn't been able to identify anything, and the venom had evaporated without a trace while he'd been investigating it.

It had reached the point where Jon was seriously considering asking for retirement, a request he damn well knew the General would honor, and one that would probably lead to his death in hours, if all he feared was true…but there was that little fraction of doubt left over, making him wonder if it was truly all in his head.

Jon sighed and shook the dark thoughts free, pulling out a flask from his inventory and pouring three drops into his coffee. He waited patiently for the color change, allowing the antidote to do its work before he dared to sip at the drink he'd had delivered over an hour ago.

He had to wait for it to go cold, or the antidote wouldn't work, and the potion made the drink taste like shit, but it provided the needed boost to his alertness.

He grumbled as he forced the cup down before putting the flask away, reminding himself to get more ingredients to make another batch soon, then got up to straighten his uniform.

He regarded himself in the mirror, observing the haggard look, the rings under his eyes, and the stubble that was starting to appear again. He sighed, deciding for the hundredth time that he should just grow a beard and be done with it. Shaving twice a day was too much of a pain in the ass these days.

He closed his eyes, drew a deep breath, then put his professional face on and marched down the hall, heading for the General's office to pass on the latest news about this Jax character.

As the door closed, he missed the small spider that crept in through the window, as nimble hands cracked it wide enough then closed it again. Dark eyes watched as the spider did its mistress's bidding and crawled along the wall, down the far side, and under the desk to wait for its victim to disturb it.

CHAPTER TWELVE

"Well, that's the neighborhood fucked, then," Arrin muttered a few hours later as we sat around eating in the new communal facilities on the twentieth floor of the Tower.

"I say we kill him now; it's the safest way," Yen added in. "Laws and all be damned. Bards are bards. Only possible way to keep everything safe when one of those thieving bastards is around is if we stitch his mouth shut and nail his hands to his knees."

"Lydia?" I asked, looking for the Optio, and I got a grunt as her cheeks reddened and she refused to look at me.

"Seriously, someone needs to give me something, here." I sat back and wiped my mouth. The roast chicken that the communal kitchen had produced was amazing, especially after the travel rations I'd lived on for what felt like a month straight.

When the chicken–which had been perfectly normal-looking and would have been right at home on Earth under different circumstances, if it hadn't been nearly twice the size of a turkey–had been delivered to the table for our group, we'd attacked it with overwhelming ferocity.

Counting my squad and Cai, there were ten of us, and even with Grizz at our table, there was still enough that I was seriously thinking that it might need to be taken away and chilled for sandwiches the next day.

"Bards…" Cai said slowly, shaking his head and wincing. "It's hard to find a more reviled class, and deservedly so, I'll add." He met my confused gaze earnestly. "While there are the occasional few who make a mistake and choose the class despite all of its stigmas, most of them are the thieving bastards we all think they are."

"Yeah, but…I mean, come on, guys. We have tales of bard classes back home," I said, shrugging dismissively.

"Describe them?" Tang suggested, popping a section of leg meat into his mouth and sighing in pleasure.

"Well, they're a support class." I scratched the back of my head in confusion. "They provide buffs to the group, making you stronger and faster. They usually have a heavy charisma build, basically relying on their luck and ability to talk their way out of shit to survive; and they occasionally either use bows or knives for defense and combat, but mainly just an instrument."

"And?" Yen asked. "Is that all they say about them?"

"Well, no…there's always a joke or two about them being horny fuckers, dogs with two dicks, that's kinda thing." I frowned, getting a snort from Yen.

"That's it," she said, nodding in satisfaction.

"What? They're horny?" I asked, more confused than ever.

"No, not horny. Grizz is horny. You and Oracle are horny. They're…they're like a fucking force of nature. They can talk practically anyone into anything. Their entire lives are built around seducing anything they fancy. They take what they want, then they move on, regardless of the situation and how many lives are ruined in the process."

"Right?" I asked, still not getting it.

"My husband told tha village I'd been with a bard," Lydia said suddenly, standing up and tossing her plate, still almost full, onto the table. "That's why nobody complained when 'e sold me." She stormed off, Oracle and Yen following her, and the rest of us frowned at each other awkwardly.

"What did I miss?" Grizz asked me quietly, looking totally flummoxed.

"You knew Lydia used to be a slave, right?" I asked, getting a nod of confused acknowledgement. "Well, as it turns out, it was her husband who sold her," I said shortly.

"Shit, that motherfucker," Grizz said, his voice a low, flat growl. "We're not gonna let that stand, right, boss? We're gonna find him, yeah? Nobody fucks with the Legion."

"No, Grizz, we're not going to let it stand," I agreed, following Lydia's departure from the room, with Oracle and Yen walking by her side. "We are going to find him, and we're going to let Lydia deal with it, and if she asks for any help…well, we're going to get creative."

"There'll be a fight," Grizz warned me. "Everyone will want to be in on it, and there won't be enough of him to go around…"

"I can heal," I countered, a low fury filling me at the thought of all that Lydia had gone through because of that bastard. "I can heal him again and again, until everyone that wants to play is done."

"Now that's a new use for magic." Grizz grinned appreciatively. "I might need to learn some healing spells."

"You will be," I said, getting up. "Part of the plan is for the Legion to learn a lot of magic over the next few months. Right; Westin is waiting for me with the bard, and I'll bear in mind what you said. I'll catch you later; enjoy your food, mate." I took my leave of Grizz and the others, jerking my head to Cai, who'd finished his meal a while ago.

Cai got to his feet smoothly and joined me, and the two of us headed out onto the first of the new communal levels on the way up. As we walked, I thought about the overkill of the precautions that Romanus had requested in dealing with the bard.

I examined the changes in the Tower as we went, marveling at the solid white, veined marble that seemed to be the standard now. The halls were clean, magelights that had been set into the walls in ages long past now gave off a gentle, clean light, and the air was both pleasantly warm and smelled fresh.

We headed up to the twenty-sixth floor, saying little at first, simply enjoying the walk as much as we ever had.

Every stairwell was now well-lit, as was all of the Tower, save those floors that weren't currently in use. With the stone that had been absorbed and repurposed throughout the Tower, the ancient structure now fairly shone with life. Where people had often moved quietly, apart from the kids, they now wandered joyfully, amazed at their good fortune in living here.

We talked of minor things as we climbed, plans for setting up a school for the kids, the new gardens, arranging a planting schedule for the new glasshouse, which I had yet to actually visit, and a dozen other things. These ranged from giving out stonemason training primers for making reasonable-sized rooms for families soon, rather than spreading out in rudimentary encampments across four floors, to plans for when the fleet arrived.

When we finally made it up to the flight deck, as it'd become known, I paused again. The sight of the two ships that were docked for work still made me pause each time I saw them. Oracle arrived silently, settling onto my shoulder in readiness for the conversation we needed to have with our prisoner.

Sigmar's Fist was berthed on the right, with a section of cladding removed from her outer hull, as two simple servitors were being guided by a complex model to both repair the ship's damage and to upgrade it.

The old design had consisted of two separate hulls, one laid atop the other with a section between, where the skeleton of the ship resided. I didn't pretend to understand why, and when Oren had asked for permission to update it, I'd just listened then nodded and waved him off.

The stocky and often serious Dwarf had whooped and sprinted away as soon as I'd told him yes, vanishing as fast as his stumpy legs could go, with Giint running alongside him.

It'd concerned me a lot that it was Giint's idea, but when Oren thought it would work, I'd just accepted it. I had no time to worry about everything, after all.

The end result was that the ships were getting a slight upgrade, as the golems put the thicker, outer hull back together in small sections, using whatever magic they possessed to bond the wood together.

The result was a hull that was lighter yet considerably thicker. The wood was apparently the local equivalent of oak, and by the time it would be done, it'd have the armor rating of more than a foot of solid hardwood, while only being half that.

This meant the ships would be faster, lighter, and more maneuverable, as well as more efficient when it came to mana expenditure.

I made a mental note to have Oracle look into the engineering skillbooks we had left; there were still more than twenty just on that subject. I also hoped to find one that covered how to make the same sort of Wisp core that Tenandra had integrated into her ship. If we could create them and set them in all the ships, along with collectors, we could make them self-sufficient.

"Jax!" Cai called. I blinked, realizing I'd totally zoned out, lost in my own thoughts.

"Dammit, sorry, Cai. I was thinking. What did you say?" I asked sheepishly. He closed his eyes and clearly tried to calm himself before opening them and looking at me.

"I asked if you'd made a decision about the bard," he repeated, and I shook my head.

"No, not really," I replied. "I don't like that he was in the Tower, and certainly not that he's been here this long, literally hiding for weeks or more, but to put him to death without a trial? It isn't in me. Add to that, he's done nothing really wrong. Yes, he's been teaching Caron a load of things, most of which, while damn annoying–like his new habit of breaking and entering locked rooms and looting them–will actually be a useful skill when he's older, if he puts them to work in the service of the Empire, of course."

"And if he hands over all his looted items," Cai muttered darkly.

I eyed him with concern. "I thought he'd stopped, now that you'd had a word?"

"He promises he has," Cai said grimly. "But Kayt got a new ring when she woke up this morning. It was resting on her pillow. Grants plus five to Intelligence as well."

"Sounds like it's time to have a chat with Caron myself, then. I don't like the idea, but if he's stealing from me, then he can swear the Oath. I'll damn well order him to stop, if that's what it takes," I declared as we walked between the ships, seeing the second ship, Oren's vessel, was being loaded for a patrol.

A dozen legionnaires were settling themselves on the deck, while Oren called out orders to Jory to "not scratch a wee hair o' ma babbies head" as he eased out to do a circle around the Tower.

"I'm still concerned that he managed to get into the Tower and hide in the first place. If he's that powerful a bard, then we can't risk him speaking in his own defense," Cai cautioned me as we approached a trio of legionnaires, who stood around a figure wrapped in chains on the deck.

The man had a gag in, and Westin stood over him, glaring down at the bard with scarcely concealed contempt.

I came to a stop before him and crouched, looking into his eyes and steeled myself as I made a decision.

"Oracle, be ready to read his mind. But for now, I want to try to talk to him. Can you hear me?" I asked, and the bard nodded. "Good. This is what we're going to do: I'm going to have Westin free you, then we're going to have a chat. You're going to tell me who you are, and how you got here, and why I shouldn't kill you.

"You're going to be very truthful, and if my legionnaires so much as suspect that you're using your abilities on me, and I do mean *suspect*…they have orders to kill you." I kept my voice even and friendly, even as the single figure I'd called for earlier arrived.

I felt its footfalls on the floor as it closed the distance, and I saw the widening of the bound man's eyes in shock.

"That's Sarge," I explained calmly, feeling the enormous presence of the complex war golem as it marched up, coming to a halt behind me. "He has orders to kill you if anything happens to me. So, if, for example, you were good enough to somehow stop the legionnaires and everyone else here, as soon as Sarge senses any form of magic in my mind, he'll hammer you into a pale pink smear on the stone. Do you understand me?"

He nodded frantically.

"That's good. Westin, release his gag, please." Westin complied, glaring down at the bard as he did so.

"Thank you…could I have a drink?" the man croaked.

I paused, waiting to be sure. There was no form of compulsion, no desire to do anything hidden in the request, so I nodded, and one of the legionnaires held a cup for him to drink from.

"Thank you." The man sighed, relaxing back into the chair as much as the chains would allow. "There's no need for all this, you know?" he said hopefully, nodding down at the bonds.

"Oh, I think there is." I smiled, though my tone was cold. "You've made it into my Tower and have been looting it, giving a child an item, then convincing him to put another girl in touch with a noble, just so she could be interrogated in her dreams. You've hidden and stolen from me. So go on, tell me why this is all just a big misunderstanding."

"It wasn't like that!" he said quickly. "I didn't trespass. Hell, I've been here for months, maybe more! The kid found me, and yeah, I used a bit of a glamor on him. I didn't want him to go screaming that he'd found me. I didn't know what you'd do, after all. But I never hurt him! I just, you know, gave him advice on the girl he likes and what to do." He searched around frantically.

"Bullshit," I said grimly. "I cleared this Tower myself. You weren't here then."

"I've been here for ten goddamn months, ever since my party found the place." He pushed back, shaking his head. "There were four of us. Maskin was our muscle, a big guy, longsword, and a long red cloak, helm with little daft wings on it. His cuirass was enchanted with some kind of sound charm, made him quieter in the woods.

"Senna was a rogue, and Barin was our mage. We found the Tower and thought we could loot it, okay? Between Senna's talents and my own buffs, we thought we could make it. We made camp on the sixth floor for the first night. We'd just had to fight some weird undead, and Senna's abilities killed the black things that possessed them easy enough. Maskin was on guard, we were asleep, and then…then it all went to shit." He shook his head, clearly struggling through the memory.

"Senna woke me, hand over my mouth, and made me flee with her. Maskin was just standing there, slumped over, letting out little gasps. Barin woke up and cast a light spell before we could get to him, and…and…" He started to shake, and I tightened my grip on my naginata, wondering if it was acting or not.

Oracle slipped down from my shoulder and strode forward, growing as she moved, then crouched before the obviously distressed man.

"I'm going to read your memories; is that okay?" she asked gently but firmly, an edge of a threat in her voice.

"Whatever. Do whatever you want," the bard said eventually, sniffling.

Oracle reached out and laid one hand against the man's head, closing her eyes, then placed the fingertips of both hands on his temples, frowning as she concentrated.

Long minutes passed, the man's breathing slowing from its ragged and frightened rhythm to one of peace as he fell into a deep sleep. Westin caught him as he slumped in his chains and lowered him to the ground. When Oracle finally released him, she stood up and turned back to me, tears standing unshed in her eyes.

"It's true," she said simply.

"What is?" I asked.

"All of it," Oracle replied. "All of it, and more. He was part of a party that tried to raid the Tower. It was his idea, and that alone is eating him up. I'm going to go back a little, so get comfy." She gazed sorrowfully at the bard who slumbered peacefully in the chains.

"His name is Ronin, and yes, he's a bard. There's some kind of block in his mind, probably an Oath or something, that's hiding a lot of his memories of more recent times, but he grew up in Himnel. Doesn't remember his parents; he lived with his older sister in a whorehouse until he was kicked out. Once he was on the streets, he used the skills he'd seen the girls use in the whorehouse."

"Sounds like fun," I quipped.

"Not as much as you think. The whores were trained in sleight of hand, manipulation, and pickpocketing, as well as persuasion and seduction techniques, as much as more carnal skills. When Ronin was thrown out, the only skills he had learned gave him three very clear paths: rogue, bard, or whore. He refused to whore and began to mix the two skills he had left, growing more and more skilled, until he was recruited by a gang.

"A few years passed with him gradually working his way up in the ranks. He has a few blade and bow skills, and has killed, but he mainly used his skills to run away or persuade people to leave him alone. Eventually, he and a friend found out about a big score, a handful of bags that were being moved from one location to another, skillbooks being part of the heist. They pulled it off, hid aboard a ship from Himnel to Narkolt, and thought they'd made it big. Then, when he was asleep, his friend stole most of the loot and tried to sell it, abandoning him."

"What a great friend," I muttered, as Oracle regarded me soberly.

"Yes and no; the people he tried to sell the books to were the Smuggler's Guild...unknown to them, the very people who had owned those goods in the first place. They tortured and killed his friend for the information on where he was. By the time they turned up, Ronin had woken, figured out what had happened, and fortunately for him, one of the bags he was left with contained an extremely valuable class skillbook. Being a street rat, what did he do?"

"He read it," I guessed, and she nodded.

"It wasn't a regular skillbook, but a class skillbook—a primer for an entire class, mind you—the changes, the memories, and the abilities it gave him knocked him out cold. The Smuggler's Guild found him, took him prisoner, and beat the hell out of him when he woke up, then realized that the only way they could make use of the class skillbook was to make use of him."

"Hold up...what's the difference between regular skillbooks and class skillbooks?" I asked.

"Mainly cost and density," Oracle said. "General skillbooks for, say, a baker, teach the basics of baking. Higher books, such as expert level volumes, might teach the intricacies of patisserie, chocolate crafting, and other things.

"Class skillbooks are like that, but they involve hugely complex details, overriding the basic skills with muscle memory, complex instinctual responses, and more. Imagine a warrior like Grizz: he gets a mace skillbook, and suddenly he knows a load about how to use the weapon, but he still needs years of practice before he's genuinely good with it, much less before the muscle memory is inbuilt.

"Class skillbooks instill that muscle memory, and more, *BUT...*" Oracle held her hand up to stop my next question. "You might not be able to make the most of it. There might be, for example, physical issues, such as Bane's build against a human's. Suddenly, he's finding his every instinct is to fight with a mace in his right hand and a shield in his left. He has two of each hand, so every single time he goes to use the weapon, he has to mentally pause and decide to do things differently. This causes a pause in every fight; how long do you think he'd survive?"

"So, they sound stupid, then…" I leaned back and scratched my chin.

"It depends. For an unskilled warrior in the right circumstances, they'd be fantastic, despite the issues with their muscles being larger or smaller than the skillbook might have been written for. The Tower wasn't stocked with them, simply because they cause as many issues as they solve, so eventually, they went out of fashion.

"This skillbook had something to do with bards, and it imparted some of their class skills. His almost instinctual need to learn secrets and his love of dealing with people actually complimented the book, which is rare as hell. He somehow talked the Smuggler's Guild into letting him work for them. They found a master to train him as a bard, and some sort of deal was struck. However, once he was trained, his master vanished. They still cross paths fairly regularly, so I think there's more to the story there, but it's hidden." She spared the sleeping man an empathetic glance before going on.

"That's literally all I can get from that section of his life. I know that he was trained, but everything from where, to the bard's face, to what the training is, all of it is protected by an Oath. Once the training period was up, though, Ronin had changed. He'd gone from, frankly, a little shit, using his persuasion and seduction skills to rob and screw everyone around him, into practically a different man.

"He was driven, searching for something, and occasionally met up with his mentor. He learned new talents, including buffs. Musical instruments that he'd simply played with before suddenly became his life, and he worked ten and fifteen hours a day to master them, playing for free more often than not in the various taverns of the city.

"He used a bardic ability called Forget, which looks like it makes people forget anything distinctive about him. Interestingly enough, he became so skilled with it that it grew to passively affect the entire area around him when he used it. I think that's what he used to hide himself from Seneschal, and a single general buff spell that essentially gives a short-term healing effect.

"That seems to have been all that's kept him alive, as he ran out of food roughly nine months or more ago. He's literally survived on that buff spell and the Forget ability almost exclusively, casting each at least once an hour, every hour. As a result, until Caron arrived and found him, he'd had no uninterrupted sleep, nor time free of gnawing hunger and pain, for the better part of a year."

"Sounds like a shitty way to live, but, well, there's a lot of that going around," I said grimly, thinking of the former slaves and their children.

"Very much so. Going back to his past, it wasn't until his handler was killed that he managed to escape the guild again. He spent the next five years hiding as far away from them as possible, traveling on a ship, the *Bounty's Crossing*. He basically played his instruments, sang, and told stories, in exchange for peace and quiet, and something else I can't get; something to do with the bard from before.

"Then his ship was taken by pirates, and he spent another year doing much the same for them, but with a chain around his neck and enduring constant beatings. Then the pirates boarded a ship that fought back better than usual. He saw his chance, and using a stolen key, he escaped to the other ship, and for the first time, he used his buffs for others.

"He made the defenders stronger, faster. The ship's guards who were hired for the trip survived due to him, and the pirates were killed, their ship taken instead. For the first time, Ronin was welcome somewhere, and when he admitted what he was, rather than being reviled, he was celebrated." Oracle gently brushed the man's hair back from his face as she regarded him sadly, and I felt a sudden, powerful surge of jealousy.

"The next three years were the best in his life. The guards left the ship at the end of the contract, and he went with them. They spent years adventuring together, and he…did what bards do. He got them into trouble constantly, as he basically tried to screw everything with a pulse, and his friends constantly rescued him.

"They raided dungeons and fought creatures that would make the Legion pay attention. They also ran away a lot, starting again from scratch a few times when things got too messy, too dangerous, or when they got too recognizable. Eventually, Ronin seduced a scout for Himnel, and she told him about the Tower they'd found. The next few months were spent in preparation and verifying the location. Then they came and tried to loot it, hoping to beat Himnel to something."

"Brave or stupid?" I asked.

"Definitely stupid," Westin replied.

"Either way, they weren't prepared for a SporeMother, especially not one that wanted to take them alive to make them hosts or guards. Maskin was captured by DarkSpore, as was the mage, Barin. Senna managed to get Ronin away, and the pair of them fled. They didn't know which way to go, and between their individual stealth skills and his buffs, they managed to lose their pursuers.

"Unfortunately for them, the dead had nothing else to do, so they cleared the Tower floor by floor, herding them upwards…while I slept." Oracle shook her head.

"Senna was practically torn apart, and he fled again, eventually managing to break into the room you found him in. He had a few weeks' worth of food, but only a few days' worth of water, and he spent the next few months in that room. He managed to get the balcony door open and drank the rainwater.

"At one point, he made a huge mistake in that he tried to make himself some health potions with the alchemy set he found in the room, using ingredients he found in a pouch. He had no idea what he was doing, and made a clumsy attempt at several different potions. Two were weak healing ones, fortunately for him."

"That's insanely lucky then, considering how hard it is to make a potion," I muttered, and Oracle nodded in agreement.

"It was a bit easier for him. After all, he had limited ingredients and simply mixed several together, assuming if they were stored together, they'd be a recipe, more or less," Oracle added.

I winced, thinking of the random ingredients I kept together.

"Point, I should really split my poisons and healing stuff up, at least," I agreed, getting a smile from her.

"Unfortunately, one of the other potions he created was a weak disease. He spent the last six months alternately sipping from the weak healing potions or using his healing buff, as the disease is permanent. He basically used all the ingredients he could find, constantly making more healing potions, but never managing to make anything strong enough to heal himself completely.

"Then Caron found him, and he was terrified. Caron, being a young boy, told him everything, including the fact that you fought the SporeMother one on one and killed it, as well as his captors. Ronin is essentially terrified of you to the point of almost pissing himself.

"He used his abilities to make Caron trust him and smuggle him food and ingredients, and he kept trying to make a healing potion, planning to sneak out as soon as he could. He also constantly used his Forget spell on the area, which somehow shielded him from Seneschal."

"So, he's a bit of a coward, but more of a greedy fool than a threat?" I clarified, considering the sleeping bard.

"Basically, yes." She sighed. "Bards are notorious for being thieves, and judging from his memories, he's that and more. Basically, he steals whatever he can get away with, and has sex with anyone he can, but he's not actually as bad as I was expecting."

"So, what the hell do we do now?" I asked nobody in particular.

"I'm tempted to suggest we give him a pack of supplies and send him on his way," Cai admitted before sighing. "But that would be a waste, wouldn't it?"

"Yeah…" I said slowly, a sinking feeling in my stomach.

"What are we going to do, then?" Oracle asked.

I scratched my head, considering the options. "We'll speak to him when he wakes up, I guess. What did you do to him? And is he still diseased?"

"No, Nerin cleared the disease as soon as she healed him. It was a really weak one, apparently, but persistent, and it would have killed him eventually. As to his sleep, well, I figured he needs it. He's not had sleep without the disease or nightmares and fear in months."

"I can't believe I'm considering this." I shook my head as I looked down at him. "If we make him swear the Oath, then I order him not to use his abilities except to benefit the citizens of the Empire, that'd work, wouldn't it? Then he could still use his buffs and so on?"

"I think so, but I think he's going to be in for a lot of grief. He's a bard, and nobody trusts them."

"But here, he's not going to get stabbed," I countered. "Plus, we damn well need someone to teach us some stealth and rogue skills, and some entertainment wouldn't go amiss."

There was a chorus of begrudging assent, and Ronin was dragged off to a nearby room, the gag replaced. His guards were given orders to bring him back to me when I called, so we could give him his choices.

The rest of the day was spent in boring tasks, confirming orders that Cai had given in my stead, approving jobs, and allocating areas for people to work in. We gave permission for people to claim various rooms, approving a thousand more little jobs, then finally, thankfully, closing the door on our small suite, with Bane and Tang and everyone else, aside from Oracle, on the other side.

There was a *shower*, an honest-to-God *shower*, built into a wall alcove, with my own toilet, a balcony with double doors leading out onto it, and a furnished sitting room, but I only had eyes for the bed.

It was massive, solidly constructed of polished wood, with a straw mattress and two pillows, a big blanket, and thank the Gods, not only was it sturdy, but it also didn't creak…despite all the attempts Oracle and I made to break it, or each other, that night.

Chapter Thirteen

I t was early the next morning when I awoke, the sounds of a ship coming in to land several floors below me echoing up through the open balcony doors. Warm sunlight streamed in, and the songs of birds filled the air.

I stretched, feeling Oracle next to me, and I rolled over, cuddling into her. Her ass pushed back against me as she made herself more comfortable, and I sighed happily.

I shifted my head on the pillow, blowing a lock of her hair free of my face. The coppery-blonde tint to it contrasted wonderfully against the plain dark sheets and pillow, and I enfolded her in my arms, letting out a little groan of pleasure as I pulled her in close. Her warm skin and a gentle vanilla and coconut scent roamed my mind as her firm flesh filled my hands, and her hand quested down, waking me fully and guiding me to her.

The gasps and groans from us both as the bed started to shift, rocking rhythmically, was the only sound that rolled through the room from then on. Short, tense orders and requests, often phrased as begging and pleading, were the only words spoken, until we collapsed back into each other's arms, completely spent some time later.

"Well, that's the way I want to wake up every morning," I panted when I could think again.

A low giggle rose from Oracle as she lay her head on my chest. "I think that can be arranged," she purred, shifting around and beaming up at me affectionately. "What about your name day, though? No special requests for then?" I grinned mischievously at her.

"There're a few days back home that are considered special." I paused, considering. "There's your birthday, or name day, as they call it here…waking me up with a bacon sandwich and a blowjob would be very much appreciated!" I finally suggested, and she grinned, her eyes alight with inspiration.

"Oh, well, if that's the tradition, I can do that. Anything else?" she laughed, pretending to make a note.

"Well, there Valentine's; basically a day when a man spoils his girl. You know, nice dinner, drinks, and a lot of sex; usually she wears something nice for him, that kind of thing."

"Like I usually do for you, you mean?" she asked.

"I'm a very lucky man," I agreed.

"Anything else?"

"Well, Valentine's is the fourteenth of the second month, February in my world, and as its basically a day we treat our girls, there's also the opposite, on March the fourteenth…" I trailed off, raising my eyebrows suggestively.

"Okay, what's that?" She eyed me suspiciously.

"Steak, blowjob, and shut-the-fuck-up day," I said, grinning down at her.

"Explain…" she said, narrowing her eyes at me.

"Well, it's basically a day where we get a nice steak cooked for us, given a blowjob…*and no nagging,*" I finished in a rush, wincing as her hand took hold of something sensitive and squeezed, none too gently.

"Do tell me more, Jax," she said sweetly.

"Ah, there's only one more!" I said, and she eased off the pressure slightly. "It's an international holiday, not everyone celebrates it for the same reasons. For a lot of people, it's a religious celebration, but for others, it's just a family one, called 'Christmas,' and everyone gives everyone else gifts."

"And that's it?" she asked me suspiciously, threatening to squeeze again, and I winced and nodded vigorously. "Hmm…okay, we can adopt those traditions." She was suddenly all smiles again. "The Tower used to have four others, as well. Summer Solstice, when the sun is at its height and mana flow is strongest; Winternight, which is the opposite. Then Cannimet and Valpurgist, the nights of souls, where all remember those we have lost. The two soulsnights are held six months apart, spread out so that the four celebrations were always no more than three months apart."

"Well, when the time comes to worry about those, and we all have time for holidays, we'll celebrate," I promised as she climbed off me and strolled to the open balcony doors.

I pulled her pillow over and put it atop my own, propping myself up to watch her naked ass as she walked away, and I let out a low whistle as I admired the view.

"You like?" She grinned back at me as she leaned against the doorframe suggestively.

I nodded firmly, when a chime rang through the room. I bolted up straight, scanning around in confusion. A bubble of silvery liquid formed on the floor in the middle of the room, then coalesced into Seneschal.

"Apologies for disturbing you, Jax, Oracle, but Decin has returned, and Legionnaire Primus Restun has requested an audience with you and Legionnaire Prefect Romanus at the earliest possible opportunity."

"Okay; where are they?" I queried, kicking the blanket off my feet and clambering out of the bed. I had a split second to wonder why whenever I saw Oracle climb out of bed–or any hot girl in my past, actually–they were always so goddamn graceful, while I made it look more like a walrus was trying to fuck the mattress into submission.

I strode to my new wardrobe. It had been looted from a room higher in the Tower and brought down by a servitor at some point yesterday. The thing was huge, ancient, and the doors creaked a bit weirdly, but it was also more than half gold and patterns of embedded gemstones, and it actually had space for my clothes to hang.

Not that I had many.

I had literally one change of outfit, as the rest had been taken away to be summarily burned or cleaned, depending on the condition. I thankfully had prospects, though, as I remembered the tailors and armorers were working on some new items for me, so I pulled on the scratchy clothing with as good grace as I could manage.

"They are landing on the flight deck now; shall I direct them to the Command Center or…?"

"We need a room closer than that, really," I said, sighing. "And it doesn't make sense to have the Creation Table down there. Is there a room nearby we can use? I'd also like to transfer both the council chambers and the Command Center up to this level, please, mate." I put more clothes on before sitting down on the edge of the bed to pull my boots on.

The fabric of my new clothes was rough and uncomfortable, and the boots…well, the less said about the fit, the better. The only description they could be given was that they covered my feet, but fuck me, they pinched.

"Okay, fuck this shit," I snapped as I stamped the floor, trying to get my foot in more comfortably. "Seneschal, once the council chambers are ready, I want them all in there. We're going to sort out some of the skillbooks and other logistics. Let's get shit sorted."

"Very well, Jax. I have diverted a golem to collect the Creation Table now, and two more are on their way to relocate the remaining items from the rooms. I estimate an hour and seven minutes."

"Then reach out to the council and instruct them to be present and ready in two hours…. Oracle, tell me we've got some goddamn cobbler's and tailor's skillbooks in there, please." I grumbled as I straightened my clothes.

"Seriously, I know they're fucked up, vicious bastards with an unhealthy fixation on death and a problem with whisky dick, but why the hell are the goddamn *Drow* the only people who have made comfortable clothes so far?" I gestured angrily at my stiff pants. "I mean, honestly…" I continued muttering under my breath as I stomped across the floor, doing my best to ignore the clear amusement on Oracle's face as she blurred into her smaller form and floated after me, summoning her clothing as she went.

I continued out into the hall, greeting the legionnaires on guard. One came with me as a bodyguard, while the other remained to guard my quarters.

From there, it was a short stroll past the quarters given to the squad, the council, and the upper echelons of the Legion, as well as a room that had been put aside specifically for Augustus (and I assumed Hellenica). I'd noticed Flux and Ame were now sharing quarters, while Isabella and Cai had rooms next door to each other. Once I was past the last few of these rooms, I reached another Legion guard, who nodded to me and my escort as Restun approached, Romanus at his side.

We took the first of the spare rooms available, ignoring the total lack of any furniture. I opened the balcony doors, reveling in the warm sunlight and gentle breezes that played around the room as I stepped outside and leaned back against the wall, facing the two men.

"Welcome back, Restun. How bad is it?" I crossed my arms, readying myself for the worst.

"It's going to be a slaughter," Restun said grimly, before a slight crack appeared in his stern façade. "For them, anyway," he finished, a small and very evil smile quirking the edge of his lips upwards.

"What?" I asked, unsure I'd heard him right.

"They're ploughing straight toward the Tower. There's no deviation at all. They come across a stream or river, they build a log bridge; a swamp, they make a road; trees, they smash through with their mages. They are drawing an almost perfectly straight line from the city of Himnel directly for the Tower, and they're moving fast." Restun pulled a length of chalk out of his pocket and began drawing on the floor.

"This is Himnel, this is the village of Dannick, and this is the Tower," he explained, marking three points about three feet apart. "They're literally running as fast as they can, almost without care for the potential issues this causes. They have two mages on overwatch, but they are clearly bored and pass their time on other things, as we got within a mile before they noticed us. They've run a road straight through Dannick, and apart from a few monsters too stupid to get out of the way, they've had it all their own way for the entire trip."

"Until now, anyway," Romanus interjected, grinning. "You requested ambushes to slow their march, and in this case, as unprepared as they are for any surprises, that's either a great big trap, or a lot of little ones. This is what we've come up with..."

The next two hours passed in a whirl of planning. Others were called in, Denny especially, as well as several other legionnaires I'd not met before, but by the time it was done, I'd had both Thorn and another Legion blacksmith named Allie alternately cursing and praising me as they wandered off to begin their jobs, sadly certain that they'd not be sleeping much over the following few days, but determined to learn, nonetheless.

It had taken Oracle almost an hour to fly up to the Hall of Memories and to select all the books we needed, even using a bag of holding, but the look on Denny's face when she handed the journeyman trapmaking book to him was worth every second.

"You've got a choice, Denny." I said, watching him as he gaped at the book he held in hands that shook slightly. "Either you can read that book, after reading this one..." Oracle pulled out the apprentice grade book as well and handed it over to him. "...and you can start training up a few people to work alongside you.

"Or you can accept the journeyman tome, which might repeat a lot of information in the apprentice one, or that you've learnt already, and you can nominate someone to receive the apprentice book instead. I need a team that can work together to make traps, not just today, but in a lot of scenarios in the future, I have no doubt. What's it going to be?" I watched him carefully, knowing I'd literally given the man a handful of temptation and was asking him to show restraint.

He looked from one book to the other, then he swallowed hard and straightened up, fixing me with a passionate stare.

"Thank you, sir! I'll be worthy of these books!" he barked out, and I nodded, feeling my heart dip a little as it seemed that he was going to take them both.

"But a legionnaire is only as good as his team...sir. I'll give this apprentice grade book to Pertin; he's also an apprentice carpenter, so..." He looked at me, waiting to see if I'd refuse it, and I gestured for him to go on. "Pertin has complementary skills, sir. He can help me, and we can craft the tools we need to make more complicated traps in the future."

"Good man," I said simply, smiling in approval. He sagged a little in relief, then turned and passed the book to Legionnaire Pertin, who grabbed it, hanging onto it for dear life as he saluted me so hard, he nearly broke his fist on his breastplate.

As Denny and his crew left, I sat back, scrubbing my face with my hands and groaning. The constant decision-making that was required as a leader was annoying the hell out of me.

One detail I'd never really considered was the fact that there was no good choice to be made in so many situations. I could have kept Denny and his crew back; they could have requisitioned the right equipment for the job, which would then enable them to do far better work, the resulting effect being significantly more effective, but by then the Dark Legion would be literally on our doorstep, and I had to assume they'd be ready for a fight and suspicious by then; more so than they already were of ships that passed them by, anyway.

Or I could have them do the job with almost none of what they needed. The traps would be far less efficient, but they'd slow the enemy considerably. Unfortunately, that would result in them arriving up to a week later, with far more troops combat capable and aware we had a thing for traps.

In a game, there'd be the ideal scenario, the one I'd taught myself through countless strategy games to look for, and here, there just fucking wasn't.

On the upside, though, Denny was excited to all hell, so I shrugged and let it go, guessing that was a win.

There was a cough outside, and I looked up. The door for this room had not been so much as carved yet, never mind hung, and I noticed Cai standing politely just outside.

"Hey, Cai, what's up?" I asked him tiredly.

"Ah…you ordered the council to gather, Jax…an hour ago?"

"Ah, crap," I groused, rising to my feet. "Sorry, mate, I got distracted." I emerged into the hallway, finding the others seated in a nearby room down the hall. I hurried over, Cai, Restun, and Romanus following along.

"Sorry, everyone," I said sheepishly as I walked in. "I was speaking to the Legion, and…"

"Jax, it's okay," Flux interrupted, his low *thrum* of amusement filling the air. "We could hear you were busy, and you are the lord here. We serve at your pleasure."

I paused at Flux's comment and instinctively turned to look for Bane, who had appeared casually in his seat, and I held up a finger warningly.

"Not the time, dude," I said, having sensed his desire to make a comment about Oracle 'serving at my pleasure,' or something along those lines.

"I would never…" Bane said archly.

I shook my head at the low snickers around the room. "Right, people! We've a plan for slowing the oncoming Dark Legion. Restun and Romanus are, obviously, in charge of this. The rest of us will move ahead on two fronts: first of all is the Tower, we're going to hand out more of the Tower's stockpile of books.

"Although a lot will be held back until we have someone that's appropriate for them, obviously, we have a need for people who can fill certain roles, and I have a goddamn need for some soft pants!" I grumbled, clearly annoyed as I attempted to shift myself to be more comfortable.

"Secondly, the local area." I gestured to the windows that let in a pleasant breeze. "We know bugger-all about it; all we know for certain is that there are ruins nearby. There are probably several buried golems, ones that would be tremendously helpful, and…" I frowned, turning to where Seneschal, Oracle, and Heph waited placidly in the center of the table, looking at me in their diminutive forms. "I saw Sarge earlier, so I take it the golems we found in Waystation Four all made it here, okay?"

"They did, laddie." Heph responded with a grin. "One of tha wee beasties out there apparently tried ta make lunch of one of 'em, though. It had a wee scratch on its armor…"

"And the monster?" I asked.

"Well, there be remains of a stain on one boot an' all." Heph bit back a chuckle, making me grin.

"What would happen if we used the golems on the Dark Legion?" I asked cautiously.

"They'd stomp 'em flat, laddie. Ain't no flesh an' blood force gonna stand up to tha war golems one-on-one," the burly Wisp said proudly.

"Hmmm, well I'll consider that, then. After all…" I began, when I was suddenly interrupted by the presence and words of Jenae, Goddess of Fire.

"I'd recommend you don't do that, Jax," She said without preamble. *"Using creations like that to destroy Nimon's forces will change your current state from–I'm sorry, but it's true–an annoyance, to someone that truly garners His attention. He will abide by the rules and will not interact to simply destroy you out of hand Himself, but He is likely to make something to counter the golems. The time to use them is when you need them most, not when you could win the battle without them."*

"Jenae…" I said, lifting my eyes upwards, although why I always did that, I couldn't explain; there was just the ceiling to see. "Thanks for the warning. It's a shame, but I guess it makes sense. What are the 'rules,' though?" I wondered aloud. "You've mentioned or hinted that there are rules before, but nothing easily understood?"

"And I can tell you no more now, my Champion. Take not offense, but the rules, and the strictures we place upon ourselves in the Great Game, are not for the ears of mortals. If, one day, you truly ascend, you may learn of them then."

"Oh…okay then," I said, feeling slapped down hard. I nearly responded with 'well, fuck you very much,' but managed to stop myself at the last second.

"Again, it is not a choice; please understand that," Jenae said soothingly. *"That being said, I have come to remind you of a Quest, my Champion. It is time to bring back my brethren, painful as sharing your devotions will be."*

You have been reminded of a Quest by your Goddess: Bring Back the Old Gods:

Bring back the Old Gods to displace Nimon and return balance to the realm. Aid each to find a champion that suits their aspect, and spread knowledge of the Gods to bring about a new Golden Age.

Gods Awakened: 1/9
Champions Chosen: 1/9
Reward: Blessings of the Gods, 100,000xp, Random local notable locations identified

"Okay…" I muttered, reading through it. Then I sighed and read it aloud for the benefit of the others, hearing low whistles at the details. "Right; that'll be my next job, immediately after this meeting…but…Jenae, what is a heliomage? Apparently, they're involved in traps? Can I give out the memory for that?" I was treated to a long moment of silence, making me wonder if Jenae had gone or hadn't heard me before She finally responded.

"A heliomage is a mage dedicated to the Sun and an embodiment of my power directly. A heliomage's memories can be given, but their power cannot. It must be earned. I will consider the individual you wish for this, and if I find them appropriate, I will grant them a simple spell. They will have to earn more, as a heliomage is no simple skill or class; they are also my Priest Guardian for my Temples."

"I was thinking of Denny, a legionnaire who is learning to become a trapsmith. I'm not sure if he's really priest material…" I hesitated, seeing Restun close his eyes and shake his head slightly, while Romanus winced.

"I shall evaluate him," Jenae responded. *"Now, I shall leave you, Eternal. Good luck."*

"And to you!" I replied automatically, respectfully waiting for the sense of Her presence to leave the room. "Okay Restun, Romanus, how badly did I just fuck up?" I asked with growing concern and they shared a glance before Romanus spoke cautiously.

"Legionnaire Denny is…irreverent, Jax. He is possibly one of the least respectful in so many ways. The only legionnaire I can think of off the top of my head that I would recommend less for divine contact would be Grizz."

"Oh shit. No…" I whispered, just as an elated cry rose in the distance.

"Yes, Goddess!" a now-familiar voice shouted, the sound echoing up the stairwell at the end of the corridor.

"She's found him already…" I muttered, rubbing the heels of my hands into my eyes. "Well, too late to worry about that now, I guess…" I straightened up.

"Okay, let's get this done, then. Training time, but first, we split the people into teams for the various professions," I said, outlining my plans. "We train the first ones, either from experienced people, skillbooks, or memories, and they train five more. Those five each train five more, until we have the required number of people. Carpenters, for example, can make a bed, or a table, or a door, or…with a little extra training…a spiked pit trap." I rubbed at my chin in thought. "Oracle, basic skills, ones that are probably useful straight away…what do we have, please?"

"Hmmmm, counting the books that you looted and those we had upstairs in my Hall, which I've now brought down…" Oracle peered into the bag, listing them as Cai made notes, occasionally pausing to let him catch up. "We have two more farming skillbooks. One is a basic how-to guide for a novice. The other is a specialist tome called 'Complementary Growths for Mana Cultivation,' and it basically teaches someone to grow certain plants in ways that will increase the mana density in an area, as each plant produces a specific flavor of mana.

"All nature does, obviously, but while all living things can make use of mana, plants use it as part of their growth cycle. Certain types also produce beneficial mana as part of that cycle. This tome would make a gardener into someone who could build up both the mana density in an area and the health of the plants being tended. This would, in turn, increase crop yields and can lead to beneficial changes in plants."

"Give the first to a volunteer from the farming team who's impressed you, and the second to Esse, the herbalist," I instructed Cai.

"Tel, our resident alchemist, has been making the most of the alchemy and herbalism training you gave him," Cai noted as he wrote. "He and Esse have been growing a considerable number of herbs and making as many potions as they can."

"Glad to hear it. Seneschal, include a section exclusively for herbs in the glasshouse, please. Go on, Oracle," I said, trying to keep things moving.

"We have one novice tome that deals with glassblowing, and a memory crystal of an artist who created stained glass windows and more…"

"Give out the tome, please, Cai," I ordered. "Save the skill memory for later and tell whoever you choose for the glass production that once they make it to journeyman; they'll get the skill memory. Their priority is glass vials for potions, for now. They'll have to make their own tools first, so I don't expect much in the short-term."

"And considerin' they'll need sand fer tha glass? Good luck to tha' end, laddie! Ha!" Oren crowed, elbowing Decin who grinned at him.

"Congratulations, Oren!" I smiled wolfishly. "You get to make arrangements for the sand they'll need. Sounds like a trip to the coast and a lot of digging to me, mate. Thanks for volunteering! Now…you were saying, Oracle?" I couldn't help grinning at the crestfallen look on Oren's face.

"Next, we have two masons and a stone carver."

"Considering the building, we could use them in making individual rooms. Cai, give them out to anyone that you feel merits them, or hold onto them until the fleet gets here. There's no desperate rush yet for those skills, but I'll admit, it'd be good to get the rooms more functional."

"Jeweler, leatherworker, and potter," Oracle listed off, reading the stack of books she'd removed from the bag and ignoring the startled gasps that their appearance had drawn. "The jeweler is novice. For the leatherworker, I have two books, one novice, one journeyman, and a skill memory for leather armor. Potter, there's a single book, but it's lord level."

"Lord?" I asked, raising one eyebrow.

"It's the level past expert. It's a level that maybe one in ten thousand would achieve back in the old Empire, but without the lower levels, it would be a terrible waste, as the person who learns it would end up imbalanced with their skill.

"They'd literally be able to make the basics without any thought and would level their own skill very, very quickly but they'd be permanently plagued with the knowledge that, if they'd gotten it after making it from novice to apprentice, the overall level they'd reach would be higher, due to the loss in knowledge that these things tend to have when the gap is too great."

"So, what you're saying is that if we give it to just anyone, they'd be an amazing potter, but it'd be a waste, but if we had an experienced potter and gave it to them, we'd be better off in the long run?" I asked, and she nodded. "Do we have any potters?"

"The one from the village died in the raid," Cai said grimly.

"Great. Hold onto it, Cai. If there's a potter in the refugees, then they get it. If not, pick someone who's interested, and they can have it instead. It does us no good sitting there being wasted."

"Yes, Jax; and the leatherworkers and jeweler?" Cai asked, scribbling furiously.

"Give out the jeweler and the basic leatherworking to someone without any skill since it gets them into the trade. Give the armor one to the Legion armorers and see what they want to do with it."

"Thorn may want to marry you," Romanus warned jokingly.

"Just wait until we get to the proper stuff. Can we have the full list, please, Oracle?" I said, winking.

"Hmmm…" Oracle muttered, shooting glares at us both before going on. "Well, there are two ranger skills, both novice; a scribe novice, covering making basic paper and inks, as well as more advanced and higher quality ones, journeyman this time. Two saddlers; a tanner; a ropemaker, including basic sails for some reason; a cobbler; three scholars, mainly focused on research; five carpenters, including an expert level; two lumberjacks; an architect; a tailor; two torturers; a teacher; a weaver; and three miners, as well as a collection of skills I don't think we really need, mainly highly skilled, like expert and lord-level, such as perfumers, painters, a jongleur, a courtesan, and a beekeeper…oh wait, I missed one. There's also a baker, expert level."

"Okay, fuck off most of the last ones. We can ignore that for now, although a courtesan would be popular, I'd imagine. That's for later, I guess, unless you know someone, Cai?" I asked, and I swore he reddened, glancing at Isabella before coughing and muttering that he didn't.

"Give out the novice books as you see fit, Cai. We need all the skilled citizens working as fast as we can get them, basically. The higher skills, like the expert carpenter, should go to someone who's at least apprentice already, and get one of them to damn well start making some doors!" I gestured to the empty doorway. "Also, use the beekeeper tome, as we could do with the honey. Leave the torturer ones entirely. Not a road I want to go down. As to the saddlers, pointless at this time; leave them as well."

"I'd take one of the torturer tomes," Flux interrupted.

I frowned at him, opening my mouth before Romanus caught my eye. He inclined his head to Flux, and I took the hint, letting him speak.

"While I agree that torture is distasteful, it is a useful skill. You wish me to deal in the shadows, creating a group that will be both bodyguards and assassins for the Empire. This skill would be useful to a team such as this, and while I do not wish to learn it, I would, and I would pass on the relevant knowledge on anatomy and persuasion that it would assuredly contain to my team." Flux explained, watching me.

I considered him for a long minute before sighing heavily and nodding in acquiescence.

"I'll be honest, Flux, I don't like it, but you're right; it would be useful, and more to the point, I trust you. The book is yours." He nodded in thanks, and I rubbed my chin, contemplating the piled books that Oracle had set out and refreshing my memory of her words.

"Give the painter book to Renna; that's the artist, isn't it?" Cai nodded. "Good. Tell her to keep working with Ame on the runes." I found Ame and grinned at her. "They really worked, and they resulted in a pair of new classes."

"You think an entirely new pair of classes being created wouldn't be memorable?" Ame asked. "Renna is waiting to see if you'll formally grant her the class, and others will no doubt want to join it as well." She sighed, though her body language seemed to convey approval. "Well done, Lord Jax. It was impressive; two new classes, added to the list of your accomplishments, is amazing."

"Thank you," I said. "And yes, of course I'll officially bestow the class on her, if that's needed. Give one of the Ranger books out but save the other...give it to Miren when she arrives," I said sadly, looking around the table. "Miren has decided that she wants to leave my personal squad. It's a decision I don't blame her for, and I'll be incredibly angry if I find she's been given any kind of abuse over that choice. She's young, and I asked more of her than I should have. She's skilled with her bow and as a hunter, so when she arrives with the rest of the fleet, make her a ranger and send her out with a small team to explore the area. She will be a trainer for a while, I think, teaching the basics to those who want to learn." I stopped and thought for a moment.

"Recruit the best of the scholars and the teacher from the people once everyone is here. I know I don't have to say this, Cai, but wait until the fleet arrives to give out some of those books. I don't want a 'them and us' mentality to start with the new citizens and the older. Arrange classes for those who want them, and make sure at a minimum, all the kids get some basic schooling. They need to be able to read and write and pick a job, at least. Beyond that, I'll leave them up to you."

"What is it that you wish the scholars to do?" Nerin surprised me by asking.

"Well, they'll do research, I guess, help Riana...would one of those books be of use to you, Riana?" I asked, but Oracle spoke up before she could respond.

"There are other, less basic skills that will suit Riana more, my love," she interjected.

"Okay; in that case, have a look through the rest of the books and memories. There are engineers coming in the fleet who are already highly skilled, and they'll need some, as well as the Legion armorers and bladesmiths." Oracle nodded at me, and I searched the faces of the rest of the people gathered in the room. "Well, is there anything else?" I asked.

"The baker," Cai pointed out delicately.

"Oh God, yes. Find the absolute best person for that role and give us all an expert baker!" I stated firmly. "That's going to make a hell of a difference to our damn quality of life, so do it, and do it fast." I regarded those sitting with us patiently, and I smiled at them with gratitude.

"I need you all to make food and defenses a priority now, please. Those who are helping out in various nonessential areas are to be diverted to help with the glasshouse. I know it's big, but I've not had the chance to see it yet." I held up one finger to Bane without looking. "Shut it, Bane," I said, and we all heard the ultra-low bass of his laugh as I shook my head.

Damn, I should never have taught him lines like "that's what she said," I reflected momentarily. "We need to get the glasshouse filled and ready to start growing crops. I know we're in late summer now, but if the storms are starting, I'm assuming that's a sign of the changing seasons here as well?"

"It is," Flux said. "As an established resident of the area, I can assure you that it grows very cold, amazingly fast. We will have increasing storms for the next month, growing in frequency and severity, until the autumn has fully arrived. Expect heavy snowfalls and much reduced hunting over the next few months."

"Then this is the priority. We have a wall, we have golems, and we have the Legion; now we damn well need food to keep everyone going. That glasshouse was a gift from Jenae, and I've no doubt it will make a huge difference. Is there anything else?" I asked and got a series of head shakes.

"There are a dozen minor matters," Cai said quickly. "Perhaps we could discuss them…"

"While we walk," I finished, sighing. "I've got a long walk ahead, though, be warned. I'm heading up to awaken the Gods, as I get the feeling they'll be immensely helpful to us, not to mention damn well needed. I'd imagine that Ame and Nerin would like to be involved in this?"

I got fervent nods as they both hurriedly rose to their feet, as did the rest of the room.

"In that case, you're all dismissed," I said, gesturing to Ame and Nerin to wait behind. Once the others had left, and both Bane and Flux had obviously stealthed and were clearly following along as well, we began climbing the God-damn hundreds, if not thousands, of stairs up, hounded the entire way by Cai and his never-ending minor matters.

CHAPTER FOURTEEN

When my legs ached from so many stairs, and my ears practically bled from Cai's recommendations, requests, and confirmations, we reached the required floor.

This floor, as high as it was in the Tower, was a single room, maybe a hundred meters or so across, with a high, arced ceiling, reminiscent of a cathedral nave.

Two sets of doors, facing east and west, led out onto an overgrown garden level. It had once been a balcony that had slowly been colonized by plants growing and dying over the centuries of neglect, of pots being alternately baked and blasted by the sun, then frozen solid in the snows until they'd broken, freeing their soil to spill across the stones.

Hundreds more years had passed, turning the mulch that fell from the trees into a thick compost that spread out, in turn allowing the further colonization of the level. Until, after more than *seven hundred years*, the entire outside had been converted into an orchard, a pool twinkling in the middle of it, with a gentle waterfall from higher up the Tower splashing down into the pool before overflowing on the far side.

I took a moment to admire the changes that had been wrought since I was last able to visit, and I smiled. The dark and depressing air of the place was gone, and where the doors on the east side had been warped and shattered, with unrestrained plants spilling in, now the debris and cluttering foliage were gone.

Instead, bright, welcoming sunlight shone in through an embellished archway. The windows that could be restored had been, and those that couldn't had been coated in a thin film of stone, granting a rough look to the light. The white marbled floor, seemingly glittering with the light of a thousand stars, made the altars glow instead of looming as they had on my first visit.

I led the way through the bright room, naming the altars as I went, until I stopped at a specific one as a sudden memory pricked at me.

"Ashante, Goddess of Nature and of Life," I murmured slowly, turning to Mistress Nerin. "You once asked if Ashante was returning, the Goddess of Life, not Lagoush, the Goddess of Healing...why is that?"

"Because She was the Goddess of my mother," Nerin whispered after a long pause. "She cried out to Her, even as she lay dying, an illness eating away at her insides, and still nobody answered. I was four." Nerin scowled defiantly at me. "My mother prayed to Her every day, as did others I know, yet She never responded, and I want to know why!"

"Right," I said, taken aback by the ferocity of Nerin's demand and by the need for it. Oracle and I exchanged a long look, and she landed, growing to her full size and placing a reassuring hand on Nerin's shoulder.

I coughed nervously. "Umm, look, I might be able to answer that, so I'm going to give it a try...okay? This might not be entirely accurate, but it's my understanding of it, so, you know, take that into account, and don't murder me. I'm saying this because you can call me an asshole if you want, and I'll be fine, but if you do that to a Goddess, even one newly awoken, it might have some…side effects."

"Believe him, Nerin. Words with Gods need to be taken seriously," Oracle whispered.

I scrubbed the back of my head with one hand, and gestured through the archway out onto the balcony. The branches of the short, fruit-laden trees swayed in the gentle, constant breeze.

"Let's go sit down," I muttered, leading the way out and sitting with a sigh as I plucked a red apple from a branch and idly polished it in my hands. "Look, when…a certain asshole…banished the Gods, They lost their link to the world.

"That meant They couldn't help Their followers, as another asshole and his friends slaughtered those followers and destroyed their temples. There are a few still standing, and others, like this Tower, that have surviving altars, but they're rare; like seriously rare. I don't follow exactly why, but a Goddess only receives your tribute if you pray in a consecrated place, or if you have a consecrated item to use…so if you prayed to Jenae right now, you're in a Tower dedicated to Her worship, and She'll get that mana straight away. You try praying to Ashante? Wasted mana, because it can't reach Her. If it goes anywhere at all, it's just out into the ether…again, I don't know exactly how or why; this is just what I got from Jenae's explanation. Ashante is asleep still, which prevents Her from answering any prayers. If She'd been getting any of that mana, even if it took a while, She'd have already awoken…"

I explained it carefully, trying not to be an asshole when I told her that her mother, and anyone else who'd been praying to Ashante, had been wasting their fucking time.

"I have to ask, considering your class, your abilities…hell, everything that I know about you, which admittedly ain't a lot, do you really want to swear to Ashante?" I pressed Nerin, cautious not to sound dismissive. "Ame is a healer and Runecrafter, and she wants to swear to Lagoush, the Lady of Water, who is also the patron Goddess of Healing. Wouldn't she…"

"No. My mother worshipped Ashante. I will follow Her teachings, even if it is inconvenient for you," Nerin snapped, staring daggers at me.

"Whoa, listen, Nerin, you do you. I don't give a shit; just do me a favor and don't pick N…that asshole. That's all I ask," I said, holding my hands up as I leaned backwards, flinching from Oracle's warning glare, as I had almost said Nimon's name aloud. "Look, you've clearly got an issue here, and you don't want to talk to me. That's fine, *BUT*," I said firmly, fixing her with a glare of my own. "I'm not sure it's a good idea to let you swear to Her today."

Nerin growled in outrage, pushing to her feet. "What! I…"

"No!" I snapped, clambering to mine and going toe to toe with her. "Nerin, you are clearly pissed at Ashante, and She's had nothing to do with this. You need to take some time to reflect on it. Speak to Her tomorrow, if you want; hell, do it in ten minutes, so long as you've calmed down. I am not having a newly awakened Goddess furious at me and my people because you're in a mood!" I drew a deep breath and then turned to Ame and Flux, knowing Bane was hiding somewhere out of sight.

"Okay, I'm thinking for now, we awaken the Gods and Goddesses two at a time, so there's not so much stress on them. Ame, you're welcome to awaken Lagoush now, if you want to. I need to consider another God or Goddess to awaken, as we've limited time, and we can't afford to pass this opportunity up. You'll get a notification of how much mana you need to tithe to Her; it was a thousand for Jenae. Stop at ten points from the limit, please, and let me know, so I can contact Jenae for help."

Ame looked from me to Nerin and back again before nodding once, sharply, and stalking off to find the relevant altar.

"Jax?" Flux said quietly, and I raised an eyebrow. "I'd suggest Tamat."

I frowned, scanning my memory for the name. "Wasn't She the Goddess of Darkness?" I asked, confused.

"Yes, and of assassination and larceny," Flux confirmed.

I regarded him with surprise. "And this seems like the perfect time to introduce more of that to the Tower?" I asked, stunned. "We've already got a kid who's been half trained by a goddamn bard, for fuck's sake. You really want to go there? And who's going to volunteer to worship Her that we can trust?"

"I will," Bane said from directly behind me.

"Goddamnit!" I shouted, practically jumping out of my skin. "I fucking swear, Bane! I will staple a damn bell to your forehead if you keep that shit up!" I backed away from him, taking a deep breath to get my heart to calm down. "You see if I don't, you evil sod."

"Seriously though, Jax, you need a team of dedicated bodyguards and assassins. I know you've not said it quite like that, but you want a group for spying and assassinations, don't you, not just bodyguards?" Flux questioned.

I sighed heavily, straightening up and regretfully letting one more piece of the old me slip away.

"Yes, damn it, I do. I need a team I can trust to take care of problems. I remember Amon and the shit He went through before He accepted that there are black deeds that need to be done. But mark my words: there's a limit to it. I won't suffer an innocent to be killed, nor children. I need a team of assassins, because nobody else can guard against an assassin as well as one who's been on both sides, but I will only send them out to be knives in the dark when I don't believe there's another option."

"And Barabarattas?" Flux asked, causing me to snort and shake my head.

"Oh, come on. If you know where that dickbag is, and you can do it? Go have fun. I don't give a shit about idiots like that. Slaughter him. I'd only regret that I didn't get to do it personally, but no; I mean someone like Alistor."

"Who?" Flux asked, then interrupted before I could respond. "Oh, the Legion Tribune who is so…unpleasant…the one you mentioned, Bane?"

"Yeah, that guy," I said, leaning back against a tree. "Seriously, he's fucking annoying, like he's doing everything he can to fuck with me and our efforts, while never doing anything severe enough that I can really call him out on it. Amon would have gutted him already, given the chance. He'd have ignored the knob the first time he did it, then He would have had his knives gut him, slowly and painfully, as an example.

"Amon was an utter bastard, Flux; He did shit…" I shuddered as I stared back across millennia, hating the memories I'd found. "But the one thing I can say for

Him is that, as the Emperor, He did it all for the good of the Empire, not for the good of Himself or anyone else. If He'd woken up one morning and believed, really believed that He shouldn't be the Emperor anymore, He'd have walked away in an instant."

"Okay," Flux murmured, watching me, and I looked back at him.

"You don't get it. I *know* Him now. I feel the echoes of who He was. Seriously, He was that straight of a guy; He believed in the Empire with everything He was, and that left no room for anything else. No lazy mornings, no wild-ass parties or sitting and talking shit with friends.

"He was the Emperor, and He was viewed as a tiny step below the Gods by *everyone*. He had no friends. His only peers were the Ancient Dragons, creatures that could destroy continents, and they thought He was fucking dangerous. You don't know what having that kind of focus, of responsibility, does to you."

"Well, you have us, and you have the Legion, not to mention the rest of the citizens, and frankly, you also have a Goddess watching over you. I don't recommend going down that route."

"That's the point, Flux. I have checks and balances, and you're wanting to bring in a Goddess of assassination? You don't think on a bad day, I might give in to a suggestion?"

"I think, if you were going to, then you would, anyway. Jax, this is pointless. You said before that you needed to return all the Gods, not just the ones you wanted, as the world and the realm needs balance."

"So shut the fuck up and put my big boy pants on, huh?" I asked, grinning in spite of myself.

"Essentially, yes." Flux hit me with a thrum of amusement that made me grin deeper.

"Fuck it; okay, Bane. You, I do trust. If you want to go and awaken the Goddess, go for it." I sucked in a deep breath as another thought came to me. *In for a penny, in for a pound.*

I concentrated, going to one knee and pulling the mana from inside myself, twisting it and withdrawing what I saw easily as strands now, specifically aligned mana. Like fire and earth, air, and water, they looked and felt like plain mana, until I grew more familiar with them. Thanks to Amon's recent brain dump, I'd learned so much more than I ever should have been capable of at this stage in my development.

I separated the fire mana, tucking it in and weaving it around the air and time. Strands of life lifted to fill in the gaps, and I felt my understanding of magic, of the nature of mana itself, deepen somehow as I pulled the spell in close, then released it.

"Jenae." I called out to the Goddess, and I felt Her respond.

"I am here, Jax. Is it time?"

"It is." I straightened up and drawing in a deep breath. "It was my intention to reawaken the Gods two at a time, as I thought that They might be confused or even distressed. Is that likely, or will your presence negate those issues?" I asked, and there was a pause.

"I cannot promise all my brethren will be polite or pleased with their lot when they reawaken. After all, they were all-powerful Gods until we were

attacked and cast out by one of our own. But I will ensure your safety against them, and I will aid them in understanding their new reality."

"Then in that case, are You ready?" I asked her. When I sensed Her agreement, I searched for the others nearby, finally picking my way across the balcony to the doors and the altars waiting inside. "Let's go wake up the Gods then, I guess." I fixed Nerin with a stern glare. "But hear me well, Nerin. You damn well show respect. I don't want to have to fight another God."

"You? *You* are counseling *me* to show respect? Wait...what do you mean fight *another* God?!" Nerin's tone melted to shock, her eyes opening wide as Oracle rolled her own.

"Honestly, Nerin, do you really need to ask?" Oracle's voice was a mixture of sadness and pride. "Who else would pick a fight with the Gods and survive, and when have you ever known Jax to learn a lesson the easy way? Trust me, darling, you don't want to see him truly angry."

"He fought a God?" Nerin asked Flux quietly.

"We had a disagreement; I wouldn't call it a fight." Jenae rumbled.

Nerin winced, scanning the room anxiously before glaring at me again.

"You picked a fight with Jenae? The Lady of Fire?! You..." she hissed, when Jenae spoke up again, exasperatedly.

"Actually, I started the fight, and we both agreed to end it." She admitted, a note of shame in Her voice.

"You fought a God to a standstill," Nerin whispered, gaping at me, a mixture of disbelief and awe with a touch of exasperation filling her voice.

"Like Jenae says, it was a...misunderstanding." I walked inside, setting my half-eaten apple on the floor. "Anyway, enough of that shit. How about we get to this...Oracle?" I asked.

She nodded as she reached out to the Tower, filtering the mana and diverting it into the selected altars, leaving out the Dickbag of Death's one, of course. The stone pedestals glowed with energy as the mana was absorbed.

It didn't take long, bare minutes, when the air changed.

It felt strange, charged, like just before a lightning strike. The pressure in the single room increased, and I began to feel sick. I checked for Flux, Ame, Nerin and Bane, as Oracle moved closer to me, reaching out one hand in an unconscious gesture, needing reassurance.

"What?"

"Who?"

"They're dead."

"No..."

"Let me sleep."

"NIMON!"

The voices were faint, weak, and confused, overlapping each other, but the last cry rang out with a level of fury that was palpable.

"Oh fuck..." I muttered as the aura in the room changed. I felt and heard Jenae as She tried to reason with the Gods, calming some, reassuring one who whimpered endlessly, but after long seconds, a growl rang out again, and the pressure changed as one of the Gods focused in on all of us exclusively.

"Who are you? Speak!" the voice boomed, and I recognized it as the one that had cried out the God of Death's name.

"I'm Jax, Scion of the Empire," I forced out, and felt all of the deity's attention on me. My legs shook with the pressure.

"He is mine!" Jenae said sharply, shoving the mounting pressure aside.

The other Gods pushed back. Where Jenae tried to erect a barrier, a protection for us, this presence tore at it, driving itself around and around the barrier, seeking a weakness.

"It is weak, as are you, sister. Give it up. Choose another champion, and I will mold it, break it, and twist it into the weapon we need," the voice demanded.

"No! He is mine! Others may choose to serve you, Tamat, but YOU will serve ME!" Jenae snarled, and the Tower shuddered as the pressure built. Cracks appeared around the room, and the newly repaired window glass detonated and was hurled away.

"Never!" Tamat screeched, and we were suddenly thrown backwards, all of us slammed forcefully across the floor. Our bodies rolled and bounced, crunching into the wall, and the Tower shook again, this time stronger. I felt my people's fear as our newly rebuilt home was being torn asunder.

"Fuck this shit!" I snarled, rolling to my feet, and gritting my teeth as I reached out to Amon, opening myself to Him and inviting Him in.

For the first time in days, Amon responded, and not simply a disinterested prick of the mental ears; oh no. I felt His cold fury joining with my own as He called out, His mental summons stretching across the realm and being answered by another.

I growled, lifting my right hand and forming a blade with it. The blade slashed down, tearing a hole in space as He guided, manipulating our mana as billowing mist poured off me. It surrounded me, shielding me as I stepped forward. Oracle lay somewhere behind me, her physical form forgotten as she bared her teeth mentally and fed the mana collectors' take directly into me; Amon grasped the stream and smoothed it out.

The world changed between one step and the next, and suddenly I was gone, vanished from the senses of the others as I stepped between realities, Amon and the one He'd called to, Tuthic, reaching out to join with me.

My foot crunched down and dust rose, the cracked and broken earth beneath my foot shattering and floating away, dust puffing with each step as I walked forward.

I closed my eyes, feeling both sets of eyelids close then whisk apart as I took the next step, seeing the realm of the Gods before me again.

It was a dead world, like the hottest, driest deserts, where mud flats had shattered and cracked. Yet it was cold, and something pulled at me, wanting to drain my life away.

Last time I'd come here, there'd been a palpable sense of danger. This time, that sense was magnified tenfold, and all around me were presences.

I recognized Jenae easily; an older woman, still in Her prime, dark red hair shifting as the wind blasted across the realm. She had clad Herself in a mixture of dark red scaled armor and an outfit I'd expect to see an action film star wearing to fight zombies, all sand-colored leather and bags.

Where She was solid and carried an aura of command and strength, the others were more like ghosts, phantasms that desperately wanted form. I sensed Their retreat before They began flowing forward, moving quickly to surround me. Their hunger leeched through as They tasted the mana flowing off me in waves. It bled off as I left the other realm behind and lost my connection to the Tower's mana flow.

I growled as a form appeared before me, a shifting haze of blackness, lit only by pulses of red and the two eyes that burned out at me, yellow and black sclera with red irises, a vertical black pupil bisecting the middle.

"You dare trespass?!" The same voice that had been fighting with Jenae snarled at me, and out of the corner of my eye, I saw Jenae regard me thoughtfully before stepping back and giving me a brief nod of approval.

"I *dare*?!" I snarled back at the formless Goddess, lifting my right arm up, elbow bent and hand held out vertically as I closed my grip around a naginata that hadn't existed a split second before.

A shiver of power flowed through me as Tuthic's enormous presence towered behind me, invisible, yet providing both power and reassurance. Silvery scales flowed over me, like they had before.

Instead of the fractured, self-hating Amon I was used to, I felt the laser-like focus of the revenant as He glared at a Goddess He'd despised in life. His scorn built as He now felt Her weak enough that, were He at His full strength, He'd have torn Her apart with His bare hands.

"Oh, I fucking dare, you bitch!" I snarled at her, stepping forward. The sound of my footfall changed midway from the clunk of steel to the silvery peal of True Silver.

The life force of the dragon Shustic, the Silver Maiden of the North, seeped out of the simulacrum of my naginata, making me shiver with the power that flooded me.

The entities around me hesitated, these fallen Gods who recognized an ancient strength and a very new fury. Tamat lashed out, dozens of claws of smoke flashing from Her misty shape to sink into me, designed to bypass my armor and sink deep into my flesh, like the knives of Her chosen had always done.

"Feel my wrath as I feed on you, mortal!" She sneered. *"Understand what it means to trespass in the realm of the Gods!"*

"Yeah, let's see how that works out for you," I hissed, pain tearing through me, only to be rammed down by my fury and Amon's hatred as I lashed my left hand into the amorphous cloud of darkness. I watched my hand as it vanished, clad in bright silver scales, the gauntlet gleaming with an inner light as claws flashed and sank into Tamat.

She screamed, both in disbelief and in pain, feeling Her own life force being torn from Her, Her divine blood being drained, even as She did the same to me.

"It's not possible!" She screamed in outrage as She felt her meager life being ripped free. I rammed the Naginata forward, the blade low, then angled it up. Amon fed pure Light mana into it, the antithesis of the Goddess of Darkness.

"JAX! Stop! Jenae ordered, but I ignored Her, feeling my lips curl in contempt at this weak godling. Furiously, I began to saw it into the cloud-like substance that She had been reduced to.

Tamat let out a terrified, pain-filled screech, then Jenae was there, backhanding me, unleashing true power into the blow as She sent me flying dozens of meters through the air. My naginata vanished into the ether like the construct of mana it was.

I slammed into the ground, bouncing and rolling, arms flailing as I struggled to form coherent thoughts beyond the pain that wracked me.

When the world stopped spinning and roiling, my head clunked back one final time, and scales of pure magic cascaded away as my dragon form broke. I felt and heard, albeit at a great distance, Jenae and Tuthic speaking. They were far enough away that I couldn't make out the words or any sense of the meaning, beyond Tuthic bowing His head in acquiescence and retreating, leaving me lying there, broken, as Amon grumbled His hatred of Tamat.

The sky overhead was a surrealist's nightmare of contrasting, frantically roiling clouds, dark and forbidding. Cracks of light and booms of thunder sounded near and far, and I lay there, stunned, until she appeared.

Jenae's face filled my vision, and She crouched down, lifting me like a child and setting me back down, straightening my limbs and healing me as she spoke softly.

"I couldn't permit you to kill her, my Champion. We need her, and another who would rise to Godhood in her place would be unlikely to share our aims with regard to HIM." She sighed as she straightened my right arm out, and I felt pain rip though me as bones, which had so effectively been shattered, were yanked back into place again and flash-healed.

I screamed in agony, before quickly biting down on it and glaring up at Jenae, as she went on.

"Think, my Champion. You know this was wrong; we need them. Though you came to my aid when I needed you most, and I'll not forget that." She added the last bit alone in the silence of my mind. "The other Gods didn't expect that. They didn't realize who and what you are, nor what you could become, and as such, are genuinely concerned now.

"They, Tamat especially, awoke confused, in pain, and vastly weakened, but they believed they were still as they once were. Your maiming and near slaughter of Tamat showed them that they are mere fragments, so now is the time to be magnanimous in victory. Trust me, it will be worth it. Remember, she attacked you first and must make reparations, for if she does not, who will worship her?"

With that, the sense of Her in my mind was gone, and She was helping me to my feet. I glanced down and saw the shimmering armor coating me again, but I also felt its lack and realized that it was an illusion, gifted by Jenae, to allow me to stand tall and salvage my pride.

I forced myself to draw up to my full height and stare imperiously at the forms that hovered in the distance, even as I tried not to reveal that my entire body ached like an impacted tooth. I reached down and casually swept up a handful of the silvery scales that were scattered about, pouring them into my bag. As I rose, I spotted, then quickly swept up and deposited something else.

A single silvery claw, from my gauntlet. A claw that was smeared with black blood.

I flexed my jaw, showing nothing on my face as I verified that I had the rest of my claws, aware that it might have ruined my march back to them, but I really didn't give a fuck what Tamat thought of me, and the rest...meh.

When Jenae came to a halt a half-dozen meters from the rest of the forms, I stopped by Her side, and She spoke to them in a clear, firm voice.

"This is not the reality we were torn from. It is a ruined, devastated version of it, as are we. None of us are a fraction of the strength we were, and that…our brother…has only grown in strength while we slumbered. We have two choices: we can surrender to entropy, return to that deep, dark sleep, and pass from the realm eternally, or we can form a new Pantheon and face our former brother and the Lesser Gods he has uplifted.

"Tamat has proven that you cannot be trusted to do what is right, and you have all seen what can happen to you now, if even an inhabitant of the lower realms, albeit an exceptional one, can injure you to the point of near death." She gestured to Tamat, now in a far tighter, denser cloud, where She laid half submerged and sprawling on the dead ground. Black, hissing spots of blood were spread liberally around Her, spots other Gods eyed covetously.

"Tamat, you started this, so you will be the first to apologize and to pledge to the Pantheon, or I will step back and allow my champion free reign. I will not interfere a second time," Jenae warned as She moved one step further to the right, away from me.

My mana continued to leech from me. The massive influx of power from the Tower, courtesy of Oracle, had stopped the moment the rent in reality slammed shut, and now, it was draining away, pouring off me in waves…and being greedily absorbed by the emaciated godlings.

However, I had enough power for this, at least, and I lifted my right hand, consciously forming the mana. For a split second, nothing happened, before my naginata shimmered back into ethereal existence.

I'd nearly failed. I'd tried to force the mana into a spell, frantically trying to remember how I'd summoned my weapon last time, only to have Amon snarl in my mind and shove that apart, leaving only my *desire* for my weapon.

In the realm of the Gods, intent was everything, and the Gods had all felt my killing intent when I faced Tamat. She'd intended the same to me, after feeding, but She'd been totally unprepared for the reality of Her weakness and my strength, and in the pain and doubt that had followed, I'd come within a hair's breadth of actually killing Her before Jenae could act.

Now, as I stood before Them, resplendent in silvery scaled armor, my naginata held in one hand, I stared coldly down at Tamat. While I was frightfully conscious that I was clothed only in illusion, and that my naginata would run out of mana any second, it was enough, barely, to break the last resistance.

"I yield," Tamat whispered. *"I yield and accept responsibility. I will pay my debt, although I must recover first, and I accept the bonds of Pantheon."*

"I accept you into my Pantheon and will levy no more than I must upon you, sister; this I swear." Jenae responded before turning to me. *"Will you permit Tamat to hold off on paying her debt to you, in the sure knowledge that your mercy will be repaid with her generosity?"* Jenae asked me, and the other Gods watched, waiting.

I paused for dramatic effect more than anything else, before nodding once. Then, thinking I'd better make a good show of it, I took one knee before Jenae, bowing my head as I laid my naginata down against the ground.

"I will, Mistress," I intoned, remembering Tuthic, the Elder Dragon calling her that. "I am your servant and ally, and I came at your need. Now, there was damage done to the Great Tower when your sister…expressed herself. May I return?"

I said it all as formally and respectfully as I could, but inside, I was screaming with the need to get back, terrified that the Tower could be collapsing after that blast of power from the mad bitch, Tamat.

"I apologize, Champion. You reawakened me, and all my brethren, and we have rewarded you poorly, injuring your people and damaging your home. I will return you, and we will discuss a suitable way to thank…"

She broke off as a sudden cold wind tore across the landscape, dust clouds billowing, and a cruel howl growing all around us.

"He is here!" Jenae spat in sudden fury and fear. *"See what your temper has caused, sister! Hide, all of you!"* Jenae spun to me, Her right hand lifting, palm flat as She swiped it sideways. The ground under me vanished as I plunged through another portal.

This time, I had a split second to brace before my boots slammed into the center of the cathedral-like room. My sudden presence drew gasps from the others as I rematerialized into the UnderVerse. Wisps of silvery-grey smoke and solidified divine power lifted from me as the last of my true armor wafted away, the need for it gone, even as Jenae's gifted illusion vanished as well.

"I know you now, mortal! I see who you serve!"

The voice rang out, a hissing fury filling the air, and notifications began appearing before everyone on the continent.

KNOW THIS!

The God of Death, Nimon, has intervened in the war between Himnel and The Great Tower of Dravith!

All citizens of Himnel may now kill any citizen of Jax, Imperial Scion of Dravith, without fear of repercussion. Furthermore, they will receive one hundred gold coins, payable by the Priesthood of the God of Death.

*

KNOW THIS!

The God of Death, Nimon, orders the faithful to stamp out the nest of heresy known as The Great Tower of Dravith! It is to be destroyed, its lands salted, and its stones sunk into the depths!

*

KNOW THIS!

The God of Death, Nimon, declares war between the Dark Legion of Nimon and the Empire! Any Imperial Legionnaire who wishes to stand apart may pray to the God of Death, will be freed of their Oaths, and may leave, regardless of any Oaths given to the apostate Jax!

"Yeah, well fuck you too, Dickbag!" I shouted into the air, glaring up.

"What the hell did you just do?" screeched Mistress Nerin as she read the wall of notifications Nimon had released to every sentient creature on the continent.

"Nothing!" I snapped, straightening up and examining the room. I was especially relieved to see that the cracks in the walls were starting to close.

"*Nothing?*" she snarled. "Boy, the God of Death personally drew a target on your head and on all of ours! So I'll ask you again, *what did you just do…?*" Her voice dropped to a growling whisper, and I scowled at her, feeling that it was all bit unfair that *I* was being blamed for all of this.

"He nearly killed Tamat in single combat, but that is a tale for another day," Jenae responded for me, before going on quickly, Her voice obviously hurried as She tried to explain. *"Nimon has found us, my Champion, and while he was irritated with you before, and wished your death, he is now aware that the Gods have returned, even if we are weak and hiding from him. He has sensed your presence in our realm and made the obvious conclusion. Now he will order the full might of the Dark Legion to muster. They will not be content with sending a minor contingent. Prepare well, Jax."*

"You really know how to have a family spat, you know that?" I groused at Her, surprised by my lack of fear or anger. As far as I was concerned, they had been planning to do this anyway, so all that had changed was that they were now coming slightly faster.

"I am sorry, Jax. I did not account for Tamat's temper, or her fury at the assumption of many regarding the aspect of her role, such as Darkness being taken by Nimon. It is difficult to explain the purview of the Gods, but we jealously guard them.

"Tamat has sworn to aid you, both in apology for her actions, and now because you are to directly face the servants of the one she hates most. For now, I recommend you move quickly. You no longer have the luxury of even a few days to prepare. If you are to survive, you must recover the slumbering golems and other forces that surround you. Nimon has shown his hand, and due to his actions, I can aid you somewhat more than I had expected to. Look to the Constellation and use your Map."

With that, She was gone, and I swore viciously. I'd been relying on the time I thought we had.

"Seneschal!" I bellowed, knowing he'd be listening. "Get Cai, Oren, and Romanus to the *Agamemnon's Pride*…and tell Denny and Thorn to get there, as well!" I added as an afterthought, before sighing as I noticed the shattered glass and broken trees strewn around outside.

"*Fucking* Gods," I snarled before turning back to the others and pausing. "What?" I snapped at the shocked looks on their faces and their body language.

"Jax…what did she mean, you nearly *killed* the Goddess of Assassins?" Oracle asked with a brittle smile and obviously forced calm.

"I'll explain on the way; come on!" I snapped, running for the stairs, the others groaning and swearing as they followed.

CHAPTER FIFTEEN

The trip back down took less time than the walk up had, but it was still a lot longer than I'd have liked. It did, however, give me time to think.

I resolved to look at the Constellation of Secrets once we were on our way, and I had some time; we had around a day before the Legion and the others would arrive with the fleet, and I couldn't wait for them.

I pulled up my map, making it damn difficult to keep myself upright on the hundreds of stairs as they flashed past, but I had no time to wait. As I looked over eight new markers that had been added to my map by the Gods, I grunted in irritation. The five waystations from Himnel to the Great Tower–apart from number four, which I'd already explored–drew an obvious, if slightly curving line.

The one closest to Himnel was too far, as was the one closest to the village of Dannick, as the last report I'd had on the Dark Legion put them near to that area. The next one was maybe ten miles out of their direct route, with the fourth already looted, and the fifth again close to their direct path.

"I'll have to get number three first; can't risk waiting for them to pass it, just in case they find it somehow," I muttered before missing a step and almost plunging headfirst down the stairs.

I blinked away the map, staggering as unseen hands appeared and helped me to stay upright. I grunted in sudden instinctual fear, then got a grip and picked up the rhythm again, calling out my thanks. I was surprised to hear Ame grunt that I was welcome.

I'd forgotten about her, in all honesty, and she wasn't really required to come to this next meeting, but I carried on, figuring if she could keep up, she'd have earned the right by the time we made it.

Dozens of floors flashed past, windows letting in streaming sunshine, though I caught a glimpse of the occasional crack in one here and there.

Two revolutions more, and we exited onto the floor I needed, the twenty-sixth, or the flight deck.

It was—as always—a bustle of scarcely controlled mayhem. At first glance, it appeared to be chaos incarnate, but in looking again, I could start to see patterns as people easily avoided each other, dancing aside at seemingly the last second without looking.

A closer look would reveal that these people were working on complementary but unconnected jobs, which meant they were always on the move.

Looking a little closer when I was here last had made me realize that the noise was them all calling out as they went, letting each other know where they were, even if the words meant nothing on their own.

This was how the engineers had learned to work in a world without safety nets, regulations, or technology that would make them safer. They'd created a system to make each other aware of their presence with ease.

I loved it, especially as Oren hurried up out of the far stairwell and let loose his customary bellow on entering the floor.

It was a song, he'd told me. A damn old one, one that they all knew, and it basically meant that he was someone with the right of passage. He called out the words as he ran through, and as others drifted close, they responded with one of two choruses. The first meant they accepted his authority and would avoid him; the second meant that they couldn't, or wouldn't, step aside, usually because the job they were doing couldn't be moved. He'd swerve around them.

It was ridiculously complicated, and I'd given up on even trying to learn it after I'd heard it a few times, but it always lifted my heart to watch.

I rushed across the floor, hearing an engineer nearby call out, making sure the others were aware that an outsider was loose on the floor. I hurried forward, as the others scattered from my path, giving me a free run to the ships, despite the dozens of people hauling cannons, items, and stores and sections of hull.

As soon as my foot hit the gangplank leading up to the ship's deck, the nearest Engineer changed his chant, calling out a new cadence, and the songs and calls changed again, signifying that the interlopers were out of the way, and work was safe to resume again.

I banished it from my mind as I approached the door to the captain's cabin, hoping the others waited inside already.

The door opened as I approached, Denny, Romanus, Cai, and Oren shuffling around the limited space as I led in Flux, Bane, Ame, and Nerin. It was uncomfortably cozy with everyone practically pressed against each other. That was before Thorn, the enormous and heavily muscled half-orc armorer joined us.

With her joining us, arriving last, the room was impossibly cramped.

I looked around and growled to myself.

"Ame," I said quickly. "You can see this is no use to us. Your job, now you've seen this, is to figure out a way to integrate my damn map with the Creation Table. You have my authority to use it, and Oracle will take you to the Hall of Memories. Search there until you find something that will help you to do it. Go," I ordered.

Clearly there was something in my voice that suggested today was not the day to give me shit. She simply nodded, then left, Oracle kissing my cheek once before flying out with her.

"Thorn," I snapped next. "My squad and I will be leaving *very* shortly to raid some ruins. Hopefully they'll be empty, but the way my life is going, I doubt it. I need armor for us all, and you're to bring anyone you need to help you to get it fitted to us. Again. Sorry, but the gear I was wearing is pretty much trashed. Thanks to you, and how damn good that armor was, though, I'm alive. I'd like this state to continue, so get a move on, and keep up the good work. I want you back here with the gear and anything and anyone you need, in an hour. Go." She blanched, her mouth hanging open for a second, before she slammed it shut with a *clop* then saluted and shuffled out of the door, following Ame.

"Nerin. You're going to start a new kind of healing when we're gone. You've seen Giint and heard about the Gnomes?" I asked.

"Yes," she said. "I found Giint, and I'm impressed with the work you and Oracle did on him already. He has issues still, many of them, but some will resolve over time, and the alterations that would be necessary to fix his brain now…well, I don't recommend too many changes in a short period of time."

"I agree with you there," I grunted. "There's another fifteen of them incoming. Giint was the worst, but he was also the one worked the hardest on, so expect there to be a lot of issues spread across them. I need them as healed as you can get them, and fast. Go set up whatever you need. Have you picked out a suitable location for yourself?"

"I have, but…"

"No time for shitty details right now, Nerin." I cut her off with a raised hand. "Do you need my help to make it into what it needs to be, or can you deal with this?"

"I can deal with it, if I have your authority to…"

"You have it. You are the Tower Healer. In medical matters, your authority is absolute; only I can override you." I said formally, then stared pointedly at her. "Don't make me regret that." I jerked my head to the door, and she surprised me by smiling and nodding her thanks before leaving quickly.

That left me with Romanus, Cai, Flux, Bane, Oren, and Denny, and I could feel Seneschal and Heph watching as I updated the map table with my own map. A wonderfully detailed 3D map appeared above the table, as though by, well, magic.

I ignored the looks of shock on Denny and Romanus's faces, well aware that they had never seen this level of detail for the continent they lived on, but not having time to fuck about.

I pulled up the local area instead, tapping each of the new symbols that flashed and pulsed.

"Okay, this one here." I tapped the one closest to Himnel. "I'm going to go out on a limb and assume is Waystation One. This would be Two, Three, Four, and finally, Five," I explained, touching each in turn.

"This is Waystation Four; we already found it and cleared it out, which is why I suspect these are what they are. As near as we can tell, they'll each be ruins, probably infested as well, Four was full of Goblins. The reason that we give a shit is that they each also house a contingent of golems; war golems, to be precise, with a single complex or level three servitor golem present to carry out general repairs.

"Thanks to the Dark Wanker himself taking a hand now, we need those Golems, as the gentleman's agreement not to use them just well and truly fucking expired. As I have to be there to exert Imperial Authority over the sites, I'll need to clear out each one personally," I said quickly.

"This means that I need to move, and fast, as number Four was heavily damaged, and the golems were long since drained. Without knowing what state the rest are in, I need time to hit them, clean them out, and activate the collectors before moving on and raiding the next site. Then we'll have to return to issue orders to the golems to 'Get to the choppa'…" I finished in a poor Austrian accent.

I resisted the urge to smack myself in the face, grimacing at the confused people in the room. "Forget about the chopper comment; it's an old joke from my home that was poorly timed, and I don't want to explain."

"Very well, Lord Jax," Romanus said, regarding me with a faint smile.

"From the Waystations, I'll need to raid the other sites. I won't be sending the Legion," I said, cutting off Romanus's attempt to speak. "The reason for that is threefold. First, I need the legionnaires we have here, and here." I tapped the Tower on the map and a point halfway between the last sighting of the Dark Legion and the Tower, creating a direct line.

"The Legion is to start this fight without me, although it galls me to admit that. I want you to set up here, Denny. Trap the hell out of the place; use the nastiest and most evil shit you can think of. After all, you only get one chance to make a first impression, and by fuck, I want it to count." I tapped the location I'd indicated for emphasis.

"I'll have Oracle bring a dozen low-level spells and a handful of higher ones. Give them out to the legionnaires you intend to use here, Romanus, as I want those Trailmasters dead. They are the priority. I'll try to get there in time to play as well, but regardless, I want them fucked up, as many slaughtered with absolute maximum viciousness as possible.

"Then the Legion is to fall back. If there are survivors that continue on, then I want hit and run tactics. Every time a Trailmaster starts casting to speed them up, kill the fucker. I'm sorry to say this, but there will be Legion deaths. I really hope we can avoid that, but I just don't see how.

"Romanus, you are to minimize the casualties, but we need to wipe out this column, no survivors. Once the Trailmasters are dead, you hit and hit and hit the Dark Legion again. Harry them and cut them down, one at a damn time, if you have to," I growled, jabbing my finger into the map. I hated the necessity, knowing that I was going to lose some damn good legionnaires, but it had to be done. We needed the time!

"Thanks to the Dark Wanker's involvement, I'm betting that this road they've cleared so far will be taken by the main force. Once they're all dead, you're to set up any traps you can, Denny," I ordered.

"Romanus, if you think it'll help, despite the tree cover and the risk, take two of the ships and use their cannons. The risk we take with those weapons is that they'll explode on even a single shot, and I don't want to use them, as we risk losing a ship, but...they can turn the tide.

"Hell, a well-placed shot can probably kill dozens of them alone, but possibly wait until the Trailmasters are dead. If they're buffing the column to move faster, you might get too many dodging? I don't know. This is your fight, Romanus; yours and Oren's."

"The second reason I won't be taking the Legion to these sites is Imperial Authority," I went on. "To put it simply, you know that if you have to face a war golem, you'll lose a great many. Well, if Oracle and I face them, we might be able to not only lose fewer, but we might also be able to capture the golem, even if they're hostile to us to begin with." I trailed off, shrugging.

"And the final reason?" Romanus persisted.

"We need the experience," I replied with a tired smile. "We've no time to grow stronger gradually; the only way I can do this, survive long enough to lead you all, to give you the home you all deserve, is to accept that every damn day is going to have to be a climb."

"It always is, if you want to reach the very top." Romanus agreed gravely. "Jax, I know this was said poorly in the past, when Alistor raised the possibility, but you are talking about facing a God. Perhaps loading the ships and aiming for another continent is an option we should consider," he said grudgingly.

I snorted, working to contain my annoyance, when Flux spoke up for me.

"Did you feel the Tower shake earlier, Romanus?" he asked calmly.

"I did." Romanus frowned. "Although, I had hoped the recent repairs would have lasted longer than…"

"That wasn't the Tower failing," Flux interrupted. "Jax reawakened the Gods. One of them took badly to the situation They found themselves in and threw a temper tantrum. Jax literally beat Her into submission and close to death. The Lady of Fire had to intervene to save Her sister's life.

"While facing a God is a terrible thing to consider having to do, and Goddess Tamat was clearly weakened at the time, if anyone is to have to face…the Dark Wanker…as Jax calls him, I will back our lord."

"You fought a *God*?" Romanus asked, stunned. I patted my pouch reflexively, answering with a slight smile. He caught the gesture, and while we didn't comment, his eyes were wide for a long moment before he grinned. "Well, we didn't start this, but it seems that it will come down to a fight, regardless. At least it will be one for the histories."

"How many chances do you get to have your name marked down in history as a Godslayer?" I asked him with a grin.

He grunted in amusement. "One point, however, Jax, and please, take this as it is meant; if you nearly killed the Lady of Shadows, Mistress of Assassins…in truth? For the love of the Empire, find a way to even the field between you and bury any bad blood. We cannot win the war if a minion of Hers guts you first."

"I know," I said flatly. "I…will."

"Pride is a hard thing to give up, Jax, but sometimes, it is necessary." Romanus rested a hand on my shoulder, smiling in understanding. "Also, you may remember we had a few discussions when we first met about proper comportment and speaking with authority?"

"I do…" I answered, eyeing him curiously.

"Well, I'm pleased my lessons hit home, as this meeting was that of a leader and a ruler. When you gave your orders, you did not request, you did not ask. You told. There are times when discussions are necessary and even highly valuable, but at times, action matters, as does the timing of it. You do well."

"Thank you," I said slowly, a faint smile lifting the edges of my mouth as I shut off the map. "Okay then, everyone, you have an hour. Bane, get your arse in gear and get the squad together, as well as Giint." I paused, then drew a deep breath, letting it out with a powerful exhalation. "And someone bring that damn bard," I growled. "He may have information on the area." Bane straightened and clapped his fist to his chest in salute, vanishing out of the door.

The others started to follow him, but I stopped Flux and bade him take a seat. Oren looked back, clearly wanting to know what was about to be said, when Cai grabbed him by an ear and half-dragged him out.

"You wish to speak with me, Jax?" Flux asked after a long handful of seconds passed in silence.

"Yes, and no," I said, sighing and internally acknowledging that Romanus was right. I damn well had to grow up and do what was best for the Empire and its people, and that meant swallowing my pride.

I drew in another deep breath, then I went down on one knee, pressed the knuckles of my right hand flat to the deck, and closed my eyes, pulling up the weave I used to communicate with Jenae.

While I usually used fire, I pulled up darkness instead, being extremely careful not to touch death, and I reached out tentatively, sending the call into the ether.

"Tamat, Lady of Shadows, I wish to speak to you. Will you honor me with a response?" I asked, and several heartbeats passed before the room seemed to dim, shadows lengthening around the edges, reaching towards me as a new presence entered.

"Eternal," came an ethereal voice. It whispered, rather than spoke, and seemed to move around, one minute beside me, then across the room. The way Flux jumped made it clear that he could hear Her moving around as well.

"You wish contact with me again so soon? I'm impressed by your bravery, if not your sense."

"I want to apologize," I said, rising to my feet slowly. "I was wrong to trespass in the realm of the Gods without invitation, and due to that choice, I was at least partially to blame for what happened. I wish to offer you a gift, as I have been told was once the custom when two parties were wronged?"

"Speak on." Tamat whispered, now clearly interested, where before, Her voice had been sour.

"I have instructed Flux," I said, gesturing to the astonished Mer, "to create a specialized group for the Empire under my authority. They are to become assassins, rogues, and spies. They will go where I cannot, kill and steal, and carry out all the clandestine operations that the Empire requires.

"My Lady of Fire and I accept that not all of those who swear fealty to me, and to the Empire, will wish to follow Her. With that in mind, I would offer you the first chance to recruit from their number, with my open blessing, provided that they are never to be used against the Empire or me."

My proposal was carefully phrased. I knew what I was doing and how dangerous playing this game was. I was sure She also knew what I was doing, but it would allow Her, and me, to save some face in the whole thing. Frankly, I needed every edge I could get.

The silence stretched out uncomfortably, and just as I opened my mouth to call out again, She spoke. I realized from the amused sound of Her voice that the bitch had been waiting for me to break first.

"Very well, Jax, Eternal, Scion of the Empire. You are a fool, but an honest one, at least. I accept your apology, and as I was not entirely blameless, I offer my own. I shall choose all those who please me, citizens of your faction of the Empire or no, but those who follow me shall know that they will lose all favor with me should they raise a hand against your faction during the next ten years. After that time, your faction is fair game, as it was long ago. Only you personally will be off-limits." There was pregnant pause while I struggled to consider the implications, knowing my companions were at risk if I accepted. Ultimately, I had to acknowledge that there would always be this possibility with assassins and their ilk.

"Very well, but bear in mind that any assassin who hunts down my people will be marked as a target by the Empire, and by *me,* " I warned. "So, if you want to keep them, I suggest you make damn sure they behave themselves as much as possible."

She didn't respond aloud, but I could feel it, the contempt for my reply hanging heavy in the air.

"I will give your people my personal attention for now," She said after another long pause. *"However, I have scores to settle, and each of my new blades will bring in much needed sustenance. I will require these blades to be given certain books and memories held by yourself, as well as some items recovered, items that are appropriate to their role.*

"I will inform your companion as to the items in your possession, and your map has been updated with three new locations. I recommend that you hurry, as a divine assassin would make short work of the Dark Legion's more...squishy...members." Abruptly, the sense of Her presence vanished, and Flux grunted, shaking his head.

"Jax, while I never fail to be impressed by your bravery, you know sticking your manhood in a meat grinder and cranking the handle just to see what happens won't end well, don't you?" Flux asked.

"Well, that's a needlessly horrible mental image." I winced.

"It's what it takes to get your attention. Please, Jax. Consider at least slightly before you do this in the future. It appears to have paid off well this time, and yes, Bane and several of the others will be deeply pleased with the opportunity this presents, but still...it could have gone badly just as easily." Still shaking his head, Flux rose to his feet and clapped a fist to his chest in salute before stalking out.

"Repairs are in hand, Jax, and I must agree with Flux; bravery tempered with luck is not a strategy that can be relied on in the long-term," Seneschal commented briefly, then the feeling of his presence faded away as well.

"Sometimes it has to be, lads," I muttered, pulling the map back up and poring over it, caught between a feeling of excitement that all the boring shit was done for a time and trepidation over what was to come.

CHAPTER SIXTEEN

I t was more like an hour and a half later before the ship, *Sigmar's Fist*, was ready to launch. The books had been given out and the various orders confirmed. Her hull was only half-converted, but apparently, she was already the fastest, and there was no reason that the golems couldn't work on her as she flew, as the numerous upgrades Oren was testing on her, with Giint's help, were ones that required a huge number of individual alterations.

As the ship wobbled into the air, the constant shuddering and swaying promising to make the entire crew vomit before long, Oren whooped in joy, and dozens of other voices rose to join his own.

"What the hell did you do, you mad bastard!" I shouted back to him, but he just laughed, waving me off as I cursed. Oracle and I made our way up to my squad, hearing the helmsman and the captain making constant adjustments.

"Asshole..." I growled as I joined the others on the deck. Thorn and her people were already working quickly and efficiently to repair, replace, and generally improve on our armor. I grinned involuntarily as she turned to face me.

"Lord Jax, please tell me that's not all of your armor," she said slowly, the missing cuirass and the heavily scarred and deeply cut vambraces being very obvious. The damaged greaves, the sabatons, all of it, didn't look much better. There was only one part of the armor that remained in decent condition, and that was the helm I pulled out of storage.

Helm of Imperial Right		Further Description *Yes*/*No*	

Details:		This helm was crafted to be worn by the Warden-Inquisitor of the Prax *"Glorious Retribution,"* and grants the following bonuses:
		    +5 to Wisdom
		    +5 to Perception
		
		Bonus Ability: Inquisition
		Once per day, at a cost of 100 health and mana, the wearer may demand an answer to a question. If the target refuses to answer, lies, or withholds information, they will feel the wrath of the Inquisition. It gives a bonus of +7 to resisting physical damage.	

Rarity:	**Magical:**	**Durability:**	**Charge:**
Legendary	Yes	99/100	1/1

"Jax, please!" Thorn practically begged, gazing at me in horror, as I pulled the remaining sections of armor out of my bag and passed them back to her. "Please tell me this is a joke!" she said in a small voice.

"I'm afraid not, Thorn, but if it helps, your armor kept me alive where lesser work would have failed," I pointed out. "The breastplate, well, I'm afraid I left it in the Tower when it was remodeling itself. I'm told it was absorbed. Sorry." I grimaced, wisely omitting the fact that it was practically useless and scrap metal by then.

"As to the helm, do you like it?" I asked, passing it to her. She caught it easily and examined it with a crestfallen expression.

"It is a work of art, my lord," she said sadly. "And it is far beyond my skill…" She broke off abruptly as Oracle took one of her massive, calloused hands and placed in it a red leatherbound book with gold lettering that covered the front. All work stopped as the other armorers stared on enviously. Thorn turned the book over and over in her hands, unable to speak.

"It's called 'True Silver, the Armorer's Love'," I said quietly. "I don't know more about it than that, except that True Silver can apparently be made from other ores that we have limited access to in the area, or in the Tower's storage. It's a level below Arcanium, admittedly, but its making was apparently lost long ago, according to the information I have. That book will make you and those you teach the only armorers in the Realm, as far as we know, who can work with it and create it." I reached up, resting one hand on her shoulder as she stared at me in shock.

"Thorn, I trust you to do this. I trusted that the armor you crafted would keep me safe out there, and it did. It took heavily enchanted weapons and powerful spells to do the damage you see. Anything less than your work, and I'd be dead. You earned this book, and more, when the time comes." I smiled and patted her shoulder, withdrawing my hand.

"Oh, and Jenae told me about the work required to get you a magma forge. Yes, the Goddess of Fire, the Patron of Smiths, and I discussed you *specifically*. You won't be getting it for a while, but there are plans in the works, so get ready, because it's coming. Now, do you have anything for me?" She gaped at me, her mouth flopping open and closed like that of a fresh-landed fish.

"Tell you what, take a minute," I chuckled, as I instead pulled the dagger, Death's Kiss, and handed it to Bane, as well as the twin swords, Hunger and Thirst, giving them back to Tang. The pair looked shocked, but I explained that they needed decent weapons, and that these were theirs to keep, waving their thanks away and turning back to Thorn. "Well, Thorn?" I asked cheerfully.

"I…uh…I…" she stammered, clutching the book between her massive hands. I could see the effort she was expending to not damage it, while holding onto it for dear life at the same time.

"Legionnaire!" Yen barked, and Thorn jumped, spinning around to stare at the speculatores, who grinned back at her unrepentantly.

There was a brief pause where Thorn wiped…dust…from her face and coughed, slipping the book into her belt pouch, then turned back to me.

"Yes…well, thank you, Lord Jax," she whispered, then cleared her throat, going on in a much stronger voice. "I have some parts for you, including a spare cuirass, but this time, please don't lose it; it's the last we have. I have a set of vambraces as well…I think…" She tugged the lid off a box, sifting through it and shoving it aside in annoyance, searching the next.

"Wait!" I said, suddenly remembering. "I got some from the Prax...now where..." I mumbled, rifling through bags, until I finally pulled them free. They'd been no use to me in the Prax, after I'd lost one of my goddamn arms, but now they were worth looking over, at least.

Vambraces of Imperial Right		Further Description *Yes/No*	
Details:		These Vambraces were crafted to be worn by the Warden-Inquisitor of the Prax Glorious Retribution, and grant the following bonuses: +5 to Dexterity +5 to Perception **Bonus Ability: Memory** Once per day, an inquisitor may shed a drop of blood of their choice upon the Plates of Question, and they will see the last sight the owner of that blood saw. It gives a bonus of +5 to resisting physical damage.	
Rarity:	**Magical:**	**Durability:**	**Charge:**
Legendary	Yes	100/100	1/1

I resolved to read the frantically blinking notifications soon, as I'd been putting them off, but it needed to be done.

"Okay, so the vambraces are compatible with standard Legion armor," Thorn mumbled, turning one of them this way and that, checking out the method used to fold the metal and more. "Maybe if I..." She rubbed one section thoughtfully before Yen elbowed her. The huge half-orc glared at the speculatores briefly before she swallowed shamefacedly at being so easily distracted and handed the vambrace back to me.

"Well, yes, that's fine, Jax," she said quickly. "The cuirass will be identical to the one you had last time. I see you need to replace the greaves as well, since they're pretty scarred and twisted now." As she continued assessing my damaged items, she unpacked gear from crates and checked the sizing against me, making small alterations as she went.

The captain of *Sigmar's Fist* interrupted the outfitting once, confirming that we were less than an hour from the first point on the map I'd given them. Thorn and her people stepped up their pace, hurrying to replace or repair the missing sections of armor before landing.

While they worked, so did I, reading through dozens and dozens of notifications. The vast majority were ones that I automatically dismissed, minor updates about my weapons, spells, or actions like running and jumping or leveling up.

Simple actions, like jumping, didn't gain an evolution until level twenty, for some reason, so I'd never had to choose anything for them, but that time was fast approaching.

Once I'd cleared away the crap notifications, I finally got to the good ones.

Citadel

Congratulations!

**Through hard work and perseverance,
you have increased your stats by the following:**

Agility +1

Charisma +1

Constitution +2

Endurance +1

Intelligence +1

Luck +2

Continue to train and learn to increase this further.

Adding those points to the ones granted by my new helm and vambraces meant I'd taken a serious jump in capability, and I could damn well feel it. Before, the word had been normal. But now, if I concentrated, it seemed to almost move in slow motion even without using my mana overdrive skill. It was a far weaker effect, obviously, and it needed me to concentrate, as I'd grown accustomed damn quickly to the new way of seeing and doing things, but hell yes.

You completed the Quest given to you by the Goddess Jenae: Bring Home the Bacon.

The Goddess Jenae has commanded you to retrieve all you can from those that skulk and raid the corpse of the Empire. Take your rightful place as their lord and bring back that which you need to repair the seat of your power, the Great Tower.

Recover Magical Artifacts and Technologies: 38/?
Retrieve Manastones: 327/100
Recruit Additional Citizens: 937/100
Recruit Skilled Crafters: 31/100
Recruit a Tower Healer: 1/1

Bonuses will be given for exceeding these numbers.

Reward: Basic functionality of the Great Tower, Rune of Fire, 250,000xp

Bonus Reward: While the crafters' section of the quest was failed, you did manage to recruit almost 900% of the additional citizens required to complete the quest. Therefore, you have been awarded the following by the Goddess Jenae:

- 1x Bonus additional structure in the Great Tower
- 1x Alchemical ingredient: Fireblossom
- 1x Notable location: Harvesting Grounds

*

You have made progress in a Quest: Bring back the Old Gods.

Bring back the Old Gods to displace Nimon and return balance to the realm. Aid each to find a champion that suits Their aspect, and spread knowledge of the Gods to bring about a new Golden Age

Gods Awakened: 9/9
Champions Chosen: 1/9
Reward: Blessings of the Gods, 100,000xp, Random local notable locations identified

I nodded in satisfaction as the knowledge of the Rune of Fire filled my mind, as well as extra tiny details, such as the way that angling it, the depth of the carving, the filling of the carving, all of them would change the effect. I was interested for a minute, before noting the complexity and actively moving on.

I sighed in relief when the damn thing finally stopped flashing, and I checked over the final details, reviewing my character sheet and assigning five points I had from my level up into Strength, as it was one of the three areas I was notably starting to leave behind, and two into Endurance, as running out of stamina was a constant concern.

It went against decisions I'd made earlier, as I damn well knew I could increase them through training and exercise, but where things like my Agility and Dexterity were rocketing ahead, my Strength was plodding, and I couldn't afford to let it fall too far behind.

Name: Jax Amon				
Titles: Strategos: 5% boost to damage resistance, Fortifier: 5% boost to defensive structure integrity, Champion of Jenae: One search for hidden knowledge every 24 hours				
Class: Spellsword > Justicar > Champion of Jenae > Imperial Magekiller > Imperial Justicar			Renown: Imperial Scion, Lord of Dravith	
Level: 23			Progress: 144,024/510,000	
Patron: Jenae, Goddess of Fire and Exploration			Points to Distribute: 0 Meridian Points to Invest: 0	
Stat	Current points	Description	Effect	Progress to next level
Agility	43	Governs dodge and movement.	+330% maximum movement speed and reflexes, (+10% movement in darkness, -20% movement in daylight)	31/100
Charisma	27 (22)	Governs likely success to charm, seduce, or threaten	+170% success in interactions involving other beings	19/100
Constitution	52 (47)	Governs health and health regeneration	1020 health, regen 69.3 points per 600 seconds, (+10% regen due to soul bond, -20 health due to soul bond, each point invested now worth 20 health)	59/100
Dexterity	62 (57)	Governs ability with weapons and crafting success	+520% to weapon proficiency, +52% to the chances of crafting success	39/100
Endurance	49 (46)	Governs stamina and stamina regeneration	980 stamina, regen 39 points per 30 seconds, (each point now worth 20 stamina)	8/100

Intelligence	60	Governs base mana and number of spells able to be learned	580 mana, spell capacity: 33 (31 + 2 from items), (-20 mana due to soul bond)	89/100
Luck	25	Governs overall chance of bonuses	+15% chance of a favorable outcome	4/100
Perception	48 (38)	Governs ranged damage and chance to spot traps or hidden items	+380% ranged damage, +38% chance to spot traps or hidden items	58/100
Strength	39 (36)	Governs damage with melee weapons and carrying capacity	+29 damage with melee weapons, +290% maximum carrying capacity	67/100
Wisdom	43 (33)	Governs mana regeneration and memory	+495% mana recovery, 6.45 points per minute, 330% more likely to remember things, (+50% increased mana regeneration from essence core)	87/100

I needed to try and balance out my build, I knew that, but damn, it just plain galled me to put points into things like Charisma. Especially when I'd *never* been lacking in willing bedpartners, and now I had *Oracle*, so I'd never need to worry about that shit again…

There was more to Charisma, I knew there was, as memories from Amon slid across, trying to fill my mind; times he'd intimidated, or in the early days, charmed his way through problems, but that just wasn't me.

Luck, though…yeah, I definitely needed that. I was fully absorbed in considering my future build when Thorn rapped on my cuirass, causing it to ring and making me feel like a bell.

I blinked in shock and frowned at her. Seeing the chagrined expression on her face, I quickly smoothed my own, realizing she'd been trying to get my attention for a while.

"I'm sorry, my lord," she started apologetically.

"It's okay, Thorn. I was just lost in thought, that's all. What's up?" I asked, reassuring her with a forced smile.

She gestured to the visible ruin in the distance that jutted from the top of a hill nearby, vines, small shrubs, and trees covering most of it. "I think we're here."

"Waystation Three," I whispered, then moved to the railing to look both behind and ahead.

The captain had brought us in low, as I'd ordered, the sure knowledge that the Dark Legion was a matter of hours ahead of us somewhere. If they saw a ship landing and working on something, they'd at the very least send a contingent to check it out.

"Get us down!" I called up to the captain, who nodded and spoke to the helmsman. The rest of the group finished any last minute gear changes and gathered together.

"Okay, people, that looks like it'll be the next Waystation. It's in roughly the right area, anyway. It's not far from the Dark Legion's marching route, so the captain is going to drop us off and move further to the west," I told them, having sorted this with him already. "Once we've done what we came here to do, we can signal him in and get the hell onto the next site. We're literally going to clear and claim as much as we can, as quickly as we can. Any questions?"

"I have a few," Yen said quietly, "but the first and foremost has to be about *him*."

"Wha…fuck," I grunted, cutting myself off as I realized what I'd missed before. In the rush to get moving and get our armor sorted, I'd totally forgotten about the goddamn bard, who'd been sitting quietly off to one side. "He's here for any local knowledge he might have. Grizz, Bane, cut his throat if he starts playing silly fuckers," I said grimly as I took a knee in front of Ronin I spoke quickly but clearly as *Sigmar's Fury* turned in a low arc, the captain picking out the best landing spot for his ship.

"Okay, you've recovered enough that, if you're really dumb, you're going to try to escape or use any class skills and abilities you've got, right away, so let's make this very simple." I met the eyes of the still gagged and bound bard.

"I'm going to give you a choice. First, you can tell me what you know about the area and any ruins in it, then you can fuck off. As long as you head west from here, you'll avoid a large band of Dark Legionnaires coming this way. Once you hit the lake, you can go wherever you want; just stay out of our way." I watched his eyes for a hint of the choice he'd pick.

"Second, you decide you don't want to run, and you'd rather be useful and live somewhere that you'll actually be safe-ish. You swear an Oath to me, the same one that everyone swears. I give you an order to not use your abilities on any Citizens, beyond entertaining or helping them. I know that's a bit vague, but otherwise, you can't really do anything, from what I understand. The kicker is this: if you choose this path, then I find out you've seduced someone unwilling, steal, or otherwise fuck with my people, I give you to *him*." I pointed to Bob, who hulked motionlessly nearby, watching us all.

The look the bard gave me was full of fear, and I believed it. Bob was terrifying to behold, at the best of times; his Naga skull and heavily layered bone-plate armor made him look like some kind of animated death knight from hell. Covered in dried blood and broken fragments as he was, he only looked scarier.

I'd not been able to fix him yet, as there hadn't been anywhere near the amount of bone required, so I'd resolved to do it once we cleaned out the nearest ruin.

"Choose quickly. I recommend you don't try fucking about, as if you do, one of us will kill you," I assured Ronin, smiling.

He nodded again, and I untied the gag and removed it, giving him water when he croaked out a whisper that was unintelligible.

Bane freed his hands, and the bard clung to the cup, draining it in seconds, prompting me to refill it again and again. When, at last, he'd drank his fill, he regarded the towering, armored figures that surrounded him, smiling hesitantly at all of us.

"Look…I think we got off on the wrong foot," he whispered roughly before clearing his throat and going on in a stronger voice. "As I said when we first met, my name is Ronin, and I'm a bard, yeah. I was…I just wanted to live with my friends, you know?" His eyes filled with tears. "We heard about the Tower, and yeah, okay, we were going to rob it, but we didn't know you were here or that it was yours. All we were trying to do was survive, okay?"

"And that's why you get this choice, Ronin," I explained as the ship slowed, the engines humming as she came in for the landing. "Oracle read your mind; she knows that you're a shifty fucker, but that you've not done anything else. Believe me, had you been using your abilities to bed unwilling partners, we'd not be talking now.

"Here's the deal: tell me what you know about the area, and we let you go. Or, you swear the Oath, you get to live in the Tower, you'll be as safe as any of us are, you'll get paid, and you can use your abilities to help us all. Choose." I turned my gaze out to the ruins higher up the slope as the ship settled onto a flat area about halfway down on the far side from where we thought the Dark Legion might pass.

"This Oath," he asked, licking his lips nervously. "What...?"

"Here," Oracle said gently, pushing the offer to him. He read as I stood up, my knee creaking from being down on it for so long.

"You've got a few minutes to think," I told him, striding over to the captain and giving him instructions on the signal and what to do in certain circumstances, including if we vanished.

When I returned, most of the others had left the ship and were getting warmed up on the grass by the side of the ship, while Grizz, Bane, and Bob still watched over the bard.

"I'll swear," he said promptly when I returned to him, but rather than going straight ahead and swearing, he took a deep breath and met my eyes. "Can I ask for something, though?"

"Depends on what it is." I said slowly.

"I want to go with you."

I started in surprise. "Why the hell would you want that?"

"I need to level; that's why my crew was out here. Hell, I *really* need to level, and you need me to, as well." He smiled nervously. "Look, you're at war, right? I don't know what you know about bards, beyond what everyone says, but we're not all dicks.

"There's a lot more of us around than people realize; we just specialize in different classes," he said in a rush, taking a deep breath. "Look, this isn't easy to talk about, okay? We're oathbound to not speak about this unless we're commanded to by the proper authorities. So, in a minute, when I swear the Oath, I'm going to need you to do that.

"And by 'proper authorities,' I mean an actual member of the Imperial House or their representative." He broke off awkwardly, staring intently at me and waiting to make sure I got it. "That's meant to be so rare that its basically the same as saying 'never,' as we know history, and the truth.

"That's part of our calling, or at least it is for a true bard. We know that the vast majority of nobles have no authority in the Empire, beyond that they have wealth, sharp steel, and will probably have us killed if they don't like our haircuts. They claim they're nobles, but they're *not*; most of them, anyway. You've claimed the continent, and the Realm itself has acknowledged you.

"I mean, even the death God refers to you as being part of the Empire, so it *has* to be true. So, I want in, okay? I want to be the first true bard in centuries, and I want the chance to redeem my class from all those damn scumbags out there. You think I don't know how untrusted we are? You think I *want* to be like this? Hated and suspected?"

"Screwing your way through every town and village you can?" Grizz interrupted, grinning.

"Hey, fuck you, legionnaire!" Ronin snapped, glaring up at Grizz. "I did what I had to!"

"Oh yeah, bet it was a terrible life," Grizz retorted, still grinning.

"You have no idea," Ronin grated out through gritted teeth. "Please, Lord Jax, when I found out who and what you were, I was going to escape the Tower, that's true, but not to leave. I was going to enter in the front door, make sure you knew who and what I was. In truth, I mean; not what everyone thinks we are! I didn't want to be found skulking, but…"

"But you couldn't help taking advantage of a kid?" Grizz slipped in, and Ronin struggled to get to his feet, staring daggers at the massive legionnaire.

"No! I was dying, and he helped me. He found me when I was trying to crawl out, terrified and diseased, and I warned him off. I told him I was dying and to stay away. You know what he did? He helped me anyway.

"He found me a goddamn healing potion and hid me when I asked him not to tell anyone about me. I wiped his memories of me each day, and he still found me every time and tried to help me. So, yeah, I started teaching him, because he's got a hell of a gift, and I swore an Oath to teach those that I could, just like my master did for me!"

"Interesting," I said, looking to Oracle. "Your master, you said?"

"Yes. Look, give me a chance, okay? I'll swear; just command me, then I can answer, but unless you command me, I can't tell you all of it, right? It's complicated," Ronin pled, looking from one to another of us desperately.

"Fine. We don't have time for this right now. You want to see what it's like with us? Swear the Oath, and you can join us for the day. After that, well, we'll see," I agreed grudgingly.

"I swear to obey Lord Jax and those he places over me; I will serve to the best of my ability, speak no lie to him when commanded otherwise, and treat all other citizens as family.

I will work for the greater good, being a shield to those who need it, a sword for those who deserve it, and a warden to the night.

"I will stand with my family, helping one another to reach the light, until the hour of my death or my Lord releases me from my oath.

"Lastly, I will not be a dick!"

As soon as the words were out of his mouth, I nodded and responded.

"I, Lord Jax, do swear to protect and lead you, to be the shield that protects you and yours from the darkness, and the sword that avenges that which cannot be saved. As the Tower grows in strength, so shall you."

I took a deep breath and augmented my return Oath. "I order you, by the Oath, to tell me the truth, and to live by the spirit of the Oath you have just sworn, not just the letter." Ronin started to shiver, then grunt as something happened to him, something related to the Oath, followed by taking a deep breath and standing up straighter and relaxing, as the ropes that bound him fell away, thumping to the floor.

Grizz and Bane tensed, but as Ronin straightened, he lifted one hand casually and revealed the slim blade braced between his fingers.

"Whoa, guys, relax!" He smiled. "I'm one of you now, right?"

"Not even close," Grizz growled, making his face drop.

"Ronin, I order you to tell me if you have any kind of hidden plans that will harm me or mine," I said, and he coughed, shaking as he tried not to answer, until the Oath forced the words out.

"I have a plan to use your status to achieve several goals that, while beneficial for you overall, will involve putting you and others in severe danger," Ronin said through strained lips before sagging and trying to catch his breath. "Damn, please give me a chance to tell you properly. If you say it wrong, you could make a request for breakfast into a threat, so let me tell you the story my own way, okay?"

"Tell us on the way," I said, marching down the gangplank and waving to the captain to take the ship to hide.

As soon as we were off, the gangplank was pulled up and the engines started to fire, the air pressure forcing us all away as we started up the side of the hill.

"Uh, Jax?" Arrin asked carefully. "What's he doing with us?"

"He's got some information for me, apparently; some big secret. Says he wants to join us, and I don't have time to fuck about, so he's getting the chance." Then I grinned at Arrin. "But that means he's actively asking to join in training as well." Arrin winced, then grinned evilly before leaning in closer and dropping his voice.

"You know Lydia has a problem with him, right?" he asked me softly. I nodded, making him nod in return as he fell back.

"Ronin, this is the team," I said, lifting my voice as we started to walk up the hill, and I pulled out my naginata. "Everyone, this is Ronin. He has some information for me and can apparently help us, but before we go any further...Ronin! Do you bear anyone in my team any ill will, and do you intend to harm them at all?"

"No!" Ronin said, the single word torn from him.

"Glad to hear it. This is the way things are here." I began pointing at people. "This is Oracle. She's my companion, and my lover; do not piss her off. This is Lydia," I said gesturing to the Valkyrie next. "She's my second in command and leads this squad. I'm going to leave any disciplinary issues to her, and she hates bards, so I really recommend you behave." From there, I named the others, including Ty'Baronn, Jian's summoned Demon. The Demon hissed at Ronin, then spat when Ronin took a step too close to him, his lips curling upwards in contempt to reveal sharply pointed teeth.

"Lord Jax, maybe we could talk, somewhere..."

"Nope. No time, no need." I cut him off. "I don't hide things from my people; not these, anyway. And we're going to be too busy soon to talk, so say your piece and get it over with." I said, squinting up at the ruins a hundred meters or so ahead.

They'd been conspicuously barren, a mere smattering of vines and small bushes covering them, with only a low line of obviously worked rock to show it had ever been anything more than a bare hill in the past.

"What's that smell?" Arrin asked suddenly, sniffing the air.

"I don't know…it's familiar, but…" Yen frowned. I followed suit and sniffed, getting a scent like vanilla and strawberries and feeling myself relax slightly. I smiled at the memories that scent conjured—of summer and sweets, and one feisty ex whose lips always had that taste.

As we got closer, though, three things became obvious. First, the normal grass, moss, and other plants ended a few meters away from the remains of the structure, with a bare ring of dead dirt around the edges on all sides. Secondly, the structure had appeared from the air to have simply been overgrown, but now that we were closer and approaching at ground level, it was clear that at some point, there'd been a fight here. Craters marked the area leading up to a low stone lintel, with a partially open door beneath it, leading inside.

Lastly, as we closed the remaining distance, weapons at the ready and wondering what was going on, the third detail was pointed out by, of all people, Ronin.

"You guys…uh, you know that the only plant that's here is the same one, right?"

"What?" asked Yen.

"Those bushes, the vines, the trees; they're all the same plant. There's no other plants on the hilltop?" he offered, a little more clearly.

I frowned, looking closely at them, and realizing that what looked like trees were, in fact vines that had grown upwards, pushing all their offshoots together to create an illusion of a tree. Then I noticed the other thing about the entrance:

Drag marks led into it.

CHAPTER SEVENTEEN

"What the hell?" I muttered, pointing my naginata at the drag marks, just as Yen screamed, and all hell broke loose.

"Get down!" she cried, shouldering me aside as Grizz jumped forward, slashing down with his sword in time to catch a vine that seemed to leap up, twisting towards him.

I staggered and swung my naginata as a vine that had been laying by the side of the too-convenient path we'd followed suddenly lifted, snakelike, into the air and struck at me.

"Yateveo!" bellowed Grizz, and Tang swore sulphurously nearby.

"What?" I slashed my naginata sideways and drew a long cut through the vine's bark-like coating.

"It's a Yateveo!" Yen screeched, starting to cast as I felt Oracle do the same.

"It's a fucking devil plant that tries to kill everything else!" Grizz shouted.

A flare of magic blasted out from Lydia as she activated her Iceshield, followed a few seconds later by Grizz whooping and activating his. Some peculiarity of the magic, a combination of the fact they were identical spells and the subconscious will of the caster when casting them, meant that the second spell formed a bubble attached to the first, giving us a short-lived dome shield. The vines that were flashing forward smashed aside, giving us a small space to breathe. Panting, we looked around furiously, finding the frantically writhing vines on all sides.

"What the hell is that?" I snarled.

Oracle shouted something, and a flash a few feet outside of our barrier showed the unfurling of Cleansing Fire, which immediately started burning a path clear.

"It's a Yateveo," Tang repeated, before being interrupted by Ronin.

"A Yateveo is a plant, a particularly nasty one that doesn't feed off the ground very well. Instead, it drinks blood. It basically kills the entire area if it's left to grow long enough. I'd guess from the size that this one is about fifty to sixty years old. According to the tales, and the reports, it should have a central bulb; it'd be at the middle of the nest. Kill that, and you kill the whole plant," Ronin rattled off quickly.

I regarded him with surprise, then glanced back out through the warped ice of the shield that Grizz and Lydia had cast around us all. I inspected the vine monster as best I could, observing the way the vines moved back quickly, staying well clear of the patch of Cleansing Fire.

"Any weaknesses?" I asked, trying to use my Greater Examine on the creature and getting nothing.

"Fire," he said quickly. "Ice works as well, but it's slower. Fire is its anathema; well, and death magic, but you know, that's the case for all life." He shrugged, trailing off.

"Well, I'd say we wait a few minutes, then get out there and kick ass." I caught sight of Jian at that point, grimly holding both scythes ready, with his

Demon standing behind him. I had a momentary pang of guilt over giving the twin swords to Tang, when they were precisely the kind of weapons that Jian would have loved and had designed his build around using. But the legionnaire was both more experienced and more deadly with them, striking from stealth. Besides, Jian loved flying the ship, so I'd consider that when it came to his birthday.

"Okay, you agree with that?" I asked Yen. She grunted then finished her spell. A massive trio of Flamespears grew in the air above the Iceshields, then flashed out, one after the other. They slammed down, blasting bits of broken vines and smoldering bark through the air. Satisfied, she took a deep breath and straightened, nodding quickly.

"Yes; I've heard of them before, but never fought one myself. They're unusual to find above ground."

"Usually found in cave systems, and around deep wells underground; they feed on the unwary drawn to the water," Ronin rattled off as though reading from a textbook. I looked at him in surprise. "I'm a bard, for fuck's sake! Look, I'll explain it all later–you know, when we're not in mortal danger–but the Bardic College has one overriding impetus and drive, okay? And despite what people might think, it's not about getting laid!" The last was called out along with a scowl aimed at Grizz, and I couldn't help but chuckle. "Can I use my buffs?" he asked, and I nodded slowly. "Oh, thank God. I was worried I'd get stabbed if I tried." He started to chant, and I felt the magic reaching out.

I tensed, watching him intently, until I forced myself to relax, reminding myself that he'd sworn the Oath and that he'd have to be fucking nuts to risk doing something that would anger us all.

Buff: Glory!

Effect: Health regeneration is boosted by 5% for 60 minutes. Strength is increased by one point for 60 minutes.

*

Buff: Aura of Invulnerability

Effect: Creates a weak shield that will deflect or absorb up to 50 points of damage. Any damage done inside the effective radius will be taken from the pool of defense first. Lasts 15 minutes

*

Buff: Speedster

Effect: Increases Dexterity and Agility by 5 points for all friendlies who hear this song for so long as the song is played.

"Shit, that's impressive," I admitted, reading over the details as they appeared.

He quirked a smile while continuing to chant. He took up drumming his hands on his thighs along with the beat and spoke quickly before going back to chanting.

"If I could get my damn lute back, I could do more, then I wouldn't have to sing constantly," he interjected. I snorted, gesturing to Bane, who sighed and pulled it out of his bag, handing it back. The Bard took it with a grin, tightening the strings and starting to play.

More buffs appeared, and I felt both relaxed and full of energy as the Iceshield began to die away, the multiple vines slamming into the frozen barrier wearing it down quickly, even if they did pull back with frost damage each time.

"Okay, people, as soon as the ice breaks, I want a run for the entrance."

"For!?!" squeaked Ronin. I frowned at him as his fingers slipped, and a series of discordant notes echoed out, making the buffs die away.

He swallowed hard and returned to playing while I started speaking again.

"As I was saying, we rush the entrance. We need to secure the site; if there's some fucking vine monster in there, then that's fine. It just means it'll be a single monster we need to kill."

"Makes a nice change, really," Lydia agreed as she squinted out at the frantically battering vines. "Yer remember tha Goblins?" she asked Jian and Bane, who both snorted a bitter laugh.

"Yeah, they were a pain," Jian muttered.

"Took days to get all the bits out of my hair, no matter how much I washed it, you know?" Arrin added in, and I caught the look of horror on Ronin's face.

"What's wrong?" I asked. "You used to adventure with others; what the hell did you expect?"

"Well, yeah, but you know…we used to…well, run away a lot," he replied shakily. "A Yateveo is kinda a big thing." He was abruptly cut off by Grizz, who started to laugh, a laugh which was quickly picked up by others in the rapidly weakening shield.

"What level are ye?" Lydia asked him suspiciously.

"Eleven," he admitted in a small voice.

"Hey, Bob!" I called, looking up at the silent behemoth. "You want to hang back a bit and help protect Mr. Squishy here, please?" Bob lumbered forward and stared down at Ronin, who swallowed and looked at me beseechingly.

"It's for your own good," I told him, shaking my head. "Okay…Oracle, renew Cleansing Fire outside in ten seconds, please. Yen, three Flamespears, one after another, to burn our path clear to the entrance, then you're behind me. Tang, Bane, lead the way, make sure there's no traps. Arrin, middle. Get ready to light them up. Lydia, you're with me, right behind the scouts. Grizz, Jian, you bring up the back.

"Giint, Bob, stay in the middle with Ronin," I ordered, getting nods, affirmatives, and anticipatory grins back from the group. "Well, let's go fuck up this thing's Tuesday!" I called out cheerfully, and I felt the dip as Oracle started channeling our mana. Yen mumbled at the exact same moment.

Just as we were about to start forward, a glow lit in the corner of my vision. I spun, gaping at Ty'Baronn, who'd set his feet and was blatantly powering himself up for a strike.

"No!" I snapped, stepping in front of him. He recoiled, then relaxed and allowed his mana to dissipate before snarling back at me.

"I don't serve you, mortal!" he snapped. "I listen out of courtesy…but…" I interrupted him by grabbing him by the throat and glaring into his eyes, resting the tip of my naginata against his throat.

"You will damn well listen, you little shit, or I'll slaughter you and make a fucking Demon-skin rug for my quarters! I told you last time, you save that blast for when I tell you!" I growled into his face.

He snarled back, his eyes starting to glow bright red as lines of power snaked up his horns, forming the outline of the disc that he'd used to launch the plasma attack in the Prax.

"Last chance," I warned, placing the naginata's tip against the underside of his chin and channeling a little ice into it.

"Die, mortal!" he snarled as his eyes flared wider, then he screamed in pain. His mana was ripped from him, the skin darkening and drying as it seemed to age a hundred years and more in a few short seconds, the almost-cast Ability being stripped of mana as well.

I stopped myself just as I was about to ram the naginata upwards, gaping at the dying creature in shock. He whimpered, turning his head and reaching one suddenly frail hand out to…Jian.

"I warned you what would happen!" Jian snarled at the Demon. "I warned you again and again! I serve *HIM*, and you serve *ME!*"

"Master…please…" Ty'Baronn whispered, his flesh desiccating more and more by the second as he was reduced to a husk of his former self.

"I told you! I told you over and over!" Jian repeated, clearly furious and ready to kill the creature himself.

"We have to go!" Oracle shouted, her Cleansing Fire spell unfurling beyond the Iceshield and forcing the vines aside as they crisped and smoldered.

"Last chance," I snapped at the Demon, dropping him on the floor, now reduced to the size of an Imp. Jian leaned down and quietly hissed something at the creature. He nodded frantically, letting out a gasp as Jian released the mana he'd pulled in, letting him feed on it again.

The Demon let out a sound that was half a groan of pain and half a moan of the filthiest pleasure before unfurling from the fetal position he'd curled into.

He looked like shit, significantly smaller and weaker, and somehow more…real. The way he had looked before had seemed impressive, but it felt like something was off, always. I'd put it down to the damn thing being a denizen of another realm and just being, well, fucking magical.

Now he looked much more real, and I growled out my discovery before I realized I'd spoken.

"It was a fucking illusion!" I heard myself say, and Ty'Baronn flinched, fuming up at me, then flinched away again from my gaze.

He was the same creature, but simply smaller, weaker, and clearly a hell of a lot older, I realized. I turned away from him, staring ahead at the flicking, frantically reaching tentacles.

"He can't use that beam weapon now, can he?" I asked Jian, already knowing the answer.

"No; it'll take him a few days to recover from what I did, I think…besides, I'm going to need time to 'talk' to him."

"Good luck with that," I told him absently, recognizing the low fury and embarrassment in Jian's voice. "Remember, you've still got that other book to use at some point," The resulting whimper from Ty'Baronn was audible to all of us.

"Shield's failing!" grunted Grizz, followed a half second later by Lydia saying the same.

"Yen?" I asked, and saw her lips moving as she whispered out the last few syllables before opening her eyes wide. I started as I saw something I'd never noticed before. Her eyes were glowing, the pupils ringed with flames that flared and popped, rotating around the central irises.

She nodded, clearly straining to hold the Flamespears back, and I glanced around, verifying that everyone was ready, except for Ronin, who was clearly about to shit a brick, and Ty'Baronn, who looked like he'd faint at any second.

"Fuck's sake," I muttered. "Bob, carry the little shit, will you!" I ordered, and he reached out, sweeping the diminished Demon up in a single enormous, claw-tipped hand.

"Yen, go!" I ordered, and as she threw her right hand forward, a single spear flew, followed by a second at the next gesture, then a third, when she slumped, panting hard.

"Go!" I shouted again, matching action to words as I sprinted at the wall of the Iceshield. I winced as I closed on it, changing the mana racing through my naginata from ice to fire and feeling the surge of heat radiating from the weapon. The shield fractured apart, cascading to the ground in a thousand pieces that shimmered from reality before they reached it. We all raced forward, the buffs that Ronin had cast unexpectedly vanishing as his fingers struck discordant notes. The terrified bard slipped in his panic, being shoved forward bodily by Bob.

We continued to sprint for the opening, feet scrambling over the loose dirt as the vines reeled from the impact of the spells.

At a series of grunts from the others, I swung at a vine that struck a pointed tip at me, aimed at my ankle. The tip of the naginata flashed through the vine, severing it a few inches behind the head and forcing the remaining section to yank back in pain as the hiss of the superheated blade passing through sounded in the air.

I pumped my arms and legs, rushing forward. My blade flashed out, wheeling, dipping, and rolling in arcs as I sliced free entire sections of the plant effortlessly. I grinned inside my helmet at how convenient it was to find out about the plant's weakness to fire.

A whoosh made me glance to the left as a quintet of Magic Missiles flashed past, blasting into the base of a particularly thick vine that had clearly decided the ruin was not open to visitors today, as it tried to seal the door.

The impact of the missiles, one after another, caused a small hole that rapidly grew with each additional impact, until the vine thrashed weakly and snapped off, crashing to the ground as other tendrils tried to keep us back.

"Well...looks like that Cleansing Fire likes us after all!" Grizz shouted over to me as he raced across the runic circle of the casting, unharmed, then jumped into the air, slashing down with all his might to carve through another thick vine that had been aiming for the door.

"Thankfully!" Bane yelled in agreement.

"Well, we needed to know!" I called back, slashing my weapon overhead and dropping to the ground, sliding as a trio of vines tried to take me down. Braced in anticipation, the blade cut effortlessly through the green and brown vines.

I dug my left foot in and popped upright, my momentum helping me along as I ran at the doorway, now only a handful of meters ahead. The flicker of a stealthed Bane slipped in, Lydia on his heels, with me following her.

The inside of the ruin was a mess; the roof and walls were bowing under the weight of the vines, only some of which were mobile, thankfully. Several stones had recently fallen, leaving a liberal scattering of dirt strewn across the floor. There was a clear path through the debris and dirt, though, complete with drag marks, and we sprinted ahead, following those.

The first intersection was clear, if tight, but when we tried to follow the drag marks, taking a right, there was an almighty creak and groan from somewhere up ahead. The vines retracted, and a handful of seconds later, before we could make it through, a section of the roof collapsed. It left us all coughing and waving the dust and dirt free of the air as we skidded to a halt, looking in dismay at the fresh cave-in.

"Well, does...this mean...we all go back...to the Tower?" Ronin asked hopefully, gasping for breath as he staggered to a halt nearby.

"Nope," I said, examining the structure and orienting myself. "Back to the last intersection; take a right, and there should be stairs." I figured they'd have built the waystations to simple specifications in the days when they'd made this.

We set off running again, ignoring the muttered complaints from Ronin and the yelps of pain from him when Bob, responding to a mental nudge from me, clipped him across the back of the head and pointed to the lute he was carrying without playing again.

The music started back up, if a little shakily, and a handful of seconds later, the buffs kicked in again.

The stairs were, thankfully, right where we'd expected. While the passages were tight, there were signs that the structure had been cleared out in the past and shored up.

The plant left us alone as we went deeper, clearly hoping we'd leave it alone in return. Less than ten minutes later, our group–much filthier after having to crawl through a section that had collapsed, with Bob digging it out in relatively short order–came to a halt in a large, open room.

The room was full of broken boxes, and at some point, someone had tried to pry the giant diamonds from several of the golems that stood in slumber along one wall. Fortunately for us, they'd failed miserably, merely leaving scratches in the stone that made up their bodies.

I grinned as the others started to relax. Bane walked to the wall opposite the golems and let loose with his worldsense in a powerful *thrum* that made everyone's teeth ache, before turning and nodding to me.

The room was solid, and there were surprisingly no signs of the vines, making me guess that it had taken root in one of the higher rooms and started to feed from there, having no interest in the deeper locations, as no food had ever come from that direction.

"You're in for a surprise!" I whispered, directing it at the plant as I strode across the room, giving out orders.

"Grizz, Jian, Lydia, secure the hallway. Arrin, Yen, you're in here; rest and recover your mana. I'm going to need it soon. Bob, get ready, as you're gonna have to do the heavy lifting, buddy. Giint, come join Bane and me. Tang, keep watch," I ordered, ignoring Ronin, who could barely stand.

He staggered over, his fingers shaking as he tried to keep playing, and I waved for him to stop. Bane nodded to the wall, and we took up station by the barrier, sweeping our hands across and uncovering the carvings that had been hidden under centuries of dust and dirt.

The filthy coating cascaded away, revealing the ancient carvings. I scanned them quickly, spotting the sunburst pattern and grinning.

I pressed the center, gradually increasing the pressure until, with a loud clunk, the latch released. Dust and dirt blasted out of the cracks in the hidden door as it shifted, making us all cough as I waved Bob forward.

The massive bone minion stomped in, working the tips of his claws into the gaps and heaving.

At first, nothing happened, and we all ignored Ronin's increasingly frantic and pestering questions, until Bane finally grabbed him by the ear and led him aside. The Mer quickly and quietly explained, and apparently threatened the bard if he didn't stop being such a pain in the ass.

Giint moved in, stepping between Bob's massive legs without concern to examine the tiny gap before rooting in his bag. He gestured Bob back, and I confirmed the order, as Giint tugged free more and more parts, laying them out on the floor and getting to work.

It took a handful of minutes, but when he was done, he held up two short rods to Bob, who took them gingerly at my direction.

"In the wall," Giint whispered, coughing and pointing. "Pull trigger."

We looked at him in unified shock, hearing for the first time clear speech from him.

"It was Nerin," Oracle said in a low voice that somehow still carried. "She helped you, didn't she, Giint?"

"Crazy old bag," Giint grunted, clearly disgruntled. "Giint not need help!"

"It's okay, little buddy," Grizz called from the doorway where he watched down the corridor, his affixed magelight casting a warm, white light down the filthy, empty hallway down to the bend, illuminating the rotten door that hung in the doorway of the room that directly corresponded to the one the Goblins had used as a kitchen in the first waystation we'd visited. "We love you as you are!"

Bob stepped in again, sliding the rods into the gaps. Once the device was wedged in place, Bob struggled with the triggers until Giint rolled his eyes and stepped up, grabbing them and yanking them back. A *clunk* sounded on the far side.

"Now you pull," Giint growled, moving back again.

Bob heaved, and the wall moved, slowly at first, but with increasing speed, the massive block grating across the floor until I called out to him to stop.

The newly revealed room was small, three meters on a side, with a table in the middle and a chair on the far side that, when used, would face the table and the entrance.

I patted Bob's shoulder in thanks as I stepped around him, slipping around the table to sink into the seat.

It was strange; the room had far less dust in it than the last had, and it seemed particularly strange in comparison to the rooms outside.

The walls were regular and undamaged, and they all rose to the center of a small domed ceiling. A magelight had been mounted on each wall in the center, and one hung overhead, indicating that, when the item was powered, the room would practically blaze with light. For now, though, it was dull and dead.

"Get comfy, people; this is the bit that's going to take a while," I said, reaching out and laying the palm of my hand flat on the table before me. It reacted instantly, and I felt the now-familiar sucking sensation of my mana being pulled from me. I closed my eyes and activated Peace, speeding up my mana regeneration and that of those around me.

"I'm going to meditate; Ronin, if you have any buffs to help mana regeneration, now's the time," I said, drawing in a deep breath and working on my structures in my mind. I heard Oracle start to explain to the others how to meditate, with Arrin helping her to describe the concepts.

The next twenty minutes or so went quickly, with the climb to the requisite thousand mana going far more quickly than ever before, thanks to the others taking turns to touch the table, donating their mana to aid my own.

When the draining pressure eased, I opened my eyes, finding the table fairly humming with power. The lights around the room slowly started to brighten as prompts began to appear.

Congratulations!

You have reached the control center of Waystation Three and have the prerequisite authority and abilities to claim this structure and the surrounding land, adding it to your territory as a claimed location. As this territory holds less than ten (10) percent of sentients that are actively hostile to your rule, it can be claimed.

Do you wish to annex this territory now?

Yes/No

I chose Yes, of course, and I felt the room responding to me until a new prompt filled my vision.

Beware!

This structure has not yet been cleared! One previous inhabitant is located in the upper structure and must be removed before full control can be bestowed!

*

Citadel

Warning!

Two hundred and eighty-seven hostile creatures are approaching the boundary of this territory. If the structure is not cleared before they enter the territory, this structure will change from clear to contested and may be claimed by any other who reaches this control room with the proper authority.

*

Repairs and restructuring options for this location are not available until hostile inhabitant has been removed and the structure deemed to be clear.

"Motherfucker!" I growled, springing to my feet and stepping around the table, bursting out into the room before grinning as a better idea came to mind.

"Okay, everyone, this won't take long," I purred, striding forward.

CHAPTER EIGHTEEN

One by one, I had the others step up and join me as I stood with my right hand pressed to the enormous stone golem's chest. They touched it, and Oracle laid her hand on theirs, generating a warning prompt, one they quickly acknowledged and allowed, giving her access to their mana for a limited time. She then sucked out a portion before thanking them and letting them step back, all the while I poured my own into the sleeping form before me.

Oracle sat half-submerged into the diamond that rested in the center of the massive construction's chest, and with each donation, the gemstone's glow grew brighter.

Another half an hour was all it took before the golem opened its eyes and surveyed the room, locking onto my gaze and pausing as everyone readied weapons.

I'd warned them that it shouldn't awaken in a mood, but, you know, just in case, be ready.

Thankfully, it accepted my authority with ease, as I'd claimed the control room.

"Find the hostile creature that's squatting upstairs," I ordered it. "Go as quickly as you can and kill it."

The enormous creation lifted its sword and shield and stepped free from the wall that had held it for hundreds of years. Dust, fragments of stone, and the buildup of the ages fell free in a shower of debris and tiny fragments as the newly awakened complex war golem stomped out of the room, striding past the others like they didn't exist and breaking into a run in the corridor.

It hit the small section that had collapsed, the same one we'd had to crawl through, like a train hitting a haystack. It blasted through the rubble, making more of that section fall in.

"Okay, people!" I said forcing a smile as I saw the looks on their faces, ranging from Ronin's shock and horror to Tang's amusement. I held up a single finger to Bane as he opened his mouth to speak. "Shut the fuck up, Bane. So, we all get to repeat the process again; sorry about that! However, the next one will be concentrating on rebuilding the walls and making it all safer, so let's get to it!" I ordered, moving down the line past the other war golems until I reached the servitor, also level three, or complex, and Oracle and I started the process again.

Fifteen minutes into it, I broke away to return to the Control Room and assumed my chair again as new notifications popped up.

Congratulations!

You have cleared Waystation Three. In clearing this location, repair and restructuring options have been made available!

*

Citadel

Congratulations!

You have annexed new lands onto your own, providing the following benefits if the land is worked:

Abandoned Village: This location has been recently abandoned, with the inhabitants relocating to the Great Tower. If the village were to be repopulated, you would gain a new tax base. Gain +5-500 gold, depending on taxation options selected and possible structures built.

Logging Camp: There is an abandoned logging camp in the borders of this territory, located close to the abandoned village. If this is reclaimed and worked, gain +10-15 hardwood logs per day.

*

Attention: Citizens of the Territory of Dravith!

High Lord Jax of Dravith has expanded his territory and has claimed an additional one hundred and four square miles of lands by defeating the previously hostile occupants!

All titles, Deeds, and Laws in the Territory of Dravith are held for review, and can be revoked, altered, annulled, or approved.

All Hail High Lord Jax of Dravith!

The last one made me grin, knowing that the entire continent had gotten it, as it had the characteristic gold edges and scrollwork. I had to assume that the Dark Legionnaires sprinting full-tilt through the forest would have been likely to have an issue with that, especially as it couldn't be dismissed to clear your vision until it had been read and acknowledged.

I pulled up the main structure of the waystation on the table, watching it grow from the liquid mana that pooled in the center to form walls and corridors, rooms and outer walls, as well as collapsed sections.

I quickly scanned through the structure, finding it more intact than Waystation Four. Of the five mana collectors, when I selected them and ordered them to deploy, three pillars responded, sliding out of the depths and punching up into the air outside.

I felt the change in the structure as they locked into place and began to draw again. The entire building, having only just settled from the shudder of the mana collectors deploying, gave a second strong quake, before the rooms were unexpectedly filled with gently growing light.

The lights that had been placed in my little room had already activated, although dimly. The rest of the structure, though, soon blazed to life as the numerous magelights still attached to the walls–despite well over half of the building being looted in days long past–flared to life again.

Outside, Oracle guided the others to continue pouring their mana into the Servitor, her voice carrying to me as I pulled up a new screen and tuned out the alternately frantic and awed questions from Ronin.

Greetings, Lord of Dravith and Master of the Great Tower.

This interface is limited by damage and capacity.

Please select from the following options:

System Repair:
Current condition: 68%
0-100% of Mana allocated

Structural Integrity:
Current condition: 84%
0-100% of Mana allocated

Golem recharging and Maintenance:
Current charge: 21%
0-100% of Mana allocated

I designated the golems as the first priority, sending ninety percent to them, with the remaining ten percent being split between the other two.

I got a notification that all the golems would be reawakened in seven hours, and I grinned, remembering that the first of them had taken six or so at the other site.

I sat back, thinking, then clambered out of the seat and kneeled before reaching out.

"Jenae, Goddess, are you there?" I asked, and I felt Her amused attention a few seconds later.

"I'm impressed at the humility, Jax. I was expecting you to be insufferable after our last conversation," She said, sounding pleased.

"Yeah, well...I thought, you know, I should behave a little," I muttered, smiling as I stood and returned to the chair.

"What is it you're looking for, Jax? This type of shouting across the realms is hard to detect, but it is still shouting, and as such, is risky."

"You offered a bonus for the over-completion of the quest to bring everyone back, specifically a bonus structure. Can I claim that, even though I'm not at the Tower?"

"What is it? I'll be honest, I likely cannot do it straight away, as it will take a large amount of mana."

"Hephaestus recommended a structure that could link up any locations I claimed; a beacon or something?"

"The Control Tower," She supplied, voice going flat. *"A structure that would be the equivalent of, for example, a foundry, a blacksmith's, and a farrier's, with space left over? That's what you're asking for?"*

"Uh, yeah?" I confirmed tentatively.

"Uh, no." She snorted, the sound extending into a long sigh, clearly trying to maintain Her patience. *"Jax, I may not have specified, but I offered a **low-level** building. I didn't, for example, stipulate that you couldn't ask for a second entire Tower either, but it was a matter of common sense. If I had that kind of power to bestow idly, I'd have simply done it, rather than sending you off to the city to raid it, wouldn't I?"*

"Well, you didn't exactly 'send me'," I pointed out.

She snorted again. *"Well, regardless, it's a no, I'm afraid. However..."*

"Go on."

"The quest to return the Gods and grant them their champions."

"The one that had the bit about getting them champions added in? You know, after I'd already accepted it?" I noted, a slight bite in my voice.

"Ah. Well, yes, that quest. That might come with a bigger bonus to you than you think."

"I'm listening."

"The champions will receive gifts, much as you do from me. While they will not gain access to something similar to the Constellation of Secrets, many of the Gods will grant an ability in addition to the more standard powers. For example, Ashante has been known to bless a location with fecundity."

"Gesundheit," I responded automatically.

"What? Champion, fecundity means the potential of something to be very fertile. For example, your people, lands, and anything you planted would grow in number easier."

"I totally knew that," I lied.

"You liar," She responded affectionately. **"Others, such as Svetu, might give gifts such as a construction bench or laboratory, simple items that are nonetheless fantastically powerful, if used to increase the Tower's potential."**

"Okay, so the quicker I recruit Champions for the other Gods, the better, right?"

"Very much so, but remember, they are Gods, and will not grant their abilities to those you choose, but those they select. Pushing the wrong people forward will achieve nothing but wasting goodwill."

"Okay, that makes sense, dammit."

"With that in mind, however, there are several close to you who would be suitable champions, very close to you, right now."

I opened my eyes, having closed them when I was speaking to Jenae without thinking about it, and I noticed three people close to me right then, which made me blink in confusion, as they were all about the same distance away, with the others being considerably further out.

Giint was examining the wall, poking at the hinges that the hidden door moved on. Bane was reclining against the wall nearby, examining the dagger I'd given him, and Lydia. Lydia stood nearby, watching Giint to make sure he didn't disturb me.

Giint was an easy one; Svetu had been the God almost exclusively of the Gnomes, and was all about creation, and therefore crafting. So, yeah. Bane...well, he would suit Tamat, the Goddess of Dark Deeds, and he was basically growing to be a dual-spec assassin and bodyguard, so I could see that, but Lydia?

"Hmm…" I mused, staring at her and making her jump when she saw I was focusing so intently on her. I didn't respond, instead flexing a mental muscle and pulling up the quest that I had received specifically regarding her.

Congratulations!

You have discovered a new Quest: A Pillar of Strength.

Your bondswoman, Lydia, commander of your personal squad and close friend, has begun to evolve into a Valkyrie. To complete her evolution, and to become all she could be, she requires four things:

Resolution of the Past: 0/1
Cleansing of the Last Valkyrie: 0/1
Find a Class Trainer: 0/1
Discover/Create/Recover Suitable Armor: 0/1
Reward: A full Valkyrie under your command, possibly more, 50,000xp

Accept: *Yes/No*

"Lydia," I asked absently. "Which of the Gods did the Valkyries worship?"

"I don't know," Lydia said, and before I could ask another question, Ronin called out from the other room, where I could hear him idly playing with his lute.

"Vanei," he offered. "The Goddess of the Air and Lady of Change."

"Thanks, Ronin," I called back, smiling and closing my eyes.

"So, Giint to Svetu, Bane to Tamat, and Lydia to Vanei?" I asked, and there was a chuckle as Jenae responded.

"Well done on coming to that conclusion entirely on your own," Jenae said mockingly. I laughed despite myself. **"But I suspect they would be useful suggestions, as would the locations those Gods might gift to you, locations where useful items might be found. Beyond that, I cannot say more and must go. Pick a simple building, one that is non-magical, if I have to say it! I'll do my best to arrange it soon, but…"** She left it hanging, until I asked.

"Yes?"

"I do need you to lead some of the refugees to the worship of the other Gods, but, well…"

"But we did all of this, and they need to understand that you're the head girl?" I asked, earning another snort.

"If you could lead some to worship the others, yet possibly make it clear that you specifically follow me?"

"And if others want to follow in my footsteps, then it'd be acceptable, got it."

"Thank you. Don't forget about the building."

"I won't," I promised, feeling the sensation of Her leaving my mind.

I opened my eyes and sat up again. A blinking notification awaited me, and I sighed, opening it quickly.

A party under your command killed the following:

- 1x Yateveo, level 26, for 11,340xp

Total party experience earned: 11,340xp

As party leader, you gain 25% of all experience earned

Progress to level 24 stands at 146,859/510,000

*

Citadel

Warning!

Two hundred and eighty-seven hostile creatures are approaching the boundary of this territory.

Beware, Lord of Dravith. Your territory is being invaded!

Time until hostile incursion: 17 minutes, 12 seconds.

"Yeah, fuck this." I pushed to my feet. "Come on, everyone, time to move on." I gathered the others up and exited into the main room, closing the control room door behind me with Oracle doing...*something*...to ensure that we'd be able to control the facility from a distance of at least a few miles.

"What's happening?" Ronin asked, rising clumsily.

"We're moving on; we've got a lot of places to visit today," I said shortly, still very much unsure of the bard, despite his help so far.

We walked out into the corridor, picking the others up and heading along the hallways, eventually passing the servitor as it worked to repair the wall.

I reached out and ordered it to stop and to instead follow along with us. While I wanted the facility up and running, I wasn't going to risk the Dark Legion finding something so valuable, not when they might find a way to convert it to follow them.

Our party started jogging, hurrying for the front door, while Oracle vanished ahead to summon the ship back.

By the time we reached the exit, she'd also summoned the complex war golem and instilled a set of basic commands to imprint onto the other golems once they fully awoke.

They were to start heading directly for the Tower after swinging ten miles to the West. That should set them far enough on a new trajectory that, unless they were very unlucky, they'd miss the Dark Legion entirely.

The other two, though, the much more valuable level three, complex versions, would be damn well coming with me.

The golem had its hands full when it arrived, six desiccated corpses, all clothed and crumbling.

"It's loot, right? You weren't going to leave it, surely." Oracle said, looking confused.

"I'm so proud of you right now." I grinned, gesturing upwards in question.

"I sent the Fireball up," she confirmed, gaining a full smile from me.

That was the signal we'd agreed on with the *Sigmar's Fist*, and while we waited, we quickly searched the remains.

Five minutes later, the ship was landing, and we guided the golems up onto the deck, dumping our gear and relaxing in safety, as Ronin and Grizz sorted through the loot.

Ronin, it turned out, was a support classer all the way, having picked up an Identify spell at some point, and was happily ranking the meager lot by value as well as effectiveness.

There were three swords, all crap, a mace that seemed to be more dangerous to the wielder than the target, a pair of daggers that couldn't cut butter, and six copper coins.

I snorted and shook my head when he delivered it all to me and asked what I wanted to do with it.

"Take the weapons and store them somewhere," I asked a passing crew member. "When we get back to the Tower, have them given to the smiths to melt down, please." The coins, I just put in a pouch and told the others I'd share out any loot once the day was done, if there was anything worth sharing out, anyway.

Leaving Ronin and the others to relax, I jogged across the deck and up the steps, joining the Alkyon pair as they watched the world around the ship.

"Captain!" I greeted as I came to halt, and she nodded her birdlike head, fixing me with one eye then the other before saluting. Once I returned the salute, they both returned to the job at hand, the helmsman charting a course off the map tacked to a board by his side, and the captain watching everything else.

"Lord Jax," she croaked. "Was your hunt a success?" I nodded, making her relax.

"It was, thank you. I'm sorry, but I can't remember your name?" I apologized.

"Kinnet. This is my mate, Raan," she said politely, and the helmsman lifted his head, exposing his neck in submission.

"Thank you both. Again, I know we were introduced; I've just never been good at names, that's all," I clarified. "So, moving on, what happened since I left the ship?"

"Little." Kinnet responded with a shrug. "We scouted the local area, saw a few caves and, in the distance, the enemy, but nothing else."

"The flyers," Raan reminded Kinnet, and she croaked, nodding her head sharply.

"There is a pair of flyers high in the mountains, my lord, large ones. Dragonkin, I'd guess, but not true dragons, judging from the evidence."

"What evidence?" I asked.

"We're alive," she said bluntly. "A true dragon would have hunted us down for flying so close to its range."

"It's probably a pair of wyverns, my lord," Raan added in helpfully.

"Fair enough," I said, unable to argue with their logic. "A problem for another day. You heading for the next waystation?"

They both nodded. "As you ordered earlier, my lord."

"Thank you. Shout to us when we are close, please." Satisfied, I headed back down to sit with the others, who were generally talking shit and enjoying the breeze as we flew.

I studied the trees as the ship left the low hills and began to fly over the forests again, watching the line of devastation in the far distance, where the Dark Legion was busily carving a furrow in the land towards the Tower.

I squinted, the occasional flash of sunlight on metal letting me pick out small parties that had clearly been sent out to scout, leaving the main body. As we soared over the trees, it was a small comfort knowing that, due to the massive canopy of green, brown, and red leaves, we were probably well-shielded from them.

The next forty minutes passed in a relaxing blur as we all talked, and while Ronin tried to draw me away for a private chat on several occasions, I shut it down each time. We'd be having the truth of his background and any secrets buried there after we returned that night, when I would have time to fully dig and make sense of it all.

"Waystation Five." I muttered as we slowed, moving to the side of the ship. The only thing visible was a mass of leafy canopy below us, the trees swaying in a gentle breeze, birds flitting from one to another as the yowl of a hunting cat of some kind echoed up to us from below.

Nothing stood out anywhere, and I quickly pulled up the map before grunting and dismissing it to head up to the raised deck where the captain and helmsman stood.

It was a short jog, but by the time I'd made it from the lower deck to the upper, we'd turned farther, arcing around, and I waved to them as I examined the small paper map they had attached to a board for reference.

"We're off by about two miles," I told them, trying to remind myself that these were green crews. The original crews had been killed when we'd taken the ships, leaving us with people that were either totally new to the whole thing and barely trained, or people who'd once held similar, although usually lower ranks, and had been bumped up to fill out the crews as quickly as possible.

The captain and helmsman looked embarrassed and immediately started apologizing. I quickly reassured them, explaining that my magical map gave me a much more accurate way to check, that was all.

I redirected the ship, and shortly afterwards, we closed in on a narrow strip of slightly shorter trees that ran southwards in the direction of the lake.

While the trees were slightly stunted, indicating a more difficult area for growth, there still wasn't anywhere we could land, the trees being, if anything, more densely packed.

"We're going to have to hike in." I grumbled, scratching the back of my neck, then gesturing at what looked like a clearing about two miles to the west. "If you can get us to the ground over there, please, Captain, and we'll see what we can find. Once we've got the area cleared, we can have the golems cut you a spot to land somewhere nearby."

I glanced down at the war golem, which still stood resolutely, while the servitor had joined its fellows happily and was below decks working on the ship, blending the hull panels together with seamless artistry.

As the ship turned, heading toward the clearing in the distance, I moved back to the others, grinning as I arrived at the end of a particularly bad joke that Grizz was telling. His unofficial lover, Yen, smacked him hard across the back of the head as the others burst out laughing.

"I'm starting to wonder which'll break first, your hand or his head," I teased, grinning at them. "Either way, get ready, everyone; we're here. Waystation Five is somewhere down there." I pointed over the opposite side, behind us, at the trees below. "The problem is, none of us know exactly where, and the damn trees are so thick, we can't land. We're heading for the clearing over there." I indicated the distance ahead of the ship and got a round of nods. "From there, we get to search."

I'd considered dropping the golems, or even just the war golem, over the side into the trees, but figured that sending a multi-ton creature to fall blindly might be a mistake, especially as it could conceivably fall somewhere it couldn't get out of, or onto solid rock, damaging itself. Equally, I'd considered flying down myself and searching for a suitable area and having it jump over the side then. Once it was on the ground, it could clear the trees to allow us to land.

The problem with that was that we just didn't know what was down there, once again, and we could inadvertently destroy something valuable. In clearing the area, we could expose the ruin to scrutiny from the Dark Legion, if their scouts found a big patch of obviously recently felled trees. In the end, I'd decided to just keep it to us, as a two-mile hike really wasn't that big a deal.

The ship managed to get down to a hundred meters from the ground once we reached the clearing, but that was as far as it could make it, due to the various trees, branches, and rock outcroppings. From there, I ferried the others down with my Soaring Majesty ability, being forced to leave Bob on the ship, much to his, mine, and Oracle's disappointment.

"As soon as we find enough bone to repair you, I will, bud," I whispered, patting one massive shoulder awkwardly. He nodded slowly, forcing me to smile through the guilt.

"I'll be back soon. For now, you protect the ship," I ordered, jumping off the side.

The captain had clear orders from me for the day. Once we were gone, she was to scout the local area, discover if there was anything interesting that she could see, and then deliver the war golem and the new servitor golem to the Tower before returning for us, given that it was an hour or so from our location to the Tower, and we would realistically need several hours, at least.

Once I made it to the ground, and we heard, more than saw, the ship making its way into the distance, we set off, my map providing a rough guide that should lead us to the right general area.

The clearing, once we were actually on the ground, was small and rocky, a bowl-shaped depression full of stone and water that shimmered as we skirted the edge, making me think of a cave system that had collapsed at some point. As we passed, a loud clicking rose from below. Something that had been lying camouflaged by the side of one of the small rocky pools dived in, making a loud splash that silenced the birds in the area.

"That's not good," Tang said in a low voice, his feelings echoed by Bane wholeheartedly.

"What was it?" I asked, as we all crouched, peering down into the small, rippling pool.

"No idea, but it was big enough that we should have seen it. The fact we didn't, and the birds in the damn trees know to keep quiet when it's about?"

"Not a good sign," Bane muttered. "I suggest we move on and quickly."

I gestured to the others, and we carefully rose from where we'd crouched and hidden amongst the rocks surrounding the depression.

"Is that a path?" asked Lydia quietly as we picked our way along, and I paused with the others, inspecting a narrow trail, appearing out of the sun-dappled forest ahead of us and leading directly down to the water's edge below.

"Looks like something comes here regularly," Bane confirmed, when Giint, surprisingly, spoke up, nudging Ronin, who was close to him.

"Good for hunting," was all he said, but following the line of his gesture, we all froze.

A small, carefully maintained structure blended seamlessly into the far side of the slope, maybe ten meters down, with clear sightlines over the entire pool.

"What the hell is that?" I asked carefully.

"It's a hunter's blind," answered Tang. "It's designed to blend in so that a hunter can sit in there and watch for prey."

"It's almost invisible to me," Bane said slowly. "It's been constructed that way deliberately."

"You think whoever uses it is hunting your kind?" I asked him, and he shrugged.

"Mine or others with a sensitivity to the world. Someone is using it regularly, though."

"Fuck. Tang, Grizz, go check it out," I ordered, and Yen snorted as Tang vanished.

"You chose one of the sneakiest and the least sneaky...you did do that intentionally, right, boss?" she asked.

I grinned, wondering if she'd called me that deliberately, or if she was picking up Grizz's habits already.

"Everyone else, spread out. I want us watching the forest as much as the blind and the water," I ordered, and everyone moved quickly. "Bane?" I hissed, and a few seconds later, he appeared, crouching next to me.

"Yes, Jax?"

"Go into the forest. If we're being watched, I want to know. Scout the area and keep back. Oracle, go with him. You can adjust yourself to blend in, and you can tell me what you find."

"I don't like leaving you," Oracle whispered, back in her tiny form and having been seated happily on my shoulder since we'd ferried the last of the team down.

"I know, but it's the safest way," I responded. "Hopefully, I'm just being paranoid, but just in case..."

"I know." Oracle sighed, leaning in and kissing my cheek. The press of her lips was as smooth as cool silk, then she was gone, her form dimming and shifting to match the darker areas between the stones.

She and Bane vanished, and I had to force myself to not track her progress using the bond.

I turned, watching as Grizz slowly crept down the side of the pit, navigating his way between large rocks and upthrust sections of stone as he closed in on the hunter's blind.

The pool below stirred again, the water rippling in a different pattern from the breeze, and we all froze.

I was putting Grizz in danger in sending him and Tang down there, literally hanging him out like a target, and he knew it. Still, the massive legionnaire was the best choice, and the way he held his shield, always angled towards the water, his short, broad-bladed gladius at the ready, showed me he was prepared.

I glanced about and found Lydia crouched with her back placed to the pit, glaring out at the forest, while Giint, a few feet from her, watched downward, his crossbow planted firmly against the rock he hid behind, ready to fire.

Nearby, I spotted Ronin. He was seated on the ground, his lips moving and fingers tapping on his legs. Even though no sounds reached me, I still felt some of the buffs activate.

Buff: Glory!

Effect: Health regeneration is boosted by 5% for 60 minutes, Strength is increased by one point for 60 minutes.

*

Buff: Watcher's Grace!

Effect: Bardic Companions are buffed for as long as the Bard continues to play, receiving +2 to Perception and +10% to Stealth.

"He might be worth keeping, after all," Arrin muttered close by, making me glance over at him. I found him, and Yen crouched, alternating between him looking down and her looking out, with Jian on the far side of them, the small form of Ty'Baronn still conspicuously keeping silent and hiding as much as possible. He'd almost managed to make me forget he was there, and I was annoyed with myself at how close the little bastard's strategy had come to working. I'd be addressing *that* as soon as we got back to the ship.

"Might be," I agreed with Arrin, going back to watching and waiting.

Grizz vanished into the structure a minute or so later, reappearing soon after and shaking his head before starting to make his way up towards us.

He'd barely covered a meter, though, before the thing that lived in the water finally made its appearance, erupting into the air with a scream of fury that echoed up from the pit, freezing us all in place as hundreds of shapes took flight around us, including the birds that had filled the trees, only to rain down in spatters of blood and feathered clumps.

CHAPTER NINETEEN

"What the hell is that?" I grunted as it roared its challenge before breathing out a blast of ice that coated the side of the pit. The gust slammed Grizz backwards against the side of a large rock, only for him to slump down, chilled and drained by the extreme cold.

His symbol in my peripheral vision shifted from green to yellow to red in mere seconds before the breath attack finished. He dragged himself backwards, his sword dropping from nerveless fingers as he tried to crawl back to the hunter's blind.

The buff fell away before being replaced by others sending our health regeneration up a few points. Our blood surged as the music started up, falteringly at first, but growing stronger by the second. I leaped to my feet and started running, slamming my naginata into my bag and yanking out the tower shield, so damn thankful for the way the neck of the bag seemed to grow and shrink as appropriate on these higher-quality versions.

I leaped from rocky outcropping to scuffed ground to rock, jumping and running as fast as I could, just as the first spells slammed into the creature below. Its camouflage rippled, making me miss a step, almost breaking my leg as I saw it clearly for the first time.

It was a lizard, a dozen meters long, but narrow-chested. Two well-muscled front legs held the body up with the chest blending into a long, sinuous tail with a ridge of spines running down its back. It was covered in light blue scales with a fan of flesh that joined the spines together, flesh that glowed with rapidly dissipating heat until it started to suck in another deep breath with a head that made me pin it as a definite dragonkin.

Its eyes glowed a bright, cold blue, highlighting yellow-slitted pupils. As it whipped its head back, sucking in more air, the fan began to give off heat again. The air shimmered around it as the wide, toothy jaw opened, exposing dark flesh inside. A trio of horns pointed back from the top of its head, protecting the back of the skull. Two more curled outwards from the temples and down, terminating on either side of the jaw, pointing forward, ready to rip into its target.

"It's an Ice-Drake!" screamed Ronin.

I grunted, my foot slipping on frosty ground as it landed poorly. Righting myself, I sprinted the last few feet to skid to halt, half-covering Grizz, in his ice-coated armor.

I reached down, grabbing onto him and hissing at the cold leaching through my own gear, until he pulled me down, jamming his shield to his right as he laid on his back. I slotted my shield in alongside his, with barely a second to go before the next attack slammed into it.

The first hit rocketed our locked shields into us, shoving us bodily across the ground to press up against a rock.

Then the cold hit.

The inside of my shield changed color, as did Grizz's, frost coating them and cold-welding them together. We both shivered, unable to do more than groan as even the air in our lungs hurt.

I reached down for the bag at my waist, trying to get my naginata out, only to find that I couldn't feel my fingers. With no control over them, the bag didn't respond to me.

"Shitty place to die," Grizz whispered. I looked over at him, seeing his skin turning blue and purple. The little of his face I could see under his helm had grown ice crystals, and even his eyelashes looked to be freezing.

"Don't you…fucking…dare!" I ground out, barely able to speak through my shuddering lips as my skin tried to flinch from the horrifically cold metal of my armor.

The breath attack stopped as suddenly as it started, and a wash of heat slammed over us, the temperature shock making us both cry out in pain as Yen hammered down with her Flamespears, swiftly followed by heals smashing into us both. I forced myself to look up, seeing a series of small glowing flashes as a barrage of Magic Missiles roared through the air, only to impact into the same black birds that had flashed upwards when the creature first made its appearance.

"Wha…" I managed to get out, before I grimaced, seeing that whatever they were, they were sacrificing themselves to intercept the missiles.

"Ice-Drake!" screamed Ronin again. "Weak to Fire and Life, with undead minions!" he cried out before diving aside and screaming again, this time in terror as a handful of the black flyers slammed into the ground where he'd just been.

Giint fired his crossbow at the Ice-Drake, and Lydia was bracing her shield over her head, blocking a veritable stream of the flyers that were intent on her.

Oracle hit me with another heal, and as soon as my fingers started to work, I forced them through the complicated gestures needed, summoning Cleansing Fire while Grizz tried to yank his shield and mine apart. Arrin was running and shrieking like a madman as the undead birds focused on him as well.

He screamed in pain, and his health bar started to empty as dozens of the flyers hit him, hurtling past to slash his skin with their tiny, sharp claws, breaking his concentration as he tried to cast.

Jian was a blur, spinning and dancing, his blades flashing through the air. Their Drow-made silvery steel shredding the birds that he managed to catch, yet doing nothing for the majority, until his summoned Demon, Ty'Baronn, appeared at the lip of the pit.

He gripped the edge of the rocks in withered claws and bared his teeth as the disc above his head lit up, red and yellow lines arcing inwards, flowing up his horns. The light grew brighter and brighter, flaring to white as the Ice-Drake slammed a massive clawed foot down atop the rocks next to us, rearing up to draw in another breath, readying for a third blast.

Tang appeared, sprinting across from my right then throwing himself down and skidding along on the icy ground before digging his foot in. A claw-tipped paw slashed through the air where he'd just been.

As the claws passed, he flipped himself up and over. In a move that would make an Olympic gymnast cry with envy, he hammer-kicked the creature in the side of its face before slashing down with both magical swords.

They carved deep gashes in its skull, opening the scaled skin all the way down to the bone, making it rear its head back to shriek in pain as it fell onto the floor.

Tang landed awkwardly, bouncing off a rock then slamming into another before managing to stop himself. One of his swords clattered loose, tumbling farther down the pit.

As the Ice-Drake lashed its head about in agony, screaming, the bird-like undead familiars flashed skyward, abandoning all other targets to form a massive wave, cresting high overhead and diving at Tang.

The next second, Ty'Baronn unleashed his attack, the disc above his head erupting in crackling, arcing fingers of plasma, when a beam the thickness of my thigh punched out, slamming into the top of the Drake's head then tracking down to take it in its right eye.

The Drake screeched in pain, its skin blackening; but its spines stood straight. The fanned flesh between them shimmered as it tried to suck the heat away somehow, channeling it and redirecting it as its right eye boiled and melted.

The familiars changed direction, the first three pounding into Ty'Baronn with wet smacking sounds as their bony beaks and claws pierced his flesh, followed by dozens more, beating the small Demon into a puddle of lifeless meat before even half had hit him.

As soon as the corpse hit the ground, they peeled away, with a handful too close to obey the silent command and instead detonating on the rocks as they tried to pull up, feathers, dry flesh, and bones flying everywhere.

Bane suddenly appeared; he'd made it behind the creature somehow, and his daggers flashed in the early afternoon sunlight as he began to carve great swaths out of the creature, made even more effective by his new legendary dagger, Death's Kiss.

I grunted as I finished my spell, the area of effect Cleansing Fire rippling out from under the Drake. The resulting wave of flames caught Bane, Grizz, and me in its radius, healing us as it began to eat at our enemy.

I looked down at Grizz as he roared in fury, and the shields finally tore free of each other, the cold welding breaking under the onslaught of Grizz's rage more than anything else.

The dagger in Bane's hand caught my attention as he struck again. The blade visibly lit up, then darkened as he staggered, and he'd fed it some of his life force to trigger the powerful effects. As it flashed down, carving a new furrow in its flesh, the Drake screeched again, batting him aside with its long tail.

Bane flipped end over end before slamming into a rock on the far side of the pit and slumping to the ground.

I checked his health, finding it at a quarter of its full, but only slowly draining. I growled, seeing that almost all of us were doing about the same.

I realized I had a damage over time effect on me, as did Grizz. The bluish tinge to my skin and shaking was draining my health by ten points a second.

I gritted my teeth, hitting Grizz with a powerful healing spell, then yanking the naginata out and slamming fire mana into it, making it blaze to life.

Lydia was using her new abilities, flashing backward and forward, covering meters in an instant. Her shield smashed the familiars from the air and protected the rest of the party, while her mace batted and crushed the creatures into bundles of bone that clattered to the ground.

Arrin had managed to get another barrage of Magic Missiles off, then was hitting Bane with a heal at the same time as Oracle hit me with another one. Giint abruptly screamed, dropping his crossbow and rushing from sight.

Yen's Flamespears slammed into the Drake again, staggering it with the first two while the third tipped it over. The beast screeched, and a white mist billowed forth from it, cloaking the entire pit in choking mist. The fog made my lungs shudder and convulse when I breathed it in as I rushed for the downed Drake.

Beware!

You have been affected by Burning Cold;

You lose an additional 5 points of health per second for the next ten seconds, and cannot breathe until this effect expires.

I staggered, my breath freezing in my chest and panic rising in me until the fury rose to combat it. A Fireball from Oracle hurtled past me to smash into the Drake's face, rocking it backwards and momentarily stunning it.

I checked Grizz's health bar, furious to see it plummeting too quickly, and I dropped my naginata, grabbing my friend instead and activating Soaring Majesty.

The additional weight of the massive, heavily equipped legionnaire made me strain harder. But as we rocketed upwards, slamming through a handful of the familiars and shattering them, we left the mist behind and erupted back into daylight.

I flipped over, dipping down to the grass that covered the top of the pit, and dropped Grizz, leaving him to roll on the ground as I desperately threw myself back into the air. Their plummeting health bars made it clear that my team couldn't wait.

Oracle hit Grizz with a heal, and I frantically tugged a mana potion out of my bag, damn thankful that Cai had thought to give them to me earlier and downed it before diving back into the mist. The bond that tied us all together aided me in locating Bane as I pulled on it, only to land hard enough that my ankle snapped, as an unseen rock was at exactly the wrong place and time.

I reached out, grabbing Bane, then kicked off and soared upwards again, barely making it out of the mist before that batshit little bastard Giint flew past me, leaping from the top of a rocky outcropping with his glowing axe in one hand and a buzzing kill-stick in the other.

He vanished into the mist, and a half-second later, the Drake screeched in pain.

I hurtled to Oracle again, gritting my teeth as I dropped Bane and yanked a health, then a mana potion from my pouch, downing them both at once. The potions mixing in my mouth in the same way that I'd once tried to mix White Lightning and Carlsberg to make a snakebite, having run out of glasses.

It ended better for me this time, as both bars jumped up, rather than making me vomit. I plunged into the mist again, seeing Tang throw a hand out to me as I closed on him. Some skill or ability of his made him able to sense my return. I rolled in the air, using my momentum to yank him up as I pushed harder and harder, erupting from the mist with him and pounding into the ground near Oracle as I miscalculated.

I cried out before slamming my mouth shut, gritting my teeth as the pain rolled through me, sending my mind reeling as I fought to recover. A symbol flashed up in my vision, which I later recognized as Stunned, although at the time, I couldn't think enough to do anything.

I heard shouts from all around me and felt something being forced between my teeth. Liquid poured into my mouth, and I coughed as it went down the wrong way, bringing most of it up.

Strong hands slammed me onto my back and another potion was force-fed to me, while screams and roars rang out, filling the air.

More cold filled the air, and I groaned when the Stunned effect mercifully wore off, the bubble of Grizz's Iceshield above me.

I blinked, seeing dark shapes, lots of them, smashing into the shield and shattering it, but not before they fell into piles of broken bones and dead flesh.

"What...?" I grunted, forcing myself back upright and looking around. A sudden flash of green light, followed by a dozen more, lit up the outside of the shield.

Oracle hit me with another heal as soon as my mana had recovered enough, and a mana-migraine flared to life, making me wince before I forced my eyes open in panic.

The squad...the squad all had less than half health. Hell, most were less than thirty percent, but the last of the debuffs had stopped. As I blinked woozily, another wave of the green lights cascaded outside.

Grizz popped the shield at Oracle's terse order, and it collapsed into shimmering ice shards that vanished before they hit the ground, exposing the forest around us.

Several massive figures stood silently in the previously empty woods, over a dozen at least, and they drew back on huge bows. The arrows were glowing fiercely with green light before they tore out and slammed into the Ice-Drake. The creature screamed a final time before collapsing, a single death's head floating up in my vision to confirm its passing.

I looked down into the pit, watching the mad little fucker, Giint, appear from the far side of the Drake, scaling its face...to bite its cheek, punching it with his right hand, while clinging on with his left.

"Uh...someone go tell Giint it's dead," I muttered, gazing around the upper edge of the pit and studying the enormous figures turning towards us.

They were clearly made of the forest, with wood and leaves in place of flesh. A strong, steady green light glowed out from between woven sections, and they stood over eight feet tall on cloven hooves. Their heads were adorned with horns and grim faces.

One of them stepped forward, frowning down at our badly battered little group as it shook its head, hair flaring out and gold rings embedded in one pointed wooden ear jangling as it inspected us.

"Weak, foolish mortals," it ground out. "You trespass in the Great Forest of Easterbrook. Explain your actions or die."

"I..." I broke off to cough, before straightening up and letting out an involuntary groan as Oracle hit me with a heal, drawing their attention to her.

"Little sister," the huge figure whispered, lifting his right hand and tracing an arcane symbol in the air. Lines appeared, floating from Oracle to me, then from me flaring outwards to each of the others, with their own lines stretching from one to another.

Some, like Grizz and Yen, had lines that flared in different colors, clearly hinting at the nature of the connections, but they dissipated before I could do more than see they existed.

The huge creature clearly read more from them than I did, though, as he hissed like a kettle and drew his arrow back, aiming it at my heart. The rest of his party did the same, covering the entire group, save Oracle.

"Little sister, move aside. We will free you," the figure replied as Oracle dove in front of me, even as the arrow began to glow again.

"Don't you dare!" she snapped at them, making them pause. "This is my love, not only my master! Lower your weapons!"

"Enslaved," rumbled another one of the creatures. "Ettin, she is a slave. Better to free her to sleep the long sleep in peace."

"Sleep...no, you bloody fools!" Oracle growled, darting forward and hovering at head height before the one they'd referred to as Ettin.

"Silence!" Ettin hissed, glaring at the creature that had spoken, before looking back to Oracle. "Explain. Your intrusion has resulted in the death of our Drake. Your deaths will be weak recompense for this debt."

"Your Drake?" Arrin muttered. "Look at the fucking state of us! If anyone's getting recompense..." Before he could finish speaking, Lydia had spun on him and grabbed him, her hand clamped over his mouth as she glared into his eyes.

I winced as I caught fragments of a low but fervent comment about tearing his tongue out by its roots.

"I am free!" Oracle insisted, growing from her tiny form to her full size, wings and all, as she landed on the balls of her feet and lifted her chin defiantly at the creatures. "I *was* enslaved to the Tower, but my love and my master, Jax, set me free. I chose my life. I bonded him, not the other way around!"

"That's true," I muttered.

"Silence, mortal!" the creature snapped at me, regarding Oracle curiously.

"Fucking 'mortal.'" I snapped at the creature, drawing its attention back to me. "You dickbags always assume that, don't you?" I stepped forward, only to have its arrow aimed between my eyes before I could take another step.

"We abandoned our patrol to come and stop the Drake from killing you, but one more word, and you can prove if you are mortal or not."

"Please, Guardian!" Oracle interjected, flitting between us again. "This is a misunderstanding! I am bound to him, yes, but he is also bound to me, and to the land. He is the ruler of Dravith, the heir to the Empire, and..."

"Another mortal with delusions of grandeur, and he has infected you with them, little sister," Ettin growled. "Perhaps they are right, better to free you."

"Wait, you are a forest guardian," Oracle interjected quickly. "Therefore, you are guarding a grove, or..."

"A grove," Ettin admitted grudgingly. "We serve and protect the Grove of Western Light."

"We have news and a warning for your grove, then: three hundred Dark Legionnaires are traveling this way, come to make War on us, and behind them come thousands more."

"Bashtokk!" one of the Guardians that hadn't previously spoken snarled, clearly cursing. "You bring war to the grove! Ettin…"

"I said SILENCE!" Ettin snarled, his chest creaking alarmingly with his fury and green light glowing through fresh cracks and breaks.

When all was silent again, he regarded us stonily before looking over the remainder of the group.

"You will all surrender your weapons, and you will plead your case to the grove."

"I don't think so," I retorted, and he drew back on his bow, regarding me furiously. "Oracle, this grove of theirs. Nature, right?" I asked and she paused before smiling proudly and nodding in confirmation.

"You just hold that fucking thought, sunshine," I growled at Ettin, going down on one knee and pressing the knuckles of my right fist to the loamy ground. I closed my eyes and reached out, separating a thread of Nature magic to build the communication spell.

"Ashante, Goddess of Life and Lady of Nature…a little help here?"

CHAPTER TWENTY

*"**J**ax, you call to me?"* came a gentle voice in my mind, and I felt myself relax, as though there was more to worry about in the world, and that all problems could be dealt with, each in their own time. I let out a long breath.

"Yes, thank you for responding, Goddess Ashante, I apologize that my first interaction with you has to be this way, but there are a bunch of grove guardians who want to kill me and mine. I figured I'd better see if they were under your protection, being nature guardians and all, <u>before</u> I started fighting them."

"You would find the defeat of such as these far more challenging than you think, Champion of my sister. Ettin alone would defeat most of your band in short order, and that would have been the case even before you were so gravely injured. Please, give me a moment."

I opened my eyes and stood up, shrugging off the feeling of relief that She would intercede and telling myself that I could have taken down the nine-foot-tall wooden grove guardian with the magic bow...honest.

When Ashante reached out to them, the entire group tensed, moving back to back and staring out at the forest, bows tracking around as they poured more and more mana into their arrows...until suddenly, Ettin relaxed his string and held up a clenched fist.

He held it level alongside his ear for a long moment, then lowered it to shoulder height, opening his hand and making a cutting gesture from left to right, as he straightened and lowered his bow to his side.

The others followed suit, relaxing their bows and glowering at us but clearly no longer intending to slaughter us. My own team relaxed in response, betrayed by the sudden jingle of armor and hushed voices.

"You have impressive acquaintances, human," Ettin rumbled, considering me with something between a glare and a sigh. "We will take you to the grove, and you will meet with the Ancient One. Gather your people."

"I'll need to heal them all first," I said firmly, turning away from him and moving to the others, ignoring his growl of frustration.

"Perhaps a little more subtlety would be in order, Jax?" Oracle whispered, and I glanced irritably at her.

"Perhaps you could explain what the fuck is going on first? After all, I'm guessing that using an Identify on them right now would be a bad idea?"

"A very, very bad idea," Oracle confirmed quickly. "Grove guardians are just that: sentient offshoots of the grove, usually a place of extremely high magical concentration. A grove typically has several guardians and a central figure, from what I remember. That central figure has an aim; the one I knew of was focused on harmony and growing the influence of the Fae, so that we would be safe. She demanded cooperation, mutual protection, and scouting of the areas we held."

"What happened, little sister?" asked one of the guardians curiously, moving closer and lowering itself to one knee so its head was the same height as hers.

"Some agreed then didn't do it. They had simply agreed in an attempt to stop the asking and begging. Then we were found one day by a scouting party of Elves. We were torn, wishing no harm to befall them, yet knowing the rules.

"In the end, the Elves swore to tell no one, and our mother wished to live in peace, so we told no one about them, lest they would be hunted down and killed. Four nights later, they came back, dozens of them, with mana-cages. We were taken, our mana channels burned out, and we were forcibly bonded to the Empire."

As she spoke, others crowded in closer, listening and scowling at me and the others.

"See!" one said, stomping closer to Ettin. "Even the little sister warns us with her words. We must kill them all."

"What we must do is take them to the grove," snapped Ettin. "It is not your place to decide this, nor is it mine. It is *his*."

This resulted in a wave of creaks and nods from the other guardians before they moved off, spreading out around the area. As I counted off, checking on everyone, I noticed we were one short. Giint.

"Oh, hell, where's the mad bastard gotten to, now?" I muttered, standing up and peering around. When I couldn't see him anywhere, I focused, pulling up the strand of the Oath that bound us all together, and followed it to the edge of the pit.

I paused there for a long minute, unsure what to do, as the others moved up to stand around me, also watching him in astonishment.

He'd not only managed to field-strip at least a third of the enormous corpse by himself already, with the skin going into his bags with bewildering speed, as were several organs that clearly glowed to my enhanced vision, but…his face was covered in gore, and he was noisily chewing on a section of raw flesh.

"I…uh," Grizz muttered, shaking his head. I grinned at him, remembering a conversation from when we'd first adopted Giint into our mismatched little cadre.

"I vote Grizz is responsible for the mad little bastard," I declared quickly, holding my right hand up. "All in favor, say 'aye'."

There was a long pause as everyone figured out what I'd said, and what it meant, before they all started chiming in with agreement. Grizz's eyes widened in horror, and he shook his head.

"Oh, hell, no!" he cried, looking to me. "Come on, boss, that's just messed up!"

"Sorry, mate, that's democracy for you." I laughed as I turned away.

"What the hell's democracy?" Grizz asked, confused.

"It's uh…it means you do as I say," I said, smiling at my sudden burst of inspiration. I could be a democratic leader, as I'd always been taught was right. It was just much easier to manage when I swapped the meaning of democracy for that of autocracy. Fuck the haters.

"I don't think I like democracy," Grizz grumbled as I stepped away from the pit.

Yen told him to make sure Giint finished looting the creature before the guardians realized what he was doing.

"It's been said that it's the worst form of government ever tried, mate," I added as I left him there, making my way back to where Tang leaned against a rock. "Except for all the others, anyway." I laughed again and moved on, healing

Tang again. Ettin gestured for Oracle to come with him, leading her off to the side to speak, clearly thinking he was being subtle.

After a few minutes, she let out a silvery peal of laughter and returned, leaning in and whispering in my ear.

"We need to get moving now; they're losing patience, and more of the guardians are looking for an excuse to kill us all. Once they realize what Giint's doing, they *really* won't be happy…"

"Okay, let's go distract them," I said, grimacing as I stood. "Tang, go get the others moving, and make sure Grizz remembers to make Giint clean himself the fuck up."

Tang nodded and set off quickly, commenting loudly that he needed to recover his weapons, and that he'd be right with us.

Oracle and I gathered the others up, wandering over to join Ettin, who was regarding us with an irritable expression, while his fellow guardians drifted off through the trees to resume their patrols.

Three remained with him, and they all looked unamused by the need, but as I approached, he gestured the nearest, who had been speaking, to silence.

"Are you ready at last, human?" he rumbled, clearly frustrated, and I nodded to him.

"My people are gathering their weapons that were dropped in the fight. I have to ask, though; there was a small blind in the pit…what was it for?"

"I am unfamiliar with the term."

"A hunter's blind," I clarified. "It's a structure that allows a hunter to hide in order to observe a creature."

"An observation post." He grunted the correction. "The Ice-Drake was a valuable contribution to the mana of the area. We often had one of our observers watch it from there, ensuring that its needs were attended to, as best as we could manage, and collecting the valuable scales it dropped."

"Can you explain that?" I asked as he gestured for the group to start moving.

"No," he replied flatly. "It is none of your business, outsider." The guardian looked around, clearly counting us, before frowning suspiciously at me. "Where are the others?" he demanded, when Tang hurried up, ostensibly waving the sword he had dropped and slotting it back into the sheath on his hip.

"Sorry that took so long," he offered, smiling winningly. "I couldn't find the damn thing."

"Then we move," Ettin growled, glaring at Giint, who tried to smile up at the massive creature, only to expose teeth that were covered in blood with bits of raw meat still stuck between them.

The Guardian froze, glaring hatefully at the little Gnome with the metal teeth, before shaking himself and turning around to lead us onwards, all the while muttering something about killing us later.

The next half hour passed quickly, with the group following a clear path through the forest. We traversed across little rises and gullies, occasionally clambering around the easiest route because the guardians insisted that we not disturb the plants that grew in those locations.

As we closed in on our destination, I checked my map and nodded in satisfaction. They were either guarding the same place, or were close enough that they had to be linked.

I'd assumed it was strange that they would be guarding somewhere so close to the waystation, but now I knew it; there was something linking the two.

The closer we got to the grove the guardians were taking us to, the more the creatures around us grew, in both number and size.

Soon we passed deer that had to be six foot at the shoulder with a staggering twenty points across its antlers, that paused to watch us regally before moving off with his herd.

"Shoot nothing, harm nothing," Ettin rumbled when he saw the stunned looks on our faces at the sight of the monarch deer. "Any harm done in the grove is paid back ten times over. You have been warned."

I nodded, as did the others, and Grizz yanked Giint closer and whispered furiously to the little Gnome, clearly laying down the law.

When we finally reached a thick ring of brambles and bushes, skirting around the outside until we found an arch to step through, we paused in shock.

The trees as we'd travelled had grown steadily taller, thicker, and stronger, but there had also been a huge number of smaller plants that filled the majority of the forest floor, stopping us from being able to see very far.

Here, there were notably less.

Once we crossed under the arch, we all slowed and gradually came to a halt at the sight of the huge, and I mean *huge,* tree that stood alone in the center of the grove. It had to have been almost two hundred and sixty feet around at the base and hundreds higher, spreading out a canopy that, while from above blended in with the others, from below, it was clear that it was mind-blowingly larger than dozens of other, smaller trees.

The grove was carpeted in verdant green grass, sun-dappled, with small brooks running here and there. There were clumps of bushes and patches of wildflowers, but where they grew, somewhere nearby each one, I could easily spot a creature like the guardians, albeit smaller and unarmed, tending the plants.

We were guided around the base of the tree to the far side, coming to a halt before a low series of rocks that were obviously meant to be seats that had been carved and placed around that side of it.

We sat as we were ordered, the entire group silent as we breathed in the air which seemed so charged with life and energy, and Yen was the first to see it.

"Look," she said quietly as two thin vines slowly lowered themselves to the seats, one for me, and one for the guardian, Ettin.

For him, the vine seemed to join to him and form a complete plant, the tips of it sinking into the creature and making it hard to judge where one ended and the other began. The other vines stopped before me and waited.

I looked around at the others, until Oracle, who had assumed her smaller form, spoke up.

"It's safe, don't worry," she assured me, and I nodded to her, her word all I needed. She'd been uncharacteristically quiet as we went, yet I'd been able to feel the strange ball of emotions that belonged to her, so I knew she wasn't scared, not exactly. More than that, she seemed to be cautiously hopeful.

I reached out my hand, and as I touched the vine, it wrapped itself around my hand, holding me gently but firmly, as I felt a pressure against the edge of my mind and was guided to sit down in the seat.

Jez Cajiao

The Arbuton of the Grove of Western Light asks to establish a link.

Will you allow this?

Yes/No

I took a deep breath and selected Yes, and the world seemed to vanish from me.

Suddenly, I was seated in a comfortable chair on a wooden deck back home. I straightened up, looking out over the houses nearby and realizing that I was on the back upper deck at one of the houses I'd lived in, in Jesmond, of all places. I could see the concrete warren of houses and yards all around me. As I shifted, I felt something in my hand, and I looked down.

In my right hand, I held a glass, a thick-bottomed tumbler that was half-full of an amber liquid. I sniffed it and smiled unconsciously, recognizing the smell of my favorite rum, and I took a sip.

It burned comfortingly as it went down, and a leaf and vine motif tattooed into the flesh on the back of my hand caught my attention.

I frowned, staring at it until a sound nearby drew my attention.

I lifted my gaze and found an old man I'd never seen before sitting in a comfortable chair next to me. He had obviously been tall and broad once, but now he sat hunched, his shoulders turned in. He breathed slowly, his breath slightly raspy as he regarded me from under massive eyebrows.

"You trespassed in my lands, little one," he said eventually. "I would know why." His voice was firm but calm, with no hint of threat, simply a rock-solid belief that he would ask and I would answer.

I regarded him for a while, then I nodded, deciding to be as truthful as I could afford.

"I was seeking the waystation," I answered, and I caught the slight tightening of his eyes. "I didn't know you were here, or the Ice-Drake, so I'm sorry if I've caused a problem in killing it?"

"You have, but that is neither here nor there. It is dead now, and we must move on," the old man replied, still perfectly calm. "Why do you seek the waystation? It has been long ages since it was abandoned, and little of the shiny metals your kind value can be found here now."

"I don't care about the metals…"

"The resources of the land, then. What have you come to beg for?"

"Uh, nothing, as far as I know, but I'm obviously interested if you want to trade?" I suggested hopefully. He shook his head, smacking the base of a walking stick down on the ground hard, making a loud crack of fracturing wood sound out. I frowned unconsciously, having not seen the stick before, and I waited for his reply.

"We have no interest in trade with the outside world. Your kind can give us nothing that we cannot produce for ourselves both cheaper and better."

"Then why speak to me?" I asked.

The old man smiled for the first time. "Through the mind of one of my guardian children, I felt the touch of the Goddess, a touch I have not felt in long ages. I would know more."

"Ashante," I confirmed, nodding. "I thought you might be interested in Her. Are you a worshipper of Hers?"

He shook his head slowly. "Better to say that we were allies in days long past. Then She and Her brethren disappeared, and the heavens rained rock and fire. We believed Her to have perished, and thus we fought to protect the realm in our own way, sacrificing much to bring safety to the groves. Now you bring word of Her, and I wonder…did she simply grow bored and leave us?"

"No," I said honestly. "That Dark Wanker, Ni…The God of Death banished the others. They were gone for a long, long time, and when They finally reappeared, it was too late. Their strength was wasted as They tried to recover before They passed into slumber. They slept long ages away, until I found the altars in the Great Tower."

"The Dark Tower," the old man corrected, and I paused, considering him curiously.

"What do you mean?" I asked.

"The Great Tower, as you call it, we called the Dark Tower, a place of terrible secrets, and finally, terrible evil. Not least of which was the mutilation of the Wisps."

"Yeah…well, I won't disagree with you there." He turned away silently, staring out across the concrete jungle before us, and sighed.

"And yet, this image, one that slipped from your mind as I created this simple place to speak, it shows nothing of beauty. I know your kind take comfort in it, but it seems dead to me."

"This is my home," I said, shrugging and climbing from my chair to gesture to the southeast. "That way is Jesmond Dene; it's a wooded area, but yeah, the city itself is a shithole. At least it's not Sunderland, though," I said with a snort.

"This land of Sun is worse?" the old man asked, and I snorted again.

"Nah, not really, just a long-standing rivalry. It just kinda slipped out, you know?" I shook my head at the confused look he gave me. "Look, I'm sorry. This was my home, but it's not anymore. My home now is the Tower. And yeah, the Empire did some fucked-up shit in the past, from what I can see, but it also did a lot of good. Frankly, it'll do more from now on."

"Because you now lead it?" the old man asked.

I nodded.

"Very well. Your Empire is well and good. A simple agreement is that you take care of yours, and we will take care of ours. Beyond that, we need no further contact."

"Whoa, no!" I said quickly, as the vision began to dim. "There's an army coming, and I need the waystation!" The vision brightened again, changing until the man, now seated across from me, looked older and rougher, his skin changing from wrinkled flesh to ancient bark, and his eyes glowing with a fierce green light.

"Explain," he demanded.

"Look, you want to know what's happening? Fine. I re-awoke the Gods, and the God of Death ain't happy about it, okay? He's sent his armored goons to kill me and those I protect, and they're currently cutting a path through the forest towards the Tower. They'll pass within ten miles of here, and I need to both warn you of their coming, so that you can prepare yourself if you need to, and I need to take my golems from the waystation."

"There is nothing that belongs to you here," he retorted, emotionless.

"You and the waystation being here can't be a coincidence," I stated, maintaining eye contact with the stone-still form that stared passively at me. "You weren't here when the Empire was at its height, or I'd know, so you set up here after the fall. You picked the place because of the waystation, that's obvious…"

"I agreed to speak with you because you have the approval of the Goddess of Nature, but be careful with your words, mortal," he warned.

"I'm never careful, mate." I grinned slightly. "It's not in my nature. You're clearly concerned now, but you know that fucking with me would be an unbelievably bad idea," I pointed out, being able to sense that much. "Whatever this link is, it's given you limited access to me. That's how you made this illusion…but it means I can sense you, as well, so let's cut the bullshit, shall we?" I asked, getting a green flare of the fierce eyes but no words from the tree creature.

"Okay, you chose this location, and you clearly need a fuck-ton of mana to live. The way you've made the grove guardians shows that, so let's take it a logical step further. You picked this place specifically because of the mana. That means that when Seneschal shut down the waystation, the mana collectors that shut down fully elsewhere probably didn't here, for some reason. Instead, with nothing to drain that mana away, it started to build up and grow. Now, you need that mana, am I right?" I asked, eliciting a heavy sigh from the creature before it finally responded.

"You are almost correct. The mana collectors, as you call them, were shut down. But even as they are, buried and unused, they draw a small amount in. Even a small increase to the ambient mana levels is noticeable. If you visit other such locations, you may find that they have also been claimed by creatures of power."

"The other two I already claimed had to be cleared out by force, so how about we take a different approach here?" I asked him, getting another hard look in return.

"Why don't we share it?" I offered.

"Share what? The mana? There isn't enough," the tree creature stated with irritation.

"There is, if I reactivate the mana collectors." I sat back, waiting.

He paused, regarding me for long seconds and nodding in thought. "You could do this? Make the collectors work again?"

"I think so; we've got them being repaired at the other sites now. It all depends on how damaged the waystation is," I said carefully.

"You said you wanted to retrieve your property," he said, changing tack. "Explain that."

"The Empire made golems, constructs that only I can command. Each site has held a contingent of golems hidden within. I'd need to charge them from the mana collectors, plus I'd need to claim the area in order to take my portion of the mana."

"This grove belongs to the forest," he rumbled threateningly.

"And that's totally fine; I'll lease it back to you."

"Lease?" he repeated, unfamiliar with the term.

"It means I own the territory, which I need to claim to repair the waystation, *but*," I said hurriedly, "I have no need of the actual land. I have plenty already, and nowhere near enough citizens to work it. Instead, I would leave the grove under your control.

"In return, you take half of the mana that the structure generates, which is usually far, far more than they do when they're shut down, and you use that. You agree to aid me if I have a need, and I do the same with you. We become allies…"

He scoffed at me.

"No," he refused swiftly. "We will not be drawn into your war."

"Fine. Instead of soldiers, or militaristic help, what about herbs and plants, alchemical ingredients…you kept the Ice-Drake in that pit because you needed the mana it gave off, right?" I asked. "You've probably got loads more creatures in the area like that. Well, you won't need to siphon off the excess mana that the creatures give off.

"You'll be taking a lot more mana from the waystation, so you can ignore the creatures out there, or hell, get more. I really don't give a shit. You're about thirty miles due south of the Tower here. Believe me, that's a hell of a long way, as far as I'm concerned. I can tell my hunters to steer clear of this area, and if you keep yours from killing any of my people, everyone's happy."

"What herbs?" The Arbuton asked after a long pause as it considered options.

"All of them." I held my hands up placatingly. "I don't mean I want all the herbs you have, but I want half of every type of herb or alchemical ingredient. We need to make potions and more, and we have a glasshouse…that's uh…a magical building that's dedicated to growing plants," I explained. "Any plants you give us, we will need cuttings that can be planted as well."

"And the Goddess?" he asked eventually, his voice a low rumble.

"What about Her?" I asked.

"You have contact with Her. You will ask Her to speak with us."

"That's a big ask," I settled back and tried to keep my excitement under wraps. "I can ask Her, but I can't offer any guarantees," I hedged.

I was almost shocked out of the communication link by the figure that appeared and sat down between us as the third point in a triangle.

She was tall and slim, with long, platinum hair that reached all the way to Her hips. A simple, long green dress, cut modestly, covered Her frame, aside from the long legs that escaped as She rested one knee over the other, and She smiled gently at us both.

She appeared elven, with the fine features and the pointed ears, but She also had sharp canines. There was a palpable aura of hunger around Her as She sat back, watching us both.

"As you are bargaining for land that is mine, I felt I should make an appearance," She said, and her voice confirmed what the feeling of her presence had me suspecting.

"Welcome, Ashante," I said, standing and taking a knee before Her, then rising and sitting back down. "I didn't want to interrupt you twice in one day," I said quickly.

"You wished to make deals before I could involve myself, you mean. Let's be clear, Jax, Eternal, Scion of the Empire. I have needs, and the mana from this site would do much to address the most urgent of them."

"Maybe," I acknowledged, refusing to be intimidated. "But I'm the Scion, and this continent is mine, with the blessing of Jenae, my Lady of Fire." I emphasized the point that I was a follower of Jenae, not Her. I was hoping She'd respect the lines between us and that She was also subservient to the Goddess of Fire.

"Noted," She said, inclining Her head.

"Well, the Waystation *is* Imperial property…" I began, and She smiled sharply, cutting me off.

"Yet you are not the Emperor, and rights so long ignored and unclaimed might as well not exist. Arbuton, do you know me?" She addressed the ancient being, and he bowed his head.

"I do, my Lady of Nature. My creatures and I stand ready to serve."

"Will you relinquish those I feel are needed to my care?" She asked gently. He paused, clearly struggling, before bowing his head. The simple presence of her Godhood was more than enough to encourage us both to acquiesce. *"Excellent. Jax, you and I will discuss appropriate rewards for your service later, as well as a fitting tithe of your new followers,"* She broke off long enough to shoot a warning glance at me, before going on.

"And in return for the mana from this site being split THREE ways, an equal share to each of us, you will be permitted that which you have asked for. Half of all production of herbs and ingredients of the grove will be gifted to you, monthly, and you may remove the golems. I trust that is acceptable?"

"No, but it is a good start," I said, smiling tightly as Her aura grew stronger. "There was a little hesitation there when you mentioned the production of the herbs and ingredients, not to mention that I also asked for several of each plant to grow my own. So, explain what I'm missing when it comes to production. Wait…" I rubbed my temple with one hand as I closed my eyes. "You don't grow anything like that, do you?" I asked the Arbuton.

"Well done, Jax," Ashante purred appreciatively. *"No, the grove produces nothing beyond the guardians and tenders of the grove. The plants themselves are pruned and guided, but only to ensure that the correct mana strains and mixes are maintained."*

"Then how about we agree to abide by the intent as well as the word of the agreement, and I'll introduce you to a member of my council who very much wishes to meet you next?" I offered. "Additionally, if you can provide some tenders and guardians to aid the Tower, I could provide some manpower, or golem-power, I suppose, should you need it? I was serious about the Dark Legion, after all."

"I have already had Nerin reach out to me, and she is one of my first worshippers in these times, but I appreciate the thought. I will provide two tenders and two guardians from the grove. They will aid you for one month, and not in war. The guardians will be present exclusively to protect the tenders. New tenders of the grove will be germinated, and when they grow to maturity, then they will serve the Tower and its gardens."

"And how long…?" I asked.

"Twenty months, depending on the land's will," the Arbuton replied calmly.

"And that'd be a no, because I might be dead next week," I declined calmly. "You give us two tenders now, and you keep those you're growing. The two guardians serve the Tower in all things; if I send them to war, they go. It is against your brother, after all," I added to Ashante.

"No, I will not have the guardians wasted, but they may be used in defense of the two Tenders. They will be our choice, and one war golem is kept here on permanent loan to the Arbuton," Ashante countered, before adding. *"And you can have half of all the herbs and ingredients in the grove now, on the condition that you also provide me with thirty new worshippers upon your return to the Tower."*

"How long do the tenders live?" I persisted, and I caught a predatory smile on Ashante's face as the Arbuton let out a rumbling laugh.

"I will provide two in the bloom of youth. They will wither in more than fifty summers, but you spotted that well," he admitted with a faint smile.

"Ha, thanks!" I grinned in return. "Okay, so I'll go one better. I get two guardians, and two tenders, all in full bloom? I get half the ingredients or loot in the territory. I claim the territory, and I'll set the waystation to repair itself and give us each a third of the mana it collects, and a single war golem. I'll need to build a Control Tower for that, though, Ashante, and I don't have the mana for that yet. I'll need you to do it somehow; get the other Gods involved, or something."

The frown formed as She started to shake Her head, so I rushed on, hoping I was right about what She genuinely wanted. "But, as I know you'd want to help by blessing the land to be bountiful and all that, how about I guide all the farmers and those involved with new life to you? Including those who currently worship Jenae? We've already discussed this, as She wanted to support you." I added quickly.

Ashante froze, Her mouth open, before closing it and regarding me through narrowed eyes for an uncomfortably long minute. I fought down the urge to fidget until at last She spoke.

"How many worshippers?" She said slowly.

"I can't guarantee any; I won't force them to worship anyone, but I'd think that forty to fifty would be achievable. A lot of the villagers that joined us recently are farmers, after all?" I said, hedging my bets.

"Very well." She eyed me warily, straightening. *"We accept."*

The Arbuton bowed his head in respectful obeisance, and She smiled, reaching out and stroking his face. Even from where I sat, I felt the power wash out from Her into him and the sigh of relief as his great weight seemed to suddenly rest easier on his roots.

"Thank you, my Lady," he breathed, and She smiled down at him.

"Ah, Lady Ashante?" I asked tentatively, and She gazed down at me. "Just a suggestion, not sure if it will help you to arrange the Control Tower." She frowned, Her expression darkening as She realized She might have been conned in Her desperation to acquire more worshippers. "I have fifteen Gnomes with the fleet that is traveling in, and they all dream of one day worshipping Svetu again.

"I'm sure He would have no problems in making the Control Tower at almost no cost, and if you were to mention that not only are there fifteen Gnomes incoming, but that I have a suggestion for a champion for Him?"

"I shall speak to Svetu, and we shall see. I promised to aid you with it, not make it entirely. Oh, and you might remember that I agreed you could have half the ingredients?" She reminded me.

"Oh yes," I agreed, smiling.

"Good. You'll note I didn't agree to harvest any of them. Therefore, any that you harvest, by logical extension, you will deliver half of to the Arbuton."

"Fuck," I muttered, scowling at Her.

"Quite." She grinned down at me. *"Remember your place, boy, but I did enjoy the chat, so I'll uphold the deal. You'll find the Tower's growing efforts are significantly improved from now on,"* the Goddess promised with a wink before vanishing.

The Arbuton and I stared at each other in silence before he finally sighed.

I was suddenly blinking at the sunlight, sitting on the seat before the massive tree. The vine withdrew from my hand as the others looked to me, waiting to see if they would be offered a vine as well.

The large guardian growled deep in his throat as he stood up, peering down at me in disgust, then stalking off.

"What just happened?" Oracle asked, frowning, as Grizz grunted.

"Yeah, boss, didn't we agree that pissing them off would be a bad idea?"

"He's always miserable!" called a warm voice from my left. I turned, seeing a tall, slim creature, built similarly to a guardian, marching over. "I'm Wo'Idiara I't'aren. The mortals I occasionally deal with call me 'Woodite,' for some reason, so it would be acceptable for you to use this name also."

"Woodite," I repeated as I looked over the tall creature before me. He bore humanoid features with elven ears, pricked upright, rather than outwards like those of the guardians. While slenderer of build and notably unarmed beyond a pair of slim wooden daggers on one hip and the opposite ankle, he was clearly strong, given the casual way he deposited a large trunk of wood on the grass nearby.

"I have been designated to be your lead helper, and I need direction. What is my role to be and where?" he asked.

"You don't mind? That you're to move to the Tower and serve me, and the Empire, I mean?"

"I was germinated to be traded to the Dwarves," he informed us cheerfully. "To instead be sent to the Dark Tower, especially to aid your efforts at growing, should be interesting. Besides, at least I'll have a better chance of not being held underground until I wither."

"Right...well, it's the Great Tower, not the Dark Tower; kinda a minor detail, but you know, branding and all that. As to what you'll be doing, well, you'll be helping us. There's a glasshouse that can supposedly aid in growing all plants, regardless of the environment needed, so you're going to be helping there, and in the fields, I guess?

"Oh, and I made a slight mistake in phrasing when it comes to the deal. I own half of all the ingredients in the territory, while the other half is to go to your Arbuton there," I said, gesturing upwards. "The problem is, I didn't specify that it was to be harvested for me."

"Ah, and now you need to harvest it. Understandable. Are these ingredients?"

"All ingredients, including alchemical," I confirmed hurriedly.

"And the priority is alchemical?" he clarified. When I nodded confirmation, he carried on brightly. "Excellent. There is an argument for including everything, after all.

"Stone is an ingredient of a cliff. Water of a river. If alchemical is the focus, I shall have my mate concentrate on that. If you have a container of some kind that you wish us to fill, now would be a good time to provide this. Moving on, I believe you wished to be shown to the ruins under the grove?"

"Yes!" I smiled gratefully at his exuberant efficiency, pleased that he was both helpful and thorough. "Yes, please take us there, and here," I said, quickly shifting things around to free up a larger bag to provide for Woodite and his partner to fill.

The personable tender led us through the grove to another section close to the base of the massive Arbuton. He reached down, grasping a large slab of rock and lifting it with a slight grunt. Once he'd set it aside, he guided us calmly down into the utter blackness. I paused, gesturing to the others to get ready while I pulled my naginata out.

"There's nothing living down here," Woodite reassured me calmly, smiling back up at us, and I grunted.

"We've fought plenty of undead lately," I countered.

He smiled again, shaking his head. His eyes glowed in the darkness as my own DarkVision attempted to compensate for the loss of light, while Grizz and several others activated their magelights.

I eventually gave up and just pulled one out as well, while Woodite continued down the corridor.

"There are the remains of several humanoids that were trapped down here, but they sleep the sleep of ages and show no signs of awakening now."

With that reassurance, he turned and led the way down the dark corridor. We followed closely, marveling at the condition of the place. The other two sites were ruined and partially buried, but here, the hallway was mainly intact. There were minor sections where the wall or ceiling bulged in precariously, but these were due to roots that had pushed through, and they had been clearly grown by the Arbuton to hold the corridor together.

"Why did he preserve this?" I wondered aloud, and Woodite glanced back at me, his eyes suddenly flaring bright green.

"Because I didn't know what was important and what wasn't. I needed the mana to continue," he said in the Arbuton's rough voice, before the eyes dimmed, and he continued in his own pitch and timbre. "The grove requires mana to grow, and while most areas have equal mana, this location was long found to provide excess. It was more efficient to germinate a grove here than anywhere else."

"So, the Arbuton has maintained the structure?" I asked as we walked along, reaching the first branching nexus of corridor and Woodite paused.

"Correct; the grove maintained the entire structure in case its decline would cost us the mana-generating properties."

"And he can speak through you any time he wants?" I questioned carefully, getting a shake of Woodite's head.

"No, the Arbuton can speak though me only when I am within the boundaries of the grove. Now, I am unfamiliar with your needs in this place, so…?"

I nodded, realizing he wouldn't have any clue where the control center was, and I took over guiding our trajectory, working from the memories of the last two we'd visited.

Due to the fact they were both truly ruins, that meant a few wrong turns, but less than ten minutes later, we had reached the middle floor and I was pressing the release for the hidden entrance in the usual golem room, trying not to worry about the missing figures in the row of golems.

While it was dusty, like the others, it was also neither damaged nor coated in filth, which meant the door easily swung free after a good, hard jab at the release.

As soon as the door was open, I strode in and sat down in the chair, reaching out my right hand to begin the long process of awakening the system.

It took just over an hour to charge the system, partially because, after everything that had happened, I wasn't pushing anyone to drain their mana, and partially because Woodite kept talking.

It turned out that he was actually excited to leave the grove, despite having been germinated there, and having never left, beyond the occasional mission to recover plants or to repair the streams that fed the grove when storms blocked one with a fallen tree.

"I've already informed my mate, and she is harvesting several of the more hardy and unusually potent alchemical ingredients now. Once Ha'AnZel Lish'I'Ara is done, we will see which of the grove's guardians we are paired with…it should be interesting to see…"

"Hanizz?" I started to say, trying to navigate the mash of syllables, and Woodite laughed, tapping one finger against the side of his head to produce a hollow *tap-tap-tap* as he thought.

Each time the finger landed, the sound would echo, and the green light that filled him, gleaming out from the cracks and edges of the wood that encompassed him, would flare slightly.

"Ha'Zel," he said eventually. "She said that some of the Dwarves have referred to her as Ha'Zel."

"Hazel," I confirmed gratefully. "That's a hell of a lot easier to pronounce, thanks."

"Uh, ah…whatever," Woodite replied after a slight pause, clearly checking through some kind of link with Hazel. The large wooden creature shrugged and leaned in, watching as the last few drops of my mana were added to the table, and it flared suddenly to life.

"Fascinating," he remarked in a low voice, the timbre echoing faintly as I read the notifications that popped up, accepting them one at a time.

Congratulations!

You have cleared Waystation Five and have the prerequisite authority and abilities to claim this structure and the surrounding land, adding it to your territory as a claimed location. As this territory holds less than ten (10) percent of sentients that are actively hostile to your rule, it can be claimed.

Do you wish to annex this territory now?

Yes/No

*

Congratulations!

You have annexed new lands onto your own, providing the following benefits if the land is worked:

Ancient Grove: This location has agreed to an alliance with you and will provide between 3-15 tons of crafting materials per month, depending on focus:

1) Alchemical: 3-5 tons

2) Consumable: 5-7 tons

3) Mineral: 7-15 tons

*

Attention: Citizens of the Territory of Dravith!

Lord Jax of Dravith has expanded his territory and has claimed an additional one hundred and seventy-six square miles of land by defeating the previously hostile occupants and bargaining with the current inhabitants.

All titles, Deeds, and Laws in the Territory of Dravith are held for review, and can be revoked, altered, annulled, or approved.

All Hail Lord Jax of Dravith!

CHAPTER TWENTY-ONE

This time, as the interface wasn't broken but rather had been dormant without mana for ages, it was a quite different system that greeted me.

The table glowed, the liquid silvery mana drawing together at the center. Then it rippled and spread out, flashing to create a map of the facility, spread over four levels, unlike the others we'd cleared, which had been composed of two accessible ones, with a third basement floor that had been flooded in both cases.

Here, the structure was remarkably similar to the others, but each floor appeared almost fully intact beyond the occasional small section that had sagged or bulged in or out.

As the map grew in complexity, it shrank in size, until standing before me, seemingly made of liquid mercury, was a detailed three-dimensional map of the entire structure.

Once this was complete, a series of tiles began to populate around an outer ring, and my breath caught. It called to mind the similar system that the Great Tower had, and how dead it had been when I'd seen it last.

This location boasted six tiles, three lit, three empty, and I spun the map with a thought to get the three lit ones into view.

The first showed a symbol like a circle with a wavy line through it, and as I reached out to tap it, the map faded from sight, showing instead a line drawing of the local area.

The territory was narrow, running to a point on the eastern side that ended just below the Tower itself, but widening as it ran west up into the foothills of the mountains and higher.

A handful of green dots popped into existence, all clustered about where we sat currently, with a fast-moving second group of green dots on one side heading towards us, roughly, from the Tower. Then a series of blue dots, dozens and dozens of them, all surrounded a single yellow, and these were indicated directly above us. I realized it was the equivalent of a threat map.

There were six red dots, two on opposite sides of the Grove, about a mile or so out, and I guessed that these were creatures that the Grove tended, like the Ice-Drake had been. The remaining four, though, they were spread out, and I made a conscious effort to link my map to the table, getting an acknowledgement a few seconds later that made me grunt in acceptance.

Two of the dots coincided with two of the locations I'd had pointed out by the Gods, so I bet myself that the third, with one much larger dot, and one small one close together, indicated a monster nest of some kind as well.

There were dozens of other dots, most of them a dull grey, with maybe forty or so clustered around a site halfway up the nearby mountains, the rest spread out across the land.

"What's this?" I asked Woodite.

He leaned in to inspect the map, lifting one finger to tap the concentrations. "The Dwarves of the Stone Thane Clan." He indicating the grey dots gathered in the mountains. "These are dryads," he explained, touching a half dozen smaller ones in one area. "Fun, but a group to be wary of. They tend to be...enthusiastic, I have heard. The male Dwarves who go to visit are often in need of rescuing within a few days but some return regularly, nonetheless."

He pointed to the respective red dots. "These are great beast lairs, tiger, bear, and I think this one is a beast...although the guardians could tell you for sure." He straightened up and went back to watching the table as I used it.

"What's the difference between a great beast and a normal one?" I asked, and he leaned in conspiratorially.

"Great beasts are intelligent, and they are often hunted for this reason. Many mortals wish mounts that can think, rather than the dumber beasts of the world. I am sure I don't need to say this but enslaving the great beasts would be an exceptionally large mistake. One the grove would not tolerate."

He eyed me warningly. "A pair bond, in which you mutually choose to live in peace, would be fine, but capturing and forcibly bonding them would result in a very different relationship with the grove."

"I have no interest in subjugation," I clarified hastily. "We might see if they want to live with us, but I'll be very careful in how we approach it; maybe ask you or a guardian to go with anyone who decides to visit them; that way, we can make sure it stays...friendly."

"That would be for the best," Woodite said, clearly pleased as he straightened up again. "The Arbuton agrees with your suggestion as well."

"Good," I said simply, realizing that having Woodite around also meant that I was at constant risk of judging from the Arbuton, at least until I left the grove. He was clearly watching how I controlled the facility, but there was no simple way to get rid of him without making it obvious, so I ignored him and went on.

I flexed a mental muscle, then another, and on the third try, with my hands pressed to the table, the symbols flowed back into place on the tiles. Satisfied, I went to the next. This time, it was a simple building, and when I tapped on it, I received a plain interface.

Welcome, Master of the Territory.

Please choose from the following options:

- Repairs
- Alterations
- Inhabitants
- Facilities

I selected the first, and a new notification popped up.

229

Repairs:

Waystation Five is currently at 88% integrity.

Mana available for repairs: 4/10,000

Ambient mana is insufficient to repair this facility.

Please deploy mana collectors.

I moved on from that screen to the next, skipping through them, though I found much the same message in the alterations menu, warning that nothing was available. In the inhabitants menu, no guests were currently listed.

The facilities menu, on the other hand, was far more interesting.

Facilities:

Mana Collectors: Disabled

Production: N/A

Storage: 4/10,000

Construction: 3/6 Available.

Golems: *See more.*

I selected the mana collectors and ordered them to deploy, gaining a wire diagram of the surrounding area and a check for confirmation. I spun the image to make sure that none of the collectors were going to damage the Arbuton or anything else, and drew Woodite's attention to a single thick trunk that was blocking one of the paths. Within a few seconds, his voice changed, and he asked me to proceed but to go slowly as he shifted that root. I complied, holding my breath as the entire building trembled.

Eventually, it was over, the shuddering subsiding as the entire structure began to glow from the gentle light of the repowered magelights.

I pulled up the options again, selecting Repair first. Seeing that the structure had dropped from eighty-eight to seventy-nine, I set it to repair itself, with fifty percent of the mana available going to the repairs and the other half going to charging the golems.

"Woodite, I know the Arbuton and Ashante want their cut of the mana, but we need to repair the facility first, so please warn the Arbuton that it's going to take…twelve hours to complete repairs, and after that, he and the Goddess will start to receive their share. I won't be getting anything until that time, either," I finished, hoping that Ashante was listening. When he confirmed that the message had been relayed, I thanked him and went back to the golems screen.

Golems:

Construction: 1x Class One, 1x Class Three.

Servitor: 1x Class One.

Crafter: 0

War: 0 (Recalled to Tower)

I couldn't help but grin at the sight of the first class three construction golem I'd found. Yeah, I'd have loved more, especially higher leveled ones, but hell, I was happy with that, even though I guessed that the war-classed golems had been returned to the Tower and destroyed long ago, considering how close this facility was to the Great Tower.

I shrugged, a bit annoyed, as I'd agreed to a golem being kept here and would need to send one from the Tower, instead of leaving one of the local ones in place, but that was a minor issue.

"Arbuton," I said, a thought occurring to me. "Are you wanting a golem for defense or something else?"

"Why?" The Arbuton replied through Woodite, the tender's voice changing and his glimmering light deepening as he was taken over by the huge creature.

"Because there are only construction and servitor golems here, no war-class ones." I rubbed the bridge of my nose as I tried to think how best to describe the differences. "There are four basic models of golems, okay? War, for fighting and defense, construction, for, well, building, obviously. Servitor for cleaning, repairing, and general duties, and crafter. Crafter makes things from scratch.

"Now, as I understand it, all of them can do things to a certain degree. The crafter could hit a Goblin and kill it, the war golem can hold a wall up while it gets attached; servitors can do basic upgrades. The problem is that they are built for one thing each and are far better at that one thing. A war golem can patrol and defend a location automatically, even as a class one, which is the lowest. However, to get it to dig a well, you need to be guiding it constantly. So, what is it that you need?"

"Craft…"

"I don't have any crafters."

"Humph, a war golem, then."

"Fine; I'll need to send one from the Tower, as there's none here. It'll take a day or so, I'd guess, but that's no great hardship. I'll make sure it takes orders from you." I relaxed as the Arbuton left Woodite's body without responding.

With that sorted out, I pulled up the bit I was really interested in, even as I called out to Bane and the others. "There're two additional levels to this facility, and it's fully lit now, so if you want to explore, you can. There are no enemies here."

Some of the group left immediately, while others just called acknowledgement and stayed where they were. I dismissed it from my mind, much like I did Grizz's constant low level of chemical attacks on the group and Giint's incessant tinkering.

I pulled up the Construction options, and the remaining three blank tiles lit up with options.

Construction:

Facility	Size	Yield (Golem)	Yield (Living)
Logging Camp	2	10 logs daily (per worker)	1 log daily (per worker)
Transport (Canal)	3	Dependent on connected territories	Dependent on connected territories
Farm	1	500-2000kg per facility/worker per month	50-500kg per facility/worker per month
Control Facility (No connected facilities, N/A for construction at this time)	2	N/A	N/A
Defensive Facilities (Siege Weapons)	2	N/A	N/A

I looked them over, not particularly excited by any of them, until I realized that this was what was currently possible to build and how many of the tiles they would take up.

The location determined the options, with the farm option being because the land here was both fertile and mana-rich; in the hills where waystation three and four were, I guessed there would be more options, especially four, with the lake.

I pulled back from the options, figuring the Arbuton would be a bit pissed if I converted his grove into farmland.

The Storage option indicated that there were four of something unidentified left behind, and the Alterations menu revealed that I could add extra rooms and grow the facility, but again, I could see no reason to do that here. This was essentially the grove only, and I didn't want to make any changes.

I ordered the golems, once they were fully charged, to return to the Tower, then named the Arbuton to have limited control over the system and the golems. He couldn't countermand my orders or take over fully, I made sure of that, but he would at least be able to control the war golem when it arrived, as I sure as shit wasn't giving him a class-three.

Satisfied with his access, I shifted the symbols again, pulling up the third and final one, a lightning symbol shot through with what looked to be layers of different liquids. I tapped on it, then frantically selected No when I read the option.

Please confirm Geophysical Seismic Charge,

current charge at 4/100 and climbing.

Fire at 100%?

Yes/No

I slammed No, again, watching the charge dissipate and wondering what the ever-loving fuck a geophysical seismic charge was and why the hell it didn't have a damn big warning attached to it. I locked the access to that to the Imperial Scion and Heir only. Then I stood, making a mental note to find out what the hell it was when there wasn't an allied sentient creature using the location as its goddamn home.

With that, I gathered the others, found that nobody had really bothered to explore very far, and quickly added the need for the golems to gather the four things in storage and bring them to the Tower when they came; then, with bugger all else to do, we left.

Once outside, Oracle took off, vanishing through the canopy to find the ship, then returned to my side, cursing. They had apparently taken several Fireballs, including one that damn near hit the ship, before she managed to get their attention.

We gathered up the team, and at our request, the Arbuton bent some of his branches aside, clearing enough of a space for me to fly people up to the ship when it arrived.

I made a point of thanking the Arbuton before the last trip up, once only Oracle and I were left, and confirmed that Woodite knew where to go. We'd agreed, when I was resting between flying people up, that he and Hazel would get their guardians and harvest until the golems were ready, then they would travel with them to the Tower.

Once I was back on the deck of the ship, I made my way to the Alkyon pair and gave them the third and final location for the day, some forty miles to the east, and the last of the closer locations.

Woodite had stated it was a village at one point, but that a monster attack had resulted in it being abandoned. He cautioned that there was likely something else living there now. It was outside of the grove's patrols, however, and they had no interest in it, considering that they had so much land to patrol as it was.

I made sure they compared the location to the one on my map, altering their own to correspond to the location where I had it, then I returned to my own group and sat down.

"Well, wasn't that fun?" I asked and got a round of grunts, a couple of grins, and an incredulous look from Ronin.

"You did well down there," I told Ronin grudgingly, getting a smile in return. "Want to tell us all a little more about what you can do?"

He shrugged noncommittally, before looking at me pointedly, as though waiting. I waited as well, until I guessed what he wanted and made it into a command.

"Ronin, I order you to explain more about who and what you are, and what you can do for me and my team." He shuddered then straightened and let out a deep breath.

"Hell, Lord Jax, you've no idea how long I've been waiting for that," he said with a groan. "I've not been able to explain almost all of it, thanks to the Bardic Oaths. Do you really want to have that discussion now? In public, I mean?" He looked around the squad.

"I trust them with my life. You, not so much," I said dryly. "Explain."

"Okay...Where to start?" He rubbed his chin and fiddled idly with his lute. "I was a bit of a scamp, once. Had a gift for it, getting into and out of places I shouldn't, you might say, but I also had a nose for gold and for secrets. I found that one always led to the other, and I started to dig, trading one for another when I had to, but I kept the secrets when I could, as they were more valuable."

"Blackmail," Grizz grunted. "You were a blackmailer."

"Sometimes, but usually, no; only when I had to. I usually kept the secrets because they were interesting. Secrets are…important. And to a street kid, to know things that nobody else did made me feel important." He shrugged.

"Anyway, I had a partner, a friend, and we worked together. He and I, we found a score that would set us up for life and give us a new chance to live, and we took it. Turned out, it wasn't what we thought it was, and when we got seen, we had the choice of running or dying.

"We ran and hid aboard an airship bound for Narkolt, some envoy or other. Anyway, we stayed hidden, and when we got there, we made a break for the city. Simple. We thought we had it all figured out, found somewhere to lay low, and Achim went out to try to find us some food." Ronin spat over the side of the railing into the forested canopy below.

"At least, that's what he said he was doing. I had one of the bags, and he had the other two. When I went to have a look at what we'd gotten, it was almost all gone. One small pouch had fallen out, but the rest he'd skimmed; he filled them full of grain so they looked similar. Bastard musta done it while I slept. Anyway, I checked the little pouch and found three books. Two were spells, it turned out, but the third? That was my mistake. I opened it, and being a street kid, I took what it offered.

"Memories of Society," he whispered, his eyes far away as he recalled the book. "I had no clue what that meant, not really, but I knew that anything that was magic was valuable. Yeah, I wanted to be special, and I was feeling pretty pissed off, I guess.

"It was a class skillbook, and it taught me how to memorize things, how to think like a bard. It held everything: how to see the links that bind us together, where to put yourself to read them better, and tricks like being able to memorize a conversation word for word."

He ignored a low comment Grizz muttered to Yen. "The real mistake, though, was that I was flat-out unconscious when they came for me. The Smuggler's Guild, I mean. Turns out, the score was theirs, and they'd sent it from Narkolt to Himnel with a plan for a specific person to use the books. Then Achim came along and tried to sell them their own gear, so they beat the story out of him and came looking for me.

"They found me out cold, the skillbook already in my mind, and the others spread around me. They were furious." He let out a short laugh, shaking his head as he looked back in his memories. "Basically, long story short, I convinced them that it was a good thing, and they gave me a job, made me use the skills for them. Took a few years, but I was valuable to the Guild, and they trained me accordingly."

"All well and good, but…" I started to say and he held up his hand imploring me for patience.

"Just a few more minutes, okay, boss?" he reassured me, and I sighed, nodding. "Right, well…it turns out that they got the book from the Bardic College, stole it along with a load of other things, and the bards sent my master to look for it.

"It took him twelve years, and when he found me, he spent a little time observing me." Ronin let his fingers dance across the strings of the lute he was idly tuning, a ripple of notes filling the air, and he smiled.

"He decided that I was worth saving and could be an asset, rather than a waste of the book he had made himself. So he got drunk and made a scene in a tavern, made it look like the Smugglers' Guild found him instead of the other way around.

"He made them think he was a bard in the manner they know of them and did a few things he wouldn't speak of, so they thought they had him under their thumb. They didn't. He agreed to train me, to pay off his debt to them, which is what he was after all along, and he spent the next year doing that."

"Why did he want to train you?" asked Tang, idly polishing a nick out of a dagger.

"Because the Bardic College isn't what you think, and neither are bards." Ronin grinned. "We're not the shifty shitbags you all believe we are, and we used to work closely with the Legion, once upon a time."

I frowned, a tickle of memory coming back to me, before vanishing as Amon refused to elaborate.

"Bullshit," Lydia growled, glaring at him.

"It's true! Well, okay, yeah, some of us are shits, and most of the bards you know are scum. But those of us trained in the Bardic College, or by true masters? We're different."

"Oh yeah, because you work for the good of the Empire and all that, not to just get your prick wet, right?" Yen scoffed, rolling her eyes while I watched him carefully.

"Let's get this clear," I said, standing up and walking to him. I drew in a deep breath and reached out, grasping his forearm and looking into his eyes as I triggered the special ability of the Helm of Imperial Right–Inquisition.

As the orbits shone with a bright white light, I gazed intently at him, with Oracle standing by my side, now full-sized and reaching out a hand to us both, watching with her power and abilities as much as I did with my own.

"I am Jax, Scion of the Empire, and I order you to explain who you are and your purpose here," I said, making it as clear and hard to hide as I could.

"I am Ronin Fer, and I am a member of the Bardic College, charged with intelligence gathering for the Empire," he confirmed, letting that hang in the air for a moment before he went on, speaking into the utter silence that had blanketed the group.

"I was recruited and trained to serve the Empire, gathering information and doing whatever was necessary to achieve my quests. I need to level, and fast, because, for the first time in centuries, the Bardic College has the chance to serve a true Imperial Master, and I can fulfill my Oath.

"I am trained to provide buffs to a group, seduce the unwary, and locate information, piecing together details from multiple sources to provide briefings on threats to the Empire. I am loyal to the Empire and to you, Lord Jax."

Silence rang out before I finally released him, the magic dying away as I shook myself and Oracle hit me with a heal.

"It's the truth," I confirmed to the rest of the group, looking around. "All of that was the truth; no hedging, no trying to hide shit. He believes it."

"Shit." Grizz let out a low whistle. "You mean they're actually not scumbags?" he asked nobody in particular.

"Bards?" Ronin asked, and he nodded. "Depends. Most bards *are* scumbags; they heard about the reputation and decided that's how they want to live, and use the class as an excuse, basically seducing anyone and everyone.

"Real bards, though–those of us that are trained by the Bardic College or by masters sent out from there–we have that reputation, and we build it up because it makes sure nobody thinks we're doing anything else. People talk when they think you're nothing. Hell, the Smuggler's Guild was the perfect place for me to pick up information for years. I passed it on to my master, who passed it back to the college. Then I took a ship for a few years, toured around and kept learning, picked up new skills, and grew my old ones."

"What skills?" I asked, leaning back against the railing, far more interested in what he had to say now.

"Well, as I said, I can buff the team, and I can give you useful information, such as details on the beasts you face. I can find things out, and nobody suspects the 'scumbag bard'." He chanced a smile at Lydia, who continued to glare at him. "Okay, look, some people will hate us because of the reputation, and, well…we do things sometimes to get the job done that aren't very nice. But we do get the job done. Always."

He looked around at the entire group one by one. "I can gather information, advise you, and provide entertainment to your people, but there's an entire class skill path that only became active for me when you claimed your place in the Imperial Hierarchy, so it's weak now.

"I haven't got more than a single level in it, but…it's powerful. Or it will be." He smiled while he looked his internal screens over. "My buffs will grow in strength the more I use them, and I can debuff your enemies, but my main class has actually changed from bard to Imperial truth-seeker."

He made his new class details appear for us all to see, before shifting it to show bard again. "It means I can find things out; anything. Given enough time, my abilities will guide me to whatever you need, and I'll only get more powerful."

I nodded thoughtfully as he sat down, smiling.

"You have no idea how hard it was to tell you all that, and how many Oaths were in place to make sure I didn't, unless it was to the right person." He sighed, shifting and bouncing his shoulders. "It feels amazing to actually have the truth known by the one person that could command it."

"You guided me to ask the right questions," I pointed out. "I mean it; you literally made me say the words you needed. How could you do that, yet not say anything else?"

"Because of who you are," he replied, smiling. "After all, what if we met and you hated bards? We're given the latitude to be able to set the conversations up with you, but only with you. If Grizz there had been in charge of whether I would have met you or not…well, it'd have come down to me seducing him and talking him around."

He gave an exaggerated grimace as Grizz straightened up, scowling. "So, yeah, thanks for not making me do that." He winked at me. "As to my buffs, abilities, and so on? Well, that's why I need the levels. It's hard to gain them when you're not a combat class, and each class quest takes six months to a year to reach me from the College."

"Where is the College?" I asked.

He grinned, a twinkle in his eye. "On the mainland, on Dai'Amaranth."

I froze, having not heard that name for a long time. "It still exists, then?" I whispered.

He nodded seriously. "From what I've been told, it was the center of the Empire of old, and it's still there. It was severely damaged; half of it was destroyed outright, and a lot more burned down or sank into the seas. But it's an island that's covered by a single vast city, over five hundred square miles, so it still exists.

"The majority of the Empire returned to it, entire Legions and more, but...it's not what you will be hoping for," he warned me. "The noble houses rule there, and they've carved it up into a thousand factions. One of the main reasons for the Bardic College to still exist is to guide the next Emperor when the time comes, as we've been watching and waiting, and the College knows all their secrets."

"My lord..." came a cry, and I turned, the conversation dying away as the Captain Kinnet approached us. "We're here," she said simply, gesturing down to the forest below and the hidden third stop of our day.

CHAPTER TWENTY-TWO

I got to my feet and led the way to the railing, seeing little to mark the location as different from the rest of the forest. Hesitant, I even went so far as to check the map to make sure it was the right place.

It was, and I contemplated the narrow gap in the trees that was visible just ahead in the last light of the day, as the sun reached the horizon and the continent sank into darkness.

"Can you get us down?" I asked the captain.

She eyed the ground uncertainly. "I can, but it will be tight, with no room to turn."

"In that case, if there *is* anything down there, you won't be able to get free quickly. Best for us to check it out, and you can land if we need you to." I peered down at the trees again. This section of land had been just over the border of the territory that contained the Grove, which meant it hadn't been included in the sweep that showed the enemies the way the rest of the territory had been.

"I could go and check it out?" Oracle offered in a low whisper, resting her hand on my shoulder. I almost refused the suggestion out of hand, my heart clenching at the mere thought of putting her in danger again. But after a long breath, I got control of myself and relented. I couldn't keep her chained to my side forever, and I had to remember that.

"Please be careful," I sent to her.

She smiled, reaching up and kissing my cheek before blurring into her smaller size, and diving over the side of the ship.

"Get ready, everyone," I called out, seeing them checking their weapons and gear. "This is supposed to be an abandoned village, but it's been highlighted on my map twice now; once when I first started exploring the area, and again by Jenae and the other Gods, so there's going to be something interesting about it, even if it's not obvious."

The few minutes between Oracle leaving and returning were nerve-wracking, even when I remembered I could relax and sense much of what she was seeing. I closed my eyes and reached out, only to be greeted with a barrage of blurring images, log walls, sagging shelves, rotting food, and weeds poking though thatch but when she returned to my side, it was with a frown on her face.

"There's something wrong down there," she said firmly. "The entire village was abandoned, and it looks like a group of monsters rampaged through it, but..." she broke off, shaking her head.

"But?"

"I don't know," she answered anxiously. "The village feels and looks wrong. It was made recently, like the last fifty years or so, and the monster tracks are recent, but there's older stonework as well, possibly from the time that the Tower was first built. There's nobody about, but there are animals grazing and crops growing. It just...doesn't make sense, I guess."

"It's okay, Oracle; you did well." I smiled before turning back to the others. "Okay then; sounds like it's time for us to go exploring, people." I held out my hands. "Who wants a cuddle first?" I asked, knowing the answer.

Grizz, of course, was the first to step up, and he held his arms out, grinning as I wrapped my arms around the huge legionnaire, before triggering my ability and lifting us both into the air with a grunt of effort.

It didn't take long, ferrying them all down to the ground, despite the awkwardness of the method, but by the time it was done, I was gasping and downing my second mana potion as Oracle healed me.

"I wish…" I panted, "there was a better way to…do that." I bit back a groan as Oracle healed the damage that the use of the ability did to me, as well as the strain on my body from carrying the others, each in full armor.

"Stay quiet and keep close together," Tang ordered in a low voice, appearing from the right of the group and gesturing to the collapsing houses we'd found. "Grizz, get the others inside." He vanished again, and I resisted the urge to swear as Grizz hurried ahead, and Yen took up the rear.

As soon as I'd dropped them off, Tang and Bane had stealthed and vanished. The lack of Bane and the terseness of Tang's words made it clear this wasn't going to be good.

The village was small and run-down. The houses had been made of huge logs, felled and drawn together, giving the buildings the look of being imposing and solid through sheer size, yet the canopy overhead didn't seem noticeably denuded, and the area was quiet.

Actually, it was too damn quiet. I couldn't hear any birds, or even insects. There was the faint creaking of the branches in the breeze, and that was it.

The houses seemed mainly intact, with one nearby having developed a slight lean but not so far as to collapse. The roof sagged, and the nearest corner of the building had come away, leaving the interior open to the elements, but overall, it looked like a few days' work would see the house put back together. Livestock bleated somewhere nearby and the familiar scent of a farmyard wafted on the air.

Which is to say, it reeked of shit.

We reached the house where Bane was waiting, and he waved us all inside. We gathered close together, the palpable sense of wrongness affecting us all as Tang reappeared and spoke quickly.

"There's definitely something living here," he said in a low voice. "There are all kinds of weird tracks, insects, it looks like, and they cover the whole village. There are no people, but the place is maintained, animals kept and tended, and there's even stuff hanging as if to dry on a line…*but*…" he whispered, pausing as he put his thoughts together. "It's all wrong. The stuff on the line is just random bits of cloth, and the line goes through them, so they can't come down and be used. The beds are left as they are, even moved around to make them look like they've been used, but they're not. Move the covers, and it's all stone and rotten leaves underneath. Whatever this place is, it's not a village."

"Hssst!" Bane whispered from the window, gesturing for us all to get down.

We scattered, moving close to the wall or crouching by the closet and table, waiting and listening.

At first, there was nothing, then a chittering clattered in the distance, followed by more silence.

Minutes ticked by, but Tang gestured for everyone to stay still and silent.

From outside, a cry rose in the distance, along with the sound of a pig oinking before being cut off with a squeal of pain.

My heart froze as a terrifying possibility came to mind. There was at least one pig here, and that meant there could be more. There might even be enough that I could have started a breeding program. Then, someday soon, I'd have been able to have bacon again, but right then, while we crouched in hiding, the last pig might have just died, and I'd lost my chance at it forever.

It was a fucking stupid thing to think, especially given the condition of the rest of the village, or whatever it was. But it was what went through my mind, and I bared my teeth in a savage grimace as I silently swore to kill whatever was out there.

A heartbeat later, something man-sized swarmed up the side of the house, the sound of dozens of legs skittering and digging into the wood as it rushed up the wall and onto the roof. It moved in that jerky, stop-start way that insects do, rushing up the wall, across the roof, then down the other side of the building, making me freeze.

I looked over at Tang, who slowly sheathed his sword and drew his bow from his bag, aiming not at the window or door he was closest to, but at the loose end of the building where we'd entered. He oh-so-slowly drew back an arrow, sighting down it.

Some of the others were watching him and making similar gestures of preparation, while Ronin crouched even lower, trying to make himself as small as possible.

Something rushed across the roof again, the sagging section bouncing slightly, and an almighty creak echoed around the room when it stopped directly over the opening we'd used to enter the building.

There was a piercing whistle, followed by a series of notes being played through what sounded like a tiny reed pipe, the kind you used to buy in the tourist shops on holiday, before answering peeps rose in the distance.

"Giint no like!" Giint growled, and we all gawked at him as he rubbed one ear, almost stabbing himself in the face with the spike on the back of the axe in his right hand.

As soon as he spoke, all sounds outside ceased, and we all glared at him.

A single tap hit the roof, then two. A burst of sound reached us from another angle as something rushed over a log. Then silence, followed by more tapping, as more and more of the creatures converged on us, the sounds coming from all angles. I growled under my breath, then straightened up, the element of surprise well and truly fucked in the ass with a jackhammer.

"Get ready," I said in a firm voice as I took two quick steps into the middle of the room and faced the open end of the building.

The others moved into place, and the air outside erupted in shrill whistles and the sound of tiny pipes trilling.

There was movement by the open end of the room, and I glared at it, settling my shield on my left arm and crouching, my naginata leveled at the gap.

"There!" shouted Arrin, and I heard the *whoosh* of a Magic Missile barrage, making me half-turn to look, before I remembered my army training from so long ago.

"On your sector, maggot!" the sergeant had screamed at me, punctuating his words with a very un-PC boot in the ass. It'd taught me a lesson, though. I half-heard his scream and felt the phantom pain as I jerked my head back in time to see a veritable swarm pouring into the room.

They were insectile, as we'd guessed, monstrous, centipede-like creatures, most the size of large dogs, though a few were nearly man-sized. I was shocked into pausing as I recognized them, then Ronin was shouting.

"They're Drach! Don't stare at them if they start to dance!" he cried, frantically starting to play as they came to a halt a dozen feet from us. More and more poured in, hanging from the ceiling and the walls, coating the floor, until we were fully surrounded.

Arrows sang, and Arrin's missiles slammed into bodies, followed by a Darkbolt from Yen, presumably because there wasn't room for a Flamespear or three.

But as quickly as they appeared, the Drach halted. Then, as Ronin had warned, they began to dance, and the fire from my team faltered then dropped off entirely.

"They're weak to fire...and to...to..." Ronin whispered, his voice mumbling to a halt. I glared at the creatures, and notifications flashed crazily in my peripheral vision.

"Drach," I growled, my fingers moving stiffly around the haft of my naginata and the grip of my shield.

"I remember you." Scraps of memory and the ancient stones protruding from the ground on the way in sparked off each other, reminding me of a dream from months ago. A dream in which these fuckers had dismembered me.

I leveled my gaze on one of the tiny figures that sat astride the Drach's back, hanging from a tiny saddle while it played its pipes and commanded the creatures. My eyes narrowed in remembrance, looking for one in particular.

"You!" I picked out one that glared at me with a special hunger, and its eyes widened as it realized I wasn't under its thrall.

I gritted my teeth and released the spell, the casting time seeming shorter than it should have been from my memories. The massive amount of mana I'd forced into it clearly increased the damage, as the lines and circles, rings and symbols of Cleansing Fire slammed out, filling the small building and pouring flames into the creatures that surrounded us.

There was a collective screech of pain and hatred from dozens of throats as the spell attacked them, while my companions flinched, the dulling blanket that had been holding their minds captive being torn free.

"Attack!" I roared, and others took up the cry, along with Grizz, Yen, and Tang's deep-throated bellows of "For the Empire!"

I rushed forward, fire flashing down the length of the naginata and bringing it ablaze as I swept it sideways across the throat of the nearest Drach, practically severing its head as it opened its mouth, its black and red carapace gleaming with flames as its mandibles flexed.

The next one lifted itself up, rearing back in preparation to attack. I slashed the naginata through the front segments, slipping between segmented thorax and severing the upper third to send it flopping onto the floor as the room erupted into insanity.

Some of the creatures attacked, others fled; still more, driven by the pain of the flames, attacked each other. The tiny creatures that rode their backs frantically clutched and played the reed pipes as they tried to hang on for dear life to their mounts.

I slashed and stabbed, kicking out and impaling one of the damn riders through the stomach. Yanking it off its mount, I dropped it to the floor, where it wailed. Disgusted, I drew back and punted the little creature as hard as I could. Its limbs snapped as its body, barely a foot tall, was hit full in the chest by my boot with a degree of force that would have gotten me instantly signed into any football team in the world, even if my lack of patience would have seen me barred soon after.

It hurtled through the air and out of the window, the damaged, old shutters that barely kept out the rain torn off the wall by a body that was already cooling before it hit.

By the time the shutters were done with it, I guessed that "lost containment" was the best description of the sack of skin. That, or a bag of jam and bone shards.

If the rest of the squad were surprised by my fury, they didn't show it. One by one, they screamed, kicked, hammered, and blasted the room clear. Ronin even grabbed a bench, heaving it up into the air with a cry and staggering under the weight, before slamming it down on one of the Drach that had fallen, burning, from the ceiling.

The rider I'd fixated on and was trying to reach had been just outside the original burst of Cleansing Fire, which meant it took precious seconds for me to carve my way towards it through milling, screaming insects. That time allowed it to goad its mount out, screeching orders and trilling them into the pipes, directing more and more to leap at me.

By the time I'd made it outside, with two of the damn things actively clinging to me, it was halfway across the village. I spotted it rushing into a collection of crates that stood, seemingly piled haphazardly, by the side of the biggest house in the village.

I stabbed the blade of my naginata into the rear section of one that was trying to run down my body, using that leverage to flip it away and into a village well. The creature vanished with a cry and a splash, followed by the frantic sound of thrashing and panic.

The second creature was trying to wrap itself around my helm, its claws digging in under the helmet and into the gaps in my armor around the neck as I tried to disengage my left hand from my shield until something sliced the thing lengthways, gutting it and yanking it free. The action tore some of my skin, but I didn't care.

The back end of the creature I was chasing vanished into a gap between the crates, while more skittered frantically after it. I yanked my mana in, gritting my teeth as I pulled together a spell I hadn't used in at least a few days. The syllables of its spoken component slid between gritted teeth as I ran forward, my fingers flashing.

I stiffened my legs, skidding slightly as I slammed both hands forward, the black, red, and bright white bolt of Explosive Compression forming and blasting into the crates. All around me, the Drach and their riders screeched and skittered as they frantically tried to escape the flames and fury.

My spell hurtled through the air, the weak spellform that made up the first layer barely holding together, until it hit the box that the first creature had vanished behind.

As soon as it hit, the spellform popped like a soap bubble filled with glue. The secondary, far more powerful spell contained within went active. Similar to the way that Cleansing Fire laid down what would, in other worlds, be called a ritual circle, Explosive Compression threw out a form. However, where a ritual circle was designed to maintain and enable a spell, this amalgamation of lines and circles cobbled together through fury, half-understood hints, and pure, undiluted hatred, was designed for one thing.

It opened out, then it pulled *in*. At the very center of the form was a bending of gravity, a twisting that grew stronger, the more power and fury I poured into it. I was livid as I recognized a creature that had not only killed me once already, but had fed the children of this village to its fucking pets in years past.

The spell unfurled to its fullest, a space about six feet across. Then it yanked inwards, catching three of the insectile Drach and one of the small riders in its radius then drawing them inexorably to its center.

At first, it was simply painful for anything caught in its influence, but as it constricted, the gravity grew, compressing harder and harder, and the air was filled with the sound of wood splintering, rocks grating, the pop of chitin as it fractured and bent, and the frantic squealing and mewling of the creatures caught inside its environs.

The spell lasted mere seconds, but nothing that it caught survived. When it ended, leaving behind a solid marble of compressed matter that clunked to the ground, there was a clear, open space that exposed a hole leading down into the ground, which the marble slowly rolled into.

I slammed the naginata into the ground, butt first, and released it as soon as I was sure it was firmly upright, then yanked the neck of my Bag of Spatial Folding open and chucked my shield into it.

As soon as the shield fell into its depths, the neck returned to normal, and I started casting again. Oracle landed next to me, glaring around in challenge, before leaping back into the air to hover a few meters above me. Her hair was noticeably disarrayed as she sputtered and hissed, her memories and mine pouring in to feed one another's emotions as we hadn't in weeks.

We dual-cast, but for the first time, we did it with two bodies, two forms united in hatred and rage, and the Fireball we created was a thing of terrible beauty.

It rolled into being between us as we both glared at the hole, flames of different temperatures painting the ball in reds, yellows, blues, and whites before it cut the air with a sound like a supersonic jet, shocking the world around us into silence.

Silence that lasted less than a second when the beach-ball sized spell blasted into the darkness and exploded, sending jets of flame erupting from a dozen hidden entrances to the underground hive scattered around the village-turned-trap.

After the flames died away, a hush fell, only broken by the whistling and hissing of my breath as I panted and tried to regain control.

I turned looking at the others, mopping up the dozens of Drach that were left. They were ambush predators, I guessed, judging by how easily they died. I didn't doubt that the others would be a match for them, but as I turned back towards the hole, I couldn't hold back a snarl.

"Lydia!" I roared as I grabbed my naginata again.

"Sir?" she called, punctuating her response with a grunt as she clearly ruined something's day…terminally.

"Clear the village and keep everyone here. This is personal," I ground out as I stalked to the edge of the hole.

"Jax, perhaps I should…" Bane said in a low voice, arriving close to me.

"Perhaps you should stay the fuck up here and clear the goddamn village!" I snapped, not looking at him. Without a backward glance, I stepped forward and dropped into the hole, Oracle shrinking into her smaller form and accompanying me.

I landed on hard-packed earth, the signs of drag marks clearly leading from behind me to somewhere ahead. I snarled, rushing toward the outer edge of the village as I figured it.

The path was narrow, barely wide enough for me to stand straight on, and I kept having to duck and twist as rocks protruded from the earthen walls and floor. But here and there, I caught traces of my quarry.

Bloody lines, small puddles, and torn sections of ground and wall let me know that something had traveled this way recently, and it was injured.

I was determined to change that state of affairs to "deceased," and I ran faster, my DarkVision making the murky path as clear as if I'd worn military-spec night vision goggles.

I followed the tunnel as it wound from side to side, rising and falling, until I guessed I was some ten meters below the ground. When I hit the first crossing corridor, to the right was another dirt-lined passageway, and ahead was the same, but to the left?

At the far edge of my vision, in the direction of the village's center, I could see worked stone. I growled, turning to follow that.

I ran faster, trying to make up for my pause, and chittering filled the air ahead, as the path turned from compressed dirt to dirt scattered across an ancient passageway.

The passageway lay canted at an angle, clearly straight at one point, then having sunk into the earth before coming to rest at its current location, badly broken, with sections of walls and roof tumbling down to partially close the path off over time.

There was enough space, though, and though it was so narrow that I struggled through some sections, others were wide enough for three men abreast to pass.

I took an adjoining corridor, seeing the option of left and right, the familiar filth and accompanying smell to the right.

I snarled and headed down that way, splashing through shallow puddles and jumping over sections that were filled with eggs and baby insectile mounts that swarmed and screeched at my passage.

I leaped across another pool, this one larger than the last few, before skidding on the dirt and bouncing off a wall, then squinting into the room that waited before me.

It was long and narrow, maybe ten feet wide by thirty deep and twelve high. The walls sloped inward to create a more triangular design than I was used to seeing, but what filled me with trembling shock was the sarcophagus that leaned brokenly at the far end of the room.

It had faint magic lighting it even now, lines that staggered and faltered as they tried to repair and refill the space within, a space that I'd vacated what was only a few months, yet seemingly years ago.

I turned, my eyes tracking along the racks and the piles of refuse that lay everywhere, to find it.

The body I'd worn was gone, though clear marks showed where the fight had been. The nearby piles of shit and racks had been smeared about and shattered, with sections of broken carapace left behind from the Drach I'd managed to kill when unarmed.

I assumed, judging from the blood spray across the walls and lack of any corpses, either mine or my opponents', that they'd dragged the bodies away to eat them.

I searched around, only turning when I heard the crackling pop of flames from the corridor and felt the furious glee that filled Oracle as she turned the miniature creche into the seventh circle of hell.

I strode out, searching down the corridor, and noted the small forms twisting and curling up in death. Cleansing Flame sought them out and killed them in seconds, their health was so low.

The small pools spat and boiled as the bodies within them were destroyed. I marched forward, the flames caressing me as they recognized their master.

I stopped on the far side, the air shimmering with heat that barely touched me, and I took a deep breath before starting again, this time paying more attention to my surroundings as I went. Spotting the tracks that crisscrossed the walls, ceiling, and floor took hardly any effort, but occasionally there were other signs: drag marks, small footprints, splatters of long-dried blood.

Those I followed, taking countless lefts and rights, until the overall size of the cave system dawned on me, right before I walked out into a cavern that was filled with the echoing music of falling water, cries of pain and snarls of hatred.

I crept forward, the exit I'd used appearing high on the western side of the cavern, and made my way to a ridged section of carapace that appeared to have been stacked deliberately to angle any breezes upwards and away.

I peered over the edge of it, using the small and simple construction for cover as I scanned the vista below.

The cavern was made up of several rings, each leading to the next one down, narrowing as they drew closer to the center. A great pool glimmered in the reflected light of enormous glowing mushrooms that colonized the entire eastern wall.

The pool was filled with Drach, dozens upon dozens of them, and they were all titans of their race, if the ones I'd fought were anything to judge them by.

Where the others had ranged from dog to man-sized, the smallest of these looked to be the size of a horse, and the largest...well, in the center of the pool was a pair of thrones placed back-to-back, with withered, shrunken occupants that occasionally moved, surprising me, as I'd thought them long dead at first glance.

The thrones were seemingly cemented to the back of a Drach that must have been ten feet across and at least sixty-five long. Its head was ridged in spikes, unlike the bare, chitinous pate of the others, and it appeared to have multiple sharp spines that gleamed and reflected the meager light as it slowly shifted its bulk about.

At the far end of the creature was a raised ovipositor, which trembled and shook as it dipped down into the water, laying clutches of eggs before lifting away.

Scattered all around the cavern were the little creatures, the riders. Some wore small leather sections of armor, but most were naked, only a few wearing the pipes around their necks. One and all, they hissed and snarled at each other, yet shied away from the occupants of the thrones and their mount.

As I watched, a Drach, made tiny by distance and comparison, scuttled out of a low passageway next to the water's edge, and on its back was a rider which slumped, left arm missing as it frantically played its pipes, directing the creature until it came to a halt at the edge of the water.

The wounded figure fell off the Drach, rolling and crying out until it touched the water. The huge one, the queen, I assumed, spun with surprising speed, rearing up in challenge.

The tiny rider cried something out, burbling and screeching, before playing a short burst, followed by a longer, more complex tune.

Its mount slowly spun in place, showing the entire sections of its legs and back that were missing. I growled, low and feral, in the back of my throat as I watched the ovipositor lifting into the air, twitching over the little creature.

I didn't want that thing to kill him.

I wanted to kill that fucker myself! I remembered the look of glee on the little bastard's face as I'd literally been eaten from the inside out by those damn creatures burrowing into me. Now it was the one screaming and shitting itself.

I wanted to attack, but I wasn't doing it, not yet. I might be about as bright as a five-watt light bulb at times, like my teachers had always told me. But I recognized now that I'd made a mistake when I'd ordered the others to stay up top.

I'd been thinking that I just needed to catch the little asshole and kill it, that they could clean up the village while I amused myself with breaking the creature into pieces, but now? Nope. I needed reinforcements, judging by that big bastard.

"Oracle, can you find your way back up to the others? Lead them down? " I asked.

She nodded, dropping a light kiss on my cheek again, before making me look her in the eyes.

"No stupid stuff, okay? Just wait for the rest of us," she warned. I grinned, leaning forward and kissing her back. She shifted her size quickly, enough that the kiss felt natural, before she shrank back down and flitted silently out of sight.

Stifling a sigh, I turned back and gazed down at the cavern, then at the walls, looking for inspiration. I needed a smart way to do this fight, one that resulted in that bus-sized thing dying painfully, along with all the others, preferably while I sipped on good rum and got a blowjob.

I was probably asking too much, but you know, better to shoot for the stars, and all that.

CHAPTER TWENTY-THREE

I remained crouched behind the concealing ridges of carapace, staring out and around the cavern. There were two more levels above the one where I was concealed, and that was concerning. Anything wandering out onto those levels would see me straight away, given the way I was lying there.

Beyond that, while there were no other exits on the level I was on, or at least not that I could see, there were three on the next level down and two on the one past that.

With the way the little bastards were swarming about, and the thrashing from the numerous Drach in the pool and laid around on the shores, I couldn't even get a straight count of them, either.

I focused on one of the little creatures and slowly built my spell, reaching it out and keeping it as whisper-quiet as I could, just in case, as the screeching and spitting from below rose in volume.

Sub-Sentient Vern

This Vern has not yet accrued sufficient levels or age to grow fully sentient and is easily directed. The Vern are known by many names; Pictsies and Du'rutkai are commonly used. Vern are simple creatures birthed from magic. They age slowly, growing in power and stature until they can no longer survive underground, usually tearing their way free into the upper realms.

Vern delight in feeding on young flesh and will maintain nurseries or small farms of creatures reared for consumption, encouraging a select few to breed continuously to provide fresh sustenance. Adult Vern are powerfully magical, but if their food source is restricted, they grow physically weak very quickly. Due to this metabolic conundrum, they are known to raid villages and steal away breeding stock.

Weaknesses: 75% weakness to physical damage. 25% weakness to Fire, Earth, and Light magic.
Resistances: Both Water and Darkness magics used against a Vern are 50% less effective.
Level: 2
Health: 11/15
Stamina: 62/70
Mana: 20/20

A loud cry burst from below, a roar of fury, and the cavern went silent. I dismissed the information I'd gotten, putting my eye back to the concealment and spying down.

The huge Drach had reared up, its body more than half out of the water as its head turned slowly. The hideous mouth gaped wide as it drew in great whistling breaths, seeming to taste the air, as opposed to smelling anything.

It turned its head this way and that, clearly searching, until it paused, rotating slowly to aim at the ledge where I was concealed.

I froze, holding my breath, then subvocalized, my fingers moving rapidly as I cast Chameleon to help keep myself hidden.

The Drach arched its back, lifting its head higher and clearly remaining fixated on the entrance I hid by, and I started to sweat.

The damn thing was more than sixty-five feet long, and as it reared out of the water, I realized that its legs were six feet long on their own.

As it reared higher and higher, it started to move, its body flowing closer in a sinuous side-to-side movement, totally ignoring the occasional smaller Vern and Drach that were too slow to avoid the huge, chitinous spear-like appendages as they slammed down. The smaller forms were skewered; their bleeding corpses flicked aside as it moved closer.

I stayed perfectly still as it drew nearer, my concerns about moving turning from a suspicion into a certainty, until it got too close. I started to creep back, glancing over my shoulder to find where the entrance to the paths lay, before looking back and freezing.

The damn thing had climbed the side of the cavern, and it'd been virtually silent!

In the handful of seconds I had inched back, and the head had been out of sight as I eased away from the ridged windbreak, the goddamn thing had started climbing!

The head lifted over the edge and peered down at the entrance, and I stayed absolutely still. Whatever mutation this thing had gone through to make it so sodding huge had robbed it of any eyes, replacing them with the ring of spikes that made up its crown, but the way it focused on me as it hovered noiselessly made my asshole twitch.

I gripped the naginata tightly in my right hand, having been especially careful to not bang it on the stone of the floor, and I closed my left hand slowly over the rock pressing against it.

I slowly lifted the rock, throwing it to the left in one sharp motion, causing it to clatter off the stone wall as it bounced out into open air, and the effect was stunning.

Where the creature had been all slow menace before, now it was flashing death. The ovipositor slammed down into the rock of the cavern wall inches from where the stone had bounced off. As it clattered down the side of the cavern, the huge Drach queen spun to follow it, her mandibles flung wide as she spat a stream of liquid at the area the rock clattered off next. She moved in a flash, ducking down out of sight, and I heard the splash of the spittle landing, and then a hissing shriek from whatever it'd landed on.

"Fuck this!" I grunted, not even realizing I'd spoken the words aloud as I shoved, throwing myself from a push-up position to my feet. Then I dove aside, feeling wind from the passage of the ovipositor as it screamed past me.

I rolled, then jumped to my feet and dove aside again, as it smashed down right where I'd been about to step. The ovipositor's sheath of flesh that had been depositing the eggs had tightened and retracted, bringing a spiked tip into view. I frantically scrambled to my feet, changing direction from heading for the passage

I'd entered through, to rushing upwards and following the circular path that led up the side of the cavern to the upper rings. I tried not to imagine what that thing would do if it hit me.

Puncturing my armor would be the least of my concerns, as, if it didn't kill me outright, it'd likely lay something inside me that'd just *ruin* my fucking day.

I sprinted as fast as I could, faster than I ever expected to be able to move in such close-fitted and heavy armor. But the only thing that was saving me for now was that the creature seemed reluctant to climb higher, as the figures on its back tilted precariously on their thrones.

A screech burst out, followed by the sound of multiple notes ringing in the air, and the Drach pulled back, settling into the pool and staring up at me with its tail thrashing.

I slowed, warily watching the creature when it retreated, and quickly learned that was a fucking mistake.

The creatures that were seated in the thrones might look like desiccated humanoids, Elves, or something similar, but the way that they moved made it clear they weren't.

The figures gestured, one casting a spell, while the other lifted its face toward me and shrilled a series of notes that hung in the air, lasting unnaturally long, like a fart in an elevator.

In response to the call, the cavern exploded. The smaller beings, which had solely concerned themselves with avoiding being stepped on by the huge creature, now erupted into movement, racing towards me. The Drach leaped onto the walls and gripped tight before starting to climb, while the hundreds of Vern swarmed the backs of the climbing Drach or raced up the narrow inclines that ringed the cavern toward me.

I spun and sprinted again. I was too far from the entrance I'd used to reach the room, but I guessed that my best chance now was to get to the top level and find a way out, preferably one that resulted in me getting onto the ship with the others and using its fucking cannons on the village. To hell with the risk they posed.

I raced ahead, feet kicking up clouds of dirt and loose scree that fountained out over the edge of the cavern, and I reached out to Oracle frantically.

"They found me. Heading up the cavern to the top. Get the others out, and get them onto the ship somehow!" I sent, sensing her fear, her worry, and her determination being sent back to me.

I desperately wanted the rest of the squad here now, damn, I did, but the thought of them coming out and getting swarmed, just as I found a nice exit up high? I couldn't do it.

Better that I was the only one at risk, especially as I was the dumbass that had ordered them to stay up top.

I raced on a second loop, then shoved my naginata back into a bag, the wrongness as the weapon, over seven feet in length, vanished into a pouch that looked to be four to five inches being just one more bout of weirdness I was slowly getting used to.

I leaned into the corner as I ran, pumping my arms faster, and started to cast. My mana had almost fully refilled, sitting comfortably at four hundred and eighty-seven points out of five hundred and eighty. I decided it was time to start thinning the ranks out and gaining myself some time. The two things, which I assumed were adult Vern, continued casting their own spells and whistling to their creature.

I flicked my fingers over and over, twisting them in knuckle-popping ways to fulfill the somatic sections of the spell, flinging both hands out a second later. The ritual circle of Cleansing Fire hurtled from my fingers to slam into the wall on the far side of the cavern, just below the lip of what I was classing as the third level. Upon impact, unearthly flames flashed out from the symbols and lines, striking at any of my enemies that tried to cross it.

A new notification flashed frantically, and I ignored it, casting a second time as I saw how effective the first was.

I kept running, casting the spell again as first a handful, then ten or more Drach fell from the stone where the circle had impacted, their bodies curling up in pain as the spell burrowed into them. The tiny Vern bodies burst alight as they tried to run through the section that overlapped the path.

I flung a second spell downwards with a grin. This one hit another area of the wall, a lower section, rippling outwards and taking an even dozen or more Drach out, as well as the milling mass of the Vern that had gathered at the edge of the path, reluctant to try to cross.

As they screeched, their pained cries rising into the air, I threw myself aside as a trio of black darts flashed through the air toward me.

I hit the wall and bounced, half coming back upright, half rolling, as I was entangled in a section of roots that grew outwards from the wall. I stumbled, the narrowness of the path where I ran so blindly suddenly making me realize my mistake.

I'd been so focused on rushing away and slamming out spells that were taking dozens out at a time, that I had not looked too closely at the higher level.

The upper levels that I'd been rushing headlong to reach were interspersed with five Vern openly drawing a bead with small bows. Their mounts, six of them, were racing down the slope as we closed the distance to each other.

I stumbled as I tried to avoid their darts, my footing crumbling as the roughly compacted dirt that ringed the cavern gave way. I tipped outwards over the edge of the cavern, arms windmilling before I managed to right myself.

Heart pounding, I glared up at the little bastards, remembering that even underground, I had an advantage they didn't. I took two steps to the edge and leaped off, activating Soaring Majesty and hurtling upwards as the next series of darts flashed past, vanishing into the gloom below me.

I jerked myself around in the air, flipping myself over as I hurtled towards the ceiling, and managed to land, or crash, if truth be known, into the small pack of creatures, killing one simply by landing on him with one knee and crushing his tiny ribcage to the floor.

I lashed out, fists flying, and sent the bodies slamming into the walls, floor, and one out into open air as he tried to leap at me, a dart held up to stab through my visor.

I backhanded him, sending the little body hurtling out to fall with a pained gurgle into the open cavern, presumably to end in a vicious splat on the floor below.

As soon as the creatures near me were dead or incapacitated, I straightened up, looking down to find that at least a hundred more Drach were incoming, and the area I'd taken, while the high ground, as certain mystical wizards might know it, was also a sodding mistake, as what had looked from below to be a passage out was instead a storeroom or pantry.

It was maybe forty feet deep, sixty-five wide, and filled with animals and people restrained in tiny cages or chained to the wall.

People screamed as soon as I appeared, a variety of pleas to help them, to save them. Guttural screeches, which I assumed were the Vern's language, were also grunted at me from terrified figures.

I swore viciously, seeing there was no way out and that I'd ordered Oracle and the others back to the surface.

I was alone in a place I couldn't escape from, with prisoners begging me for help, and Gods, yes, five pigs in a pen on one side.

I turned back to the doorway, peeking outside and seeing the oncoming horde, and made the conscious decision to hold this place.

"Oracle," I called, and she responded with a burst of fear and hope. *"I love you,"* I cut the connection, unable to risk the distraction as she questioned me.

Panic burst from her, but by the time she'd fed that through to me, and her direction changed, I'd already started casting.

The first spell was another Cleansing Fire, right over the entrance to the cave. The positioning forced anything that entered the storeroom to come single-file, thanks to the narrow entrance, and take fire damage as they came.

The second spell was Explosive Compression, fired from the edge of the cavern and aimed down at the twin figures that rested on the thrones atop the queen Drach.

It hurtled away from me as I started casting the third one, and the last I'd be able to afford for a while.

Even as Explosive Compression slammed into an unseen shield and burst, taking a handful of tiny Vern that were too close, but doing no real damage, the third spell finished. I had a split second to read the details.

Adult Vern Queen

This Vern has reached the third stage of their life cycle and has begun to birth new Vern through mixing its essence with that of a male or King Vern. The resulting physical and magical drain has weakened the pair dramatically, forcing them to pause in their growth cycle while they spawn.

Weaknesses: 50% weakness to physical damage.
Resistances: All magical attacks against an adult Vern are reduced in strength by 65% due to their magical nature, with their species-specific shield spell needing to be defeated before any assault on their physical forms can begin.
Level: 31
Health: 114/200
Stamina: 54/80
Mana: 648/1200

I'd barely finished the basic details; knowing the bastards had a shield would have been incredibly useful before I'd used the last spell on them, but hey, shit happens.

A pulse of power flashed out from them, and I realized for the first time that their mount wasn't just a mount. The ring of spikes around its head flared with shimmering heat before a circle of lightning flashed out, crackling from the points and bouncing back and forth to build for several seconds as I tried to build another Cleansing Fire spell.

It beat me to it, and by beat me, I mean beat me like a red-headed stepchild. It unleashed its spell, and I was forced to dive aside as the charged lightning bolt slammed into the space I'd just filled.

I was thrown backwards, trembling and thrashing, my brain sparking as the world dissolved into pain. The mixture of my own failed spell backlash and the close impact of the Vern's spell sent horrific pains wracking through me. I flopped involuntarily and tried to curse, while my jaw clenched and my teeth gritted so hard, I nearly broke them.

It was the screams that broke me out of it, the world rolling and twisting, making me want to vomit as my entire body roared at me in pain, and my health bar flashed a dull red warning, depleted to only a quarter of its usual size.

A new sound layered over the screams and begging of the prisoners; the screeching, screaming sound of the Drach being burned to death yet still coming, as the last guttering dregs of Cleansing Fire began to wane from the doorway.

I'd been blown backwards down the passageway, deeper into the larder and away from the edge of my Cleansing Fire spell, dammit. I reached out, trying to reignite the spell before giving up with a whimper as my singed and frayed mind rebelled at the attempt to use my mana.

Instead, I staggered upright, the heat fading from my armor as I took one, then another, then a half dozen uncertain steps towards the edge of the spell.

I managed to get just inside the ring as the spell died, absorbing nearly three seconds of healing and feeling my body being soothed by the flames. Sighing at the momentary relief, I pulled out my naginata and planted my feet, yanking a potion of healing out as well.

It was a low-level one, weak as hell and about as useful as a sodding cup of tea compared to what I could craft, given some time and ingredients, with my new alchemical understanding, but it was *something*, at least. I sank my teeth into the cork, yanking back and spitting it aside to pour the potion into my mouth.

I swallowed the liquid as fast as I could, throwing the glass through the last few flickering flames on the far side of the doorway as the first wave of Drach rolled forward, their multitude of spiked limbs crunching across the charred chitinous plates of their fallen brethren.

They hissed in pleasure and hunger upon seeing that the flames were gone. They raced at me, one in the lead, but dozens more crowding in from behind.

The tip of the naginata skewered the first one through the face. A simple, fast, and efficient kill, but as I yanked the blade back, it caught in the chitin, and I had to yank again. That single act gave the next one in line the chance to make it a few inches closer. When I stabbed at that one, careful this time to not hit too hard, I'd already had to take a step back.

Rather than fighting as I'd intended before the lightning bolt, on the far side of the doorway, with room to back up, I was now halfway back into the space already, and the room opened up a mere three feet behind me, meaning that if I retreated too far, I was, to put it plainly…fucked.

I stabbed the second through the mouth, and its mandibles clacked shut on the haft of my weapon, its body spasming and twisting in death. Then I struck forward with my right foot, Sparta-kicking it off the end of my weapon. Adjusting to a better combat style for the tight quarters, I used the weapon as a short spear instead of the polearm that it was.

I grasped it halfway up its length with my right hand, my left diving into my bag and yanking out a shitty round shield.

My Olympic level of strength allowed me to use the naginata creatively, combined with the small shield in ways that would have made a Spartan warrior weep for joy. I stabbed forward, again and again, using the shield to bash the creatures as they tried to surge in, and the bladed tip of the swordstaff to cut through necks, to punch through chitin, and to carve through the softer internals of the mouths into their brains.

I fought and I stabbed, occasionally kicking, shouting, and cursing, until I couldn't hold any longer, and I had to take a second step back.

Once I'd gained that space, I stabbed forward again, finding it easier, but as the flood of insectile creatures poured in, pushing the piled corpses of their dead ahead of them, I was forced to fall back again and again, inch by inch, just to get room to stab at the living rather than the dead.

I could see the roman numerals of the notifications changing regularly as new ones were added, but I ignored them, fighting frantically to clear just one more from the doorway, stabbing forward each time. I cursed myself internally, realizing just how goddamn stupid my urge to cast that spell had been.

I was a spellsword build at heart, relying equally on might and magic to survive and win, and after the spell backlash, the damage of a failed spell that still left my limbs trembling, I was reaping the consequences.

I wasn't strong enough to go toe-to-toe, not in the long term. Even now, while I'd managed to avoid the majority of the injuries, thanks to my weapon's longer reach and the narrow confines of the entrance, I'd taken some, and my regeneration was nowhere near enough to heal me in the middle of a fight.

All I needed was a Cleansing Fire in the doorway right now, as I blinked sweat away from dripping into my eyes. But I might as well be asking for a goddamn claymore mine or a Ma-Deuce heavy sodding machine gun.

I stabbed out again, sweat getting into my eyes and blinding me for a split second to make my aim wander.

Instead of a clean punch through the mouth that worked best with these things, it deflected off the mandible, carving into the chitin on the side of the Drach's face. The creature went berserk, twisting and thrashing, tearing the weapon from my tired grip.

I tried to grab it as the haft was yanked free, but a descending pair of mandibles made me yank my hand back, saving my fingers and costing me my weapon.

I hesitated a second, my hand hovering between the sheath I still had across my back and the bag on my waist. In that one second, I started to lose the fight.

The buildup of bodies in the doorway had been helping as well as hindering my attacks. It had slowed the Drach as they were forced to scrabble through or over them, their frantically digging claws pushing the corpses backwards, but they'd built a veritable wall of their dead over time, and it toppled forward on the left. As I hesitated, a dozen corpses rained into me, and I slammed out with the shield, deflecting most of them and making my second mistake.

The sight of the falling creatures spurred me out of my indecision, and my hand finished its travel to the hilt of the right-hand sword on my back. I grasped the leather grip and yanked, before releasing it and grabbing the blade itself a third of the way up its length.

It was a stupid thing to do, but the way the blade got stuck again and again meant I'd developed this strategy to get it out faster. I yanked and released, whipping my hand forward and down to catch the hilt again as the blade came fully free. Frantic, I slashed downward at a Drach that leaped for my leg, the blade slamming into the chitin halfway down its length. The heavy tip punched into the creature, even as the chitin kept it from going too deep.

I twisted my grip on the blade and thrust down as the Drach wrapped itself around my leg, its mandibles clamping around the knee-joint of my armor as it frantically chewed and bit.

The blade dug deeper. It took several seconds, but I eventually found one of its multiple hearts and severed the nerve column.

While I'd been rooting with the blade, I'd been using the shield to good effect, battering and smashing the others that tried to get to me, but the shield was cheap, and wherever it'd been made, it certainly wasn't crafted to Legion standards.

The top half bent under the impact of a Drach that flung itself at me, exposing my helm as the stunned creature fell to the floor.

I tried to pull the sword blade up to block the one I saw preparing to spring from the corpse of its brother before me, but as it bunched, then leapt into the air, its slavering mandibles held wide and all its legs spread out to grasp at me, the chitin held the sword in place. I was forced to release it, bringing an empty fist up instead.

The Drach locked its mandibles on my fist, wrapping its centipede-like body around my arm. Its legs dug in, drawing blood in numerous places where the armor left gaps for movement. I slammed my shield across, trying to beat the Drach off my right arm with the edge of the shield.

That distraction was enough, and more of the creatures flooded in, pouring over me like a tidal wave.

I fell, my armor clanging off the floor, and I screamed in pain and rage inside my helmet as my sight was blocked off by scrabbling creatures piling over me.

The shield was pinned down by multiple bodies, forcing me to either release it or have my wrist break. I twisted, trying to roll, as I lashed out with right hand, battering the Drach that gripped that hand against the floor.

With the first blow, the creature bit down harder. On the second, it released slightly, as I had clearly stunned it. But the third came down on one of its scuttling brethren, and it robbed the strike of force, making the damn thing tighten its grip all over again.

I rolled over on the second attempt before being driven helm-first into the floor by the weight of a particularly large creature landing on my back.

I twisted, planting my right hand firmly, fingers wrapped around the Drach's face. Its mandibles clamped either side of the gauntlet, the little bastard's teeth scraping and scratching on my palm, and I closed my eyes for a second. The entire world seemed to recede for a heartbeat as I reached down inside and triggered Mana Overdrive.

I pulled back my right hand, slamming the back of the Drach's skull into the ground and feeling something crack. Using that arm as leverage, I twisted, reaching up and grabbing onto the fucker on my back. A long, claw-tipped leg twitched beneath my questing fingers. I twisted and yanked, feeling the spasm of pain, the scream of agony as I ripped the limb free, and a gush of fluids spattered across my back.

I whipped the disembodied leg around and slammed it into the smaller Drach that was holding onto my right hand, the claw punching through weakened chitin to pass clean through the head of the creature.

It spasmed, and I flicked my hand, the dead thing falling free. As I heaved myself up, the screams of hope and pleading in the room changed.

I forced myself to my feet fully and started to strip the fuckers off. The biggest one, clinging to my back and chewing on my helm in an attempt to literally behead me, was next. Both hands came up, grabbing a mandible each, and I *pulled*.

The crack rang out in the air as half its face came away with the mandibles, and its legs spasmed, letting me shuck it off my back.

It fell, landing on its back and writhing around in insectile panic, until my booted foot came down hard, shattering its carapace and making two eyes pop out.

The body stilled, and I went on a rampage, weapons forgotten as I started lashing out. The nearest Drach leaped at me, legs flung wide, mandibles reaching, chittering rising from the back of its throat...until my fist slammed into its head.

It was like the thing had been hit by a semi. The body flipped forward, tail arching up into the air as the corpse tumbled past, landing in a quivering heap on the floor to bounce and roll into the darkness.

I kicked, punched, and at one point, grabbed both the head and tail of one Drach, held it over my head, and pulled, tearing it into two uneven chunks. The rain of viscera stunned the collection of small Vern that had crept in around the piled dead.

Some of the tiny humanoids were armed, but most held nothing more than dull claws on spindly arms, and I attacked them with animal ferocity.

The first barrage of darts and short arrows were like hail, rattling off my armor. A few got through, lodging between sections of plate and in lighter areas meant to allow for movement, but the majority bounced and fell, broken.

I rushed forward, prompting squeals of terror from the diminutive creatures. They ranged from a few inches high at their dumbest, barely able to walk despite slavering to hurt the world, to three feet tall for the biggest, and that one stood at the back in the doorway. I raced forward, the remaining two living Drach that were still attached to me and the three black darts embedded in various joints were all but forgotten in my desire to rip its fucking head off, when I hit their shield.

I bounced back, staggered, then struck out, feeling my punch, then the kick, slamming into something that felt like a goddamn stone wall.

I'd managed to push them back into the short passage that led back into the cavern, and I growled as they gathered behind the shield, preparing. I slammed my fists and knees against the barrier, making it flare with power as I warily eyed my plummeting health and mana. I had a handful of seconds left before I lost my overdrive skill, and...

"Fuck, wait, what?!" My health was dropping even faster. I looked, wasting precious seconds, as I tried to figure out what had happened, until I felt another itch.

I'd felt them continuously since the little bastards had managed to get me with the darts, and...I looked at the site of the itch, finding that the shaft had broken off, but it'd left the head embedded...a head that was sodding hollow!

It was literally bleeding me dry, and if I had to guess, I'd say it was working its way deeper with every second!

I roared in utter fury and spun, booting the shield as hard as I could, making the whole thing shudder and turn black before it returned to normal, and I saw it.

My naginata was maybe six inches on the other side of the shield, but each blow I leveled against it was shoving the shield, and everything else on that side, back. That meant I was moving the very weapon I needed to pierce the shield steadily away from me...

I grabbed at my bag, quickly pulling out a potion of health and one of mana as I glowered at the fuckers on the far side, moving virtually in slow motion as I thought.

I had maybe ten seconds, and that was only because I kept downing the mana potions. This was the third, I realized, seeing an empty vial on the floor and not remembering taking it.

I needed mana, as I desperately needed both to heal myself as soon as I could, and to fly again, ideally soaring across the cavern and up one of the other passages, escaping to the upper levels...

But I couldn't.

I regarded the gaggle of filthy, emaciated figures chained to the back, and...yeah...the pigs, although the prospect of a bacon sandwich meant a lot less when compared to the state of those people.

I growled with frustration as I spun back, looking at the cackling, dancing dozens on the other side, and I grinned inside my helm.

"Okay, fucknuts, time to play." I kicked the shield, then punched it, then kicked it, again and again, pounding it and making it flare as it came close to failure, but I didn't want that.

I paused, giving it a half second more before I hit it again, then I planted my feet as solidly as I could, the uneven ground working to my advantage. With a grunt, I braced myself against the shield as the blackness receded, making the barrier appear as a faint haze. I smiled maliciously at the sudden look of horror on the adolescent Vern's face as it finally realized what I was doing. I bunched my muscles and shoved with all my might, sending it and the other creatures on the far side of the shield backward...and cascading out into the empty air of the cavern.

As soon as they were gone, and I had a handful of seconds left, I cut the mana to Mana Overdrive, grunting as the debuff hit me–minus eight to every stat. With the increase in efficiency I'd chosen for the evolution, that still took my health from a hundred and seven points left...to twenty-seven.

And falling.

I backed down the short passageway, reaching into my bag and pulling out the last health potion, followed by...no more mana.

"Shit!" I growled, tearing at the clasps on my armor. Once I'd popped the cinches, I yanked the cuirass free, exposing myself, but also revealing the three holes that bled like a tap.

I pulled a dagger free of my bag, bit the cork free of the healing potion and spat it out, before dragging the dagger over the first of the spots where I could see the slowly moving head of the dart.

It popped free in a gush of blood, and I gritted my teeth, the pain tearing into me. Bracing myself, I repeated the process on the next. The one from under my right pauldron, where it met the cuirass, and the one that had gotten through the links that covered my stomach were easy. The last, buried in the meat of my neck on the right side?

That was harder.

I dug the tip of the knife in, unable to see but going off the feeling. It caught on something, making me grunt in pain as it drove the dart deeper.

I shifted the knife's tip, coming in ahead of the dart and cutting down, feeling the flow of blood wash the dart out, and I sighed in relief, then downed the potion.

I looked for my cuirass, desperately hoping, but the chittering and clattering of claws on stone informed me I had no time.

I'd lost my naginata over the edge when I'd tossed the creatures over, and I reached into my bag, hunting for a weapon. There was only one left, besides the multitude of daggers.

My kill-stick.

Giint had recharged and upgraded it, seeming pleased that I wanted to keep the weapon. Now, as I yanked out my full-size Tower shield and lifted the kill-stick, I couldn't help but grin.

The little bastard might be batshit crazy, but he did good work. I flicked the activation lever, and it roared to life, a subtle blue and green glow flooding the weapon. In place of the three levels of rotating blades, there were now three heads close together at one end. Somehow, they faced each other, forming the points of a triangle. They revved outward, forcing any bits out, rather than crushing them into the center to jam the machine. They seemed to flow through each other, like they broke the laws of physics, reminding me of a Mobius strip. But I didn't give two shits about breaking natural laws, not anymore.

I could sodding fly when I decided to, and I lived in a Tower that was over two miles high, not to mention I was fucking a Wisp.

Nature could go suck a bucket of dicks.

I revved the kill-stick, locking my left arm in tight to the back of the shield and started forward.

It was time to go fuck some shit up.

CHAPTER TWENTY-FOUR

I burst forward, the last few Drach falling back as I slammed the kill-stick on top of a Vern trying to crawl away.

The ferociously chewing blades raced outwards, tearing the body into shreds that rained across the passageway. Its gurgle of terror erupted into a high-pitched noise that sent fear through the rest of the pack, causing them to instinctively fall back.

It was the third wave since I'd changed to this weapon, and it was getting low on charge. I chose to stop it between each attack, in fear that the damn thing would give out entirely. But between the terrifying sounds it made when it dug into a target and the way I probably looked now, I had apparently managed to instill a level of fear in the creatures that was buying me time.

As the blood dripped from me, I reached up, casually searching and pulling free a strip of Vern that had gotten stuck to my razor plume somehow. They cowered fearfully, while I stood tall and straight, shield at the ready, still fully armored, bar my cuirass, and watched the short passage as I tried to catch my breath while simultaneously looking as though I did this every day.

I'd managed to cast my first spell and the comforting flames of Cleansing Fire added to the overall image of terror I was cultivating for the Vern. The flames jumped and licked over me, happily repairing the dozens of fresh, minor wounds I was covered in, while they devoured any of the Drach or Vern that were foolish or brave enough to set foot in range.

I slowly got control of my breathing again, staring ahead and risking it all by meditating and using Peace, but I couldn't afford to do less. I needed every edge I could get, even if it did slow my reactions as I changed from meditation back to war.

The increased mana and health regeneration was worth it, and I'd managed to somehow anchor the Cleansing Fire to myself. Using the combination of the remote activation ability and my growing familiarity with the spell, I could now maintain it indefinitely, provided I had the second level of meditation and Peace going at the same time, anyway.

The outer ring of the spell crossed over the path at the end of the passage, so the only way they could reach me was to basically set themselves alight.

The two attempts they'd made to attack from the Drach's back across the cavern had failed miserably. Not only was the range excessive for their short bows and weak stature, but all I had to do was step to the side, out of sight, and it rendered their attacks pointless.

I'd not been wasting my time, though.

"We're nearly there." Oracle whispered in my mind, recognizing the need to not interrupt my meditation as she brought me up to speed.

And it was true, I acknowledged with a separate section of my mind, one that watched dispassionately as I focused on the glowing box of light I had constructed around myself.

She was getting closer, that was for sure.

I could hear the occasional crunch and grind, the crack of stone as they dug at the ground overhead. I smiled as I envisaged the terrible surprise that was coming for the fuckers below.

"A few more minutes, my love. I'm nearly with you now." Oracle whispered.

I opened my eyes, fully awakening from the mediation as I sensed a change nearby.

I could feel Oracle, her love, her irritation that as soon as she turned her back for *one goddamn minute,* I got into trouble, and her desperate need to be with me, not because of our shared life and mana, but because she was determined that whatever we faced, we would face it together.

It wasn't that, though.

I reached out cautiously, the heightened mental state that always came from meditation having alerted me to it, and I searched, seeing past the stone walls, past the dirt and roots, the literal tons of corpses and gallons upon gallons of bodily fluids that were stinking the place up.

I pushed my mental senses past the twin impressions of awe and terror that the prisoners regarded me with, the almost supernaturally fast and deadly fighter that had battled its way into the room where they were held, to protect them alone from all those terrible creatures, or so it seemed to them.

No, it was something else. I reached out further, my mind scanning, following the traces in the air, the hints that pulled my mind down until I hit the shield, and I finally registered something I should have known all along.

The Vern, the adult king and queen, or whatever the fuck they were, weren't here by accident, not in a location that contained a summoning chamber for a mana-wight.

No, the people who'd set up their village over the site had been the only ones there by luck, as even shitty luck, is, by its nature, luck.

The Vern were there to secure something, something that the summoning chamber had been built as a last resort to protect, or to defend against.

They had built their nest atop it, and it was still here.

Whatever it was, it sang to me, and I growled low in my throat at the thought of them defiling it with their presence.

I took an involuntary step forward, followed by another, as I sensed the shield below flickering…weakening.

I blinked, dismissing the trace elements in the air of all I'd seen and sensed. With my mana refilled and my health full, I stared at the Vern below and at the huge Drach as it prowled and thrashed, stomping here and there in the pool at the bottom of the cavern.

The Vern watched me, even as they siphoned mana away from their shield, building it down there.

The people and animals behind me bleated in terror and prayer. I turned back, walking to them and crouching nearby, eyeing them all carefully.

There were three women and one man shielding six small children behind them. All were desperately filthy and malnourished, chained to the wall, and further encased in a roughly built cage. They gaped at me with a mixture of terror and hope.

Since I'd arrived in the small larder, as I guessed it was, I'd done nothing but fight, heal, and meditate, then rinse and repeat.

I'd been careful to keep the Cleansing Fire ritual circle clear of them and the animals, but beyond that, I'd essentially ignored them.

They'd spent their time trying to get my attention, one way or another, different languages, calls, shouts, pleading and I'd blocked it all out, simply because I'd not been able to afford the time or distraction.

Now, with what was coming, I took a few brief seconds to speak to them.

"There's backup coming. They'll help you," I said slowly, pulling my cuirass to me and starting the awkward task of reattaching it, as it was meant to be put in place before the other sections.

"But…"

"Please…"

"Free us…"

They called and begged, and I shook my head, twisting latches, trying to get them to lock into place. I severed the connection to the spell, letting it rely on its own mana, and started a mental timer as it began to run lower by the second.

"I can't," I said simply. "I need to finish this. They're doing something, a new spell, and I can't wait for them to attack any longer."

I felt the catch click at last. The pauldron and its attached vambraces and gauntlets suddenly felt lighter as they locked into place properly. I sighed in relief before attacking the last latch on the left. Another thirty seconds, and it clunked into place, making me sigh once again.

"Oracle, how long?" I sent.

A few seconds later, she replied. ***"Looks like another few minutes, that's all."***

"They've weakened their shield, and they're gathering their mana," I warned her.

"I know. You need to get out of there. Vern have some insidious spells and abilities. Please, Jax."

"I'm not leaving these people," I said firmly.

"We'll be there for them soon, and if you leave, there's every chance the Vern will stop."

"You really believe that?"

"No," she admitted after a long pause. ***"I can sense the mana from here. They're already past the point that they'd have released for a normal spell, so whatever it is, it's powerful."***

"Exactly. I'm going to go make a pest of myself. Get down as soon as you can."

"Jax!" I cut the connection to her and stood, rising to my full height before the cowering group. Reaching into one bag, I pulled out a handful of the dried trail rations the legionnaires swore by…or at. I passed them over then turned, shaking my shield to make sure it was comfortably attached as I drew in a deep breath and shook my head and shoulders, loosening them up as I got ready. I drew the kill-stick out, verifying that it was working with a little flick, then started down the passageway again.

It was time to end this.

Whatever the Vern were working on, a spell that size couldn't be allowed to build further.

The fact they were putting so much effort into it meant I had to stop it. Logically, it was either designed to reach whatever was secured below, a desperate attempt to stop me from getting there, or it was an Armageddon spell, something they believed I'd never survive, even hidden out of sight as I was.

I couldn't risk any of them.

I strode out, ready to fight, only to find that the Drach and the Vern had fallen back all the way down to the third level and were sinking lower as fast as they could.

"Fuuuuuck," I growled, dropping the kill-stick into my pouch and raising the shield to deflect the hail of tiny darts smashing against it and bouncing off. Most broke and tumbled down. In the meantime, I started to cast as well.

I hunched behind the shield, fingers flashing and mouth chanting as I formed the various elements of the spell, before sticking my head around the corner to aim and launch a dual-cast version of Magic Missile. Ten bolts, one from each finger, flashed out, hurtling down.

I'd targeted four for the small sub-sentient Vern that were hissing and screeching at me, firing dart after dart, and even as weak as the glowing missiles were, hitting such tiny creatures practically guaranteed a kill.

The other six hit the shield, spread out equidistantly around the royal pair, in the hope that it might be a one-sided spell somehow.

It wasn't, I realized, as the shield flared to life, absorbing the bolts and making me wince.

I quickly tried again with Fireball, charging it with a full hundred and fifty mana before firing it at the shore of the small pool closest to the creature.

It exploded in a bright white and yellow bloom of magic and fire, tossing the thickly clustered Drach and Vern into the air in chunks of singed chitin and bloody limbs, respectively, but the flames slammed into the barrier and bounced off, making me growl in frustration.

"Okay, so you have a dome," I muttered, firing another Fireball into the growling, spitting mass gathered at the base of the cavern closest to me.

It hit and exploded, sending bodies tumbling. The smaller Drach and Vern were dying easily, but my mana was vanishing quickly. The larger, far more dangerous versions were getting singed and maybe losing a limb, at most.

I glared down at them, wishing I'd brought Bob or a load of mana potions…or hell, the entire team. For the hundredth time that day, I cursed myself for a fool, telling myself again and again that a leader didn't have the luxury of foul-tempered grudge matches.

Not when I didn't know for sure what I was walking into.

I ducked back out of sight of another hail of darts. The smarter ones were trying to get them up and over the shield to fall on me. Crouched as I was, and without the benefit of force behind them, they were an annoyance, little more, as I worked myself up. I had just enough health and mana for what I knew I needed to do.

At least I hoped I did.

I held on for another ten seconds, debating the sense of the move, when Oracle reached out to me.

"We've hit a pocket of stone; it's slowed us down," she warned me.

"Looks like its nut up or shut up time, then," I sent her.

"Be careful," she sent back, knowing the limited options I had and that none of them were good.

"I love you."

"I love you, too."

With that, I stood, backed up then started running, outwards and down.

I sprinted as fast as I could, though the curve of the narrow, beaten dirt path made it awkward to hold the shield on my left, and the path also curved to my left. But that was par for the course, the way this day was going.

I gritted my teeth as the little bastards got over their shock and started firing again, the darts smashing against the stone and embedding themselves in the dirt all around me. I saw the gleam I'd been looking for among the remains of the last Fireball's victims.

I glanced ahead and firmed my resolve, seeing a section where the path narrowed, and a large stone jutted out.

If I was a sensible man, that would have been a great place to hunker down to rest from the barrage and hope the little sods ran out of ammo before the spell finished.

But, as I wasn't a sensible man, I used it as a jumping off point instead.

I planted one foot firmly on the rock and pushed off as hard as I could, deliberately flipping myself over and triggering Soaring Majesty for all of two seconds.

It was enough to massively increase my speed, driving me headfirst toward the ground. I angled my shield, then triggered it again, flipping myself over as darts hurtled by. A *whoosh* and splash, followed by sizzling and pained screeching, told me that the Drach queen had sprayed the area again, the gust of air letting me know just how near I'd come to being made into a puddle.

My boots slammed into the mass of bodies and scuttling creatures, one of the Drach under my right foot absorbing most of my momentum and practically bursting. My right hand shot down, catching the naginata six inches below the bladed section.

I ripped it up, cutting deep into the Drach that spun to face me, flipping it into the air in a shower of ichor.

I hunched down, pointing the naginata and bracing my shield before feeding light mana into the weapon and banishing the darkness. The cavern filled with a pained screech as I triggered Soaring Majesty again.

I hurtled forward, slamming into the shield over the royal pair, and felt it resist for a quarter of a second before it popped like a balloon, as the naginata's shield-penetrating ability came into play, powered by the magical anathema to their kind.

I flew forward, aiming the blade for the chest of the Vern queen, where she sat immobile on her throne, her withered arms and legs seemingly fused into place. Only her eyes moved, great orbs of yellow and black malevolence.

I was going to drive the naginata straight through her chest and through the king's back…the last few feet seemingly taking forever to cross…

Until I blinked, realizing that it *was* taking forever, several seconds already at least, and it wasn't a facet of adrenaline!

I had a split second to realize what this meant before the Drach queen completed her spin and slammed the ovipositor spike down, smashing me from the air. I bounced and clattered across the ground, air driven from my lungs. Juvenile Drach and Vern surrounded me, screeching in hatred as I teetered on the edge of the small pool, then fell in.

I sank fast, pulled down by the weight of my armor.

The world spun as I tried to adjust to the sudden shift. I opened my mouth, my mind reeling from the blow, and I sucked in hot, foul water instead. Panicking, I thrashed involuntarily as I sank deeper.

I forced my eyes open, trying to make out which way was up, and saw nothing but a churning mass of bubbles and frantically stabbing black chitinous legs. As I sank farther, I suddenly realized that the damn Drach queen was keeping to the shallows…an entire section in the middle of the pool was horrifically deeper, and I bounced off a ledge, twisting and rolling, before being dragged to the depths, the weight of the armor and a sharp tug from an unseen current enough to wrench me over the next ledge and into blackness.

I tried to calm myself, tried to get control, to stop my lungs from spasming as they filled with water, but I couldn't.

I'd always been a terrible swimmer, always. I'd nearly drowned twice as a child, and that was in a normal swimming pool.

I opened my mouth and screamed, water rushing in to replace the last dregs of air, and the world turned to night as I lost consciousness.

CHAPTER TWENTY-FIVE

H er presence enveloped me like a warm blanket, clinging to me, reaching out, even though she was too far away to speak.

I blinked, turning onto my side and coughing weakly, bringing up water and vomit. It hit the inside of my helm and spattered back, covering my short beard and face, going up my nose and even into my eyes.

I retched again and reached up frantically, yanking and shoving at my helm. My fingers scrabbled across the bottom as I missed in my haste, the tips of my gauntlets bouncing off and scraping the side of the helm instead. Desperate, I returned them to shoving, tearing the skin on my chin and right cheek in my frantic need to uncover my face.

My helmet came loose, and I heaved, another wave of watery vomit erupting from my mouth and splashing into water I could hear and feel, but not see, blinded as I was.

I thrashed my arms in the water, feeling a shallow depth where I lay, but my questing fingers dropping off into deeper water mere inches away, brushed by a fast-moving current. I backed up, blindly, before almost falling off what turned out to be the other side of a small island, barely three feet across.

I spun, hands reaching, feeling the world as my eyes adjusted. Blinking fast in an effort to swipe the last vestiges of stomach acid free, I finally saw the clean water to my right, ignoring the soiled…chunks…that floated to my immediate left. I plunged my face into the water, shaking it then coming up for air and frantically rubbing and my eyes and cheeks to send foul water and droplets flying.

I collapsed back, flopping down on the raised hump of land and looking around blearily. Shock and the near brush with death made my mind sluggish, even as I sensed her again.

Oracle.

She was reaching out to me, too far to make out any words, just a sense of reassurance, of love, of a powerful desire to hold me, to screw my brains out, and to scream at me for scaring her so.

She must be frantic with worry, I realized, the mash of her emotions blurring together and reinforcing my own confusion.

Then it changed, a flare of relief coming through as she sensed me calming. I forced myself to catch my breath, sucking it down a throat that felt red-raw and into lungs that felt bruised to shit.

I panted, clutching at my chest, then quickly slammed my hand down, twisting as I thrashed my hands around in the shallow water flowing past the raised section of ground that had undoubtedly saved my life.

I was alive, but both my naginata and my shield were gone.

Fuck.

I crouched on the shore, squinting around. Even my DarkVision did little, barely allowing me to make out the walls of a cavern cut out by millennia of rushing water carving channels, a roof a handful of meters above me, and the little knot of land I laid upon, surrounded by fast-moving water.

I swore as I realized that, wherever I was, it wasn't somewhere I could stay.

I reached out, grabbing my helm as it shifted in the shallow current before an errant surge nearly pulled it from me, and I turned it over, grimacing at the smell and state of the inside.

I quickly washed it clear then put it in my bag. Sighing, I stood to strip off, slipping each section of armor into the bag and shivering as I did.

Once I was down to my underwear–the padded undergarments that held the armor were waterlogged and weighed almost as much as the metal, after all–I began searching around the small area I could see.

The water crashed down from somewhere higher up and to my right. I had vague recollections of bouncing off rocks and worse, of underwater stalactites and stalagmites sending me careening from side to side. I felt the hundreds of tender spots across my body as I looked up then to my left, where the water vanished, curving around to the right again and out of sight.

"There aren't a lot of choices here, are there?" I whispered before sighing and casting Surgeon's Scalpel. It identified dozens of wounds, the cracks and minor breaks, the bruises and internal bleeds that made up my body, and I realized that, without my armor, I'd have been dead long before I got to this island, and with it, I should have drowned.

I was a lucky sonuva bitch, and I needed to accept that, even if I wasn't where I wanted to be right then.

A new notification flashed, and I grunted in irritation, then sat down and began pulling them up, figuring I might as well get them out of the way before I tried to leave and possibly drowned.

Congratulations!

You have raised your spell Cleansing Fire to its First Evolution.

You must now pick a new path to follow.

Will you choose the path of DESTRUCTION or that of HEALING?

Choose carefully, as this choice cannot be undone.

DESTRUCTION:
Your spell has healed you for small amounts, and occasionally larger, over long periods of time. However, that was always a secondary benefit when compared to the damage the flames have wrought in your name!

Evolving Cleansing Fire to Flames of Wrath will remove the healing element and will enable it to be far more effective as a weapon, doubling the damage from ten points per second to twenty, while increasing the mana cost from fifty points to one hundred. As a bonus, the spell length will increase from 60 seconds to 75.

HEALING:
You have found that, while the Cleansing Flames dealing out punishment is welcome, it is less important than the healing properties it provides. You may now choose to increase this side effect, raising the spell from a mere two points of healing per second to five, although such a large boost does come with a shorter lifespan and higher cost to the spell.

Cleansing Fire will evolve to Flames of Renewal, costing one hundred points of mana for 30 seconds, healing 5 points of damage per second to all friendlies within the sphere of effect.

I looked over both options, and frankly, thought they were both shit. I loved the spell primarily for its utility; the fact I could heal myself while injuring anyone else that stepped into range, had literally saved my life during my altercation with the Vern and Drach. Both evolutions took one side of that away, heavily reducing the usefulness of the spell.

I glared at the screen, trying to dismiss it, and when, like so many times before, it came to a CHOICE like this, I couldn't. I swore loudly.

Fuming, I splashed down, sinking onto my ass in the shallow frigid water and shivered, too pissed to acknowledge the cold as I glared at the screen again.

Healing or damage. Healing or damage…well, the healing equated to three hundred points of healing over a short time, and was a hell of an improvement over the original hundred and twenty, and the damage was going from six hundred to fifteen hundred…

I had no idea why the damage levels were so high on that, for such a low cost, comparatively speaking, but it wasn't something I could pass up. Growling under my breath, all the while resolving to make a new version of the spell with Oracle, I accepted the change.

You have selected Destruction for your First Evolution of Cleansing Flames.

Your Spell has evolved to Flames of Wrath and can now be used scour away your enemies with even greater effectiveness!

For a cost of one hundred mana, and a casting time of ten seconds, you can now deal up to fifteen hundred damage to a single enemy or spread the damage out across multiple enemies who cross the threshold of this ritual circle.

I cursed again, long and loud. The old version did the same level of damage to everyone inside the threshold, for the same amount of time, so no matter if one enemy was in it, or if there were twenty enemies, they'd all receive the same six hundred damage. Now, it was more expensive, and the goddamn spell was weaker! If there were three enemies inside the circle, they'd get less damage overall.

I seethed, remembering something that Yen had said at one point when we'd talked.

I didn't remember exactly what she'd said, but it'd been something about our usages deciding our evolutions. So, basically, I had been using the spell wrong, and it was trying to evolve in the direction I was guiding it subconsciously. The evolution itself was powered by a combination of my experiences, my knowledge, and my abilities, which was why the basic spells, such as Firebolt, were fairly common, but higher-leveled spells were so rare.

Anyone could make a Firebolt, in theory, but once I'd leveled it up to whatever its highest evolution for me was, that spell became unique to me, and I could teach it. I would be passing on a weakened version, yeah, but still a spell that nobody else could have created, as nobody else had the exact life and knowledge I had.

That meant that the change to the Cleansing Fire spell that had practically fucked it was my own fault, as I focused mainly on fire for damage and healing spells for, well, healing.

That meant that my only mixture spell had been tied to one of those channels exclusively. If I'd been using lightning more, the way Oracle liked, or ice, for example, I would have gotten totally different evolutionary choices.

"Well, that's just peachy," I groused. "Not only do I have to try and spread out the spell usage now, I have to plan for complementary evolutions!"

I sat there shivering for long seconds that turned into minutes, until finally, I pulled up the next notification, figuring it was best to get through them before I died of sodding hypothermia.

Congratulations!

You have killed the following:

- 91x Drach of various levels for a total of 38,350xp

- 136x Vern of various levels for a total of 4,975xp

A party under your command killed the following:

- 26x Drach of various levels for a total of 17,100xp

- 17x Vern of various levels for a total of 835xp

- 2x Royal Vern, level 31 for 42,000xp

- 1x Drach Queen, level 28 for 14,800xp

Total party experience earned: 74,735xp
As party leader, you gain 25% of all experience earned
Progress to level 24 stands at 208,867/510,000

I nodded in satisfaction, pleased that the others had cleared out the problem while I was napping, killing both the adult Vern royalty and the queen Drach. I puzzled for a minute over the different levels of experience that the party and I had received for the smaller Drach, then grimaced, guessing that the difference in the experience per kill was probably because I'd been swarmed again and again by little ones, while they'd had to fight the full-size suckers.

I dismissed the class options before they could fully form as I'd been doing for the last few days. Once they were clear, I'd be stuck accepting one of them, and couldn't trust myself to look, just in case.

I moved on, skipping through the usual notifications. I'd leveled up my swords, my shield, my naginata–though that was lost somewhere underwater now–and my unarmed skill, which was at level nine, as was my brawling. Weirdly, I had a skill I'd not noticed before, armored combat, that was at level seven already.

I checked through them all and sighed as I caught the common detail.

They all involved me beating something or someone, but because I did it in armor, the experience earned points in that category, unarmored in another, and in mixed gear, which was probably when half my armor was trashed, in brawling.

It was annoying as all hell, because once they reached level ten, they each granted a single point into the overarching field of unarmed combat, and that was what would make me deadlier. Until then, though, I was stuck plodding along.

I dismissed them again and looked out over the water, trying to build up both the courage and the interest in getting in, as well as risking my goddamn life again.

I watched the water rushing past for several seconds before sighing and scooting forward, sliding out of the shallows and ducking my head under water. Blinking as my eyes adjusted to the horrible feeling of water pressing against them, I started to search.

I had to swim against the current, as I figured it was best to be sure, but by the time I'd swum upstream to where the roof lowered to join the water, and I no longer had space to breathe, I mentally drew the line.

I would search from here and no further up. If need be, I could send a damn golem down later to search properly.

I took a deep breath and dove, swimming against the current and thrashing until I reached the bottom of the river. I searched for as long as I could, moving from left to right, before finally going up for air.

I grabbed onto a low stalactite and caught my breath, diving and repeating the process four more times, until I was confident I'd searched the entire area, up to the shallows.

There was no sign of the naginata or shield.

I dragged myself out of the water as far as I could. Shivering, I huddled on the bank, casting a Fireball and holding it as long as I could in an effort to warm myself up.

Once I'd recovered, I grudgingly accepted that I couldn't afford the time I needed to search properly. I had to get out of here and reach the others, as well as preparing for the fight with the Dark Legion. Sitting in here for days just wasn't an option, especially when I had very limited rations and no real options for warmth or a safe place to sleep away the time until the others could find me.

I slipped back into the water, diving and searching as I was pulled along by the current. Up and down, up and down.

Eventually, I was dragged in a large circle by the stream, the cavern seemingly a giant sinkhole that swirled like a drain. As I went, I passed through faster and slower sections, catching glimpses of monstrous eels and great jagged scratches that marred the riverbed.

I passed low-roofed areas and sections where the ceiling was too high for my DarkVision to reach. While I could feel myself being dragged farther and farther from Oracle, I also knew her rough location, and that stayed reasonably constant, letting me know that while I was steadily descending, I wasn't being dragged huge distances.

I worked out that I'd done three revolutions of the massive spiral when I saw my first glimmer of hope.

It was the battered, split carapace of a Drach, a large one, and it was pinned in place between a section of flat rock that had fallen recently, and the river, being slowly worn away.

I swam down to it, bracing myself against the current, and reached under it, flipping it up to bounce and float away, carried by the current.

It'd been stripped of most of its mass, either through the current or the eels and random fish darting about out of the corner of my eyes, but under it was the treasure I sought.

My tower shield.

It, and several other bits, things I recognized once I made it back up to the surface and found somewhere to rest. Arrow heads from the Vern had clearly been dragged by the current until they'd hit this pocket, where they'd been waiting for me.

The shield was scarred, dented, and battered, and its durability was down to thirty-six, but still, I had it again, and that alone was a massive relief.

I secured it in the bag, then dived again.

There was another section a few minutes later, this time housing a collection of bones that were definitely humanoid, but not human, short and stout, thicker than I'd have guessed, and almost stone-like in their strength. I guessed at a Dwarf, as I searched through them, finding only a simple gold ring, battered but intact.

I pocketed it, went up for air, then returned to the bottom. Time and time again, I cursed myself for a fool, having held a damn potion of water breathing in this very bag only a few days past. I'd put it into the general pool of items so I had space to stash more later.

I was grimly aware that my greed might very well kill me in this case, but I went on, scouring the cavern, being careful to return to the surface for air before I got too desperate, just in case.

Three hours passed like this, resulting in two damaged swords, a stone axe, a few clubs and a pouch, several dozen coins, and hundreds of bones, and a dead Drach, before I found something.

Unfortunately, I found it by following a long, carved scar in the stone, shiny with recent making, all the way to a dark hole.

The current here was powerful, and I guessed it was an exit from the speed and pressure as I braced myself and stared into the darkness.

Even DarkVision needed something to work with, and up until now, there'd been lichen and tiny glowing bugs on the ceiling, or cracks that reflected faint light in from elsewhere. Now, there was nothing, nothing nearby that could illuminate the black crack, and I couldn't even cast Fireball down here. I'd tried once and had earned myself horrifically scalded arm for my trouble.

I braced myself, and hoping I wasn't about to get bitten, I reached into the darkness.

My hand was numb from the cold, making it harder to feel. Hell, my entire body was numb by now. Where I was, I desperately needed air, so I couldn't afford to be cautious.

I reached in, flailed around, and let out almost all of my air in a silent scream of pain as I slapped the flat of my hand onto the tip of a curved dagger, impaling it.

I dug my fingers into the rock where I hung, gritting my teeth and shaking, as I forced my fingers on my right hand to close enough to lift it out, dragging something with it.

A golden chain, covered in silt and set with a blue stone, came out as well, caught on the hilt of the weapon. I made the pair of items vanish into my inventory, even as I kicked off from the wall, pushing myself upwards.

I pressed my right hand to my chest, now almost blue with cold, bleeding heavily, as I struck upwards, desperately searching for air…only to find the cavern roof.

The water was filling the tunnel now, and I was dragged faster and faster along it, slamming into a wall and rolled along, head over heels, as I tried and failed to keep myself upright.

I started to panic and asphyxiate as I saw, just for a split second, a section of water that appeared to have an air bubble trapped in it, before I flashed past it and was dragged down to a tight hole, a meter wide by half a meter tall.

I smacked off the edge of the hole, banging my head and, of all things, my goddamn funny bone, before scraping along a short, narrow tunnel as the world began to darken again.

This time, I hit something before I could go any farther, falling into something that bound me tight before yanking me to one side and out of the flow of the water. My head reached sudden cool air, and I dragged down a breath before coughing and bringing up what felt like half the river again.

I jerked around and swung, bouncing as I heard a bell tolling in the distance. I felt myself being dragged, but all I cared about was the air, the blessedly clear air as I sucked it down.

It took several long minutes for me to recover, to get enough of a handle on myself to look around and make sense of the world, enough to see that I was caught in a net, rolled tight, and dangling clear of the river, while being slowly drawn along on a rope.

I twisted, trying to determine how tangled I was, finding that I was suspended a good three or four feet off the ground by a rope attached to a winch, one that was slowly dragging me through the air in a line along with a dozen other…things…in similar nets.

I looked back, observing a huge section of netting over the mouth of the river. Seemingly, from what I could make out, if something solid hit it, its own thrashing and weight rolled the net around it. Then the weight triggered the section of net to move along, lifting it out of the water.

Then a fresh piece would move back across the mouth of the river, ready to catch the next piece of flotsam.

Looking at the bundles ahead, I made out one that was weakly twitching, three that were clearly full of dead things, and one…one that held my naginata!

It was stuck clean through the remains of a Drach, a big one, despite all the missing legs and battered sections. I sagged in palpable relief that I'd not lost it.

I twisted slightly, feeling the rub of raw skin on the net, and I tried to find an opening, without any luck. After that, I decided that the net, while I was sure it was valuable to whoever made it, could go fuck itself, and I reached into the pouch, pulling the dagger free.

It was a short thing, small enough that it was sized more for a child than a man, with a serrated back and curved blade, but the edge was wickedly sharp, and

I put it to good use, cutting enough of the net that I managed to tumble free, landing with a smack and a groan on the cool stone floor below.

I laid motionless for a time, listening to the net creaking overhead as it slowly moved along, and I forced myself to my knees, grimacing at the bloody imprint I had left on the stone.

I let out another groan, using my Surgeon's Scalpel spell and fixing the disgustingly large sections of missing skin, fractures, and internal bleeding, not to mention my cut-open palm.

It took longer than I would have liked, but by the time I was healed, the naginata slowly vanished around a corner ahead.

I forced myself to my feet, pulling clothes out and dressing quickly as I went. I reached the corner, peering around it before backing up slowly.

I dressed fully, taking the time to put my armor on. It was a process that took literally just over a quarter of an hour, as inexperienced as I was with it all. But once I was done, I felt a hell of a lot more prepared as I moved up to the corner and peered around it, right into the blind, white eyes of a startled creature that had sidled up to see what was making the noise.

It screeched in shock, somehow still seeing me, then turned and raced away, barking and screeching, as I hit it with an identification spell.

Dark Kobold

Dark Kobolds generally live in the deep places of the realm, surviving in the abandoned homes of more successful creatures. They are known for their cowardice, aggression, and love of pain.

This particular variant of the Dark Kobold has developed undesirable mutations, resulting in a much shorter lifespan only enhanced by the creature's natural stupidity.

Weaknesses: 10% weakness to physical damage, 50% weakness to Fire, Earth, Water, and Life magics.
Resistances: Dark Kobolds have a natural affinity for Dark and Death Magics, granting a 25% resistance to attacks by these elements
Level: 4
Health: 37/40
Stamina: 52/80
Mana: 10/10

I cursed as it ran, the entire cavern echoing with its cries, as three more Kobolds popped their heads up.

They weren't the almost-cute creatures I remembered from the online games, no, these were fugly little things. They had stunted frames and were completely hairless, with sightless, milky white eyes and antennae that would be more at home on an ant than anything that walked upright. Their hides were covered in sores, with short legs that ended in wide paws and four arms, all of which looked to be spindly and weak.

Where the others ran, one at the far end of the line hissed at me in challenge before spitting and barking something, gesturing quickly with short, sharp movements.

It took only a few seconds, time I used to take in the cavern, before the creature finished, and a grey, spectral form, encased in glowing black and red chains howled and rushed me.

I hefted the shield and my new dagger, slashing at it and making it scream as the dagger passed through it. But before I could draw back, it struck at my forearm, making me drop the dagger from suddenly numb fingers.

I backed up as it clutched at its torn-open stomach, the spectral flesh slowly resealing as I tried to make my hand work.

I released an identification spell at it as I backed up, thankful, not for the first time, that it was possible to cast when you still held something; in my case, a shield.

Kobold Spectral Minion

A spectral minion is just what it says it is: the spirit of a creature tortured to death by the Kobold or another creature. It is then forced by the use of Death magics to serve its new master.

Weaknesses: Spectral minions, like all Specters, cannot be injured by non-magical physical weapons, but are particularly susceptible to Life and Light magics.
Resistances: 100% resistance to non-magical weapons
Level: 3
Health: 120/120
Stamina: N/A
Mana: N/A
Time: 76s remaining until imbued mana expires and spectral minion is dismissed.

I grinned, having resolved earlier to use more of a range of spells, as I started to cast, quickly building the spell. Aiming through the Spectral Minion at the Kobold beyond it, I wasted no time in firing the lightning bolt at it.

The bolt injured the minion, shoving it back and tearing a hole in its form. Unfortunately, it began to repair itself immediately as it shrieked at me in hatred.

The bolt continued, however, to smack the Kobold that had cast the minion spell from its feet, slamming it back against a rotting wooden crate and dropping it, stunned, from its feet.

The Specter hissed, and I grimaced, running to the right. I felt a thrill of relief at seeing the corpse of the Drach dangling, half-freed from its restraining net. The naginata was jutting out, and I grabbed it and pulled hard, yanking it free.

I pointed at the Specter, weapon in hand, and took a deep breath before acknowledging the feeling that was bubbling within me.

I stepped back and slammed the butt of the naginata down against the ground, eyeing the spirit that was closing on me slowly, hissing its hatred, clearly being forced to obey its master's desires.

I could feel the pull, the *need* to do it, and I had to just hope I would have the time to finish it.

I reached out to that feeling, to the power in my chest, and I tugged at it, pulling it into me. All the while, I stared into the hate, and I recognized the despair-filled look in the eyes of the Specter.

The power filled me, the mana in the area changing as it was pulled into me, and I shook as it coursed through my arms and legs. Tiny bolts of it flickered from finger to finger, and my naginata flared to bright, glowing life, making the Kobolds tremble and yip in fear as they hid behind boxes and rocks in the distance.

I focused on the spirit, my anger over what was done to it growing, filling my heart as all fear of it vanished.

I no longer saw an undead Specter, a spirit I had to defeat, to kill again. I saw a victim. A shadow of the person it had been, tortured, beaten, and murdered, then their soul forced to stay and serve their murderer.

I saw it all in a brief second, and I grew incensed at it. This Specter before me was a child of my Empire. It was born and had died while the Empire slumbered, yes, but that didn't make it any less of an Imperial Citizen in my eyes, and neither was it less in the eyes of my power.

I leveled my naginata at it, and it flinched. Then I spoke new words to it, words its soul had longed to hear, but had never known consciously.

"Be free," I said simply, my order, my simple words full of power bridging the gap between the tip of my weapon and the cowering shade as a blast of blue-white lightning hurtled down the naginata.

It howled in pain and joy, and my power raced on, streaking across the room in crackling strands that completely bypassed the remaining Kobolds, only to vanish down the passageways that led off the cavern.

The world spun. My body, beaten, stressed, and nearly drowned twice over, collapsed as I fell into unconsciousness.

Fucking AGAIN.

CHAPTER TWENTY-SIX

I awoke slowly.

The room was quiet, the floor where I lay sandy and bare, but comfortable. I blinked groggily as I looked around, finding nothing amiss.

My memory returned gradually, and I shifted, finding that not only was I free, but I still held my naginata. I was equally pleased to find that, while my body was sore, it wasn't the soul-sucking cold I'd felt when the spectral minion had clawed at me. It was more of a full-body toothache. Clenching my jaw, I forced myself to my feet and searched around grimly, ready to be attacked again. I couldn't help cursing myself for my stupidity at using a power I knew I couldn't control in the middle of a damn fight.

I was incredibly lucky that the Kobolds had left me be; in fact, I was…

I wasn't alone.

The Specter was still there, and it was watching me. The form changed to that of an old man, defining details growing clearer as it glided closer.

I glanced from it to the space behind it in the distance, where the summoning Kobold had been, and saw…a mass of shredded flesh and blood.

I shifted my gaze back to the old man's spirit as it came to a stop a few feet away and bowed its head in thanks.

"Eternal, you freed us." he whispered.

I blinked in surprise. The voice seemed to come from a great distance, thin and frail, but clear.

"I…you're welcome…wait, us?" I asked, and he nodded.

"All the enslaved nearby; we were torn free of our bindings, our souls scoured and healed, and our memories returned. Many struck out aimlessly at first, filled with fury, but as our minds settled, we bonded, our shared experiences finding common ground where none had previously existed between the species."

"Were there many of you?" I asked, and he grew solemn.

"There were, but no more. The others have moved on now, their revenge taken, and their souls ready for the next step, but we remained. We few."

I looked away from him as others moved into sight, a scarce handful. But soon, more appeared, until just under a dozen stood there, their faces wan and drawn. The shapes of the crates and rubbish behind them were indistinct yet still visible.

"Why did you stay?" I asked.

He smiled, a gentle, wistful expression, as he shook his head. *"You think we would abandon you to the darkness? You who freed and healed us? No,"* he said, shaking his head more firmly. *"No, Eternal, Scion of the Empire, we would not leave you alone to wake in the cold and dark places of the realm. You saved us, and we will save you,"* he declared, gesturing back over his shoulder.

"We know not who built this place, but the city behind us is old, older than the Empire herself, and long abandoned. The Kobolds were but the latest

inhabitants, and they are scoured from its streets now. We have sealed the great doors and killed all who called it home. Now, only we remain, the unquiet dead, and soon, we too will move on. Before then, though, we would guide you free."

"Thank you," I said fervently. "You know a way to the surface?"

"The Vern traded us long ago to the Kobolds in exchange for powerful trinkets. Paths existed then, and still may, although my soul was bound to a stone that passed through many hands over the long years. We will guide you out."

"Ah, thank you. One question...if you don't mind?" I asked, shifting awkwardly as I thought about how to phrase it.

"Of course." he replied, waiting.

"You all killed the Kobolds, right?" I asked, and he nodded impatiently. "So...uh...you said powerful trinkets...?" I attempted not to make light of all they'd suffered, but I certainly wasn't wanting to pass up loot, either.

"The city was filled with many races over the thousands of years it stood here, and many items remained when the Kobolds came. Some still do, or at least some powerful sources of magic still linger," he whispered. *"One such source is close to the path we must take. Do you wish to visit it?"* He smiled as I nodded quickly, and at his gesture, two of the spirits turned and started off, and I fell in behind them.

"What's your name?" I asked, and he shook his head.

"I don't know," he admitted sadly. *"Many things are lost in passing over the veil. I remember a daughter, her hair like sunlight, but names? No, I remember no names."*

"What should I call you?"

"Call me whatever you wish. Once you are free, we shall move on. It matters not to us what happens beyond that." He smiled gently.

"Okay then, spirit," I glanced at him to make sure he didn't take offense to the label. When he smiled, I relaxed and went on.

"Well, I'm at war above ground, so if there's any kind of loot, weapons, gold, magic, or whatever that could help, I really need to find them," I said, wincing internally at the total lack of subtlety.

"There are many magical items remaining, but the dead do not see the way the living do. Many items are embedded in the stone or are intrinsic to the location. I can tell you only that there are many sources of magical power. Some were worn by those who held us captive, but the strongest, by far, is the source we lead you to now. It would take many weeks to unearth all these sources, and we have not the strength to last that long."

"And I've not got the time, even if you did," I agreed. "Okay, thank you. Take me to the most powerful source, then lead me out, please."

They picked up the pace, leading me quicker and quicker, until I was running, ducking down corridors and passageways, dashing through massive rooms, past huge tables which ran down the length of them.

I passed through narrow doors, clearly designed to slow attackers, where the defenders could secure great stone blocks into place. Ancient murder-holes in the walls, floors, and ceiling provided multiple opportunities to kill anyone trying to pass.

I rushed through rooms with purposes at which I could only guess and covered my nose as I passed through sections filled with foul-smelling scum floating atop stagnant pools.

Everywhere I went, there were bodies, or parts of bodies. Hundreds of Kobolds lay everywhere, torn into thousands of pieces.

I checked my notifications as I entered one long corridor, and I had to stop myself from cursing.

Warning!

You have activated an Imperial Ability without sufficient authority and now must pay the price!

All stats have been permanently reduced by two points, and your body has been damaged in ways small and profound. Think carefully before you overreach again.

I pulled up my stats sheet and gritted my teeth as I saw it laid out in all its damning truth.

Name: Jax Amon				
Titles: Strategos: 5% boost to damage resistance, Fortifier: 5% boost to defensive structure integrity, Champion of Jenae: One search for hidden knowledge every 24 hours				
Class: Spellsword > Justicar > Champion of Jenae > Imperial Magekiller > Imperial Justicar			Renown: Imperial Scion, Lord of Dravith	
Level: 23			Progress: 208,867/510,000	
Patron: Jenae, Goddess of Fire and Exploration			Points to Distribute: 0 Meridian Points to Invest: 0	
Stat	Current points	Description	Effect	Progress to next level
Agility	41	Governs dodge and movement.	+310% maximum movement speed and reflexes, (+10% movement in darkness, -20% movement in daylight)	53/100
Charisma	25 (20)	Governs likely success to charm, seduce, or threaten	+150% success in interactions with other beings	31/100
Constitution	49 (44)	Governs health and health regeneration	960 health, regen 64.35 points per 600 seconds, (+10% regen due to soul bond, -20 health due to soul bond, each point invested now worth 20 health)	63/100
Dexterity	60 (55)	Governs ability with weapons and crafting success	+500% to weapon proficiency, +50% to the chances of crafting success	44/100
Endurance	47 (44)	Governs stamina and stamina regeneration	940 stamina, regen 37 points per 30 seconds, (each point invested now worth 20 stamina)	11/100
Intelligence	58	Governs base mana and number of spells able to be learned	560 mana, spell capacity: 32 (30 + 2 from items), (-20 mana from soul bond)	92/100
Luck	23	Governs overall chance of bonuses	+13% chance of a favorable outcome	7/100

Perception	46 (36)	Governs ranged damage and chance to spot traps or hidden items	+360% ranged damage, +36% chance to spot traps or hidden items	63/100
Strength	37 (34)	Governs damage with melee weapons and carrying capacity	+27 damage with melee weapons, +270% maximum carrying capacity	74/100
Wisdom	41 (31)	Governs mana regeneration and memory	+465% mana recovery, 6.1 points per minute, 310% more likely to remember things, (+50% increased mana regeneration from essence core)	90/100

I gritted my teeth and reminded myself that it was the right thing to do regardless. I dismissed the notification and moved to the next in line.

Quest: Return the Rule of Law, Bring Freedom to the Enslaved, and Peace to the Unquiet Dead III

Note: This Quest cannot be refused without losing your class as an Imperial Justicar.

Punish Breakers of Imperial Law: 511/250
Free Unjustly Imprisoned Citizens: 104/250
Grant Uneasy Revenants their Eternal Rest: 1,287/250
Reward: 1,250,000xp, Access to Fourth Tier of Evolving Quest

*

Congratulations!

Forces set free by your hand have destroyed the population of an entire city down to the smallest and weakest.

You gain a new Title: Kobold Ravager!

You gain +25% damage to all Kobolds due to the terror you engender in their race!

Due to your lack of control over these forces, you receive no experience for their kills.

This time, I really did curse, swearing violently as we ran. Not only had I essentially captured an entire city, but all the inhabitants, a race of dickish little bastards who'd been murdering and enslaving souls, no less, were all dead through my actions. I'd lost literally three levels' worth of stats, and because I was unconscious through the damn expenditure of power, I'd gotten nothing!

Okay, yeah, so I wasn't directing them, but I wasn't directing my party when they fucked up the Drach and Vern, either.

I suspected it had something to do with the fact that the others were in my direct party, while the spirits weren't, just like the legionnaires weren't when they captured the rest of the ships, and Mal, when he'd saved me before, wasn't...but fuck me sideways, it was galling.

I shook my head and carried on before slowing as a familiar feeling washed over me.

I stumbled, then caught myself as it passed, recognizing it as the feeling I'd experienced when I was higher up, and I'd felt the Vern doing something.

They'd been trying to use their power to tap into this, I suspected. From the half-seen threads and weaves of magic they'd been using, they'd definitely been trying to reach something below them, anyway.

The power I felt up ahead made me suspect that was all they could be after, especially when a second wave of power washed over us, and the spirits fuzzed, losing their distinct edges and dimming.

"Eternal, we run low on time, you must hurry!" the old man begged me, hovering close. I stored the naginata away and dug down, pushing harder and picking up speed despite the terrible weakness I was left with as a result of using that power earlier.

They led me through countless doors and along corridors, up two levels then down three more before we eventually broke out of a passageway into a central area, and I almost fell in shock.

At first, it looked like I was outside, free above ground again, rather than buried under rock, until I saw the tower that led upwards, vanishing into the ceiling of a massive cavern to my right.

I slowed then stopped, gazing about in astonishment at the effects and feeling the pleasant breeze that blew across the grass. Bits of rubbish and general detritus were being blown along, and an artificial sun shone down, blanketing the city in its gentle warmth.

I stared about, stunned into immobility, as the spirits gestured, bidding me to keep moving.

"What the hell is this place?" I asked slowly.

"It is all that remains of our lives and the Great Cities that once covered the realm," an ancient, grim voice answered me, sadness clear in each syllable, and the spirits grew noticeably weaker with every word.

"Please, my lord, we must hurry," the spirit of the old man whispered before fading further.

"You may leave us, little one. Take with you those who follow you, with my thanks," came the first voice. The spirits wavered, then vanished, as though they were naught but fog blown by a stiff breeze. There was an overwhelming sense of peace and relief, then they were gone. I turned, looking towards the center of the city and the source of the voice.

"Who are you?" I asked.

There was a long pause as the owner of the voice considered how to respond. *"I am...Malthus,"* the voice said eventually. *"Or at least you may use that name. It is inaccurate, but so would be any other description I could give you in your language. I was once the Administrator of the city of Peleth's View."*

"That's what this city was called?" I asked, uncertain. "Peleth's View?"

"Once it was named so. The fractious creatures that have squatted in its corpse for so many eons have named it many things in their time. I usually ignore them; all leave eventually."

"And me? Why speak to me?" I eyed the tower and what I assumed was the way out.

"Because you freed the little ones. It was old magic you used, magic I thought long lost. I suspected its use recently, on several occasions, but was unsure. Now I know. I wish to regain its source, and in return, I will gift you with power."

"Its source?" I repeated, glancing around warily. I was getting the distinct feeling that whatever was here was used to getting whatever it wanted. "It's a magic that's part of me and of the Empire..."

"The Empire, yes. I remember a mage from your Empire; he sang me such wonderful songs." There was a long break and suddenly humming, and a faint voice singing in a deep baritone rose at the edge of hearing.

"Uh, okay?" I said, shrugging. "I don't sing."

"You must know some songs of your people?" the voice asked.

My mind went totally blank. "I...no, not really..." I frantically wracked my mind and found only three songs in there that were complete enough that I could sing them. Not a single one would be appropriate, especially as I tended to sound like a cat with a weight on its tail when I tried.

"Please, a single song, then I will answer your questions." the voice whispered, sounding more alive.

"Look, you need to understand two things, okay? I'm a terrible singer, and I've got a terrible memory for songs, right?" I said insistently. There was only silence while the voice waited.

Resigned, I took a deep breath, and regarded the three songs I could remember in their entirety, dismissing "Charlie Had a Pigeon" as being too short and "Barbie Girl" as being too goddamn annoying. That left me with only one...

"Frrrosty the perrrvert...in a trenchcoat he did go...." I started to sing, my voice terrible as always.

By the time I reached the end, the silence continued for a long while, and I started to think I'd offended the formless spirit with my poor taste in songs and terrible voice.

"That was...memorable." The voice came back eventually. *"I suspect parts of the song are lost on me due to cultural differences, but the gestures and words were amusing, thank you. You had questions. I will answer as best I can; however, I ask for one thing in return."*

"I sang!" I stated firmly, my face still red with embarrassment.

"And it was...interesting...but the ages are long, and I find myself wishing for things I cannot have. It is no difficult request?"

"What is it?" I growled out.

"Company," the voice said simply. *"I sense you have a settlement nearby, from all you said to the little ones. I will open the pathways, enabling you to leave the city and me behind. In addition to this, I will answer your questions, as best I can. All I ask is that you grant me company now and then. Even if another band of creatures moves into the city, I can hide you or those you send."*

"Can't you just seal the city up? And yeah, I'm sure company can be arranged." I thought of Decin's engineer, Riana. She loved ancient ruins, and, well, this place was also impressive to me, which meant I'd happily come and explore at some point. "Uh, the breeze and the warmth, is that permanent?" I asked, getting the mental equivalent of a nod.

I grinned, thinking about taking future holidays down here, getting a damn tan when it was deep snow up above.

"I could seal the entrances to the city, but then I would be alone again. The company of even dumb creatures is better than the long ages of silence. Even ignoring them is better than being entirely alone," the voice acknowledged sadly.

I swiped a section of the grass clear, making myself comfortable. "Well, sounds like we could make a deal, then," I said, grinning.

Five hours later, I staggered up the final flight of stairs and stepped out into the verdant forest, pulling off my helm and drawing in a deep lungful of fresh air as I looked around. My DarkVision faded away as I emerged into the dappled sunlight.

I sensed Oracle hurtling toward me, and I stepped out of the doorway, turning to face that direction as she emerged at high speed from between a grove of short trees.

She flew at me, not slowing until the last possible second, then transforming into her full-sized version and hitting me with her exuberant hug.

"You're alive!" she cried. I burst into laughter, staggering back a few steps, before spinning around while holding her and feeling her legs flying out from me.

I spun her three times, laughing, before setting her on her feet and kissing her thoroughly. When I finally surfaced from the kiss, gazing joyfully down into her bright green eyes and huge smile, I couldn't resist going back for more.

She was blonde now, despite the brunette she'd been earlier, busty and excited, practically throwing herself atop me in her excitement and relief. I damn well knew I was either in for a hell of a night, or I'd need healing by morning. Or both.

"What happened?" she asked me breathlessly, and I grinned, kissing her one last time before nodding towards the distance, when the sound of breaking wood filtered through the trees.

"I take it that's the others?" I asked, and she nodded impatiently. "I'll have to explain it all over again once they arrive, so why don't you just read my mind for now?" I asked, grinning and trying to keep her from guessing why.

She frowned at me, clearly suspecting something, but she obediently reached up a single hand and closed her eyes before letting out a gasp then a throaty giggle.

The mental image I was holding in my mind, knowing that it'd be the first thing she saw, was both filthy and fun, and I knew she loved doing it for me and having me do a similar thing for her.

She opened her eyes and grinned, her right hand reaching out to cup me. I looked down, and she pulled the front of her suddenly loose top outwards, exposing a beautiful slope of firm breast, and the rapidly hardening bud of flesh atop it.

"Want me to do you here? Quickly, before the others arrive?" she offered, her voice a low purr. "You can owe me 'til later?"

I started to nod, my right hand lifting of its own accord and slipping into the front of her top, cupping her in return, when a voice whispered aloud, and we both froze.

"How interesting…is it a mating ritual?" Malthus said, clearly curious. I sighed, my rapidly rising sex drive abruptly derailed. Oracle quickly covered herself as she glared around furiously.

"Seriously, read my mind," I prompted her, the tone and excitement of a minute ago totally ruined.

Citadel

Ten seconds later, and Oracle, being the avid seeker of knowledge that she was, was happily chatting away with the spirit, finding kinship on several levels while I sat morosely on a mossy boulder, enjoying the view and thinking about what might have been.

I'd been watching the threads that bound the others to me. I saw the two that broke away from the others, circling around and closing on me from either side.

I waited until they were both close before standing up and pointing out to each of them, making finger guns.

"Bane, Tang!" I grinned when they both became visible, clearly annoyed that I'd spotted them. "You're losing your touch, boys!" I called gleefully, lying through my teeth.

Even when I'd been able to sense exactly where they were, I'd barely been able to find them, and they'd moved through heavy underbrush to reach me. Any sounds they'd made had been masked by the crashing of trees as a golem appeared in the distance, an enormous sword slashing sideways and clearing a tangle of brush in one clean strike.

"Either you got much better, we got worse, or you learned a new trick," Bane said suspiciously as he became visible and closed in towards me.

"I'm betting a new trick. He's not that good, and we clearly are," Tang finished.

"All I'm saying, boys, is that I can find you anywhere now." I laughed, shrugging.

"See, new trick," Tang confirmed, crossing his arms. "Not earned, so it doesn't count."

"Fuck you both." I laughed, shaking my head.

"So, you have fun on your own?" Tang asked.

"No, and I shouldn't have done that," I said with a sigh of regret. "Bane, I'm sorry for being a dick and ordering you to stay up here. I'll explain everything when everyone's here, okay? It's not so fun a story that I want to go over it again and again. What happened up here while I was fighting for my life?"

"Oh, you know, the usual. We fought as a team and killed things." Tang settled down with his back against a tree and grinned at my uncomfortable expression. "And if you think Oracle gave you a hard time, just wait 'til Lydia gets ahold of you," he finished, grinning.

My mind froze. "Uh...what?"

"Oracle, she was furious. Did she not give you a hard time?" Tang queried. I swallowed as things slipped back into place and made sense again.

"Yeah! Whoo, yeah, she gave me a hard time," I said enthusiastically, grinning.

"Yeah, clearly," Yen called, coming into view.

"What?" I called innocently over to her where she led the others through the bushes, frowning.

"Elven ears, remember?" Tang whispered.

"Fuck's sake," I growled. "Fine, I'll tell all...most...of the story when you all get closer." I made a face, looking at Tang again. "What happened with the Vern royal pair and the Drach queen?"

He snorted, shaking his head. "Well, the golem dug through into that chamber, we rescued the prisoners, then Oracle ordered the golem to jump off the top level of the cavern and land on the Vern. Easiest battle ever."

"Really?" I asked, surprised.

281

"Oh yeah, multi-ton golem jumping from like a hundred meters up, landing on a small fleshy creature with both feet first? It popped like a cockroach. Only one of the Vern's bodies was lootable; the other…well, it was a mess. It burst, basically." He grimaced, as if to rid his mouth of a bad taste.

"After that, it was just cleanup. Took about twenty minutes; you should have waited," Bane said slowly.

"Yer damn right he should have!" Lydia stomped over and glared furiously before grabbing me and pulling me into a hug. "Yer goddamn idiot!" she snarled into my ear. "Oracle told us ye were drownin'!"

"I did," I whispered, hugging her back. "Twice."

After that, the others all crowded in, aside from Giint, who still glared at me suspiciously and Ronin, who was too new to be so handsy with me, especially while hearing Lydia grumbling about the "Lord o' fuckin' Stupidity," as she kept calling me.

"Okay, people, I'll give more details later if I need to, but basically one of those little Vern shits, the one that I followed down that hole? Well, that bastard killed me a few months before I came here. I saw him, remembered it…it was a sodding painful death as well, by the way, and I kinda went a bit nuts," I admitted, scratching the back of my neck.

"Did he just say he *died?*" I heard Ronin whisper to Tang, who shrugged.

"He's weird; just go with it," Tang advised laconically.

"Anyway, I expected to find a summoning hall down there, and little else, not the miles of tunnels and the damn thousands of assholes. I got spotted by the royal pair and their mount, found the prisoners, and tried to hold the line.

"Then I felt the magic building, and once it got into the 'fuck this is big' levels, I figured I couldn't let them finish the spell, mainly because I had no fucking idea what it was going to do. I flew down, tried to ram my weapon through the pair of them, and got smacked down by the Drach, thanks to their magic freezing me in place. When I hit the water, I found out it's a LOT deeper than it looks. Cue whirlpools, underwater tunnels, and drowning, et cetera." I sighed heavily, then gestured back behind me with a thumb at the freshly risen building containing the stairwell.

"Once I got drowned a few times, I got caught in a Kobold net. They dragged me out, and I found they had a city down there."

"A city?" Ronin gasped in shock. "Kobolds are a nightmare. An entire city…oh God…"

"Well, they're all dead now. There were only a few hundred, I think, according to the notifications." I glared briefly at him for interrupting me. "Anyway, I freed all the spirits they'd enslaved, and they went on a murder spree; killed everything in the city…oh shit, wait a minute…" I paused, turning back to the building.

"Malthus, were there any prisoners held by the Kobolds?" I asked.

"Almost a hundred prisoners of various races were held by the Kobolds."

"And where are they now?" I asked, wincing.

"They were killed by the little ones," Malthus informed me blithely.

"Ah, crap," I whispered, closing my eyes and shaking my head. "I just killed a hundred innocents." I rubbed at the bridge of my nose as my stomach dropped.

"Incorrect. Most of those prisoners were captured Goblins from the settlement to the north. Three were dark Elves, and one was a human of similar ancestry to yourself."

"Like me?" I asked, opening my eyes wide. "How long was he down there?"

"Seventy years. He was responsible for the net system you mentioned, as well as several other facilities around the city."

"And I just got him killed."

"Yes, the spirits you released killed him and the others. However, judging from their behavior in their cells, none were what I believe you would class as innocent. Each of them, at one time or another, killed others, performed violent acts, and consumed the flesh of the dead."

"Cannibals!" Ronin squeaked out, rubbing his hands together. "This just keeps getting better!"

"Better?!" Lydia snapped at him, and Ronin nodded emphatically.

"The Lord of Dravith just killed an entire city of Kobolds and their cannibal slaves. Do none of you see what this is? It's a tale for the ages! This is AMAZING!" he cried, and Lydia scowled at him, spitting on the ground in disgust and turning away.

"So, they were all dark Elves, Goblins, and a human that came from my world?" I confirmed. "And they were all assholes?"

"I can only judge on their actions while inside my sphere of influence. While detained inside this city, however, they were…unpleasant."

"Oh, well, fuck those guys, then," I said, relaxing.

"Anyway, I set the spirits free, they killed everything in the city, and got the attention of Malthus, who is, basically, a sentient section of the city; a spirit, is that right?" I asked, and Malthus responded calmly.

"Incorrect, but acceptable. I suspect your current lack of appropriate phrasing is due to your species' age and experience. Until you have achieved transcendence, this failing is common. I will accept 'spirit' for now."

"Wait…what?" Ronin whispered in awe. "You can…"

"Thanks, Malthus," I responded, having put up with nearly five hours of the spirit's confusing chat, oblique hints, and refusal to make any goddamn sense on topics when pressed. I suspected he was actually a lot dumber than he let on and was putting on a front.

But, as his role was basically being an AI assistant to an underground city, one that we could use as an ally in times of desperation, I didn't give two shits. "So, Malthus has agreed to cede majority control of the city to me in exchange for certain things. He has also sealed up every entrance to the city bar this one, so we now have somewhere to retreat to if we need it."

"And access to the manawell," Malthus reminded me.

"Yes, access to the manawell," I agreed, glancing at Oracle, who still looked stunned, but shook her head once, opening her eyes in warning. I frowned then moved on, dropping that particular subject.

"Anyway, what happened after I left you guys in the village?" I asked.

Arrin snorted, shaking his head. "Yeah, subtle topic change there."

"Shut it," snapped Grizz, and I gaped at him in surprise. The normally happy-go-lucky legionnaire was glaring at Arrin. "He's the boss; if he doesn't want to discuss something, you accept that and move on. You don't draw more attention to it." He fixed Arrin with a warning stare before forcing a smile and picking up the thread of the story.

"Well, we hunted down the remaining Drach and secured the village, then Oracle came for us. We were nearly halfway when you ordered us to fall back, then we heard you were in trouble. Oracle sensed the ship nearing, so she directed us to the surface and took off. We made it out with a few minutes to spare, before they dropped him." he said, nodding towards the golem that was carving a section of trees down.

"It's making a clearing big enough to land the ship," Oracle explained.

"We followed it down, then boom. The fight was over in minutes, most of it spent mopping up. I know the golems weren't really used for monster hunting as much as war, as they're slow, plodding things, but damn, boss, you're not going to replace us all with them, are you? I don't know what I'd be, if not a legionnaire."

"Nope," I said, shaking my head. "Legionnaires will always be needed. The golems are, like you say, slow, and they need constant guidance. Without that, well, they're pretty useless. I could order them to go wipe out the Dark Legion, I guess." I scratched my beard contemplatively. "But the outcome of that, well, let's think about it logically. A girl I once dated was a programmer, and she always said that the best thing about computers was also the worst thing: they do exactly what you tell them."

I looked around and sighed at the blank expressions. Damn, I missed having Tommy around to understand my references.

"If I set them loose and told them to kill all the Dark Legion, we don't actually know what they'd do. They might decide to cut their way through an orphanage to get to the Dark Dicks, killing hundreds of kids, or they might miss the Dark Legion entirely, wander around and fall off a cliff. They might all pile into the ocean and start off walking in the direction of the largest concentration of them on another continent, or they might just totally ignore us because they can't see any Dark Legionnaires at the time of the orders being given. Then a few months later, one of you walks past a Golem all covered in dried black blood. Suddenly you're a "Dark Legionnaire" and they all converge, smashing you into paste." I sighed, then shook my head.

"That means that we use the golems where they can be specifically directed, mainly in construction and where the Wisps can control them, or a higher-level golem can be given the orders and kept under tight watch. As far as possible, until we get a golem to lead them, at least a class five, I don't want the legionnaires and war golems involved in any fighting together. We will have the golems to protect the Tower, as they can be controlled directly by Heph. Outside of that, it's down to you guys."

"Oh, thank the Gods," Yen said, grinning. "Can you make a point of telling the rest of the legionnaires please, boss? I get pestered constantly about this, and I didn't know what to tell them."

"Fine, remind me later," I muttered, squinting up and trying to make out the ship above us as it slowly lowered itself down, slipping between the trees to land with a low thump. I let out a sigh of relief.

"Malthus, seal the entrance for now, please, but make sure to listen out here, and I'll make sure you have some company soon," I promised, heading away from the small pagoda that had torn its way up through the sod of the forest to allow me to exit from the subterranean city.

"Acceptable." came his voice, and the entrance slowly closed, a huge slab of stone acting as a door and clicking into place to seal the passage down. The ground shivered, and the building slowly lowered itself from sight again, like a reverse mushroom.

"Now there's something you don't see every day," Ronin said in a stage whisper to Giint, who just grunted. Tang laughed and clapped him on the shoulder, shaking his head while watching in fascination as the peaked roof slowly corkscrewed from sight.

"Trust me, stick with us, and this kind of shit becomes normal," Tang told Ronin. I shrugged in agreement as I walked up the gangplank.

Once aboard, I paused, sighing as I realized the real reason I was feeling low, now that the day was done. It was guilt.

I walked across the deck, taking a deep breath and gazing up at the towering figure of Bob. I'd had to leave him behind for most of the day, as he'd either been too big, or too damaged to make real use of, or too loud and unsubtle.

"I'm sorry buddy," I whispered, looking him over. "I kinda neglected you today, didn't I? And I have for weeks." I reached up and patted him on the shoulder.

"Are you ready?" I asked him, getting a surprising nod in return, and I grinned, glad that he could understand me so well. "Right, then; let's get you fixed up a bit. I don't have many bones available here, but…hmmm…Okay, how about a redesign?" I suggested. Bob simply stood there, waiting, as I grinned, the new plan flowing together in my mind.

While I considered, I noticed Captain Kinnet approaching, and I waved her in.

"Back to the Tower, my lord?" she asked, head twitching as she looked at me from different angles, clearly wondering at all the scratches and dents in the new armor I'd been wearing only that damn morning.

"I wish, but no, Kinnet. You know where the legionnaires are setting up to intercept the Dark Legion?" I asked, and she nodded once, sharply. "Good. Take us there, and keep low so the Dark Wankers won't know we're coming." I got another sharp nod from her before she beat her wings and returned to the upper deck. I turned back to Bob and looked him over again, settling the new idea in my mind as I worked.

"Yeah, this is going to help a lot, I think," I muttered, summoning the magic to my hands as Oracle moved up to stand next to me. The rest of the squad gathered around, making themselves comfortable and watching.

I let the power build for several seconds, pulling the image I wanted into my mind before I started to work. I used Bonemeld first, repairing the bones, as many of them were cracked, chipped, or fractured. That, unfortunately, reduced the bone mass I had to work with, as I needed more material than I had in my bag, but that was okay.

I kept the Naga skull, as that was intimidating, if you didn't know him, and the Tower's citizens were used to it, seeing the outer form more than I did.

I looked over the current design, pulling sections apart and gathering the bones to one side, keeping only the skull, a spine, and legs.

The legs were massive, encased in solid, thick plate bone armor, and I stripped them, making them smaller, narrower, but still strong. As I worked, I let my instincts loose, sensing Oracle guiding the magic into the bones as I went.

I gave him a basic humanoid structure, but rather than all long, solid bones, I made them shorter, able to flex in ways we couldn't, adding in extra joints to the legs and arms.

The torso was slim but solid, interlocking waves of bone wrapping around a hollow core to reduce his weight. But again, I compressed the bones as far as I could, forcing them into a kind of solidity the natural world couldn't come close to. As I worked, the bones drank in the magic, responding both to my intended shape and altering slightly to match my will.

I created a new form of bone armor across his legs, torso, and arms, closer in but physically attached everywhere I could to the main structure. I fixed the seams where they met, smoothed points that might grind, and increased flexibility and speed over strength and solidity.

I scrapped the long arms from the SporeMother that had served Bob so well until now, arching up and over his back to use as stabbing spears. Instead, I shortened and compressed them, giving them wicked edges and grips, resulting in dual shortswords and a pair of daggers.

I narrowed his skull, keeping the overall shape of the Naga, but altering the wide cheeks and narrowing his face more, making his features appear closer to a dragon than a snake.

I continued shifting and changing, twisting sections and fixing others, making his upper body broad and his waist slim. I narrowed his feet, but added bony pads that mixed the best of stability with a lower chance of being heard.

I worked endlessly, until I felt the warning of an incoming mana-migraine building. I took a break, meditating then starting up again, adding, removing, and enhancing. I had Bane and Tang weigh in with suggestions, and Yen, surprisingly, but by the time we slowed for the final approach into the Legion camp, he was done.

As we sank into the trees, landing at the small camp by the river that the Legion had set up nearly a mile from the planned ambush site, I watched Bob move.

He stalked back and forth, his movements more sinuous, more graceful than ever before, and I couldn't help but grin. He'd become an assassin. Sure, he didn't have the skillset yet, but that would come.

He'd been born in the tower, made of fused bone and my will alone, and he'd dedicated himself to protecting me and mine.

Well, now, he'd have that chance. I saw Bane moving with him, speaking quietly and leading him as they started to run, circling the ship.

Bob would make a hell of an assassin and a bodyguard, and my people would make him into the best version he could be.

I turned away as the pair raced, jumping and running along the railing of the ship, at least until Bob missed and fell off. A few legionnaires present in the camp stepped forward to see what we were doing there.

It was time to get serious.

CHAPTER TWENTY-SEVEN

"You sure you want to be here, boss?" Denny whispered for perhaps the tenth time. I snorted, digging into the ground with the others.

"Denny, seriously, dude, I fight the same as everyone else. Why would I be too good to get dirty by making traps?" I asked.

He shrugged, barking an order at someone on the far side of the gully, who was apparently digging in the wrong section before turning back to me.

"I know you're not too good for this shit, boss, but seriously, isn't there something else you should be doing?"

I nodded. "Yeah, there's about a million things, especially as the fleet will be arriving at the Tower any minute, but this is the best use of my time right now."

"Okay..." Denny accepted uncertainly, shrugging.

"Look," I grunted, lifting a chunk of wood with the others and slotting it into place, holding it as steady as I could while Denny slipped a dead mana crystal into it and muttered a few words of prayer before looking up to the sun as it peeked through the foliage overhead.

He reached up one hand, placing the other atop the crystal and chanting, seconds becoming minutes before he stopped. By the time he did, a brightly glowing crystal sat embedded in the wood where the dead one had laid before.

"Okay...move it!" he gasped, gesturing tiredly, and we packed the earth in around the tree, creating the illusion of an old deadfall.

"What...were you...saying?" he asked, half bent over and bracing his arms on his knees as he panted.

"What I'm saying, Denny, is that in order to make things right, to get things put together, and to make sure that everyone is safe, we need this fucking column stopped. I could sit in the Tower and wait, or I could come help. I don't think my shitty skills in traps are going to do much, but a day of helping here might just make the difference. Are you okay?" I asked him curiously.

"I...will be..." he huffed, straightening up and pressing his hands into the small of his back and groaning as I heard audible clicks and pops, even encased as he was in armor.

"What the hell happened to you?" I asked.

"Remember the...Heliomage memories?" he asked with a grin, and I nodded. "Well...the Goddess Jenae...accepted me." He sucked in a deep breath and shook himself out, then sounded much stronger as he went on.

"Sorry, Lord Jax, it just takes...a lot out of me, that's all. Okay, so a Heliomage is a warrior-priest-mage class, meant to both guide the faithful of Jenae, and to protect the temples. The Goddess blessed me with the ability to imbue the sun's rays into certain objects, then have it release when I want. Sounds simple enough, but when I used the memory crystal and it linked up with the books I've read, well, it was clear." He gestured to the valley we stood at the far end of.

I followed his gesture, seeing the other legionnaires and a dozen helpers from the Tower working to conceal things, replacing cut brush and sweeping dirt over tracks.

"When even a tiny piece of the power of the sun is released all at once, well, it has explosive consequences." he revealed, winking at me, and I took another look around the shallow valley.

"You made the entire valley into a kill-box, didn't you?" I asked, impressed, and he nodded firmly. "You done other valleys out there as well, or just this one?" I was well aware that even with the best and most careful projections we could make, we might be hundreds of feet off when the Dark Legion came through.

"Nope, just this one," he said, scratching one cheek. "We looked at it, and found this was the perfect spot. We could have spread ourselves out, maybe gotten a few more of them if we got lucky, but we figured once they're aware of the possibility, they might take precautions, so better to take them by surprise once and for all."

"Right." I nodded, waiting.

"So, we decided to mix and match the plans you recommended. You gave us three objectives out here: kill the Trailmasters, kill as many of the Dark Legion as possible, and slow the survivors down, making it a lot harder for more to come in the future."

Denny sighed as he pointed to the right, where a thick collection of trees blocked off the view.

"That way, it's all narrow paths and heavy cover, great for ambushes, but their Trailmasters will just blow it up from a distance," he said, then pointed to the left. "That way, it's more open, harder to ambush, and as soon as the attack happens, it will be damn hard to get clear, as the sightlines are longer."

I nodded, grasping what he meant easily enough.

"This area here, this is the best for an ambush, but it's also obvious, if you know what to look for, not to mention if the Trailmasters let loose with a spell or two, they might slaughter us all accidentally if they set off one of my little surprises early."

"Right," I said, watching as the others moved on, getting the next tree into place.

"So, I decided that the best way to deal the absolute maximum amount of damage was to make sure our guests are in the middle when it goes off." He gestured to where two legionnaires were assembling something made of metal in the middle of the trail below.

I looked at it, observing rough and quickly made sections of metal joined together over mesh…

"Is that a cage?" I asked, raising one eyebrow.

"Maybe it used to be. Now it's a heavily reinforced safe area."

"Doesn't look that safe to me," I stated dubiously.

"It's as safe as we can make it for now," he said. "Besides, it's a volunteer mission; what could go wrong?"

"Explain," I ordered grimly.

"We've worked out that they'll set up camp about an hour's run to the south of here. We'll hit the Dark Wankers—I love that name, by the way—" He grinned before going on "So, we'll hit them with a barrage of heavy spells, crossbows, and arrows when they're resting and tired after the long day, focusing on taking out the Trailmasters wherever we can. Once they've been hit, we form a phalanx and pound them, doing as much damage as possible, as quick as possible, before we turn and run, pretending to be broken by a counterattack."

"There are three hundred of them, and they're at least as heavily outfitted as we are, plus they have the benefit of near-unlimited funding and opportunities for progression," I interrupted. "What makes you think we'll survive the counterattack? There's thirty of us."

"Well, first off, there's only twenty on the attack," Denny said, eyeing me. "The assistants from the Tower aren't in on it…"

"No, but me and my team are," I said.

Denny shook his head "That's not a good idea, Lord…"

"Then tell me the rest of the plan, and we might adjust it."

"Right." He sighed in resignation. "Well, we hit them hard, taking out their mages as fast as we can, then we sprint into the woods like our arses are on fire." He picked up a stick and swept a section of the ground clear, starting to draw, showing the probable location of their camp and this valley, marking an indirect path to it.

"While the rabbits—that's the group the wankers will be chasing—run them this way and that, the rest of the squad slip away, setting up in hides we're making along this route. These are our most stealthy people. If a Trailmaster survives and tries to follow, they hide until they get a chance, then they take the mage out. It's the most dangerous job, as once they strike, they will be exposed. Therefore, it will those we can most afford to lose."

"Go on," I ordered, arms crossed as I listened.

"The rabbits lead them into the kill-zone. Once inside, they slip away, and I'll be in the middle of the trail," he said, tapping an 'x' he'd drawn. "I need to be close to the crystals to control them all at once. I'll jump into my reinforced safe box, close the door, and set off the trap. Once it's over, we mop up, depending on how many of us survive and how many of them there are. Or we run like buggery and get back to the Tower with our cocks in hand."

"You paint a pretty picture," I said, forcing a smile.

"Well, it's the realities of war, sir. They started this, they wanted to face the Empire, and now they need to be taught the error of their ways."

"And our losses?"

"Depends very much on the way things go, sir," he responded. "If they have a full watch set up that's paying attention? Could be high. Hell, it could be as many as ninety percent. There are two rabbits reserved for leading them if the main team is wiped out, and I'll unfortunately need to be waiting here."

"Best case?" I asked.

"Could be that we get lucky, they have no sentries, they panic, and we all live. Realistically, though, unless there's a lot of fucking idiots that chase us blindly, I'd expect around half the legionnaires to die," he said grimly.

"Half." I stated coldly. "You expect half of all these people to die and you're okay with that?"

"Yes, Lord Jax, I am," Denny snapped. "I am okay with it because sometimes there's no better way, and to lose ten or even twenty of the Legion here, to lose our assistants as well, if need be, to take out ten times our number of the Empire's enemies, is well worth that cost. Hell, I'd pay that a hundred times over if I needed to. You forget, *Scion of the Empire*, that this isn't about *us!* It's not even entirely about *you*." His eyes flashed with righteous indignation.

"It's about the EMPIRE, about making sure that the sun rises on it tomorrow and sets on the farmer that's still alive, because we made sure those fuckers out there don't get to him. That's what this is all about!

"I don't want to risk losing my men! I want to see them all die of old age, setting around arguing over whose wife makes the best bread and had the best tits, but it won't happen, not unless we *make* it happen. The only way to do that is to take risks, to fight the fight, and to make damn well sure those fuckers run screaming to their momma every time they even think of facing the fucking Legion, *sir*!"

I held my tongue, considering him for a long minute before nodding in respect.

"Okay, I can see that," I agreed, watching the fire die from his eyes as he caught his breath after dressing me down. "The thing is, though, if you had more men, truthfully, would that help?" I asked.

He paused, eyeing me cautiously, before sighing and nodding.

"It would, but the risk…"

"The risk would be lessened by our joining you. We don't know the route, but you can have the rabbits do most of the leading. We'd just be there to aid in the assault then in leading the Dark Legionnaires, that's all. I have Bane, Tang, and Yen in my team, all skilled scouts and assassins. I have Bob, who's admittedly new to it, but he's also the only one of us who'll take having his legs blown off as a mere annoyance," I pointed out.

"Seriously, sir, if I survive and you don't, Prefect Romanus would murder me," Denny said quietly.

"Yeah, there is that; not to mention that Restun would be annoyed because he didn't get to murder me through excessive training, but this is the way it has to be, Denny. How long do we have?" I asked.

"We're planning on hitting them tonight, about fourteen hours from now."

"And how are we fixed for potions?" I asked, before quickly adding, "And poisons…I have to think they'd help…"

"They would." He paused, taking mental stock. "All the legionnaires have two health and two stamina, with the few casters we have carrying a mana potion each. We have no poisons."

"Then that sounds like a plan for me and my team; we'll scour the area for any ingredients, and I'll use what I have and what they bring me to make up whatever I can for you. Tonight, we do this, and if need be, we fall back and hit them again and again. Hell, a few small changes to the plan, like adding poisons to the mix, and deliberately taking as many of their leaders out…Hmm. Give me a minute…" I said, thinking fast.

I started sketching designs on the ground, then pulled up my map and zoomed in before going back to the drawing.

"What if we made a few little changes…" I pointed out choke points, or places where they could be created with a little work.

Citadel

"They're going to kill me. Prefect Romanus and Restun will kill me." Denny groaned as he shook his head twenty minutes later.

"Only if you live long enough," I clapped him on the shoulder, getting a weak smile in return. "I'll leave you to it, and I'll get the potions and poisons going. Unless you can think of a better plan?" I asked.

"Not really; all plans change when there are new options, I guess…"

I grinned encouragingly at him, turning and making my way back towards the camp and gathering up the rest of my people as I went.

"Okay people," I finished loudly as we walked, having filled them in on the plan while making sure they could all hear me. "What that means is that we need every damn potion ingredient we can get. Ronin!" I snapped, and he straightened.

"I need you to do your best with a perception-enhancing buff. Everyone else, these are the plants I know of that we should be able to find in the forest, but remember, I'm new to this," I described them, occasionally getting a recommendation or correction from the others, depending on the plants they'd seen in the forest so far.

For the next hour, I worked with the team, and we scoured the local area, working the borders of the gentle river, under fallen trees, and picking flowers, searching for anything and everything that could be useful.

At the end of the hour, as agreed, we all met up at the camp, and with Yen and Giint, who was surprisingly good at finding "smelly plants" we sorted through everything we'd found.

More than half was useless, simply pretty, damaged in the picking, or worthless, but what we found was still plenty.

I separated them into the two piles, the discard lot and those to concentrate on finding more of before giving the others their orders and moving on.

I also pretended not to notice Grizz sneaking a handful of the flowers from the discard pile aside and adding in some green grasses and long white stems. He listened while I spoke, but surreptitiously worked, slipping it all into his bag of holding and eyeing Yen with a speculative air.

I shook my head in despair at his antics, fairly sure he was either going to get stabbed or married, the way he was going, and it was even odds which, at this point.

Once the others had their orders, I sent them on their way and sat down at the table that had been provided, the ship having long since returned to the Tower, instructed to return an hour before sunset to be ready in case we needed to make a fast exit.

I looked over the piles of ingredients, including a dozen that dripped and oozed, thanks to Giint's habit of harvesting anything he killed for parts. Surprisingly, a significant portion of the animal and monster parts he'd accrued were actually ingredients, so I had to think he was either gifted as a gatherer, knew more than he was letting on, or was utterly fucking batshit and basically had the entire carcasses in his bags, pulling out only what he'd already identified as likely to be useful.

I suspected all three.

I started with a plant that looked like a very distressed flower; it was basically a long stem, thick rubbery leaves leading off it, with a…bulb…at the tip of the stalk, minus the flowery petals.

I looked at it closely and couldn't see anywhere they'd been attached and fallen free, so I had to assume that a plant that looked just like a pair of testicles hanging on the end of a stick had ended up evolutionarily attractive to something.

Against all sense, when I used my new Organic Examination spell, cycling mana through the plant, I was left with a definite urge to sniff the balls and I did without thinking about it consciously, pulling back quickly when I realized what I'd done.

"Holy shit, they smell like..." I had sudden memories of being a teenager and adverts assuring me that using a particular deodorant would make me irresistible to women. It hadn't. In fact, not smelling like that had worked far, far better for me, but the scent that emanated from the...nutsack...basically made me feel sorry for an entire generation of women back home.

I shook my head and went back to cycling mana through the plant, getting several conflicting impressions, before using the Greater Identify skill as a last resort, then working out what each feeling of the mana was attuned to.

Perrin's Jewels		Further Description Yes/No		
Details:		These memorable seed containers are both rare and extremely potent. Beware of cross pollination. **Uses Discovered:** 1) Fecundity 2) Fortify Stamina 3) Hallucinogen 4) ?		
Rarity:	**Magical:**	**Durability:**		**Charge:**
Rare	No	88/100		N/A

I couldn't help but grin at the plant, as I recognized the pattern for two of the effects eventually. There seemed to be five separate patterns that made up the plant, but I settled for the two I could recognize, hallucinogen and fortify stamina, realizing that both would be particularly useful.

I moved onto the next plant, stripping the dried outer leaves and examining what was hidden inside, nearly being sick as a thick green fluid started to leak out. It made my head spin and my throat tighten as I smelled the residue on my fingers, and I worked quickly to examine it before summoning clean water and blasting it off my hands.

This stuff was awful, yet as I grimaced, realizing what it'd done, despite me not feeling a thing, I knew I needed more of it.

Trinair's Bane		Further Description Yes/No		
Details:		This plant produces the much-maligned Trinair's Bane, a numbing agent that both poisons and dissolves its victims. **Uses Discovered:** 1) Acid 2) Hypoesthesia 3) Confusion 4) ?		
Rarity:	**Magical:**	**Durability:**		**Charge:**
Rare	No	63/100		N/A

Whatever, or whoever, Trinair was, this being their bane was understandable. It had made me feel sick, but it wasn't until I washed it off my hands that I found the entire top level of my skin had been eaten away in seconds. I hadn't felt a thing.

I checked, and a series of status debuffs had indeed appeared. I healed myself thoroughly before picking up a second stalk of the plant and examining it without peeling the outer leaves off.

I kept at it until I was sure I'd recognize the effects, then moved on, spending the next three hours on familiarizing myself with ingredients.

By the time I'd finished with the pile of plants I'd set out, the others had come back several times, piling on more and more ingredients. Most were ones we'd found already, some were utter shit, and some were well known to me already. I still made sure to check before popping a handful of the forest strawberries into my mouth.

They had little use as ingredients, but were damn tasty, so I was happy with that. I asked that the others find certain plants and remove them intact, not storing them in the usual pouches, but in the herbalist's pouch I lent to Yen for the remainder of the day. Better not to have the plants killed by being in the weird other dimension of the standard bags, after all, not when I could grow them later.

Once all that was done, I set to making some new potions.

I started with the healing, figuring that they were always needed. If I was going to give out poisons, I damn well needed to give health potions out as well, just in case.

I'd found eleven ingredients with what I thought involved sections of the healing pattern, and I put them all together on the table before me with my alchemy set ready as I started to examine them. The first few, I felt I knew well enough, and I had over a dozen of each, so I set to work.

In the past, I'd used ginseng regularly, simply chopping it up and boiling it, but this time, I kept my Organic Examination spell going, and I watched the effect that had on the plant. I was annoyed to find it weakened the healing part of the pattern, sections that made up that part of the weave within the plant fraying and dissolving, holes appearing in it. But I also noted the way that the fortify stamina section of the pattern seemed to strengthen, and I made a mental note of that before going back to the beginning.

I boiled the root, chopped it, used it raw, cut it lengthways and burned it to a blackened mess, before I found that boiling the potion with a segment of ginseng in it, then crushing the ginseng and discarding the root, keeping only the sticky liquid that dripped free, strengthened that portion of the pattern.

I was ecstatic as I realized I'd managed to figure out the best use for it, when I noticed it was getting dark.

"Wait…how long did that take me…?" I muttered, and Bane answered from my left, laconically.

"About six hours."

"Holy shit!" I cursed, dismayed.

"Yeah," he said slowly, walking over and inspecting the mess I'd made of the table. "Have you actually made a potion yet?" I shook my head, annoyed with myself. "Might want to fix that?" I gave him the finger, took a few minutes for the necessities of life, and returned.

This time, I picked out a few dozen ingredients that I knew had strong healing bases and started work again, determined. I used the majority of them the traditional way, using only the ginseng and some berries differently, mainly because I found the berries were more potent by squashing and straining them, discarding the seeds, and that was the first thing I tried.

Less than an hour after, I found myself staring bleary-eyed at a batch of potions that sat before me, gleaming redly in the light of the magelights set up around the camp, and I pulled up my notifications.

Congratulations!

For staying true to your choices and for walking the Path of the Creationist, you have gained a point of Intelligence!

*

Congratulations, Apprentice!

You have taken further steps to a wider understanding of the art of the Alchemist! Continue to experiment, to push back the boundaries of ignorance in your search for the truth!

The Path to Healing Pattern Mastery has begun! 5/100

Healing Potion		Further Description *Yes*/*No*	
Details:		This healing potion is more concentrated and powerful than the norm, yet was made by an apprentice, limiting the possible effects. Regain 150 health on imbibing, with an additional 5 points returned per second for ten seconds.	
Rarity:	**Magical:**	**Durability:**	**Potency:**
Rare	No	100/100	4/10

I read it over and over again, annoyed that the potency wasn't fantastic, but to regain a hundred and fifty health on one go was seriously good. I sat contemplating that for several seconds, realizing that the massive jump in strength of the potions might be a better use of my time than anything else, or better yet, teaching a few people to use my newly discovered spell and having them working away.

That would bring a lot of issues, not least the fact that the scientific method had yet to be discovered here, and I had only the faintest clue what I was doing myself. But, if I were to spend some time teaching someone these skills, then have them create a book including all those details, a skillbook, that would be amazing.

I lost myself for a few more minutes, fantasizing about the kind of potions that could be made, before a clear cough made me straighten up, and I looked over at Tang, who sat on a log nearby.

"Bane gave up and went for a nap half an hour ago," he said quietly. "He told me to make sure to wake you up if you zoned out, and as you clearly have no concept of time passing…"

"So you decided to interrupt me while I was thinking…" I replied.

"You could have made a handful of potions while I've been here," he pointed out. "I know you've found something new. I heard you muttering about it, and believe me, that's great. You found a way to make stronger potions. Fantastic. I'll have some, thanks very much, but you know what, boss?"

I grunted at him, gesturing for him to go on.

"You know what'd be more useful? More useful than a handful of fantastic poisons?" he asked again, staring pointedly at me, and I sighed, nodding.

"A lot more that are weaker," I responded flatly.

"Yeah, boss." He nodded, giving me an encouraging grin. "Look, stronger poisons would be awesome. I'd love that, I really would, but there's ten of us in this team alone, and you're running out of time. Making a handful of poisons that each kill one person, or a few dozen that help us to kill multiple people?"

"Yeah, alright, you dick," I replied, sitting upright and rubbing my eyes. "I get the hint."

"Good." He grinned. "Because if you burn yourself out working then can't fight later, that's going to suck for the rest of us. We've got six hours before we need to start this little party off. It'll take an hour to get there, and you need to stop staring into space and make some potions. You got, what, three hours' sleep before we started helping Denny?" he asked.

"I'll sleep when I'm dead, mate."

"Well, keep this up, and it'll come around a lot faster than you think," he warned me, moving over to stand next to my table. "Look, I know shit-all about potions, not interested either, but tell me what to do to help you prep them, and I'll do it."

His offer made me smile. "Okay, mate," I said, pointing to a collection of black and grey berries. "Take those and peel them. Don't break the flesh if you can help it, just peel the outer skin off, then…"

CHAPTER TWENTY-EIGHT

"**A**re you ready?" Centurion Musset asked quietly, staring hard at me in the darkness. We were less than a half mile from the enemy camp now and had gathered together, preparing before we started the party. The majority of the stealth-based fighters were already in place, and I felt the loss of Bane, Tang, and Yen fiercely, despite Bob's comforting presence in my mind and by my side.

"Yes, Centurion," I whispered. He frowned before turning away and starting forward.

I stifled a retort and followed along like a good boy, well aware that, in terms of skill and experience, I was one of the very few fighters who hadn't done this kind of thing before. My entire squad was the weakest link in the plan tonight.

Musset clearly didn't want me here, though he was pleased with having Bane, Tang, Grizz, and Yen. He'd made no bones about letting me know that I was putting everyone else at risk with my "idiotic demands to play a part." I'd asked him if he had a greater chance to succeed if I was there and to tell me straight if having me and my squad, including the bard's buffs and the magic we brought to the fight, weren't needed.

He'd just grunted and stormed off.

Now we were sneaking through the woods toward the camp of the Dark Legionnaires. For the first time, I was actually intentionally putting myself at odds with the Dark God of Death, Nimon, and I couldn't decide if I was excited, or really, really shouldn't have eaten that wrap with all the chilies that Grizz had offered me.

I crept closer, the firelight of the camp's torches ahead, while the others moved slowly around me, and for just a second, I almost felt like I had Tommy there with me too.

We reached the marker Musset had made, a line he dragged his foot across to leave stark and clear, and we stopped as he pointed at me and at the line.

I was to wait here with my team.

Musset would lead his legionnaires in the attack, carefully coordinated with the stealth types, and our role was to stand behind this line and throw everything we could at one tent in the middle of the camp, while the "real legionnaires" showed me how it was done.

I watched as they got ready, waiting until the guard changed and for a signal from Musset. In the meantime, I worried over the sheer number of damn guards the Dark Wankers had at the ready, standing at attention every ten paces, ringing the entire camp.

Personally, I'd hoped that they'd be lazy fuckers, maybe only a couple of sentries on watch, not the nigh-on sixty who stood there, fully armored and ready, and I looked at Musset in question.

He stepped in close and whispered in my ear, seemingly so annoyed that I was daring to be here that he was entirely ignoring that the orders had, in fact, come from me.

"We've orders to take this fucking camp down, and we're going to do it. Now, either you get ready, or you start running home to your mother and hope to fuck that the real legionnaires hold the line long enough for you to get away. What's it going to be?"

"I'm going to kill more of them than you do," I whispered back, and he sneered before moving away.

On the count of eleven, he raised his hand once and gave the first signal. Everyone in the two lines with him took a knee, with their crossbows and bows loaded and aimed.

Five more seconds passed, and he signaled the second phase, and those of us with magic started to cast, an assistant each from the camp shielding us with an oil-impregnated canvas to muffle the light as we worked. A faint sound lifted from the camp as stray glimmers escaped, making it clear that they suspected something was out here.

I concentrated on the spell, building it as fast and well as I could, my lips moving soundlessly and fingers weaving like I was trying to make a damn net.

Out of the corner of my eye, I saw it, as Musset lashed his arm down. The various bows all fired at once; each arrow and bolt was aimed for a different Dark Legionnaire, flashed out and hit them with powerful smacks and crunches.

Every single one of the heads had been dipped in the watered-down deathbloom poison I'd provided. The finished potion had gained an extra effect with the miscellaneous poisons I'd diluted it with. But in spreading it out, it had grown weaker overall. Still, it was enough, and I was only glad I'd remembered the three original vials were still in my inventory and had thought to test the mixture.

Deathbloom Poison (Diluted)		Further Description *Yes*/*No*	
Details:		This poison is one of the most reviled in the realm. Not only does it commonly kill its victim, doing 12 points of damage on contact, but it also lowers the target's health and mana pool by 5 points per second for sixty seconds. This reduction is permanent and cannot be healed. This poison has been diluted into a solution of Asp's Kiss, adding in a damage over time effect of an additional 3 points per second for twelve seconds and hyperemesis for one hour.	
Rarity:	Magical:	Durability:	Potency:
Special	Yes	100/100	3/10

In the end, I'd managed to spread it out to make seventy doses. While it was far weaker than the original, something about the overall interaction between my own home-made poison and the severe one cultivated by the Drow had resulted in the last effect being particularly nasty.

Hyperemesis was a reaction that a woman I'd known back home had when she was pregnant. She'd ended up in the hospital because she was sick constantly and couldn't keep any food down. This was similar, but it condensed what she experienced over nine months into a single hour of vomiting hell.

Even if the damage was nothing to someone who'd specced themselves into a tank, pouring points into Constitution like water and ending up with thousands of health, they still would end up fucked, because being unable to stand through vomiting and the world spinning like a waltzer gone wrong made it kinda hard to fight.

If I'd had more time, I'd have experimented with it loads, but with the constraints we were under, it was all I could do.

I lifted my hands, and the assistant, Harp, I think his name was, pulled the oiled tarp aside. I let fly with my spell as he ran to join the others and get the hell out here.

My spell, an overcharged Explosive Compression, hurtled into the camp, joining the dozen others in hammering into the tent of the Trailmasters.

We'd decided at the last minute, when our scouts had reported the way they'd made their camp, that there was just no goddamn way we could make sure of the Trailmasters with the assassin team as we'd hoped, so we'd made this adjustment instead. Now that we'd fired our magic into the tent, killing as many as we could, we changed our targets, ignoring the few sentries nearby who were still standing. Instead, we began aiming for the bodies that were rolling out of blankets and reaching for armor and weapons.

We threw everything we had at them, a savage glee filling us as we killed one after another, aiming for heads, throats, and groins with spells and projectiles dipped in poison that made it almost impossible for the afflicted to apply pressure and keep it.

A handful of skulls floated up at first, followed by dozens more before Musset gestured, and the archers shifted their arm again, taking out the few figures who staggered from the Trailmaster tent.

"Flame!" he shouted into the night, and those of us who could cast fire started to build those spells, while those who couldn't began to throw the vials and containers he'd prepared earlier into the camp. They smashed against the caravans at the middle of the camp, and our fireballs landed seconds later, setting the entire site ablaze.

Then he turned and started to run, and so did we.

The original plan had been to try to fight them, to kill as many as we could to get their attention, then to run, but once I'd made the poison, that had changed everything.

Half of it was given out amongst the archers. The other half was given to Bane and Tang, and they stayed well-hidden as the camp erupted in fury, Dark Legionnaires chasing us as we ran.

I'd thrown my last spell and was running with the rest when the arrows started falling, followed fast by the spells. For the first time, I was on the receiving end of a Magic Missile barrage, dodging as best I could. One of the darts slammed into my shoulder, cracking the pauldron, the second hitting my right elbow, and the third hit my right knee.

I staggered, grimacing over the skill of the bastard mage before righting myself and running on. A Firebolt flashed past me and slammed into a tree ahead, setting it ablaze and showing us clearly as we ran.

Another barrage followed, this time a pair of Icebolts. One missed, and the other took a legionnaire in the back of the neck. He collapsed with a clatter, twitching.

I started to slow, only to have Grizz appear on my right and Lydia on my left, each grabbing me by an arm and shoving me on.

"He's..." I started to argue, and Grizz locked eyes with me, our gazes meeting through the thin visors of our helms, our eyes reflecting the firelight.

"Dead," Grizz finished, half-carrying, half-shoving me forward.

I stumbled then started to run again as arrows hammered into the trees on either side of us. A single Magic Missile slammed into my shoulder again, the others deflected by Grizz's shield.

I cried out, cursing as the pauldron shattered, the cracks making it fall apart when the second hit landed almost atop the first. I bit my cheek as we ran, determined to make them pay for that. Another legionnaire to my left screamed, flash-cooked inside her armor by a green-laced Fireball variant that hit her dead on.

I raced after the others, fury making my feet fly over the ground as spells, arrows, and the occasional crossbow bolt flew after me, along with the rising cries and taunting of the Dark Legion.

Legionnaires staggered, the Taunt ability forcing them to start to respond, before their training and resistances kicked in. I raged internally at the coordinated way the next round of bolts and spells were used, as three Taunts were used at once, and the ones who faltered were targeted by the flying messengers of death.

I changed direction, scrambling to the right as I recognized the bark carved off a trio of trees ahead to mark the turn, and I dug down, forcing myself to run faster.

This time, the Taunt skill hit me as well, the first wave of those who'd been targeted having mainly fallen, resulting in a heavier effect blanketing those of us who were left in its range. I slowed, turning again, rage filling me, until I was hit in the stomach and hoisted into the air.

I grunted, falling forward, then banged my helm into the broad back below me, and I realized what had happened as I saw Lydia running next to me.

"God damn it, Grizz!" I shouted as I struggled to get down.

"Stay still!" he snapped, pushing himself and picking up speed. I cursed then accepted my lot. Grizz stopping to let me down was inevitable; I was, after all, fully armored and not a small guy, but the time it would cost him, after he'd already diverted while running to pick me up, meant we were falling behind the main pack.

That left me with two choices.

I could struggle and squirm. He'd have to drop me, then we'd start running again. Knowing that noble asshole, he'd probably insist on falling back to buy us some time...or I could do what I was good at.

I started to cast a spell, weaving it as fast as possible, dropping it behind us just as Grizz groaned and twisted his hips, flipping me forward and letting me down.

"Run, you mad bastard!" I screamed at him as he staggered, and Yen was there, grabbing his arm and dragging him back upright as he almost fell over. I stumbled before Lydia grabbed me, and I straightened, running again and looking about frantically for the next sign. Cries of pain and anger lifted from behind us, as the Dark Legionnaires were introduced to my new Flames of Wrath spell.

Judging from the sounds, there were a fuck-ton of them, if not the entire camp, chasing us, so it'd not do much damage, but hey, even a little could ruin some fucker's day.

I pushed Lydia away, gesturing for to her to run, and called to her as we went.

"I can damn well fly, remember!"

"Then do it!" she snapped. "Get tha hell out of here!"

"And ruin the surprise for them?!" A grin forced its way onto my face, despite nobody being able to see it.

Explosions went off behind us as spells hit the ritual circle, and I grinned again. They weren't that smart, after all; they'd either stopped or diverted spells aimed for us to destroy the circle I'd laid down…I'd have just run around it.

I soon saw others ahead of me, and I turned when they did, angling to the left this time and following the path that had been clearly marked, to those who know what to look for, at least.

It got trickier as the narrow ridge we ran up was rocky and covered in loose shale, slowing us down and allowing the wankers to close on us again. But just as they did, we made it to the top and barreled into the trees, as they, in turn, were slowed by the shale.

Once through the thick strand of trees, I saw Ertun waiting, facing us. I'd been introduced to the big bastard earlier, and I was still in awe that Thorn had made armor that size, never mind that he'd somehow managed to blend into the rest of the Legion, considering he was damn near eight feet tall and about the same across the shoulders.

The man was mountainous, with shovels for hands and a seemingly near-unlimited level of stamina, if a slow overall speed.

He waited until he was sure I'd seen him, then gestured sharply to his left. I nodded, biting my tongue as I went.

He'd volunteered for this, I reminded myself, and if anyone was going to do it, he was the best candidate.

Ertun stood in the middle of the narrow trail, his enormous greatsword held easily in one hand. We ran past, taking the path to the right and up to safety as he readied himself. I forced myself not to look to the sides as I went, knowing that Bob, Giint, and Arrin were hiding there, ready.

This part of the plan was the worst, as it relied on too many things that had to go right.

Denny had explained, using small words, that in any pursuit, three things happened. Some people didn't bother and fell back at the first opportunity.

Some people saw the runners, and if the runners were rabbits, they became like greyhounds, fixated on the rabbit and, thanks to tunnel vision, ignored everything else, simply chasing for the sake of chasing.

Then there were the professionals. The soldiers of the group, they'd be doing a mix of both. They'd chase, but if they saw no chance to catch the target, they'd fall back and lick their wounds.

We couldn't have that.

Ertun was there to intercept the greyhounds, and provided there weren't too many, to slaughter them, while we made it to the top of the path.

Depending on how many of them were in sight when we reached the top of the path, as we would gain a clear view of Ertun's position, we would either pause and wait for him to catch up or fire down at them. If there were too many, we'd fire upon him, using him as the target for the most destructive spells we could.

I hated that idea, but as he'd said, it was better than what would happen if they took him alive.

I'd been violently opposed to leaving him behind, but when the rest of the group, including my own squad and Ertun had argued for it, I'd been forced to accept it.

We needed to make sure the remainder of the group followed and came to the final section, bunched up. Triggering the trap with three people in it was pointless, after all.

I scrambled around the narrow collection of trees then up the defile, grabbing onto rocks and heaving myself forward. The whole time, I hated the fear that raced through me for the rest of my people.

Oracle's touch was a soothing balm on my mind, hovering high overhead as she was, ready to guide us if we got lost, her sadness and her desperate love for me a constant companion as I went.

I saw the others reach the top, and I pushed harder, my breathing ragged as I cleared the grey stone and slippery moss. Heaving, I skidded to a halt and actually bounced off Grizz's armored shoulder. I turned to look back down, thankful for the DarkVision that made this so much easier for me than most people.

I easily spotted Ertun, standing in the middle of the path, flicking his sword to one side to get rid of the blood. The three bodies that laid about him were practically naked, and I looked over at Lydia, who spoke up without being asked.

"Seventeen seconds," she said, and I nodded my thanks.

He was to hold for a full minute, then fall back. That forty-three seconds had passed in the blink of an eye was impressive, but so was the fact he'd killed three men in that time.

I saw movement as another form, a woman clad only in her underwear, hurtled out of the darkness, leaping at Ertun. He swung his sword almost lazily, and I felt the shock he must have experienced as she twisted mid-air and kicked off the flat of the blade, using it to flip herself over. Instead of being cut in two, she slashed her own swordstaff across and plunged it into the edge of his cuirass, the tip slipping under the edge of his pauldron, judging from the grunt of pain.

She landed, rolled, and sprang back to her feet, her own weapon eerily similar in design to my own naginata, save for its shorter haft and narrow blade.

Ertun grunted again, then briefly attacked, jumping back as Giint made an appearance. The little Gnome fired his crossbow, taking her in the leg.

She screamed in pain and outrage, grabbing the bolt and yanking it free as Giint ran.

A flicker of movement came through the trees, and I sent the contingency order to Bob.

The bone minion broke from his hiding place, rushing the woman, only for her to spin, slashing at him and knocking him from his feet, one arm lighter, though she staggered again, thanks to Giint's bolt.

Arrin cast Magic Missiles at her, and she dove aside, rolling and coming to her feet, then stabbed out, driving the tip of the swordstaff through Ertun's neck. The wet blade appeared under the back of his helm, and I snarled as I fired my own Magic Missiles. The trio flashed down, making her dive aside as her wounded leg gave out, and she bellowed in pain, grabbing at the injury.

More movement resolved into a trio of figures, kitted out in full armor, who raced forward. I sent a new order to Bob as he rolled to his feet. He'd raised his sword, about to stab the woman, when he got the order, and he spun quickly, racing to Arrin's position, the daft bugger still standing there in plain sight with his tongue held between his teeth in concentration.

Bob swept him up in a fireman's carry about half a second before he released his spell, and the lightning bolt flashed out, slamming into the strand of trees. Someone screamed as their armor became a superconductor.

While Arrin cursed, and Bob and Giint ran, I started casting, hitting the area with a Flames of Wrath first. The woman screamed as a figure in full armor sprinted in, diving down and discarding their mace and shield to grab her, then rolling to one side to carry her out of the effect.

I cursed, fixating on the figure as they threw her out of sight and looked up, clearly spotting me on the ridge.

Others appeared, but thanks to my spell, they funneled to either side of the ritual circle, clearly unsure as to the effect and unwilling to cross the glowing red lines, hemmed in by the fallen trees we'd arranged earlier.

I wove the Fireball quickly, but as quick as I was, he was quicker, and a trio of blue-green Magic Missiles hurtled from his hands, headed straight for me.

I released the Fireball moments before the missiles would have hit me, diving back out of sight. I could not avoid snarling in pain and fury as his missiles detonated the spell, blanketing me and the stand of trees in flame and exposing us to the figures below.

Grizz and Lydia had backed off and were calling for me to do the same. But from where I lay, I could see what they, and the assholes below, couldn't.

Bob, Arrin, and Giint. They were racing for the patch of flaming ground I stood in, and they'd be picked off easily if the other side had ranged attackers, now that the entire area was alight. Considering the patch of shale and unstable ground they'd have to cover, now well-lit and in clear view, they didn't stand a chance.

"Get them to safety!" I shouted, sprinting forward quickly enough that neither Grizz nor Lydia could catch me, leaping into the air.

I hurtled forward, making my movement look like an Ability, something like a Bullrush, rather than true flight. With a grunt, I deliberately landed a half dozen meters from the figure in black-enameled plate armor.

I steadied myself, pulling my naginata from my bag of holding and pointed it at him. He took two steps to the side as the flames of my spell ran past, reaching down to sweep up the woman's swordstaff, then moved back. Though he grunted as the flames burned him slightly, he was quick enough to avoid most of it, and he stood facing me, armed and ready.

Others closed the distance, and the woman shouted something to the figure who faced me. I ignored it and lunged.

I led with the tip, and he swept his across to block, his footwork good as he shifted his weight. Countering, I twisted, dipping the blade and intending to take his hand.

My blade slid down his, but he twisted his weapon in turn, making the blades spin in a circle as we both tried to get our weapon to slide down the opponent's, aiming for the wrist.

He spun his, and I spun mine, before we both stepped in closer. He abruptly dropped to one knee, releasing his weapon with his right hand and firing a Firebolt. The spell hit me in the chest as my own strike flew over his head, the loss of resistance making me grunt in surprise.

I took a step back, the Firebolt causing me little damage in my armor but heating it and shoving me off balance as the figure threw the swordstaff at my face.

I blocked it instinctively, then brought my knee up as he rushed forward, aiming for my waist.

My blow connected, the thick metal of the knee slamming into his helm and sending him rolling. I twisted, slashing my naginata down and aiming for the back of his neck as it was exposed.

Just before the blade would have hit, punching deep into the neck and ending the fight, a huge figure ploughed into me from one side, crushing me into a tree. I barely kept my grip on my weapon as a huge orc grabbed both my arms and forced them back, holding me spread-eagled against the trunk while he roared in my face with bestial bloodlust and headbutted me.

His helm was impressive, all lacquered steel, but it had a large, open section over the front of his face. While his first blow landed solidly, knocking my head back against the tree, my right knee took him in the balls before he could capitalize on it.

The moment of weakness gave me the chance to return the favor, and when I ducked my head and drove it into his face, he got a terminal surprise. My helm wasn't topped with fancy plumes as it appeared to a casual observer at night.

They were sharp, bladed points, like the tips of a steel porcupine's quills, razor-edged. As they punched into his flesh, I whipped my head back up, shredding the big bastard's face.

He screamed, a new sound, considering he'd made it without lips or half the flesh on his skull, and he released me as he reached for his ruined face.

I shoved him back and slashed my naginata sideways across the space before me, starting to cast at seeing the first figure I'd fought was back on his feet. He was shaking, growing larger by the second as he activated some kind of ability, his muscles bunching and swelling.

The Dark Legionnaire roared, throwing his head back. His helm struggled to stay atop his head, as his fingers reached up to yank it off. I glanced aside, noticing the others closing in on me, weapons raised. I grinned ferociously, shouting to them all.

"Yeah, fuck you too, dickbag!" I fired the spell downwards between my feet as I shoved off with all my might, activating Soaring Majesty and hurtling into the air, Explosive Compression slamming into the ground as I soared away.

It tugged at me, but a second later, I was out of its range. The huge orc, his face shredded, screamed again, being close to the epicenter of the spell that dragged the group inward.

I flew higher, bones breaking and screams tearing free of those I'd left behind, but only one skull lifted in my vision. I swore in fury, tempted to hold my position there and Fireball them into submission, before I remembered the real plan, and I forced myself to land atop the bluff, making sure I could be seen, before I staggered from sight and into the darkness.

CHAPTER TWENTY-NINE

Shouts rose behind me, pleading for help, and a deep-throated scream of fury and hatred that I just knew was that asshole I'd fought, but I ignored them. The pain of the fight ate at me, combined with the cost of the short use of Soaring Majesty. I forced myself into a stumbling run and headed down the valley toward the safety of the far side and leading the fuckers into the valley of death.

Denny stood proudly to my right in the middle of the small clearing, and he lit a cigar from the torch he held, giving me a wave. I waved back and ran on, grinning as I thought about what they had coming as he nonchalantly puffed a cloud of cobalt blue smoke into the air.

I scrambled up the far side, shoving the bushes aside as they swung back, one smacking me in the face as Arrin carelessly released it. I spat out leaves, cursing him, as Grizz and Lydia closed in from either side.

"Look, I know you're pissed, and you know I'll do it again tomorrow. That asshole caster down there wasn't in the plans, and he'd have killed Giint, Bob, and Arrin, and you know it, not to mention being too close for us to be able to pull this damn trick. No, I didn't want to do it, and yes I'd like a fucking beer and some popcorn to watch this bit. Does that answer all your questions?" I growled.

They both opened their mouths to argue but took one look at the glare I was giving them and shut them again.

"Seriously, I know, all right? Let's just move the hell on to where you both accept that I'm going to do what I goddamn need to," I muttered, following the others to lie in a panting heap on the far side of the ridge below a raised stone bulwark that should block most of the damage.

"Who did this, anyway?" I asked around, and I got a weak wave from a slim elven figure who was trying to catch her breath on the far side of the bodies.

"I did…my lord…" she wheezed. "Stone…singer…"

"Well, that tells me fuck-all but sounds amazing," I replied, grinning wolfishly. "But it sounds like the guests of honor are arriving, so you'll have to tell me more later!"

Taking my leave, I moved to where another legionnaire had let out a low whistle. I poked my head up, aligning my sight with gaps woven into the wooden barriers and staring down through the foliage at the group of clearly furious Dark Legionnaires who were sprinting into the shallow valley below. Denny had moved out of sight behind a small barrier.

He had four crossbows lined up and ready, and he used them one-by-one, so quickly it looked like they were simply firing without coordination.

As per the plan, Arrin and Yen waited at the end of the valley and fired off their attacks next. Arrin's was a bit more pathetic than I'd have liked, considering he was barely in position in time and was exhausted, but Yen's Flamespears...well, the Dark Legionnaires didn't know what hit them.

The small force I'd faced wasn't there, or at least, I couldn't see them yet, but there were at least a hundred others crowding into the valley. Where Denny's first attack had made them pause, Yen's had knocked them back. I'd taken advantage of the handful of seconds the shock engendered to move into position. I joined four others, stepping forward into sight to let loose with our own Taunts.

"Fight ME!"

"Face ME!"

"Come on!"

The other three were more traditional, and had obviously been trained in the same way, but–and I knew I'd be forever proud of him for this–Grizz had become more used to my relaxed and altogether more contemptuous methods of dealing with my enemies.

"SUCK IT!" he screamed, his hands braced on the back of his head while helicoptering his cock round and round, thrusting his hips in time to a rhythm only he could hear. Where he'd found time to halfway strip out of his armor, I had no idea, and I just knew that Yen was going to murder him later for risking her favorite part of him, but I could barely keep from laughing as I used my own Taunt.

"Your mother was a hamster, and your father smelt of elderberries!" I bellowed into the rising fury below. Yes, it wasn't the most impressive of Taunts, but it was traditional from my homeland, as I'd explained on several occasions, and anything I did after Grizz's was going to be ignored, anyway.

The clearing erupted in screams of abject fury as the entire mass of black-clad dickheads raced forward, waving weapons at us.

We turned and ran, or in Grizz's case, staggered, latching his armor while giggling like a schoolgirl, then dropped down behind a defensive barrier just as Denny activated his Ability.

The night was suddenly lit by a terrible bright light, and a blast of stinking, insanely hot air, like an explosion from the devil's arsehole after a phaal curry, roared over the edge of the barrier.

The sound was insane, as all the crystals detonated at once, creating a similar effect to a fuel air bomb going off. Competing pressure waves slammed outwards and, more devastatingly, inwards to the center of the clearing.

Trees that weren't vaporized instantly were instead converted into claymore-like detonations of splinters that tore in every direction through the forest, shredding the foliage for hundreds of meters and sending canopies collapsing in a wide arc.

"Fuck me!" I screamed, ducking my head down as the searing white light erupted overhead, followed by the most horrific sounds I'd ever heard. Dozens of trees were turned into weapons and well over a hundred Dark Legionnaires became mincemeat.

The barrier above us, solid rock and half submerged into the soil, tilted and shifted. For a terrifying second, I thought we were going to be killed by our own trap, until it stopped.

I looked around, finding the others looking just as stunned and shaking their heads. Most people had done as they'd been told and had laid flat on the ground behind the barrier, and they were covered in shredded foliage and dirt, but a few, either hardier or more stupid than the rest, were up already and were peeking over the barrier.

I caught one of them waving to get my attention, then pointing in the direction of the clearing. I shook my head, the world feeling weird and filled with an irritating buzzing.

I shook my head again as I shifted, feeling the dirt cascading off me, but in silence, and I frowned, trying to make sense of the situation. I could just hear him, at the edge of my range, and he was pointing down into the valley, gesturing for us all to come, then leaping over the top.

"Jax, what happened?" Oracle sent to me. *"Is everyone okay?"*

"I think so." I still shook my head intermittently and moved to my feet. "The world sounds funny, though. I must have burst my damn eardrums," I realized with a grunt, starting to cast. As soon as Surgeon's Scalpel washed through me, a thousand tiny perforations appeared, most so small I'd not noticed them, but they all contributed to my general feeling of lousiness. I quickly washed a healing through myself, my ears popping and shifting weirdly as they were flash-fixed.

I made it over the barrier, only to stare down into a scene of devastation. The center of the valley looked like it'd been hit with a fucking *nuke*, a mixed mess of shredded bodies, metal, and scoured earth, while the air was filled with a mixture of fresh-cut sawdust, burned meat, and freshly turned soil.

I swept my gaze up and around, taking the wide clearing that looked clean up to the stars, and I grinned involuntarily.

"Hell, waste not, want not," I said to Oracle through the link. *"Get the captain to come and pick us up here."* I waited for her to send a quick acknowledgement before I left the connection, then realized what the legionnaire had wanted…Denny!

I rushed forward as well, skidding down the side of the valley. Exposed roots and splintered wood made the footing treacherous, but I quickly caught up with him and started digging into the middle of the valley floor.

It was where Denny had insisted on being, saying he needed to detonate all the crystals at once. He'd built a buried bunker to hide in, as well as enlisting Oracle to help him by acting as a bridge for Grizz to teach him the Iceshield spell.

We frantically threw sections of bodies and metal aside, splashing through mulch and pooling blood to reach down to the half-exposed and partially melted container he'd been sheltering in.

The legionnaire who'd led the run grabbed the handle then immediately released it with a curse as he shook his burning hands. Then, growling in fury, he grabbed it again and pulled, ignoring the pain to rescue his friend.

It held for a few seconds, the metal seam flash-welded closed, before he screamed and *heaved*, and the top popped loose, sending him staggering back.

Inside, Denny lay curled up, and I hit him with Surgeon's Scalpel, wincing as I absorbed the details.

He was alive, but only barely. Third-degree burns covered most of his body, his eyes were, well, they were fucked, as were most of his externals, and even his muscles were registering as pretty much well-done on the fucked-meat-ometer.

I poured magic in, healing him as fast as I could. Concentrating on his brain and heart first, I desperately tried to lower his rapidly rising internal temperature.

Several legionnaires pulled him out, grunting in pain at the heat of his armor as they touched it. Yet they set him down gently, and I alternated the next round of healing with a fountain of cool, fresh water.

The water sizzled and hissed, steam rising from the armor in places where it retained the most heat. The nearby legionnaires cursed at the well-liked man's mangled state.

Countless minutes passed while I worked on him, and the others quickly moved, gathering in around me with their weapons out and ready.

"Jax, I'm nearly there," I sensed from Oracle, and my heart jumped, knowing how much better than me at healing she was. I snapped out orders quickly.

"The ship's incoming; be ready to get him aboard as soon as they land. We're heading back to the Tower."

I got a few rounds of acknowledgement and heard others shouting the order into the faces of deafened legionnaires. A few minutes later, we were staggering up the gangplank, Denny carried on an improvised litter while I continued to pour magic into him.

"I've got this," Oracle said, appearing next to me, and I sagged, accepting a mana potion as it was handed to me and downing it in relief.

"Jax!" a voice called, and I moved to the side, looking down to where Grizz was indicating.

I leaned over the side of the railing as we climbed past the canopy of trees, squinting down at the handful of Dark Legionnaires below.

Less than thirty remained, and they were gravely injured, or most of them were, at any rate. I snarled as I looked down at them, calling out for anyone with ranged weapons.

Several people moved up alongside, and crossbows, bows, and spells were quickly readied, firing down in a continuous barrage at the survivors as they frantically limped away.

At the last second, I saw the berserker I'd fought, standing over the slumped and partially cooked body of the woman, surrounded by a pile of corpses. He held a shield in either hand, sheltering her and two others, protecting them as my people fired on the injured and practically defenseless Dark Legion.

My heart dropped, then I gritted my teeth. These fuckers had come to me; they'd come looking for a fight, and if word got around that fucking with Jax meant pulling back a bloody stump with no body attached? Well, maybe I'd save some lives in the long run.

I felt Amon's approval and felt even sicker as I considered what anyone from my world would think of me now, flying away on my ship and leaving all of those people to die there in the mud.

Swallowing hard, I turned away, gesturing to cease fire before stumbling across to sit on the deck next to the legionnaires.

I closed my eyes and meditated as best I could, blocking out the world and activating Peace as I sensed movement around me. Injured people were being healed by those who could heal, while Oracle worked tirelessly to save Denny.

It took seemingly forever to return to the Tower, and when we did arrive back finally, Lydia shook me from my meditation. I found Oracle shrunk down to her smallest form, curled up in my lap, clearly trying to provide me with reassurance as she felt my barrage of doubts and self-recriminations.

I opened my eyes and sighed as my momentary sense of peace was washed away by the feeling that I'd done something very wrong, despite this being war.

Taking a deep, calming breath, I gently roused Oracle. Her form shifted from the one she'd been wearing, tiny and fairy-like, with her "combat gear" of black leggings, a tight red top, with two tiny lines of camo paint on her cheeks, into her stunning, full-sized form.

I took Lydia's hand and let her help haul my armored form to my feet, clapping her on the shoulder in thanks and looking down into Oracle's eyes.

My companion nodded as if to tell me she understood, despite everything. I forced myself to put it all aside, straightening my back and looking around. Nobody needed to see their lord doubting himself.

I strode along the deck to stand at the fore, gazing up at the Great Tower, outlined against the departing night by the wash of warm light glowing from the windows within, and the faint light of dawn. The ships that had finally arrived last night, gathered about the Tower's base.

The battleship took up most of the space in the courtyard, huge and dark, its form barely distinguishable from the darkness of the surrounding canopy, save for a handful of small lights that were lit aboard her deck.

Others were berthed about her, reminiscent of remoras around a great white shark, faint calls drifting on the air from the birds that rose to greet the dawn.

I sighed, a lot of the stress subsiding as I took in my home. I saw the distant movements inside, the flickering lights and the shadows dancing as people went about their business. The newly rejuvenated Great Tower was clearly alive again after being an abode of death and nightmares for so long.

"It's beautiful," a voice said softly.

I glanced to the side, finding, of all people, Giint. I spoke quietly, so as not to disturb the others, who were generally relaxing.

"It is, mate, and it's our home."

"It's so big, and the potential!" he said, his eyes glowing. "Look, we could make turrets there…and there…and launchers for Badunkas on the side of the hull, and…"

I blinked in surprise, following the direction of his finger. The mad little bastard wanted to be able to fire the Badunkas into the sodding air.

"We'd have to figure out the process, maybe strip an airship or two, but we could do it; we could make them smaller…flying Badunkas!" he let out with a moan of avarice, and I had to look away, torn between laughing and worrying that the little bastard was getting off on the idea.

"Yeah…well, no taking our ships apart," I said firmly. "You want to do that, you do it with enemy units. I don't know, test it with a captured ship or something." I looked back towards the others, walking to another part of the ship.

I used a burst of Soaring Majesty to fly across the intervening distance and land next to Captain Kinnet on the upper deck.

"Captain, thank you for coming for us, and for being fast about it," I said, getting a raised head that exposed her throat, along with a fist to heart as a greeting.

"Pleased to serve, my lord," she said.

"Well, still…thank you. Now, can you land inside the Great Tower for me, please? I have things I need to do."

"Of course, my lord." She frowned slightly as she inspected the open area of the landing deck on the twenty-sixth floor. She grunted in satisfaction, and directing the helmsman to take us in. While Kinnet prepared for landing, I moved down to the lower deck, making my way over to where Denny and the others were gathered.

"You look a little better," I said, crouching next to Denny and gently grasping his shoulder.

He grinned up at me weakly, still looking rough as hell, but significantly more alive, and I smiled back.

"Never had that many levels or skill upgrades in one go before, that's all," he quipped.

I snorted. "Yeah, nothing at all to do with nearly cooking yourself to a crisp, right?"

He shrugged, looking a little embarrassed, but also damn pleased with the effects. "Well, I'm a heliomage now, and a trapsmith; what do you expect me to look like?" he asked nonchalantly.

"Asshole," I laughed, and he threw me a cheery wink as I stood up, turning away and moving to the railing to admire the Tower again as we closed in on her.

I pulled up my notifications, grunting as I looked them over, quickly dismissing them one-by-one.

Congratulations!

Through hard work and perseverance, you have increased your Intelligence by one point. Continue to train and learn to increase this further.

*

Congratulations!

You have killed the following:

- 3x Church of Nimon Sanctified and Blessed Soldiers of various levels for a total of 18,650xp

A party under your command killed the following:

- 63x Church of Nimon Soldier-Aspirants of various levels for a total of 214,200xp
- 153x Church of Nimon Sanctified and Blessed Soldiers of various levels for a total of 1,093,650xp
- 14x Church of Nimon Sanctified Sergeants/Officers of various levels for 136,500
- 11x Church of Nimon Trail-Mages of various levels for 102,905xp
- 1x Church of Nimon Legionnaire Prefect, level 41, for 13,290xp

Total party experience earned: 1,560,545xp

As party leader, you gain 25% of all experience earned

Progress to level 24 stands at 617,653/510,000

*

Congratulations!

You have reached level 24!

You have 7 unspent Attribute points and 0 Meridian points available.

Progress to level 25 stands at 107,653/570,000

I felt pleased as I read over the details, then did a little mental math. It was much easier than it ever used to be, requiring far less effort, where I'd always been crap at math before.

We'd managed to kill two hundred and forty-five of the Dark Legionnaires in that raid, leaving fifty-five alive, and who knew how many of them were actually combat capable after that.

My stomach churned over the fight again, and I stamped the feeling down, resolving to speak to Romanus or Augustus later. Hell, maybe both.

I glanced over at Denny, knowing that the vast majority of the experience came from his ability and efforts. I had to guess he'd hit at least a few levels from it.

I relaxed as he laughed at something that one of the others said, and I turned to observe our final approach of the Tower. The hull of the ship slipped over the edge of the balcony and glided in somewhat smoothly to the docking cradle ahead, empty and waiting.

I looked back, seeing the pair of Alkyon at the helm doing their species' equivalent of sweating as they constantly fluffed and ruffled their feathers while guiding us in. I turned away quickly, not needing the extra doubt in that moment.

As the arch of the Tower's thick outer wall passed overhead, along with the narrow clearance for the height and width of the cruiser, I let out an involuntary sigh of relief, joining the others gathering by the space for the gangplank.

I noticed as the handful of people milling about began to grow, as word reached the masses that we were back from our first fight with the Dark Legionnaires. I couldn't help but grin at the sight of Augustus, who appeared thoroughly stressed by the way people kept bowing to him, clearly unsure of what they should be doing.

He snapped an order at a pair of legionnaires, who saluted smartly then sniggered when he looked away, letting me know that at least some of the overly deferential attitude was deliberately performed to wind up someone they saw as one of their own.

Once the ship came to a full halt, settling into the cradle with a creak and groan of pressurized wood, and the engine's omnipresent *hum* wound down to a much more pleasant low drone, I waited at the side of the ship. A deckhand slid the gangplank down with a grunt, and I jogged down it, coming to a halt with Cai, Romanus, and Nerin all waiting for me. Augustus strode over with a frown that he carefully smoothed away, and the rest of the ship disembarked behind me.

"Welcome home, my lord," Cai said formally, voice pitched so that it would carry. "How went your first encounter with the Dark Legion?"

I finally realized the reason so many people were present, seemingly doing a million minor jobs, coiling rope, moving boxes, and generally doing make-work at this time in the morning, and I smiled, damn pleased to have Cai, as he'd clearly seen this coming long since.

"It was a success!" I declared loudly. "We lost several good legionnaires, and I'm sorry for that, but for each of our number we lost, we killed thirty or more of the Dark Wankers. I'm proud of my legionnaires," I finished with a firm look at Romanus, who nodded seriously.

"I, too, am proud of the legionnaires," he stated loudly. "I knew the team we sent with you would serve you well, and they will have done all they could for their brothers and sisters in arms."

"They did Romanus, they really did." I stepped in closer and dropped my voice to speak normally. "I'm sorry to have lost so many of them. They fought damn hard, but still, of the twenty I had, we lost eight."

"Thank you, Jax," he said sadly. "Any loss of my...sorry, your...legionnaires is heartbreaking, but..."

"They'll always be yours, Romanus," I said firmly. "Never doubt that. We need to talk, and soon, but first–and I'm sorry for this–we need to have a quick AAR, and then I need to sleep."

"AAR?" he asked, and I winced.

"Sorry; carry over from my days in the military back home. It stands for an After Action Report. I'm not writing it up; never was any good at that side of shit, but I need to go through it with you while its fresh in my mind, as well as make arrangements for the various sites we visited and claimed.

"Once that's done, I can get some sleep, and you, and Cai, and Augustus...I see you there, mate..." I shot a grin over at the massive legionnaire. "...get to make the plans into reality. No point in everyone waiting for me while I sleep. Nerin, thank you for being here. I healed the majority of those who were gravely injured, and several of the minor ones, but there are still dozens of smaller wounds scattered about. Please make sure they're all healed properly, and check on Denny for me. He was in an awfully bad way, and our skills are nowhere near yours."

I got a nod from her as she headed up to the group that was disembarking, waving her hands and shouting orders to them.

"The Council Chambers are ready, Jax, or..." Cai said quickly, stepping in, and I shook my head.

"The Command Center," I said firmly. "I need to see where we are with things, and get the next phase moving while I explain what's happened."

I gestured towards the stairs, and the others saluted, falling in behind me as I called out to Lydia to join us. Bob had slipped into his long-accustomed position, ghosting along behind me. Bane and Tang were nowhere to be seen, and I knew from past experience that one was ahead, and one behind me, even now.

I was tempted to change direction, just to fuck with them, but I dismissed the childish thought with a grin.

It only took us a few minutes to jog to the Command Center, now located on the same floor as our living quarters, finding, as always, that a lot of thought had been put into things. As I arrived, I was overjoyed at finding a tray of warm, freshly baked bread, a jar of butter, and several jugs. The jugs were filled with everything from warm milk to fresh water, to something that smelled like it would strip paint at a hundred meters.

"Gods, that smells good!" I muttered, taking a slab of bread as Augustus sliced it free and slathered it with butter deep enough to leave teeth marks in it.

"Well, we got the bakery up and running; properly, I mean," Cai said, smiling as he took a slice from Augustus as well. "I diverted a pair of golems to work on it. Integrating the steel sections, which the blacksmiths had managed to make, into the actual structure of the Tower was surprisingly easy with their abilities, and though the result was a few hours added onto their standard jobs, now we have fresh bread and somewhere for our bakers to work."

Augustus rolled his eyes in remembrance, letting out a little groan.

"You remember that you told me to give out the expert-level baker's skillbook?" Cai asked, and I nodded, taking another bite.

"Worth it," I mumbled around a mouthful of bread.

"That's from his apprentice…one of three, to be exact," Cai said. "Joha was an apprentice baker himself, although he ran the bakery in Dannick. The limited opportunities and ingredients kept him from moving higher in his art. With the book, well, he created these yesterday…" Cai produced a small bag out of his bag of holding, offering it to me.

I opened it and picked out a fluffy, baked ball, popping it into my mouth before letting out a groan.

"A doughnut! Fuck my life, an actual honest-to-God doughnut. Get that man a raise…hell, I need to speak to him. I have needs…and I never thought I'd say this, but that man is going to satisfy some of them, at least.

"Also, we got some pigs while we were out on our little adventure, and they just became highly valuable property to the Tower. If I can make things work so that I can get a goddamn bacon sandwich for my breakfast occasionally and some sodding doughnuts, then I'll view this as all being worth it," I declared adamantly, to resounding laughter and grins.

Over the next twenty minutes, I filled them all in on the details, answering questions and asking my own where needed. By the end of the conversation, I was yawning, and the others took it as a clear invitation to leave me to rest, promising to continue integrating the newly arrived people into the Great Tower and get everything moving along, as well as a scouting trip to keep tabs on the Dark Legion.

I waved them out, resting back in my chair and staring at the stylized Great Tower that revolved slowly on the Creation Table before me.

"Seneschal, Heph, join us, please," I said eventually, still staring at the image, and they both phased into existence as I sat there. "You don't need to wait for an invitation, you know." I finally looked aside from it to make eye contact with them both. "Much as I expect Oracle to come and go to these things as she wants, yet to be here if there's a good reason, I expect the same of you."

"Aye, laddie, well, ah'll know fer next time, right?" Heph grumbled, but he nodded his thanks.

"Thank you, Jax," Seneschal said.

"Fine. I take it you both heard all of that as well?" I gestured randomly around the room to indicate the conversation I'd just had, getting a pair of nods again as Oracle stood by the side of my chair and rested her hand on my shoulder in silent support. "Good," I said, reaching up and taking her hand in my own. "What you know, and the others haven't really thought about or considered yet, is that there's more to the story that we need to figure out."

"The Night King," Seneschal pointed out.

"In part, yes." I rubbed the back of my neck absently. "Oracle was told by the old inhabitants of the Tower that you were here to act as a bastion for the people of the continent and for the Empire as it expanded and fought the Night King. She, and I suspect, you…just accepted that, am I right?" I got a trio of nods in response.

"Fair enough; that's understandable. However, there are problems with that. First of all, the mountains. Oracle told me that there were mountains in the past, but they were lower before the cataclysm and didn't go all the way to the sea. Is that what you remember as well?" I asked, getting more nods.

"Great, well, let's look into that. This Tower, supposedly a horrifically expensive thing to construct, was placed here for a reason. In a time when the first Prax had been raining death and destruction on the enemies of the Empire for nearly fifty years already…"

There was an awkward pause as they considered that.

"Add in that none of you knew about the city of Pelath's View. That's too damn close for it to be a coincidence, yet far enough away that you could get some warning if it decided to attack. They were in contact with the Empire, or at least Malthus—who holds a similar position to you, Seneschal—was in contact." I took a long drink while I was thinking before nodding to myself.

"Malthus seems to be alone and essentially bored off his tits. He was happy for me to make contact and claims that the Empire once stole heavily magical artifacts from him. He wants them back…yet is content to allow us to loot the city, so somewhere, he's bullshitting us.

"He also agreed to allow us access to the manawell that's located under the city. It appears, from what I could tell, to act much like your own manawells do, but it's old, incredibly old, and it's been absorbing mana for millennia. It apparently draws its power from far beneath the surface, and he doesn't believe we could use enough to make a dent in a century, let alone a few weeks, which is all the time I intend to run the risk for," I said adamantly.

"Seneschal, you said that the collectors that we're feeding down into the ground can harvest up ores, assisting the Tower in growth and improvements…can one of them be changed into a siphon and dipped into the well?" I asked hopefully, having considered this ever since Malthus had told me about the well.

"It could, but the risk…" Seneschal said slowly.

"What risk?" I asked.

"The risk to the Tower, if Malthus is not the honorable creature he appears…"

"Then he could get access to the Tower," I finished for him, nodding my head. "He knew about the Tower, and it was wide open to magical influence while the SporeMother was in charge here. If he could have physically reached out, he already would have. Next concern."

"Could it be that he's trapped? Needs the siphon to escape?" Oracle asked slowly.

"That's a possibility, but I kinda give it a low chance. No offense, but if he wanted to be up here, I get the feeling that he would be. He tried to explain what he was a few times, and I couldn't understand it. He's something like a mixture of a Wisp, a spirit of a mage long dead, and something else.

"Claims our Gods are just 'the latest to rise' and that the city was built by a long-vanished race. From what I could see, that fits, as the city was definitely alien beyond anything I've seen. But again, I've also been here like five minutes."

"What is it you wish to do with the city, if you have claimed it?" Seneschal asked, and I shook my head.

"I haven't, as I didn't know what to do with it yet. He seemed not to give a damn either way. He wants people to watch; he likes interacting with 'good beings,' according to him. I think that might be bullshit as well, but that's all we have to go on for now. I want the place checked out; any mana we can make use of should be siphoned and magic, well, nicked."

I frowned contemplatively. "I know he's playing his own game, so I think we should be as well, but I can't help but think that whatever the real reason was for this Tower, it had something to do with that city.

"There were Vern surrounding it, breeding, a royal pair, apparently, and they were trying to reach the city. The Kobolds that held it were bargaining with them, but there was clearly something the Vern wanted. I want to know what it was…" I broke off with a jaw-cracking yawn, and when I could see again, blinking away the exhausted tears, Oracle was kneeling before me, making me grin tiredly.

"Yeah, baby, yeah…" I muttered, and she snorted, shaking her head.

"Like you've got the energy!" She shook her head. "Come on, let's get you to bed." She pulled me to my feet, and I groaned a little as my back clicked, before waving to the other Wisps.

"Seneschal, Heph, thank you, guys. Have a think about what I've said, and I'll go sleep. I'd appreciate it if you would come up with some plans and keep things going," I said over my shoulder as Oracle led me from the room and across the floor to my quarters.

Once we were inside, with a legionnaire standing guard a little way down the hall, I called out into the seemingly empty room before me.

"Right, you perverts, get out unless you want a moustache ride!" Tang straightened up, his stealth falling away, and he headed past me towards the door, patting me on the shoulder as he passed.

"I'd have left once I knew that you were settled; nobody wants to see *that*, after all." He grinned, and I turned to where Bane still crouched in the bathroom next door, having gone ahead of us and slipped inside.

"You too, Bane!" I called, and he slunk out.

"You're getting better," he congratulated me.

"Or you're getting sloppy," I replied, grinning. Only Oracle and I knew that I'd used the strings of the Oaths they'd sworn to me to see where they were.

"I'll report to Flux to make arrangements for an expanded guard from now on, and one of us will be outside at all times." He ignored my jibe, heading out of the room. "Try not to be too much of a freak though, Jax. It's hard keeping quiet about things like what we caught you doing on the ship the other day." He winked, then closed the door before I could respond.

"That asshole!" I grunted, shaking my head and knowing he'd just started the rumor mill up. When they found there was nothing, it was inevitable that someone would create something.

Then I remembered squatting over an ice-cold fountain and helicoptering my cock at Oracle, who was perched, naked, on the wall at a forty-five-degree angle.

"Okay, so *maybe* that had looked a bit weird, but still..." I mumbled, as Oracle led me through to our bedroom and started to strip me off. Her ability to become semi-incorporeal made it much easier for her to get at the awkward latches and clasps, and in minutes, I was stepping gratefully from the last section of armor and plodding into the bathroom.

The shower that Seneschal had put in for me was heavenly, and it was made even more so, when, after a few minutes of soaking in the hot, almost painfully strong flow of the water, Oracle's hot hands slipped around me from behind and reached down.

I let out a little moan, turning around to take her into my arms. Kissing her long and deep, my hands reached out to her as well. She felt amazing, firm muscles, bouncy, and hard buds of flesh, all covered in skin that was smooth as silk. As she slipped down, the heat of her mouth on me, my groan seemed to release all my pent-up needs.

From the shower, we moved to the bed and played for a short while, wet and exhausted as I was, before she slipped from the bed and left me to dream.

Hours later, when I reawakened, it was to her, working me again. This time, I was fully awake in seconds, spending my time returning the favor and more before we collapsed back into a spent pile on the tumbled bedding.

CHAPTER THIRTY

When I finally woke up again, and my brain was rebooted and ready, I dressed quickly, before making my way out of the set of rooms. I was pleased at finding a familiar legionnaire on duty outside as I exited.

"Holt, right?" I asked.

"Yessir!" he replied, straightening.

"Good to see you, mate," I said cheerfully, clapping him on the shoulder, then patting my bag on my hip. "I'm off to sort some details. Make sure things are going well, then I need to find Thorn. Gotta get my damn armor fixed...*again.* Any idea where I'd find her?" I was fairly sure I could find her through the bond, or by asking Seneschal, but it was worth the conversation.

"She's working on the new forge; it's on the ground level for now, north section. Oh, and errr, my lord?" He paused, and I nodded for him to go on. "That priest, Martin, came looking for you; said he wanted to discuss the worship of the Lady...."

"Right." I frowned. I didn't remember a priest, not beyond Denny being made one to take the heliomage class. Then I vaguely remembered Oren complaining about some mad bastard of a priest, and I shrugged. "What about him?"

"Well, he showed up a few times while you and the Lady Wisp were.... uh...resting..." he stammered, blushing furiously. "Then the last time he came, the Lady Wisp was just leaving, and he told her he has to instruct you on how to worship the Lady."

"Oh, fucking does he?" I growled, frowning deeper.

"And the Lady Wisp told him that you didn't need any instructing on how to worship a lady, beyond occasionally letting her get more sleep."

"Wow," I muttered, seeing Holt go even redder and trying to keep my grin to myself, considering that I damn well knew Oracle didn't actually sleep.

"Yeah...well, he didn't know how to respond to that, and the Lady Wisp said that she'd take it up with Jenae personally if the Goddess wanted to have you give her a good worshipping. Then she told me to make sure you weren't disturbed and flew off."

"And the priest?" I asked, trying not to grin.

"He...ah, well, he left, too. Looked a mix of angry and worried, to be honest. I just left him to it, but I figured you should probably know."

"Thanks, man. Yeah, that's gonna be a weird conversation, I think." I grinned as I started to walk away.

"Well, good luck with it, Lord," he called after me, and I waved to him over my shoulder.

I strolled out of the reserved quarters section, then headed down a few floors, heading in the general direction I remembered the kitchens had been set up, with the intention of a bit of breakfast, preferably before something happened to turn my day to shit.

"Morning, Oracle!" I sent to her, and immediately, I got a sense of a smile and a mental kiss.

"Morning, Jax! Are you ready to start the day?

"Well, I'd kill for another few hours of sleep, to be honest, but that's just me being a lazy bastard," I admitted. *"What's this about a priest?"*

"Oh, that prick," Oracle responded darkly, and I felt a hint of irritation and exasperation flow along the bond.

"Basically, he's a worshipper of Jenae, which is fine, but he's also a bit of a, well, a bit of a weirdo. All he's done since appointing himself a priest of Jenae is poke his nose into places he shouldn't, because 'the Lady is interested in what's hidden,' and he's tried to tell people how to lead their lives. He does push the worship of Jenae, and I think that's the only reason She hasn't hit him with a Fireball Herself yet, but he's going to cause some problems sooner or later."

"Yeah, fuck that. Let's nail his knees to his ears as soon as possible," I said. *"The last thing we need is some asshole causing problems. I'll get some breakfast, then I'll go speak to the Gods."* I sighed and shook my head as I started to jog rather than walk, snorting as I realized that it took one damn minute before there was a problem I needed to step in with.

I picked up the speed, fairly flying down the stairwells, grinning as a plan occurred to me. All I needed to do was make sure that there was a balcony next to the kitchens, and I could literally fly from my rooms down, no running through corridors or anything.

"Good morning, Lord Jax!" a bellow rang in my ear, and I almost fell in panic, a move that would have sent me falling down the stairs for at least fifty of the damn things.

I staggered, then slipped, and a firm hand reached out and grabbed me, yanking me upright and keeping me there almost effortlessly until I had my balance again.

I looked over at last, ready to blast whoever that had been, and felt my balls shrivel in fear.

"Restun," I greeted, and my voice definitely didn't go into an unmanly squeak, no matter what anyone said later.

"Lord Jax," he said smoothly. "Where are you off to in such a hurry?" I gaped like a landed fish before coughing and mentally shaking myself.

"I'm off to get breakfast, Restun. I've got a busy day ahead, after all," I said firmly.

"Excellent. Good job I caught you, then, as you'll not want to waste the effort the cooks put in, will you!" He grinned evilly.

"Uh…no?" I replied weakly. "I *do* have a lot to get done today, Restun…and reports to get, and, uh…."

"And you asked me to take over your training and swore to make yourself both available and responsive to my efforts," Restun said firmly. "Now, as you'd not want to break your word, which would be a terrible example for a leader, especially one who desperately needs this help, we'll start with a gentle warm up: a run!"

With that, he took off, picking up speed and sprinting across the central corridor of the floor we'd just entered. I raced after him, only to slow in surprise when he slowed on the far side, resuming jogging as we entered the next stairwell.

"What's the plan?" I asked him, confused. "I thought we were running?"

"And we will, Jax, but while a jog is acceptable downstairs, to run is a foolish risk, one we don't need to take. Instead, we shall sprint across each floor to the next stairwell and jog to recover as we go down."

"Okay…" I told myself I could do that.

"Then, once we reach the ground floor, you can join the rest of your personal squad in their training session before I release you to Flux for work with your personal weapon, followed by an hour of training with Augustus on your sword technique."

"That's going to be a problem," I cut in before he could add anything else. "Seriously, Restun, I know this is important, I do, but I have shit I need to do, and…"

"You sent for me, Jax?" Cai interrupted, hurrying over as we crossed the floor.

"Perfect timing, Cai," Restun said, smiling widely. "Jax was just saying that he needs to get up to date on various details and make some decisions, but he has limited time to do it. In that light, I asked for you to be brought to the training grounds to give Jax your reports while he works."

"Oh no," I whispered, seeing Cai's face light up as he clutched at his little book.

"Oh, that's wonderful! Thank you, Restun. That's a fantastic idea, Jax; that way I can go through all the details we never have time to discuss."

I broke the rules straight away. Sod jogging on the stairs. I sprinted, intending to outdistance Cai and that evil, sneaky bastard Restun.

By the time we made it to the ground floor, and I staggered out on weak legs, I had long since lost Cai, his stamina thankfully too low to keep up for long. But where I was wheezing like a bellows, Restun looked to be slightly pink, as though refreshed by a brisk stroll.

The bastard.

I let him lead me down the final wide flight of stairs and across the main floor to the huge stone slab doors, running across a surface that had been cracked and broken stone, covered with the detritus of ages, mold and mildew coating everything that wasn't taken over by fungus, shit, and death.

That same floor had been transformed into something clear and light, the beautiful, white-veined marble floor crossed by several huge shafts of sunlight streaming in through windows high on the walls, making me smile up at them. This entire floor had been in ruin, a place that gave me a subconscious automatic fear of being crushed whenever I crossed it, due to the tremendous weight of stone over my head and the general terrible state of the place.

Now, it was beautiful, supported by graceful arched columns and inconceivably thick outer walls. The entire space made me feel better just by walking in it.

Restun allowed me my few minutes of silence to catch my breath before we left the Great Tower and jogged down the stairs onto the grass outside.

"Wow," I murmured in surprise, looking around. "What happened here?"

When I'd been down here before, the courtyard had been a mainly grassy area, with a few hardy trees that had forced their way up through the cobblestones.

Now, the grass that had been waist high in some places was cut to a short fuzz, barely two inches, and legionnaires were running in the distance with rotating blades on wheels, making sure the massive area–several miles in all, considering the width of the Tower and the fact that the courtyard ringed it–was maintained.

Then there were the walls. I'd seen them when they'd lifted into solidity again, born from the massive bounty of mana crystals we'd looted and used to repair the Tower. But still, I'd been kind of overwhelmed at the time. The walls rose, clear and perfect, around the courtyard, and the massive battleship hulked just inside, perched on the freshly cleared section the golems had arranged for the ships to land.

I took in all of this in one fell swoop, glancing around as we started to cross the grass, before I noted the dozens, if not hundreds, of people milling about and carrying things in and out of the Tower.

We'd passed them on our way down, but in all honesty, I'd been concentrating on not coughing a lung out, which meant they had not registered fully.

"To the left, Jax," Restun directed, and I followed his instruction, seeing a group of at least a hundred people exercising. I couldn't help but smile as I recognized many of them.

"Those are the original citizens that make up the majority, aren't they?" I asked.

He nodded, picking up the pace and leading me in a steady jog to join them.

He gestured to a section that was left conspicuously empty, and I sighed, moving into place as he took his position on an impromptu stage.

"Good afternoon, everyone!" he called.

I winced, abruptly aware that I'd slept the morning away through a combination of battle exhaustion, which was totally acceptable, and staying up late screwing Oracle's brains out...which wasn't so much.

"Now that we're all here, we can begin. Flux and I have agreed to split the daily exercise between us and will be further dividing you into individual groupings after the general start is done!" he explained, standing with his hands clasped behind his back.

"There will be three groups: Improve, Maintain, and Excel. Improve will be for those who are starting out. We will train you to grow your confidence with weapons and with your body, building your Strength and other physical characteristics to make you into healthy, happy people who can stand tall in any situation! Your focus will be mainly fitness, with basic weapons handling."

I discreetly scanned the crowd, seeing a lot of the general people looking pleased with this and nodding to each other.

"The second group is for those of you who are already at the first level: for my legionnaires and for any soldiers amongst you. You will be training to maintain your edge, exercising to make sure that you continue to reach the legion standards, and are kept fighting fit. You will have a focus primarily on weapons skills, with a lesser focus on fitness, simply maintaining."

I looked again, noting with surprise that the original group of a hundred or so was rapidly swelling, with a ring of legionnaires joining in, and many of the refugees from the city wandering over, asking what was happening, and generally following along.

"The final group, the group that will be right here at the front," he said, gesturing as the rest of my squad was led through by a grinning Augustus, as well as a dozen or so additional legionnaires, and surprisingly, Mal, Soween, and Nigret.

"This group will be training to excel. Their training will only truly start when the rest of you are broken and have given up. Watch them, see the way they push, striving higher and harder, and you will be inspired!" His voice carried over the murmuring crowds, and he glared down at us, as though daring us to do anything less than he had said. "Their focus will be to push their bodies past the limit of mortality. They will become physically perfect, then they will spend another two hours a day in fighting training!"

I gritted my teeth, closing my eyes before reopening them to the awed looks that the people who were being moved around were giving us.

At some point during his speech, legionnaires had started filtering through the crowd, and the centurions started to bellow, guiding people into set areas, depending on which grouping they fell into, and starting their exercises.

Restun stepped off the edge of the platform and grinned at our small elite group, then clapped his hands together, looking us all over.

"Well, now, I think the warm-up is done, don't you?" he asked us all, before bellowing out orders and leading by example.

"A hundred pushups!" he ordered, and Augustus dropped to the ground beside me, making me flinch, until I realized that everyone else was already on their first, and I'd not yet started.

I dropped down, starting to pump along with them, before redoubling my efforts when Restun called out a new promise.

"Each day, to make sure you all understand just how much effort you need to put in, a single person will be picked from each group," he shouted, climbing back up to where everyone could see him. "That person will be the tail, and the tail gets beaten! Nobody wants to be the tail! In Improve, they get a full extra lap of the outer walls with a legionnaire to explain what they did wrong all the way around!"

That got worried looks from most of that group, but they all accepted that it was fine, and they could live with that. After all, they could stop at any point, if they decided this wasn't for them.

"In group two, Maintain, they get an hour's additional sword practice…with Primus Augustus!" he bellowed, and I saw looks of true concern flashing across the faces of numerous legionnaires.

"Finally in group three, Excel, you get a simple run, with exercises to improve your strength. With me. To the top of the Tower, followed by a series of pushups, sit-ups, and, a new exercise recently taught to me, proving that we can all learn, no matter our age, burpees! Twenty of each—on each floor—all the way to the top!"

I paused, gaping up at Restun in disbelief, then started frantically pounding the ground, desperate to make damn sure I wasn't last.

Cai joined us soon, smiling amiably as he started to explain the issues he'd found and his recommended solutions, ranging from sewage to a girl who'd been found stowed away on the ships. Eight years old and unable to speak, it had been impossible, so far at least, to make sense of where and how she'd ended up aboard.

She'd seemingly been caught stealing from the stores, and someone had asked why she wasn't simply going for her meals like everyone else. When she'd been unable to respond, she'd been passed to the nearest person of authority, then upwards gradually as people discussed her, until she'd reached Cai.

Most of the decisions were easy, but the girl, not so much. I worried that she'd been dragged along accidentally, and that we'd basically kidnapped her from her family.

Between panting for breath and trying to decide if Restun was actually a secret assassin trying to kill me through sheer fucking overwork, or just the evilest being in all of creation, I summoned Oracle and sent her to change into full size and read the little girl's mind.

A few minutes passed, then Oracle returned, told me tersely to keep going, took Augustus and two others, and set off in the direction of the ships.

Nearly an hour later, as I practiced a spin kick with Flux's aid, and much laughter from the others as I kept missing, Oracle returned. She now led a dozen legionnaires, all surrounding a small group of three people, two men and a woman. The little girl was clearly afraid, shrinking back at the sight of them, but Oracle held her hand firmly and brought the group to me.

"I won't share the details of what these people have been doing, but they are stowaways as well. They haven't taken the Oath, and have killed at least one of our citizens who caught them stealing from a storeroom. They also...hurt...the girl. This is why she doesn't speak. She was brought aboard by them and has no memory of a family, just being...used...by these creatures. They were intending on sneaking in and setting up in the Tower, stealing, and pimping out those they could force into that life."

I had stopped to listen to Oracle, but by the end, the mix of her absolute fury and my own had almost robbed me of the ability to speak.

I took my leave of Flux and started walking, jerking my head to the legionnaires to bring the group along.

I ordered Restun off the raised platform and took the center, speaking to everyone within hearing distance, my voice a growl as I repeated Oracle's statement.

"No, we ain't!" argued one of the men, a flat-faced little bastard who spat on the grass and sneered at me. "We was promised a new life. We swore an' everythin'! Ain't done nuffin' wrong, so yer can't do nuffin', not unless it's all a lie, eh? All this swill about you bein' better than the rest of the nobles?"

I stared blankly down at him and gestured for him to be brought up to stand alongside me as I pulled out my new helm and took a deep breath.

"I'll give you one chance; one!" I called out so that all could hear it. "You didn't swear, but you now have the chance to tell me everything. Admit to your crimes, crimes this child experienced, witnessed, and *suffered.* You will serve with your life to replace the citizen's life you took. All three of you will. If not, if you force me to make you prove it, then you all get to climb the Tower with me, and we get to see just how far I can throw you off it."

"She's mute! Can't talk, so can't say nuffin!" the man snarled triumphantly.

I glanced from him to his cowering friends. "Does he speak for all of you? Do you want to admit to the crimes now, or will you stick with him?" After a minute, when it was clear they wouldn't respond, I turned back to the crowd and spoke again, loudly enough for all to hear.

"You all know who I am by now. Some of you have met the Wisps, many of you are familiar with them, but for those who don't know, let's make this clear. Oracle is my companion, my lover, and the Lady of the Tower. Seneschal *is* the Tower, and he sees all that happens within it.

"Hephaestus is the heart of all the golems. What they see, he sees. There is a final Wisp that some of you may meet, Tenandra, and she is the *Interesting*

Endeavor; where Seneschal is the Tower, she is the ship. Any and all Wisps have the ability to read your memories and mind. They can teach you magic, should you deserve that gift, but they can also see memories of your past and observe what has been done.

"This little girl was kidnapped, smuggled aboard a ship, and made to steal by these fucktards. Oracle was forced to see what they did to her when she searched the child's mind for her home and family. She witnessed them murdering a citizen, and you have all witnessed me offering them the chance to explain themselves and their crimes."

I turned to the three grimy people, who now looked even more angry and scared. One of them spoke up, this time, the woman.

"Look, we'll go, right? We didn't do nuffin, but you don't want us here, so we'll just go back to the city, okay?" she bargained, clearly terrified.

"The last detail you should all know…" Oracle called out in a clear, firm voice. "Is that one of Lord Jax's classes is that of *Imperial Justicar*. He can sense the truth of crimes brought before him and will dispense justice on behalf of the Empire."

With that, I pulled my helm on, and activated its special ability, Inquisition.

"Since boarding my ships, have you broken my laws, harmed my citizens, or stolen from me?" I asked, aiming my ability at all three of them.

"No!" snapped the first, while the other two glared and refused to answer. Seconds passed, and I noted the way they started to sweat, then tremble.

The light around them seemed to warp, drawing in as pressure built, and everyone watched in silence.

After a minute, the third of them, the man who'd refused to speak, cried out, falling to his knees, grabbing at his head, and pulling at his hair. "Make it stop!" He cried, shaking. "Yes! Okay, I admit it! We took some food, then Din killed the guy what came lookin'!" he shouted.

I felt the truth of his words as the Inquisition ability verified them and left him to sag in relief.

The first man, Din, broke next, shaking his head and tearing at his skin frantically, begging me to stop before admitting it was true, that they'd killed a man, amongst other things, and they'd hurt the girl.

The woman lasted another two minutes before shrieking and falling to the ground, babbling. It took several moments before she made sense, but when she did, it was a litany of the crimes she'd committed, one that I cut off with a gesture only a handful of words in, as disgusted as I was.

Silence reigned as I glared down at them, pulling my helm off and stowing it away before turning back to the crowd and speaking again.

"They have admitted their crimes and will be taken to the top of the Tower and dealt with. However, this raises a point. I will not be a noble who rules by whim. I will not decide alone who lives and dies, simply because I have that power.

"The law applies to us all equally, and as such, I will have a justicar and inquisitor both on my council and to turn to personally, should you feel the need. Speak to Cai if you wish to apply for the position," I commanded before turning back to the three who were being held by the legionnaires.

"Take them to the upper floors of the Tower. I won't have them defile the Hall of the Eternal, but just below the top, there's a long, narrow balcony. Take them there and wait for me," I ordered, turning back to the people.

"Is this everyone?" I asked aloud, getting a sense of most sent through the bond with Oracle, and I knew suddenly that those who were out on the ships or ranging and hunting for food were all already sworn.

"It seems this is most of us, standing here before the Great Tower. I'm sorry that this morning had to be defiled by these scumbags, but as it has happened, we will learn from it. Several people who arrived on the ships did not swear the Oath. Some of you who joined us from the Village of Dannick haven't had the chance to swear yet, and I've been made aware that several of our children have reached the age of sixteen, the age I have set as the minimum age to swear to the Empire and directly to me. We will take the Oath first, then we all know who has sworn and that you are all safe from the others, just in case…"

I felt Oracle acting as a conduit, reaching out and tapping into the Great Tower's mana channels to filter out a seemingly tiny speck of power to aid me in this, even as the first voice rose in swearing the Oath. Predictably, it was Oren's thick baritone that rang out the clearest.

"I swear to obey Lord Jax an' those he places over me; I will serve to tha best o' ma ability, speak no lie to him when tha truth be commanded, an' treat all other citizens as family.

"I will work fer the greater good, being a shield to those who need it, a sword for those who deserve it, an' a warden to tha night.

"I will stand with ma family, helping one another to reach th' light, until tha hour o' ma death or ma Lord releases me from my Oath.

"Lastly, I will no' be a dick!"

I felt the mana pulled through me, reaching out to those who'd not yet sworn, creating new bonds between them and me, as well as reinforcing the bonds that already existed, tying my people to me and helping them to feel welcome and trusted, not to mention safer after the shock of the small group in our midst.

"I, Lord Jax, do swear to protect and lead you, to be the shield that protects you and yours from the darkness, and the sword that avenges that which cannot be saved. As the Tower grows in strength, so shall you," I said, ending the Oath and giving them my promise in return. "Wisps, who did *not* swear the Oath?"

There was a long pause before Oracle, smiling and still holding the little girl's hand, stepped forward and spoke in a loud, clear voice. "All but four spoke the Oath. Of those who did not, three are honored guests and were not expected to swear," I glanced at Mal, with Soween and Josh standing next to him. All three were covered in a sheen of sweat, but they nodded to me, and I nodded back, resisting the urge to flick Mal the finger.

"And the last?" I asked loudly, disliking the theatre, but knowing it served a purpose.

"She is being brought to the Tower," Oracle said. A sudden shout echoed out, and a woman I'd not seen before was hoisted into the air by a golem servitor.

It picked its way through the clustered people easily, its multiple legs and heads guiding it without incident into the Tower to disappear.

"I will question her, and if she chooses not to swear, then she will be free to leave. If she is a spy, well, we shall see," I said clearly once again. "Next, the matter of the Gods." I figure that we might as well get that dealt with. "There are ten Greater Gods, despite what you may have been told by priests, and…"

As I spoke, a fat, greasy man pushed his way through the crowd, beaming around self-importantly. I assumed this was Martin, the priest, and I promptly dismissed him from my mind, moving on.

"Nine of those Gods have been sleeping, ever since the God of Death caused the Cataclysm. They were wounded, attacked by one of Their own, and are finally returning. They ask for your worship and devotion. I am a follower, and the Champion, of Jenae, the Lady of Fire, Exploration, and Hidden Knowledge, and the Great Tower is dedicated to Her worship, as well as that of Her Pantheon of the Flame.

The remaining Gods, for those of you that are unfamiliar, are Ashante, Goddess of Nature and Life; Cruit, God of Earth and Stability; Sint, God of Light and Order; Tamat, Goddess of Darkness, Assassination, and Larceny; Vanei, Goddess of Air and Change; Lagoush, Goddess of Water, Healing, and Alteration; Svetu, God of Invention and Creation; and finally, Tyosh, God of Time and Reflection." I took a deep breath as I finally got Them all out.

"I…" I meant to continue, when the fat little shit tried to climb up to the platform I was on, while calling out and speaking over me.

"And the Lady of the Tower, *Jenae*, is a worthy Goddess!" he cried, giving me an honest-to-God reproving shake of his head as he stated that Jenae, not Oracle, was the lady of the Tower. "The true Goddess, Jenae, Mistress of the Flame is the worthiest of all Gods for your devotion. She rules here, as She should anywhere a flame burns in our hearts and across the realm! The Lady…"

"Yes, thank you," I snapped, cutting him off with a glare, starting up again. "I am the Champion of Jenae, it is true; however, the worship of all Gods, save the God of Death, is encouraged here, and…"

"Yet the Tower is home to Jenae, and therefore the Lady should be worshipped first and foremost," the priest said, stepping in close to me and grinning moronically out at the crowd. Then the cheeky little shit actually stepped in front of me!

I reached forward, almost casually, and grabbed him by the neck of his self-sewn rough robes, then dragged him to the side and shoved him off the platform to land on the cobblestones with a squawk of protest.

"Restun," I called, and the legionnaire stepped forward and saluted sharply. "I believe this priest and I will discuss his beliefs, and the correct way, and time, to speak about them.

"Please escort him up the Tower and hold him for me on the level *below* the cathedral to all the Gods. When I have time, I will see him, and then I'll discuss it with Jenae and the others." I tried not to look like the damn power-mad lunatic that I'd probably started to portray.

I was also trying extremely hard to not kick the living shit out the goddamn priest, as I suspected that would be a very bad idea.

"As I was saying..." I called out, to the immensely shitty backdrop of the priest being led away by one of my top legionnaires, his face bloody where he'd apparently busted his nose on landing. "We respect all the Gods here, and you may choose who you worship.

"I encourage the worship of Jenae, not least because She is the head of the Pantheon, and my own mistress, but because She fits with my choices. I am interested in exploration, in finding that which was lost or hidden, and so I follow Her. Others, such as the Gnomes..." I gestured to one side, where, in an example of cosmically perfect timing, all the Gnomes were standing together, looking smart and as though they were paying attention. "...were followers of Svetu, and they may choose to follow Him again." At that declaration, Frederikk collapsed, hitting the ground face first. A few of those around him fell over as well, and I realized that the little bastards were stoned all to hell.

"Oh for..." I rubbed the bridge of my nose, sighing and dropping the attempts I was making at respectability. "Someone, get the Gnomes somewhere to sleep that off, please," I growled. "Look, we're all at war, and we need to make this place as safe and successful as possible, alright?

"The way to do that is for everyone to work together, and not to cause fucking problems, like that wanker of a priest is sure to do. All I ask is that you follow your trade. If it's a trade that we already have a lot of people doing and no need for more, then we might ask you to take up another. But, if you prove yourself, I swear I will support you. Where's the baker?" I called down to Cai, who shouted out a name, and the man waved an arm, revealing where he was.

"What did you get a few days ago?" I asked him, and he grinned so widely, the top of his head looked like it was in danger of coming off.

"An expert-level bakery skillbook!" he called out. "Thank you! Thank you so much, my lord!"

"You're welcome. Remind me later, and I'll explain what a sausage roll and a Cornish pasty is, and you'll be set for life," I replied dryly. "Now, as you can see, I have access to skillbooks. You've all seen this morning that there's martial training, and more on offer.

"Hell, those who want to be mages, talk to Arrin; he's the little guy in my personal squad, the one who's not a permanently stoned Gnome, but looks like he's dying from the exercise still." I gestured to him, and he waved weakly.

"I'm...alive," he gasped, and a round of nervous laughter lifted from those near enough to hear him.

"Seriously, we need more of everything, and that includes mages. The legionnaires will be getting magical training soon, which will include a handful of spells; then, so will those who want to help in the fighting. After those two groups are sorted, we will open it up to anyone that wants to be taught magic, for basic healing spells, at least." I offered, thinking about the sheer madness of teaching children combat spells.

"So, in conclusion, I want you all to work, basically. Those who need healing or guidance, speak to Nerin and Cai, respectively. The rest of you, help out where you can, and you'll be sorted out over the next few days." I dismissed the crowd without preamble, leaping down from the platform.

THOMAS

"Don't you fucking dare die on me, Bella!" Thomas growled, slapping Sergeant Belladonna across the cheek and shocking her into awareness again.

"Wha…" she mumbled, eyes rolling wildly.

Thomas hissed with frustration before raising his voice to the rest of the squad…the survivors of the squad, anyway.

"Move it, you worms!" he shouted, grimly working to tie the tubing off so that it wouldn't waste any of Nimon's Dark Gift.

Thomas didn't know if it would work; hell, it might kill her outright; she'd not been blessed the same way he had, after all, but it was all he had left.

Their potions were gone, long since used up. The bandages were useless, not with that jagged spear of wood rammed through her stomach. And as to magic, he didn't have any healing spells, not anymore, not since the Dark Gift had corrupted his mana channels.

None of the grunts were given any of the spells that *would* work. Fool that he was, he'd only taken the one, the single time he'd had the chance at them before he came to this realm, believing instead in bandages, his unnaturally fast healing, and his own skill to see him through. He'd chosen instead to take an additional offensive spell rather than a second healing spell.

Thomas grunted, nearly stabbing himself with the impromptu needle he'd made as he stumbled over the uneven ground. Coran's quick grab was all that had straightened him out in time.

"Thanks, man," Thomas mumbled, wiping his mouth and calling out to the bedraggled team. "And slow!" he ordered, the running teams of stretcher bearers slowing from a full-on run to a steady jog instead, then to a measured walk.

"We don't have time for this!" Felis snapped, falling back and glaring at Thomas. "We must make a report to the Church!"

"I only need a minute to make the connection, then we can start jogging again," Thomas assured him as he lined up the thin, hollow vampire's tooth attached to the tubing with the vein on the back of Belladonna's hand.

"Seve, when I get it in, I need you to bind it, make sure there's no kinks in the tube, or the blood won't flow," Thomas repeated for perhaps the fifth time.

Seve glared at him, just as tired, dirty, and hungry as Thomas was. "I'm not a fucking idiot, Thomas. You told me already; now either do it or admit we've carried her this long for nothing!" Seve snarled.

Thomas growled at him, baring his teeth, even as Felis interrupted.

"I'm in command here. Thomas, we're moving out!" Felis snapped.

Thomas bared his teeth at him instead, in a parody of a smile. "Of course you are, Felis, and we'll be along soon; now fuck off, before I tear your head off and shit down your neck."

Felis backed up, having seen the Dark Berserker's temper once before. "Fine; you have until I reach the front of the line." Felis beat a hasty retreat.

"That's going to come back to bite you, boy," Seve muttered, eyeing the retreating form of the single functioning sergeant they had left.

"Yeah, well, they can all go fuck themselves," Thomas took a deep breath and jammed the hollow tooth into his own vein in the crook of his arm. The blood flowed immediately.

Something about the properties of the vampiric tooth made sure that the blood flow was uninterrupted. Thomas smiled grimly, shaking a few drops out of the end of the line, making sure there were no air bubbles. That was all he needed, after all, to send a damn embolism into her brain or heart.

He nodded to Seve and jabbed the tip of the other end into Belladonna's hand, letting out a sigh of relief as he massaged the vein, noting that the skin didn't bulge or distort; the flow seemed to be contained.

Seve moved quickly, binding the tooth into place and checking again to ensure that the line was free of obstructions as it flowed. Thomas called out to the others that it had worked, for now.

"Will she live?" croaked the voice from the stretcher to Thomas's right, and he looked over, forcing himself to make eye contact with the sheer mess that was Turk.

The huge orc lay awkwardly on the stretcher, maimed. His bandages leaked constantly, the blue blood of his race no longer smelling of oil and eggs combined. Now he smelled of sickness, of infection and disease, and despite the greyness of the orc's skin, sweating, and fever, still, he only asked about Belladonna.

They'd offered him one of the only health potions they could find, and he'd refused it, insisting it be given to her instead. Thomas was convinced that Turk was only alive now through sheer fury and a determination to see Belladonna safe.

Thomas glanced at the blanket that covered Turk's remaining leg, or the mangled mess that had once been a leg, before he could stop himself.

Whatever that spell had been, it'd made a hell of a mess of the group. Only their armor and blind luck had kept them alive, and Shen Thingals-Bane had died less than an hour later.

The compression had forced them all together, and only Turk's prodigious strength had allowed him the seconds of forcing his way up Shen's body that had saved him.

Torin had been folded and mutilated, compressed into a ball half the size of a family suitcase, while before, he'd been over six feet tall and the kind of man they had in mind when they coined the phrase, "Olympian," and Shen…

Thomas blinked away tears and glared ahead as he responded to Turk.

"I don't know, mate, but we've done all we can; it's up to her now," he said, trying to keep the rough edge from his voice.

There were long minutes of silence before Turk spoke again. He'd laid back on his stretcher, clearly thinking hard. When he spoke, his voice was rough.

"I didn't mean to kill him, you know?" he said in a low, harsh voice. "Shen was my friend for thirty years. The first to see just another Dark Legionnaire, instead of a filthy orc."

"I know, man; save your strength," Thomas mumbled, and others nearby added their comments in consolation and understanding as well.

There'd been three hundred of them that set out, but now there were nine. Sixteen had died since the ambush that had claimed two hundred and fifty of them, and the handful who'd fallen and been trampled to death in the march? Well, they'd given their lives for the Dark Legionnaires to make all speed. They'd died, believing that the Legion would win again tomorrow.

Instead, they'd been slaughtered.

Thomas had seen what pride and determination, belief in the Dark Legion, got you, when so many of those in higher authority were fucking idiots. He'd have killed the fool who ordered the attack himself if someone else hadn't already done it.

A single officer had survived out of twenty-two, and when he'd denied knowing any magic, only to be caught using the last of his pitifully weak healing spells on his own foot, having twisted his ankle? Well, Gor had slammed his mace down into the man's skull, killing him with a single blow, right before the geas kicked in and killed Gor.

It was a fucking joke.

Thomas opened his mouth, planning to try to reassure Turk. As he glanced over again, he saw Turk pull free the blanket that concealed his body.

The flesh was mangled, the armor bent and twisted, unable to be removed, and the big orc's guts had been pierced, judging from the smell and the literal shit that oozed out of the edges of his cuisses.

Turk glared over at Thomas before calling out in a loud voice to Felis.

The man flinched, then picked up the pace, moving deliberately ahead so that he could claim he'd not heard later.

"Coward," Turk growled, then coughed, a wet, tearing sound, and let out a little whimper that everyone would later deny to their dying day the big orc could ever have made. "I claim the role of Sergeant, declaring Belladonna to be incapable of carrying out her duty," Turk snarled over his obvious pain, and the rest of the squad, including Thomas, spoke the ritual words.

"I declare Belladonna to be incapable and accept Turk as Sergeant," they thundered as one.

"Now, I name Thomas to Sergeant of the squad, declaring myself to be incapable," he wheezed out, and Thomas stumbled, shocked.

"No, man, that's you. You take over from Belladonna," Coran said quickly, the grey color of his skin indicating he knew what was coming next.

"Hear me and obey!" Turk snarled, and the others around Thomas responded to the ritual as it'd been drummed into them.

"I hear and obey," they all chorused.

"Turk," Thomas said haltingly, before Turk leaned his head back, his breath coming out in a whistling gasp at the pain that motion caused.

"Set me free, lad. Only a higher rank can dispatch a lower without repercussions, you know this," Turk whispered, looking up into Thomas' eyes.

Thomas could see tears there, although Turk would never allow them to be shed. Tears of pride and of shame, tears over his own actions, his instinctive response in trying to save his own life, and those of pain and fear.

"Turk," Thomas whispered as they all slowed, and the bearers set the stretchers down, gathering around. "I...I..."

"You'll do it…Thomas…" Turk grunted, biting his cheek and stifling a moan before going on. "You'll save her, do you hear me?" He reached out his right hand, shaking and barely able to grasp Thomas'. "You save her, boy, or I swear I'll fucking haunt you 'til the day you die!"

"I will," Thomas promised grimly, tears of his own rolling unashamedly down his cheeks as his friend nodded, relieved and accepting his word.

"Thank you, boy, now…make it quick…let me die a warrior…it's the only way you'll make it in time, if you're not carrying me as well."

"Turk…" Thomas started again, and the orc glared at him, the fire that Thomas had grown to know shining through one last time.

"Don't let me down, boy…let me do this one last service for her," Turk half ordered, half begged.

"Turk…" Thomas said again, before swallowing the lump in his throat as he drew his dagger free.

It had a long blade for a dagger, chisel-tipped and designed for fighting men in armor. As Turk leaned his head back, exposing his throat, Thomas squeezed his friend's hand one last time, ramming the blade up under the orc's chin and into his brain with the other hand.

The orc twitched, then the last breath left his body, and they all felt his passing. Thomas furiously shoved aside the experience notification for killing his friend.

They remained there for long moments in silence before a groan from Belladonna roused them. She was far gone again, deep in a delirium-filled dream, and Thomas left his blade in Turk's body, taking the orc's blade instead and ramming it home in his sheath.

"I'll get him for you, Turk. Whoever that fucker was, I'll gut him with your blade," Thomas vowed.

He stood, glancing around, and called out the orders.

"Gather her up; break's over," he said simply. "We've got days ahead of us, and he gave his life to give Belladonna that chance. The first of you that even thinks to waste his sacrifice dies by my fucking hand," Thomas snarled, starting them off, jogging steadily as he resettled the tubing, glad that he'd not managed to tear it free yet.

The color was returning to Belladonna's face, he noted grimly as they picked up speed. He could only hope that his regeneration didn't give out before her bleeding did.

CHAPTER THIRTY-ONE

"**V**ery inspiring," Cai said flatly as Oren grinned maniacally at him.

"Oh, bless yer, tha wee kitty be a wee bit stressed!" he cackled.

I grinned. "You get to sort out all those who are interested in serving in the fleet, organize the ships, get the goods and so on that we nicked stowed away in the Tower, and even get to send someone on a nice trip to the sea. We need a fuck ton of sand, apparently, and that won't be you, now that I've had time to think about it. No fucking chance are you slacking off and leaving Barrett to sort this out!" I told the Dwarf, leveling one finger at Oren as Barrett stepped up, grinning.

"Actually boss, I came to thank you for letting me take a step back from training the troops, especially after seeing the legion lead it. I know you wanted me helping to arrange people, but any chance I could go back to the fleet instead?"

"Fine, go on, then; make sure you tell Romanus and Flux, though. And thank you, Barrett. I know I asked a lot of you here," I said, having seen that coming already before turning to the last five people that were waiting calmly for my attention.

"Mal, Soween, and Josh, you're with Oracle and me; we're heading up to get you sorted out, and we can talk on the way. Augustus, what's up?" I asked frankly, already starting to approach the Tower.

"I'm looking for my role in all of this, Jax," Augustus said simply. "Am I to continue as a legionnaire, or am I to do something else?"

"Yes," I said, grinning. "Yes, you're a legionnaire and yes, you're going to be doing something else. First and foremost, I need two things: someone to go to Narkolt and meet the Legion there. Try and bring them to my side. That's going to be someone they know, and I've no fucking time, so it's either you or Romanus.

"Secondly, your role is to work with my Legion, or *Legions,* as it will become. You're to integrate the normal people who want to be soldiers into the Legion structure. The Empire of old had the Legion on one side and the nobility on the other, supposedly as a balancing force for each other. But the nobles grew and grew, until they ruled everything under the Emperor. To hell with that," I snapped, walking up the outer steps of the Tower and entering the blessedly cooler areas inside.

"The new Empire will incorporate the noble houses still. At least, those who surrender and know their place, but everyone is to support the Legion, from farmers to craftsmen. For the short term, their only goal is to support the Legion so that the Legion can bring order to the land. No more of this 'only a legionnaire' bullshit."

"I'll not complain at that! So, am I staying or…?"

I grinned. "I trust you, Augustus, or I wouldn't have made you my heir. Take a ship, take a dozen legionnaires, and go to Narkolt. Take that asshat, Hannimish, with you, and any of the researchers who want to go. Return them to their city and see what kind of a deal you can strike with the Lord of Narkolt. Bring back any support you can, and here…" I reached into my bag and brought up the menu, seeking the gold and platinum I had to hand, I took half of it and transferred it over to him, making him grunt in amazement as it just kept going.

"Take the gold and buy any skillbooks, spellbooks, memory crystals, food, and crafting supplies that you can. The priorities are, in this order: recruit the Legion, achieve peace with Narkolt, bring back refugees and supplies."

"When shall I go?"

"Go as soon as your ship is ready, and you've either convinced Hellenica to leave her kids at home and go with you, or to stay here herself with them. I'll need the stronger ones to scout the area, after all, but until the ship returns with word on the Dark Legionnaires, there's not much we can do."

He saluted then peeled off and jogged over to Romanus.

Mal stepped up to my side and glared at me. "So, what was all that shit about?"

"Which bit?" I countered tiredly.

"Narkolt, the priest, the little show trial, you pick," he said, his mouth set in a grim line.

"The trial wasn't a show trial."

"You can make anyone say anythin' with magic, son. Seen it done before. Woman convinced Jay he was a chicken," Mal said firmly.

"That's because Jay has a brain the size of a chicken's," I replied dryly. "They really did all that I said, though. Two minutes..." I grabbed the arm of a passing legionnaire. "Find whoever is in charge of the Speculatores and send them to me," I ordered, and he clapped his fist to his chest in salute, sprinting off.

"The what?" Mal asked, and I smiled.

"The special scouting branch of the Legion. They deal with all the general sneaky shit, and they used to deal with nobles who got out of hand. I don't doubt they still could, or in this case, can, act as enforcers of the law. Anyway, next question; what was it...?"

"The priest," Mal muttered.

"Yeah, no idea there. Comes across as a dickhead. I'll have a word with him, then if need be, with Jenae. If I have to slap him down hard, I will."

"Saw the way he helped himself to the crowd when you were talkin'. Might be a better idea to make it a permanent solution..." Mal warned casually.

"That's damn tempting; he's a rude little fucker," I agreed.

Mal regarded me seriously. "He damn well is, and if there's somethin' I can't abide, it's a man with no manners...what?" he asked, noticing the way I was looking at him incredulously.

"Never mind," I said after several heartbeats. "And Narkolt, what do you mean about that?"

"You really sendin' a ship there?" he asked, and I nodded. "You know that's my next stop..."

"I do, and I know both that it'll cost me a fortune and that I need to be able to get the others back as well. Can't do that very well if you bugger off from there to head somewhere else or decide you like the look of the mountains and change your mind halfway..."

"Are you sayin' you don't trust me, boy? Because that's a mite hurtful, especially after all I did for ya," Mal said in a low voice.

"Like getting me to fight in the arena so you could pocket a ton of gold?"

"You got half!" he snapped.

"I got half of the gold from the bets I won. I got nothing from the arena tickets or the entrance fees, and I seem to remember something about manastones..."

"That's not important. Look, we split the money; we were partners, fair and square...besides, let's look to the future, not the past. Can't change it, after all." Mal smiled widely.

"Go on," I said, shaking my head in disbelief.

"Anyway, let's say we come to an agreement, sort of a deal between us, as equals..." He peered around at our surroundings and the people that hurried about, doing their jobs.

"Go on..." I said again slowly, ignoring for a moment the fact that I was basically the Emperor-to-be, and he was a smuggler.

"Well, we could possibly make a deal; more of a long-term thing, you know, in exchange for a position–outside the standard chain of command, mind you—I won't be taking orders..." he amended quickly, looking at me and checking to see how I was taking this.

"Uh huh," I said noncommittally.

"So, we...I...was thinkin', you're going to have some jobs that you don't want to entrust to your legionnaires, things that are delicate, like explorin', or travelin' to other lands. Maybe it's takin' a spy somewhere interestin'-like. Those kinda jobs, that's what you'd need me an' mine for."

"So, you want to travel and explore the realm, but you want me to pay you for it, basically?" I asked, and he scowled irritably.

"Hey, if you ain't interested, all you have to do is say so!" he snapped, straightening and looking as though he was going to storm off.

"No, I'm interested, but I know you now, Mal, and you're a sneaky bastard. If I shake hands with you, I need to check to make sure I've got all my rings afterwards, not to mention my damn fingers." I fixed him with a glare in return, one that was entirely ruined for both of us when Soween laughed.

"What the hell?" Mal snapped. "This look funny to you?"

"Yessir, it does." She chuckled, before smiling at me. "We're in, sir. You make a deal with Mal, one where we get to fly around, explore, and have adventures, then we're in."

"Hell, woman, you don't say shit like that when I'm tryin' to make the damn deal!" Mal snapped, shaking his head.

"You're taking too long, and this way we all know what the others want out of the deal, in our case, its spellbooks, sir. Five preferably, but we'll settle for three."

I nodded respectfully. "Depending on the level of spell, I can go with that," I said. "Always a pleasure making a deal with you, Soween. I take it I'm paying you two to make sure Mal keeps to his bargains and survives whatever gets thrown at him in the course of the job?"

"That, and we make sure that the deals with you and Mal go smoothly, fix the incidentals, and give you a generally positive reputation, sir. Think of us as the grease that makes the wheels go round." Soween gave me a brief smile.

"And this deal for these spellbooks is good for how long? I can't afford to pay this for each job..."

"Just the once, sir," she said with a smile. "Although, a bonus now and there won't go amiss...speaking of which, here are your ingredients, and I threw in the bags." She handed over two lesser bags of holding, each filled with ingredients for alchemy when I checked inside.

"As I said, pleasure doing business with you, Soween, Josh." I smiled at them both before turning back to Mal. "Come on, then. What's the cost to me, you conniving bastard, and where's my goddamn change?"

"Well, that's just plain rude," Mal said, pretending to look shocked. "I can't believe that's your attitude but if that's how it has to be, well, maybe the Gnomes let slip about a core, a little device that means a ship need never resupply with manastones. Might be that would be needed, you know, for the long missions an' all," he suggested. I held up one hand, stopping him.

"We have one, and it's in use. Can't be removed from the ship," I said firmly.

"You sure? Gnomes said it might…"

"And it might kill Tenandra," I stated flatly. "Not happening…but…"

"But…?"

I scratched my chin, thinking hard. "But…it's basically a heavier duty core than the ones the golems use. Much heavier duty, don't get me wrong, but it's something I'd be willing to work toward, as I could do with them for the rest of my ships, too." I said slowly. "Leave it with me, and I'll see what I can come up with."

"And in the meantime?" Mal asked bluntly.

"Well, for now, you–well, Jian, too, but that was an accident–have the only crew that have fired a cannon and survived to tell about it. Speak to Riana, see what she can sort out, then in a few days, take your ship and escort Augustus to the city. Separate out if you want to, pretend not to know each other, whatever. Just be there when he needs you."

"And what do I get out of this?" he asked coldly.

"You get to be busy while I make my own enquiries into the core. You get practice with the ship and have an excuse to bugger off and enjoy flying around, as well as go where you were going anyway. Last of all, I'll let you have a Gnome to work on your ship for a day, with a golem servitor."

"What the hell would I want one of those crazy bastards back on my ship for!" Mal snapped, and I grinned at him.

"Because we've cured some of the madness, and the servitors can make real, serious upgrades. You've seen the *Sigmar's Fist*, right?" I asked. When he nodded, I went on. "Well, she looks the same, but the hull weighs nearly half what it did, and if the hull armor was classed as level one before, it's now around a five, far stronger than it was. One day, that's all you get, but they can make a hell of a difference in that time, believe me."

"Fine, but I want that memory as well," he grumbled, and I nodded, Oracle's hand slipping into my own as we walked.

The trip to the Hall of Memories took nearly three hours by the time we stopped for Josh every few floors to let him catch his breath.

Along the way, I dealt with administrative details, gave orders to those who found me while I was walking, and got a nasty surprise when that miserable bastard Alistor turned up, only to tell me he was in charge of the Speculatores.

"Great. Wonderful," I said, forcing a smile. "In that case, I want a judicial system put in place. Next time, I don't want to have to do a show trial when something comes up; I want to be able to deal with them nice and quietly, not to mention permanently."

"And what do you need me for?" he asked slowly.

"The Speculatores used to mete out justice, investigating and hunting down the truth, as well as cutting out corruption. Your new job, as you're apparently the head of them, is to plan how to set up a facility for that."

"Details, Lord Jax, I need details. Spell this out for me, please, so that I'm very sure where my role starts and ends," he requested grimly.

"Fine," I said, glaring at him. "I want you to create a facility to watch over the Empire as it stands, so basically this part of the continent, then make sure it's able to be scaled up to whatever size we need. You are to investigate everything from thefts to willful disregard for the spirit of orders. So, oh you know, if I were to order something to be done, then someone did exactly what was ordered but no more, deliberately not carrying out what was clearly fucking intended, just to be an asshole, I'd like to know why. Just as a wild example, that person could be sent to the arse-end of the empire to do the most thankless jobs imaginable. If you get what I'm saying." I raised one eyebrow.

"I suspect I do...Lord," he responded slowly.

"Glad to hear we understand each other, Alistor. Now, some utter assholes were abusing a young girl on one of the ships, thankfully not sexually, but everything from hitting her to deliberately making sure she was on the brink of starvation and never allowing her to sleep, all because it amused them.

"That kind of shit would result in a very harsh ass kicking, like a group of legionnaires taking that person for a long walk and a discussion, and a warning, up to banishment in my eyes. If they'd sexually abused her, it's death. Plain and simple. In this case, they also killed one of my citizens, so yeah, that's death as well. I'd like this to be a remarkably simple and easily meted-out justice system, Alistor, because the more complex, the more assholes can twist it."

"And for theft?" he asked, pulling out a notepad and writing details.

"Confiscation of double the stolen item's worth, given to the treasury to mete out to the injured party, any damages to the victim paid out of the thief's pocket, so if they broke a lock getting in, not only is the item returned, but the lock is also replaced, and all that."

"And if they don't have the wealth to take?" Alistor queried.

"Then they work the debt off, on top of their actual job. Food is free here, and housing is provided, so you better understand that theft is for luxuries and tools, etc.

"Don't get me wrong; if you find that there's a genuine reason, then come to me, and we'll discuss it, but at the end of the day, I want a group of justicars who are ready to investigate and mete out justice. If in doubt, use the old Imperial Laws, but ignore the sections about nobles being above the laws, because they're not."

"And you? Are you 'above the laws'?" he asked quickly, glaring sharply.

"Well, that depends, doesn't it?" I asked, coming to a stop and staring at him. "Because I decide what the goddamn laws are, so I kinda am, above them, I mean. But, if I break one, it's going to be for the good of the fucking Empire. Now, you seem to have a problem with me, so either spit it out, and we can talk about it right now, or put your big boy pants on and get over it."

We stared at each other for several seconds, time in which I heard the creak of his armored gloves as he clenched and unclenched his fists, before he finally looked away.

"No, my lord," he ground out through gritted teeth.

I snorted, turning away. "Then get over whatever your fucking problem is, Alistor, because I'm sick of your shit, and I've got no time to deal with it anymore." I stalked off, climbing higher into the Tower.

"What is your problem with that fella?" Mal asked after a few minutes.

I let out a grunt of annoyance. "He deliberately does the absolute bare minimum, argues with everything I tell him to do, and seems to be making every job he can ten times harder. Boils my piss," I muttered.

"Two options there, then, well three, but unless you want to kill him…"

"Oh I *want* to, I really do, but no," I grumbled before shooting Mal a grin.

"Then you either boot him or promote him," he said, shrugging.

I looked at him in surprise. "Boot, I can totally understand. Hell, I'm tempted to make an example out of him by making Restun take over his personal training the way he's damn well breaking the rest of us, but you know…hey, why did you join us for that training session, anyway?"

"Didn't mean to," he replied. "Was on my way to ask you for the books an' stuff, saw the session, and thought I'd see what it was like. Now I can laugh every time I look at the clock and know you're being punished like that." He grinned, miming holding a drink. "I'll even raise a beer to you in memory."

"You bastard." I laughed, shaking my head.

"Anyway, the other option is that he's actin' out of boredom; is he any good at his job?"

"According to Romanus he is, yeah," I admitted grudgingly.

"Then promote him. Give him a chance to not be bored and to prove himself."

"I'd rather stab him," I admitted with feeling, getting another laugh from Mal and a grin from Soween. "But I'll think about it," I promised.

We passed the last dozen floors to the Hall of Memories in amicable chatter, including me learning from a laughing Mal that yes, the field we'd landed the battleship in was the lower meadow for the herbalist he was buying from, meaning that I was pretty much blacklisted by that herbalist and would now have to send Mal to satisfy any purchases from them.

I was still cursing him, and he was laughing, when we reached the Hall of Memories, and I waved the crystal door to open.

Mal's laughter cut off abruptly when the door evaporated, the polished, impenetrable crystal dissolving into apparent mist before slipping from sight into the doorframe.

"What the everlivin'…" Mal mumbled, staring wide-eyed as I led the four of them into the room, Lydia also looking around in utter awe.

I knew how they felt. The Hall of Memories was a place of wonder to me as well, not least because, where the rest of the Great Tower was trashed, this place had been pristine. Had been, because I'd bled all over it, conjured fountains, and generally lived in it for a few days, but that was the way these things worked.

The room was filled with bookshelves, dozens and dozens of them, each holding hundreds of predominantly magical books. I'd looked through them several times and had Oracle advise me on what we had, and it was an utter treasure here.

Unfortunately, it was also a very awkward treasure, as, like all knowledge, if it wasn't used right, it would be totally wasted.

There were books, skillbooks and normal, not to mention spellbooks that ranged from the extremely basic to the insane. There was a grandmaster spellbook that I couldn't even get the cover to make sense, let alone be able to read. Some things, like a master-level tailoring book that was dedicated exclusively to working with Aldebrainian Silk, were both amazing and useless.

If I gave that book to an average tailor, they'd learn a few new tricks but without the damn silk, they'd never be able to make use of the book properly. And if they were, say, a novice who read it, they'd find almost all the techniques were totally beyond them. Without the basic skills to build upon, they'd forget the knowledge in weeks, occasionally being able to get a little bit to work instinctively here and there, but remaining a novice, basically.

Most of the room was like that; exceedingly valuable, but filled with skills that were basically useful to an Empire of luxuries that ceased to exist seven hundred plus years ago.

"Right, Mal, you were promised a memory crystal," I said, gesturing to the wall ringing the room. Far more valuable than the skillbooks, these were the actual memories of the person who had made them, and they included a hell of a lot more information.

Oracle set off flying around, reaching out and tugging one here and one there from the wall, before returning to where I stood. I caught Mal's arm, stopping him from going to search through them.

"The deal was that I'd pick," I reminded him, and his look soured, before I shook my head at him. "Don't be an ass, Mal; I won't rip you off. Oracle's looking for the most appropriate ones for you now. She'll narrow it down to five, we can discuss them, and you can tell me what would be best for you. But I pick, as I said. I'm not losing something powerful and irreplaceable that you won't be able to use, just because you got greedy. Also, you're not taking it out of here and selling it. You use it. Well, you or them, anyway," I finished, gesturing to Soween and Josh.

Oracle led us to a table and a series of low couches before spreading the crystals out.

"We have five here that I think are useful to you, Mal, or to your team," Oracle started. "The first is Bee's Seafaring. Unsurprisingly, it's the memories of being a seafarer who worked his way to captain. He was on a normal ocean-going ship at the height of the Empire, but as you're running a ship now, and will be doing a lot of the same things, such as steering by starlight, I think it would be useful.

"Secondly, Valerie Santos's memories of being a merchant dealing with the Islands of the Sun. Yes, the chain of islands is probably very different now from what they were, but its value lies more in the nature of the merchant skills and the various charts that might be useful." She indicated two crystals, sliding them to one side.

"Next, we have the memories of Master at Arms Baloo. Baloo was the enforcer and right hand of Bee on his ship, the Secret Crossing. He was skilled with most weapons that were used aboard ship, but especially a mace and the ballista, as well as his iron fist. He was known for his meticulous skill at running the ship, and that one, I'd recommend for Soween," Oracle said with a smile.

"Last of all, two mage's memories: one, Gillen, was an apprentice air mage. Doesn't sound that impressive, I know, but that's because he spent all his life using three spells: Gust, Downdraft, and Turn. By concentrating on these spells exclusively, he gained a fundamental understanding of air magic and could speed his own ship's crossing of the oceans, becalm his opposition, and even nudge storms and hurricanes aside; not stop them, you understand, but push them enough that his ship always made it through to safety," Oracle said, tapping that one and looking at Josh, who was gazing at the crystal in awe, even as I considered the usefulness of that one.

"Last, and by no means least, the memories of Artem Featherfoot," she said, tapping a glittering crystal. "Artem was a thief, a pirate, and a smuggler, known for sneaking past blockades and for his downright vicious behavior. He was caught and given the option of life imprisonment for his crew, and a memory read and execution for him, or for the entire crew to be executed.

"Surprisingly, he gave up his memories, and this was stored until it was to be given to an Imperial Captain. This crystal contains the memories of a pirate who hid most of his loot…"

At those words, Mal sat straight upright, a wide grin on his face.

"BUT!" Oracle cautioned. "This was in the last days of the Empire. The landmarks and all that he used might be long gone now."

"Take a few minutes to think about this, Mal, and tell me what you want and why, then I'll decide," I instructed before standing up and leading Oracle and Lydia to a stack of books on the west wall.

"Lydia, I know you're going to go for Valkyrie as your build and class, so I brought you up here, because only you know what you need. Work with Oracle here, look around, and pick skillbooks or spellbooks, then tell me what you want." I smiled, patting her on the shoulder as she looked around in awe, stunned at the offer I'd just made.

I turned, leaving her to it, and tuned out the excited babble from Oracle as I walked back to Mal and his team.

"So, any decisions?" I asked the three of them, and Mal nodded grimly.

"First of all, you're a bastard." He gestured to the table and the room. "You show us all this, and these, and then say you'll pick, that's just…"

"Mal…" Soween said in a low, warning growl.

"Anyway," Mal said, after glaring at Soween. "Yeah, we'd take any of these. If the choice is up to me, and you're not just going to be a dick and take out the one I pick, then I'd choose either Baloo or Gillen's memories." I saw the smiles that flitted across both Josh and Soween's face as he chose for them, rather than himself.

I nodded and smiled before passing the memory for Gillen over and nodding to Josh as he took it.

"I'll give you this one, Josh, mainly because I know Soween is already amazing at her job. While I'm sure you're good, the ability to force another airship down, aside, or to speed your own up, well, it'll make a hell of a difference to you reprobates actually surviving when I have missions for you," I said, seeing the looks on their faces.

"Right, well, about another crystal…" Mal started, and I gestured to the door, walking that way myself.

"We can talk about that in the future. I know it looks like there's a lot, and there is, but most of it…well, as an example, there are three crystals in there that apparently are the memories of highly skilled seamstresses." I paused, looking at Mal, who frowned in confusion.

"Only one of them has anything to do with sewing, and the others apparently just called themselves seamstresses in polite company. Seriously, there's not that much that's usable. One memory crystal is for perfectly training a specific breed of cat to hunt out beans, then turning the cat shit into the best kind of coffee."

"What?" he asked, stunned.

"I know, who first tries shit like that?" I asked him in disgust, shaking my head. "I mean, seriously, who watches a cat take a shit and goes, 'hmmm, I bet that'd be an appetizing ingredient for a drink' crazy!"

"No! You have a memory for that, I mean?" Mal asked seriously, staring at me hungrily. "For the coffee?"

"Uh, yeah?" I responded, looking at him askance.

"I'll take it," he said quickly. "You think it's worthless; I'll take it."

"No, because I know you, Mal," I said slowly. "You've got some angle here, and you think you can make serious money, so we'll make a deal for it. But right now, I need to go deal with a priest, some Gods, and throw some assholes off the Great Tower, so do me a favor and sod off, okay? Come up with an offer for the cat shit memory, and we can talk later." I rolled my eyes, reminded nevertheless that, just because it was worthless to me, didn't mean it was worthless.

"Fine, but I want that memory, and before I leave to go to Narkolt," Mal grumbled, stalking off, a bemused Soween gripping my shoulder and smiling at me once in thanks, while Josh stumbled past, already staring into the depths of the crystal.

CHAPTER THIRTY-TWO

I left Lydia and Oracle in the Hall, knowing that Oracle could let them in and out easier than even I could, and I continued up the stairs, coming to the floor below the Cathedral at the same time as Restun, who was now dragging the fat priest up the steps, despite the time I'd spent with the others.

Restun looked furious, but when I arrived, he straightened and saluted, fist to chest, while the fat little priest whimpered on the floor, rubbing his legs.

"Thank you, Restun, and I apologize for cutting our session short," I said formally. "I need to discuss the realities of life here, however, so if you'll wait a minute, then you can escort him back down the Tower."

"Of course, Lord Jax." Restun barked, deliberately being formal and respectful while I looked down at the sniveling priest.

"You can't do this," he whimpered. "I'm a priest, the first priest of Jenae, and…"

"And I'm her champion and ally, and you just made her commandments to me regarding worship and aiding her brethren ten times fucking harder than it needed to be," I snapped. "I'll be discussing you directly with her in a few moments, while you get to walk back down the Tower, taking the time to think about how you should be acting around your future fucking EMPEROR and the chosen champion of your Goddess, you little shit."

I stopped myself, taking a deep breath and letting it out in a long, slow exhale. The priest could be useful, and I had to start trying with people more, or I'd end up screaming "off with their heads" a dozen times before breakfast by the time I hit thirty.

"Look, Martin, right?" I asked, and got a weak nod. "What did you do before this?"

He sniffed. "I was…I was the village tax collector…" he said, and I looked him over. Fat, weak, and blatantly wearing far nicer clothes than the others had been.

"And who were you to Isabella and Lorek?" I asked carefully.

"Reeve Lorek was my master…my lord?" he said in a quavering voice. "I went to Master Cai and offered to collect taxes for him, and he shooed me away. The villagers didn't like me, so I just…made do. Then I heard the Goddess speak, and she filled me with a need to spread the word, to help her!" As he went on, I noted his voice growing stronger and more impassioned.

"And when was this…?" I asked carefully.

"When she spoke to us, she spoke to us all!" he exclaimed, nodding fiercely.

"And to you; did she speak to you directly? Did she choose you as a priest for her? Hell, what's your class? *Are* you a priest now?" I asked suspiciously, seeing his head dip and tears starting to drip from the end of his nose.

"Oh for…" I grumbled, sighing as I pinched the bridge of my nose and closed my eyes. "I know I'm going to fucking regret this. Restun, bring him along."

I headed up the stairs as Restun dragged the protesting "priest" across the floor until he got his feet under him.

We continued up the last spiral of stairs and out onto the level I'd taken to thinking of as the cathedral, both because of the high, vaulted ceilings, and the fact that it held all the altars to the Gods.

I strode out into the middle of the floor and went down on one knee, the knuckles of my right fist pressed flat to the floor as I cast the spell to speak to Jenae.

Several seconds passed before the sense of Her presence joined me, along with several others. I took a deep breath before rising to my feet, the overwhelming presence of multiple Gods being akin to the pressure in the depths when diving past your limits, it made it hard to breathe, to think, and certainly to react coherently.

"Mistress Jenae, my Lords and Ladies..." I said respectfully, aware of the others being present, but not what it meant or specifically who had come, as there was no physical form to look at.

"Jax, you called, my Champion?" Jenae asked, and I felt Her deliberately softening Her Aura to make it easier to breathe.

"I did, thank you," I said. "We have several details to discuss, but first of all, and so that we don't need to clean the floor, I need to introduce you to Martin. He has named himself your priest, and has been haranguing people to follow you, not to mention sticking his nose anywhere he wanted in your name. That being said, he seems genuine in his desire to help, just dickish in carrying it out. First, do you want him to be a priest for you? And second, I need some advice on how to spread your worship, and that of the others. I'm assuming that you don't want everyone trooping up to this room every day to pray?"

"No," She said firmly, and there was a pause as Martin whimpered. *"No, I don't think having everyone traveling all the way up to this place to worship is a good idea. As to Martin..."* There was a long minute of silence, then Martin flinched and fell onto the floor, prostrating himself and shaking.

A few more minutes passed, then longer. Just as I was about to open my mouth, a new voice spoke, directly to me, rather than into the air so they all could hear.

"Jax, Jenae speaks to her supplicant directly, so I shall use this time to put forward my own plea," the voice whispered, a sense of cold, of high places, and peace filling my mind.

"I am Vanei, Goddess of Air," She introduced herself, moving along quickly. *"And I have a need, a powerful need. I am aware that you have a quest to reawaken us and find us champions. Several of my brethren have already begun to reach out, searching for those who please them the most, but I already know what I need, and you do as well."*

I nodded, speaking mind to mind with Her. *"Greetings, Lady Vanei. Yes, I think you want Lydia, is that right?"*

"Yes, but I must admit, I want more. I wish for her and her sisters to return. Much as Sint had his Paladins, and Jenae had her Seekers, I had my Valkyries, and their loss pains me more than you can know. You have one who treads the path of the Valkyrie now sworn to you. I sense her devotion, and her worship is to you and to you alone. Therefore, I cannot reach out and draw her to me, but if you were to set her aside? I would reward you."

"Not a chance," I said firmly. *"Lydia is my friend and my Optio, the leader of my personal Squad. I'll not put her aside for anyone, Goddess or not. It would break her heart, not to mention I damn well need her."*

There was a long pause as I waited to hear that I'd been added to another God's shitlist, when She finally spoke again.

"Then I am pleased three times over," Vanei said sweetly, a note of amusement in Her voice. *"A single Valkyrie is not a being alone. She must have an earthly master and will draw power from that master, based on her beliefs. I had to test you before I could allow you to continue. Lydia would fall, should you put her aside without the strength of her sisters to draw upon. I wish for her to ascend, to become a full Valkyrie, and to take me as her patron, to ultimately become my Champion and gain my favor. To do so, however, she must complete her class quest."*

"Go on."

"I cannot aid her in her class quest, though her companions could," She said carefully.

"There would be a deal to be struck between us then, Vanei," I said, phrasing things the best way I could.

"Oh?" She asked, and I swore the room dropped by a few degrees.

"I have need of a location, a location that might, for example, just off the top of my head, contain some armor?" I hinted, not explicitly stating it, but leaving it hanging. There was a long period of silence, while I sweated internally, before Her voice returned, and She sounded amused.

"I will grant you two locations, one is in payment for the other, as my Valkyrie requires something from that first location to serve me better."

"Thank you, Goddess Vanei." I released an explosive breath, reaching out to Oracle as the sense of Vanei's attention left me. *"Oracle, bring Lydia and whatever she's chosen to the cathedral."* I asked, and I received a quick sense of agreement and excitement from her.

I looked around, finding Restun standing at parade rest, staring straight ahead, while Martin remained on the floor, mumbling as Jenae no doubt discussed things with him.

I shrugged and pulled up the prompts and the map, noting the two site locations that Vanei had given me. Thankfully, they weren't far from one another, and they were both needed. One was in the forest, and about thirty miles or so further to the east was the other one, seemingly in a ruin on the far side of the village of Cornut.

I intuitively sensed which was which. Lydia's most-needed site was the one in the ruins, making me think that needed to be a priority.

"Eternal, I would speak with ye." came a new voice, and I jumped, shocked, before stifling a curse. *"I am Svetu, and I believe Ashante might have struck a bargain with ye, one that included my assistance."*

"Ah, Great Svetu, yes; thank you for speaking to me. I am aware of the deal," I said carefully.

"Ashante did not discuss this with me, and now I feel a need to honor my sister's word, yet I've little to do with this. As ye be going to carry out a quest for Vanei, and for others, I've a special task for ye."

"Of course, Lord Svetu. I am in need of your help, so I will gladly help as I am able," I said carefully.

"Excellent. Your map is updated to show a location, one that once contained much that my chosen people valued. It is infested now, but clear it, claim the location, and I will aid ye in joining it and other claimed locations to this central Tower.

"It contains much we both need, and I will permit the Empire to regain control of it, provided my personal facilities are returned to me, and the production facilities are shared between the Empire and my chosen." With an impression of cautious satisfaction, I felt Him leave, and I sighed again, my head already starting to feel like a drum from all the pressure.

"I'll do as you request," I called out, but only silence came back, and I let out a grunt of annoyance, rubbing my temples and reflecting on the way the Gods all had to shout inside my skull. No simple sodding conversations, oh no; it felt like They were trying to do dental work through sheer vibrations alone.

"Jax," Jenae said in my head, and I jumped.

"Holy fucking shit, Jenae!" I snapped aloud, before scrubbing my face with my hand and speaking to Her in my mind again.

"Sorry, Jenae. I've had one after another of your brothers and sisters at me this morning. I mean, I needed their help, but fuck, my head feels like a drum now," I explained, feeling better when She started to laugh aloud.

"I apologize for startling you, my Champion," She said aloud, and I let out a relieved sigh as She went on. *"Martin and I have discussed his desires, my own needs, as well as his proper place and the need for control, patience, and goodwill. I have accepted him as a priest, and he will now begin to work upon his quests and aid you when he can. I, however, have a request of you, if I may?"*

"Of course, Goddess." I said, straightening up and staring forward into space.

"I ask that the shrines of my brothers, sisters, and myself be moved, and that instead, we be given a new home in the Lower Tower, within a room that I have marked on your map."

I pulled it out and scanned through the Great Tower, nodding appreciatively when I saw the size and location of the room. It was a huge space on the ground floor, behind the stairwell, and I'd been wondering what the hell to do with it, as it could accommodate the entire population of the Tower and more with ease.

"Not a problem," I said carelessly, nodding as I thought about the logistics of getting the shrines down, before pausing and looking over at Nimon's shrine. "Ah, Goddess, considering we're at war with the Dark Prick, do you really want His shrine, or altar, or whatever down there?" I asked. There was a tangible pressure change in the air before it vanished.

"No, Jax, we do not," Jenae said flatly.

I nodded in understanding. "Are the altars special? Like are they especially strong, or magically protected or anything?"

"No?" She responded with confusion after a few seconds.

"Last question: is it going to do anything fucking weird to me if I touch it?" I asked carefully.

"Again, no, Jax. Why?"

"Awesome. Restun, open that fucking window, will you?" I asked, nodding towards a large glass-filled opening on one side of the huge room, closest to the respective altar. He grinned and complied, sticking his head out to make sure it was clear below before pulling back and nodding to me.

I strolled over to the altar, a great ugly thing of black stone and shiny depths. Grabbing it, I pulled, finding it heavier than I had expected, but not unbearable. I grunted with the effort as I carried it to the window and chucked it out, before pulling the window closed again, and rubbing my hands together in satisfaction.

Shocked silence filled the air, then Oracle and Lydia arrived. They took one look around, noticing the stunned look on Martin's face, the silence of the room, and the feeling of the Gods watching in horrified amazement. Both women instantly fixated on me as I brushed the dust from my hands.

"What did you just do?" Oracle asked me suspiciously as a bunch of new notifications popped up for me.

Congratulations!

You have received a quest: My God is Better Than Your God (3)

For each altar or sanctified place of worship dedicated to Nimon, Ardat, Asmodeus, Baphomet, or Illoth that you destroy, you will receive a Mark of Favor and a random blueprint for your crafters from the Goddess Jenae.

As you have destroyed an Altar to Her most hated brother, you will receive a bonus item.

*

Beware!

You have reached a new low.

You are now HATED by the God of Death, Nimon.

He will encourage all those who worship Him to seek your death ever more fervently! Beware the Knives in the Dark!

An audible growl split the air, before a final notification popped up.

Know this!

The God of Death, Nimon, has been declared a HATED ENEMY of the Goddess of Darkness, Assassination, and Larceny.

Tamat issues this challenge to all those who would gain her favor: take the lives of the followers of the God of Death, and you will receive a personal bonus from the Goddess.

*

Nimon has personally intervened to declare any follower of the Pantheon of the Flame as an Enemy of the Church.

**All sanctified soldiers of the Church will receive +3 to Strength, Agility, and Endurance when facing the forces of the Apostate and his hated Gods.
Killing any member of those forces will make this buff permanent.
Furthermore, this buff will increase by +1 for every additional kill those soldiers make.**

Kill on, Holy Warriors!

"Jax, seriously?! What the hell did you just do!" Oracle shouted as, for the first time in recorded history, Restun laughed.

"He threw the God of Death's altar out of the window," he said proudly, still grinning.

"That asshole has claimed my role, he claims my Knives, he claims my element. Jax! I. Want. My. Champion!" Tamat snarled.

"Bane!" I called out, and without pause, Bane appeared, crouched by the door, watching everything.

"Yes, Jax?" he asked, and I smiled at him, before speaking to the exceedingly pissed off Goddess.

"I think that Bane is the most skilled of my stealth warriors at this time. Flux will be able to train more, but right now, he is the best by far, and he carries a Legendary Dagger that is a particularly evil damn weapon."

"BANE!" Tamat snarled. *"Will you worship me? Will you dedicate every kill you make to my glory, and send the souls of my enemies screaming unshriven into the darkest night?"*

"I will, Lady Tamat, but I am sworn to Lord Jax as his bodyguard, and I will not forsake that Oath."

"He is the next Eternal; that is accepted," She snapped, letting out a low growl after a few seconds. *"But yes, he is your mortal...he is your Master, as I am your Divine Mistress, and you are my Champion!"*

With Her pronouncement of his status, Bane stiffened, letting out an audible groan as he started to shake, then change.

Before, Bane was big for a Mer, almost six feet tall when he stood straight, although that was damn rare, considering he spent most of his time skulking around. His skin was a dark grey, black, or green, depending on where he was, some kind of natural camouflage aiding him in that way.

Now, though, an inky marking spread through his skin as he shook and groaned. Audible pops and clicks came from his body, and with each one, his health in my party sense would dip, before being healed again. He occasionally let out a groan of pain...or pleasure...as changes were made to him.

By the time She was finished, and Bane stood on his own again, a little shakily, but breathing heavily, he looked different in a thousand little ways, yet was still clearly himself, weirdly enough.

His body had natural edges and ridges, such as the areas around the knuckles, where the flesh was harder. That now had tiny serrations, making even a casual blow from him able to tear flesh. His muscle tone was more defined, and his skin seemed duskier. As he crouched, my gaze slid off him, and I grunted in surprise at the speed of the change. Usually, I could track him for a couple of seconds before I lost him, but now, he was just…gone.

"Bane?" I asked, and he blew in my ear, making me flinch, before darting away, thrumming. I concentrated, and even my Oath to him was altered; it was still there and still as strong, but cloudy and hard to track.

"You asshole; just as I figured a way to be able to find you," I growled, and I felt that subsonic *thrum* of amusement from him again.

"I will require you to furnish my champion with appropriate equipment and skillbooks, Eternal." Tamat growled, still clearly furious, and I said nothing as two new markers popped up on my map, making me grin.

I had five places now that I needed to visit, and in short order; two for Vanei, two for Tamat, and one for Svetu, and I nodded, before speaking.

"Very well, Lady Tamat, I will do as you ask and leave the reward to discuss later." As I mentioned a reward, I felt the irritation of Tamat building again, so I tried to move quickly along.

"So…"

"No. What do you ask of me, Eternal? Resolve this now," She ordered grimly.

"This is Bob; he's my summoned minion and my friend. I'm aware that the realm of death isn't darkness, but he's undead, so neither alive nor dead. You are the closest I could come to an appropriate Goddess to ask…" I said slowly, weighing my words.

"To ask what?" She prompted musingly.

"To grant him levels and life," I said. "We can all level, and I know that eventually he'll be able to, as he grows. But he will always be tied to me, alive only so long as I live. I want him to be alive in his own right, to be able to choose his path, and, should he choose, to become a dedicated counter-assassin and bodyguard, to assist Bane in hunting down the enemies of the Empire."

"Oh, this I like." Tamat whispered, examining Bob.

"You'll do it?" I asked in surprise, and She grumbled before answering.

"Give me some time to think on it, and I'll decide, but remember, Eternal, you'll owe me on top of the deal we just struck." She warned. I nodded, hoping I'd be able to pay the bill when it came due.

"Lady Vanei, this is Lydia, commander of my personal guard and soon-to-be Valkyrie."

"Well met, Lydia, as you are sworn to both Jenae and to the Eternal, I required an introduction to you, as you did not come to me first. As an aspiring Valkyrie, your allegiance would be more suited to serving me. Jenae has agreed, and the Eternal has also, on the provision that you are his, first and foremost. This is acceptable to me, as a Valkyrie without a Master or Mistress is only half-ascended. What say you? Will you serve me and complete your quest to become my Champion?"

"I…well, aye…but…" Lydia said, looking overwhelmed, and I took pity on her.

"It's all sorted, Lydia. This way, you get to be the first of a new group of Valkyries, you gain the blessings of the Goddess of the Air, and you get to stay with me and lead your squad, should you want to. I'll understand if you don't…"

"No!" she snapped, quickly turning in the direction the voice had come from. "I accept! I don't want my life to change, not from this…I…I want to grow! I want to be all I can be, but I don't want to lose this!"

"Then welcome, Lydia; as an Aspirant-Valkyrie, you have much to do, but I have faith in you and will watch your trials with great anticipation." With that, the sense of Vanei's presence receded, followed by most of the others, until only two remained: Jenae, and one other.

"Jax, my brother Sint has asked for an introduction to give you a quest in turn," Jenae explained.

"Well met, Jax!" came a voice, and for the first time since this conversation started, there was a shimmer in the air, and one of the Gods appeared where I could see Them.

Sint was tall, broad-shouldered, and heavily muscled, dressed in shining steel plate highlighted with gold, with a white tabard that ran down his chest and cinched on the sides.

Where I expected a broadsword and shield to complete the outfit, however, instead He bore a book and quill, and He stared down at me from a height of at least nine feet.

His hair was blonde streaked with grey, and while a moustache normally made someone look like a sex offender from the 80s, in my opinion, His actually made him look distinguished. He conveyed a sense of calm and patience, tempered by strength and a force of will that was frankly terrifying.

I dropped to one knee instinctively after meeting His gaze, feeling for the first time since coming to the world–hell, in my life–that I wasn't just in the presence of a powerful being, but actually seeing a God in truth.

Where the others bludgeoned with Their presence, He was a rock, one that was calm and solid, even as the waves of an ocean storm hit it, unmoved and unaltering, simply stating that it *was* and always would be.

"Lord Sint," I said, bowing my head in reverence.

"Thank you for the show of respect, Eternal; now stand, for we must speak," He said.

"I have observed your situation and your intentions regarding the rule of law. I find this pleasing and would offer you a bargain and a boon, if you will?"

"Please, go on, my Lord." I bowed my head to the massive figure, who smiled slightly.

"You need not use honorifics with me, my child. I am but another of the Pantheon of the Flame now," He said calmly. *"There are many excellent soldiers in your forces, but as you have stated, you need more. You need a true justicar and paladin, one to lead your forces in doing what is right, not simply what feels right at the time, as I am sure you are aware of the difference?"*

"Well, yeah, I am," I grumbled.

"Excellent. I have already selected him and called him to my service. His bloodline is ancient, and he is long-lived, having seen much in his years. He will require your aid to reintegrate into the Legion and to join into your council. But the one you have selected to oversee the rule of law is not suitable. This will, I believe, bring balance to you. Someone that you may speak with, and who will teach you, even as he learns from you."

"Okay, thank you, I guess?" I mumbled, confused, as I received another notification and checked my map, finding yet another marker had flared to life. I blinked, realizing that it was far, far to the south and deep in the mountains.

"It, ah…might take a while to get to him there, Lord Sint," I said slowly, and He nodded equitably.

"I understand that, Jax; however, please, send someone to him soon. He will be a boon to you and your forces. If you will take him, and make him welcome, you will benefit greatly, not least because I will grant you a boon to aid the Great Tower in the upcoming battles with Nimon." With that, He stepped back, smiling before bowing His head and fading until only Jenae was left.

"You did well, Jax, and my brother likes you. Believe me, that was always rare for Sint, and considering your lack of respect for the rules, it's a bit of a surprise, to be frank."

"Yeah, to you and me both," I muttered, blowing out a breath and straightening. "Thank you, Jenae. I know you made things run a lot smoother than they could have there."

"Well, you are always interesting to watch, my Champion. Now, I must leave you, for I have much to do. Please, encourage the others to pray to the Pantheon, and soon?" She asked, and I nodded.

"I will, don't worry, and thanks for whatever you said to Martin." I flicked my gaze to the priest, who was still sitting on the floor, legs splayed out, his face tear-streaked and awestruck.

"Anytime. Oh, and Jax, have you thought on your building?"

"A forge," I said nodding. "I think that's for the best."

"It is. I will begin the growth of the forge on the ground floor for now, outdoors, and I will gift you a basic blueprint for a moonstone forge as your reward for the destruction of that altar.

"This is far lower in level than a magma forge, but it is one that has the potential to grow and to be upgraded, piece by piece, even if it will take many years. It will be more than sufficient for your blacksmiths and weaponsmiths, not to mention being of higher quality than the forge the legionnaires left behind in the city. Use the simple forge I will build you to make the parts to build this one, and I promise, your smiths will be pleased."

"Thank you, Jenae," I said appreciatively. "I'll go deal with those assholes above us, and I'll arrange for the altars to be moved." I took a deep breath and let it out with a sigh.

"Then I think Martin will get to speak to the people, after all. We can hold a ceremony in the new cathedral, and I'll get started on the quests for the other Gods. I don't suppose you know what Tamat's going to do to Bob, or when?"

"Tamat works in her own time. I suggest you allow him time to rest and repair him. Keep him close, though."

I nodded, and the sense of Her presence faded away as well. I turned, looking around the room and smiling at those gathered there.

"Well, congratulations to you both, Bane and Lydia, and to you, I suppose, on actually being accepted as a priest, Martin."

"Tha…thank you…Lord…" Martin stammered, scrambling up and bowing in an awkward bobbing fashion.

"Yeah…well, anyway, Martin, go to the ground floor and find the largest room, behind the staircase; you'll know which one, as I'll get the golems to start taking the altars down there soon. And get it ready for a ceremony tonight, I guess. We'll have everyone in there, but it'll be short and sweet, give everyone a chance to swear to the Gods, or not, then boom. I'm going to bed. First thing tomorrow, I'm leaving to fight some more, so get it done," I ordered flatly, eyeing him.

"And Martin?" I said, waiting until he looked me in the eye. "Don't be a fucking dick again, right?"

"I…no, my lord…" he said in a small voice. I nodded to him, doing my best to forgive and forget, then gestured to the stairs.

"Good man, now fuck off." I turned back to the others.

I looked at each of them, smiling, before reaching out to Seneschal.

"Seneschal, mate, I need the altars…"

"I heard, Jax. I already have a pair of golems on their way."

"Ah, brilliant. Thanks, dude. Pass the word to Cai to sort food or something, and get everyone to the new cathedral tonight once it's all set up, say about three hours' time; that long enough to get it all done?"

"Should be."

"Coolio, thanks, man." I cut the connection off, looking to Bane, Oracle, and Lydia.

"Right; what did you pick, Lydia?"

She looked embarrassed, holding out three books nervously.

I took them, reading the spines then passed them back. "Novice-rank Leadership and two spellbooks, Lightning Storm and Healing Wind," I noted, smiling and passing them back.

"I…I dinna really know what I need," she admitted shamefacedly. "I don't want to take these, in case I need somethin' else…"

"Take them," I said. "If you need more, you'll get more." I mentally resolved to have Nerin look over all the team for any signs of the injuries that using too many of the books had caused me. Knowing now that she could reverse the damage meant I was far less concerned about that.

I suspected my issues had been down to the mixture of the Valspar infecting me and the multitude of spellbooks in one go. Lydia had already used three, two that were several weeks ago, and one a few days back, but it was better to be safe than sorry.

"When you're ready to use them, ask Nerin to watch over you. If all goes well, once you've had the chance to use them a few times, Oracle will bond us together, and you can teach me, and I'll teach you some fire magic."

Lydia stared at me with her mouth open, and she tried to speak a few times before closing it and nodding firmly, her eyes full of unshed tears.

"Lydia, you're worth this and a hundred more. *Never* believe any different," I insisted. "Now, go find Jian and check on him, make sure that Miren is alright and she's settled, and check on the rest of the team, make sure they get armor and whatever they need sorted.

"They're your responsibility, and the next few days will be hard. We'll be sending the legionnaires to mop up the Dark Wankers while we quest and work on the Gods' requests. We haven't got enough hours in the day, so make them count," I ordered.

She straightened, clapping her fist to her chest in proud salute.

"Restun, go with her and give her whatever aid she needs. Make sure people understand that she's my right hand; if they fuck with her, they're fucking with me." I said fiercely, giving Lydia a wink and turning to address Bane and Oracle.

"Bane, you scary fucker, where are you?" I had seen him a few seconds ago, but he'd gone again. He reappeared a few feet away and looked at me in question. "We're going up to take care of those assholes now; use this time to think about what you need, then tell Oracle. If we have it, we can sort it," I said, and gave him a quick smile. He blurred from sight again as Oracle stepped in close.

I took her in my arms, kissing the top of her head as the others left the room.

"Are you okay?" she asked quietly.

"I am; are you?" I replied, getting a nod.

"Are you okay with doing this?" she persisted, leaning back and looking into my eyes. When I frowned, she jerked her head towards the stairwell that led up to the next floor. "Dealing with them, I mean, considering that you've had the time to calm down. I know a lot of things are easier when you're filled with adrenaline."

"Nope," I said, shaking my head firmly. "I'm not 'okay' with it, but I'm damn well going to do it. As the former Lord of the North said, 'if you make the rules, you can carry out the arsekicking.' Though, he said it with a bit more flowery shit, admittedly." I broke from her reluctantly and made my way across the floor with her striding by my side in silence.

We took the next few floors in companionable silence, Oracle reaching out and worming her fingers into my hand making me smile as I squeezed and felt her squeeze in return.

As we reached the final floor, I considered the sorry little group before me then the group of legionnaires standing around the three criminals. I felt Oracle's concern, but as I searched my own feelings, I found no doubt.

"Bring them," I ordered flatly, opening the door to the outside and striding through.

The balcony beyond was long and narrow, a meter or so wide at the far end, two meters as you stepped out of the Tower. It had railings on either side that ended abruptly, leaving a gap that led out into open air as an access point for beings who could fly.

I looked down, squinting, and reassured myself that there was nobody down below that would be put at risk. My memories of the Tower's orientation had been correct; this was the back of the Tower, the place farthest from the doors and the areas that people would be walking, but still…

"Seneschal, is the bottom of the Tower here clear? I'm not going to hit anyone with a falling body, right?" I asked.

"There is nobody in the area at this time, and I am observing it carefully."

"Thanks, man."

I dismissed the connection and looked back to see the legionnaires pushing the three out. The first of them, the man who'd been most vocal and aggressive, grabbed at the doorframe and frantically tried to hold on.

"All right, all right!" he called out suddenly. "I'm fuckin' scared, I've learned my lesson, right? I'll be good and won't do nuffin ever again!" He clung tenaciously to the doorframe as a legionnaire tried to peel his fingers free.

"Come here," I growled, punching the terrified man in the face and stunning him momentarily. As soon as his grip lessened, I grabbed him by the throat, yanked him out, and threw him off without pausing, even as a streak of yellow piss escaped him.

I turned to the other two, who were frantically pushing back, looking stunned and terrified. A despairing shriek rose up to us from below, their most abrasive member falling quickly out of earshot.

"You killed a citizen, you abused a fucking child, and God knows you've done worse in your time. You've one choice left to make…"

"Anything!" said the man, quickly.

"We'll do anything!" the woman agreed, relaxing slightly, thinking she was getting a last-minute reprieve.

"Meet your end with good grace or bad," I said grimly and pointed to the end of the walkway, a few meters out.

They'd stopped struggling for a second, and the legionnaires had managed to manhandle them out. When they heard my words, they started to fight again, and they were quickly restrained, arms held behind their backs while the legionnaires looked to me for orders.

"Give him here," I said, stepping forward and spinning the man around. I gripped him by the back of the neck and his belt as his arms were released by the legionnaire. I lifted the man bodily into the air, taking two quick steps, then spun, building up momentum, and flung him out as far as I could, seeing him go much further out that the first man, who had impacted the side of the Tower a few hundred meters down, leaving a bloody streak that the rain would have to wash away.

I turned to the woman, who by now was feral with desperation and panic, alternating between offering sexual favors, power, gold, and more, and trying to knock everyone else off the barrier.

The legionnaire who held her eventually released her wrists and slammed a fist into the side of her head, stunning her. I grabbed her, flinging her out into the open air as well.

The scream that echoed up wasn't pleasant, but I gritted my teeth and waited, making sure to verify her impact before I stepped back, regarding the legionnaires, Oracle, and Bane.

"I was taught to never hit a woman, to be polite, and that to take a life was a terrible thing," I stated above the whistle of the wind. "Those weren't people, though. They weren't lives. They were fucking scumbags who thought they were predators. They thought they could lie, cheat, murder, and steal, and there would be no consequences…well, fuck that."

I grunted and looked over the side before shaking my head and gesturing for the others to step back inside.

"Tell any who'll listen," I said to the legionnaires. "That's what happens to those who hurt my people. Now, I'll let you go, and thank you all."

They saluted and set off walking down the stairs, while Oracle and Bane both stepped in closer to me, Bane becoming visible as he looked me over.

"Are you okay?" he asked quietly.

"I am, actually," I admitted, surprised a little myself. "They had to die, and to be honest, that's kinda all there is to it. It's not helped that, for a lot of people, that was their first interaction with me, seeing me condemn those arseholes to death. But at least they all know where I stand when it comes to crime and fucking punishment, I guess." I shrugged then gestured to the stairwell that led up to the final couple of floors.

"Let's go; the few rooms above were for the elite, the rulers of the Great Tower, right, Oracle? Well, now I'm the boss, and we can fucking loot those rooms before checking the Hall of the Eternal. Then it's back down the Tower, some goddamn food, and a quick ceremony for the Gods." I pointed to Oracle. "Then, I'm going to take you back to our rooms and try to snap you in half." I gave Bane a dismissive wave. "You can go stab something or whatever you do when you aren't with me."

"I'm so glad he pointed to you first," Bane quipped to Oracle, getting a grin from us both.

"Ah, you love it, you fugly bastard," I muttered, starting up the stairs with the other two on either side.

"I'll have you know I'm considered exceedingly handsome by others of my species," Bane said, the subsonic that he used to indicate humor lacing his words, making me grin.

"Yeah, well, you are all blind, I suppose," I shot back.

"We can feel the true shape of the world, Jax, which is why I know that you will forever be a disappointment to females of your race, despite your protestations otherwise."

"I don't even know where to start with the fact that you've used your sonar to check out my junk, man; it's just wrong." I shook my head as we climbed, stopping when we came out onto the third from top floor.

"Okay, I can have Seneschal simply open these doors with a word, but it's a chance to practice my lockpicking," I said, grinning and pulling out a pack of picks I'd managed to get from Mal. Unsurprisingly.

I strolled to the first door, crouched, and examined the lock, noting the scratches around the keyhole.

"Wait a minute," I muttered, and I tried the handle, finding that it opened easily. As I looked around the room beyond, I started to swear.

"Motherfuckers!" I shouted as I realized what had happened.

It'd clearly been ransacked, and as I moved to the other doors, I found they were all the same. I moved up to the top floor and found every last room open, with only the Hall of the Eternal still securely locked.

CHAPTER THIRTY-THREE

"Seneschal!" I bellowed, striding into the room after I dismissed the crystal doorway and looked about. "What the hell, dude?!"

Seneschal appeared, flowing into existence, and paused, bowing his head to me before speaking.

"I was unaware the rooms had been tampered with, Jax. It must have been done by someone who had knowledge of my methods of observation, and either has an ability to prevent that or to make me forget about it...

"Caron," I muttered. "Caron and the fucking bard!" I found myself angry beyond reasonable measure, not so much that, at some point, they'd broken into the rooms–although, yeah, I wasn't pleased about that, considering I'd been looking forward to doing that myself.

No, I was pissed because we all knew there would be gear inside these rooms, and they'd neither admitted and handed it over nor fucking apologized for it.

Caron had been handing some of it out to Kayt, trying to make her happy by giving her my goddamn magical, valuable loot! Who knew who else the little sod, in all his childish stupidity, had given the gear to!

I looked around the room again, finally seeing the Hall of the Eternal properly, and I felt my anger subside somewhat at the sight.

The Hall of the Eternal was the very peak of the Great Tower, and it was a strange but beautiful room. The stairwell terminated in the huge door leading inside, but once I stepped across the threshold, there was gleaming brilliance.

The Great Tower was both bastion and noble homestead. The results of hundreds of years of sporelings plastering the walls in their shit, literally, and the Tower itself crumbling away, damaged by erosion, storms, and the simple fact that no structure this size, unaided by magic, should damn well exist, meant that, while I understood it, I'd never really experienced it before.

The Hall of Memories was fantastic, but despite the plush carpets, the reasonably soft couches, and the intact drapes and bookcases, the real treasure was, and always would be, the knowledge it contained.

Here, though, this was designed to be the heart of the Tower, the refuge for the Eternal, the old Emperor, or now me, I guessed, if we ever came to visit. Failing that, it was the place the entire Tower was designed to be maintained from, plans made, and if need be, great spells cast from.

I walked inside a few steps before coming to a halt and slowly looking around. With the doorway behind me, the room took up three-quarters of the final level of the Tower, and I guessed it was about twenty meters across, with the final quarter of the Tower reserved for the room I'd used as my refuge when I'd first arrived.

The main room was semi-circular, each of the three walls paneled with a single set of arcing windows that lifted gracefully into the air, bending inward at their apex to vanish into a rose pattern high above.

Between each section of windows, fluted columns rose, the stone now visible as perfectly polished marble inlaid with gold and silver motifs, patterns, and fanciful designs that made me drop my jaw in wonder.

The Baron, dickish bastard that he was, had liberally coated the hallways of his citadel in gold and gemstones as an obvious example of "I'm so wealthy I need a special wheelbarrow to carry my wallet."

The Great Tower was more of understated elegance. The sheer mastery of the work was enhanced by the gold and silver, not plastered in it, and I couldn't help but be impressed.

The fourth and final wall had a second crystal door set into it, and as I opened it, glancing inside, I raised my hand to my mouth in awe.

As part of Seneschal's renovation efforts, he'd clearly removed the remains of the sporelings, a feat I was grateful for, as they'd have been reeking by now, and the room was left spotless.

This was, I guessed, meant to be a place of reflection and somewhere for the Eternal, or the lord of the Tower, to relax.

The walls were solid, with spaces set aside for seats or tables that had disintegrated over the years, as well as dozens of magelights set into the walls, giving the room a pleasant, warm light.

The walls were covered in fantastic carvings, and they, in turn, had been enameled, coated, and polished until they shone with vibrant color.

The central frieze was as I remembered it, although far more beautiful, now that I could see it clearly. It was a forest scene with the Tower in the background. Dozens of races had gathered in awe as a giant dragon flew overhead.

There were two figures in the center of the glade, a man and a woman, holding their hands out in friendship to the others.

They offered their hands, but they were heavily armed. In the background, now discernable with the proper light, were dozens of legionnaires, war golems, and more standing half-hidden beneath the trees.

The message of the image was clear and unsubtle.

"We can be friends," it said. "Just don't fuck with us."

I liked it. Hell, I loved it. It made the Emperor's position clear, and that of the Empire. I decided I needed a copy of this done where people could actually see it.

I looked around the walls, admiring the various scenes of woodland tranquility, of mountains and lakes, and I winced at the scratch marks left on the walls from where I'd gouged lines from my wild strikes with my naginata in the sporeling fights. I opened my mouth to ask, before realizing that in the refurbishment, they could have been fixed and that they'd been clearly left to show that even here, the Empire kicked fucking arse when it was needed.

As I wandered back out of the small room, Bane flowed past me then back out, following me as always, and I moved to the feature that dominated the room, the staircase.

The middle of the Hall of the Eternal wasn't on the floor you entered onto, or rather it was, but perhaps it was better described as suspended.

The stairwell led up from the center of the room; spiraling around, it opened out onto a smaller platform fifteen meters up, which was perhaps a dozen meters across.

I climbed up, amazed at the single column of fluted ridges that held the platform aloft. Here and there, scratches and gouges remained, caused by my tumble down them. I winced, remembering the confusion, shock, and pain I'd felt.

When I'd arrived in this realm, I'd leaped through from a fully-lit, professionally built, if insanely full of magic, arena ante-chamber on earth.

The experience of having an incorporeal body rammed into gateways protected by spells–through a bunch of portals, before one had opened to permit me access, had been jarring to the point of slamming me across galaxies.

When I'd arrived, the spells protecting the portal had shredded, allowing me access. However, because, like everything else here, they and the structure that housed them were failing, I'd arrived shocked, stunned, and finally rammed into a terminally unlucky sporeling who'd happened to be crossing in front of the portal when it opened.

The light of the portal had burned, seared, and blinded the creature and its kin, allowing me to hit it, tumble over, and fall down the stairs. I'd come to a semi-concussed rest against the wall at the bottom, fortunately close to the door into what had become my refuge.

I'd managed to get this very door open, mainly through blind luck, and closed again, locking myself in the pitch darkness of the smaller room with several sporelings, who were fortunately as blinded by the light as I'd been by the dark.

The resulting fight had ended with me panicked but alive, them not, and a lot of blood and scratches everywhere. I'd basically hunted them by smacking my weapon off everything until I'd felt and heard them die.

It'd been a bad day all around, I had to admit.

Now, though, I could see the portal and the sheer bloody artistry that had gone into it.

I walked up onto the platform and slowly toured it, the windows still arcing above and casting a warm light over everything.

The portal itself disappointingly didn't have a control panel or a magic disc like a certain fictional interplanetary portal. Instead, it was ringed with numerous small slots. I could recognize the size and dimensions for the keys I'd been given by my noble asshat of a father and others.

Admittedly, I'd traded his for the one from Falco at the first opportunity, but even as reasonable as Falco had been, I wasn't opening it. Not now, and probably not ever.

I also had a handful of keys in my bag from other houses, the Sunken City having provided these, so I had options, but considering that they led back to the nobles trapped in my world?

Nah. They could burn in hell.

I reached out, gently touching the portal and tracing the line of the outer rim. Just as the Great Portal they'd kicked me through to come here, and the smaller one in the Sunken City, this appeared to only have one edge.

I put my finger on it and traced it, determined to prove to myself that it was an optical illusion, like a mobius strip. But try as I might, I couldn't find another side. Every time I reached out, I just touched the same place. Reach to the right, and my hand landed on the same spot; the left, and yeah, same.

I tried it with both hands and even closed my eyes in case they were playing tricks on me, only to find that my hands ended up pressed one atop the other.

After a long minute, I gave up and inspected the rest of the platform, finding a railing that ringed it and little else, if one discounted the view.

I didn't. Instead, I leaned against the railing and stared off into the distance, gazing across the hundred plus miles of the realm that were visible from such a height. The ship was closing with the Tower as it returned from scouting, and the still-rising plume of smoke trailed off from the devastation yesterday when I'd fought the Dark Legion.

I watched the ship almost lazily, admiring several huge birds that flew around her as though checking on this sudden rash of interlopers into their territory, before speaking aloud. Smiling to myself, I recognized that a lot of the flying figures, tiny dots though they were at this distance, were actually Alkyon, Djinn, and probably the little handful of Imps that we'd accepted.

"It's beautiful," I said, seeing the lake a good seventy miles to the south. "Do you ever wish you were back there, Bane?" I asked.

"Not really," Bane admitted, appearing and leaning against the railing next to me, watching out over the distance. "I assume you mean with the pod back at the lake where we met?" he asked. I nodded, gesturing through the window before realizing my mistake.

Bane saw things through a form of sonar, and he could sound or sense things up to a few hundred meters with it.

Up here, I could see for literally hundreds of miles; the sparkling expanse of the eastern sea was visible, as was the bay that Narkolt and Himnel glared at each other across, while he could see nothing.

"Why not?" I asked him curiously as I shifted, trying to get my back to crack.

"Because I was a simple hunter there. I was literally just on the verge of adulthood, meaning I was trusted to hunt alone, but not given the freedom to hunt where and when I wanted. I had weapons that, while useful and adequate, were only that. Since meeting you, I've seen more of the world, travelled to interesting places, and met interesting creatures…"

"And killed them," I finished for him, grinning.

"Well, yes, there has been a lot of that, have to admit it. But, at least, unlike you, I'm generally classed as a likeable sort."

"What do you mean 'unlike me,' you cheeky bastard?" I gasped, pretending to be offended.

He pretended to cough. "Ahem, murderhobo."

"I told you…" I growled.

He held up his hands, counting on his fingers. "The Prax, the Grove, the waystations, the underground city, the…"

"Oh, fuck off," I grumbled, straightening up and walking back to the portal. "Seneschal, is there any way to make sure the portal can't be used by others?" I asked the room at large, and seconds later, the cloaked and armored figure of the Wisp stood by my side.

Citadel

"Reach out and lay your hand on the frame, Jax," he instructed, and I complied. "Now focus and think 'restrict.'"

A notification popped up, making me snort at how ludicrously easy it was.

Greetings, Master of the Great Tower.

Do you wish to restrict access to this Portal?

Yes/No

I selected Yes, obviously, and a second prompt arrived.

Please select level of restriction:

- Fully Locked
- Key access only
- Restricted to members of a designated group
- Open to designated individuals
- Open to all connections

I selected fully locked. I didn't have anyone I needed to be able to access it for now, so I saw absolutely no need for anything else. With quick thanks to Seneschal, I released him to get back to whatever he was doing.

With that done, I took a few minutes to walk around, admiring the view and thinking about what I could do with the space, not least of which was turning this room into a sodding awesome bedroom and screwing the hell out of Oracle pressed up against the windows.

I indulged the thought for a minute, even getting Oracle's attention when she sensed my rising ardor. But eventually, I shook my head, putting my arm around her shoulders as we walked back out into the Tower with a palpable sense of regret in leaving the Hall of the Eternal.

We carried on down the stairs in silence, finally reaching the open balcony where I'd just thrown the three dickheads off, and I grinned at Bane.

"So, want to walk down, or are you coming for a cuddle?" I asked him, getting a sigh and a shake of his head.

"You really need to have a word with yourself, you know. I'm handsome, I know, but please, try to date within your own species. I'm really quite flattered, but not interested," Bane quipped.

I laughed before telling him to climb on my back.

"Oracle, could you sort things with Seneschal and get the council to the council chambers, as well as Augustus, and get some goddamn food brought up, please? My belly thinks my throat's been cut." I muttered, she graced me with a smile and a kiss, then vanished, diving over the side.

Once we were ready, and the obligatory "that better be a dagger I can feel poking me" comments were done with, I stepped up to the edge. Knowing Bane was a little uncomfortable with heights, I did what any friend would do.

357

"That's strange, I can't make my flying skill work, oh well. Maybe it'll start working on its own once we get going fast enough?" I muttered just loud enough Bane could hear me over the wind.

I felt him tense, and I stepped off, diving forward into the air.

The air whirled around us, the sound accelerating from a faint susurration of a breeze into a howl of passing wind, suddenly so loud I knew I'd have to shout to be heard as we plunged towards the ground. Bane latched onto me so tightly, I could barely breathe. I grinned as I twisted to the left and *pushed*, activating Soaring Majesty and sending us flashing forward even faster.

We circled the Tower, searching, and when I saw the great hanger-style doors of the flight deck on the twenty-sixth floor, I slowed, bringing us in for a smooth landing.

As soon as I was down, Bane slipped off my back, growling that he would "get me for that."

The ship docked ahead was apparently the *Summer's Promise*, as I read the emblazoned lettering on the side of the hull. She was one of the three ships dispatched to the Tower with me when I'd needed to get here fast, and she was damn fast when she wanted to be.

"Captain!" I called up, spotting him striding along the deck. He gave me a salute and hurried to the gangplank.

He wasted no time in coming down and nodded to me, Romanus alongside him and clapping his fist to his heart in salute as they came to a halt. The older legionnaire looked grim.

"Jax, we need to talk."

"Okay, clearly a fun flight," I said, gesturing to the stairwell. "Come on, the council is being assembled," I said to Romanus, before turning to the captain of the *Promise*. "Captain, thank you for your fast flight; we can chat another time." I quickly apologized for calling him down, then not inviting him to the council meeting.

"Of course, my lord. The *Promise* stands ready for any and all missions for the Empire," he said, smiling widely. I grinned at him, taking my leave. The captain of this ship had been a cabin boy, thrown into the slave pens for reasons that had never been clear to me.

He was only seventeen, but his experience had ranged from assisting the ship's cooks to plotting the navigation to handling the wheel and considering the desperate lack of any real experienced ship's crews, he'd been given the command, along with a seasoned centurion named Othello to help him maintain order.

So far, I'd heard Othello was having a great time. He was basically relaxing on the ship all day, while the captain, Oliver, was sprinting around the ship, training people. I'd had visions of needing to remove the boy, or of Othello spending all day every day cracking heads.

I'd been totally wrong. Oliver had picked a crew from the younger members of the volunteer pool, and he'd even replaced the half-trained Alkyon helmsman with a tall elven girl, so that all the crew, save Othello, were his friends.

They were so far one of the fastest-learning crews in the fleet and certainly one of the most enthusiastic. I made a mental note to get them a skillbook or two, or train one of them as a mage, just to see what a crew this inventive could come up with.

I set off jogging with Romanus and called out to Seneschal as we went.

"Seneschal, ask Thorn to make sure my armor is as fixed as it can be, please." I got a sense of acknowledgement from him that made me smile.

Seneschal had been a dick when he first awoke, upon finding the Tower he loved so dearly had been trashed and infested. But as time went on, he'd mellowed, until finally, he seemed to relish speaking to people.

I'd noticed this and had taken to asking him to pass messages along. While he made a show of occasionally grumbling at the job, he also sent a feeling of contentment when he did it, making me smile.

"Is there a problem with your armor?" Romanus asked me, and I shook my head.

"Not so much a problem as a hell of a lot of damage. I clearly have a lot to learn still, because the others generally get occasional scrapes and scratches…mine tends to look like I've been in a slaughterhouse that rolled over ten times then fell on me," I grumbled. "Honestly, I think Thorn is going to kill me if I ask her to replace sections one more time…"

Romanus paused before catching up and phrased his next question much more carefully.

"Jax, have you been having problems with your armor, and to be clear, I mean: is it faulty?"

"No, why?" I asked, confused, then suddenly realizing that he had a reason for phrasing things that way, even if it wasn't clear to me. "My armor is the best I've ever had, and I'd be dead several times over if I'd been wearing the shitty stuff I used to wear, so no. My legion armor is fantastic. Why?" I repeated.

"Because part of the issue that the legion had before my time–yet it's still an effort to stamp out–is that certain people are worth more than others. Certain races, for example, should be the only ones to do certain jobs. Elves for scouts, humans for warriors, Dwarves for armorers, and so on." He fixed me with a very careful look.

"Thorn has been in command of the armorers a short time and has done fine work. But if others are seeing her constantly making you armor that seems to fall apart, it reinforces the image that a half-orc should not be in the smithy."

"And that's bullshit," I said firmly.

"It is, but there are those who see it that way. They are not necessarily bad people; it's conditioning, that's all. I have great hopes for the Tower and the new Empire, Jax, one of which is that you are so uncaring of racial issues. As such, we need to make the point that it is not a failing of Thorn's that you can't wear armor properly," he finished with a smile. I gave him the finger, making him laugh.

"Well, I spoke to Jenae, anyway," I noted, as we exited onto the floor we needed.

"Oh?"

"Yeah, she's giving us a building; non-magical, unfortunately, but it was a quest reward, so we're basically getting a smithy and a set of plans. We can use the plans and the smithy to make a much better smithy, one we can use to build upgrades for other things. It's a bit complicated, but hey, shit happens."

"Well, Thorn might forgive you, then, if she's getting a smithy," Romanus acknowledged as we slowed to a walk.

"Here's hoping," I said, forcing a smile then letting a real one out as a handful of people, led by Isabella, came running up the stairs behind us, carrying a bag of holding each.

"Isabella!" I said as she staggered to a panting halt nearby.

"My...lord..." she gasped, leaning over and breathing heavily, before forcing herself to straighten and speak. "I apologize...that we didn't...manage to...get food and...drinks to...the room in time." She gulped in air, and I held up a reassuring hand as the others staggered off in the direction of the Council Chambers.

"Whoa, seriously? I called this meeting only what, ten minutes ago? Don't kill yourself trying to sort it. We can wait." A look of uncertainty crossed her face, and I straightened up, forcing myself to appear more serious and in charge. "Isabella, I don't want you and your people injuring themselves to bring me food and drink. You are to slow down, and that's an order."

She looked up at me in shock before recovering and smiling.

"Thank you, Lord Jax. I fell back on old habits. Reeve Lorek would..."

"That shitbag would have been an asshole no matter what you did, I bet. Isabella, seriously, relax. There's too much to worry about without risking you falling and break your neck rushing to deliver a cold sodding drink."

"It's bacon sandwiches...lord?" That last response was called in confusion, as I'd turned and started running for the council chambers.

CHAPTER THIRTY-FOUR

Fifteen minutes later, with my most immediate needs met, as well as those of the council all finishing our food and drinks, the last few people staggered in on rubbery legs. I sat forward, brushing crumbs from my hands and nodded to Romanus.

"Okay, mate, it's time; tell us all what you saw," I ordered, having instructed him to wait until everyone was present.

"The forest was a scene of devastation," he said, standing up. "The trap set by Legionnaire Denny and his people was both horrifically powerful and terrifyingly effective. When we arrived, I tracked the survivors first and returned to examine the damage later. We landed, and I took twenty legionnaires and followed them. They were easy to track, forced to abandon their wounded as they died. It took us less than twenty minutes to backtrack them to their camp."

"Felt like it took us a lot longer, and we were running," I muttered, getting a raised eyebrow from Romanus. "Sorry, I'll be quiet." I grinned sheepishly.

"Thank you, Lord Jax," Romanus said formally, smiling slightly. "So, as I was saying, we essentially followed the trail of their dead back to the camp, finding it severely reduced in size, with a single tent back up in the center. I'd guess they're either tending to their wounded and holding place while they wait on reinforcements, as they must have known that a force of three hundred was insufficient for a siege, or they're preparing to run."

"Okay, next steps please," I requested.

"Either we ignore them and prepare for the inevitable follow-up group to arrive, or we go hunting for that group."

"Right." I muttered, scratching at my chin and mumbling without realizing I'd said anything. "Gods, what I wouldn't give for a decent barber…"

"I can help you with that if you wish, my lord?" Isabella said. I blinked, realizing what I'd just said aloud.

"We have a barber?" I asked.

She hesitated for a moment. "I trim my family's hair; I always have. I could do yours, if you wish?"

"Gods, yes please, after this meeting." I scratched furiously at my neck where the beard hairs were being pushed back under the skin by my constant use of armor. "Right. Talking seriously, though, I truly doubt there aren't more of the Dark Legion coming, especially after my last little discussion with the Dark Wanker, so we need to act as though they are.

"Waiting for them to arrive gives them a certain amount of control over the battle, and that's not a good idea, generally, but frankly, neither is trying to go toe-to-toe with them, considering they're supposed to be our equals…" I caught the expression on Romanus' face, and I paused, looking from him to Augustus, who were clearly trying to figure out how to phrase something. "Okay, out with it. What don't I know?"

"Well, Jax, the Dark Legion isn't exactly as straightforward as we are. First of all, while anyone can apply to join the Legion, the *Imperial* Legion, I mean," Augustus said carefully, sitting forward and leaning his massive forearms on the edge of the table. "Very few actually make it to legionnaire status. They join as an aspirant, and then, through many different events, the majority fail.

"They might not be physically strong enough, training might break them, or they might receive injuries that result in them leaving. Some very brave aspirants simply fall apart when they kill for the first time, or they see others killed. Some break when they are among the first at the scene of a monster attack, and they leave. In the old days, they'd have been hunted down and forced to return, but frankly, we haven't the manpower." Augustus shrugged, and I read the look of old pain on his face.

"The Dark Legion, on the other hand, recruits far more...forcefully than we do. Not only do they recruit through the standard channels, but they also recruit from the prisons, they purchase slaves, and their church offers loans to those who need them, with outrageous penalties.

"When people inevitably fail on the loans, they take their children, indoctrinate them into the church, and raise them as unthinking soldiers. Finally, there is a small but growing group that, from what we can see, are literally an elite faction amongst their ranks: the bastard children of noble houses, the third and fourth sons of merchants, and so on. They've made the Dark Legion a more socially acceptable place to deposit the useless children that were given over to drink and debauchery."

"Sounds fun," I quipped.

"Yeah, well, the issue that's comes of that," Augustus replied, smiling faintly, "is that this means the Dark Legion is unofficially split into three groups: fodder for the monsters and for battles, actual warriors, and the social elite who do as little as possible, but have access to spells and other valuable benefits.

"I'm willing to bet we faced little of the actual fighting class here, probably only a few squads; the rest who charged in so blithely and were slaughtered were those trained and intended to do so. Last of all, we took out a good swath of their magically-inclined social butterflies."

"Riiiight..." I said carefully.

"So, we basically killed a lot of recruits they consider expendable and a handful of those they really don't. We can expect a much more serious push next time around." Augustus smiled humorlessly.

I sat back, grimacing as I recalled the crazy bastard I'd fought, remembering how fast and deadly he was, and that he'd been using the half-naked female legionnaire's swordstaff, not his own mace and shield that he'd dropped to save her.

"That's concerning," I admitted. "The ones I fought, well, they were good."

"They will have been *actual* legionnaires, their true ones, I'd bet. From what we know, they're split internally into slaves, slave-aspirants, aspirant-soldiers, soldiers, then legionnaires, with the officer class above the legionnaires. The nobles were likely killed by the first wave and finished by the rogue attack once the main force pulled out to follow you," Romanus said.

"It's true," Augustus agreed, reaching into his bag of holding and casually pulling out a greatsword, then another, and laying them on the table, accidentally shattering a jug and sending fruit juice pouring across the table. "Dammit," he muttered, shaking his head as everyone moved to contain the spill.

He flicked the tip of the first sword, sending a clear chime of shimmering steel into the air.

"You hear that?" he asked, waiting and repeating it until everyone had it fixed in their minds. Then he moved to the second sword and did the same. At first, the sound was the same, but as he passed one to Restun and they began to alternate, I noticed subtle differences.

"The second one," I muttered, pointing to the sword that Restun bore. "It sounds...different."

"It's enchanted," Ame said flatly, reaching out and putting a finger on the sword to stop the sound. "And a word of advice to you all: such noises are...unpleasant for our kind."

"Ah, my apologies, Ame," Augustus said formally, bowing his head, with Restun doing the same.

"It is no great thing, young lord," Ame answered, bowing her head slightly in return. "I simply wish to avoid the sound continuing. As to the difference in the swords, one is enchanted, one is not. Both are good steel, though. I suspect the first is from those you define as fodder, while the second has had additional work put in? Intended for the true legionnaires amongst their number?"

"We believe so," Romanus said, nodding.

"What's the difference between runecrafting and enchanting?" I asked, realizing it'd been digging at the back of my mind for ages.

"Enchanting requires little skill," Ame said firmly, folding her arms. "Runecrafting is the opposite."

"And that's a singularly unhelpful answer, thank you, Ame," I responded dryly.

"Fine." She sighed. "To enchant an item, you use a trapped soul or mana crystal and force a basic rune into it. Once its charge is used, it will gradually absorb mana from its surroundings to recharge itself. Then it may be used again. True runecrafted weapons or items can be used continually, and they will use the mana that is connected to them, either by crystal or user, or in the case of the Great Tower, the structure itself."

"So, why are enchanted items more common than runecrafted, then?" I asked, confused.

"Because they are children's toys; simple to make and easy to replace!" Ame snapped leaning forward and gripping the edge of the table. "Runecrafting requires years of study! Understanding why a single misplaced line could have dire consequences or tremendous boons! Understanding the rune means that you can adjust it, alter it, adding in secondary effects and beyond. Simply chaining together a few enslaved symbols and powering them up is as likely to result in the death of the wielder as anything else.

"This is why you see a thousand swords that do a minor amount of additional damage, but only one sword that kills trolls with a single, fiery blow, then slays a Demon with an ice attack. It is skill and understanding that matters, not simply repeating the same thing over and over! This is why the runes are so rare, because the few who have any idea try to hide them!

"A shield that was inscribed with a true rune would drain mana from its bearer at less than a quarter of the rate of an enchantment." She poured scorn into the very word. "It is cheaper and considerably quicker to simply enchant an item with a shield rune then layer a concealment over the top, when a true runecrafter might use a dozen or more complex runes, but the difference is night and day to the wielder!

"Additionally, an enchanted shield is weak against everything. You should instead enchant against fire, frost, or physical damage on top of the original rune. A proper runecrafted shield will resist all damage or permit you to focus against one kind at a time. Runecrafting is art as much as anything else. Enchanting is for the lazy."

"Ummm…" I rubbed the back of my head. "Did I give you that Shield rune yet?" I asked cautiously. She turned smoothly and slowly, like a warship's cannon tracking a target.

"What Shield rune?" she said in a calm, controlled voice.

"Give me a minute." I reached into my bag and rooted around, then moved to another, and another. "No. Damn it, what the hell did I do with it?" I mumbled aloud, before looking up to find Ame inches away, all her tendrils extended out, focused on me with laser-like intensity.

"Uh, remind me at the end of the meeting. I've grabbed a few magical items; you might like to go over them." I leaned back and fought the urge to pull a normal shield out to hide behind.

"You have multiple magical items, and you simply forgot about them?" she asked in a low hiss.

"Uh, yeah." I decided not to point out that I'd been back just over a full day and had been buried under responsibilities nearly every waking moment. "Sorry. Oh, and I got a Fire rune from Jenae as a quest reward. I think I've got the details for that somewhere, as well…"

"You…" she started, only to have Flux grab her and forcibly drag her back to her chair, whispering furiously. Every so often, outbursts rose from the pair, her gesturing at me and saying "but he…" and "the fool…" and Flux shushing her and calming her down.

"Moving on. So, we've found that the Dark Legion is egalitarian; they take any fucker, then they train them, right?"

"More or less," Augustus confirmed. "They accept more than we do, and where we fail out those who can't reach our standard, they have three options: fail and be worked to death, held to the same standard in exercise as those who can do it, but be thrown against targets as fodder. Achieve and be granted a relative level of freedom, but still be owned by the church, essentially. As mentioned before, this level is called a Soldier, while the first group is either a Slave-Aspirant or a Soldier-Aspirant, depending on if they manage to move up and get considered for better things. Then from Soldier, they move to Legionnaire. At Legionnaire, they have the basic gear replaced with enchanted and are given more specialized training, as well as a few rare individuals being granted additional blessings from their God."

"We believe the one you faced was one of the blessed, Jax," Romanus interjected. "We've heard that they are standard classes, such as scout, and such, but blessed–or cursed–with a warping of the bearer. A scout becomes a dark scout, for example, more easily able to hide and receiving more assassin-based skills and training. But whatever the alteration they make, it damages the bearer considerably, both shortening their lifespan and resulting in side effects that often require them to be culled after only a few years of service."

"Culled?" I frowned.

"Executed. I faced a dark warrior in a fight long ago," Restun said grimly, shifting the neck of his cuirass slightly to show the tip of a scar at the base of his neck.

"And?" I pressed, both confused and curious.

"It was a barfight that got out of hand," Restun said shortly. "My team and I were sent in to aid the guard. Twenty-seven died that day. The dark warrior killed them indiscriminately, from the person who started the fight to the serving girls to the boy peeling potatoes in the kitchen. Once they lose themselves in the bloodlust, they become more animal than man."

"What kind of fool would accept that?" I asked shaking my head.

"I doubt it's a deal they're offered," Romanus said. "From all we know, it's a rare thing. Some simply go that way, so I'd imagine it's something that done to them or an effect over time. We really don't know, but ultimately, it's an example of why you shouldn't do deals with a being who feeds on death. Any death adds to its strength, and it seems not to care about details like combatants and innocents."

"Either way, it's definitely something we need to know about, as that one almost killed me. Had there been more of them like that, my team would have been overwhelmed in short order," I said grimly.

"Unfortunately, it is simply the way of the Dark Legion. One silver lining to the cloud, however, is that those who go 'to the dark' as some call it, are often the most unstable, meaning that a single push might send them over the edge." Romanus smiled a little.

"And that's a good thing?" I grimaced. "Dude, seriously, we need to talk about your optimistic outlook on life."

"It's a very good thing, since we might be able to trigger the change when there's none of us to fight," Romanus said, smiling openly now.

"Go on." I responded, frowning.

"Control is the essence of all things to a Dark Legionnaire. They live with rules like lesser men do with fleas, I suspect to prevent exactly this. If we started to fire a few spells or crossbow bolts into their tents every time they made camp, we'd kill or injure one or two, but keep the rest on edge. We might be able to not only slow them and wear them down, but we might be able to set off a few unstable ones into using their powers on each other. Once they use their power on another Dark Legionnaire, they are culled."

"So, we harry the next force they send, lots of little things, with hit and run tactics, and let them cut out their strongest fighters for us?" I asked, grinning as it finally clicked.

"Exactly," Augustus said, matching my grin.

"This assumes that they will be sending more," Nerin pointed out, and the room went silent. "Yes," She sighed, looking around. "I know it is extremely likely, but that does not mean it is definite. They may choose to hold their position or to bring in more ships and face us in an airship battle."

"But it's unlikely…" I said carefully.

"It is, but if you send everyone out to face one possibility, then we will have issues if they perform another. You know this, boy," Nerin snapped, smoothing her skirts and adjusting a pouch on the wide bandoliers she always wore.

"True," I grumbled. "Look, people, we need to make this Tower as secure as possible as quickly as possible. To do that, we need three things, as I see it."

I sat forward, taking a drink and flicking the spilled juice from Augustus's earlier jug assassination aside, before counting them out.

"First, we need to secure the Tower itself. That's in hand, thanks to the golems incoming, the militia we're training, and the Legion, but we do need to secure the local area. That means clearing out any monster nests, wiping out the dickbags who are heading for us, and generally laying claim to the nearest few hundred miles.

"Next, we need to secure the lives of our people, which means a focus on the economy, crafting, and food, as well as the little luxuries, like making sure everyone has beds and clothes on their backs." I said sardonically, making eye contact with those around the table.

"Third, we need to secure the air, meaning we need the airships up and running, the crews trained, and the ships themselves ready to fight. That's down to you, Oren, Decin, and Riana," I said, looking at each of them. "Oren and Decin, get the ships ready, get the crews training constantly, run drills, and have them exploring the local area. All the things usually done on a ship need to be practiced, then add in things like boarding each other. Make use of the Alkyon, both as boarders and to make sure nobody actually falls off and dies. Riana, where are we with the cannons?"

She sighed, glancing to Ame and back before answering. "The cannons, well…"

"The cannons are death traps," Ame said firmly. "The runes they use to generate the power are sloppy, the containment runes appear to have been botched repeatedly, and everything from the dimensions of the projectile to the range are imperfect."

She looked around, and, seeing that everyone was waiting expectantly, she stood up and started to pace, her hands gesticulating as she explained. "Imagine you have a patch of smooth sand. You draw out a word, a long one, and ask your younglings to copy it.

"Then you leave after looking over what they draw once, and you erase your example. As you leave the cave, you tell them to draw this word one hundred times, and that they are skilled indeed. This wonderful encouragement makes them brave, and they start to draw. None of them understand what the word means, but they can repeat it."

She started to draw symbols in the air, a simple one that looked like a stylized A then went on through the alphabet, as near as I could tell. "As time passes, the younglings relax, they talk, they unintentionally stop faithfully repeating the symbols, and errors creep in. Gaps that were necessary become shortened; others that didn't exist are created.

"Still more symbols are entirely created in error...or repeated back to front..." At this point, she drew a b followed by a d in the air. "The perfect example the elder has drawn is long gone, leaving the younglings to compare against their own earlier examples, each other's, or–should they have access to it– the original device, one that has systems built in to prevent exactly this. This results in the students' creation being mimicked, not the master's. Soon, the variations are all that are left, and we reach the point which we are at today."

"We think...that is, Ame and I agree..." Riana said carefully.

"We need to scrap all of the cannons," Ame said firmly.

"What?!" I gasped at the same time as Decin and Oren.

"They are *all* dangerous to use. Months of training is given to those who fire them, and that is almost all in gauging the likelihood of a critical failure that would destroy the ship, almost none is given to actually aiming and using the weapons.

"If we could start researching how to build such a device, using the runes we know and keeping the best of the cannons for examples, while smelting down the rest, we would have magically charged metals ready for casting into the new cannons, greatly speeding up the production."

"And how long would production take?" I asked suspiciously.

"As you were sensible enough to send the engineers with skillbook training from the Old Empire to us, without us losing days searching for them," Ame said sarcastically. She had no eyes, yet *still* I could feel her glare. "I would estimate three weeks."

"Three weeks to replace the cannons?" I mused, rubbing my chin. It wasn't as bad as I'd feared.

"Three weeks to build a prototype," Riana clarified, shaking her head apologetically. "After three weeks, we should be ready to test the prototype. Then, if all goes well, we could start production, as soon as a proper smithy is built."

"Fuck." I slouched back in my chair.

"Quite," Ame agreed grimly.

"Yer canna be serious, lassie!" Oren snapped, sitting forward and swinging his short legs in agitation. "Three weeks wit 'out any cannon be three weeks tha' could lose us tha war!"

"You have cannons now, Oren, but you can't fire them," I pointed out. "Three weeks of waiting with the cannons removed from the decks that are useless, or three weeks of sitting, with them able to explode at any time?"

"Laddie, tell me yer no' be considerin' this!" Oren growled, tugging on his beard.

"They're right, Jax; we need to be able to fight, and if it's dangerous, well, that's the nature of war," Romanus said quietly, his calm voice cutting through the rising hubbub.

"And if it exploded the first time its fired and takes out the ship, then it's pointless," I retorted firmly. "Oracle, how many Fireball, Firebolt and similar spells do we have in the Hall?"

"Ah," She closed her eyes, checking over the details before coming back. "Sixteen," she said definitively. "There are almost a hundred in total that could be used as you think, but most are higher leveled spells, and unless the user has a sufficiently large manapool, they either wouldn't be able to use them, or they'd only get one spell off."

"Fine; get those sixteen and give them to Augustus," I said. "Augustus, I want you to pick sixty-four willing volunteers from the pool. Make them healthy and ready to fight; you've got a week. At the end of that time, give the sixteen best the spellbooks and take them out hunting. Once they've used the spells a few times in a fight, Oracle, you'll form a bridge and aid them in passing what they know to the remaining forty-eight. I know it's hard work and wipes you out, so I'm sorry to have to ask you to do this." I shot her an apologetic glance. "But it needs to be done."

"I know," Oracle said bravely, forcing a smile. We both remembered how exhausted she got after teaching just three spells in the past. "I can get Heph to help me, probably."

"Once you have these, they are to replace your cannons," I said to Decin and Oren. "You are to hand the cannons over to Riana and Ame, who will make damn sure they are as fast as possible with the replacements; am I understood?"

The group nodded at me.

"Jax, you had tasked me with a trip to Narkolt?" Augustus reminded me.

I swore. "Fine, okay, hell, I'm sorry to do this, both to them and to me, but Restun, this is now your problem. Pick out your volunteers and train them. If need be, keep them alongside my team during training," I said, before adding hopefully, "We could go a bit easier for a few weeks, after all…"

"No, I can achieve this as well as your own training. Never fear, my lord," Restun said placidly.

"Joy," I muttered before forcing a smile and thanking the Primus. "Moving on. Hanau, I want you to shift your focus in the short term, at least, possibly over a longer period, so consider a second to help you; Barrett, possibly. Make sure the ships are all outfitted and stocked, then you're to hand it over to another and take over trade and the economy. Take stock of the treasury and assist Cai there. You told me before that you were the trader on your ship, made the deals, and so on? Do that for us."

"Umm, Jax, we were mainly smugglers." Hanau winced slightly.

"Then you know where to look for additional markets. I don't care what the local wankers' laws are. We're under Imperial law. If something is banned under the Empire, it's for a good reason, like slavery. Otherwise, we deal in it. Make us money, Hanau," I said firmly.

"Yes, my lord." Hanau said, smiling.

"Cai, Isabella, and Nerin, look after our people. Make sure everyone has a job, somewhere to sleep, and food to eat. Beyond that, work with Hanau to figure out the internal economy. We need a form of taxation so we get back some of the gold we hand out in wages, but beyond that, we need to make people happy and safe." I got a trio of nods and two sets of smiles, with Nerin sniffing loudly.

"Yes, I know you don't do economy and would have made people safe anyway, Nerin, so here," I said, sliding a book I'd retrieved earlier across the table to her. She stopped it and picked it up, eyeing me warily.

"This is Magical Gardening, boy," she said slowly.

"Yes, and you once told me how much you wanted to learn that," I replied. "I need the herb gardens growing and producing fast. Woodite should be joining us in the next day or so; he's a tender from the grove and will be bringing his

Citadel

partner and two guardians. Once here, they'll probably take over a lot of the glasshouse. I need someone who won't back down and will be able to kick his arse across the continent, if need be. That's you if you hadn't guessed." I grinned. "That book is so you know what you're talking about."

"Hmm. I dislike learning from books, boy, but I will. This once," Nerin said, giving the lie to her dislike by the way she stroked the cover gently.

"What will you be doing, Jax?" Augustus asked me politely.

"Well, seeing as you asked so nicely, I'll tell you. I'll be questing, checking out the locations the Gods have given me, along with our slowly spreading mapping ability, and I'll be doing what that asshole keeps accusing me of..." I said, pointing at Bane. "I'll be being a murderhobo."

It was over an hour later, with the sun dipping behind the mountains and casting huge shadows across the land, when the council meeting finally broke up.

In addition to the minor details of who I was going to kill and where, we'd also covered the Gnomes and their need for catnip–which was apparently their version of seriously hard drugs without the side effects–the assigning of a team of a hundred people from the pool and a class-three servitor to the *Interesting Endeavor* to get Tenandra sorted out, and a crew to be put through rapid training to help her.

Finally, we'd set up a rotating watch to make sure that we knew what the hell was going on with the Dark Legionnaires, and a place for a ship to be stashed. In an emergency, they could fall back to the Tower with whatever news they needed to share.

With all of that sorted, we split up, taking a bit of time for ourselves to manage several individual jobs, the weirdest of mine being a meeting with Horkesh.

"Lord Jax!" the little spider cried, bouncing up and down in excitement, rushing for me with that insane, breakneck speed that arachnids had, making every instinct in me scream that I needed to Fireball her into the next zip code.

"Horkesh!" I replied, forcing a smile, amazed at how hard it was to build up a level of tolerance to her kind and how easily that accrued accustomedness vanished when I was apart from them. "How are you? I hear your crew is happy?"

"Very!" she warbled, slamming to a stop a few feet away and bobbing like a puppy that was about to piss itself in excitement. "My crew wish to stay!"

"Really?!" I asked, stunned. "I mean, that's great...but..."

"When we took the ship, there were issues...especially with the flying ones that we had, the...Alkyon? They did not wish to stay, but those we freed from the cages, they were pleased to learn and wish to stay as permanent crew."

"And the original crew?" I asked, remembering that I'd assigned her to Bateman's *Star's Glory*. It was a ship that was practically dedicated to slavery, working as a mixture of taxman and enforcer. They'd taken to enslaving the prettiest from the villages they visited if they couldn't pay their taxes to Barabarattas. Considering that most of the villages between Himnel and Narkolt tried to be free of them both, they were taxed heavily and regularly by both instead. That had resulted in a situation where they were regularly raided for slaves, slaves who had no hope left.

369

Then, the giant spiders had boarded the ship and stolen it, freeing the slaves. Unfortunately, they had been thousands of feet up by the time the slaves were free, so they couldn't just get off, and they were surrounded by Horkesh, who was the size of a Great Dane, and her soldiers, huge spiders that stood the size of horses.

"We put some in the cages, imprisoning them the way they imprisoned the others," Horkesh explained.

"And the others?" I asked.

"We split them between the former caged and ourselves," she said calmly. "We ate ours, but the former caged liked to throw theirs over the side of the ship. It was a waste, in our eyes, but they were theirs to do with as they pleased."

"Soooo, you ate some of the former crew, then put some in cages as, what, a larder? And the slaves threw their portions over the side?"

"Essentially," Horkesh confirmed, unconcerned. "You said that we may not feed on the citizens of the Empire, but they were slavers, and as such, food, yes?"

I paused as I thought it through, before nodding my agreement.

"Yeah, actually, fuck it. Feel free to eat the slavers," I said, my hackles finally settling as I got used to having Horkesh around again.

"Thank you. We had feared we had misunderstood."

"Nah, but remember, slavers *only*, or those who attack the Empire; they're fair game. Okay, I'm going to be making an announcement in the cathedral soon; might as well introduce you all there, so can you bring just one of your guards with you?"

"Of course!" Horkesh said, shivering with pleasure that I was asking her to do something.

"Fantastic…uh, what have you been doing since you arrived?" I asked cautiously.

"Mostly leaving your people be. We have stayed close by, and the ship is very convenient, thank you, but mainly, we have been exploring the surrounding area, looking for a new nest site."

"That's fine; any idea when Ashrag will arrive?" I asked, bracing myself.

"My Mother is at least a touch of risings of the daystar away."

"A touch?" I asked, and she raised her claw tipped feet, tapping each once, then looking at me to see if I understood.

"A touch, the times I could touch something without using the same limb twice…"

"Ah, eight days, then. Coolio."

Just over an hour later, I followed the last servitor into the newly cleared, relit, and frantically scrubbed cathedral on the ground floor.

I moved quickly through the crowd, people making way for me and my small entourage, until I reached a small platform and climbed it, coming to face the people gathered in the massive room.

It was hundreds of meters across, circular, and even now, alcoves were slowly growing from the living stone of the Great Tower, alcoves that were filled with the altars of the Gods, the last one being carried into place by a silent, hulking servitor golem.

I nodded in satisfaction, knowing that while it'd been done at my order, Jenae had been guiding Seneschal as well, as motifs of flames rose up the walls. Hundreds of magelights had been repurposed and installed. The cathedral, despite it being on the ground floor, now gave the impression of light and space, rather than the millions of tons of stone that were overhead.

There were just over twelve hundred people sworn to me now; well, around that anyway, and I couldn't be bothered to check right now, but Oracle had told me as we entered the room that almost all of them were here. Those few that weren't were out on patrol, and she said over and over not to worry about how many there were, but to speak from the heart.

I stood there, staring out at the sea of upturned faces, and my mouth went dry as the last conversations fell silent, and every eye fixed on me. I felt a sudden desire to tell a bad joke or to let out a truly tremendous burp, anything to break the reverent silence, I shook myself, forcing a smile as I pushed down the urge to do a little dance.

"Citizens of the Great Tower and of the Empire!" I called out, my voice echoing slightly in the empty reaches of the room. "This place has been set aside for the Pantheon of the Flame. The nine Gods will hear your prayers, your pleas, and should they judge you worthy, they may bestow their blessings upon you. But before they will do any of that, you must choose."

"I understand that some of you may not wish to follow a God, and that is your right. You don't have to worship any of them, and so long as you live in peace with your other citizens, I don't care, frankly," I said. Oracle covered her eyes with one hand, making me pause before soldiering on.

"Also, before we move to the Gods, I want to direct you all to the great big patch of space over there." I pointed. "Yes, that's a huge fucking spider, and a smaller one. Yes, I know a lot of you screamed the first time you saw her, and that doesn't help. The smaller, more *beautiful* spider..." I forced the words out and tried to make the point that I accepted her, and therefore, everyone else better damn well follow suit, "is Princess Horkesh. She speaks excellent Common and is here as an ambassador of her kind.

"The soldier behind her does not speak, as far as I know, but it's the size of a horse and extremely lethal, so please, don't piss it off. Horkesh's mother, Queen Ashrag, is on her way here, along with her hive. She will be living close by as my ALLY, and has sworn to never harm a citizen of the Empire, on pain of death. You are safe from her, and she is safe from you.

"She and her kind can produce excellent silks for clothing, and poisons to aid us, as well as being able to slaughter anything that pisses her off. She and her people are, and I can't stress this enough, honored ALLIES. Be respectful, behave yourselves, and you might even be friends, like Horkesh and I are."

Horkesh bobbed and danced a little in excitement, and I shook myself before moving back to the matter at hand.

"For those who do wish a divine boon and wish to aid the Gods and myself in this fight, I ask that you choose your God. Take the time to touch Their altar and reach out to Them, swearing your fealty. Once you have sworn to that God, whenever you choose, you may come here and pray to Them, as this location is dedicated to all the Gods, not just my Lady, Jenae." I risked a glance at Oracle, who smiled and gestured for me to keep going.

"The Gods each have Their own focus and Their own gifts to give in exchange for your devotions. I need to stress one thing, however, and that's that the devotions are entirely between you and the Gods. I would appreciate it if you would make it a part of your day to come here and take a few minutes to pray to your God specifically, because the Gods gain power from our devotions. They were weakened by that asshole Nimon's betrayal…"

The air seemed to grow darker, as everyone felt the pressure of the God of Death's attention drawn by being named, and I paused, looking up.

"And yes, I'm talking about you. Just because you're a God doesn't mean that you're not a complete wanker! You started this, and it'll be my boot that finishes it! Now, go on…fuck off!" I called out, glaring upwards. There was an immediate pressure change as Nimon's anger made itself known. But something that Jenae had let slip in one of our conversations was that the Gods themselves were restricted in what They could do, somehow. He'd used His followers to go after me, and I'd fought them, so for some reason I really didn't get, that meant that this fight had to be dealt with between us pawns, rather than by a giant thumb appearing and me being squashed flat by it.

Seconds passed, and the God of Death was forced out, the pressure leaving, as a different weight replaced it, the feeling of nine divine souls watching us.

"And there He goes!" I called out, shaking my head as though in contempt, while feeling my asshole twitch a little. It'd been a calculated risk, but I had decided on the walk down here that if I kept being respectful when I spoke about Nimon, it gave the wrong impression.

I didn't really do respectful well, anyway.

"So, when you come and pray here, you might feel a sensation of draining…that's your mana being siphoned to help the Gods. The thing is, and those who've been with me the longest can confirm this, I know…" I said, hoping for all hell they could. "…when you do this regularly, it helps you as well.

"The drain on your mana can help to increase your Intelligence and Wisdom stats, respectively. This means you'll have a better chance of being picked when it comes to giving out magical training, as we will be doing over the next few weeks." I finished, looking around until I spotted a familiar face in the crowd.

"Whatever you do, though, I don't want you to keep going when your mana gets too low, as I know you've been doing, Jory!" I said, pointing at him. "Jenae warned me that you've been pushing too far again." This was actually true; She'd not mentioned it recently, but whenever I'd heard about the devotions, She'd pointed out that he kept going until he almost passed out. "So, stop when you get down to the last ten or so. You'll know when because you'll start to feel fuzzy-headed and tired. Rest a few minutes, and you'll be fine, and you'll have helped the Gods in Their fight against the Wanker of Death and His followers!" I called out before pointing to the altar behind me in pride of place.

"Now, *this* is the altar of Jenae, Lady of Fire, Mistress of Hidden Knowledge and Exploration. I am the Champion of Jenae, and Martin here…" I gestured to the side for him to step up onto the platform, and he did.

"Martin is a Priest of Jenae. All the Gods need priests, and he is Her first. He has been given gifts and will aid you where he can, as well as carrying out the quests the Lady of Fire has given him. As I am a worshipper of Jenae, I suggest Her as your Patron if you wish to follow these paths. But all the Gods, save the Prick, are welcome here, so please, follow your heart!"

I turned, looking at the altar of Jenae, and as She'd agreed when we discussed it on the way down, She appeared.

It began with a flicker of fire, one that grew in the air, then descended to form a line, then a pillar of flame. The pillar split down the middle and rolled to either side, becoming a doorway, and She stepped out of it.

Jenae wasn't in the usual outfit of dusty leathers and metal armor I usually saw Her in. Instead, She wore a mixture of beautifully crafted red plate armor, chainmail of the blue found in stars, and Her hair floated around Her as She appeared in a corona of fire.

She hovered there for a few heartbeats as the crowd gasped and fell to their knees, before She settled atop a throne that appeared for Her.

"Rise, my children. My champion must introduce my brethren," She called out in a smooth, strong voice.

I bowed my head, gesturing to the altar a dozen meters to the right of Her.

"Next, we have Ashante! The Goddess of Nature and Life, a Goddess of growers and those who love the lush flora all around us." The air shimmered over Her altar as Ashante stepped into view, clad in green plate that ran from light to vibrant to so dark that it was almost black, with hints of flowers and vines adorning the metal.

A long cloak of ivy hung from Her shoulders, Her black hair gently caressing the leaves. Ashante paused, smiling down at the figures gathered before Her, then She reclined gracefully onto a throne that appeared as She sat.

"Cruit!" I called out. "God of the Earth and Stability, Lord of Stone and Strength!" The figure that appeared wore armor of plain black and grey, which looked battered and dusty, seemingly made of slate. He wielded a massive warhammer in one fist. With a grunt, He nodded in satisfaction at the Dwarves in the crowd, who had sank to their knees at the sight of Him. Where the two Goddesses appeared twenty feet tall and slender, yet gave off a sense of implacable will and strength, He was maybe fifteen feet tall and ten wide. His shoulders alone looked as though He could lift an airship without noticing, and as He set the hammer down on the flat plate of its head, resting one hand on the pommel while seated on His own throne, He gave a single nod of approval to me.

I couldn't help but bow my head in response before moving on.

"Sint!" I called out. "Lord of Light, and God of Order." With my words, He appeared, the flare of bright white light making everyone shield their eyes. As it died away, a massive figure in full silver plate armor appeared.

Where the others adorned their armor or colored it, and in Cruit's case, it was seemingly made of the mountains themselves, Sint wore plain steel with a blue tabard that ran down the front and tied at the sides, carrying a huge broadsword and tower shield. He removed His helm–He'd been the only one to wear one so far, a Y-shape cut out of the otherwise unadorned helmet–and let His short, golden curls free, nodding to me and giving me a faint smile before resting His sword and shield against the sides of His throne and sitting back.

I bowed again to Sint, feeling that, despite His formal and sensible outlook, besides Jenae, He was probably the one I got on with the easiest.

I moved to the next altar, the last on the righthand side of the room, as Jenae was at the head, and the door at the foot as people entered.

"Tamat, Goddess of Darkness, Lady of Assassins and Larceny." When Tamat appeared, I paused unconsciously.

Her hair was long and black, curls bouncing with every step, Her lush figure encased in black leather with blades strapped to Her practically everywhere I could imagine. Straight, curved, twisted, and angled, the blades themselves seemed to hug Her figure, as though they loved to be close to Her. I blinked as I realized just how much I'd been staring.

"Glad to know I can still turn a pretty boy's head," She whispered to me in the silence of our minds, blowing me a kiss as She seated Herself, crossing one leg over the other and staring around at everyone in challenge. "I…uh…welcome, Goddess!" I forced out, hurriedly. She was one that might have the least overt followers, yet I needed Her to be as powerful as possible.

"Tamat, the Goddess of Assassins, is also the Goddess of those who hunt in the night, of those who protect us from plots, and Lady of the Knives in the Dark," I said, not wanting to go so far as to admit I was training assassins of my own. "If you wish to go down the path of the rogue, She is the Lady for you." She smiled at me, inclining her Head and winking before I moved on to the other side of the door, starting to run back toward Jenae.

"Vanei, the Goddess of Air, Lady of Change," I intoned as a beautiful woman in light blue chainmail and white hides appeared, a long spear in one hand, Her hair a mass of blonde curls, which was pinned high on Her head by an intricate tiara. Huge, white, feathery wings sprouted from Her back as She smiled gracefully at the room and sat down on a specially altered throne to accommodate Her wings. I glanced over at Lydia and saw the look of awe and the way She'd already taken involuntary steps in Vanei's direction as soon as She appeared.

"Lagoush, Goddess of Water, of the Depths, and of Healing and Alteration, Lady of Peaceful Passages," This Goddess was clad in greens and blues, a scalemail outfit that hugged Her figure fantastically and made me think that the creators of the underwater superhero franchises all owed Her royalties, or Her them.

Her hair was a peculiar grey, green, and brown that made me think of seaweed or fronds more than hairs. She locked Her eyes on me and smiled, nodding once and sitting on a rock that rose to meet Her. A spear with five tips laid out like a trident but mimicked the cardinal points of the compass with a single central tine, which She gripped casually in one pale hand.

I smiled back at Her, then moved to the final pair of Gods.

"Svetu, God of Invention, and Lord of Crafters and Creators!" I called out, and the figure that appeared almost made me laugh.

Where the others were huge, not just physically, but gave off an imposing sense of will, Svetu appeared to be a normal-sized Gnome, topping out at just under three feet, carrying at least of a third of His weight in bags, pouches, and tools that hung off Him.

He wore simple leather pants and tunic, heavily reinforced and padded, with a monocle stuck over His right eye, and He'd perched Himself atop a comfy old stool before He blinked, seeing the disparity in sizes. He mushroomed to twice His size before sighing and making an 'up' gesture that made His stool grow so that He could see over the heads of the gathered crowd.

"I was busy," Svetu said, an edge of irritation clearly tamped down as His voice echoed around the room.

"Then I apologize for interrupting you, Lord Svetu," I said quickly, then moved to introduce the final God, who stepped forward as soon as I spoke his name.

"Tyosh, God of Time and Reflection, Lord of the Everlasting Chime." I introduced the figure that stepped forward, who wore a single orange robe. His head was shaved, and His beard ran to His stomach, knotted and braided in intricate ways.

He was smooth-skinned, but each movement conveyed a sense of peace and of power. Strangely, I felt that He was one of the most dangerous of the Gods, despite appearing to be the least overt threat of them all, seated unarmed atop a pillar that appeared for Him.

"These are the Gods, the Pantheon of the Flame, and They are ready, should you wish to meet Them, for you to worship Them, and to learn Their ways." I finished formally, stepping down out of sight.

For the next twenty minutes, we remained as people spread out, moving to the figures that called to them most of all. I made eye contact with Jenae once, getting a sense of Her thanks, before I took Oracle's hand and left the room.

We all headed our separate ways, although Flux went with Bane and me, filling me in on the progress of recruiting some sneaky types for the assassination and bodyguard teams.

It was in progress, but it wouldn't happen overnight, was the general theme.

Once Flux left us, and we finally reached the living floor again, I forcibly evicted Bane from our room once he had satisfied himself it was clear of any threats, then let out a sigh of relief.

I stripped off, thankful beyond measure that the legion tailor and armorers had delivered new gear while I was out: two full sets of clothing, replacements for the damaged parts of my armor, including a stern letter from Thorn not to fuck this set up, and joy of joys, a new and improved belt.

This one was designed to be worn over my armor, where the last one had been an impulsive addition, so hopefully this one would last longer. As I checked, the toggles came loose, revealing the razor wire hidden inside.

Jax's Surprise		Further Description *Yes/No*	
Damage:		25-100	
Details:		This belt contains a deadly secret, a length of high steel razor wire crafted by a legionnaire weaponsmith with far too much time on their hands!	
Rarity:	**Magical:**	**Durability:**	**Charge:**
Unique	No	100/100	N/A

I smiled, reading the description, then grunted as I felt the wire. It was sharp, yeah; the tiny teeth drew blood with ease, but I pulled on the toggles, drawing it taut, and grinned even wider.

I'd been impressed at the sheer lethality of the razor wire before, but now? Pulling on the toggles made the teeth slide out of seashell shaped recesses in the line, swinging them up into a one-up, one-down layout.

I nodded in satisfaction, stowing the line away, then turned, opening my mouth to speak, and froze.

Oracle was seated facing me on a low chair, the back was to me as she straddled it. Her arms were braced casually across the top of the chair as she watched me and waited.

She'd changed again; her hair was long and blonde, cascading down her right shoulder and onto her chest in a wave of loose curls, while she peeked up at me from behind heavily-lidded eyelashes, green eyes sparkling. Her lips were full, and her figure…

The way that she straddled the chair, with the back between her body and my eyes, meant that she was mostly concealed, but as I watched, she stood up, revealing the tiny bra and panties set of silken wonder in black and dark green, the straps and stockings that shimmered slightly as she walked towards me. My mouth went dry as all the blood rushed elsewhere.

She reached up and drew my face down for a single, hot kiss, and then she was gone, sauntering past me to sit out on our balcony. The cry of the birds flying past at dusk and the occasional joyful shout of a child from below floated up to us, as she leaned back against the railing and crooked a finger at me.

"I believe you owe me those lips and tongue," she whispered, and I grinned, the failing light outlining her against the oncoming night as I went down on one knee, feeling one thigh coming to a rest over my shoulder.

CHAPTER THIRTY-FIVE

The next morning found me stretched out on the bed, sheets half thrown off, and brain as rumpled as they were. I blinked and tried to clear my mind, wondering what had woken me.

I lifted my head in time to see a fantastic peach of an ass walking away from me towards the door. A white shift appeared, clinging to her skin like weighted silk. Oracle spoke quietly to someone, then returned, setting a tray on the rickety bedside table that had appeared from somewhere.

"It's time to wake up," she said softly, tucking one leg under her and sitting on the edge of the bed before leaning down to kiss me, her hair falling across us both and shutting out the world like the curtain of night.

I reached up, wrapping my arms around her and half-rolled, half-flipped her onto her back, holding her under me as I admired the view.

She looked up at me with a brilliant smile. Her hair was black with a hint of blue and her eyes caramel this morning, her face flatter, with a button nose, and I knew that no matter what form she wore, I'd always know her instantly. The thin layer of silk that separated us evaporated, her skin warm against my own.

"We should be getting up," she warned me between kisses. "It's after sunrise…" I lowered my face to a nipple and kissed it before sucking it into my mouth and making her gasp.

I moved up after a few seconds of kissing and teasing and gazed deeply into her eyes again.

"We're supposed to be joining the others for breakfast," she protested, triumph in her eyes as I glanced to the side, noticing a pot of coffee waiting on the tray.

"Well, you've got two choices, then," I whispered, rising to kneel beside her.

"Oh?" she asked huskily, looking down and back up.

"We're either going to be late," I said, moving the tray onto the little bedside table where it'd probably be safer.

"Umm hmm?" she responded, talking with her mouth full.

"Or very, very fucking late…" I groaned.

An hour later, we finally arrived at the agreed room, a handful of doors down from the council chamber, less than twenty meters from our bedroom.

As we walked in, hand in hand, interrupting the low murmur of conversation, I spoke up quickly, holding up one placating hand.

"Hey everyone, I'm sorry we're late. You wouldn't believe the traffic this morning," I said, straight-faced.

"Probably not." Grizz smirked knowingly as I took a free seat next to him and reached out for the coffee pot.

This was one of the best things I'd found since returning from the city. Not only was coffee a thing there, but some fantastically helpful soul had kept the best coffee beans, which were exclusively for the use of the nobility, close enough to the stocks that Mal had ordered them stolen with everything else.

When he'd found out about their existence, he'd apparently started an uproar as everyone frantically sought to find the bags, six of them, all huge sacks. In the confusion, he'd had to hint at what they were, quietly, to a legionnaire.

That legionnaire had denied all knowledge, and with a straight face had promised to hunt out Mal's "cheap but favorite family blend" for the few coins Mal had tried to bribe him with.

He'd then passed word to an Optio, who dropped everything, and, after passing word up the chain of command, had every ship searched for the missing VIP packages.

Five were then delivered to my personal stash as a gift from Romanus, one having been given to the legionnaire who'd raised the alarm with wholehearted thanks.

I'd never been overly fussed on coffee, thinking it was all good, and had initially accepted the beans with a confused and lukewarm word of thanks…one that changed to me pressing a platinum coin personally into the hand of a stunned legionnaire with my personal thanks, as a second bag was gifted back to Romanus for himself and his close team.

Another was given into the regular stores, for a special occasion, or when someone was in particular need.

That left three bags, and they were kept firmly under lock and key. I'd gone so far as to explain in no uncertain terms to Caron and Ronin what would happen if any went missing, and that they would thoroughly regret breaking into the storage room.

They, of course, had professed total understanding and had vowed to watch out for any "shady types," then tried to break into the locked room less than an hour later.

I looked over at the barely conscious bard and grinned at the evil look he was giving me.

"So, I heard someone tried to break into Praetorian Primus Restun's bedroom last night…the poor, brave fools," I said innocently.

"I hate you," he muttered, before perking up as I passed him a cup.

"I did tell you that you'd regret breaking in," I reminded him, getting another glare over the rim of his coffee mug.

"Too soon, boss. Seriously, that's just too soon. The poor guy hasn't even been sitting an hour yet," Grizz jumped in gleefully.

"What happened to Caron?" I asked casually. Yen spoke up.

"We rescued him from the Primus after two hours. The little bugger couldn't see straight for his tears and kept falling over."

"Ah, well…" I winced, having not wanted it to go that far.

"He's learned a valuable lesson, boss," Grizz said soberly.

"And it's one he'll remember, rather than getting stabbed the first time he gets caught," Ronin admitted, idly tapping his stomach. "That's how I learned."

"A stabbing?" Lydia asked.

He nodded sourly.

I smiled, it was the first time I could remember Lydia speaking to the bard without barking an order or growling.

"Yeah, see, I got stuck in the window of a..." Ronin started to say enthusiastically, before I raised a hand, cutting them all off.

"Sorry, guys, we can talk about random shit later. We need to get a move on, as we've got a lot to do today."

"Would have been easier if someone wasn't so late," quipped Bane. I gave him the finger, carrying on as though nothing had been said.

"*ANYWAY*, we're going back out to do some more questing, some more levelling, hopefully, and to explore some of the places the Gods have made me aware of."

I spread out a sheet of parchment on the desk, and, with multiple derisive comments from Bane, Tang, Arrin, and Giint, who sniggered constantly, I drew a basic map of the continent.

Then I marked out the Tower and a few other notable locations, and shaded in a full line down the middle for the mountain range. Once this was done, I started marking arrows on the map.

"This one and this one," I mumbled, measuring distances off and checking them against my actual map as I tapped them, "are both sites for Vanei, and I suspect they'll be damn important to you, Lydia," I said, pausing and making eye contact with her. "So, they're getting hit on this trip." I thought a moment before closing my eyes and sighing.

"Seneschal..." I called out, and as I felt the surge of mana nearby that preceded his physical form building itself, I went on. "Which ship has Oren put aside for us to use today?"

"The *Sigmar's Fist* is in dock, awaiting your orders, Jax."

"Fantastic; can you get the captain to come up here, please?" He nodded once, vanishing. "And the navigator!" I called after him before going back to the drawing. "Now, we need to decide on the order we hit these locations, as some are fairly open, and I'd assume have been raided before. What we need either wasn't found or wasn't recognized for the value it actually held.

"This one here..." I tapped a location that was almost due south of the Tower, in the hills on the far side of the lake where I'd met Bane and the others. "...is apparently one of two that holds either weapons or something we can use for training our assassins, as it was mentioned by Tamat. The next one, due west of that, is a cave in the mountains, which apparently contains items Svetu needs for his chosen people."

"Gnomes," Grizz interjected in a low whisper to Giint, nudging him and grinning. "You know, your lot."

Giint glared at the huge legionnaire, jabbing him in the leg with a narrow scalpel that passed through the links in the chainmail, making the massive man grunt.

"I wouldn't irritate him, Grizz," Yen said dryly. "He's been making weird shit every time I turn around. He's also carrying a lot of herbs; might even poison you."

"Not going to happen," Grizz said firmly, smiling down. "Giint and I are friends. He wouldn't poison me!"

"He might if I pay him enough," Yen declared offhandedly, staring pointedly at her lover and fellow legionnaire.

"Nah," Grizz started to say, and I tuned him out, checking details on the maps.

A little while passed while I tried to figure out distances and timings, before Captain Kinnet arrived, along with Raan, her mate and helmsman–apparently also her navigator–bearing her map.

I spread it out on the table and started marking the same points on theirs as on mine, before asking for recommendations on which we could realistically hit in short order.

"Awkkk!" Raan grunted, shaking his head around a central point, like a dog, rather than side to side like a human.

"What's wrong?" I asked, and he tapped the farthest south marker, the one that indicated Sint's incoming champion.

"This one, it is at least five days there and back. These…" he said indicating the two that were for the quest for Lydia, were the next to the south, and about forty or so miles apart. "These will take a day and a half to reach, with several hours flight between the two, and this one…" indicating the next northernly from the last pair. "Is about four hours' flight from these."

He looked to Kinnet, who nodded and back at me in confirmation.

"If you wish to go to all of them, my lord, this will take at least a week," Kinnet said hesitantly.

"No chance then, unfortunately." I frowned, rubbing my chin in thought. "We could do two days, three at the most." I decided, considering the options. "We know the Dark Legion are down to a handful. Even if they dispatch their full strength now, they won't reach the Tower for at least a week, not with the road only halfway cleared. Hmm…" I idly measured off distances on the map with a pair of fingers, until Kinnet handed me a compass.

I spent a few minutes measuring, calculating, and muttering to myself.

"Okay Kinnet, Raan, how long until you're ready for a flight?" I asked.

"We're ready now, Lord Jax," Kinnet said straight away.

"Good. It'll be the long flight, so prepare for a week, including the time to search at the other end," I said firmly.

"A week?" Kinnet asked, clearly confused after my insistence that we couldn't afford the time.

"Yeah, you're flying with us, but as an escort only for the first bit. Then I'll update your maps, and you can head to pick up Sint's Champion. I'll get him to update you with a description and greeting protocols, so the champion will recognize you." I reached out and patted the confused Alkyon on the shoulder, and she straightened, eyeing me. "Don't worry; just go and prep the ship, please."

Once she was gone, and Raan with her, I spoke aloud to Seneschal.

"Seneschal, old buddy, got a question for you." I waited as he formed his body and looked expectantly at me.

"Yes, Jax?" he asked politely.

"Before I move to the meat of the issue…Tenandra," I said carefully. "Can she hear us?" There was a long moment of silence before Seneschal spoke again.

"No, but only because she is not currently listening," he revealed eventually. "She can sense my interest in her now, but she is busy with her body. Oren has a small crew going through practice exercises on her deck, and she is fascinated by them, the people scrubbing her body down, and the servitor I have working on her lower hull."

"Is she stable?" I asked, and he was quiet while he thought about the question.

"I'm afraid not," he said eventually. "Could she be? Yes. Is she currently? No."

"You need to explain a bit more than that, mate." I snorted, sitting back and taking a swig from my now-cold coffee.

"She has just found her purpose, and she is desperately trying to hold onto it, to appear straight and sensible, despite hundreds of years in the dark, tormented and starving. While we were ordered to sleep–and she was ordered to as well, I'll point out–she was awoken regularly by outside forces, she received confusing input, and felt her structure failing around her."

"So did you," I said, glancing at the newly repaired walls.

"Not exactly. I was still connected to my body, so when I was awoken by you, I set about establishing control again and finding out the state of things as I went. She was consumed by fear, separated from the Prax by the vault, and able to sense only the barest details. Plus, she spent years being tortured by the Lich. To answer your original question, and, I think, the reasoning behind it: no, she is not stable. Yes, I think she can fly and do missions for you," Seneschal clarified carefully.

"Go on."

"What Tenandra needs more than anything is a purpose, and especially to be free, to be moving, exploring, and realizing that she is not about to be returned to the dark, if you intend to take her with you."

"I do."

"Then she will excel, because this is exactly what she needs. She needs to be useful, and she needs reassurance. What are your intentions?" Seneschal probed.

"Oh, they're entirely honorable," I quipped, snorting and sitting up. "Sorry, man. No, seriously, though, I'm thinking that we go on the *Interesting Endeavor*, with the *Sigmar's Fist* as backup, just in case of any issues, until we reach the second farthest point. We then let *Sigmar's Fist* go, they continue to collect Sint's Champion, and we start questing.

"As it'll take more than a day to get to that point, we've got plenty of time for the crew to get some practice in on a ship that has only a minor need for one, but it keeps Tenandra busy and happy, it trains the crew, and it doesn't interfere too much with the ship's repairs."

"Perhaps; are the Gnomes to remain aboard?" Seneschal asked, and I groaned.

"Seriously?" I asked rubbing my temples. "The mad little bastards are aboard her?"

"They are living there," Seneschal confirmed. I shot a frown at Giint, who shrugged, glancing at me from under seemingly burnt-off eyebrows.

"Giint lives wherever," he grunted.

"What the hell happened to you?" I asked him, frowning, as I spotted the shortened length of beard and moustache that he was trying to hide behind a mask he had pulled up around his neck.

"Explosion," he said tersely.

"I didn't hear it."

"Want me to make it bigger next time?" he asked in a low growl.

"Not really, you fucking nutter." I stared at him for a moment before grinning, and he shrugged. But I caught the hint of a smile at the edges of his mouth, and I felt better about him.

"There are still significant areas of the ship available for habitation and storage, due to the relatively small crew aboard," Seneschal pointed out, and I massaged my temples.

"Fine. Might as well give the rest of the Tower some peace, I guess," I mumbled.

"There are three Gnomes currently working on Mal's *Falcon*, as well. They are apparently doing upgrades that you authorized?" Seneschal said off-handedly.

I shook my head as it registered. "Sneaky bastard, I agreed to only one." Then I chuckled, smiling evilly. "Hey Giint, fancy dropping off a little bag of treats with your friends on Mal's ship before we leave?"

"Give it to me," Bane said, holding out a hand. "You know Giint will only keep it."

"Point," I pulled one of my last three sticks of the super catnip out of my bag and handed it over to Bane. Then I snapped off a tiny bit of another and tossed it to Giint, feeling like I'd been handling dog chews with a puppy watching me, and now I had to give him something, or I'd feel guilty all day.

"Can you get Tenandra's attention for me, Seneschal, and can she manifest here?" I asked, making him consider, then nod. Several seconds went by before a figure slowly grew from the floor up. At first, she stopped at around six inches, which seemed the standard "small" size for a Wisp, but once she spotted that Oracle and Seneschal were full-sized rather than treat-sized, she *shifted* again.

This time, she stopped at just under six feet tall. Her hair was a light reddish-brown, her kitsune ears and foxlike tail twitched from side to side, and she stalked about restlessly, getting used to the new body. She wore a blue fitted suit, a white blouse, and a tricorn hat with gold edging, making her look both insanely respectable and alluring. It was hard to miss the way the others watched her, and not just the men, I noted, catching Yen's look of approval at how tight Tenandra's pants were.

"You summoned me, my lord?" she asked me after a few seconds of settling into her form, and I nodded.

"Yes, how's the ship, or your body, or whatever?" I asked, and she looked at me, then down at her chest, then back up, confused.

"I mean your ship-body," I clarified, and she nodded as though that made sense.

"I am intact and receiving a lot of repairs right now. The servitor in particular is proving extremely useful...might we arrange a trip to the Prax to retrieve more?" she asked hopefully. "There were over a hundred aboard; many were class four, and..."

"Ah, damn," I muttered, shaking my head regretfully. "No, we just don't have the time. Not to mention, we'd still need to clean it out fully and start the repairs before we could get them. It's not like it's just a case of 'land and pick them up,' after all."

"But..."

"Not right now, Tenandra. We both know it'd take weeks of work to get through the Prax to the point that we could even charge the various golems, and there's at least one SporeMother aboard her now," I said firmly. "I've summoned you for a different reason."

"I live to serve," she said formally.

"Well, what I need to know is, are you ready for a flight? From here to here…" I indicated on my drawing. She furrowed her brow, holding her hand out and summoning a topographical map into the air that she settled over the table.

"Is this easier, my lord?" she asked, and I gaped at Seneschal and Oracle.

"Why didn't you guys do that?" I asked, getting embarrassed shrugs from them.

"I didn't really think of it, to be honest," Oracle admitted shamefacedly. Seneschal nodded.

"Right," I said, showing Tenandra my own map, which she transferred details from, revealing the entire continent, including a hell of a lot more ruins than I had any idea were there.

"I have populated the land with the details I can remember," Tenandra said quietly, gazing over the map as a red outlay appeared. "This was the shape of the land before the Cataclysm, and these were cities, holdings, and structures commonly known of." Another dozen destinations sprang to life, mainly on the far side of the mountains, and many of them were ringed with red light.

"These were enemy-held cities; the Night King and his minions may still hold them, and…"

"We're getting distracted," I said, shaking my head and holding up one hand. "We can discuss the Night King and all that later, as you clearly know some things we don't. For now, my intention is to take quarters on your ship. We will all fly to this point…" I indicated the second farthest-out marker from my map, and Tenandra made it flash on hers.

"From that point, *Sigmar's Fist* will go on alone, and you will stay with us, continuing to train your crew, as the servitor works on you. You will ferry us from these points around…" I marked each point on the map, then drew a line back to the Tower. "Then you'll take us home. If there are any problems, you and Oracle can communicate at distance, I seem to remember; what range is that?"

"About ten miles without difficulty, then it grows increasingly more difficult the farther out we go. Our maximum range is around sixteen miles," Tenandra estimated, looking uncertain.

"Right, but Oracle and Seneschal could reach each other over several hundred miles, it just took a lot of mana. Hell, Seneschal managed to reach her on the Prax, and that was what, four hundred?"

"Well, yes, but they're from the same species," Tenandra stated.

I stared at her in incredulity. "You're not?"

She frowned at me. "Of course not!"

"What…" I started to ask before holding my hands up to stop the inevitable discussion. "You know what, fuck it. Doesn't matter." I waved a dismissive hand and smiled through gritted teeth. "I don't need to fucking know; you can tell me another time. You can communicate, even at a distance, that's the part that matters. Can you be ready to leave in an hour?"

The ship-Wisp nodded. "I am in a cradle on the flight deck. It should take no more than half an hour to gather the supplies needed, and we will be ready to leave."

"Fine, do that. Seneschal, get Romanus, Augustus, and Mal to meet us there," I ordered. Tenandra vanished, while the others stood and gathered their gear.

"Am I still welcome? After, you know…" Ronin asked me awkwardly.

I nodded, gesturing to the door. "Yeah, that's fine, mate. Just sod off, and we'll meet you on the ship, although you and your little buddy will be giving me all my damn loot back when we return." I fixed him with a warning glare as Lydia grabbed him by the shoulder and hauled him to his feet.

"Jian, a word before we go," I said, and everyone else left the room.

"What can I do for you, my lord?" he asked respectfully, and I glared at him.

"You can quit that shit, for a start." I pointed one finger at his face, and I got a wan smile in return. "So, I need to know what's going on with you and your Demon."

Surprisingly, he went bright red. "I...I...Uh...I didn't mean for it to happen..." he stammered. "It...well, we just..."

I frowned and waited. I was about to say something when Oracle's hand, which had been lightly holding my own, gripped harder in warning. I shut up, returning to watching him and feigning patience.

Several seconds passed, then Jian broke, slumping forward and picking at the edge of the table, then taking a swig of cold coffee and grimacing at the unexpected temperature.

"Look, Jax..." he started. "After Ty'Baronn was dispelled, I tried to reach him, and I got nothing, I tried a couple of times, then I remembered that you'd given me both books to use, and I thought maybe he was too weak, you know? So I used the second book, I reached out to him...and it all went a bit wrong."

"Explain please, Jian." I groaned internally, wishing I'd taken the book back when we found out they were likely to summon the same Demon. From what Ty'Baronn had explained, he would make a deal on the far side, in the hells, and get a Demon subservient to him to act as a second bonded creature, as the book only linked to him, but...

"Look, you know that Miren and...we broke up, right?" he said uncomfortably.

"Not really, but I knew there were some issues," I said, carefully not referring to the way that he and Tenandra had looked at each other.

"Well, yeah...turns out that by the time they got here, she hadn't waited for us to try and sort them out," he said darkly. "She has a new legionnaire 'friend,' and he's teaching her all about the stuff I couldn't..." I couldn't help but raise my eyebrows at that last bit, and he glared at me. "About hunting and tracking, you asshole."

I had to fight to not grin, seeing the real Jian again for the first time in days. He was usually quiet and respectful, but always had a smile. Of late, he hadn't as much, and the last day he'd just seemed entirely exhausted. I'd put that down to the loss of Ty'Baronn.

"Go on," I said, feeling Oracle squeeze my hand in warning that I wasn't to give him grief.

"Well, Ty'Baronn was on the other side, yeah, but, well...he was too weak to reach the summoning circle in time," he admitted, his face growing red.

"So, what...you bonded another Demon?" I guessed, sitting upright and finding myself suddenly far more interested.

"Yeah," His face went even redder as he hung his head.

"And who is it? Can we meet him? What kind of powers does...he...?" I faltered as Oracle started to giggle.

"It's not a male Demon, is it, Jian?" she asked, and Jian shook his head, focusing on his hands.

"Can you summon her?" Oracle asked. He sighed heavily, starting to whisper under his breath, his hands tracing sigils, and his fingers leaving a trail of light behind.

After thirty seconds or so, a portal appeared in the floor, and a new Demon rose out of it, with a weakened Ty'Baronn visible on the far side, squeaking furiously to be resummoned "in place of *her!*"

I blinked, surprised at the figure who rose into the air, then settled back down on cloven hooves, grinning at Jian then looking both Oracle and me over in clear approval.

"Now this is more like it!" she said, grinning and licking her lips suggestively. "Who do I get to play with first?" the Succubus asked, and I slowly pulled my gaze away to stare at Jian.

"You kinky bastard," I murmured, caught between shock and wanting to give him a high-five.

CHAPTER THIRTY-SIX

The Succubus was taller than Jian, at nearly six feet tall. Her legs changed from those of a goat mid-way up her calves and were human by the knee, with a pointed tail that flicked and danced in the air from just above her ass.

Her skin was pale, her eyes black with red irises, and two small horns, curled like those of a goat, grew from her temples. Her fingers ended in sharp, short claws, and her canines were longer than a human's, but the rest of her...

"Wow," I said slowly, looking her over in appreciation. The rest of her was voluptuous and toned, her ears were long, like those of an Elf, and her large, bat-like wings were furled behind her back as she grinned around before pointing at Oracle.

"I want to play with you first. They can watch, then..." She purred seductively before Jian broke in quickly.

"Sehran!" he cried out, waving his hands in negation. "No! For fuck's sake, it's not like that!"

"But why not?" she asked, confused. "You're here, they're here; you summoned me, so?"

"I think Jian is going to have to explain a few things to you later, Sehran...was it?" I asked her, unashamedly admiring her figure.

"It is. I am Sehran of the Second Circle, Ninth Fortress of Az'kalett," she declared proudly. "Eleventh of my name, I am skilled and willing, and I sense your bonds. You are his master, and therefore mine as well. Maybe we could..." She raised an eyebrow, a sultry smile coming to her lips as she looked at my crotch suggestively.

"No!" Oracle spat, suddenly between us, and I felt the mana in the area shift as she drew heavily on the Tower. The light shining from the magelights dimmed, and she fairly crackled with power, lifting one hand that suddenly ended in clawed tips, warningly.

"He is MINE," she growled.

Sehran backed up, her face blanched of all color, even her ruby red lips suddenly seeming wan and dull.

"Yes, mistress," Sehran whispered, dipping low into a curtsy and spreading her wings wide as she ducked her head. "This one regrets the misunderstanding."

I reached out and slowly drew Oracle back, feeling the shift as she released the Tower's mana collectors.

"Now, now, Oracle," I said gently. "Sehran, I hadn't intended to make the point quite that forcefully, but no, I'm not interested, sorry. I have all I need. You are obviously...serving...Jian. I'm just worried for him, as in my lands, we have tales of Succubai and the consequences of tying yourself to one."

I tried not to smile as Oracle sat back down. On my lap. I risked a glance over at Jian, who looked mortified, and I couldn't help but grin. "You split up with Miren, so you summoned a fucking Succubus to take care of your pecker, mate? Seriously, that's a fucking legendary break-up move right there." I laughed. "Just wait until Grizz hears about this."

"Please, Jax, do we really need to tell anyone else?" he asked, his face bright red.

"We'll see mate," I said, feeling instantly sorry for him, but still highly amused, having screwed someone I shouldn't have after a break-up on a few occasions myself.

"I can be useful, my lord," Sehran said quickly, her tone respectful. "We Succubai are not just pleasure mates. Yes, we enjoy our traditional roles, but after the third Demon war, there were too many Succubai left, and too few males. We were forced to learn to fight, rather than simply servicing our masters' needs. I can glamour opponents, distracting them. Or I can entice them; if they are weak enough, I can even convince them to join my side permanently."

"And I assume you have armor?" I asked, glancing at her figure again before shaking my head. "Because if so, please put it on. You are seriously distracting."

"It is part of our gift, Lord. Even now, when you are aware of my powers, you cannot help but be drawn to look." She grinned, reaching out and carving a symbol in the air before her. A small rift opened after a handful of seconds, and her hand dipped inside, pulling forth a bundle of clothes.

She quickly dressed, and while she was no longer naked, she was still distracting.

"Can you stop that as well?" I sighed, forcing myself not to look. A second later, she was just another person around me, and I let out a relieved breath.

Yes, she was quite beautiful, and yeah, her armor hugged her body amazingly, the daggers and whip on her hip completing the whole look. But she was now in the same category as "hot girl at work who's dating my mate, and less hot than my girl," meaning she was still noticeable, but in more of a noticeably pretty way than a *me must fuck now* way, as she was before.

"I can distract your enemies, aid your allies, and serve as a last line of defense. I also have a sonic shriek attack that, while indiscriminate, I can aim. While it will cause pain and disorientation to anyone inside its radius, my allies will receive less damage than my enemies," she offered, smiling calmly, seemingly pleased to not be required to work as a full-on sex kitten.

"Anything else?" I asked her.

"Lastly, lord, I will grow in power with the stronger and more numerous souls I harvest."

"Explain that, please," I ordered.

"My bond requires that my master and those he designates are protected from me. I cannot harm him, nor you, so please understand that you are safe from me. But I suspect the stories you have heard regard our harvesting of souls. It is how we grow in strength. You level, the experience you gain from each kill serving to improve you, but for Succubai, we harvest, gaining points from stronger souls, instead of experience."

"Points?" I asked carefully.

"Stat points." She smiled, the tips of her canines showing over her lips.

"How many?" I asked.

"It depends on the creature; sometimes it's a single point or none. Other times, if they are powerful, well, it could be two or three."

"Uh huh," I said, nodding. "So, Jian, you summoned a Succubus, and that's why you've been looking so worn-out? I mean, seriously, dude, you look terrible." I pointed out, switching to him.

"I've uh…not been getting much sleep." His gaze pointed squarely at the floor.

"My fault," Sehran agreed, shrugging. "It's kinda my job, as well as my favorite hobby."

"She could swear the Oath; then we know she's safe," Oracle offered, and I nodded as she explained the concept to Sehran.

It took a few minutes of back and forth and explaining details, such as intent as well as the exact wording. By the end of it, Jian looked relieved that he wouldn't have Sehran taken away from him, and he grinned the entire time as she spoke her Oath to me, adding in that he was her secondary master, as he made some changes to the bond between them that I really didn't understand.

Once all that was done, Sehran was grinning like a fool, having been apparently more than a little convinced that, unless she played the dumb sex kitten role, she would be banished instantly. I dismissed Jian and Sehran, who was ecstatic to be able to see more the Tower and this realm than just the inside of Jian's bedroom, and I turned to Oracle.

"You think this will work?" I asked, nodding at the recently closed door.

"Her becoming a citizen that's bonded to Jian, rather than his Demon slave?" she reiterated. "I'm not sure, to be honest, but it's definitely what they both wanted. Considering the fact that she needs his manapool to survive here, much like I do yours. She's not entirely free, but she's no longer in one of the hells, and did you catch the change in speech?"

"When she went from 'me gonna fuck you and you and you,' to…fuck, I don't know the word, means literally 'to speak properly,'" I muttered, rubbing the back of my head in embarrassment.

"To articulate," Oracle said, smiling at me.

"Yeah, that," I agreed. "She suddenly started speaking far nicer and more carefully."

"We will need to watch her, Jax, but between the Oath to you, the bond to Jian, and his very clear orders for her to not harm a citizen of the Empire, I think we're safe from her," Oracle said, twisting around to rest her chin on her hand and watch me.

"So, 'suck it and see', basically?" I asked, and she purred. "I actually meant 'let's see what happens.'"

"That's a shame," she muttered.

I laughed, lifting her from my lap and standing up, twisting and popping my back.

"Well, you nearly broke it this morning, anyway. You know the phrase 'could suck a golf ball through a hosepipe' isn't meant to be accurate, right?"

"I took it as a challenge," she replied loftily, and I made a show of adjusting myself while shaking my head in mock sorrow.

"Seriously, I think you did some permanent damage," I whined, playing along.

"So, *don't* do that again, then?" she asked.

I threw my hands up, palms facing her and patting the air soothingly.

"Whoa, whoa, let's not go that far. Definitely do it again, DEFINITELY, just…maybe go slower. I thought the back of my skull was going to pop from the pressure of the vacuum." I grinned mischievously, and she punched me, shaking her head as I started to laugh. "Okay, okay! You're the best, seriously…and yeah, I love you," I said warmly, sweeping her up into a kiss.

A few seconds later, I set her down. We left the room, headed back into our own room, where I swept up my gear, made sure I actually had a change of clothes packed, considering it was going to be a full day or more before I even got to fight, and we'd be gone several days. Then I headed to the flight deck.

On the way, I had a short conversation with Seneschal and Heph. Oracle flashed off to retrieve the books with one of my pouches, and Cai ambushed me and badgered me incessantly about various minor issues that needed to be dealt with.

It was a necessary evil, but damn I hated all these details. Finally, just before I reached the flight deck, I made everyone stop, and I cast my bodged-together spell to communicate with the Gods, explaining my intentions to Sint, who, surprisingly, seemed amused and promised to give the *Sigmar's Fist* some guidance.

Augustus was waiting for me on the flight deck, along with Romanus and Restun. The conversation was a fast one with Mal sidling over to listen in.

"So, to confirm," Romanus said carefully. "Primus Restun is to give out these books to the new magical ranged squad he is to train." Romanus gestured to the stack of books that Oracle had taken out of my pouch and handed over. The entire floor came to a halt as they watched in awed silence over the sheer number.

"Augustus is to take a ship to Narkolt with Lord Hannimish and the Researchers who wish to leave, and both attempt to achieve peaceful relations with the lord there and to recruit and return with their branch of the Legion. He is to also spend as much of the fortune you gave him as needed to secure spellbooks and skillbooks we don't have."

"That's right," I said, smiling.

"And I am to keep watch over the Dark Legion, work on the defenses, maintain order here, and continue with the daily exercises, while Alistor is to maintain the rule of law. Cai is to run day-to-day operations, and we are to integrate the majority of the people as best we can?"

"Integrate everyone," I said firmly. "They are our citizens, and we have a hell of a lot of jobs that need doing. I'd also like you to start to recruit from the pool any who want to be legionnaires. Train them, start to work on the long-term plans here, as frankly–and I can't believe how shitty this sounds, but I'm still going to say it–we'll run out of legionnaires before we run out of enemies."

"I seem to remember a deal for the catshit?" Mal interrupted, grinning hopefully.

"Thank you all," I said to the others, and I held up a hand to halt Lord Hannimish, who was hovering off to one side, then turned to Mal and sighed irritably.

"Right; Mal, you're desperate for the catshit coffee memory. I know you, so what's the deal here?" I pressed, getting a look of utter innocence that made me instantly double the price in my head on general principle.

"It's just somethin' I'm curious about, that's all," he said placatingly, spreading his hands. "Seriously, Jax, can a fella not just be curious about the world?"

"A 'fella' can be, but you fucking can't, you shitbag," I said dryly. "You've got an angle here, and you're looking to ruin someone's day. I'm fine with that, I just don't need it to be mine, so come on, give it up."

"Look, maybe there's a similar business in the village of Sarat. Maybe, just for the sake of argument, my father had been tryin' to purchase some lizards that did the same thing, because he deals in coffee, or would like to. Maybe I'm just a dutiful son tryin' to look after his aged father," Mal said, the utter picture of trustworthiness.

"And maybe pigs will fly," I said, sparking a confused look from him. "It means that's bullshit."

He shook his head firmly. "Nope, all true. There're just a few maybes in there, that's all..." he said, grinning roguishly. "Look, kid, I'll level with ya. That coffee plantation south of Sarat is insanely expensive to buy, or it was. They were makin' a fortune, until there was an attack. Bunch of people died, though the animals survived.

"There're a few people who sort of know what they're doin' there, but it's all trial and error now. Yeah, you say the memory deals in cats, and this is some kind of lizard that they're usin', but that's fine. I'm bettin' the memories given to the right people would turn the village right around. They start makin' stupid money again, they need protection, and I can arrange that with my father. They're thankful, and they need us, so we get the good shit and a percentage of the profits. Everyone wins."

"Everyone"? I asked suspiciously.

"Well, we do, as we get the good coffee and half their profits, and the villagers get protection. Actual protection I mean–hired guards, not a bunch of guys threatenin' them–as well as their livelihoods back."

"So, who loses out?" My eyes narrowed, waiting for the other shoe to drop.

"The nobles." He beamed. "Because my father will double the price to them for shits and giggles, and once they know he has control over it, they'll go sniffin' and try to buy it back. The entire village has been up for sale for years since the attack. He'll buy it, we all make the profits, and we get to laugh at the nobles over amazing coffee."

"Two things," I said, holding up two fingers. "First, who's 'we' in the 'we take half the profits'?"

"See, that's just hurtful. I mean you and me...and my father, and my crew," he said, slowly adding in the others as I watched him intensely.

"And its equal shares, so I get what? Be exact, Mal," I said warningly.

"Well, we'd have to buy the village, so you'd get one share, same as me, and my crew..." He started calculating, still smiling, and I snorted, shaking my head.

"Nope. I get half. Half of ALL the profits, Mal. In fact, you know what," I said, breaking off as I saw just the person. "Hanau! Get your arse over here!"

The tall Elf jumped over the railing of the ship to the floor, landed beautifully, and jogged over, coming to a halt and smiling pleasantly at us both.

"Hanau, there's a village to the south, grows some kind of fantastic coffee..." I started to explain, and he nodded knowingly.

"Sarat, though it had a monster incursion and it was trashed; most people left." He rattled the details off without a thought.

"They left, eh?" I said, studying Mal carefully. "That's interesting. Well, Mal here wants us to do a deal with him for a memory crystal that includes the information they need to set up a new operation.

"He wants the Tower to give it to him in exchange for one share, and thinks that the other shares should be spread out between him, his father, and his crew, so here's the first deal you get to make for the Tower. Whatever deal you make on our behalf, you get five percent for the next year and a bonus, depending on how much you make Mal cry. Have fun!"

I chuckled, then I patted Mal on the shoulder, and Oracle gave me a kiss on the cheek before flying off to the Hall of Memories to retrieve the Crystal.

"Hey, no, wait!" Mal started to complain, but I was already striding away.

"Lord Hannimish," I greeted the nervous noble, nodding to him as he bowed to me. "I'm sorry I've not had time for you. It's been…busy…since we met in the Prax."

"No apologies are necessary, my lord," Hannimish said smoothly, shaking his head and forcing an obviously sad smile. "I wanted to apologize again for Joshua's actions and assure you that he is not indicative of my house or my relatives. I was authorized to try to seek an understanding with you, or arrange a meeting, preferably, between you and the Lord of Narkolt, Lord Rewn…"

"I haven't the time, frankly," I said, cutting him off with a sigh. "I would meet with Rewn if I could, honestly. But days spent in travel when I have enemy forces practically on my doorstep and more coming is impossible. I'm sending my heir, Primus Augustus, Duke of Himnel, in my place.

"Considering all that has happened so far between Narkolt and my forces, including the fact that a mixed fleet from both cities, bearing fucking *SporeMothers* as enslaved weapons, tried to attack me, I'd appreciate an explanation. Failing that, Rewn will be formally stripped of his position, and a second declaration of war may be issued. I'd prefer to avoid that, so when you go with Augustus, I suggest you be very convincing when you speak to your Lord."

"Lord Jax, please!" Hannimish begged, shaking his head. "Please understand: Lord Rewn would not have done this. Yes, he rules with a looser hand than Barabarattas does…did. But he would never permit anything like this. It must be a third party; a supporter of Barabarattas, perhaps. Narkolt would never…"

"Then I look forward to you proving this and brokering peace between us." I cut him off with one upraised hand. "I'm sorry, Hannimish, both for your loss and for being so short in our dealings, I really am. But my experiences with your people have been pretty shit so far, so I suggest you do your utmost to persuade your Lord of the need to be friendly. Now, I need to leave. Have a good flight, and good luck."

I took my leave of him, walking toward the *Interesting Endeavor*. I'd taken three steps before Cai appeared, smiling.

"I've included rations and tents, as well as half the alchemy ingredients we had, as you requested. Tel has sent you a copy of his notes and asks that you check them over to see if you can improve his recipes. Oh, and Thorn and the others are fighting with Heph over the production order for the new smithy, once it's complete. He wants to work on parts for the other facilities, while Thorn and the other smiths want to start work on the parts for the upgradable smithy, saying that was your direct order?"

"Hmmm, well, yeah, I guess. Split it down the middle. Let Heph work on the parts. Thorn is to work on getting some spares for the Legion made first, then we need some armor for everyone else; the militia forces, I mean, and Legion recruits. Once that's done, and only then, she can work on the forge upgrades, as that's weeks of work alone. I know the resulting armor and weapons from a higher-class forge would be better, yes, but the weeks we'd lose, when there are assholes incoming already?" I shrugged. "We have to be sensible."

"True. With that in mind, I'd like to send a party to scavenge the site of the fight with the Dark Legion," Cai said hesitantly. "Yes, I know that's likely to get them attacked, so I'd need to send Legion guards with them. But there's likely to be a lot of armor and weapons we could salvage, and even if it had to be smelted down, it's still good metal."

"Talk with Romanus, and if he agrees, then get it done. It's a good point, and you're right, there have to be parts that can be salvaged. Okay, Cai, I'll be gone a few days. You've got enough ships. If you need us back sooner than that, we'll have someone watching the skies. Send a barrage of fireballs up when its dark, have a second ship relay the signal as well, repeating it every hour. Even if Oracle can't hear the others for whatever reason, we'll be able to see that, and we'll return."

"Good luck, my friend," Cai said, clasping my wrist, and I grinned, returning the gesture.

"And to you, Cai, although I think you need it more, all things considered!" I retorted, winking at him as I let go and boarded the ship. As with every time we got to fly, I found myself grinning as the gangplank was pulled up and the ship hummed to life under my feet.

I turned, looking over the ship, and breathed a sigh of relief, knowing that, in the next few days, I only had near-death experiences, libidinous demons, and alchemical explosions to contend with, rather than the shitty pestering of command.

"Come on!" I called out. "Let's get the fuck out of here!"

Chapter Thirty-Seven

We cleared the flight deck a few minutes later, Tenandra and Jian happily working the ship out, with the supposed captain of the ship and his helmsman looking a little pissed as they were temporarily put out to pasture by the pair.

I checked on them, examining the warped and damaged spells that had created a way for the helm to be controlled from inside the wheelhouse. The runes had been masterfully repaired by the servitors, and they now gave an excellent view all around, as opposed to the faulty and contradictory imagery they had provided before.

I made sure they were okay, then left them to it, joining the rest of my team and chatting for a few minutes before leaving them to get themselves situated in their various bunks. Satisfied that the trip was comfortably underway, I turned my attention to Ronin and Lydia, who had hung back to speak to me.

"What's up, Ronin?" I asked.

He coughed, looking uncomfortably at Lydia, then leaned in and whispered to me.

"Is it true?" he asked furtively.

"What?" I asked him, in a normal voice.

"You know...that Jian, well..." he hedged, waggling his eyebrows suggestively.

"Yes, he has a Succubus. Her name is Sehran, and she's going to be with us for a little bit, mostly as a trial. You know, like you are," I said pointedly. "Is that it?"

He grinned, undeterred, then ran off.

"That's goin' to be fun," Lydia spat, shaking her head in disgust. "A Succubus an' a bard on a small ship for days on end."

"Point," I responded, sighing. "Besides that, what's up?"

"Well, two things. First of all, I, uh...thank yer." Lydia mumbled, looking at the floor, then up at me, red-faced.

"What for?" I asked her, confused.

"This whole mission, the quest; it's my quest isn't it?"

"It is, but don't worry about it."

"Don't...we're leavin' the Tower, we're flyin' days to tha south..." Lydia sputtered.

"Lydia, we're on a quest given by several Gods that will vastly strengthen the Tower. Yes, you gain from it directly, but hell, so do I! You're a frigging Valkyrie. I'd be insane not to make the effort and get you some goddamn armor and training, wouldn't I?"

"Well, still, thank yer." She blushed and smiled, clearly embarrassed.

"Any time, right; what was the second thing?" I asked, smiling back. "I need to get a move on, if I'm to make sure we don't all run out of damn potions this time around." I gestured to the ladders leading down into the hold, where I'd set up my alchemical station during our last flight.

"Well, that's a point," Lydia smirked insidiously. I paused, suddenly feeling that something was wrong. "Primus Restun said tha', as he be stuck at tha Tower, I'd need to run today's trainin' for ye."

"Now, wait a minute…" I protested, and she blatantly ignored me.

"An' 'e said to remind yer that yer swore to obey 'im, an' any trainers he places over ye for two hours of each day as a minimum, provided there no' be a real reason not to. Alchemy might be important, but it'll only take a few hours, so…" She reached into her bag and pulled out a gauntlet I recognized.

"Wait, is that…?" I froze, my mouth going dry and bladder suddenly seeming very full.

"The special weighted armor Restun had adjusted for ye, yes." Lydia confirmed cheerfully. "Time to get into yer gear, Jax." Her smile grew predatory. "The others be gettin' changed for their workout as well."

The next two hours were hell on earth, as Lydia stood in the middle of the upper deck with Bane on the lower. They both screamed at, kicked, and cajoled the rest of the squad into running, jumping, burpees, and more in circuits of the ship.

To make it worse, the others were in plain workout gear, while I was in full weighted armor.

Even Grizz admitted afterwards, when I was sprawling in a puddle of my own sweat, trying to remember my name, that he felt sorry for me.

After ten minutes more, I managed to crawl to the room I'd put aside, and I laid motionless on the floor, muttering about the things I was going to do to them all, including making it law that punishment of the Scion like this was to result in it being dealt back to them later, ten times over.

I pulled up my notifications, as I could do little else, and read through them.

Congratulations!

**Through hard work and perseverance,
you have increased your stats by the following:**

Agility +1

Strength +1

Continue to train and learn to increase this further.

I groaned, glad that at least I was getting something out of the damn exercises, then dismissed the prompts, moving on.

You have made progress in a Quest!: Bring Back the Old Gods

Bring back the Old Gods to displace Nimon and return balance to the realm. Aid each to find a champion that suits their aspect, and spread knowledge of the Gods to bring about a new Golden Age.

Gods Awakened: 9/9
Champions Chosen: 4/9
Reward: Blessings of the Gods, 100,000xp, Random local notable locations identified

"Wait a minute," I muttered, then hissed sharply as I forced myself up off the floor and glared at the next screen.

Congratulations!

The Goddess Tamat has agreed to your recommendation and has accepted your sworn bondsman Bane Ter'Jax as Her Champion!

Rewards: Improvement of Bob (in progress), 100,000xp, notable locations marked on your map.

*

Congratulations!

The God Svetu has chosen your sworn bondsman Giint as His Champion!

Rewards: Improvement of Tower facilities (in progress), 100,000xp, notable locations marked on your map.

"Holy fucking shit with a cracker on top!" I gasped, reading the details over, before letting out an incredulous laugh. Svetu had actually chosen Giint! The mad little bastard, utterly batshit as he was, was now the Champion of his people's ancestral God. I couldn't *wait* to introduce Svetu to the rest of His people, the ones that weren't completely mental.

I laid back down and wasted a few minutes fantasizing over taking Him to the villages we'd been told existed far to the south, just for shits and giggles. Then I sighed, dismissed the details, and frantically closed the Class choice screen before it could open fully, barely managing it in time and letting out a relieved breath when it faded from view, deciding I'd ask Jenae about that the next time we spoke.

Then, I checked my character sheet, remembering I had seven points to assign, as well as needing to check where my experience was after that unexpected two hundred thousand extra had dropped into my lap.

I read through it quickly, then put five points into Constitution, gaining another hundred health. The remaining two points, even though I hated doing it, went into Luck.

Luck was once a dump stat for me, like my Charisma, in games at least, because I could never see any physical change or result that I could point to and say, "there it is, that's my points at work." That said, I could definitely see when I fucked things up and blamed bad luck, so I bit the bullet and hit accept, stiffening up as pain tore through me, my body altering at a genetic level.

I sagged back a few seconds later, panting again, but as the torment of a full-body toothache died away, I let out a sigh, definitely feeling healthier, if not markedly luckier.

Name: Jax Amon	
Titles: Strategos: 5% boost to damage resistance, Fortifier: 5% boost to defensive structure integrity, Champion of Jenae: One search for hidden knowledge every 24 hours	
Class: Spellsword > Justicar > Champion of Jenae > Imperial Magekiller > Imperial Justicar	**Renown:** Imperial Scion, Lord of Dravith
Level: 24	**Progress:** 307,653/570,000
Patron: Jenae, Goddess of Fire and Exploration	**Points to Distribute:** 0 **Meridian Points to Invest:** 0

Stat	Current points	Description	Effect	Progress to next level
Agility	42	Governs dodge and movement.	+320% maximum movement speed and reflexes, (+10% movement in darkness, -20% movement in daylight)	4/100
Charisma	25 (20)	Governs likely success to charm, seduce, or threaten	+150% success in interactions with other beings	47/100
Constitution	55 (50)	Governs health and health regeneration	1080 health, regen 74.25 points per 600 seconds, (+10% regen due to soul bond, -20 health due to soul bond, each point invested now worth 20 health)	71/100
Dexterity	60 (55)	Governs ability with weapons and crafting success	+500% to weapon proficiency, +50% to the chances of crafting success	49/100
Endurance	47 (44)	Governs stamina and stamina regeneration	940 stamina, regen 37 points per 30 seconds, (each point invested now worth 20 stamina)	68/100
Intelligence	60	Governs base mana and number of spells able to be learned	580 mana, spell capacity: 33 (31 + 2 from items), (-20 mana from soul bond)	17/100
Luck	25	Governs overall chance of bonuses	+15% chance of success a favorable outcome	32/100
Perception	46 (36)	Governs ranged damage and chance to spot traps or hidden items	+360% ranged damage, +36% chance to spot traps or hidden items	72/100
Strength	38 (35)	Governs damage with melee weapons and carrying capacity	+28 damage with melee weapons, +280% maximum carrying capacity	15/100
Wisdom	41 (31)	Governs mana regeneration and memory	+465% mana recovery, 6.15 points per minute, 310% more likely to remember things, (+50% increased mana regeneration from essence core)	99/100

With that done, I forced myself to my feet and stripped ʋ at the wolf whistle that came from the door as Oracle slippʰ softly behind her.

"Where've you been?" I asked, and she shrugged.

"I didn't feel like watching you sweat–not when it's no fun–ʲent t̮ to Tenandra. We got Jian to summon Sehran, and the three of us haʲrly ch̟

"I bet that scared the hell out of Jian." I sniggered.

She laughed. "It really did!"

"What now, then?"

She tapped her chin thoughtfully. "I thought I'd come work on sonₛₚₑₗₗₛ, maybe try to figure out a decent shield while you work on your alchemy?

"That'd be useful."

I put the last section of armor away before stretching and letting out a grunt as a muscle twinged from overexertion.

Oracle settled herself on the wall, floating four feet off the ground, her lithe form stretching out as though lying on a bed and looked distractedly into the distance as I started to set up.

It took me twenty minutes to get the gear organized properly, the various beakers, boiling apparatus, mortar and pestle and more, not to mention preparing a bunch of vials and sorting out the second desk for the ingredients. But once it was done, I settled onto a stool and started to work.

The first two hours I spent making traditional health, mana, and stamina potions. I managed to make thirty of each, allowing our little team of ten to have three of each available at all times. They were weaker potions than I'd have liked, restoring only a hundred and fifty health, two hundred stamina, and two hundred and eleven mana, respectively. But I was determined not to waste the damn opportunity this time around.

Once those were done and the last batch sat cooling in the rack, ready for the corks to be added to the vials, I started the *real* work.

I'd skimmed over the notes that Tel had sent me, nodding when I found something right, or something new, and occasionally adding in corrections or advice in-between lines, but now I turned to a clear page, and I started to make my own notes.

I began with the ingredients that were known to make poisons, separating them out and choosing five of them. I spread them on the table before me and worked left to right, picking each up and examining it with everything I could: my new abilities, my spells, noting everything from the smell to the texture. Finally, after making sure I had a general-use antidote available if I needed it, I ate them, one at a time.

By the time I was done, I had a better picture in my head of the various sections of the plants that were needed, which were stronger or weaker, and surprisingly, which sections could be used as cures or ingredients in health potions. Satisfied with the usefulness of my research, I took a break and checked my notifications over.

Jez Cajiao

Congratulations!

For staying true to your choices and for walking the Path of the Creationist, you have gained a point of Intelligence!

*

Congratulations, Apprentice!

You've taken further steps to a wider understanding of the art of the Alchemist! Your dedication to your art has taught you that no ingredient is one-sided. Poisons can heal, and healing potions can kill, depending on the circumstances.

The Path to Healing Pattern Mastery has continued 11/100

I sorted through the ingredients as best I could, working them in every way I could think of and making notes on which methods improved what I'd come to think of as the poison pattern.

It was peculiar; where the healing one felt like a warm blanket being slowly stitched together as I built more sections, the poison one made me feel sick.

It began with a single ball in my mind's eye as I regarded the pattern. As I learned more, I found additional balls appearing. As I made another tiny step, followed by one more, then more and more, connections started to form, linking one section of the pattern to another. In my mind's eye, chemical symbols half-remembered from childhood started to grow.

As the hours passed, I felt the pattern growing section by section, and I became almost frantic, pawing through the rest of my ingredients, searching for more and more segments.

After five hours, my eyes sandy and aching, my mouth as dry as a litterbox, I finally sat back, one hundred and forty-seven ingredients wasted.

The vast majority *had* been truly wasted. I'd reverted to the most basic methods of preparation I knew, boiling and chopping, rather than the careful examination and improvement I'd started with, but I ignored the flashing notifications in favor of the single vial that sat before me, glimmering slightly.

At some point in making it, I'd channeled my mana into the mixture. I had no clue when or why, but by the end, I was down almost a hundred mana, and I was left with a potion that shimmered and bubbled gently in its glass prison.

Viridian Night	Further Description Yes/No		
Details:	The potion of Viridian Night is rare and costly to procure, having a threefold effect on those that are infected with it. First, the victim is struck with a sense of reassurance that all is going according to plan. Second, they develop an extreme lassitude. Third, and finally, they begin to lose their health at a rate of 3.7 points per second for 60 seconds.		
Rarity:	**Magical:**	**Durability:**	**Potency:**
Legendary	Yes	100/100	6/10

I stared at the description and wondered over the damn ingredi
I started to parse them out, discarding the failures, being damn thankf
in my desperation-induced state, I'd continued making notes.

I added up what I had, included what I could remember of the proces
sat back, shocked.

To make this single potion had taken forty-seven separate ingredients.
lemons were the weirdest part; why the hell had I included four whole lemons?
shook my head and pulled up the notifications, getting my second shock of the day.

Congratulations!

For staying true to your choices and for walking the Path of the Creationist, you have gained a point of Intelligence!

*

Congratulations, Apprentice!

You have taken further steps to a wider understanding of the art of the Alchemist! Your dedication to your art has taught you that no ingredient is one-sided. Poisons can heal, and healing potions can kill, depending on the circumstances.

The Path to Poison Pattern Mastery has begun 23/100

"Twenty-three points?" I muttered in shock, then concentrated, pulling up the mental map of the poison pattern which I'd so painstakingly constructed. I studied it, glowing there before my eyes. It was beautiful and terrible, with the vast majority missing still, and I shook with fervor.

I had to do this! I *could* do it. If I could find all the ingredients, all the ways they linked together, I could create a poison that would kill even Gods.

I could level the playing field between myself and Nimon in one fell swoop, and it wouldn't be the way that everyone expected, certainly not from blundering me.

They all thought I was thick as fuck, and I didn't care.

I'd never been the smartest, and that was fine, because I had my brother, and it was always us against the world. But without him?

Well, it was time to start taking steps to make sure that I could win, that my people could survive, and if that included poison, then so be it. I didn't like it, but I didn't have to. I disliked losing and death more.

I had a momentary sense of agreement and kinship from Amon as I leaned back on the stool, and I heard Him speak to me for the first time in what seemed like forever.

"We do what we must; we blacken our soul 'til naphtha seems like sunshine, and in return, the little child can see that light. They can condemn us, curse us, and revile us, but because of the things we do, they live to do these things.

"Welcome, my heir, to adulthood."

CHAPTER THIRTY-EIGHT

I sat in silent contemplation for countless minutes, until, of all people, Arrin came to rouse me, Oracle having slipped out to get him.

"Hey, boss," Arrin said, smiling amiably as he leaned against the table and looked down at the potion. "How's it going?"

"Arrin?" I muttered, startled out of my dark thoughts. Amon retreated, the seemingly intact mind starting to drift apart. Fragments of songs, pictures, and the smell of a rose garden in full bloom next door to a bakery drifted through our conjoined minds.

I stamped down on it, forcibly blocking him away again, and squinted up at the mage.

"Uh…what, sorry?" I mumbled, scrubbing my face and blinking myself awake.

"I asked if you were alright?" Arrin repeated, looking me over.

"Yeah, yeah, I'm fine, man. Just working, you know?" I said, forcing a tight smile.

"Yeah, well, we've been talking, and this is the result," he declared, gesturing me up with one hand as he grabbed my arm, pulling firmly. "Come on; on your feet, boss."

"What's wrong?" I asked getting up. "What's happened?"

"You did," he said grimly. "Come on…" He led me from the room and out into the hall, turning me into a small stateroom at the end of the hall, where the rest of the group waited with their bedrolls out.

"What…?" I asked again as I stepped inside, only to have Lydia intractably point to a seat in the middle of the group.

I took it and the glass Grizz pressed into my hands, before Lydia spoke.

"Jax, ye've not stopped in weeks. Ye always be runnin', runnin' from this job to that fight. Tha only times yer ever stop, yer either workin' on a new potion, a new spell, or unconscious from an injury."

"Well…"

She silenced me with a look, passing me a bowl of stew from the pot that hung on a tripod, gently swaying with the motion of the ship.

"No, Jax," she said firmly. "The sun went down three hours ago, an' yer need an actual night of sleep, an' I do mean *sleep*!" she specified, glaring from me to Oracle. "Yer to leave 'im alone, Oracle!"

"Hey!" I protested, and she rounded on me, when Oracle piped up in agreement.

"She's right, Jax," my companion said, smiling sadly.

"No," My argument died on my lips as Lydia spoke over me.

"Seriously, Jax, yer need to rest, to relax, an' to actually be around friends. Tomorrow, we might all die, an' we're fine with that, because our lives are good. "Hell, they're…what's the word you use…? Oh! Awesome! That's it, our lives are awesome, thanks to you an' what you did an' continue to do. I'd be dead or full of baby sporelings if not for ye, and tha rest of tha team. But between fights, we get to relax. Yer hardly ever do that, so to well will!" Lydia insisted, and Yen spoke up to one side.

"Ronin, play us a tune," she said calmly, and Ronin smiled, pulling a . and settling himself comfortably.

"Play a tune?" he said, his fingers rippling over the strings like a waterfall o. music. "I think I can go one better than that, my friends." He strummed a tune I'd never heard, and a few seconds in, he started to sing, lifting his face and closing his eyes as he swayed slightly in time to the music.

He wandered back and forth in the small space, seemingly with his eyes closed, though he never bumped into anything. As he sang, the small magelights in the room suddenly felt like warm hearth fires. My seat seemed that little bit more comfortable, and the darkness that had been building silently in my heart receded, just a fraction.

I let my gaze wander around the room, seeing them there, all of the squad, from Lydia to Yen, Grizz to Bane, Giint to Arrin, and even Jian sat in the corner with Sehran on his knee, one arm around his shoulders as she smiled and tapped a foot in time to the music.

Tang's fingers danced on his daggers in time to the music, and I studied the slow movements of Bob. While I grimaced for a second at the fact I'd still not taken the time to fix him from his last injury, needing more bones unless I wanted him to shrink again, I suddenly didn't feel as alone.

I felt happier, stronger, and calmer, and I felt at home.

I turned back to Ronin, listening to his song, then the next, and the next, until we all turned in a few hours later, and I slept like a damn log.

The next morning, I woke up to the echoing sound of Grizz farting. It filled the air, along with dead silence, the kind where everyone is frozen in shock, ripped from their dreams and gentle sleep until we heard his voice.

"Well, I don't remember eating that," he mumbled before being punched, hard, by Yen.

"You filthy animal!" she hissed. Giint evidently stabbed him in the leg with his little dagger again, making the flatulent legionnaire scream in shock.

"He fucking stabbed me!" Grizz shouted, grabbing his leg and inspecting it. "Right, you little..." he growled, one fist balling up as he glared at the unrepentant Gnome.

"Enough!" Lydia barked.

"He stabbed..."

"Yer deserved it!" Lydia snapped before gesturing to Arrin. "Go on, heal 'im, but next time 'e does that, no healin'. And I'll be usin' my mace, yer dirty bastard." She shook her finger at Grizz as Tang made a show of searching for a way to open the porthole.

"It doesn't open!" he wailed theatrically. "We're all going to die!"

"Just don't light any fires," Arrin muttered grimly. "I swear, a canary would be dead already."

"Thanks for that wake-up call, Grizz," I growled at the grinning and totally unrepentant legionnaire.

"Anytime, boss," he said cheerfully. I groaned as I stretched and started to ove around, before looking over to Jian, finding him gone.

"Anyone know where Jian is?" I muttered, raising on eyebrow in question.

"He snuck off to the wheelhouse," Yen said, shaking her head ruefully. "There's a bed in there, and if you don't mind Tenandra watching you, it lends some privacy from everyone else."

"Seriously? He dragged Sehran off for a shag where Tenandra could watch them?"

"Well Seneschal sees everything in the Tower, so there's no difference for him if we're in our room or on the balcony or in the Hall of the Eternal," Oracle piped up. I lifted one hand, quickly stopping her from elaborating.

"I really didn't need to know that," I said uncomfortably. "Seriously, didn't need to know, don't want to know, and I'm going to try my darndest to forget it."

"So, wait, he's…" Ronin said slowly, grinning insanely as he put it together.

"I'm outta here." I dumped my bedroll and the rest of my gear away, hurrying down the hall to clamber onto the deck, then headed over to the wheelhouse.

I knocked and waited a moment, rather than barging in, then opened the door as no response seemed to be forthcoming. Jian was hurriedly covering himself up and looking slightly embarrassed on the bed at the back of the room, while Sehran sat on the edge of the bed, naked and unashamed, talking to Tenandra, who was also full-sized and…naked.

"I really don't think I need to know what's going on here…" I started to back out when Tenandra spoke up quickly.

"Sehran was advising me on my physical body, Lord Jax. Do you approve? Do I look good?" she asked innocently, bouncing in place.

I looked from her hopeful expression to Sehran's openly lustful one, to Oracle's unreadable expression, and finally to Jian, who looked like he wasn't sure if all his Christmases had come at once or he'd made a huge mistake.

"Ah, very nice," I said, blanking, then coughing as my brain seemingly finished its reboot. "Tenandra, how long until we reach the first location?" I redirected the conversation to safer topics.

"Three hours, my lord." she said crisply. "I do not seek to steal him, Oracle, don't worry; but could I ask his opinion on how my body feels to him?"

At that point, I spun on my heel and walked back out of the door.

"Thanks, Tenandra!" I called over my shoulder. "Jian, have fun, you crazy fucker!"

I strolled past the titular captain of the ship, who was making his way to the wheelhouse, and I shook my head in warning.

"I wouldn't bother," I said. "Seriously, just go back to bed. Today is not the day for this shit."

Abandoning the confused man on deck, I returned to the alchemy kit, glancing over it and deciding I'd make more mana potions, as I could always heal people if I had enough mana, but I couldn't do as much with health potions.

I really wanted to lose myself in the search for more patterns, but I didn't dare, resolving not to waste precious time, and that I'd work on it later.

The three hours passed in a blur, or two hours and forty minutes did, anyway. At that point, I finished the batch I was working on and started to pack away my equipment, hoping that the potions would be cool enough to put the corks in before we landed.

As the engines fired and the descent started, with Oracle frowning at me in disapproval, I finally managed to put the cork into the last vial. I sighed in exasperation, giving up on the endless discussion we'd had for nearly the last hour.

"But, as she's not wanting you in that way, I still don't see the problem with you giving her feedback on her body?" Oracle said plaintively.

"And as I told you, Oracle, it's one thing to look at her and say, 'yeah, that looks good,' and it's another to give her guidance on how she feels physically. I mean, come on, where do you draw the line? If I tell her 'your boobs feel great,' then she asks me to feel her elsewhere, or give her advice on her seduction techniques? What if she wants advice on sex?"

"But that's my point!" Oracle exclaimed. "She understands that I'm yours, and you're mine, so just touching her, because there's no emotion, shouldn't be an issue, right?"

"There's always emotion!" I groaned.

"I can take care of you first, if you want...Or I can..."

"Nope!" I said before she could say anything else. "End of discussion, Oracle. Seriously, please, just leave it."

"Okay," Oracle said slowly, frowning with clear dissatisfaction. "Tenandra says she's asked Jian and Sehran, and they seem happy to help her. She's thinking about asking Ronin, as well..."

"Oh God, no," I whispered, putting hands over my ears and walking out of the room.

There was only one way to deal with this shit, as a man.

I was going to leave it the hell alone and pretend not to know anything about it. Then when it all went wrong, I'd let Lydia kick their asses.

I walked down the hallway, smiling as I saw a Gnome hard at work, half-hidden under a table to one side in another room. The ship had changed drastically since we were on her last. Between the cleanup crew, the servitor, the Gnomes, and the regular crew that had been assigned to her, and the way that Tenandra was learning to control her new ship-body, it wouldn't be long before the *Interesting Endeavor* was at least up to the level she'd been as a brand new, fully finished ship.

A month from now, I suspected that she'd be far, far better...or a crater.

I clambered up the ladder and out into the morning sunlight for the second time, this time finding the deck bustling with people running back and forth, carrying out the million jobs required to get us safely landed and deployed.

Lydia and the rest of the squad were finishing up getting their armor in place and testing weapons, and I joined them, dressing quickly as I looked over the bow at the gently wooded, grassy valley and the ruins it contained.

"Looks like they're off," Tang said from my left. I followed his gesture.

"*Sigmar's Fist*," I grunted, nodding in understanding. Where we'd dropped lower and lower, she'd stayed up high, on overwatch, and now that we had reached our destination, she'd peeled off and was steadily increasing speed to the south, aiming for Sint's champion.

I silently wished them a good journey and turned my attention back to the ruins.

The closer we got, the more details resolved, and I couldn't help but frown as I studied the collapsed buildings.

The center of the ruins was marred by a huge crater, making it look like something had fallen from an insane height and smashed into the ground. The trails of devastation that led outward from the crater made it clear that whatever the thing had been, it had survived that impact.

I called out to Jian to circle the ruins without thinking, and whether it was him or Tenandra, or the redundant captain and helmsman that made it happen, the ship slowly circled the village, letting us get a closer view.

The houses had collapsed in the center, and farther out, they were slumping. But beside the obvious destruction, I couldn't identify a reason why the village wasn't thriving.

The land around the village had obviously been cleared, with indications of fields once, hundreds of years ago, judging from the stone walls and scarce trees in certain areas. While the houses encircling the crater were collapsing, they'd clearly been built of thick stone and designed to last.

"What the hell happened here?" I muttered, only to have Lydia explain.

"It be tha Tale of Valkyrie's Fall," she said sadly, and Ronin, who stood nearby, splitting his attention between Sehran and the vista below, nodded his head in affirmation.

"It's likely that some of it is true," he agreed.

"Okay, give me the short version," I ordered.

Ronin strummed his lute and took a deep breath. "So say the bards, and the tales of men, that in the last days…" he began, his voice sonorous and chanting.

"Nope, no fucking time for that shit," I said, cutting him off and ignoring his glare. "Give me the short, short, fucking short version!"

"Fine!" he snapped. "The last of the known Valkyries died fighting a Demon. They crashed into a village, and neither of them could fly after the injuries they took. The Demon killed the entire village, and the Valkyrie drew it away.

"Once the villagers were dead, it followed her and ate her. Or she killed it. Or one of a thousand other endings. All anyone knows is that the villagers all died, and now they haunt the village. There have been countless people who have tried to find out why, but nobody ever comes back, so who knows."

Quest Discovered: Wayland's Crossing!

Find out what happened at the Village of Wayland's Crossing. Bring peace to the unquiet dead, and end the terror that stalks this territory.

Kill the Terror: 0/1
Bring Peace to the Unquiet Dead: 0/307
Find out the Truth: 0/1
Optional Bonus Quest: Use Clairvoyance instead of an Imperial Ability
Rewards: Dependent on success, 50,000xp, Title, Progress in your Quest: A Pillar of Strength.

I frowned at the details, noting that the option to accept had gone again, and I shrugged resignedly. Oracle was right; I would have accepted it regardless.

"Clairvoyance," I muttered, pulling up the details for an Ability I'd gained ages ago, yet had never used. It allowed me to speak to the recently dead, costing ten mana to cast, and an additional one mana per second, so I didn't really understand how that was going to work, but Jenae always seemed to have a hand in my quests, so either this was her helping by giving me a hint or something else.

"Fuck it. Land at the south end of that field," I ordered, pointing at the clearest overgrown meadow to the east of the village. "But be ready to take off quickly, if we need to."

I was going to try to clear the village without resorting to using my Imperial Ability, as the quest hinted, but if it was an arse, I wouldn't hesitate to use it and clear out any ghosts or whatever happened to be roaming about…then I realized what the quest's phrasing was hinting at.

I couldn't use the ability, as it would remove all the ghosts…and I clearly was supposed to speak to them, or I'd fail the quest, most likely.

Fuck.

"Okay people, good news and bad," I said for my team's ears only, waiting as Jian joined us. Sehran stepped away from the admiring looks that most of the group were giving her to stand by his side, smiling at him.

I glanced from her to the others, noting the lustful looks and knowing damn well she wasn't using her ability on them to make that happen. Ronin in particular looked like he might start humping her leg at any moment. This was all I needed.

"People!" I snapped, clapping sharply and getting everyone's attention. "Sehran is with us as a trial. If you can't function because she's here, then she'll be kicked out, so I hope you at least fucking try to behave." Several pairs of eyes dropped to the deck, abashed. I sighed, pressing on. "Right. The village is indeed haunted, and I've got a quest to find out what the hell happened and lay the spirits to rest."

"Cool," Grizz said, then he nudged Ronin. "You'll want to make notes. When he does this kinda shit, it's amazing!"

"And," I went on, shooting a pointed look at Grizz, "I can't use my Imperial Ability, because then there won't be any spirits left to question."

"Shit." Grizz winced. "Sorry, boss."

"So instead, it sounds like we need to make our way through the village to the center and fight any revenants and such as we go. Does everyone have a magical weapon?" I asked, checking for each individual to confirm and waving for Ronin to be quiet when he started to open his mouth, shaking his head.

"My swords aren't magical, but the metal the Drow use is, so I should be fine," Jian said, shrugging.

"I have magic," Yen added.

"I have this?" Grizz held up a little dagger, and I directed him to sheathe it again, before nodding my thanks to Tang as he passed him one of the two magical shortswords I'd given him.

"I want that back later," Tang insisted, pointing at Grizz, who just grinned back at him.

"Bob doesn't, but he can remain in the middle of the group," Oracle pointed out.

"Ronin, you stay with Bob. Add any buffs you can on the group, and, well, try not to die," I directed the squishy bard.

"Most of my abilities and spells won't work against the undead," Sehran said, looking embarrassed.

405

"Okay, Bob, Ronin, and Sehran, stay in the middle of the group and try not to die," I amended, leading the way to the railing by the gangplank.

The ship slowly settled at the south end of the field, landing in as open an area as I'd been able to spot, while simultaneously being close to the village.

Once the engines powered down, and the full weight of the ship settled onto the landing struts, there was a loud creak, followed by an almighty crack, and the entire ship sagged to the left, throwing myself, Jian, and Grizz over the side to tumble to the ground.

I panicked and triggered Soaring Majesty...for all of the last two feet.

Instead of landing with a grunt, as Grizz did, or a curse, like Jian, I blasted off at a slight angle and tore a ten-foot-long furrow in the field.

When I finally figured out what was happening and stopped, hauling myself free of the vegetation and soil that had somehow made it inside my goddamn armor, I swore at the laughter from the rest of the squad as I stalked back towards them.

It didn't help when Oracle reached out and plucked a dandelion from the middle of the crest on my helm and handed it to me, telling me with a smile that I had an entire bouquet up there.

I swore again, reaching up to tug my helmet off when the first screams reached us, and I spun, leaving it in place.

The entire group went on the defensive, including Tenandra and her ship, as they frantically searched for what was making the sounds while a servitor examined the broken strut.

The crew were the first to see them, higher up as they were, with the remainder of my squad clambering down to join us.

"It's the dead!" someone cried before another crew member pointed us in the right direction.

I spun, peering over the tall grasses and squinting, seeing the movement before anything else, as the grasses rippled, and the sound of a ladder being thrown over the side accompanied the others coming to play as well.

Essie Valern, Spectral Villager

Essie and her people were killed in an event immortalized in song as Valkyrie's Fall. She and her kin were slain in the massive outpouring of power. Shock, horror, an unknown creature, and the ambient mana combined to force her and those she and her kin slay to guard this site.

Weaknesses: 50% weakness to Life and Fire Magics
Resistances: Both Death and Darkness magics used against a Specter are 50% less effective.
Level: 14
Health: 1,100/1,100
Stamina: N/A
Mana: 190/190

"Okay...a creature, eh?" I mused before calling out what I'd seen to the others. Ronin went one better.

"They're bound Specters!" he cried, jumping down from the ladder with a grunt. "If you kill the Specter that bound them, they'll be destroyed as well, and it'll take a few days for them to reform."

"Any idea how to tell which ones are the binder, the bound, or, well, you know?" I called back, glancing over at him as he shook his head. "Great. Okay, people, fuck them all up. If a bunch vanish, then you got a Specter lord or boss or whatever." With no better plan in place, we readied our weapons and waded through the tall grasses.

"There's more coming!" came a voice from on high again.

"Can you take off, Tenandra?" Jian shouted up, and a second later, the form of the ship's Wisp stood at the railing.

"We're impaled on a rock. It'll take a few hours to get free and make the repairs," she stated grimly, her eyes flickering beyond us toward the village. "And they're coming from different directions now."

"Joy," I said, shaking my head. "Bob, help with repairs as Tenandra directs you. The rest of you, spread out and start killing things."

I backed up until I was ten feet or so from the side of the ship, and took aim, when Oracle fired, and a Fireball immolated a section of the field off to my left.

I sighed, carefully releasing the half-woven spell and instead concentrated on the Specters that I could see drawing nearer.

They didn't look like I'd expected; no shambling forms like zombies or ghostly apparitions like the ones from the movies, dragging clinking chains behind them.

Instead, the first to step out of the grass where I could get a good look at her was a tall, elven woman. She strode forward, her face distracted as though she was simply deep in thought. Her lips moved soundlessly, a furrow in her brow, until she saw me.

She'd been drawn by something, but when she saw me and the others, she let loose a hiss, and her face changed entirely.

The mouth suddenly stretched, blackness spreading, and sharp, needle-like teeth erupting into sight as her pale skin turned the bone white of old parchment. Her eyes went entirely black, with no differentiation between pupil and iris. Thick veins of black blood radiated out from the orbits, twisting her already freaky face.

I grunted in shock, and she screamed, her voice a wail of fury and terrible hunger as she leapt for me, hands suddenly tipped with claws and reaching for my flesh.

I spun the naginata, sweeping it from right to left, and she brought up her hands to block, screeching in pain and hatred when the blade dug deep into her body.

She grabbed the blade, hissing at me, and dragged herself down the length of it, continuing to reach for my face hungrily.

I froze, having expected a bit more of a pained reaction, until Oracle shouted at me.

"Jax! Snap out of it!" I shook myself, then poured mana into the naginata, watching as it flared with a warm golden light.

The pure life magic flooding through the weapon tore into the Specter, making it shriek and writhe as it frantically tried to pull itself free of the naginata. I lifted it, finding the Specter had almost no weight.

To the left, I glimpsed another one rushing forward, and I slashed sideways, the blade finally tearing free of the first Specter. It collapsed to the ground as the light crept out from the wound to tear the creature apart.

My next attack missed as the creature threw itself to the ground, skidded, and leaped up inside of my weapon's reach. I kicked out and grunted in pain as the seemingly solid creature became insubstantial. My boot passed through it when it struck.

I gritted my teeth as it sank its claws into my leg and opened its maw wide, lunging forward, as if about to savage me, when I managed to sweep the butt of the naginata across my body.

The life magic-infused weapon hit the Specter like a truck, sending it flying to the side, sprawling in the grass.

It lay there motionless, and I stabbed the other fucker first, making sure of its demise. Then I flipped the weapon end over end and slammed it down hard, butt-first, into the Specter's skull.

It burst in an explosion of soundless light, and the figure vanished, sinking silently into the ground as I looked for the next one. This one was a child, a little girl about four or five, but the way she moved...she hopped and ran on all fours, her plain dress marred with old, black blood, the furious creature hissing in hatred as she ran at me.

I stabbed out, the blade skewering her from front to back, and the combination of her speed, her insubstantiality, and the magic's effect left her dissolving into wisps of light and dark that flowed past me before settling to the ground and sinking in.

The fight was fast and frantic at first, but once everyone realized how weak the Specters were, and Oracle threw a few Fireballs and Flames of Wrath circles down to break up the larger concentrations of them, it changed from a fight to a slaughter.

Barely thirty minutes after we'd started, I was pulling up the quest to look it over again, pleased at what I saw.

Congratulations!

You have made progress in your Quest: Wayland's Crossing.

Find out what happened at the Village of Wayland's Crossing, bring peace to the unquiet dead, and end the terror that stalks this territory.

Kill the Terror: 0/1

Bring Peace to the Unquiet Dead: 237/307

Find out the Truth: 0/1

Optional Bonus Quest: Use Clairvoyance instead of an Imperial Ability

Rewards: Dependent on success, 50,000xp, Title, Progress in your Quest: A Pillar of Strength.

CHAPTER THIRTY-NINE

"Okay people, there's still seventy of the fuckers left, as well as something called the Terror, so keep your eyes open," I called. "We stay around the ship until it can take off and get to safety, then we move in." I got a collection of affirmative replies, settling in.

The next hour and a half passed slowly. The occasional Specter turned up, making me think it was definitely worth staying in position. Otherwise, the ship would have been overrun, but by the time the ship actually lifted into the air some time later, it really had become commonplace for us to slaughter the Specters.

As the ship gained altitude, maintaining a height of around a hundred feet, we gathered together, and Oracle healed the few minor injuries that had slipped through the net. We ate a quick bite of hard, tasteless bread, had a slug each from the fountain I conjured, then we set off.

The half mile through the long grass to the village was strange, almost silent, apart from the wind, but as we drew closer, we noticed more and more metal strewn about.

At first, it was a sword. Old, badly rusted, and with the hilt rotting away, I stepped on it and quickly yanked my foot back from the decaying arm attached to it.

I crouched, examining the corpse, and found it to be the remains of an adventurer or explorer. Half the corpse was gone, presumably broken down by the wind and rain or scavengers, but as I examined it, I glimpsed another corpse a few feet beyond the first.

Then as I stood up…another.

"Stop," I called out, a vague sense of foreboding filling me as I looked around, realizing what I'd taken for mounds of grass and dirt, weren't.

They were corpses, dozens upon dozens of them.

A quick count gave me at least thirty bodies in sight, and that meant that either we'd stumbled into an area where the majority of the adventurers entered, or…

"Look out!" cried Arrin, and a full spread of Magic Missiles flashed out from his hand, each missile slamming home unerringly into a different skull as the bodies started moving.

The movements were slow at first, and the corpses were easily dispatched. A single swipe of my naginata severed the spine of a corpse. It collapsed back to the ground, until it twitched, and unlike the other undead I'd fought, the skull rolled back to the corpse.

As soon as it was near enough, the corpse reassembled again and struggled against its grassy prison, tearing chunks free in an attempt to reach us.

"Oracle!" I shouted, looking around. "Wrath!" I ordered, pointing to the left. "Yen, Flamespear!" I pointed to the right, then I marched forward, my naginata glowing again as I hacked and slashed, driving the dead back down as soon as they started to rise, again and again.

"Bane, Tang, search the fucking village," I directed. "Grizz, you've got the rear. Lydia! With me! Everyone else, stay in the middle and break those bones!"

We stormed into the fray, weapons slashing and smashing as we laid about ourselves. The undead weren't difficult to defeat, even when they got to their feet fully. Most of the time, they were missing limbs or weapons, and they just staggered forward.

The threat wasn't from the undead themselves. A group of kids could probably do them damage, and in the areas I'd grown up in, *those* kids would have had a field day with them. The real problem was stamina.

Beating them down only took a few seconds, but it was effort. The undead didn't need stamina; they just rose again and again and again.

We hurried on, passing the outer ring of houses and moving inward. Each time, we stepped over the bodies of more undead, and they began to rise.

I looked back, going so far as to get a boost up to climb onto a roof to check, and I discovered that hundreds surrounded us already.

"Fuck! Okay, hurry up, people!" I shouted. "We've lots more incoming!" I ran to the edge and jumped off, landing on a skeleton's back and smashing it into the dirt it was rising from, before shouting again.

"There's a mound in the center of the village; the ring around the crater looks fucking dangerous, but I'm betting that's where we need to go. Oracle, Wrath behind us; everyone else, pick up the pace!"

I felt Oracle weaving as I started forward, jogging and slashing, when a sudden pain in my leg made me stumble. A glance down revealed a Specter fading back into a pile of rocks, and I understood the sudden danger we were in.

If the Specters that were left were hiding, ready to slash at us and fall back, then we might be well and truly fucked after all.

I conjured a quick Fireball and threw that at a flicker of movement I'd seen beyond the shift of bones. The impact rewarded me with a scream, before Arrin howled in pain from behind me.

I spun, my naginata flashing out almost by rote to take a head that was just rising from the mulch, and I saw him fall.

Arrin pitched forward, his arms flailing as the spell he was casting ripped into him. The backlash simultaneously tore at his mind and burned his mana channels, as the shock from the Specter that was clinging to his back, its claws digging into him, made him lose control.

"Shit!" I cursed. The others rapidly formed a circle and contracted in around the fallen man, while Sehran shrieked in rage and laid into the Specter with her claws, killing it and freeing him.

Arrin lay there moaning, though, shaking in pain and shock as the aftereffects of the spell continued and I rushed back to him, grabbing him under each arm after shoving the naginata into my bag.

"Go!" I ordered the group as I kicked off, flashing into the air and heading for the ship, which now gently circled the ruined village.

It altered direction as soon as my feet left the ground, and I raced for it, Oracle following and staying behind as I dumped Arrin on the deck.

I felt her casting the healing spells as I dove off the side again, streaking down and tearing a line through the decomposed bodies. My weapon was back in my hand and extended as I slammed through them in a single fast loop. The weapon flared with healing magic as I turned at high speed, keeping the blade extended towards the ground to carve a loop around my friends.

I lifted the blade, twisting around and looking for a likely victim before grunting as I verified what I thought I had seen a few minutes before, and several times since, now that my brain had processed the oddity.

There was a corpse that didn't move when all the others around it rose.

It was older than the others, barely a pile of bones, bleached by the sun and crumbling. But when the others lifted themselves from the earth, it just sat there, and now that I'd directly observed it, I could pick out others, making me guess that these were the corpses of the Specters.

I flipped over again, diving for the group and reaching out while I slid the naginata away.

"Giint! Ronin!" I shouted, and the pair who struggled along together looked up as I hurtled in for a rough landing.

My boots carved dual furrows in the ground, and I reached out, sweeping Ronin into a princess carry as Giint made his glowing axe vanish and grabbed onto my knee, wrapping his arms around my leg like he was going to go for the world leg humping championships.

I kicked off, rocketing upwards just as mildew-coated, rotting fingertips reached out, grabbing onto his boot.

We soared into the air; the split second's drag that resulted from an extra arm coming along for the ride slowing us not at all.

Tenandra arced the ship overhead, hovering to one side, making it easier for me to drop them off. After having to practically kick Giint off my leg, I returned, grabbing Sehran as she lifted her arms joyously into the air for me.

"My hero," she purred into the side of my helm. I grunted, dropping her onto the deck from a few feet higher than necessary, eliciting a squawk of protest. I immediately plunged back down to collect Bob, who grabbed onto Yen at my unspoken order, allowing me to lift them both at once, even though I grunted with the strain.

I deposited them seemingly seconds later, arcing over the far side of the ship to grab Lydia's outstretched hand.

Her wings were fully visible now, and something about them seemed to be driving the undead wild as they fought to reach her, a surging tide of bones and grasping spectral fingers.

I twisted, yanking her straight into the air before releasing her higher than the ship and letting her glide to the deck on her own as I dove back down for Grizz.

Once I'd firmly grasped the massive form–the only one of the group who seemed to still be enjoying the damn fight–I kicked off into the air, frantically searching and failing to spot any sign of Tang or Bane.

I dropped Grizz unceremoniously and shouted over the side to them.

"Get on a roof or something; I'm coming for you!" I swept my gaze toward the ruins, focusing on the threads of the Oaths that bound us.

It took a few seconds, but I eventually managed to trace the first one through the maelstrom of the surging undead below, and I spotted a slight blur in the air over one roof as Tang crept along it.

I didn't hesitate, jumping straight over the side and flying at him, seeing him become fully visible a handful of seconds before I arrived.

He headed to the highest point of the sharply angled roof, clinging on with one hand as he stretched the other out to me.

I grabbed his forearm, feeling his fingers tighten around mine, and I rolled, hauling him up and onto my back before rocketing upwards. As we arced above the ship, I flipped over and dropped like a stone, flaring out the landing at the last second and dumping Tang, gasping air into panicked lungs, onto the freshly washed and polished deck of the ship.

"Asshole!" was all Tang managed to get out before I was off again, leaping over the side and scanning the tops of the buildings.

I flew lower, grimly aware that I was burning through my health and mana too quickly, but terrified I'd be too late to reach Bane if I didn't.

I searched the village, my head flashing from side to side as I cursed whatever Tamat had done that was concealing the bond between Bane and me. I concentrated on the undead below; the rising wave of bodies, now easily numbering in the hundreds, if not a thousand, roiled up out of the ground, clambering over each other and spilling from doors and windows.

Here and there, I could see remains that stayed, corpses that didn't so much as twitch, and I grimly marked them in my mind, determined that they held the key to all of this.

I banked sharply as something moved on a building to my left, then banked again, peeling away. The corpse of a Trigara, like Nigret, hauled itself up and into view, its claws allowing it to scale the building easily.

I twisted, aiming back towards the center of the village, now that I'd covered the outer ring, and I shouted down, my voice almost lost in the roar of bones and crash of rusted armor as the undead rolled and fell, disassembled and merged into a swiftly growing colossus.

"Come on, Bane, you dick!" I snarled, searching frantically. Suddenly, a huge edifice of bone, a creature that looked like a mixture of a human knight, but built on the scale of an elephant, collapsed to the ground, the skull toppling down to shatter against a stone. A trio of huge tusks bounced and clattered away, crushing smaller undead that weren't fast enough to escape.

I spun in the air, aiming for that the commotion, and finally spotted him, a black blur racing down an alleyway.

He waved frantically, and I shifted slightly, locking in on him in my mind and picking up speed. He sheathed his blades, locked spears onto his back, and jumped, kicking off the flat surface of a wall to his left, grabbing the ledge of a window higher up on that wall and pulling himself up. Planting his feet under him and kicking backwards, he somersaulted away from the building.

I reached out, and he caught my arms, making me grunt in pain at the sudden weight and angle, but I managed to heave him upwards, applying more mana.

We jetted into the air, Bane grunting as he kicked at a skeleton that was clinging to his ankle, before we twisted around, lining up on the ship.

Seconds later, we cleared the final roof between us and the ship, and Bane landed with a clatter of bones as he let go of me, rolling across the deck to kill his momentum.

I landed running, planting my feet hard and skidding the last few feet to catch myself on the railing on the far side of the ship. Steadying myself, I turned back in time to see Bane smashing the arms off the skeleton.

"Don't kill it!" I shouted, waving frantically.

Bane paused, looking at me in confusion, before yanking free the arms that frantically tried to reconnect again, tossing them over the side.

Lydia did the same with the legs, and suddenly we had a rolling torso encased in rusty chainmail with a skull that snapped and bit at the air trying to reach us.

"Where to?" Jian called to me. I turned my head, fixing him with a look.

"Away; just get us the fuck back from here," I snapped, before turning my attention back to my people.

The others, Gnomes and crew included, were gathering round, staring at the limbless undead creature that was desperately clacking its teeth and wriggling in an attempt to reach one of us.

"Now that's just disturbing," Oracle said, landing next to me and shuddering.

"It's wrong, is what it is," Tang insisted, getting a general chorus of assent, before he started pointing out details. "Look there…this isn't a mindless undead." He indicated the way it obsessively followed him, yet ignored one of the Gnomes that was inching closer, seemingly fascinated.

"But it's also as dumb as a rock; look at the way it's trying to get to me." He held his hand out a few inches from its face.

The skeleton went berserk trying to bite him, and he pulled his hand back, nodding at the Gnome on the far side of the corpse.

"Now you try; don't get too close," Tang warned the Gnome, and he inched his hand closer…then closer again.

He eventually flicked the back of the skull, sending a section of matted, rotting hair and old flesh sloughing off, to everyone's disgust. The creature didn't respond, though.

"Crewman," I said, nodding to a sailor to one side and gesturing to the corpse. "See if it responds to you?" I requested.

He swallowed hard before shuffling in close. He waved his hand in front of its face, then moved closer and closer.

Eventually, buoyed up by the calls of his friends, he flicked the skeleton on the forehead, his strike ringing against a patch of clean bone, and still, the skeleton ignored him, trying to reach Tang, who was the closest of the group who had entered the village.

"What the hell is going on?" I asked, confused.

"It's a sentry," Tang said grimly. "There must be a line or something that we crossed, marking us magically as a target, but it's not interested in them at all," he muttered, jerking his head to indicate the crew.

"Why the hell would they be guarding the village?" I asked.

"No idea, boss. All I know is that they are; I mean, it's logical, right?" He straightened up and looked over the railing at the tide of undead that was tearing itself apart, as well as some of the sagging buildings, in its attempt to reach us.

The colossus was now almost fully formed, rising to its feet and staring malevolently at us, before scooping up over a dozen undead in one hand and hurling them at the ship as we flew away.

The undead thrashed as they flew, clawing at the air, desperate to reach us…then collapsed into a shower of bone, falling apart midair a few feet from the stern of the ship.

"Hey, no fair…what did you do?" someone grumbled from behind us. I spun, finding them frowning in disappointment at the pile of bones that had been a frantically thrashing undead thing on the deck mere seconds before.

I raced to the side, peering down to see that the collection of undead below that had made it out of the houses had stopped at a seemingly invisible boundary around the village, a village that was falling farther and farther behind as Jian and Tenandra fired the engines hard.

"Stop!" I shouted, aiming my voice both at the wheelhouse and internally at Tenandra the way I did to Oracle, Seneschal, and Heph.

There was a moment of indecision, then the ship slowed. Jian appeared, looking confused, from inside the wheelhouse.

"Jax, what?"

I pointed at the retreating undead. "Get us back there but be ready to turn and get us away again," I ordered.

He saluted, disappearing back inside.

"They're guarding the village," I agreed with Tang. "They're guarding the village, and whatever keeps them here is preventing them from dispersing and slaughtering the countryside. I was starting to worry that we were going to drag them along behind us for miles and have to keep picking them off."

We watched the undead slowly dispersing. They returned to the places they'd been before we awoke them, and I checked the bones of those that had been thrown outside of the invisible ring around the village.

They lay there, motionless, just a collection of bones spread across the grass.

"I wonder…" I mused, looking from them to the huge colossus that was starting to disassemble near the center of the village.

"Jian! Take us in closer, slowly! Be ready to take us back out again," I ordered, and the others gathered around the railing to watch.

We flew in slowly, crossing the invisible line we guessed to be the outer edge of the village a few minutes later, continuing on when there was no response.

The colossus had completely crumbled, most of the bones returning to their previous resting places. Here and there, the flicker of Specters showed them returning to their routines as well.

"Hold here!" I shouted as the ship neared the crater.

We were hovering over the inner ring of houses now, the village having been set up as three rings. The poorest and smallest had been set on the outside, the richest and largest in the middle, all surrounding a crater that had destroyed whatever was in the center.

I looked down at the rim that ran around the crater, noting that the fresh-turned earth was made primarily of bodies.

There were hundreds of them, and the occasional flicker from inside the nearby greater houses suggested that Specters still patrolled inside them.

"They lie where they fell," Tang said eventually.

"Explain that," I ordered. The last handful of corpses were making their way into place listlessly, laying down, seemingly fitting themselves into slots that were almost carved into the ground for them.

"Look at the way they move, the way they return," Tang said, pointing at one. It still wore a bell-shaped helm and a cuirass, but one of the pauldrons was missing, as well as a gauntlet. As it staggered along the side street and up a small bank, it was obvious where it was headed. The missing pauldron lay half-buried in the soil, and the shape of the ground where it had torn itself free fit perfectly when the body lay down again, becoming totally still as the animating force seemed to leave it.

"These are the adventurers, explorers, and others who have tried to investigate the village over the years?"

"It looks like more and more got killed as they tried to reach the center, causing the pile up of bodies there, with the weakest dying farther out," Tang guessed, gesturing to different points around the crater.

"They were trying to reach the center, assuming that whatever was causing it was there, and that was their chance to stop it. Just like we were," I mused. Others around me nodded.

"Don't want to call your plan shit, then, boss, but it wasn't exactly original," Grizz whispered to me, and I glared in annoyance at him.

"Well, you'll like this next bit, then," I muttered, stepping up to the side of the railing and hopping off.

Gasps and cries rose from above me as I flared my ability, landing gently on the ground below. The earth immediately shook as something seemed to pass through it, and the dead began to rise again.

I grabbed a corpse from behind, stomping on its arms to rip them free, then jumped, firing the ability and flying up to the ship.

As soon as I landed, I dumped the corpse on the deck, observing the way it was coming to life, its teeth flashing as it tried to get to me. But this time, it ignored everyone else, even Grizz when he smashed it back down and proceeded to rip its legs off, tossing them over the side.

"Get us back outside the village, please!" I called to Jian, and the ship started up before he had even reached the wheelhouse.

We watched the corpse for the next few minutes as the ship slowly kited dozens then hundreds of the undead toward the outer edge of the boundary.

As before, the undead were slow to rise but became more and more awake as the seconds passed, until the colossus began to form then tumble apart, as we crossed the line.

I'd been watching the undead on the deck, as had most of the others, including Ronin, who started to speak as soon as it fell apart.

"Before it died, well, you know," he said, pausing as though embarrassed. "It showed as Undead Village Guardian…but now…well, now it's just a corpse." He reached out and poked at it.

"Okay, back over the line, please!" I called out. We watched the remains as we passed over the invisible line before Ronin shook his head, even more confused.

"It's just a corpse now. Whatever animated it is gone." He nudged it with his foot, and I nodded, picking the bits up and throwing them over the side before flying down and walking around them, back inside of the village danger zone.

Other corpses started to rise again or turned from their slow meander back to their graves to head for me. But this time, I stayed on the ground, and I set off jogging.

As soon as I crossed over the line, they turned away from me. I stepped back over it, and they turned back. Curious, I waited until one was particularly close, then ducked its clumsy attack and shoved it bodily over the line, where it collapsed into a pile of bones again.

I kicked them back across, waited until the undead had dispersed a bit, then reassembled the body on that side of the line as best I could.

No life returned to the bones.

I flew up, landing on the ship as the few nearest undead lost interest and wandered off. I took the opportunity to look around at the group. While I got a few glares from Yen and Lydia, they'd apparently given up on berating me for doing this kind of thing by now.

"So, what have we learned?" I asked the team.

"The undead are only undead inside the village; outside they're just...dead," Grizz said.

"And they're not smart or cunning," Tang added. "They just rush at you. As soon as you step outside the line, that's it. They just return to their graves. I mean, we could literally just keep drawing them to the end of the boundary, pull them over the line, and boom."

"Yeah, but it'd take all day," I grunted, then I checked the notifications and found nothing waiting. "And there's no experience...?" I said wonderingly. "Like none at all, for fighting them all?"

"Oh, that's something else." Yen said quickly. "They count as part of something, like a swarm or minions of something, so you get the experience if you kill the main creature, but nothing for the bits like this, as they're counted like arms or legs, not sentient enemies."

"Okay, yet another way this is all kinds of fucked up," I muttered. "Right; did anyone else notice the corpses that don't rise?" I asked.

"You mean the ones outside the village or inside?" Bane asked, and I pointed in at the center. "Then yes. There's a handful of them all over the village, corpses that are fully dead."

"The next stage is to get one of those," I said firmly. "I'll have a walk about down there, and everyone keep an eye open for any of the permanently dead bodies, preferably as fresh as possible." I stepped up to the edge of the railing and braced myself before plunging off the side.

I timed it perfectly, flaring the power of my flight ability with the pull of gravity, to land in a pristine three-point superhero landing without breaking my knee or *anything*. I straightened up and couldn't help it; I clenched my right fist and pumped it hard.

"Fuck yes!" I grunted, grinning around at the undead struggling to their feet. I strode forward, starting to pull my naginata out, when I had a thought.

"Hey, Yen!" I called up.

"Yeah?" Her voice floated back down to me.

"What about fighting? If I use my weapons against them over and over again, once we kill the boss, will I get weapons and training experience for this?" I questioned. There was a long pause, before the others started calling out to get them down there.

I grinned as Lydia leaped over the side, her wings flaring before she slammed into the ground, slowing her nicely.

"Let's find out!" Lydia said, grinning excitedly.

"Oh, hell yes." I thought about the skills I rarely used before hunching down and leveling my naginata at an oncoming skeleton. I triggered Lunge, a new Ability I'd not yet had the chance to train with, and blurred across the several meters between us, ramming the blade through the forehead of the undead and sending the body clattering to the floor.

This time, I swept the blade to the right and left immediately after, severing the heads of those corpses closest and proceeded to kick the skulls across the line.

Once they crossed that line, the bodies stopped trying to reform, and I grunted again, grinning.

"Okay, people!" I shouted up. "Looks like it's training time! Anyone who needs some skill, get down here and get some practice in. Jian...land her there!" I ordered, gesturing to a spot a few dozen meters back from the invisible line of the village boundary.

As soon as the ship was down, the entire crew and the Gnomes poured off, joining my team. We spread out, with Grizz in the center, bellowing orders to the new trainees.

"Nobody goes beyond this line!" he ordered, slicing a line in the earth before him. We followed suit, creating a visible maximum range. "Now, you strike, kill, and retreat when you need to; any injuries will be healed by Oracle." He pointed her out, and she smiled. "Once you've had enough, you retreat properly. If you find yourself getting overwhelmed, you shout out, and we'll help you. No heroics!" Grizz glared round as he said that last bit at the ship's crew and the Gnomes.

"This team is professional; you're not. We're armored, and you're not, so no risks! This is a training opportunity like I've never seen, so we're going to make the most of it. Pick a weapon, practice, and rest. When it gets too busy, we *all* step back over the line and let things calm down. Last of all, when you can *safely* do so, you get the skulls over the line."

I watched in my peripheral vision as Grizz got nods and sloppy salutes from the newcomers. I grinned, putting the naginata away and switching to the weapons I always ended up relying on.

I clenched my fists, gauntlets creaking as I tightened them, and I stepped forward, watching the nearest undead.

It staggered toward me, hands outstretched, rotten fingers twitching in need. Flesh hung in ropy links from its bones, and I grinned, huffing a few quick breaths in and out before lunging.

I swept my right arm forward, bent at the elbow at about forty-five degrees, hand rigid in a blade, and struck. Moving left to right, I swiped its frantically reaching arms aside then twisted around behind it, grabbing its chin with my left hand and turning again to rip its head free.

I used the skull to slam into the next one's face, staggering it back as the one behind me collapsed to the ground. As I kicked this one's legs out from under it, I twisted and punted the skull of the first one to the left, sending it flying in a long arc that ended up outside the boundary.

"He shoots...he scores!" I shouted, spinning to build up momentum and lobbing the skull in my hand in the same direction. The reanimating bones behind me clattered to the ground, suddenly robbed of life again. "And the crowd goes wild!" I shouted, thrusting my fists triumphantly in the air before twisting myself around again and starting the process over.

The onslaught of undead reduced with amazing speed from an unmanageable threat that would overwhelm us all into a simple training opportunity. I fought for another fifteen minutes before we all backed over the line at Lydia's shouted command. We took the time to rest before having the ship, and the entire group, move twenty meters along the boundary, getting clear space to fight away from the massive pile of bones we'd managed to build up.

"Okay, people!" I called as we relocated. "Grab some bones; Bob needs a rebuild!"

We dragged entire corpses across the lines, adding to the dozens of skulls, and laughter started up as the undead suddenly lost interest. The relief was palpable in the new crew and Gnomes as the dangerous, but potentially rewarding, training opportunity was paused.

I gathered the bones into a massive pile and had Bob stand next to them as I looked him over. We were going for a stealthy motherfucker design, and yet, it seemed such a waste with all these bones.

I shrugged and went back to the drawing board, deciding I'd slim him down again once this mission was done.

I took the overall design for the knight I'd created previously, minus the two stabbing legs over the shoulders, and I scaled it up. By nearly doubling the overall size, Bob topped out at nearly sixteen feet tall and became nigh-on solid in terms of bone density.

I partially listened as the others started again and again, fighting the waves of undead. Each time, I heard the bone colossus rearing up again. But, as more and more bones were piled ready for me, I couldn't help but grin as I turned Bob into a powerhouse that could take the colossus on.

I named the new form Titan and nearly crowed at the new pages I was presented with as soon as I finished. I swiped them aside, holding them ready to examine, as I looked Bob over. I had to admit, I'd done a hell of a job on him.

His sixteen feet in height was complimented nicely by being nearly ten feet across at the shoulders, the outer edges of which were coated in solid bone armor that looked like it'd come from a dragon.

Bob was humanoid still, but his legs were each as thick as my torso with their attached bone-armor plates. He bore a mace that was tipped with spikes made of solid bone and a tower shield that ended in twin spikes designed to be driven into the ground to help him hold against larger foes.

His head was the coolest. I'd altered his skull again, shifting it even further from the Naga skull that it had started as. Having to make it larger anyway, I added high cheekbones, more teeth, and a more humanoid overall appearance.

I'd left him with long, pointed canines but generally made him look like a giant vampire knight, and I damn well dared anyone to come and face him without requiring a change of underwear.

I looked through the notifications again. Luckily, the one I'd hoped to see was only a few notifications in.

You have selected Titan as the name for this form. Reconstruction will require 1.6 metric tons of bone to complete from scratch. This form has received the following bonuses:

+7 to intimidation

+5 to damage against Darkness-aligned foes (due to consecrated bones used in construction)

+ 1 bonus ability to be chosen

Bonus Ability:

Due to the nature of this minion, the parts incorporated, and the blessings bestowed, Bob may now be granted one of the following:

1x Class or 3x Abilities

I didn't even have to pause. Abilities were cool and all, but a class would follow him, and as I rebuilt him over and over, it would adjust. An ability might be totally inappropriate to his next form and become useless, anyway.

Plus, I couldn't see what they were without choosing the option first.

I selected Class and read on.

You have selected Class choices as your bonus for this minion.

Beware, these choices are permanent, unlike mortal Class choices, and cannot be changed.

Revenant: This Bone Minion is becoming more and more self-aware. The price of this, however, is that a past of conflicting memories, places, names, images, and lost connections will occasionally make themselves known to Bob.

Bob will be tormented by these memories unless he is given rein to explore them, to follow and make sense of his past, so that he can be at peace with who he one day may become.

Bonuses:

- +5 to Intelligence
- +10 To Constitution
- +1 to Charisma

Bone Priest: This Bone Minion has been blessed by not one, but two Gods, each of the Pantheon of the Flame, and he has been granted limited sentience. This sentience has come with a desire to serve the Gods' will, however, and he will be freed from all ties to you, possibly still holding you in high regard, but no longer as his master.

Beware this choice if you have misused your Minion.

Bonuses:

- + 5 to Intelligence
- + 10 to Wisdom
- + Ability: Choral Summoning – Summon 5-15 spectral worshippers who will aid the Bone Priest in times of danger.

Stalker: This Bone Minion has grown in mind as well as body; however, the violence that ended his previous existences have become a permanent part of his psyche, making him lust for war, for the thrill of the fight, and for the opportunity to test himself against a worthy opponent!

Bonuses:

- + 5 to Constitution
- + 5 to Strength
- + 5 to Dexterity
- + Ability: Face Me – Single-target Taunt skill that lasts up to 30 seconds, and costs 300 stamina.

I read the choices again and again before making my decision and accepting the revenant. The priest was cool, but honestly, I didn't want to give Bob up, not yet. While the stalker was more in keeping with what I wanted as a bodyguard and assassin class, the lust for war wasn't. I decided that helping Bob come to terms with himself was the better choice and was greeted with an Ability choice for him.

Please select from the following Class-specific Abilities:

Charge: One of the reasons Bone Minions are so rare is that, despite the potential of their forms, they are often slow to move and easily damaged. Charge allows a temporary 300% increase to speed for 5 seconds, usable once per 90 seconds, for a cost of 50 stamina per ton of bone.

Necrotic Harpoon: Your Minion has discovered the joy of Ranged Magical Combat! Necrotic Harpoon summons a spear of solid Necrotic energy that can be hurled at an opponent. If the Harpoon hits, a magical chain will link the two beings pouring necrotic energy into the target, siphoning life-force out to repair the caster.

Chain may be used to reel in the target.

Chaotic Firmament: Your Minion has learned a spell of the Rift! For a cost of 50 mana per square foot, Bob can convert a seemingly solid section of the realm into a Chaotic version of itself. Will the earth become Mud? Solid Gold? A portal into the Dark Places of the Cosmos that allows the end of days to begin? There's only one way to find out.

Needless to say, there wasn't a cat in hell's chance I was risking destroying all of reality just to see what happened, so I scrapped Chaotic Firmament immediately, all the while wondering at the madness of giving a chance at spells like that to the kind of lunatic who wanted to raise the dead in the first place.

Next, I re-read the two others and settled after a few seconds on Necrotic Harpoon. Giving Bob an attack that was both ranged and magical ticked all the right boxes for me.

Congratulations!

You have raised your spell Skeletal Reanimator to its Second Evolution.

You must now pick a new path to follow.

Will you choose to continue to follow the path of the REANIMATOR, or will you seek to become a LORD OF THE DEAD?

Choose carefully, as this choice cannot be undone.

Reanimator:
In its first evolution, the Path of the Reanimator allowed you to weakly sense certain differences in bones, catching the occasional hint that a bone might be better for this function or that. But by deepening your connection with the realm around you, you will gain two important new Abilities:

Sense Bone: You may now sense the remains that lie all around us. Within a range of 5m, you will sense bones, should they be unshielded, and touching them will grant a greater understanding of their potential, not to mention who and what they were in life. (Additional Quests may be discovered along this path.)

Magically Active: Bones that have long been infused with magics will reveal themselves to you now, and you will sense ways to tease the power from them, granting your creation unique Abilities and Bonuses dependent on the materials used to upgrade it.

Lord of the Dead:
With this Evolution, you gain the chance to grow your forces again. As your first Minion reaches for sentience, freeing you from part of the cost of maintaining it, this permits you to use your expanded understanding of the Veil between Life and Death to pull fragments free, tearing them from the souls that sleep inches away, and impregnating your creations with them.

Beware!

Many of the dead do not wish to live again. Forcing them into a new, and far stranger form may have devastating effects on their stability.

Small Unit Tactics (Undead): Summon up to ten undead minions, provided you have harvested enough soul fragments to imbue them with life. These risen creations will act as you will it, but beware of their festering hatred for those they perceive as having all they have lost.

Bonus Ability: Lich's Bane

You have been instrumental in destroying not one, but two Liches. The knowledge of a Lich is tremendous, and while dark, each repository lost to destruction is a loss of knowledge that could have been used for other purposes.

Now you can interrogate a Lich, should you find their phylactery, and your Intelligence and Wisdom prove higher than theirs.

Beware! Should you prove no match for the Lich mentally, you will be consumed instead, granting the Lich a second chance at life. You have been warned!

I grimaced at the bonus ability, which just seemed fucking stupid to me, but hey. I didn't make the prizes. I barely even considered the Lord of the Dead option. Yes, it was cool; ten more Bobs, all in Titan form, would slaughter this place, for a start, not to mention making short work of the Church of Nimon, I was sure, but I'd have to tear souls apart outside of a fight. Combat was one thing but reaching through the Veil meant that harvesting the slumbering souls of the innocent became as likely as destroying the guilty.

I remembered the memories that Amon had shared, the recollections of a lich's filthy claws piercing through, indiscriminately injuring and stealing souls to serve them, and I instantly wanted to kill something.

Nope. Not the path for me.

I selected Reanimator and screamed in pain as I was blinded, my eyes almost eaten out of my head by the sheer concentration of death magic that surrounded me.

CHAPTER FORTY

O racle, thankfully, was nearby, and managed to repair my eyes, but when I could see again, I was being supported by Bob. My limp body lay reclined on his hand, with the rest of the team and the others circled around me, ready for anything.

This time, I carefully opened one eye, then immediately shut it, looking deliberately away from the village.

It took a few seconds for me to learn how to tamp the new ability down, much like the way I could turn my DarkVision on or off at will. When I finally managed that, I breathed a sigh of relief as I sagged back and rubbed my eyes, which ached like hell from being regrown.

"What happened?" Lydia asked, beating Oracle to the question, and silence spread around the group as I explained. While I spoke, I experimented with adjusting the magic's severity, trying to see just a faint glow, instead of staring at the magical equivalent of the sodding sun, but it was no good.

By the time I'd finished, I'd managed to tamp it down enough that I could finally look at Bob without him blinding me, but I still felt like I needed magical sunglasses.

I looked him over, examining the various bones, and found that I could now pick out the handful that were left from the consecrated priest of the light that I'd fought at the end of the fight for the Tower.

That raised an interesting question in my mind, as I had spoken to, and for that matter, reawakened Sint, God of Light, and I knew for a fact that he couldn't have consecrated the priest. In addition, considering that the dickbag was involved with slavers and was one himself, Sint would have squashed him flat, given the choice. I resolved to ask a few more questions of the Gods when I got the chance next.

I slowly looked towards the village again, and shuddering, I turned the ability off again.

I knew, just goddamn *knew* that there would be something I could learn from using the Ability on the village, but at the cost of my eyes being burned out every time before I could even focus? Nah. Not happening.

I stood up and looked around, finding that the undead had returned to somnolence while I was being healed. I nodded in satisfaction at the piles of bone that lay strewn about, now completely inactive.

I turned and looked up at Bob, who was kneeling behind me, and yet still rose taller than my head, and I reached up and clapped a hand on his armored shoulder, nodding to him in thanks and observing the newly awakened sentience that glowed in his blue eyes.

"Can you talk, Bob?" I asked. He hesitated before opening his mouth to expose a dark, swirling mess of light deep in his throat. He tried to speak several times, but all he managed was a crackling sound and a hiss before giving up.

"That's fine, man, we'll work on it. I guess that today is kinda your birthday, big lad, as I can see that there's a lot more awake in you than there ever was before. Welcome to the world," I said.

He nodded carefully.

The others said similar things, and I watched him closely, sensing the confusion that emanated from the ball of emotions and intentions that was now Bob in my mind.

I concentrated, sensing blurry memories, bits and pieces, occasional images, and the entire gamut of emotions running through him, albeit weakly.

I gave everyone a few minutes to talk as I hugged Oracle and thanked her for healing me, as well as reassuring others that I was fine, before straightening my back and turning to regard the village.

"Okay, people," I said. "The sun is starting to go down, and I expect the Specters will get stronger with the darkness. We need to figure out what the hell is going on, so…" I gestured to the group around me. "Half of you can stay here and guard the others while they practice; the rest of you are with me. We need to find a corpse that's not rising."

"What are you going to do with it?" Yen asked.

I grinned at her "I'm going to steal it, and we're going to find out what the difference is between them, of course."

The entire team volunteered to go with me, but in the end, I decided to limit it to Bane, Grizz, Lydia, and Jian, with Bob, of course.

That gave us mainly melee fighters and one scout, so when we needed to fall back, the magic wielders would be in place to bombard the enemy.

I waited a few minutes while everyone tightened straps that had come loose and had a drink and addressed any pressing needs before we set off back into the village.

As soon as we crossed the boundary, I felt the same wash of power ripple out, and I cursed myself for an idiot, gesturing everyone back across the line as I remembered what I'd learned before.

Once we were all back, and the undead began to settle, I made sure I knew where the nearest truly dead body was. Leaving my escort behind, I flew into the village.

Flying didn't trigger the undead; it was only once I touched down that it had the effect, so I searched for the body we'd agreed upon, thirty meters away. The bones slumped against a wall that was itself sagging precariously. The figure's clothes had long since rotted away, the surface of the bones exposed to the sun, but unlike I'd expected, they were pristine. I landed, setting off an immediate reaction from the area, as undead all around me stirred, but this one remained unmoving.

I reached down, fingers gently touching the skull before me, and I reeled back in shock as a scream of terror lashed through my mind, sending me staggering into the wall opposite.

I quickly shook myself, brought back to reality abruptly by the claw-tipped fingers scratching at my armored boot. I blinked the alley back into focus and growled in displeasure at seeing the shambling forms moving in. I tore the skull from the one that was touching me, flicking it up into the air and punting it as hard as I could into the distance before turning back to the pristine corpse on the floor.

It had tilted, sliding down the wall after being disturbed by my touch, but remained, somehow, intact, held in place as though flesh remained, despite it being centuries-long-lost.

I took three quick steps, went to one knee, and reached out, sweeping the still form up and blanking my mind to the screams as much as I could.

I spotted the narrow band of sunlight that still shone between the sagging roofs overhead, and I hurtled into the sky, reorienting once I was above the rooftops and heading straight for the ship and the others.

As soon as I crossed the line, the corpse collapsed, and I swore viciously, feeling the spirit fleeing the body. Yet, I also felt a sudden sense of relief and a slight lessening of the pervasive sense of death that surrounded me.

I landed and reached out, little hope in me, and confirmed what I expected; the soul was gone. While much more powerful clairvoyance might be able to reach the girl or young woman it had once been, I sure as shit couldn't.

I growled with frustration, waiting with the others as the village reset itself, ready for the next victim.

Ten minutes passed, time mainly spent getting everyone aboard the ship and ready. Then we were off, flying over the village and searching the streets, fields, paths, and alleyways, until Giint spotted the next body, seemingly in a better place for retrieval.

This corpse was laid across a small table outside what looked to have been a stable. We circled it, and I warned the others to be ready for anything, then commanded Bob to remain where he was, seated cross-legged in the middle of the deck.

I jumped over the side, dropping and flaring out the magic to land atop the table. I swore profusely when our hoped-for sidestepping of the rules failed miserably, as the same pulse rippled out, despite me being on a stone table and not on the ground.

I hopped down, pulled the corpse free, and gritted my teeth against the incessant moaning and screams that filled my mind as I flashed back up into the air. I set the corpse down on the deck and went for plan number two: racing to the edge of the village, exiting the invisible barrier, then returning, landing on the deck of the ship where it hovered just inside the barrier.

This time, there was an effect, but rather than the undead going back to sleep as we hoped, they kept moving, prowling, and slowly gathering below the ship. They seemed confused and disoriented, but they clearly knew something was wrong as well.

I ordered the others to watch over them and to keep an eye out for the colossus, as I moved to the corpse and cast Clairvoyance.

It was the first time I'd used the spell, and the description stated it worked on the recently dead, but when the long dead were still screaming in your mind even without a spell...?

Yeah, it worked, all right.

I felt the bridge forming, a connection between us, the magic letting our minds and memories reach each other.

It started with a barrage of fear pouring out of the corpse, a nameless terror, a sense of pain and unending torment, of something playing with the soul and others, stalking the night, and flaming whips searing the skin from the boy's back.

I knew him suddenly, as a barrier between us broke. Argyll, third son of the carpenter Min, he'd been apprenticed to the stableman Bart. While his master was a lazy sod and spent more time drunk than not, he was also kind and provided a safe place to sleep out of the cold, regular meals, and relatively few beatings.

Argyll was happy; he'd just plucked up the courage to ask Betti to go walking with him by the oak tree, and was just about to go to her, when the sky fell.

It'd started as a flare of light, high above the clouds, like the rising of a new sun. Only seconds later, it flashed again and again, and terrible lightnings filled the previously calm, drizzling sky.

Thunder rumbled, a sudden storm building from nowhere, and Argyll stared open-mouthed as a creature fell from the sky, plummeting towards the village.

It was huge, colored black and red, with enormous wings of bone. When it crashed into the headman's house, right at the center of the village, there was a scream of pain and fury from the wreckage, followed by the light, the glorious, terrible light of the storm high above.

A figure flew down, hovering over the village, clad in silver armor with huge wings that shimmered and brightened the world with their whiteness. She lifted her right hand high, and the light flashed to her, hitting something she held and making Argyll cover his eyes as he gasped in terror. She flung it down, striking the creature that was even now climbing out of the pit.

The blast hit it, a solid pillar of burning fire and cleansing white light, and it screamed, making Argyll grab at his head as his eardrums burst and blood ran over his fingers.

The creature stood up again as the blast ended, and its mouth moved, but Argyll couldn't hear anything now. It pointed at the figure floating above it with one hand and lifted an orb of green fire in the left.

There was something, a ripple, a wave in the world itself, and something passed through Argyll, like a breeze, but infinitely colder. The force pushed outwards from that orb, and he staggered, his hand going to his chest, a sudden pause as something that he'd unknowingly felt his entire life stilled.

He let out a single surprised grunt before collapsing, his face bouncing off the stone table before him. The wave returned, tearing his soul and anchoring it to the suddenly cold prison of flesh and bone that had been its home.

A part of him was torn away, used as fuel, and he sensed the counterstrike lashing up at the floating figure and the terrible pain it caused.

Then he was screaming as he was torn from slumber, his soul being fed upon by something else, some scavenger that stalked the night.

He saw the others; some of them were people from the village, like fat old Mithelas and his miserable wife who everyone knew was screwing the baker. Fern, the merchant from the big city was there, too, and they were all gathering round.

Argyll tried to speak, to call for help, but the others were huddled around the creature that hunched over him, and he couldn't move, couldn't speak. He could only watch as the creature let fall…bits…of him, fragments of his soul, that the others greedily snatched up and consumed.

The creature fed until the world started to dim for Argyll, and the tiredness returned before it barked at the others. They moved on, leaving him at the very edge of the eternal death he craved.

Years passed, then centuries.

Argyll saw them come; each time a new life force entered the village, he felt his soul being clawed at, energy siphoned away to start the chain reaction.

He sensed them falling all around him, bodies being added to by the dozens and by the hundreds. Some, like him, were left to be fed upon, while others were used to trap more and more souls.

As the centuries passed, he learned to sense when it was near: the black thing, the creature that fed upon him, the wails of the others as it prowled the area, feeding.

Sometimes, it would move to a location where he could see it, and his soul quaked as the thing fed. Its long, black arms and legs were like those of a spider, clicking as it appeared, scaling walls, its body flattening to pass into crevices in the ground then enlarging as it exited them.

The only constant thing was the face, its three red eyes and the tentacles that it grasped its prey with as it fed. Where the body bulged and shrank as it squeezed through gaps, or passed through windows, the head remained the same, watching, radiating hatred for everything.

Sometimes it would stalk him for hours, driving his terror to a fever pitch. Other times, he had no warning, and he was struck suddenly, his phantasmal form being torn and consumed by the creature as he wailed in silence, begging for the final release of death.

A release that never came.

I shook myself as I stepped back, gazing down in horror at the corpse of Argyll. I snarled in overwhelming rage, stalking to the side of the ship and searching through the village below.

"I know you now, you fucker!" I screamed. "I know you. I saw you. And I'm GOING TO FUCK YOU UP!" I roared, my mind reeling at the onslaught of knowledge and Amon's shock as He examined detail after detail before going strangely silent.

I glared out at the buildings and bodies, suddenly seeing more than before, as the pieces slipped into place.

"What happened, Jax?" Lydia asked me.

I replied tersely, my voice filled with a cold fury. "A Valkyrie was fighting a Demon. A powerful one. The village was just unlucky and got caught up in the fight. The Demon used something to kill everyone, an orb; it tore their life force to use as a weapon, and it counterattacked the Valkyrie.

"That was the last thing the boy saw before he died," I growled. "Then something else came along, something from the forests. It found the dead, saw an opportunity, and used it to make a nest, a trap.

"It feeds on the corpses, on their fucking souls! And it found willing slaves in some of the villagers and some of those who came looking; that's who the Specters are. They're the shitbags of the population, the nasty ones who'd do anything, looks like the creature made a deal with them."

"What does it look like?" asked Ronin.

I furrowed my brow, trying to visualize it. "The boy, Argyll, rarely saw it, and his mind was clouded with terror and pain when he did. It climbs the walls like a spider, but on four legs or arms or whatever. The head is a mess of tentacles and three red eyes. Beyond that…" I grunted, shaking my head.

"Anything else?" he pressed, and I started to say no, before remembering it sliding up out of a crevasse.

"Yeah, actually, it can change its size. Looks like the head stays the same, but the body gets bigger or smaller to fit through gaps."

I was cut off by a powerful roar of red-hot fury. It echoed in my head, taking me to my knees, and Amon tried to seize control of my body.

He was screaming incoherently, his voice making no sense. His spectral fingers reached out, curling into fists, and my right hand did the same.

"Run." I groaned through gritted teeth.

"What...?" Lydia asked, and I forced myself to my feet.

"Get out of here!" I roared suddenly, Amon releasing control of my mouth, allowing me that much control, as we reached a sort of agreement.

His consciousness was too ready, it had struck too fast for me to counter and was spreading throughout my body at a rate I couldn't match.

"Jax..." Yen protested, when Oracle and Bob screamed in joint pain. The skeletal construct collapsed, unable to maintain himself as my power was torn from him, and Oracle cried out in agony as our bond was torn asunder.

I had milliseconds to act, and I could either fight for control of my body, or I could save them.

I chose Oracle and Bob, frantically reaching out, gathering the strands of the bond and tying them deeper. Forsaking the bond to my body, I instead tied them directly to my soul, chaining them to me and me to them as searing pain ripped through me.

I sensed the weaves of fire and air, of water and life that emanated from my soul, and I used them, layering one atop the next frantically.

My desperate actions stopped Bob's deterioration. As his bones fell away, crashing to the deck, I barely managed to protect his heart and head. The massive form had slumped forward, sections falling free to tumble to the ground below. As his skull bounced, I managed to tie it to the chest, strengthening and replacing the initial weave that held him intact.

I didn't know what he was supposed to look like, not in here; not his soul. I sensed the fragments of souls in the bones he'd used, and I remembered the section about his class, about how these fragments that were already lost to the original souls would serve to increase him, to teach him and form part of the bedrock of his future.

I sensed the original kernel of my soul which I'd given him, to begin to grow to sentience, and I took it all in. In just a second that felt like a century, I desperately pulled and frantically pushed fragments.

It was like a jigsaw, one whose edges shifted and flowed, constantly in a state of flux, made of burning light and terrible dark; memories of deaths, of pain and hatred, and the occasional bright flare of happiness, of a loved one singing in the dark, a babe being comforted, the taste of milk fresh on her lips, the warmth of a mother's caress.

I found the sections that matched. I found the love, seeing the way those fragments shifted, the patterns they made when those feelings surfaced, and I pressed them together.

They fit! As soon as they joined, the flux stopped, and I realized that these were, in truth, kernels of souls. They were the building blocks of who these people had been. Every memory, every event had left a signature. As I pressed them together, they changed others. Like a magnet drawing iron filings, more fragments shifted as they examined each other, sensing similarities, where before there had been only a barrage of jumbled input.

I moved like lightning, pushing, pressing, twisting, and smoothing, adding in all the elements, balancing out the form as it grew. Fire and water, earth and air, light and dark, life and death, all combined to create a being that was slowly holding *itself* together now.

I reached out, feeling for the final pieces, the fragments that would make Bob more than he was, more than an unthinking automaton. These changes I made were in danger of wiping out the slight fragments of him that had grown, and I couldn't allow that.

I called out into the night, into the space between seconds, and I felt Them answer: Tyosh, God of Time and Reflection, and Svetu, God of Invention and Creation.

We shared without words, and I looked on amazed, as Tyosh showed Bob…to Bob. He reflected all that Bob was and the instincts that made him into himself. Svetu took them, binding them into the whole that I'd created. The addition of the Gods made the crochet tea cozy that I'd made into a tapestry that was suddenly made of a million billion glowing threads, threads that billowed in the wind for a split second before affixing themselves to the heart and head of Bob.

He opened his mouth and screamed. Time started to pass again, and I felt Oracle.

Where Bob was without a true soul, and had only just begun to grow, she was her own self, her own being with a soul, and her own mind.

Saving her, binding her back to me, was both easier and harder than fixing Bob. As I reached for her, I found her fraying, the golden light dimming as she started to slip away. I frantically gathered her to me.

She had no additional soul fragments to use as building blocks. The parts that were gone were now gone forever, and every millisecond, more fell away as the destruction increased in pace.

I desperately reached out, discarding all the external parts, the extraneous shards of her, and I held the heart of her tight. I bathed her in my love, and I declared "this far and no more" as I fixated furiously on her.

Milliseconds passed as I poured myself into her, using the life force and pattern that made me, that made a human, even as fucked-up as I was. I mimicked it, tearing out from my own form to fix hers.

Her love, her belief in me survived, then I felt the Lady of Fire. Her power poured into me as She forced my soul back together as I tore it to save Oracle.

"You will not fail me, Eternal!" Jenae screamed into my mind. *"I have plans for you, boy; you don't get away that easily!"*

I screamed in agony as white-hot magma seemed to pour through my soul, stitching me back together and leaving me raw. Oracle collapsed to the deck of the ship, unconscious but alive.

I watched, a passenger in my own body, as Amon stepped up to the railing then off the edge of the ship, plunging through the air to the ground below.

He didn't bother to catch himself with air, landing atop the roof of a damaged building like a stone from heaven, sending the roof, the supports, all of it crumbling inwards as He lashed out with pure power.

He commanded my mana, but He pulled from the air around us as well. The ambient mana that was everywhere, that refilled every mage's reserves, rushed almost joyously to do His will, and the building detonated.

The walls were thrown outwards in a spray of disintegrating stone and dust. The roof simply vanished, and as the dust that had been a crumbling house was banished from existence by mana's true master, Jenae's distant voice spoke from the ship above and behind me.

"Leave the area now. Amon is in ascension, and he will brook no interference."

The others asked questions, but I dismissed it as my body puppeted forward. Amon stalked out of the last remnants of the building.

There were three hundred feet or more to the village proper, and all around me, the bodies started to shift, rising to do the will of their dark master, before a blast of air rippled out.

Amon hadn't needed to use words. He had not cast a spell; He'd simply told the air that it was a blade infinitesimally thin, as hard as granite, and sharp enough to make an atom split without it noticing.

The ripple flashed out, and all around me, for more than six hundred feet in all directions, solely excluding the direction of the ship, this blade flashed, making the air warp as it rotated.

Half a second later, it was done, and my foot came down as we stepped forward again. Everything, from brick walls to corpses to ancient wood to copper pots, collapsed into tiny slivers on the ground.

For a split second, the world seemed to hold its breath in sheer terror, before the ground shuddered, and Amon leaned forward, digging my feet in and jumping.

The jump was powered in part by mana and in part through the utter certain knowledge that Amon had done this before and, therefore, this body *would* do it again.

Muscles snapped, tendons ripped, and in less than a second, they were all repaired again as if they were never damaged.

We landed, standing atop the edge of the crater and looking down, as Amon growled low in hatred, seeing all the signs His idiot descendant had missed.

The scent in the air, the sheer darkness and presence of the void and its attendant, voidal magics.

In the center of the crater was a single speck of void crystal, a fragment of a fragment, what the Valkyrie had been fighting the Demon for.

At some point in her fight with the greater Demon, it had lost the fragment, and it had pursued her as she ran, injured, unaware that the entire reason for their enmity had been left behind, slowly spreading and corrupting reality in a way neither would have permitted.

The crystal quivered, then twisted, burrowing deep into the ground, seeking to flee Amon's wrath, and He gestured once.

The crystal stopped instantly, vibrating with a terrible intensity as it tried to flee. When it failed, when it could no longer move, or hope that it would be missed, it *shifted*.

The void crystal flexed, opening a planar gateway, as its true form entered the realm. The creature Argyll and the others had seen and the evil souls had worshipped was as a gnat to the form the creature used when it felt its existence was truly threatened.

Long legs protruded first, thick as tree trunks, covered with bladed hairs and ending in scalloped claws that sank into the ground, as Amon released the pressures holding this creature–a true creation of His ancient enemy–captive.

Amon wanted it free. He wanted it to stand tall and ready, fully in this realm.

The creature dragged out its head next, the three-eyed face, a mass of tentacles and proboscis, of tiny, snapping jaws and tendrils that burrowed into bones to crack them of the marrow, simply for the pleasure of the sound its victims made as they expired.

As the nightmarish face slid into the realm, my body shook, not with fear, as my damn soul was, but with utter outrage that this thing still dared to exist at all.

Whatever had constrained the creature here, forcing it to take millennia to feed and grow, rather than running riot, Amon didn't know, and He didn't care. As the long spines of the ridged head slid through the portal, unfolding into the air, the body followed. It was ovoid, thin, and seemed to serve as nothing more than a place for the rest to join together.

Where the head was massive, the eyes seemingly big enough for me to stand inside, the body was small, little more than the torso of a child. As if that thought had been a spark that triggered it, the body *shifted,* becoming more childlike as a distant wailing filled my mind, sounding as though a child was being tortured somewhere close by.

The creature pulled itself closer, leaning in, seeming to grow in size, yet paradoxically appear smaller than it had before. Hands I'd not seen before sprouted from under the tentacles that surrounded a slobbering, jagged-toothed maw.

It reached forward as though to caress me. A tongue flickered, something…tugging…at me, seeking to pull my soul into it, consuming my essence as much as flesh. Voices spoke at the distant edge of madness.

"Fleshsonicesosweetsopinktoeattotastesolong," it mumbled and groaned, the voice rising and falling in pitch and tone.

Amon growled. "I remember you!" He screamed, a spear carved of fire that appeared in his right hand at will suddenly leveled at the creature. "I remember you, Tho'th C'hit'e!"

The creature froze, looking at us in surprise before recoiling in horror.

"Itisdeadyesitisdeadnoitcannot," it started to whisper, to howl in outraged denial.

Then Amon struck.

He moved almost faster than I could see, my mind unable to make full sense of the blurred movement, registering only the infinitesimal pauses as He repaired the damage done to me, healing me and strengthening my body, forcing it to endure the next burst of speed and the next.

The flaming spear slashed through limbs with a shudder, then my ears ruptured at the screams. Fluids that were never meant for this plane of reality cascaded upon me, wet and cold.

The touch of something so alien should have carved through my bones, splitting my cells, but Amon willed it to be as the gentle kiss of rainwater, and so it was.

The massive, grotesque creature, the Valspar, collapsed to the ground, its limbs severed. Amon stalked forward, batting aside a tentacled slash–which should have carved boulders in two–with a contemptuous backhand.

He stepped over the mewling creature and glared down at it, His fury making my head want to explode. He reached out, the flaming spear no longer in existence, my fingers digging through solid bone and horn as if it were nothing more substantial than over-ripe banana, to the brain in the center.

Amon grabbed a handful and tore it out into the air before us, staring at the sticky mess of pseudopods and hooked, frantically reaching claws.

It hung from my hand, twisting and reaching back at the rest of its body which lay still. As more pseudopods reached up for the section he held, Amon took a deep breath and changed one last time.

Silvery scales flowed over our body, coating us from head to toe in less than a heartbeat. Our fingers were tipped with claws of pure onyx, razor-sharp and impervious to any diamond drill as the heat rose.

It was like a cool wave of water, yet solid, as the scales flowed up our neck and closed across our face, the ridges forming the bulkier jaw and longer faceplate needed to accommodate the new form as our face grew, our teeth lengthening, even as our gullet changed, our tongue becoming forked and long.

The world changed, and I saw it anew, heat maps overlaying everything, even as it was washed out by the creature before me. The depths of space's absolute cold radiated off the creature's soul as I leaned forward and released the dragonfire.

I bathed the creature in it, the fats popping as they were flash-fried and rendered to ash, which was then vaporized into its subatomic makeup.

Countless seconds passed as I flooded the creature before me in the cleansing flames, removing its incursion into my reality before Amon released me, a sense of satisfaction filling Him as the shimmering scales fractured and fell away, exposing my humanoid form that lay waiting beneath them.

I staggered back, my mind reeling, shock over the ease with which Amon had altered, well, everything! I couldn't help but feel insanely inferior to Him, especially at the way He'd literally bitch-slapped a creature of nightmare into the grave.

I sensed the remnants of His feelings, of His memories, before His mind was subsumed into madness again. I knew, I just *knew* that He'd been stronger than even this in life. He'd truly been a single step below the Gods in his time, and He'd done all of that with just my body.

My vision was frantically populated by popups, and I dismissed them as quickly as I could, but one; one, I was too slow to dismiss.

Congratulations, Eternal!

You have reached level twenty-four and have a Class Choice waiting.

Class Evolution Recommendations

Common:

Exploratory Alchemist: You've found that the secrets of life may very well lie at the bottom of a bottle, after all. Choosing this as your latest evolution will grant you a one-off bonus of ten points to Perception, a randomly chosen recipe, and a chance to automatically discover a recipe by drinking a version of it in potion form.

Monster Slayer: The hundreds of creatures you've slain since entering this realm pay mute testament to your skill, Slayer! Choosing this as your latest evolution will grant you a one-off bonus of five points to Constitution and five points to Dexterity, as well as a single skill-boost of five levels to the weapon handling skill of your choice.

Experimental Magician: Magic is no science; it is an art, and you have the skill to be so much more! Choosing this as your latest evolution will grant you a one-off bonus of ten points to Intelligence and five points to Wisdom, along with a boost of one level to the School of Mastery of your choice.

Rare:

Dungeon Diver: You spend as much time in ancient ruins as out of them, teasing the secrets of the past forth to serve you in the future. Perhaps you're an explorer at heart? Choosing this as your latest evolution will grant you a one-off bonus of ten points to Dexterity and ten points to Perception.

Tactician: You have given guidance and orders to the Imperial Legion that has led to battles being won against superior numbers, superior forces, and situations you should have been eaten in! Perhaps you're a tactician extraordinaire in truth? Choosing this as your latest evolution will grant you a one-off bonus of fifteen points to Wisdom.

Paladin: You're on first name terms with a variety of Gods, as well as being a Champion for one. Perhaps it's time to take the plunge? Choosing this as your latest evolution will grant you a one-off bonus of ten points to Endurance and five points to Strength, along with a boon from your chosen God.

Unique:

Imperial Overlord: You have claimed dominance of the continent, but as yet, your claim is still contested. Perhaps a boost is just what you need?

Choosing this as your latest evolution will grant you two Titles of your choice to award to your followers.

Please see the examples below:

Arch-Priest: You are currently the highest ranking member of the Pantheon of Flame. Laying claim to the position of Arch-Priest formally will create the ability to induct others into the priesthood, granting them bonuses, depending on their deity of choice.

High Inquisitor: People lie, even the best of them. Perhaps it's time to bring the burning light of truth into the darkest places of the soul? Using heat, pain, and sheer brutality, you shall scour the land of their filth! Granting this Title will give access to the repeatable *Quest: Renounce thy Sins.*

I fell back to a sitting position on the edge of the crater, reading it over, once I realized I couldn't get rid of it. I sat for an indeterminate amount of time thinking, trying to decide, but ultimately, as much as I wanted to gain these points for myself, I was no longer a man alone, and I needed to accept that.

I chose Imperial Overlord, and my mind spun with ideas, with the possibilities of the titles. I felt a kind of buyer's remorse instantly; the dungeon diver class would have given me twenty damn points, or the exploratory alchemist would have made me capable of learning new potion recipes by drinking them, or…I shook my head. Sometimes, it was just a case of making a choice and sticking to it.

The titles were a huge boost *if* I used them right. Granting, say, Lydia a title of Imperial Asskicker was possible, and she'd gain plus five points to a stat. That was all well and good, but if I choose to give a noncombatant a title, such as Chancellor, they would gain abilities that were directly related to his role. Doing this meant a non-combat member of the Tower could become hugely helpful, rather than me becoming a little faster or stronger.

Case in point, the evolution that I'd chosen for my swords skill a few days back. I'd been given the chance to pick an ability that would work well with my naginata too, a single weapon boost, Lunge, that allowed me to cover the distance to a fight faster, doing double damage when I hit my target.

I'd spent hours idly arguing with Grizz and Bane over this decision since then, as they would have both selected the second choice, Storm, that would have enabled me to land a Flurry of Blows instead.

As I'd explained to them, yeah, I could have taken that choice. I could have used the Flurry skill several times in a fight, while Lunge was limited to a single use, but I didn't tend to fight with multiple weapons. It was generally my naginata, then my fists, then my forehead, then spare blades in any fight I was in.

Choosing the other skill would have required changing the entire style I used to fight. Plus, when I infused my naginata and struck? Doing double damage could be over two hundred points, and that would kill a hell of a lot of things, or at least take a serious chunk of their health, even if it was simply their little finger I managed to catch.

I liked swords and all, but I loved my giant murder-stick. Add to that, the damage that the naginata was accruing was getting frankly insane, and it could be imbued magically.

I glanced at the weapon, reading its stats, and couldn't help grinning. I was three souls away from a new evolution, and hell, was I ready for that.

Naginata		Further Description *Yes*/*No*	
Damage:		24-40 +47	
Details:		This two-handed weapon was built from a combination of modern Earth techniques and traditional Japanese skills, creating a weapon that is truly deadly in the hands of a skilled user.	
		Enhanced: This weapon has been enhanced through silverbright and has absorbed some of the souls of its victims. Current capacity: 47/150	
		Bonus ability: Magical infusion: Casting your spells through this weapon will infuse it with that ability for the duration of channeling and cause X damage where X is equal to the damage done by the cast spell.	
Rarity:	**Magical:**	**Durability:**	**Charge:**
Unique	Yes	90/100	N/A

I dismissed the prompt and brought up the next one, feeling drained but pleased as I read it over.

You have completed your Quest: Wayland's Crossing!

You have found out the truth of the past, discovering why the last Valkyrie destroyed a village in her quest to slay a Demon Lord. In doing so, you have cleansed her soul of the stain it bore.

Kill the Terror: 1/1

Bring Peace to the Unquiet Dead: 307/307

Find out the Truth: 1/1

Optional Bonus Quest: Use Clairvoyance instead of an Imperial Ability

Rewards: 50,000xp, Title: Valspar's Bane, Progress in your Quest: A Pillar of Strength. Training Arena design gained!

I nodded in satisfaction at that. Yeah, the fifty thousand experience seemed low when considering the Valspar and the hundreds upon hundreds of undead, but I could have also freed all the undead with the Imperial Ability of releasing souls, and Amon kinda did all the heavy lifting in the fight.

I literally just felt exhausted, and that was it. Satisfied, I moved onto the next notification.

Congratulations!

You have made progress in your Quest: A Pillar of Strength.

Your bondswoman, Lydia, commander of your personal squad and close friend, has begun to evolve into a Valkyrie. To complete her evolution, and to become all she could be, she requires four things:

Resolution of the Past: 0/1

Cleansing of the Last Valkyrie 1/1

Find a Class Trainer: 0/1

Discover/Create/Recover Suitable Armor: 0/1

Reward: A full Valkyrie under your command, possibly more, 50,000xp

Once that was out of the way, I looked up, seeing the ship incoming. The railing was packed with faces who were clearly either upset or happy with me. At this distance, it was even odds.

I exhaled forcibly and moved onto the remaining handful of notifications, grunting as I read them, as one after the other dealt with the changes Amon had made to my body.

Congratulations!

Through hard work and perseverance, you have gained points to the following stats. Continue to train and learn to raise these further.

Agility +4

Constitution +2

Dexterity +3

Endurance +2

Perception +2

Strength +5

Wisdom +1

*

Congratulations!

You have killed the following:

- 105x Unquiet Dead Specters of various levels for a total of 97,465xp
- 611x Risen Dead (Enslaved) of various levels for a total of 202,750xp

A party under your command killed the following:

- 202x Unquiet Dead Specters of various levels for a total of 210,148xp
- 348x Risen Dead (Enslaved) of various levels for a total of 114,750xp

Total party experience earned: 324,898xp

As party leader, you gain 25% of all experience earned

Progress to level 25 stands at 739,092/570,000

*

Citadel

Congratulations!

You have reached level 25!

You have 7 unspent Attribute points and 1 unspent Meridian point available.

Progress to level 26 stands at 169,092/640,000

I sat back, shifting my shoulders in the dirt of the crater and squinted as the ship blocked out the last rays of the setting sun. I gave a little wave, letting them know I was okay.

They were all staring at me, including Oracle and Bob. I sighed, dismissing the last few notifications regarding skill growth and leaving my stat points and meridian point to allocate later as I slowly clambered to my feet, looking around the remains of the village.

We'd completely trashed it, and I mean completely. There wasn't a pair of bricks left intact, let alone standing atop each other. I kicked off, jetting upwards on the wings of my ability and feeling like hammered shit.

I landed on the deck, surrounded by glares, and I held my hands up.

"Look, that wasn't my idea. That was Amon; you think *I* can do that kind of fucking magic?" I pointed out, gesturing over the side. "That was a Valspar. You know, the little thing I tore out of myself? That was an adult version of those things, so yeah, Amon lost his temper, took control, and fucked shit up. I spent all my time as either a passenger or fixing the bonds between myself, Oracle, and Bob," I explained, meeting their gazes one at a time.

Bob's massive and really cool-looking titan form was gone entirely. Now instead he was very much a humanoid, standing with arms crossed as he regarded me. Hell, he was even wearing clothes. The trousers were on backwards, and it looked like his shoes were on the wrong feet, but he was clearly trying, and I couldn't help but smile.

"You should have let me die," he said into the silence of my mind. *"I was never alive, so it would have been no loss."*

"It would have been a loss to me, mate, and to the world," I insisted, clapping Bob on the shoulder. Oracle snuggled into my side, holding me tightly.

"You shouldn't have done what you did," she whispered.

"Of course, I should," I said quietly, frowning. "I love you, and I'm not going to lose you."

"You tied us even closer together." She searched my expression for something. "Did you mean to do what you did?"

"To save your life?" I asked. "Of course."

"No, the other thing?" she asked carefully.

I tried to remember, getting a vague conflicting memory of overlaying my lifeforce pattern over hers and forcing the patterns to share…somehow.

"What exactly did I do?"

She shook her head solemnly. "It's something to talk about when all of this is over," she insisted. "In private, and very, very seriously."

Jian walked over to join the rest of the group gathered around me as the first spatters of rain began to fall on the deck, and the wind began to rise.

437

I looked into the distance, spotting a storm far away on the coast. Even here, a hundred or more miles in, the rain was starting, as were the first blustery gales.

"Lydia," I said slowly, glancing over at her furious expression.

"Yes, oh Lord of Fuckin' Stupidity?" she snapped, then shook her head and attempted to be polite. "What do yer need, Jax?"

I smiled. "You came from a village over this way, didn't you?"

She nodded, frowning with thinly veiled trepidation. "Cornut. It be about thirty miles east by north-east; why?"

"Excellent," I replied and gestured to the wheelhouse and the entrance to the belowdecks areas. "Come on, people, let's get out of the rain. We're all off to Cornut. There's a tavern there, I hear, and after that shit, we all need a fucking drink."

"No, Jax, yer can't be serious!" Lydia gasped, freezing.

"I damn well am, Lydia. You've unfinished business to deal with, and we all need a fucking drink and some hot food."

CHAPTER FORTY-ONE

W e all filed indoors, with Lydia trying desperately to change my mind. "Jax, yer don't understand. Cornut be a borin' place. Look, we're not that much farther from Baneth, that's a bigger village. Hell, it be practically a town…"

"What does the quest say about your past, Lydia?" I retorted firmly, sitting down in the wheelhouse and trying not to scream as my muscles ached and adjusted.

I'd gained eighteen points through excessive damage to my body in a matter of seconds, which normally would have taken me months, even under Restun's diabolical torture. Amon had needed to heal and practically rebuild me again and again, simply for walking the way he did, let alone striking out and fighting.

It'd been terrifying in many ways, both because I'd functionally lost control of my body—which came with its own attendant horrors that would be waking me up in sweats for months to come—and because I'd *thought* I was becoming something impressive.

I could almost hold my own against the better legionnaires, after all. Okay, yeah, I might get my ass handed to me by the likes of Augustus, or Restun, or probably Grizz, or…or that wasn't important.

I was getting better. I won most of my fights, and yeah, they were often close-run things, but that's the way the world was.

In comparison to Amon, though? A being who, even constrained by the limited capabilities of my flesh, had managed to move so fast and strike so hard that he'd actively torn through my muscles and bones, not to mention the damn thing he'd been fighting?

It just proved to me that I was nowhere near as powerful as I'd imagined.

Even though I'd been healed, and my body had been repaired supposedly perfectly, adding in the changes of the stat points meant that I ached everywhere. The last thing I needed, after such a horrific reorienting of my worldview, was the leader of my personal squad complaining and trying to prevent us going to her home.

"It says I have to resolve my past," Lydia admitted in a small voice.

"Yeah, and considering that your past, by your own admission, was fine, until you were summarily sold by your asshole of a husband, and your friends turned on you, because of a bard's supposed actions," I said, catching the way that Ronin winced and ducked, trying to stay out of sight at the back of the group. "So, you tell me, Lydia, where's the past you need to resolve likely to be?"

"In Cornut," she admitted softly before taking a deep breath and squaring her shoulders.

"What do you think it refers to?" I asked.

She paused, thinking about it for long minutes before smiling suddenly.

"My mother." She seemed to relax. "My father an' that feckless piece of shit of a 'usband were on a caravan that was raided, I 'eard, so they'll probably be long dead. But my mother, she was a washerwoman in tha village. Jax, if she wanted to, could we bring her to tha Tower?" Lydia asked quickly, suddenly animated.

"She was a good woman, tha only one who stood up fer me, an' I worried that it'd cost her. She was ignored, sent home by my father, while tha slavers took me away."

"Your father believed that piece of shit and let you be sold?" I asked grimly, rubbing my thighs. Even through the metal plates of the armor, it seemed to relieve the aches slightly.

"He said I brought dishonor on tha family, an' I deserved worse," Lydia said flatly. "Six years later, when Albrecht ended up in tha same work gang as me, he told me about tha caravan he was in bein' raided, tha others prob'ly bein' killed an' his capture. Well, I worried about my mother, then realized she'd be better off without us all."

"So, you think it's likely that the quest relates to you finding your mother and giving her a safe place to live, then?"

She nodded happily. "Jax, I never let meself think about it, I just wrote tha' section of my life off, tried to forget it. This is fantastic, I could…I can't wait!" she exclaimed, turning to Tenandra, who stood at the back of the room, behind the control chair, where Jian sat guiding the ship.

I smiled as Jian spoke up before Lydia could ask.

"Full power to the engines," he confirmed, smiling. "We'll be there in an hour or so."

"Will it be dark by then?" I asked. "Fully dark, I mean? This ship's a bit different, and the last thing we need is people asking questions before we get an idea of how the village is run now."

"Are yer goin' to recruit 'em?" Lydia asked.

"Fuck no. They turned their backs on you on the word of that cock Goblin of a husband of yours; why the hell would I give them the chance to do the same again? Lydia, this is what a family is; all of us. Unless you vouch for them, anyway." I leaned forward as I met her gaze, resting my forearms on the table.

"The entire Great Tower has your back. We're all on your side. You know what Grizz asked the day you told us about what happened to you? After you walked away from breakfast, I mean?"

She frowned, glancing over at the massive legionnaire. "No…?" she said carefully.

"He asked if we could take a ship and find that fucker," I said, vaguely remembering it as being something like that, but viewing the overall demand as more important than the details. "He wanted us to find him and kill him. For you."

I stood up and put my hands on her shoulders, forcing her to look at me. "We're your family now, Lydia: The Tower, the Legion, and hell, the Empire. We've got your back, and anyone who fucks with you, fucks with us."

"And anyone who fucks with the Legion pulls back a bloody stump with no body attached," Tang said laconically, idly twirling a dagger around his fingertips.

"We're here for you, sister," Yen declared, rising from the table and putting her hand on Lydia's shoulder. I stepped back, releasing her as the others clustered in, each taking their turn to reassure, to praise, and to reiterate their support.

Even Sehran stepped up and whispered something in Lydia's ear, making her blush furiously before the Succubus returned to standing behind Jian's left shoulder, with Tenandra on his right.

I looked the group over, smiling at the way that Grizz had moved unconsciously to stand next to Yen, the way that Tang and Bane were crouched, half in stealth, by the door and porthole respectively. They were always watching but also exchanging jokes with Arrin.

Giint perched nearby, occasionally interrupting their conversation, but welcome enough that he could interject while he played with a small cube of shining metal, slipping segments from position to position, occasionally twitching when they aligned correctly.

I noted the way that Bob stood at the back of the room, watching us all, with Ronin near to him, quietly speaking to the…well, he wasn't my minion anymore, was he?

"Bob, how you doing, buddy?" I asked as I walked over to him, leaving Lydia surrounded by the others, thanking them for their support as she tried to hide the tears the gestures had drawn forth.

"I am…okay?" Bob responded to me, his voice cold, yet confused and uncertain in my mind.

"Do you need anything? Do you have questions?"

"Yes…why?" he asked, straightening and staring at me intently.

"Why what?" I repeated, confused.

"I live…why?"

"Don't you want to live?"

He paused, clearly considering the question.

"I live…I wish to live, but…I did not before…I simply was. Why has this changed?"

"When I was changed, when we faced the creature back there, the old Emperor, Amon, who is a part of me, took control. In the process, you and Oracle were cut off from me, and I could no longer sustain you. My mana and health that gave you and Oracle the chance to live were ripped away, and you were both dying," I explained. "I didn't want you to die, so I did what I could to help you."

"Why did you not do this sooner? Why was I kept a slave until now?" Bob asked me bluntly.

I froze. "You were never a slave, Bob. You were a minion, yes, but that was because you weren't alive."

"I am not alive now," Bob accused me. *"You have flesh; I do not."*

"Okay, fair point. You aren't alive in the biological sense, and as to me changing you, well, I didn't know I could," I said truthfully. "You had to grow to be who you were first. Add to that, the bones that I used to build you contained fragments of souls, and I used those to bring you to this state."

"I have many questions…about life, about…why," Bob said flatly.

I sighed, nodding and settling into a seat next to the skeleton and trying to mentally prepare myself. Surprisingly, Ronin and Giint joined me, and I frowned at them in question.

"This kind of debate is one of the reasons I love being a bard," Ronin crowed, grinning. "I spent most of my time drunk with idiots talking about things like this and why they can't be kings. Explaining why a skeleton can't be alive? Child's play."

"Giint has problems, too," Giint said glumly, then shrugged. "Giint help Bob, maybe Bob help Giint?" Bob nodded.

I smiled, noting the odd cadence and structure of Giint's speech was still there, in part at least. When he was stressed or defensive, it was always "Giint thinks this…" instead of "I think…" but on the other side, we had a warlock swordsman who seemed to be banging his pet Demon, and if I wasn't very much mistaken, also doing his level best to seduce the very ship we were aboard, which was also a Wisp.

I couldn't really comment on the fucking weirdness of someone talking about themselves in the third person.

The next half an hour passed both in the blink of an eye and oh so slowly as we attempted to explain life to Bob. It was over quickly, because I felt we achieved nothing but to confuse him more, and yet, it took forever as he seemed fixated on little details we all took as unimportant, like why food had flavors. I pointed out that fruit tasted nice to encourage animals to spread the seeds wide. He then asked me if meat was nice, and when I nodded, he asked if the animals I ate had the same plan, and did they grow from seeds.

I explained that they didn't, and that they were just tasty…because. As soon as he asked me about sex, and about Oracle, and why, as a skeleton, he didn't have a dick, and could I make him one…I just shut that conversation down.

I was deeply grateful when Jian called out that the village was just ahead, and we turned our attention to the enchanted walls of the room, watching the lights of Cornut begin to shine through the rain.

I sighed in relief, telling everyone to get ready. Knowing we had only a few minutes until we landed, I asked Ronin and Giint to get Bob some clothes and a cloak so that he could try and fit in and watch people, which gave me a few minutes of peace, while Oracle leaned against my shoulder for a kiss.

"You've still got some notifications," she reminded me gently, and I sighed, bringing them up.

Congratulations!

You have raised your skill Unarmed Combat to level thirteen.

You may now choose your first evolution of this skill.

*

Congratulations!

You have raised your skill Unarmed Combat to its first evolution.

You must now pick a path to follow.

Will you choose GRACE, reflecting the martial artists of old, or POWER, recognizing your pugilist tendencies?

Choose carefully, as this choice cannot be undone.

GRACE:

Your fighting skills may be raw and barely trained, but still, you are a fighter who has claimed many victories, dispatching your opponents with a mixture of training, aggression, and innate skill. Selecting GRACE as your first evolution will improve your Unarmed Combat abilities by means great and small, as your movements are smoothed out in a thousand tiny ways, resulting in a slight increase to Dexterity, Agility, and Endurance of +1 to each.

POWER:

Your heart revels in the joy of the fight, of beating an opponent down with little more than strength and aggression. Perhaps what you need is more Strength to make the beatdown even more satisfying? Gain +6 Strength, at a cost of -2 Agility.

I selected the power option, as, while grace suited me better, fighting style and all, it meant I gained three points overall, while for some reason, smacking the shit outta someone with my fists would gain me four.

I shrugged and accepted it.

I pulled through the other notifications quickly, seeing a collection of minor skill bumps and one more that had reached level ten, making me smile.

Congratulations!

You have raised your skill Medium Armor to level ten.

You may now choose your first evolution of this skill.

*

Congratulations!

You have raised your skill Medium Armor to its first evolution.

You must now pick a path to follow.

Will you choose FLOW, reflecting the smooth motion of the body, as you learn to move more fluidly in your armor, or STAMPEDE, showing your determination in battle?

Choose carefully, as this choice cannot be undone.

FLOW:

You have learned to move in Medium Armor with a level of grace and proficiency that would seem incredible to your unskilled self, mere days ago. Selecting FLOW as your evolution to the skill highlights the simple tricks and increases you have earned, the ways you move in battle, and when moving, naturally settling into your armor and thinking of it as a second skin, to be preserved and protected, flowing between the grasping hands of your enemies and dealing death to those that foolishly close with you.

Gain +2 to Agility

STAMPEDE:

You have learned to move in medium armor, training your body to carry the weight of your new steel shell as if wearing gossamer silk. Now you choose to take true advantage of that experience, embracing the Ability: Stampede!

Gain the Ability: Stampede. Once per fight, you may force 100 stamina into your body, overcharging your muscles and driving yourself forward at tremendous speeds. Where others would use petty abilities such as Shield-Bash, you use Stampede, and hammer them flat with the power and weight of your entire armored body!

I chose Stampede without a second's pause. First, points were all well and good, but you know, an Ability was a whole different thing. Secondly, I liked smashing the shit outta people, even if I would only admit that to myself. I'd chosen Lunge to get my speed up, enabling me to close the distance to my targets faster. Stampede, combined with Lunge? Hell yes.

"Jax?" Oracle's soft voice pulled me back to reality, and I dismissed the last of the screens, getting a smile as I quirked an eyebrow at her. "I wanted to warn you," she said as she jerked her head to indicate the rest of the group, who were all pulling cloaks and hoods from their bags. "Lydia asked everyone to try not to be too threatening."

"Fair enough." I stood, rooting around in my bag until I found what I'd been looking for.

When Thorn had given me my armor, in addition to a small repair and maintenance kit and some spare padding just in case, she'd also given me a wax-impregnated cloak; the Legion standard, apparently.

It was a dark grey, almost black, and I pulled it out with a grin, glad to have the chance to finally wear it, as it looked cool as fuck. I paused, noticing that everyone else was putting ratty, worn ones on.

I sighed, stuffing it back in, and retrieved an old red one that I'd gotten from the Tower, pulling that on instead and feeling grimly determined to make sure people got decent fucking cloaks, at least. I wasn't wearing brand new awesome gear when the rest of my people simply made do.

I followed the group outside, grateful that the adventurer whose corpse I'd taken this from had been a big guy, and…fuck. I risked a glance and caught the sad look that Ronin had been giving me, and I felt a twinge of guilt, remembering that, yeah, the adventurer in question…had been his friend.

"He'd have laughed at you wearing it, boss," Ronin said quietly. "He would have been pleased that it was getting good use, rather than being scrapped." He paused, as though wanting to say more, before clamping his mouth shut and moving away.

I clenched my jaw and stalked down the gangplank, my previously good mood now black as I realized that, in trying to just be one of the guys, I'd unconsciously made Ronin face up to his friend's death by wearing his mate's fucking gear in front of him.

I grimaced, feeling both an idiot and pissed off, as I tried to think about things I'd always just bulled my way through before. Tonight was going to be a long and painful one if I had to damn well behave myself.

CHAPTER FORTY-TWO

"**W**elcome to Cornut, stranger!" came a voice, and I glared at the man who faced me officiously as soon as I stepped off the gangplank. "I am Pertwin, tax master of the village, and I deal with incoming travelers, making sure they pay the Reeve's tax on arrival."

"What tax?" I grunted, already annoyed.

"Why, the tax that is levied to pay for our soldiers to protect us all, of course," the man replied, forcing a smile and trying not to look at the two men who stood with him in mismatched, rusty chainmail.

I glanced from one to the other. The first had a staff, despite the obvious screws and damaged end of the post that used to hold a spearhead, while the other...

The other was carefully excavating one nostril with a gauntleted finger. When he noticed I was watching him, he wiped it nonchalantly on his tunic, adding to the multitude of already present stains.

"So, half a copper piece should fucking cover it, then," I ground out, reaching for my pouch.

"Ah, no, it's…. uh…three gold and a silver piece," Pertwin stated, looking us over and taking in the wetly gleaming copper of the ship behind us. He smiled, clearly having just hiked the cost massively, judging from the stunned look on the guards faces and the gasp from Lydia behind me.

"The fuck it is," I rumbled, clenching my fist and preparing to start an argument, when Lydia stepped forward.

"Tha taxes don't apply if tha travelers are welcomed in by a member of tha village as travelin' family, though," Lydia said, pushing her hood back and exposing her face. "I lived here, does my mother still?"

"What? Who's your mother?" The man snorted, confused, but then he shrugged. "Anyway, it doesn't matter; the Reeve did away with that rule."

"He can't, it was part of tha Town Charter," she said flatly.

"Less than half of these bumpkins can read," Pertwin sneered. "Can you? I doubt it; either way, pay the tax or leave," he demanded, smirking.

I glanced at his guards and considered just killing them both, along with the officious little shit before me. But, in the end, that wasn't why we were there. As Lydia stepped forward, growling, I reached out and put my hand on her shoulder.

"It's not worth it; remember why we're here," I ordered her, digging into my pouch.

"It's gone up, since you were all so rude," Pertwin said loftily. "It's now four gold pieces."

"Whatever," I said, pulling the coins out and tossing them at him. He scrambled, frantically catching the coins, and I strode forward, making them stumble back to let us pass.

"Who are you, anyway?" the prick asked.

I ignored him. "Lydia, where's the house then the goddamn tavern?" I asked grimly. "I need a fucking drink."

"There; we go past tha tavern an' down tha street." She pointed at a large building across the square from where we'd landed at her direction. Lights shone out of multiple windows, firelight and the sound of voices faintly escaping as we approached.

I led the way across the roughly cobbled street, our armored boots clattering on the wet stones, and I glanced around at the village that Lydia had grown up in.

The tenements that surrounded the square were a mixture of stone and wood, with obvious shop fronts beneath the majority of them, and the occasional face that peered out at the unexpected commotion.

The tax wanker had scuttled off somewhere, while the two guards had split up as well, one running ahead and slipping into the tavern as we passed it. The other vanished in the opposite direction, ducking into the maze of small houses down one side street.

"Where would your mother be?" I asked Lydia.

"Truth be tol', I don't know, Jax. She used to be in tha tavern when me Da would let her. Depended on his mood; if not, she might be at home, but..." She shrugged disconsolately.

I slowed, coming to a stop in front of her. "Do you want to check the tavern first?" I offered.

"No; best to check on tha house. Ma might not be able to afford tha tavern anymore."

"Shit," I said eloquently as I started off walking again, Lydia pulling ahead slightly in her concern. "What do you mean, 'not be able to afford it anymore'?"

"The old Reeve was a bit crazy, but 'e didn't care much for anything but his bit o' gold and the servin' girls. As long as you didn't catch 'is eye, you were safe..."

My mood darkened even more, biting back epithets as she continued.

"There obviously be a new one, though, judgin' from that fool back there, and tha 'guards,'" she said, contempt thick in her voice. "If he's raised taxes, well, me ma wouldn't have much, not with 'er wage as a washer woman. Maybe she's all right, married again, but I doubt it." She sighed, her expression strained and anxious as we turned first one corner, then another, before finally cutting across a street and entering a short alley. "I shoulda come sooner, Jax. I shoulda asked."

"You've been with me all the time you've been free, Lydia. You've had no time for this, and you know it. I should have offered," I said grimly as we turned the final corner and faced a small house that was clearly run down.

While several houses in this alley were lit, the one at the end wasn't. The thatch sagged, the stone looked filthy, and the bench that sat outside was broken in half with the door firmly closed.

We came to a stop, the surrounding houses sprouting faces at the windows like mushrooms after rain. Nothing stirred behind the windows of the darkened house at the end. Lydia swallowed hard, calling out.

"Ma?" she croaked, then swallowed again, and went on, her voice growing stronger. "Ma, it's me, Lydia. I come 'ome ta get ya."

Silence met us in the alleyway for long moments, before a door to the right, the last house before Lydia's, cracked open slightly.

"Lydia?" a weak voice asked, cracking as though rarely used. "Be that you, girl?"

"Aye!" Lydia turned toward the voice. "Dennet, I see yer hidin' there. Where's me ma?"

The door opened fully, and the woman, Dennet, stood in the doorway, clearly unsteady on her feet as she blinked at the group arrayed in the dark.

"She be gone, lass. Ain't nobody here thought yer'd be back after tha thing that were done ta yer." Dennet sniffed before shuffling forward, clearly afraid, but forcing herself to stand tall. "Mayhap none but me'd even 'member now, after all tha' happened since. But I saw yer ma after-like; she were broken by yer bein' sold. Never doubted yer fer a minute, no matter all that prick said 'bout yer."

"Where?" Lydia demanded, taking a step forward and putting her hand on her mace as she swept the long cloak back, exposing the heavy armor underneath. "Where be me ma?!"

"Sold," Dennet said, sighing. "Sold like ma man were, like tha young'uns ma an da were." She gestured back into the house behind her, two small, sandy-haired children peeking out of the window at the front of her house.

"Who sold them?" I asked, my voice a low growl of fury. "What the hell happened here?"

"New Lord Resheck, Reeve o' Cornut," Dennet said grimly. "Ye ain't payin yer taxes, yer gets dragged away an' sold, then put on tha next ship bound fer Himnel, sold tha 'ouse an' more, given away all yer owned, like yer were never 'ere."

"And where would we find this shitbag?" I asked darkly.

"Th' Reeve'd be with his cronies in tha tavern at this time o' night...always is," she said bitterly.

"How many of them?" I asked.

"Full tavern, 'bout thirty of 'em, not countin' tha guard. He lets all 'is friends eat an' drink fer free; rest 'o us ain't welcome no more."

"So, basically, everyone in the tavern is his close friend and supporter?" I asked, getting a sharp nod. "Well fuck me, that makes things a lot easier. Lydia, let's go fuck up that tavern and find out straight from the resident dickbag where your mother went and when."

"Pack yer shit up, Dennet," Lydia ordered as she threw back her cloak fully, making those hidden around the narrow alley gasp as the rest of us did the same. "All of yer: iffin yer do need a second chance, iffin yer want safety, clothes on yer back, and food in yer bellies in exchange fer a fair day's graft, pack yer bags an' tell others yer know. Spread tha word wide. Be in tha square by dawn, an' yer comin' to tha Tower. Ye'll all be safe under Lord Jax."

"How'd yer know? Why'd such as that give two shits about us?" Dennet asked, uncertain. I slammed the base of my naginata down hard into the cobbles, igniting it with a wash of blue-white lightning as I tossed my cloak back.

The others behind me did the same, exposing Legion armor, weapons that glowed with the light of enchantments and more. Without discussion, Oracle lifted into the air, hovering overhead as twin fireballs ignited in her palms. The others followed suit, calling their magic forth for all to see.

"Because *I* am Lord Jax. And I care," I declared loudly. "Gather what you need; anything else will be provided to you. Bring your friends, those who are honest, those who need a helping hand to reach the light, those who have been shit on from a great height by these fucking assholes. Be at the ship come dawn and see justice done as we leave this shithole behind."

With that, I turned from them, extinguishing my magically glowing weapon and closed my cloak against the rain again, striding back along the alley with the others following.

I reached the end of the street, took a left, then paused, turning to Lydia.

"Lead the way, Lydia. This is your village; you get to do the honors," I said, smiling at her.

"Plus, he's lost…" A low chuckle rose from Tang.

"Look, that all looked cool as fuck," I said, looking around in the dark and rolling my eyes. "But once you all joined in, now I can't see shit in the dark, okay? My night vision is officially fucked up."

"Haven't you got DarkVision?" Tang asked.

I squinted into the shadows as Lydia led us down the next few streets, and I consciously activated DarkVision.

"What's the plan?" Grizz asked.

I shrugged, turning to my Valkyrie. "Lydia, this is your village; you want to lead?" I offered.

"Nah. If I do, it'll be a bloodbath," she said, her voice a mixture of strain and hope.

"What the hell do you think I'm planning on?" I asked her, baring my teeth in a vicious snarl. "Seriously, Lydia, as far as I'm concerned, that tavern is full of fuckheads who are complicit in slavery, and now, because they chose to be in there? I'm not going to be able to get a quiet fucking beer and a meal. If anything, you leading on this one means *less* chance of bloodshed, because I'm seriously considering sealing the fucking doors and windows and just burning the place down."

"There'll be kids in there, workin'," Yen pointed out.

"And that, as well as the fact the beer's in there, are the only reasons I'm not going with that plan," I said firmly. "Lydia, lead the fucking cleansing of this village."

We turned the final corner and found that a dozen people had spilled out of the tavern and gathered around the ship, with one gaudily dressed dickhead shouting up at the ship that they were to lower the gangplank and prepare to be boarded in order to be searched for contraband.

The four guards that stood with the group, nosepicker amongst them, looked excited, and it was clear that "contraband" was going to be discovered either way.

I grinned and pointed at the group before speaking quickly.

"Dibs!" I called, striding forward. "Oracle, fill Tenandra in on what's happening, and you all go have fun in the tavern. Jian, let Sehran play tonight. She can pull any stragglers who try funny shit, and provided they're bad guys, she can eat her fucking fill."

As soon as the words left my mouth, I heard a giggle and caught movement nearby. Sehran appeared on a rooftop, blowing me a kiss.

"She was following us, eh?" I asked, shooting him a grin as the others peeled off to deal with the tavern.

"What can I say; she was on the ship when I left, must have gotten bored!" Jian called back. He smiled, rolling his shoulders as Lydia hauled back and Sparta-kicked the tavern door off its hinges.

"Oi!" I heard someone scream, followed by the meaty thwack of a steel gauntlet impacting flesh.

"So, which one of you dickheads is the Reeve?" I asked the drunken group blinking owlishly at me, spread out around the base of the gangplank to the ship as I strode up to them.

"I am Reeve." declared the gaudily dressed fat man, right before I punched him in the face. As I'd walked towards him, I'd seen something I'd missed when we arrived. In an alley leading off the opposite side of the village square were cages with a sign above them that was illuminated by the light of the torches the guards bore.

Slaves: Cheap deals, see Reeve Resheck

That was enough confirmation for me. As the Reeve staggered back, I slammed my naginata down into a crack in the cobbles, jamming it nice and tight before stepping forward and confronting the figures standing around me.

I grinned at them, seeing some of them hefting rusty knives, makeshift clubs, and more shoddy weaponry. I clapped my hands together, rubbing them sharply.

"I think I'll break a leg next," I said conversationally, activating Lunge and blurring across the middle of the group to grab the officious little shit Pertwin by the throat.

I yanked him into a headbutt, one that was far less gory, as I wasn't wearing my helm, but the blow splattered his nose like a tomato dropped from fucking orbit.

I shoved him back, sweeping his leg and reaching down to catch his flailing leg by the ankle.

I twisted it to the right, looking down at him, then punched him as hard as I could in the side of the knee, making the most of my heavily augmented strength, and adding just a touch of mana overdrive, because I could.

The result was him screaming as I literally smashed the bones of his knee into paste, fragments rocketing out of the far side as I half tore the limb off.

He flailed backward, going into shock. I yanked, more out of curiosity than malice, ripping the last segments of flesh free and standing calmly in the middle of the group, holding the leg I'd just torn off.

"Well, guess you didn't put many points into Constitution, then?" I asked the man on the floor as his blood jetted out to paint the street vermillion.

I looked over the remaining people, only one of which was dressed as a civilian. I smiled at them then sniffed and spoke in a chiding voice.

"Come on now, we're all adults here; who shit themselves?" I asked curiously. "Not that I care overly, mind you, but still."

At that moment, a scream rose from one side. We all looked over just in time to see the heaviest-set man of the group, a guy with rolls of fat and wearing fucking slippers in the damn rain, getting his throat torn out by Sehran, who fixed us all with a bloodthirsty grin as she sucked the bastard dry. The corpse withered as she assumed her true form, wings unfurling and eyes glowing as she drank his life force greedily.

"I'm thinking…" I idly shook the half leg at them, spattering them with blood and adding to the stink that rose from the group by a good factor of three. "I'll beat someone's face in with this next, unless anyone wants to surrender?" I asked pleasantly.

The rest of the group fell over themselves surrendering.

"Drop the weapons, then," I ordered grimly, the cheerful façade gone in an instant. I threw the leg over my shoulder and blurred to the side of the prick of a Reeve and hauled him upright with one hand, even as screams and shouts burst from the tavern behind me.

"Let's go have a chat with the others, shall we?" I projected a friendly tone once again, knowing it was confusing and terrifying him all the more. "Oh, and who has a key to the slave cages?" I shot over my shoulder, glancing back.

"R-Reeve...Re-Re-Resheck..." one of the guards stammered, struggling to get his words out through shaking lips.

"Oh, well, that's fucking convenient, isn't it!" I said, flashing a feral grin. "Saves me having to rip it apart with my bare hands." I couldn't, even boosted as I was and running out of time with every second, but the impression I'd given them was that I was some kind of superpowered *thing*. As long as I did nothing to break that image, I didn't need to slaughter them out of hand.

I had *plans* for them, after all.

I led the way to the slave cells, finding them to have been recently emptied, judging by the fresh excrement in the bottom. I growled, turning the full fury of my attention onto the Reeve.

"Where are they, Reeve?" I asked him slowly and distinctly. "Where are the people you sold into slavery?"

"Gone," he whimpered. "Gone three days..."

"And where the fuck did you send them, you useless shitbag?" I roared in his face. A wave of stench informed me another of the group had joined the brown trouser brigade.

"I...I..." he stuttered, panicking.

"Fine." I yanked the key from his belt and passed it to one of the guards. "All of you, strip. Clothes, belongings, everything, pile it up there," I ordered gesturing to a spot about five meters from the cages. "Then get the fuck into the cages."

"But...but what did...we do wrong?" Nose-picker asked plaintively. "Slavery's legal...and 'e's the Reeve! We just did what 'e said!"

I fixed him with a cold stare, making him strip faster.

As soon as they were all naked, already being sluiced down by the cold rain, I hurried them inside and locked the door, confident that none of them would be going anywhere, now that they definitely didn't have a key or any weapons.

Unless they commonly kept them in their prison wallet, anyway.

I dismissed that thought with an angry shake of the head and leaned forward to the cage, glowering at the men and one woman huddled miserably inside.

"First off, slavery is an offence punishable by death in the Empire, you little fucks. Secondly, you were trying to rob me. And third, I don't give two shits about what this jumped-up little prick told you to do!" I yelled that last bit at them, shaking the Reeve by his collar like a mastiff shakes a kitten.

"Most of all, though, you're in there until the villagers decide what to do with you...but this fucker? He's going to answer for his crimes to me. You want me to judge you all, too?" I asked, my left hand igniting with the beginnings of a Fireball. The group pushed themselves back against the rear of the cage, falling over themselves as they screamed that they didn't.

"Good," I said grimly, walking back to the tavern. Resheck fell a few steps in, and I let him hit the ground, ignoring his attempt to drag himself away on the rain-slicked cobbles as I grabbed him by one ankle and started dragging him along effortlessly.

I had nearly reached the door when a shuttered window was smashed out, a broken body falling onto the ground and letting out a moan of fear and pain as blood mingled in the drain, being drawn away down the street.

I glanced down, seeing a man in rich clothing with a thick gold chain around his neck.

"Who was he?" I asked the Reeve conversationally, and he gibbered and pissed himself in fear. "Fine, be like that." I dragged him inside, shoving the door open and discovering that the rest of the team had indeed let their anger and frustration out on the place.

The tavern was a long, low-ceilinged room with the door in the middle of the wall on the right side, stairs at the far end of the floor to the left presumably leading up to rooms, with a dozen or more tables set around the middle of the open floor.

The bar was at the back, a long well-polished affair with a door leading back into the kitchen. A rat-faced man who fit the image of a bard the way the squad had described them to me far more than Ronin did, sat on a stool against the back wall on a small stage, clutching a reed flute and whimpering in fear. Meanwhile, Grizz and Tang leaned on the bar, calmly discussing something in a friendly manner with the bartender.

The rest of the room was a mess of blood, broken bodies, and three clearly dead people who were dressed as real guards. Their presumed employer sat in a chair, shaking as Yen questioned him, and Lydia...well, Lydia was busily kicking someone to death.

I found Ronin and Giint, along with Arrin, setting a few tables back upright and gathering some chairs when Jian strolled back down from the stairs at the far end of the hall.

Out of the thirty or so people who were apparently the village dickbags, seven or eight were dead, while the rest had come down with a severe case of bad-tempered legionnaire and were variously crying, moaning, pleading, or unconscious around the room.

I glanced over at the barman and shrugged, pulling up the Reeve and dumping him atop one of the dead guards.

"You stay there, and we'll talk later," I told him firmly, then paused and pointed to Lydia. "Or, you know, you can run. I won't chase you. She will."

Lydia turned slowly, huffing with the exertion, and blew back a stray lock of hair from her bloodstained face, shooting a death-laden glance at the Reeve while the man she'd been beating whimpered behind her.

"Oh please...*please,* do fuckin' run," she growled, turning back to punch the man on the floor in the face, knocking him out.

"So, what's going on here, then?" I asked cheerfully, clapping my hands together then rubbing them as I took a stool at the bar, looking at the barman and the others that stood with him.

"Turns out, the tavern was claimed for 'non-payment of back taxes' when the owner tried to charge the Reeve and his friends for their drinks. Then, the owner and his family were used as slaves in their own tavern." Grizz explained, pointing to the chain that was wound around the man's leg, attaching him to a railing nailed to the floor.

I followed along its length, seeing two more chains leading off into the kitchen.

"Your family?" I asked him. He nodded, clearly still scared. "Well, I take it the Reeve has the key?"

He shook his head. "Reeve sold me an' tha lad to 'is friend," he said carefully. "'E'd be a big, fat bastard, gone out there wit' tha others, before yer friends arrived."

"Red robes with blue?" I asked curiously. "Little piggy eyes? Wearing slippers?"

He nodded.

I leaned back and watched the doorway as both Oracle and Tenandra walked in out of the rain.

I smiled at the fact that Tenandra had found some way to move around beyond her ship, and I called to them.

"Hey girls, can you ask Sehran to bring any keys…actually, better to make it anything at all that her dinner had on him? Looks like we need it."

I heard retching and looked over at the Reeve, my lip curling in disgust. "You can clean that up as well. In fact, you have cleaning supplies?" I asked the barman. When he nodded, I smiled. "Then the Reeve can make himself useful." I gestured for the supplies before calling over to the quivering Reeve.

"Well, former Reeve Resheck, you see how quickly your life can turn around? This morning, you thought you were in charge of the village, and tonight, well…tonight, you get to mop up your friend's remains. Funny how these things work out, isn't it?"

"We'll get you unlocked as soon as we get the key back in," I assured the barman. "In the meantime, can we get some food, a few drinks, and you can bring us up to date with what's been happening here?" I arched one eyebrow.

"Uh, okay," the barman said slowly, still wide-eyed at the devastation. I looked around and grinned in understanding. We'd spent the last few weeks battling practically all day, every day, fighting more most days than a real city guard, for example, would fight in a year or more.

As a group facing the kind of people that oppressed a tiny village and the local bullies that supported and loved them for it, they were laughably weak in comparison.

My squad was made up now of a mix of highly trained legionnaires, three divine champions, a skeleton who was sitting in the corner playing with the fire, totally unconcernedly, and a couple of ex-slaves who'd been given a level of training that was far above and beyond the average for a soldier. Not to mention, our number included arena fighters and more, armed with magical weapons and getting essentially power-leveled through the ranks by the rest of the team.

I snorted as I realized that Lydia could have done all of this herself, easily, if she'd allowed herself to let her wings show. So, the rest of the team now making themselves comfy and getting drinks on the go, well.

It was normal.

"Looks like we get that dinner and a drink, after all," I said, smiling, then looking over at Ronin and nodding my head at the bard on the stage.

Ronin went up to talk to him, spending a few minutes in quiet conversation as we straightened the tables and pointed out jobs to the now-sobbing Reeve.

I'd released my mana overdrive skill as soon as we stepped inside the tavern, Oracle's surreptitious healing banishing the debuff and making me sigh in relief.

"What's the plan, boss?" Grizz asked, taking a seat next to me as I winced, hearing a bone crack. I turned to find the source as the sound echoed in the air.

"Two minutes, Grizz," I mumbled. "Lydia!" I called, and she looked up at me in question, standing over a feebly crying figure. "I know you're a bit on edge, and I did say have fun, but you're going to kill him," I admonished.

"Can ye heal 'im fer me?" she asked quickly.

"Why?" I asked with a frown.

"He's me da. Booted me ma out when 'e got hisself some new fancy bit, an' left me ma to be sold as a slave."

"He sounds like a slaver to me, then," I said calmly. "I'll heal him once, Lydia. After that, you either beat him a bit and stick him in the cage with the rest," I said firmly, tossing her the key for the slave cages. "Or you kill him."

"He deserves it," she growled, and I sat up straighter, considering her as Oracle started to heal the man.

"He does, and I don't give two shits what it would do to him if you spend the next ten years torturing him and healing him over and over. Fuck, I'd teach you the spells myself and give you the torturer skillbook but I care what it would do to *you*." I gestured once to the man and then to the door. "Take him outside and do what you want, Lydia, but pick a side. Either you're a Legion Optio, and you're dispensing justice, or you're torturing him. You can't be both."

"Optio," she muttered, eyes widening.

"Fuck's sake, Lydia, we've all been waiting for you to declare it, you already do the damn job."

She paused, clearly thinking, making sense of my words, before glancing at Grizz and Yen, Tang, then the rest of the group, seeing smiles and proud nods.

"Aye, aye, Ahm Optio o' tha damn Legion! Ah be the leader o' yer damn squad!" She declared, standing straighter as we all smiled, standing and clapping fists to our chests, nodding in respect and pride.

"Damn right you are, and I couldn't be prouder of you," I promised her, feeling the prickle of tears at the corner of my eyes as I stared at her.

I saw the grim, distrustful slave who'd glared at me, expecting me to try and make a deal with her, only to throw her away. I saw the brave fighter, the Valkyrie, and the Optio. She nodded, coughing and looking away from the emotions welling up in her before glancing at the others and letting herself have a small smile. Oracle moved to her side, hugging her.

Lydia stared at me, her breath huffing out for long seconds, before Oracle healed her victim then nodded to her.

Lydia took a deep breath, then grabbed the man by the throat and dragged him towards the door as he choked and begged for help and for mercy.

"Mercy." I repeated his last word as the door banged shut, shaking my head in disgust. "Where the hell do people like that think they'll get that from?"

Sehran entered the room two seconds later, smiling radiantly. She'd shifted back to her lovable sex kitten persona, and she strutted across the room, pausing only to kiss Jian on the way and whisper something in his ear that made him blush bright red.

"Thank you for the meal, master," she said to me, bowing her head and laying a handful of goods out on the table next to ours.

"Not your master, Sehran, you know that," I replied with a smile as Oracle took my hand possessively.

Grizz rummaged through the various bags and junk she'd brought in. "Here," he grunted, holding up a triangular wedge with black runes carved into it.

"Weird-looking key." I inspected the unfamiliar object, frowning.

"Death magic key," Grizz corrected. "You try to get free of a lock sealed with this, you die, and the one who sealed it gets some of your stats."

"Motherfucker," I growled.

Sehran laughed suddenly.

"What?" I asked, my fury simmering.

"I wondered why he tasted so weird; must have been this," she said musingly. "He had really high stats, but his body…it was so fatty, you wouldn't believe…" She grimaced slightly, wiping the corner of her mouth, prompting a terrified look on the face of the former Reeve.

"You're going to feed us to *that*?" he asked, aghast. "That's what you're going to do, isn't it? You're some kind of bandits, or a Demon-worshipping cult!" he started raving, when he was abruptly hit in the face by a well-aimed potato.

We all looked to the side and saw a small boy, maybe ten years old, trying to hide. I started to laugh.

"Ah, man, perfect timing there, kid!" I called to him.

"Me da said food'll be a minute," the boy yelled, vanishing from sight just as Lydia walked back inside, her face hard, but a slight smile twitching at the corners of her lips.

"Lydia, do you want to do the honors and free the barman and his family?" I offered, waving the key at her.

"Aye, thanks, Jax." She suddenly smiled widely.

I paused, trying to think of the best way to ask her about what had just happened.

"I'll go free 'em, then I've got good news," she hinted, still grinning. A handful of minutes later, Lydia was back, the barman and his wife were happily pouring drinks and setting down platters of food for the group, and the boy was out running in the rain, going from door to door and spreading the word.

Cornut was under new management.

CHAPTER FORTY-THREE

W e all looked at Lydia expectantly, and she smiled grimly.
"First, the best news. Me ma be alive, or at least she were a week ago;
that be when tha caravan left. She were bein' taken to a slave market
at tha mouth of tha river. It be on fer tha next two days still, so iffin we be fast,
we might find 'er yet."

"That's fantastic!" I said, smiling genuinely for the first time in what felt like
days. As soon as Amon had taken me over, and so easily, I'd been fighting not to
give in to depression, and it occurred to me that the dark violence I'd settled into
with the village had reflected that.

Arriving and finding that a village that, because of their treatment of Lydia, was
actually suffering the same fate? It had both elated me and pissed me off hugely.

I'd been elated, because I loved it when someone got a taste of their own
medicine, and I'd already decided I didn't want people like this in the Empire. Then
I'd felt depressed, because arguably, it wasn't the entire village that had treated
Lydia like that; it'd been her husband and family, then learning it'd been her father,
and that he'd practically sold her mother as well? That the shitbags that ran the
village and were all okay with it were here, leaving the good ones out there?

I was filled with a need to save these people, while secretly wanting to boot
them all as well.

Good news was just what I needed, and if it came with a side order of saving
a bunch of slaves and probably slaughtering the slavers? Fuck yes.

"It gets better." Lydia grinned round. "Me da didn't wanna tell me, musta
thought I'd be pissed, but ye were right, keeping 'im alive be worth it!" Lydia
practically sang to me as she looked around the small table.

"Go on?" I prompted, as the others leaned in, breathless and grinning in
excitement as well.

"Ma 'usband!" She said, joy dancing in her eyes. "'E be alive!" She gripped
the edge of the table in one gauntleted fist before drawing a dagger and letting the
light glint off it. "An' tha fucker be due back 'ere tonight! It be him tha were sent
to tha slave market. He sold me ma, and 'e be on his way back, should be a few
hours away, at most!"

"Well, fuck me…" I said wonderingly. "The Gods really do love you, Lydia!"
I beamed as I looked around, the rest of the squad grinning just as darkly.

"What…forgive me, my lord, but what are you going to do?" came a timid
voice. I followed the sound to see the barman's wife watching us.

"We're going to catch them, we're going to kill them, and we're going to
have a damn well-deserved sleep," I said sincerely.

"And what about the slaves?" She watched me carefully.

"We're going to go and free them."

"They are usually held in the market, then they're transferred to the twin ships that moor off the river's mouth, if they're not bought by the locals. If you storm in there and just attack the market, they'll sail away, and the caravans will split up. You won't get them all," she warned us. I frowned, tilting my head at her.

"Go on." I'd planned to figure out the details on the way, recon it, and possibly pull in reinforcements, if need be.

"I was bought there," she said quietly. "Harmon was a guard on a caravan that attended. He bought me, freed me, and quit the caravan, and I married him three years later." She reached out, gripping the barman's hand tightly in hers. "That's why I know about the market. You storm in, you'll lose at least half of them, but…" she said, moving in close to explain.

Ten minutes later, we were all smiling and relaxed as the first of the locals started to drift in by our invitation, looking nervous and ready to run. But as soon as Harmon's wife, Julia, greeted them, they calmed. Once she explained the plan, and as they saw the sniveling former Reeve being forced to clean the pots, they came onboard willingly.

It was three hours more, damn near the start of the new day, before Tenandra sent me the message that she'd seen the caravan coming in. I stood up, swaying slightly, and tried to speak.

"Hey! Itsh times!" I mumbled, then swore as I shook my head and the room spun. "Er…any chansh of a heal?" I mumbled to Oracle, who was seated across from me, grinning.

She hit me with a Cleanse, then Surgeon's Scalpel, making me grunt as I was forcibly sobered, hitting Arrin in turn with the same combination. He was slumped over a table, barely coherent as he tried to chat up a serving girl.

His brain going from alcohol-filled mush to perfectly alert and clean took him by surprise, and he fell off the chair, making the girl laugh and lean down to haul him upright.

Then, she took a step back in shock as Arrin straightened and grinned at her, fully sober. He winked and whispered, "To be continued later!" before joining me in moving through the team, cleansing them all.

In a handful of minutes, the entire squad then the entire room was stone cold sober, everyone grinning at each other.

We were well spread out, and I placed my back to the door, posing as a guard for the shitbag fat guy, who was actually Dennet with a couple of layers of extra clothing on under the robes.

The rest of the room had been similarly outfitted, with everyone playing a part, either as entertainment, such as Ronin, up on the stage, or Oracle and Sehran, dressed suitably provocatively while carrying a tray of beers through the crowd, or as patrons, with everyone else dressed as guards or the various village dickheads.

Lydia alone wasn't dressed up; instead, she wore her full Legion heavy plate armor with her hood up and cloak wrapped around it.

The Reeve was seated at the table closest to the fire, facing the door, while Lydia sat with him. Lydia waited impatiently with her back to the door, glaring at her father, who was seated across from her, utterly terrified, and he kept staring at her, open-mouthed.

The last few minutes as the caravan clattered into town seemed to take forever, but when Oracle met my gaze and grinned, I knew it was time.

"Tenandra says they'll be at the door in five...four...three...two..." I smoothed the smile from my face and turned, making sure I wouldn't give the game away. The door creaked and dragged on the cobbles as someone pulled it open roughly.

"Harmon!" came a rough, sneering voice. "I told yer to fix tha damn door!" I froze, waiting, as Harmon responded.

"And I told you, Berrin, you feckless piece of shit, that when you take a man's inn from 'im, what's to make 'im maintain it? Besides, I can't even reach the fucking door, you dick," Harmon snapped. The entire room paused for a second until Berrin started to laugh roughly.

"Should have fixed it when 'e 'ad tha chance then, shouldn't he, my Lord Reeve?" he called out towards Lydia's table.

"Y...yes!" The Reeve stammered, lifting his cup high and spilling half of it, he was shaking so badly.

"Made a good profit on that lot!" Berrin bragged as he marched in, missing the tension completely. "Thought yer mighta been in bed already, but...hey, who be this?" he said, suddenly interested as he noticed Oracle.

She sashayed across the floor, tray held easily in one hand, beers stuck to it like they were glued in place, and she stepped around Berrin easily, pretending to serve someone a few tables over, closer to the door.

She looked up at me, winked, and sent the mental message I'd been waiting for, just as Berrin reached out for her ass.

"They're all in the room," she confirmed, totally unconcerned.

I rose to my feet.

Lydia and the others had been waiting, watching me or each other, ready to respond. As soon as I stood, they followed suit, and the forced conversations stopped dead as people shifted to watch, knowing what was coming.

I grabbed the man nearest to me by the scruff of the neck, swept his feet from under him, and slammed him face-first into the table next to us, filling the air with a crunch of breaking bone and wood.

He didn't even get off a scream when the death's head floated up from him, and I grunted in irritation.

I'd only meant to knock him out, but I was clearly still more on edge than I realized.

Oracle had moved forward, just far enough that Berrin had to shift, leaning further over to grab at her. As the noise stopped and the others pushed back their seats, a gauntleted fist closed over his outstretched wrist.

"Hi, honey," Lydia whispered to him through gritted teeth, her face inches from his. As he froze in shock, she grabbed him by the back of the head and nutted him.

Berrin gave a cry as he staggered back. One of his fellow villagers stuck out a leg to trip him, grinning as the big man went down, blood running from his broken nose.

I took a step to the left and rested the tip of my dagger against the nearest man's Adam's apple just as he reached for the club he kept on his belt.

He froze, eyes wide as he stared up at me, desperately trying not to so much as swallow.

"I'll take that," I said calmly, tossing the club aside. The rest of the squad had begun moving as well, disarming the seventeen men who had entered the room with Berrin.

Ronin had continued to play, simply changing the music and injecting his mana into it.

The chorus of "Luck's My Mistress" rang out, the notes rippling through the air as we all received bonuses to our luck stats. Berrin and the others received suddenly noticeable bad luck as they fumbled their clubs.

While I'd killed one thug and threatened the other, Sehran had dazed the one closest to her with her magic, and Oracle had summoned a lightning bolt and blasted one across the room and into the fireplace, where he screamed and thrashed, filling the air with the sickly-sweet smell of roasting flesh.

The rest of the group had used more conventional tactics. Bane and Tang had grabbed theirs with daggers to throats, Giint producing his crossbow and grinning maniacally. Grizz and Yen just stood up and pulled their cloaks off, revealing that they were heavily armed legionnaires. Their opponents dropped their weapons and held their hands high instantly.

Bob had yanked his in close, staring into his eyes and hissing, making the man literally shit himself. Jian had placed the tip of a scythe at the throats of the two men that faced him, making them both stay very still indeed.

Arrin had started to summon a brace of Magic Missiles, then had realized that there was nobody left for him to play with, and as he felt that he'd shown off his great magical prowess, simply returned to trying to seduce the same serving girl from earlier.

Berrin grunted, shaking his head and spitting blood to the side, then snorting out a blast of bloody mucus from one smashed nostril by covering the other, glaring up at Lydia as she cast the cloak aside.

"You!" He grunted, then spat on the floor. "What ye be doin' here, yer whore?" he asked, then realized the rest of the room was frozen, with only me and my team moving, casting our concealing cloaks aside.

"What? She been doin' her trick fer yer all? Made yer all come 'ere to teach me a lesson?" He scoffed, standing up and laughing. "I know tha laws, Legion! By tha law, she be ma property. I can 'ave her sold iffin I want, or I can fuckin' kill 'er! None o' yer can stop me. By yer Oaths, yer 'ave to stand back. This be tha law, and tha Reeve be tha man who can order yer all to leave, and yer 'ave to obey!" He straightened his shoulders, confident in his position.

"Berrin," the Reeve whispered weakly, shaking his head. "Don't make this worse."

"Just ye do what I said, Reeve. Yer tell 'em all to leave!" He grinned cockily at his 'friend.' "Tell 'em to leave an' to leave ma property wit' me." He leveled a hard stare at Lydia and cracked his knuckles. "That armor be worth a pretty copper, lass. Best take it off now, lessen yer want me to take tha cost of cleaning it out o' yer hide."

"I think that's enough of this shit," I said coldly, and I fed mana into the pronouncement I'd prepared.

Attention, Citizens of the Territory of Dravith!

High Lord Jax, Imperial Scion, Master of the Great Tower, and High Lord of Dravith, today and effective immediately, revokes the title of Reeve of Cornut, Resheck Dumbarton, stripping him of lordship of the Village of Cornut, all additional titles and possessions, and declares him outlaw.

Let no citizen offer the criminal Resheck succor, lest their titles be stripped from them and their lives declared forfeit.

All Hail High Lord Jax of Dravith!

The declaration flared before everyone in Dravith's eyes and had to be read to the end and understood before it would vanish. Fortunately, I'd told my team to expect it, so they merely glanced at it and dismissed it, understanding and aware beforehand.

The rest of the room, on the other hand, took longer, and the wail of denial from Resheck alone was worth the trip.

"What...?" Berrin mumbled, confused.

"Feel free to enforce the law, Lydia," I ordered. "This man is a self-confessed slaver, and while the others are useful...for now...he probably doesn't know much they don't."

"Yes, Lord Jax!" Lydia saluted, joy filling her face as she stepped forward. "Well, oh 'usband of mine? Nothin' to say?" she asked sweetly through gritted teeth.

Berrin growled and threw a clear and obvious punch at her face with his right and drew a dagger with his left hand, slashing it across and driving it toward the junction of Lydia's armored forearm.

Lydia leaned back, her training coming through. But, at seeing the anger and hatred on his face, she froze momentarily. The dagger hit its mark, cutting into the meat of her wrist.

We all stood by, desperate to step in as he yanked the dagger to the side, widening the wound and making Lydia cry out, but we didn't dare, not for the long-term damage coming to her aid could cause.

Oracle hit her with a heal, though, making her grunt as the dagger was pulled free.

"Lydia, snap out of it!" Yen called, echoed by Grizz, who'd drawn his sword and smashed it against an armored forearm, the crashing sound ringing clear in the silent tavern.

Tang and Yen followed suit, as did the rest of us. Lydia straightened, staring at the man who'd beaten, abused, and finally sold her. The same man who'd sold her mother into slavery literally days ago. Her fighting instincts flared back to life, and she let out a low hiss.

"So that be it, eh? Need yer friends to back yer up? Can't handle a man on yer own, little Lydia? Yer always were fuckin' usel..." His words were cut off by Lydia lunging forward. Her weapons were still attached to her armor, but she didn't bother with them, instead catching the expected dagger strike on one armored forearm, blocking the punch that came from the other arm, and hooking her leg behind his, tipping them both to the floor.

They hit hard, Berrin grunting in pain and shock as the weight of a fully armored legionnaire landed on him. She shifted quickly, pinning his arms and leaning back, glaring down at the man she suddenly had immobilized.

He looked fairly strong for a human. He was likely stronger than most villagers would ever grow to be, but compared to a Legion Optio? Fuck no.

She shoved back from him, climbing to her feet and looking scornfully at the man who'd tormented and broken her. Disdain etched in her features, she spat on the floor.

"Nah. Yer scum, and I'll no defile my armor by getting' yer blood on it. I'm taking it off, then we be takin' this outside. No need to get blood on tha walls." She reached into the crook of her left elbow and unclasped the connections, shaking them loose as she undid the gauntlet, popping the full forearm and glove onto the table next to her.

She repeated the process with the right, then started on the revebrace and the pauldrons. It took her a few minutes, but soon, she stepped out of the last section of armor and stood in her padded underarmor, facing her husband.

"What's this, yer whore…" he scoffed, when Bane grabbed him from behind, the tips of two daggers less than a millimeter from his eyes.

"You'll be silent until the fight starts, or I'll make sure the only sounds that escape are screams about why you've gone blind…understand?" Bane asked him quietly.

"Y…yes…" Berrin mumbled, frozen in place.

"Good, because I'm a legion torturer, and I'm *exceptionally* good at it. The only thing that's keeping me from demonstrating this is respect for my friend and the desire to not have to eat my next meal in a room with blood dripping from the ceiling. Speak one more time, and I'll cross that line."

While Bane had been having that friendly discussion, and Lydia had been stripping down, the rest of us had disarmed the newcomers, and we led them, and the rest of those in the tavern, outside.

We formed a ring around the pair, standing in the middle of the cobbled courtyard, the villagers moving quickly to light braziers around the outside to bathe the ring in flickering firelight.

The rain was coming thick and fast now, drumming on our armor and hissing as it hit the braziers. I stepped up next to Lydia as she stripped off the padding, leaving herself in her trousers and shirt.

"Are you ready for this?" I asked, putting my hand on her shoulder and looking into her eyes.

"Oh, aye. Never been more ready fer anythin' in my life," she growled.

"In that case, Lydia, I suggest you show the entire village what you are. There's nothing to be ashamed of; show them your power." She looked at me then grinned proudly.

"Oh, I'm savin' that fer a final shock. But aye, don't yer worry, Jax. This willna take long."

I smiled at her and stepped back as Bane shoved Berrin into the ring with her. I called out, having to raise my voice above the din of the rain, now thundering down.

"Lydia and Berrin, once a married couple in the eyes of the world, I hereby, by my authority as Overlord of Dravith, declare your marriage null and void, broken by the man who should have been Lydia's shield against the night.

"All that he owns is forfeit to Lydia, but to make this a bit fairer, should he win this fight, I won't simply cook the fucker to death or allow the Legion to beat him into bloody paste. If you win, Berrin, you'll get an hour's head start to escape justice."

"I want two!" he called out, blowing more congealed blood out of one broken nostril.

"Fuck, you're an idiot, aren't you?" I asked him. "When this is over, I seriously doubt you'll be alive. But here's the deal: you survive, you tell us everything. Where you took the slaves, who you took, who you see, the lot. Hell, if you win? I'll give you a fucking week's head start."

"A week?" Lydia growled, looking at me.

"Deal!" he snapped quickly, and I met Lydia's gaze.

"There's absolutely no fucking chance he wins this fight," I said smiling. "Now, go fuck him up, and I'm sure his friends can tell us anything we need to know, so don't worry if he dies."

Lydia grinned and stepped forward, gesturing to Berrin.

He lunged at her, thinking to use his greater height and reach to end the fight fast with a savage punch to the face.

Lydia blocked and lashed out in response, her own punch taking him in the gut before she stepped back, his counter flashing past her face.

She swiped his fist aside and punched him in the side, once, twice, then brought her knee around into his gut when he slammed his elbow down hard on the side of her face, sending her reeling back.

"Yer been workin' on that," Berrin muttered, rubbing his stomach before grinning at her. "Yer 'member when the 'ealer told us yer had a girl in yer belly? You 'member how I fixed that?" Lydia blanched, her hands shifting to cradle her stomach protectively, instinctively, and Berrin struck.

He grabbed her head in his left hand, both squeezing and holding her in place. Before she could break the grip, he punched her in the mouth, then the chest, then brought his knee up, slamming it into her gut and sending her to the floor with a last elbow strike to the back of her head.

She went down, hitting the floor hard, stunned.

"What's her life worth to ye, then?" he spat as he moved to stand behind her, kicking her hard in the lower back, then the side. He grinned at me. "Yer want 'er death on yer 'ands? I want gold, my gear, an'…"

Before he could finish his demands, Lydia twisted around, lashing out with her right arm and trapping his leg in close. She planted her left foot for leverage and flashed her right upwards, using a move that Flux had taught the group in training, heavily modified, to kick Berrin in the face.

He staggered back, and she tugged on his leg before releasing him as he fell. She rolled to her feet and kicked out as he started to rise, taking him across the face and sending him reeling.

"Yer really think that be it, Berrin?" she snarled. "Yer think that a wee beatin' like that is gonna break me? Yer used to give me worse on a fuckin' night when yer came 'ome an' couldn'a get it up!"

Berrin rolled away and pushed back to his feet, glaring daggers at her.

"Hey everyone, I give you Berrin Softcock!" Yen called out, and the crowd started to laugh.

"Shut it!" Berrin scowled. "Iffin I couldn'a get it up, it were 'cause yer so fuckin' ugly…" he started, but Lydia was already in motion.

She stepped in close, three quick strides, and blocked his right punch with her left arm, wrapping it around his forearm and jerking the limb straight. Clamping her grip in tight on his wrist, she blocked his left fist with her right and did the same before planting one foot on his slightly extended left leg and kicking off, clambering up his body in two quick steps.

She braced her left foot firmly against his chest, hauled back with both arms, levering herself out at a ninety-degree angle to his own, and stamped out as hard as she could into his face. Then she released him and fell onto her back, rolling to lessen the impact. He staggered back, clutching his already smashed nose and swearing as she rolled to her feet again.

She kicked off, three fast strides reach to him, before throwing herself onto her back, swiping his legs out from under him and sending him crashing to the floor. As she jumped up, she rushed past him again, punching him in the face as he struggled to rise.

He rolled, stunned but not yet out of the fight, and lashed out blindly, a punch then a clumsy kick.

She easily avoided them both before stepping back scornfully. "What be wrong, Berrin?" she taunted. "Can't see?"

He wiped the blood and rain from his face and blinked, glaring at her. "I can see…" he snarled.

"Here, let's make it a wee bit brighter, eh?" She stood straighter and clenched her fists, taking a deep breath.

The transformation was almost instantaneous. Her wings had been hidden until now, but as soon as she no longer consciously willed them to disappear, instead intentionally pouring magic into them, they grew.

The light started in the small of her back and the depths of her eyes simultaneously, a bright, white light tinged with gold that poured out, and she changed.

The haggard, battered woman shifted, blurring as her power flowed. Her injuries were suddenly clearly minor, the blood seeming laughable. Her skin fairly glowed with health, her muscles standing proud. As she shook her head, her hair flew free to be blown back in a slight breeze as the wings grew.

They were golden white, easily ten feet long, and where they'd been comprised entirely of light when they'd first appeared, now they were filled with distinct feathers, long white plumes that ruffled and twitched as they formed.

She flared them out to either side, a wingspan of more than twenty feet. Lydia flapped them once, lifting herself into the air before landing lightly on the balls of her feet and grinning at Berrin and the other villagers, who looked on in stunned amazement.

"Oh, aye, Berrin, did I no mention that I be a Valkyrie?" she asked mockingly. "Must'a slipped my mind."

"Yer be a useless, ugly…" Berrin huffed, when she slammed her right fist into his mouth, sending him staggering back to spit out teeth and blood.

"Shut yer face, Berrin," Lydia snapped. "Only one useless here be ye. A real man lifts his wife up, teaches her to be all she can, and is proud of her when she achieves it! A *real* man is no threatened by a wife who's smart!"

She stepped in, blocking his punch, and leaned back, her right foot flashing upwards in a high kick to nearly tear his ear free. Then she flexed, beating her left wing and flipping herself around to plant her right foot flat on the ground again. Her left foot slammed into the opposite side of his head, staggering him forward to fall to one knee.

"Yer be a useless sack of shit, Berrin, an' I wish I could'a seen it before now," she snapped, taking two quick steps, punching him in the temple and sending him reeling to the floor.

"I spent ten years as a slave, forced to work day an' night, torturin' myself each night, wonderin' where I went wrong, what I should'a done better, how I failed as a wife and as a woman. Fuck that." She grabbed him by the throat and lifted him up with one hand.

"I didna fail as either, it were my husband who failed. No' only was he a useless sack o' shit in bed, but 'e were in all tha rest of his life, an' I just couldn'a see it!" she snapped, shaking Berrin as he lashed out weakly, trying to hit her. Finally, he brought his fingers to the hand that clutched his throat in a vice-like grip.

"A real man doesna need to make his wife feel small so he can be big. No' even a feckin' Goblin be that stupid; only scum be that weak, and I'm no havin' it no more!"

Lydia punched him in the face once, then twisted him around, as he staggered, stunned, grabbing the back of his belt and lifting him high into the air over her head, holding him flat.

"I be tha first Valkyrie! I be Optio of tha Legion. And more, I be strong! I be worthy, and of more than this shit were ever worthy of lovin'!" She cried aloud, then shifted her grip, glaring up at him, then around at the crowd, at the other slavers.

"Yer men standing there, assholes who 'elped this sack o' shit condemn me and sell me in tha first place, 'ear this now! Ah be more than all that. AH BE LYDIA, AND AH BE MA OWN WOMAN!" she shouted, dropping to one knee, the other braced before her. She pulled Berrin down, hard and fast, to slam into her knee. His lower spine, just above the pelvis, impacted her kneecap with a crunch that echoed around the square, meeting the return of her declaration that hung reverberating in the air.

As he screamed, his back fractured, Lydia shoved him forward to lie broken on the street. She straightened up, gazing up as she sensed something a split-second before the rest of us did.

There was a sudden silence, a feeling of weight, of divine attention, and the entire square held its breath, even Berrin, shocked out of his pained grunting and screaming by the obvious presence of a God.

"I AM PROUD OF YOU, MY VALKYRIE, AND I ACCEPT YOU FORMALLY AS MY CHAMPION. ARISE, LYDIA VALKYRIE; ARISE AND SERVE YOUR GOD."

The voice of Vanei echoed around the square and in all our minds, and my heart swelled with pride.

Vanei had said She would not accept Lydia as Her champion until she'd completed her quest, but clearly the Goddess had been watching her progress and had decided, as the rest of us knew, that Lydia was fucking amazing. Accepting her here and now, before the very eyes of those who'd once broken her, was the time to do it.

I went to one knee, and the others of the squad. A heartbeat later, the village followed suit. Lydia lifted into the air, her wings fully formed and beating slowly, wafting her higher as a gentle light illuminated her, wrapping her in power and transforming her.

As Lydia vanished into the light, I heard the sound of running feet, and three of the slavers made a break for it, hoping to escape in our moment of distraction.

"Kill them," I ordered flatly. A heartbeat later, the deep *twang* of Giint's crossbow went off, followed by the whoosh of Arrin's Magic Missiles and the deeper strum of Tang's longbow reverberating. Projectiles flew through the air to slam into the fleeing men.

One made it a dozen feet, the other two considerably less than that, then all three were dead. Bane appeared a handful of steps from one as he fell, Giint's crossbow bolt firmly lodged in the back of his skull. The Mer sighed, shaking his head and clacking his teeth in irritation.

"I was going for that one!" he called to Giint, who replied with a giggle.

"Giint faster than Bane!"

"Fuck you, Giint!"

CHAPTER FORTY-FOUR

I grinned, hearing both the edge of irritation in Bane's voice, and the clear acceptance of Giint in the group, as well as picking up on the subtle notes of music that wafted around us. I checked my notifications and dismissed them, seeing a brief note about being affected by the event I was observing, and knowing damn well that Ronin was helping that along by somehow increasing everyone's sense of awe.

Much the same as hearing "Eye of the Tiger" playing during a training montage made the training easily two hundred percent more effective.

I watched as the light dimmed and the sense of divine attention faded. Lydia hung suspended for a few seconds in the air before dropping like a stone.

Just before impact, she flared her wings and landed in a perfect three-point stance, then looked up at me, raising one eye and grinning her question.

I strode forward, pulling her up into a tight hug, and I simply held her. At first, she seemed shocked and froze. Then she closed her arms around me and held on as though for dear life. I held the embrace for a few more seconds before whispering in her ear.

"Awesome superhero landing."

Lydia grinned proudly at me as I stepped back, and the others moved in, hugging and congratulating her. I inspected her closely, seeing a thousand tiny changes and none.

She was still the same person, still Lydia, her honest, good intentions and determination shining from her stronger than ever. But she'd been changed by Vanei's touch.

She'd always had a raw-boned grace about her, hardly any fat, and had been wiry when we'd met, then quickly growing more and more muscled as we traveled and she ate and trained better, but now…

Lydia had a subtle glow about her, a sense of good health that almost shone from within. Her edges had been softened, and if I was any judge, she'd also had her biological clock rolled back at least ten years, considering how much younger and healthier she appeared.

She'd gone from mid-thirties, if not older, and a damn hard life, into early to mid-twenties, with the impression that she worked damn hard for a living, and despite what every fad dieter would try to convince you of, she ate both her greens and her meat, resulting in a glowing, clearly healthy person.

Her wings shimmered and reflected the light. As I pulled up the quest log, I noted that we still hadn't managed to complete her 'Resolve the Past' section, but I was betting that after everything that had happened here tonight, we were damn close.

I gave the squad a few more minutes, noting the panicked faces of the remaining slavers, and I spoke up firmly as I walked toward the weakly twitching form that was frantically trying to drag himself away.

I put one foot down on Berrin's hand and leaned in, but spoke loudly to the other villagers first.

"Take the slavers, strip them of everything, and put them in the cages," I ordered, tossing the key to Harmon. He caught it out of the air, grinning, and gestured over his shoulder toward the figure that was still manacled to his seat inside.

"What about Resheck?" Harmon asked hopefully.

I flashed the barman a smile. "What, you think he's getting a reprieve?" I shook my head. "He's a slaver; in the cage with the rest."

"Yes, my lord!" Harmon shouted joyfully as he turned and vanished into his tavern. The other villagers stripped and dragged the slavers and assholes in their midst to the cages, ramming them into too small a space, and enjoying every damn second of it.

"Please," Berrin whimpered, and I looked back down at him.

"Whoops, forgot about you there, didn't I?" I muttered. "Well, now, what to do about you?" I reached out and grabbed a fistful of hair, yanking his head back and staring into his eyes.

"I can help. I know things," he whimpered.

"You will; in fact, you probably know a fuckton of useful stuff, don't you?" He tried to nod, whispering that yes, he did indeed, and he'd tell me everything.

"There's one thing, though," I said, leaning in as though speaking conspiratorially. "I think your friends probably know at least as much as you do, and if I use you as an example, well, they might want to share everything with me as quickly as possible. Tell me, Berrin. You ever hear of being hanged, drawn, and quartered?" I made no effort to hide my absolute fury at the things he'd done to Lydia, my emotions still raw and very much prompting me down the road of uber-violence.

"Please...please, no," he whispered, and I reached for the dagger on my belt.

"Jax." A voice from my right made me pause, and I looked up to find Bane standing there.

"What's up?" I asked. "I'm a little busy here, but this won't take long."

"No, it won't," Bane agreed, stepping forward and crouching on the other side of Berrin. "Give him to me. I'll make it take longer, and I'll get your answers."

"No...," I started to reply, wanting to deal with the scumbag myself.

"You remember the Drow?" he asked. "You remember the things you did to him? To make him tell you the truth?"

I froze, remembering snatches of that furious, desperate conversation, half out of my mind in fear for Oracle, and so, so desperate to share the pain I was feeling.

"I do," I answered flatly.

"You remember what we agreed?"

"He deserves this..." I started to protest.

Bane reached out, gently laying his three-fingered hand on my forearm.

"He does, and I promise he will pay in full for all he did, Jax. But you know what that did to you, and you also know that the Drow still didn't tell you the whole truth. This could be the same."

"He's not as strong as the Drow," I argued.

Bane shook his head. "No, I don't think he is, but that's not the point. You will be the Emperor, Jax. You will lead us all, and doing this, sometimes it needs to be done, but doing this with anger in your heart isn't justice. It's revenge, remember?" Bane said, squeezing my forearm, once.

I barely felt it through my armor, but I knew what he was saying. I'd traveled the realms, across a hundred billion miles, or a few millimeters, across realities. A year ago, I'd never seen the like of Bane, a mixture of the predator, a smooth-faced alien, and a damn ninja, a creature I could never have imagined. Yet, I knew I had a friend here, one who was trying to help me, to take a burden from me, and to make sure I didn't give into the darker side of my nature.

I drew in a deep breath then let it out with a long, slow exhale, forcing myself to relax.

I moved my foot off Berrin's fingers. Bane stood with me, as I reached out, placing one gauntleted hand on his upper left shoulder and squeezing.

"Thank you, Bane," I said quietly. "Be careful, my friend; I can't lose you to this as well," I warned.

He inclined his head. "I know, and never fear that. Now, I'll take him someplace quiet and private, and we can have a little chat...perhaps you could keep Lydia and anyone else from interrupting?"

As soon as I assured him that I would, he reached down, grabbing Berrin and hoisting him like a sack of potatoes over his upper shoulders, heading off down an alleyway in search of a private place to "talk."

Relief and a faint burn of desire to do it myself warring within me, I made my way across the square and clambered up the gangplank. Tenandra had landed again during the fight, and I paused at the top. I'd been intending to talk to the Wisp, but the figure standing at the end of the bow, watching the villagers, drew my attention, making me pause.

I stepped up next to Bob and looked down, seeing the square below us was surprisingly full now, before speaking softly.

"You were welcome down there with us all, you know?" I said carefully.

"I'm not like them," came the reply.

"None of us are."

"I am not alive. I am not flesh." Bob rounded on me sharply.

"And Giint's not sane. Lydia's a fucking Valkyrie, the only one of her kind. Bane's a Mer, Oracle is a Wisp, the rest of the squad is human, Elf, half-Elf, and I don't even want to try and pin anything on Grizz. He'd turn out to be a damn demi-God or a sapient golem or something," I muttered.

"But they live!" Bob insisted. *"I do not!"*

"Really? Because I'm pretty sure you're alive. You're certainly sapient; you think, you care, you question..."

"I was created by you." The skeletal being refused to be swayed. *"I'm not alive like them."*

"Bob, buddy," I said carefully, understanding this was important to him. "Okay, you're not like them. You're the only one of your kind, as far as I know. Well, I'm not human; not really.

"Let's face it, kids are made by their parents. It doesn't make them less alive. We've got a damn Succubai in the gang, who literally ate someone a few hours back, then commented on the flavor. Bane's off torturing someone to death, and Giint, well…" We both looked at the mad little bastard, who looked to be drinking a bottle of boot polish.

"Look…" I started again, my train of thought thoroughly derailed as Giint burped and showed every sign of enjoying the boot polish, going so far as to stick a finger into the pot and lick it afterwards.

"We're not a normal group. Hell, we are about as far from normal as you can get. You are alive. No, you don't have flesh, but you have a soul. You are aware, and you have feelings; I can sense them. Yes, I created you, and now I've given you life and a soul, partially with the help of a God. But you need to decide if this is what you want, Bob. I want you with us, but if you want something else? If you want to be a ranger or a gardener, a cook, or to just go sit in a cave and watch the seasons pass, tell me. I'll make it work."

Bob stared at me for a long minute, before nodding and looking back down at the group below.

"I know you feel like an outsider," I said gently. "But I'm telling you, absolutely everyone does at first. Go down, join in, and see how it feels. Ignore the villagers or speak to them, that's your choice, but try to talk to some of the group. I promise you, there's not one of them that's normal." With that, I continued my trajectory to the wheelhouse, stepping inside and coughing as I came to a dead stop.

"Uh, guys?" I said after several seconds, knowing damn well that Tenandra, at the very least, was well aware I was there. Jian jumped, and Sehran spun around, letting go of Tenandra to see who'd interrupted her fun.

"Jax!" Jian gasped in panic, quickly stepping behind a chair to hide the fact that he only had socks and a scabbard on. I shook my head, not wanting to know about the rapidly developing little thruple's kinks.

"I don't care what you're all doing to and for each other," I clarified, holding my hands out and shaking my head. "I just need to know how long it would take us to get to the slaver market and how long for Tenandra to get to the Tower from there, then back here with reinforcements. Tell me that, and I can leave you all to your fun; just try not to crash the ship, okay?"

"I would never crash, but I take your point," Tenandra said musingly, while Sehran winked and tossed a flirtatious wave at me.

The door thumped behind me, and I turned, just in time for Oracle to walk in and freeze. I looked back over my shoulder, noting that yes, Tenandra was still totally naked, and all Sehran was wearing was Jian's other scabbard.

"Any chance you could put some clothes on?" I asked the three of them, looking to Oracle and shrugging awkwardly as her eyes flashed from them to Jian, to me. She ultimately opted for stepping in close, putting her arm around my waist as I rested mine across her shoulders.

"You knew this was going to happen, right?" She asked me under her breath. I shrugged again, not really caring either way.

"Whatever. Tenandra?" I asked, and she coughed politely, suddenly dressed in her prim blue and white suit.

"Yes! Of course, my apologies, Lord Jax. To reach the market would take us three hours, less if we have favorable winds. From there to the Tower is around eighteen hours. With a fast turnaround, we could be back here in say, forty?"

"Too long," I decided. "Okay, thanks Tenandra, I'll let you guys get back to…well, you know." I pointedly did not look back as I walked to the door. "I'd consider a lock for the door, guys, especially with the Gnomes aboard, but that's just a suggestion."

With that, Oracle and I crossed the deck, stopping at the railing to look down at the group below. The tavern was clearly staying open all night now, and judging from the tables and chairs that were being moved out into the square, people were going to party, regardless of the rain.

"What's the plan?" Oracle asked quietly.

"You know me, I like simple," I replied with a shrug. "With the details that Julia gave us, we rock up, pretend to be slave traders, then we slaughter the fuckers. I don't like the idea of selling some of the team to them as she suggested, so I'm going to run the risk of losing their sailing ships. We can chase one down with the airship, maybe both, but we're too close to Himnel. If they have ships in the air, that option is off the table, and we just make do with what we can get."

"Okay," Oracle said slowly, then reached up and pulled me down for a kiss. "I actually meant, did you want to go join the others for a drink or chase me around the cabin below for a bit?"

"Now there's an offer I sure as shit ain't going to pass up." I laughed and kissed her back. "Get that ass down there, quick, before someone finds us and gives us a problem to solve!"

The next morning arrived only a few hours later. Really, even though there had been a compelling argument for us to either set off at first light to go after the slave encampment or to head off to the second of Lydia's markers and see what we could find, the entire team was exhausted, and it would look suspicious if we were to head for the camp straight away. Arriving in an obviously Gnome-crafted ship at first light would have the slavers all standing up to pay attention, considering the Gnomes were a desperately traded group.

Instead, we loaded one of the cages onto the deck, full of the former slavers, planning to act the part of the sellers, dealing in sentient misery.

I walked out of our cabin and into the corridor, then immediately was accosted by Frederikk, who tried to blackmail me on the subject of his distress about the slaver cage on the deck of his ex-clan's ship. I'd have believed in his claims of distress a lot more, if he hadn't started by asking if I had any of the stash on me.

I sent him off with an absurdly tiny section of the sticks the Gnomes were so addicted to and resolved again to try to figure out how the super-strength catnip was actually made.

Moving along the hall and up the ladder to the deck, I was accosted by Gnomes three more times before I made it to the railing. Each used almost the same argument, practically word for word, until I told each of them that I'd already given Frederikk all I had.

By the time I made it to the railing, and Giint sidled up, I just snapped off a section of a stick and handed it over, not saying a word.

Yeah, it was preferential treatment, but fuck nepotism. Giint was going to be fighting for his life soon, the same as the rest of us, while the majority of the Gnomes would be cowering below decks.

"Make sure you only have a little of that." I warned him. "Three hours, and we'll be in the shit again."

"More reason to have it now, then." Giint grunted and popped the entire thing in his mouth. I swore, and for a brief second, I considered grabbing him and trying to get it out of his mouth, like I'd once had to do with an ex's dog when it'd grabbed a chocolate bar and started wolfing it down.

It'd thrown up everywhere in the end, ruining my chances of getting laid, and I'd only had a savaged hand to show for it, not to mention the blame from the girl for "traumatizing the poor thing." Fucking chihuahuas.

I dismissed the thought and walked down the gangplank, passing the last of the former slavers being led up to the cage. I nodded, smiling at the former Reeve, who looked absolutely terrified, then continued my trek into the tavern.

"Wondered where you got to," Grizz muttered, nursing his beer at the bar.

"Oracle," I admitted, unashamed. "Why are you in such a bad mood?"

"Can't get drunk," he sourly informed me, nodding toward Yen, who was sipping a glass of milk a few seats further down the bar.

"I ordered him not to get drunk before the fight," she clarified.

"You're evil," Grizz growled. "I could have had Arrin sober me up!" We all looked over at Arrin, who was laid half-on, half-off a table in the corner, his face resting in a puddle of either drool or flat ale; it was impossible to tell which at this distance.

"Yeah, he's not going to be much help to anyone," I pointed out, shaking my head.

Lydia was nowhere in sight, but I soon spotted Tang leaning against the wall, watching over me. Giint was probably passed out on the ship, Jian was almost assuredly still in the wheelhouse, leaving only Bane, Ronin, and Bob unaccounted for.

"Where's…" I started to ask, and Yen shook her head.

"Nobody knows where Bane is, Lydia is upstairs in one of the rooms–I seriously don't recommend you interrupt her right now–and as for Ronin and Bob, well, one of them is upstairs with Lydia, three guesses which?" the legionnaire said with a wink.

"Well, considering I just rebuilt Bob, and I don't remember giving him the equipment he'd need, my money's on Ronin, but seriously?" I asked in shock.

"Ha! Nope." Yen gestured to the floor behind the bar, so I stood up and peered over, discovering Ronin, who was passed out drunk.

"Wait…" I mumbled.

"No, nothing like that," Yen said. "Although, I like how easily you believed she was getting her rocks off. Turns out the tavern has a bath. She's up there now, and Bob's guarding the door for her, as every few minutes someone turns up and wants to talk to her.

"She should be down anytime soon, but seriously, unless we need to, I think we should give her a few more minutes. She couldn't stop staring at that prick Berrin's blood on her hands, so I made her go clean herself up. After everything that happened, he's still dug in her brain pretty deep."

"Yeah, makes sense, I guess," I said. "Okay then, guys, let's round the others up and get a move on. We can leave Lydia until last." Satisfied with the plan, I cracked my fingers and started firing off Cleanse at everyone in sight.

It was a weak spell, and I almost never used it, but in this situation? It was a godsend. Hell, if I'd been able to use it at home before all this had started, I'd have been a damn billionaire. It purged any poisons from the system, so alcohol was removed like it'd never been ingested. On top of that, a general heal took you from hungover to fully functioning in under a minute.

Ten minutes later, I was removing locals from the ship or pushing our own people back onto it, when Lydia and Bob showed up. I nodded to them both as they walked aboard, nobody saying anything, until Lydia paused and squeezed my shoulder in thanks.

"I told 'em we'd be back after tha slave camp; we are still offerin' 'em the chance to join tha Tower, right?" Lydia asked me quietly.

"I hadn't intended to originally, to be honest, not after hearing about the way they'd treated you," I answered with a frown. "But meeting a few of them made me realize that not all of them were assholes, just a select few. So yeah, as long as they swear the Oaths, I'll send a few ships back, and we can evacuate them all."

"Not that I don't think the Tower is tha best place for everyone, but why not leave 'em here until we've got some time?" Lydia asked slowly.

"That'd be fine, normally. However, to prevent that prick of a Reeve from causing any problems I'd have to overrule, I formally stripped him of power. That means that anyone who puts two and two together will guess that I was at least somewhere close to this village, which will likely result in a force being sent here from one of the cities. With that in mind, it's best to bring a few ships and offer anyone who wants it to come to the Tower. They can always come back once we've sorted the area out," I said grimly.

"Can Oracle pass tha word to tha Tower?" Lydia asked.

"She's gathering herself to do it now; once we get high enough, she'll send the information. She tried to explain it last night, but, well..."

"But ye were fixated on her tits and didn't listen?" Lydia finished bluntly with a knowing smirk.

"I don't know what you're talking about," I said loftily. "Anyway, all we need now is to find Bane, and..."

"Seriously, Jax?" Bane said from the railing next to me. "You are so unobservant."

"Fuck's sake, Bane!" I snapped, jerking back and glaring at him. "A full goddamn jester's outfit; bells everywhere! I swear I'm going to invent electricity just so I can tag you and make you beep when you get too goddamn close! I'm..." I raved on at him, as Lydia left my side, walking over to the wheelhouse and sticking her head inside, giving the order to take off whenever Tenandra was ready.

My tirade of abuse floated along in the air behind the ship as we set off yet again, this time to raid the slave camp.

NARKOLT

"**S**ix hours!" Augustus grumbled to Centurion Brina. "Six goddamn hours, they've had me cooling my heels here. Never in all the years we've been sworn to the Empire have I been so thoroughly ignored, and to have it done by the Legion General!"

"Sir, Tribune Jon would have normally been here to greet you, but…"

"But?" Augustus growled.

"He disturbed some kind of spider, Lord Augustus, something nobody has seen before. It bit him, and well, it's not looking good for him," Brina admitted grimly.

"I'm sorry for that, Centurion; truly, I am. I remember Jon as an impeccably conscientious legionnaire, but that doesn't explain a damn thing. The Legion General and Prefect are neither of them a healer. From what I remember, neither would be so broken by Jon's loss that they'd be unable to handle their roles, so why don't you go ahead and just say what you need to outright?"

"I…uh…" Brina winced visibly before straightening up and shaking her head in negation. "I apologize, Lord Augustus. The Legion General will be with you when he can. I simply wished to make you aware why Tribune Jon hasn't greeted you personally in the interim."

"Fine, thank you, Centurion." Augustus said, forcing a smile before sitting back down in the small office he'd been ushered into as she walked away. Six hours ago, he'd arrived after a long flight aboard the *Ragnarök*. That bastard Mal had looped out and around, making it appear he'd come from farther down the coast, from the *south*, for Jax's sake, and he had still beaten them here.

The speed difference was insane between the two ships, and the *Ragnarök* was even classed as a fast cruiser. Augustus shook his head in disgust. They'd landed and paid some truly eye-watering bribes to secure a decent berth that they could launch from in a hurry, if need be. He'd hastened to the Legion Enclave halfway across the city, fully expecting to be met with rejoicing over the resurrection of the Empire and the Imperial line.

Instead, he and his escort had been greeted with suspicion, and he'd been ordered to leave his men in the barracks and to await the Legion General's pleasure in this shithole of an office.

Another hour passed before the door was finally cracked open, and a single legionnaire stepped in, saluting fist to chest, before asking Augustus to follow him.

He was led deeper into the enclave, along corridors he'd not walked before, but which he knew were leading him away from the more populated areas.

Each enclave was a mirror of the others, mainly due to the standard camp outline which the Empire had established. The enclaves had simply made that layout more formal within permanent structures. Of course, there were slight differences between Narkolt and Himnel; Narkolt housed more legionnaires, for a start, almost double the number. So, while the enclave was still sparsely populated in comparison to its potential, it was both busier and strangely quieter than Himnel's had been.

That being said, the section he was being brought to was behind the tannery vats, and he knew damn well they'd not been used in living memory by either force, so why...

"Legionnaire Augustus," the man leading him asked quietly, breaking his line of thought. "The ship you arrived on, was it expensive to charter?"

Augustus froze, gazing sharply at the man who seemed unaware that anything was wrong, while every instinct in Augustus' body began to scream two things.

First, this was a legionnaire, only one step above a trainee. Despite being from different Legions, being addressed as a simple legionnaire by this man as though they were equals, instead of by his rank of Primus or even his formally granted one of Lord or Duke, made Augustus want to beat respect into the man.

Secondly, something was very, very wrong here, and this was the voice Augustus had learned to listen very carefully to, the one that usually warned him of daggers in his back and axes flying at him in combat.

No properly trained legionnaire would dream of questioning a superior officer so casually, and he'd told none of the Enclave about the ship.

"It belongs to a friend," Augustus responded finally, watching the man and getting a simple shrug in response.

Augustus reached down and slid his sword out of the scabbard half an inch before returning it, making sure the blade was free. As much as he'd loved his old gladius, the Commander's Sword was both a serious upgrade and a literal gift from the Scion of the Empire, making it literally priceless to him.

Loosening his blade was an old habit, one drummed into every legionnaire over and over again by experience, especially after they'd spent a few winters in the Legion.

Rain or sleet, driven by the wind, got everywhere in winter, despite the various attempts to stave it off, and the weapons could get iced into the scabbard depressingly easily. The last thing any legionnaire needed was to try to draw his sword and find the hilt frozen to the scabbard.

Thus, the habit, at the first sign of danger, at the first instinctual risk he felt, to make sure his sword was free.

The legionnaire guiding him didn't appear to notice, continuing to lead him down a short, narrow alley between buildings, and then directing him into a dilapidated office.

"Please go on in, legionnaire; the Legion-General is waiting for your report." The man smiled blandly at Augustus as he paused at the door and gestured for Augustus to enter ahead of him.

With every instinct screaming that something was wrong, yet still *knowing* deep down that no legionnaire could actually harm him, thanks to their Oaths of service, Augustus complied. He was surprised to find seven men waiting for him in the small, dimly lit room, with one of them outfitted in full plate armor.

"What..." he started, when one of the men barked an order, cutting him off.

"Silence, legionnaire!" snapped the man. "I am Legion-General Shin, and I order you to sit and be silent."

Augustus snapped his mouth shut instinctively, responding to the order that was ingrained in him. Further bound by Oath, he stepped forward, taking the single seat in the middle of the room and sitting straight-backed, trying his hardest not to glare at the older man.

"I order you to stay completely still and offer no resistance."

Augustus's eyes widened, and chuckles rose around the small room as the Legion-General gestured to one of the men to lock the chains attached to the chair into place on Augustus's wrists and ankles before relieving him of his sword and pouch.

"Nice," the man who'd taken the weapon commented idly. "I'll be keeping this. I'll need it to pass as him, after all." The others in the room grumbled at his good luck.

"You'll damn well keep your looting for later, Asha!" the Legion-General snapped at him before turning to Augustus. "Very well; I order you to speak only the truth and answer my questions as accurately and fully as you can. Attempt to hide nothing, and warn me if I need to know anything."

"You'll regret this," Augustus said flatly, compelled by the Oath to speak. "You need to know that you've made a huge mistake, Legion-General Shen, as…"

"Silence," the man barked irritably, and Augustus grunted as his throat locked up, preventing him from speaking. "I don't care about your opinions, human! Tell me all you know about this imposter Jax, especially his personality, habits, and security measures."

Augustus braced to fight the impulse before grinning as he settled back and remained silent as the Oath searched for the levers to compel him and found none.

"Well?" the figure demanded. "I gave you an order!" After several seconds had passed, he sighed and rephrased the order, seeing his mistake. "Tell us everything you know about the one known as Jax, the Imperial Scion."

Augustus's traitorous mouth opened, and he clamped down on it, pain tearing through him as he fought his Oath of obedience to the upper ranks of the Legion. At the same moment, his Oath of fealty to Jax kicked in to prevent him speaking to one he now suspected was an enemy. Several minutes passed before Augustus passed out, blue in the face, the combination of Oaths preventing him from breathing until his autonomic bodily responses took over.

When he regained consciousness and looked around blearily, the Legion-General asked him the question again, resulting in the same effect.

Two more hours passed before Augustus awoke to arguing instead of orders.

"…telling you this won't work!" one voice snarled. "Better to accept it and move on than keep wasting our time with this."

"The Lady orders, and we obey, Ishik!" another voice snapped coldly. "Do you regret your Oath? Does it wear heavily on you after all these centuries? Speak the word, and I will relieve you of such concerns!"

"You know I am faithful, Morta!" the first voice snapped back. "His soldiers will be concerned by now, and we cannot replace them all. I say we send the three we have, with Asha to replace him, then they return to the apostate and do what needs to be done!"

Apostate. That title…Augustus stiffened as he received the final confirmation he'd needed. No true legionnaire would refer to the Scion of the Empire as "apostate." Only the Dark Legion, or someone sworn to Nimon and his Pantheon, would call him that.

Logically, that meant that these men weren't legionnaires, not really. Their Oaths of service wouldn't allow them treat him in this fashion…so either the entire Legion was…no, why take him to this dark corner of the enclave if they were all corrupt…and how the hell did a bunch of corrupt legionnaires even happen these days? Their Oaths were supposed to prevent this from happening!

The Oaths.

The Oaths did prevent this, and they would prevent them from harming him, as well. Clearly, they planned to replace him somehow, and probably kill him, and he'd wandered right into the spider's web.

Spiders. He blinked as more details came together for him: the spider that had taken down Tribune Jon, a spider nobody had seen before, which had nearly killed him.

These were a small cabal of people that seemed to believe that they could replace him and leave nobody the wiser. That meant some form of changeling or concealment spell, most likely. The spider, the names, and the arrogance all suggested Drow, a race known for their skill in subversion and assassination.

Augustus's mind continued racing as he frantically worked his way through it all, making the connections and feeling more details just out of reach.

The legionnaires couldn't do this, but a few months back, Jon had sent word to the Legion General of Himnel, and word had filtered down through every Primus that something weird was going on here.

Tribune Jon had warned that the new legion-general and prefect were acting strangely; nothing in particular that he could report. But he'd felt it was his duty to warn someone, and it'd been passed to the Legion of Himnel. With everything that'd happened, Augustus had remembered it, but only as a brief warning that they might be a bit odd.

Now the behavior, the assault and questioning, the theft of his personal weapon and pouch–which Asha, he could see out of the corner of his eye, was literally rummaging in now.

"By the Lady!" Asha swore, staring bug-eyed into the inventory of the bag.

"What?" one of the other figures grunted curiously.

"Twenty-seven *platinum* coins, eleven hundred and forty-four gold, a thousand and six silver, and ninety-three copper!" Asha said in tones of awe. "I'm rich!"

"I'm in charge of this expedition!" the Legion-General snapped. "Give it here!"

"This meat sack must have had the money for a reason! I will need it!" Asha countered, baring teeth that gleamed as he stepped back, clutching the bag and shaking his head.

"I don't care!" The Legion-General crossed the room. "I order you to hand it over in the Lady's name!"

"You're no priest, Vellin!" Asha snapped back. "You're in command only so long as you live. You want this wealth? Try to take it, and I'll take your head and your place!"

Augustus suppressed a grunt as the last pieces fell into place for him. They were Drow, and they'd usurped the Legion leadership. He didn't know what they were trying to do, but they clearly intended to assassinate Jax, using himself as the method, or his face, at least.

That knowledge, the various steps linking it up, and the logical belief was enough. He felt his Oath activate, searching his mind for falsehoods, before settling in. All resistance to him vanished as, at last, his Legion Oath and his Oath of Imperial Allegiance meshed again, providing him with a single truly clear directive.

Kill the Drow.

Augustus couldn't help but grin slightly as he twisted his right hand, and the blade he'd kept in his vambrace since childhood slid out of its sheath and into his waiting palm. It was barely two inches long, a tiny thing, really. He slowly pressed it to the chains and began to saw, the magical blade slicing through the cold iron like butter. He didn't need anything else.

His family heirloom might have seemed peculiar to anyone who saw it, but when you had a knife that could cut almost anything, well, it didn't matter how big it was.

Augustus felt the sickening feeling of his mana being torn from him in the huge quantities the magical device required, but thankfully, just before the migraine got a good grip, it was done. Taking significant pains to keep the loose restraints quiet, he carefully slid the blade back into the recess of the handle, pushing it back up into the vambrace.

It was uncomfortable; the damn thing wasn't in properly, which meant it was pressing on the inside of his wrist and causing a low throb that would make his hand go numb if he didn't adjust it properly. But the cuffs of both sets of chains were literally hanging on by a thread, so he only needed to wait for the right...

"Wake up, maggot!" someone grunted, and Augustus's world erupted in stars as a heavy sabaton slammed into the side of his head, almost tearing his ear free and stunning him momentarily.

"Hey!" Asha snapped at whoever had kicked Augustus. "Stop that, you stupid fuck! We need the flesh intact. Now I'm going to need to heal him, fool!"

"Ishik, Asha, get him upright. We'll sort out the spoils later. For now, let's get his pattern copied, then we'll keep him for a while. We'll need to question him," the Drow playing the Legion-General ordered. Augustus was dragged to his feet, his hands dragged down by the too-short chains embedded in the floor.

He stood there, hunched over, and glared up at them, making a plan. If he failed and died here, and the Drow tried to board his ship, they'd be in for a terrible shock, permanent even. Nobody but him and his personal guard knew Hellenica and several of her children were aboard and hidden in his cabin and the one next door.

He had no doubt that Hellenica could wipe the floor with the Drow, especially aided by her children, being fully rested and healed as she was now. But a gentleman never expected a lady to sully herself with such matters, so he'd make sure to slaughter them all first, if there was any way to manage it.

Augustus exhaled slowly and smiled at Asha as he stepped in close, relishing the look of confusion on the Drow's face and knowing now that it was some kind of illusion.

"Hi," Augustus said brightly. "Thanks for coming so close."

As Asha's face screwed up in sudden realization, Augustus' right hand flashed forward, the shackles cracking and barely slowing his hand as it landed on the hilt of his sword. Asha looked down, shocked, before Augustus's left hand smashed free of its restraint as well and closed around Asha's throat with crushing force.

Augustus yanked the blade free of the scabbard that was now tied to Asha's waist and slashed it blindly behind him, feeling it dig deep into cloth and flesh. The blade's signature ability triggered, blasting out a wave of fear that staggered his opponents.

Not all of them were affected; not even many of them, in truth, as most had high enough Intelligence, Constitution or Charisma scores to overcome the terror effect. But the brief moment of hesitation was all the distraction he needed.

The Primus twisted around expertly and kicked out, shucking the severely wounded figure off the sword before flipping it over and driving it up into the belly of Asha.

Augustus grunted, twisting the hilt as he searched internally until he felt something flutter, like a bag of butterflies pressed against the tip of the blade.

With one thrust, he skewered Asha's heart.

The rest of the room erupted in screams of dismay, shouts and demands, and the clank of the fully armored Drow in Legion plate as he rushed forward to engage Augustus.

"Let's get this over with, shall we?" The Legion Primus asked, grimly ripping the sword free and dropping Asha's corpse to the floor before dodging a bolt of lightning fired at him from the back of the room.

CHAPTER FORTY-FIVE

It was a little less than the three hours Tenandra had estimated when we began our descent to the landing field on the outskirts of the slave camp. Even as I looked down at it, I couldn't help but glare at the gaily decorated tents and snapping pennants. The encampment below appeared to be part slave market and part fair, making my blood boil at the overt spectacle as much as anything else.

"How did this happen?" I asked Grizz, who happened to be next to me. He shrugged and scratched one massive shoulder. The leather armor we'd found to outfit him and the rest of the party, in place of our Legion gear, strained to fit the man's musculature.

"Truthfully, I don't know," Grizz said slowly. "I think it was a gradual thing, like these things often are. I doubt anyone just woke up and said 'Today, I'm going to enslave my fellow citizens.' They probably started out with little things, like thefts, banditry, that kinda thing. Then they progressed, raiding small settlements, there are hundreds out there, after all."

"Really?" I asked, confused. "My map..."

"The map, if it's like most others, shows places that are important, along with the bigger villages or small towns. Most of the settlements out there are homesteads, two or three families that wanted a better life and went marching off with high hopes for the future," he explained.

"And?" I prompted.

"Then this happens." He gestured down at the camp. It was a sprawling affair composed of eleven wagons and a single ship moored in the mouth of the river. The other ship, which we'd been warned would be there as well, was steadily sailing out of sight already, headed to the south and the distant islands.

"If the slavers don't get them, the monsters often do, or the bandits, or the winter. I lost track of how many times we traveled out to a monster attack, passing through little homesteads that were empty again a few weeks later. A few months down the line, they had filled back up with new families. Worst were the ones who fell for 'resettlement,'" Grizz growled.

"What's that?" I asked.

"Nobles selling the homesteads," Grizz said grimly. "The settlements are on their land, so if they're empty, well, they belong to the noble. We always suspected that there were a few nobles selling the homesteads to the optimistic idiots, then selling the details to the slavers and selling the newly emptied homesteads again.

"Couldn't prove it, and there are too few of us to patrol the entire lot. So, instead, we'd take patrols out along the river near these markets when they sprang up; maybe we'd move into a newly 'abandoned' settlement. Have a few people standing around playing farmer. It worked now and then; the slavers would attack, and we'd slaughter them, then a new law was passed requiring us to inform the gate guards as to the destination we were headed for."

"And?"

"And the slavers started either not raiding or the teams we sent out didn't come back," Grizz said grimly.

"Fucking hell, man. You're saying that these bastards might have legionnaires as slaves?" I asked in a low growl.

"Nah, I doubt it." Grizz said grimly. "They'd have to take us alive for that, and I seriously doubt there's many of the Legion that they managed to do that with."

I shook my head in disgust, then raised my voice, addressing the group. "Remember, people, we have no idea about customs here nor about rules. All Lydia and Bane managed to get in specifics was that the slavers are split into three groups: the guards, the merchants and the *habieen*, or slave-masters." I worked to keep my voice outwardly calm, while inside, I seethed at their presence below us.

Amon's fury ate away at me as much as my own, and Oracle reinforced us both, creating a feedback loop that made my knuckles itch for someone to punch.

"We'll be approached by the guards when we land, and they'll decide if we should be allowed to join in. Slavers are a touchy lot, apparently; must be something to do with everyone wanting to slaughter them," Bane quipped.

"Once we get them to leave us be, probably with a bribe or two, we should be able to send out a couple of small teams to act as merchant and guard pairs. Apparently, the habieen don't move around much, preferring to stay together and make deals. The merchants deal with the day-to-day transactions of the camp, and the guards keep the peace."

"Peace?" I grunted. "What would slavers know of peace?"

"The habieen don't like to be bothered with the sounds of the camp, so the slavers are incredibly careful to keep their goods as quiet as possible. An irritated habieen tends to order people either maimed, muted–which is to have their tongue ripped out by pliers–or sent to the arena," Bane said.

"From what we learned from tha assholes," Lydia interrupted, jerking her thumb toward the caged group, "they usually deal with tha merchants an' guards almost exclusively. But when a new slaver arrives, they have to be checked to make sure they're not raiders. Us bein' in an airship means both sides are goin' to be incredibly careful. They'd do anythin' to get their hands on tha ship, as that would change things massively for slavers. That also means we, as another group of slavers, have to be ready to fight 'em off at any sign."

"So, there are lots of chances for things to get out of hand, then." I grimaced. "Tenandra, are you ready to hide things?"

"I am, Jax. Shall I begin?" she asked deferentially. I nodded, watching as the ship rippled. A slight wave of magic flowed over it, dulling the shine of the copper that she'd worked so hard to bring back and making the decks look dirty and damaged again.

"I'm sorry, Giint, but you know it'll raise too many questions otherwise," I said as he looked around mournfully one last time, then heading to the forward hold with a sad sigh.

I shook my head as he went, wishing I hadn't had to order this part of the plan. But the Gnomes were relentlessly hunted by slavers, their gifts making them ideal targets, so having a group of them wandering about the ship was just too much.

Instead, I had ordered them to hide, meaning that, for the next several hours, if not a day or more, while we searched the camp, they were to stay still and quiet in the bilges of the ship, a place filled with general sludge and crap.

Worst of all, I couldn't even give them drugs to make them happy, because I hadn't had the time to make more up. I'd spent the entire flight making a brace of healing potions to replace those we'd used in the fights earlier.

As soon as they were shut away, I nodded to Tenandra, who vanished, becoming a tiny, dark leech-like creature that made my skin crawl to look at. She was picked up by Arrin, who slipped her into his helm, where she'd be able to speak to him. She could also relay messages to me, should the need arise, via Oracle, who had done something similar and was getting comfortable inside Lydia's gear.

I could reach out to Oracle at any time, after all, so this way, if we needed to split up to search the camp, we could maintain contact between three teams.

The ship coasted down smoothly, arcing around and being guided to a clear space at the bottom of a bank, surrounded by caravans, by a large guard who flashed a mirror at us to make sure he had our attention.

I stood at the edge of the railing, watching as we came in for the landing. The ship's crew, who normally had little to do, thanks to Tenandra doing it all magically, began rushing about in a panic, adding to the impression that we'd only recently captured the ship.

The engines fired chaotically, the ship veering slightly off course before being corrected. We closed the last dozen meters, coming to a rest at the bottom of the slight gully. It was a little disconcerting to find that the sides of the bank were now higher than our deck, removing our defensive advantage should we need to make a quick getaway. If the ship had been a normal one that required crew to make the various adjustments, anyway.

Jian strode to the edge of the railing, one of the regular crew sliding the gangplank down for him and flinching as he aimed a casual kick at him for being too slow.

It was all part of the act, but still, Grizz and I followed Jian down the plank, with Lydia and Yen following us.

Once we reached the foot of the plank, Jian stepped off, and he stared coldly around as we spread out on either side, ready to protect our "master."

"Well?" Jian called out after a few seconds. "I have slaves to sell, who wants to buy?" At his proclamation, a small contingent of guards moved into view at the top of the bank to our right. We turned to face them and strode forward a few feet, ignoring the flickers of movement all around us as more and more people appeared. Some were simply curious about the new arrivals and the ship, no doubt, but others, heavily armed, were clearly considering trying their luck.

"State your business!" came a call from the group farther up the bank, and they parted to let a figure stride forward. He was rail-thin and tall, easily six and a half feet in height, dressed in gaudily colored robes and a long wrap that obscured his face.

"I am Jian Al'bayar, captain of this ship, and I want to sell my slaves. Who are you?" Jian called up, putting his knuckles on his hips and striking a pose.

"I am Saieed," the figure said smoothly, pulling the wrap back to show his face and making a few of those watching flinch away. The speaker was elven clearly, but where most Elves I'd met so far were either of the woodland variety and had tanned healthy skin, or they were Drow, with their characteristic grey tone, this individual was albino, with dead, white skin that practically glowed and strikingly pink eyes making me stare unconsciously.

"Just Saieed?" Jian demanded.

"That is all you need to know. Go, search their ship," Saieed ordered one of the guards next to him. He took off, followed by three others, marching down the bank toward us.

"Jian, make a show of trying to stop them; we'd never just let them board the ship if we were real slavers," I ordered in a low whisper.

"Halt!" he ordered. "I did not risk everything to capture this ship, just to have it taken by you! Your men are not welcome on my vessel!"

"I am Saieed. If you wish to sell your wares here, my men will search your ship. If not, take the rusting scow and leave."

"Rusting scow!" Jian snarled, taking a step forward. "My ship is a work of art! I will not have the likes of your men damage her, trying to steal whatever is not nailed down! No. You wish to search her, you may board with one guard!"

"I do not sully myself with such tasks." Saieed's response was cool, almost careless. "You wish to do business?"

"I do!" Jian insisted, puffing out his chest. "I am…"

"You are Jian; yes, I heard," Saieed remarked dryly. "This camp is the property of the habieen, Jian. As such, there are rules. These rules are simple: when a member of the habieen speaks, it is as law. The guard carries out these laws. If you wish to live to make deals with the merchant class, then you obey. Understand?"

"I do…" Jian started to reply, and Saieed waved a hand, making him stop as we all froze.

As soon as Saieed had gestured, the crowds around the gully had been roughly pushed aside, and over a dozen armed men stepped forward, all brandishing crossbows capable of punching holes in even Legion plate at this range, never mind the flimsy leather armor we'd donned to hide our identities.

"I have ordered that your ship be searched. Choose now, Jian; accept my order, or my men will search your ship over your bolt-riddled corpse."

"I…accept," Jian responded through gritted teeth.

"Very well." Saieed gestured, and a group of eight guards set off down the bank, passing us quickly and boarding the ship. Saieed beckoned Jian forward.

"You may approach, Jian Al'bayar, with one guard only."

Jian jerked his head to me, and I accompanied him, the others staying with the ship as we strode up the bank, coming to a halt at a gesture from one of the guards a few feet from Saieed.

"You wish to buy in the camp or sell?" Saieed asked, motioning for an aide to step forward, setting a table down at his side. The aide opened a ledger, flipping the book to the correct page and laying out a quill and inkpot before retreating.

I glanced at the aide, idly observing the bright white robes and silver bangles at wrists and throat…as well as the black filigreed manacle on the ankle that glowed subtly as I forced myself to look away from them.

I realized suddenly that I'd seen the person as an assistant first, then as a slave, before looking back and realizing that it was a man, last of all. Stunned, I wondered if that was how the slavers did it, seeing them as assets, rather than people.

481

I briefly met his kohl-lined eyes, finding a dull acceptance there, before looking away. If I saw more, I'd have too hard a time controlling myself.

"…raided a village of those my master had sworn protection to." Jian was saying. "Now my master has sent me to purchase back those sold in error and to sell those who raided the land to cover the expense."

"Who is your master?" Saieed asked carefully, noting something down.

"I am forbidden from speaking his name," Jian insisted, improvising for all he was worth. We'd expected, from what we'd been told, that we would be greeted by a few guards, we'd hand some coins over, and most of the team would watch over the ship, while the rest of us would go searching the camp. Instead, we were being questioned to shit, and Jian was having to make up a story on the spot to explain our presence.

I cursed inwardly as Jian spoke, realizing with hindsight that while the group would have probably accepted that from a small caravan without any issue, the ship made us either bigger fish or prey, and they were clearly trying to decide which we were.

"You cannot name your master, a master who offers protection to villages?" Saieed pressed, raising an eyebrow in suspicion. "You cannot reveal a being that clearly must be named or no village would pay for his protection. You also claim that a village was raided, and you bring the raiders as slaves to trade. Clearly, you have no issue with slavers, yet your guard stares around like he wishes to be at war…"

I had to stop myself from glaring at Saieed as the man went on.

"Perhaps we will examine the slaves you bring," Saieed said slowly. "Slaves can bring many solutions to problems, and occasionally, answers to our questions, provided they are asked in the right way." He smiled slowly, and the guards around us laughed, the sound disturbingly sycophantic.

"What about the slaves we wish to purchase?" Jian asked quickly. "Might we examine them while you examine ours?"

"Perhaps," Saieed said cryptically before looking down at the ship. A guard paused at the cage that held the former slavers from Cornut, then he spoke quickly to Tang, who lounged next to the cage. Tang looked up at us in question.

Jian glanced to me, and I gave the slightest of nods before he gestured grandly to Tang to open the cage. I found Saieed watching me, and I looked away again as though unconcerned, the entire time swearing at myself internally to use Oracle to speak through Tenandra, despite the time delay that would have caused.

I flicked my gaze down the bank to Grizz, Lydia, and Yen and made eye contact with each of them, visibly gripping the hilt of my sheathed sword.

Not only was our armor swapped out for this low-quality leather, but to allay suspicion, our real weapons were stowed away in our pouches and bags. We bore either the rusty, shitty steel taken from the slavers or the few average bits we'd collected from the guards we'd killed back at the village.

The others shifted, readying themselves just in case, in response to my subtle—*or as subtle as I ever got*—hint.

The guard on the ship yanked one figure out of the cage, dragging him across the deck, down the gangplank, and up the bank towards us.

As he came to a halt, I realized it was Berrin, Lydia's ex-husband. Oracle had healed his back this morning, despite our feelings on the man, simply because he was sod-all value if he died before we used him to get her mother free.

After being bodily hauled for several yards, he stumbled to a halt and fell on the ground when the guard shoved him forward. Trembling, he tried to get up and failed, looking up at Saieed imploringly.

"Well, well, Berrin," Saieed gloated softly, looking down at the figure before him with cool disdain. "I believe I warned you that those who steal from me have a way of becoming my property, now didn't I?"

The guard reached forward and ripped the gag free before I could stop him, and Berrin started speaking frantically.

"Saieed, it be a..." he managed to get out before the same guard punched him in the kidney, cutting his words off with a grunt of pain. Oracle had healed the broken spine, but out of respect for Lydia and all that Berrin had done to her, she'd not healed the rest, leaving him badly bruised and injured both internally and externally.

"You'll have plenty of time to explain things later, Berrin," Saieed purred, before turning to the guard captain. "Is the ship all it appears?"

"It is, Habieen Saieed." he said, bowing his head.

"Then I accept you, provisionally, into the first ring," Saieed said genially to Jian. "Both you, and your guard who is not a guard." He carefully regarding me.

I met his too-discerning gaze and inclined my head to him slowly.

"I do not question why the charade, for I do not care. I would have refused you access to the camp, despite the slaves you have to sell, as well as buy, but for two reasons."

"And those are?" I asked as Jian stepped back, letting me lead.

"First, this one." Saieed gestured to Berrin as the guard captain put a blade to his throat, keeping him still and silent. "Last time he was here, he cheated me. I had begun looking into his home, planning to raid it for him and his fellows. I would teach them a lesson. Are there others of his caravan below?"

"His entire group is in the cage on the deck," I confirmed before shrugging unconcernedly. "Those who survived, anyway."

"Excellent. I will purchase them all, at three silver per head."

"Ten gold," I negotiated calmly, having absolutely no idea what their worth was, but being damn sure that less than that was insane.

"Twenty silver," Saieed countered, raising his hand to stay my response. "I will give twenty silver per head, if they are in truth the group he was last seen with. In return, the slaves he brought, each of which, save one, were sold for the mines. In this light, I will negotiate with their new owner for you to obtain a fair price for them."

"Who was the one that wasn't sold to the mines? And what's your other reason?" I asked.

"The last one was sold to the Slavers of Menneheim to replace one bound for the Arena at Skeld, and they have already departed. I understand the one that they replaced was to be part of a matched set. Regardless, that ship has already sailed. The other reason is that I believe in investment."

"Oh?" I asked cautiously.

"You are his master, yes?" he asked me, and I nodded. "Excellent. Your name?"

"Thomas." I said without hesitation, knowing damn well that Jax would get too much attention.

"Very well, Thomas. I believe that, if you are already charging villages for protection and have captured a gnomish airship, then I wish to know more about you. Until now, I had been unaware of your existence."

"You're one of the habieen?" I asked.

"I am; I rule the Great Plains," he declared proudly, watching me.

"Not heard of that," I said noncommittally.

"Not many on this side of the dagger have," he admitted. "It is a long journey by foot, even longer by ship, despite it being more comfortable."

"The dagger...the Great Plains are on the far side of the mountain range?" I started in surprise.

He nodded, appearing pleased.

"I'd like to hear about the lands there." I forced a smile, while the albino stared into my eyes, watching for something. "Perhaps you could summon those who were taken, and you could tell me more while we wait? In exchange, I believe I'll accept the offer you made of twenty silver for each of the slaves I have, all sixteen, save this one and one other." I said, gesturing to Berrin.

"And your price for this one?" Saieed asked slowly, his eyes tensing as he studied me.

"This one is free. A gift to you that I hope you'll take your time to slaughter as painfully as possible." Berrin's face paled as I pasted on an ingratiating smile.

"I accept your gracious gift," Saieed said, smiling widely in return. "Captain, take Berrin to the center of camp and nail him to the board of disobedience. We will be along shortly to discuss his future." Saieed gestured to the side, and a short woman appeared with a pitcher of wine and two golden cups, pouring one for him and one for me.

"The other one that I have is a bit more costly," I said, accepting the cup of wine and gazing into its depths, noting it was a deep carmine with a slight glow to it.

"Oh?" Saieed regarded me with curiosity, reclining back on a seat that was quickly produced for him. I accepted the one that was offered to me, noting that the guards around us hadn't relaxed in the slightest, despite the sudden 'friendly' atmosphere and that the crossbow wielders were still hanging around.

I got the distinct feeling we were being played, but I went along with it.

"He was the Reeve of the village of Cornut," I said. "If you wish to buy him, well, I think ten gold is a fair price, considering his worth to his family?"

"I am not his family," Saieed pointed out, taking a sip from the wine and gesturing for me to do the same.

"Neither am I," I stated, smiling. "But I'd imagine you would have contacts in the city that could deal with such a detail? I find myself unwilling to return to Himnel, what with my business taking me south and out to sea shortly."

"Perhaps," Saieed mused. "What do you think of the wine?"

I lifted the cup, smelling it and swirling it around like I'd seen them do on TV, and like the assholes that used to try to show off used to in the bars where I worked. It smelled like wine to me, and as I took a second sip, it tingled for a brief moment before my tongue went ever so slightly numb.

I looked down at the cup again, bringing up my screens and searching, finding the notification I knew was going to be there.

Beware!

You have been poisoned with a concoction of Asp's Venom and Nightingale Leaf. This dual-layered poison has the effect of being both tremendously painful and forcing the target to tell the truth for 37 minutes.

-30 health per second for 60 seconds.

Oracle went to work, the Cleanse spell almost, but not quite, getting rid of the poison. She had to hit it again before finally using Surgeon's Scalpel and practically burning it from my system in her diligence and annoyance. My mana dipped slightly, as did my health, but the notification vanished as she made whatever adjustments necessary. I smiled placidly, meeting his falsely solicitous gaze, while Oracle spoke in my mind.

"Easily removed, now that I know what it is, but he doesn't know that." she pointed out.

"Thanks, my love!" I sent to her, then answered Saieed aloud.

"It's interesting; a nice little bite to it," I said nonchalantly, passing it to the server, who offered me a crimson healing potion in its place. "Do you drink it often?"

"Often enough that I have become immune to its effects. Sadly, building up the resistance needed was costly and painful, yet it has paid for itself over the years. You understand your position, yes?" Saieed asked, leaning forward.

"I understand that you've poisoned me and that you think this will get you what you want, which is what, by the way?" I asked, wishing for another drink of the wine, finding that it was actually tastier than the wine I'd tried back on Earth. For the first time, I'd actually found something I'd drink on a date without having to choke it down. Well, if not for the whole poisoned thing.

"You, of course," Saieed's reply was eerily calm. "You will now tell me who you really are and what you planned to do here."

The next ten minutes were spent with me spinning an amazing bullshit whirlwind of a story about being a bandit who'd lucked into an airship, taking the chances that life offered me, all the while sipping from the healing potion and keeping the charade up by wincing and pretending to have to force the words out occasionally.

Oracle passed the word to the others about what had happened, and to be ready. When I finally wrapped up the magnificent fable, she whispered to me in my mind.

"I think he actually believed all that rubbish! Where did you come up with the details from?"

"Movies; tens of thousands of hours spent watching movies!" I sent to her, having to stifle a grin.

"So, what happens now?" I asked eventually.

"Now, we make a deal for your future, and perhaps you will even be permitted to leave here as captain of your ship again, after an Oath of subservience is extracted, of course," Saieed said, his smile predacious. "It was indeed my lucky day to have been watching when your ship arrived."

"Oh, you'll be surprised!" I said, smiling back at him as I caught sight of the guard captain running back toward us. "Is that your man?" I gestured over his shoulder.

As Saieed turned to look, I sent the order to Oracle, and she relayed it quickly.

"NOW!"

As soon as my message was received, three things happened practically simultaneously.

Jian, who had been playing the part of the figurehead, dressed in silks, and by now almost completely ignored, saw my nod and the way my hands filled with magic. He plunged his hands into the pockets of his robes.

Pockets that led straight to the open necks of the pouches he'd stowed beneath.

They caused his robes to ripple slightly as he yanked both silvery scythes free, spinning and beheading the guards on either side of Saieed.

Arrin leaped into view, both hands full of Magic Missiles, ten glowing darts in all. He'd been holding the spell in readiness for the last couple of minutes, ever since Oracle told him the plan we'd come with was screwed and to move to plan F. F, predictably, for one of my plans, stood for "fuck it."

He released all ten spells, four at two of the guards who were still aboard the ship, two each. The fiery bolts slammed into their open-faced helms, killing them instantly.

One of the other two guards who had stayed aboard was gutted by Tang, the other smashed into paste by Bob, who'd taken a liking to a warhammer back at the village.

Arrin's remaining six darts slammed into six separate guards on one side of the bank that surrounded the front of the ship in a rough V shape.

Only two of them were crossbow wielders, but the aim was as much to disrupt them all as it was to pick off the crossbowmen themselves. After all, this was a slaver camp. The only innocents here weren't going to be standing around, armed and watching the ship with a lascivious attitude.

While those attacks roared out, I stood, channeling my own mana into a rapidly growing ball of flame between the palms of my hands. The blazing sphere left my hands with a roar, slamming into the onrushing captain's face to send him hurtling backward, screaming. The Fireball exploded and surrounded him in flames, setting light to at least a dozen others.

"Slaves on the ground, NOW," I ordered, my voice carrying an unmistakable aura of command. In light of not being countermanded by their actual owners, who were too busy with other things, they all dropped, fast.

"You know, I think he was coming to tell you that Berrin knew something he thought you should know." I said, frowning at Saieed.

"And what would that be, fool?" Saieed asked me, seemingly totally unconcerned.

"Possibly that this was a trap?" I suggested.

Yen unleashed her Flamespears on the other side of the bank, the massive projectiles detonating and sending people flying.

I heard crossbows firing, screams, shouts, and spells going off all around us, yet Saieed just shrugged.

"You think this is the first time a rebellion has been attempted? Or that this is the first time we have been attacked?" he scoffed, slowly standing. "We of the habieen have been raided more times than we care to recount. In fact, many of those who serve as guards were once raiders..."

I glanced down at one of the guards, then across at the others that were slowly drifting into view. Caravans, tents and makeshift pavilions opened. Surprising numbers of guards and heavily armed slaves marched out, many of them screaming as cramped muscles from long hours in constricted conditions were forcibly made to move.

"You kept them in boxes?" I asked, stunned as the side of a caravan opened. Men and women fell out, glowing manacles fixed on their right ankles and daggers clenched in their fists.

Behind them, small chests, spaces I know I couldn't have squeezed into were revealed. The men and women inside started whimpering as the magic forced them upright, weapons held at the ready to defend their masters.

"We keep the unworthy in many ways," Saieed explained nonchalantly. "Some are permitted sunlight and the freedom to control their own bodies; others are not, but are simply fed and watered once per day and exercised for an hour each at night to maintain their usefulness. Beyond that, a simple enchantment keeps the smell down, and we have the luxury of hundreds of battle-ready slaves at hand, men and women we need never pay, never free, and never fear disloyalty from.

"And now we have an airship, which will accelerate our plans for this side of the dagger nicely, so thank you," came another voice. I turned my head, seeing another Elf stepping forward from the shadows. His dark grey skin and bleached white hair allowed me to identify him immediately, and I looked back to the albino and grunted in recognition.

"A goddamn Drow albino; bet you fuckers are rare." I nodded in sudden understanding.

"Surprisingly so, despite every effort made. After all, an albino is assumed to be a regular weak Elf, rather than a glorious follower of the Lady of the Night," the new Elf replied, smiling and revealing pointed, perfectly white teeth.

"Yeah, still a waste of skin, as far as I'm concerned, motherfucker." I chuckled.

"Now, you will order your friends to cease all resistance, or we will kill them. If you are incredibly lucky, I may add you to my guard. After all, it seems I need a new captain," Saieed said placidly.

"You think that providing evidence that you're even more of a gang of colossal shitheads than I thought you were means I'll surrender?" I asked, incredulous. "Why would that be?"

"Because I lied." Saieed's smile deepened. "There's nothing for you here. Those that Berrin sold were never going to be returned to you, and your ship is surrounded. You cannot make it back to your vessel alive, and your friends will die without your help."

"And if you think that was all he lied about?" the other Drow crowed, "It wasn't! The poison you ingested is a wonder of alchemy; once you have permitted it into your body, you will never be free of it. You must take an antidote morning and night for the rest of your life, lest it return to…"

"Oh, is that all?" I interrupted with a laugh. "Well, that's a fucking relief. Luckily, I'm a filthy, lying bastard, too!" I leaned forward conspiratorially as the roar of spells flew past outside. "I'm not Thomas!" I confided, smiling broadly.

"You think we care about your name?!" Saieed asked, curling his lip in contempt.

"Oh, that's not all. You see, I didn't come to buy the slaves; I came to free them, and believe me, that's an important difference!" I rolled my shoulders and straightened up in anticipation, followed by stretching my hands out in front of me and interlocking the fingers, cracking them as I prepared.

"You see, Fuckface One and Fuckface Two," I said, nodding to Saieed and the other Drow as I named them. "I'm even more of a filthy, lying bastard than you, because I lied *twice*!" Even knowing they would never get the reference, I shrugged, took a deep breath, and reached both inwards and outwards, triggering the ability that I continually swore I'd lay off using. It was so effective, it might as well be crack, with how hard it was for me to avoid.

The magic rippled through me as Saieed and his brother, friend, lover, or whatever, threw up their shields. The bright blue lightning that sparked to life, cracking across my skin and flowing up and down my frame, brought a new light to the dreary day. As it jumped across my body, it also flowed into the dirt, grounding itself and leaping across the short distance to the shields. The crackling beam flickered across them, turning them dark for brief seconds.

"Is that it?" Saieed jeered from behind his. "You are weak, and so are..."

On her way to me, Oracle passed Jian as he ran for it, both getting away from me and hurrying to help the others as fast as he could. I saw the way that two of the guards at the back of the group collapsed like puppets with their strings cut as Bane released the grip he'd had on them, He recognized what was coming and ran for it as well.

Oracle reached me in seconds, slowing and twisting around, hovering directly behind me, attaching to me by our magic, as she completed the link. Her form had shifted from the leech she'd reluctantly mirrored back to a tiny humanoid as she flew.

She floated there with her back to me, watching outward as the lightning flowed into her and back into myself, no longer grounding out and being wasted. Her senses fed into me as the world around us changed, the magical senses she was naturally blessed with augmenting my own more mundane ones.

Power flowed through us, as our mana burned to provide the first spark, then the Imperial Ability gifted us with more. Where my mana should have bottomed out, instead, we started to lift from the ground, and her appearance changed again.

Her hair floated free, beginning to glow with a bright, blue-white light, as did her eyes, until all of her began to shine.

Lightning crackled down my arms, tiny arcs flashing from finger to finger, flooding through my body as my eyes lit with blue fire.

I reached out, the surrounding threat gone from my mind as the building power demanded all my attention. I sensed on the very periphery of my mind dozens then hundreds of people who had been running toward us. I sensed the fights faltering as people turned to stare at the expanding source of the bright light. I felt the enslaved people, easily nine in ten of those around the ship, faltering as their masters ceased giving them orders.

I slowly lifted higher in the air, the mana around the mouth of the river swirling and pouring toward me as I sucked at it greedily, funneling it into the mana construct. Thinking quickly, Oracle formed some of the power into a shield.

The lightning flashed from me to Oracle and back again, growing stronger and stronger as we floated higher, tugging upon the strands of the lives below me.

Each time I used this power, I learned more, I *understood* more. For the first time, I sensed the threads of life that ran from people. I sensed them reaching out and linking themselves to others, the infinitesimal gossamer-like strands of emotional connections, the thicker, spidery silk of family ties, the hints of love and rivalry, the million connections we all make with people around us, reinforced by the thick strands of the bonds my Oathsworn had to me, and I to them.

Thin, steel-strong connections radiated throughout me, but not from me to everyone, so thick they almost obscured reality, numbering in the tens of millions.

Then I sensed the bonds of slavery.

Where the bonds of sworn Oaths were thick, they were also shot through with the gold of love, the silver of duty and honor, and the thousands of colors and combinations of reasons people swore their lives away.

I saw hints of prayers for power, of whispered begging for the strength to defend their loved ones. I felt the relief, bordering on adoration, of those I had saved, and the frantic screaming in the depths of those I hadn't yet, and many that I never could.

I sensed it all, and I searched for the bonds of slavery, thick and grey, dull as stone, and ten times as strong and enduring. The weight of them crushed those beneath, and I opened my mouth unknowingly.

"I SEE YOU," I said, wonderingly. "I SEE YOU ALL. I FEEL YOU AND YOUR SOULS."

My words echoed through the air, reverberating in a way that was both terrifying and unnatural. Yet, for those imprisoned, those who begged silently for mercy, for relief, and for the release of death, my words brought comfort as well as deadening their terror.

"I AM JAX, SCION OF THE EMPIRE, HIGH LORD OF DRAVITH, AND I AM YOUR LORD. I CLAIM YOU NOW AS MY OWN, ALL WHO WERE WRONGFULLY IMPRISONED." My voice crackled with power, the gnat stings of fireballs and other combat spells fizzling against me as fast as they were hurled at our twin floating forms.

We slowly spiraled around each other, and the magic grew, the light bright enough that it would be visible for tens, if not hundreds of miles, as we climbed higher.

"I AM JAX AMON, HEIR TO THE EMPIRE, AND I CLAIM MY RIGHTS TO THIS LAND. I CLAIM THE BLOOD THAT IS SPILLED AND THAT WHICH YET SHALL BE. I CLAIM THE LIVES THAT ARE NOW AND THOSE THAT ARE YET TO BE BEGUN."

I heard the rumble of my voice, like thunder from a clear sky, as it rang out.

"I CLAIM MY RIGHT OF EMPIRE AND DOMINION, AND I SWEAR BY MY SOUL TO HONOR, PROTECT, AND SERVE. I SHALL FREE YOU, AND TIE YOU. I SHALL LIFT YOU UP AND BIND YOU TO ME. I SHALL HEAL YOU AND SCOUR THE DARKNESS FROM YOU."

I felt them, the living and the unquiet dead around me, for dozens of feet, then hundreds. Then, as the miles passed, as the lightning lashed outwards from me, flashing up into the heavens and down into the earth, the power slammed out, only to be replaced by the swirling, frantically building vortex of the land's ambient mana for dozens of miles, all of it being sucked into me.

"I SEE YOU, AND I KNOW YOU. I FEEL YOUR BONDS, AND I DECLARE THEM TO BE NO MORE. WITH THE BEGINNING OF THE NEW AGE ARE ALL BONDS BROKEN AND FORGED ANEW!"

I felt the vortex tugging at other concentrations of mana, unravelling them, ripping them free of the graceless, pathetic forms they had been bound into. I sensed with the last faint extremities of my mind that weren't consumed by the building crescendo, the shields of dozens upon dozens of asshole Drow and their fellow beings popped like soap bubbles as the mana forming them was whipped free and the storm grew.

Tenandra reached out frantically, trying to pull the power back into her core as it was sucked dry, and I fueled the core with a fragment of my mind. The sphere blazed into overpowered life as the entire ship shook, its mana channels scoured free of all damage. The subroutines which Tenandra had been carefully hoarding flared to life in a sudden blaze of glory.

"I SEE YOU ALL, AND I REMEMBER. I KNOW YOUR WEAKNESSES. I KNOW YOUR FAILURES. I DECLARE THOSE WHO HAVE BEEN TAKEN TO BE FREE. I DECLARE THOSE WHO HAVE BEEN ENSLAVED FOR NO CRIME AGAINST ME AND MY EMPIRE TO BE FREE.

"I PASS JUDGEMENT ON ALL SLAVERS INSIDE THE BOUNDAIRES OF THE EMPIRE. I DECLARE THEM ALL TO BE ANATHEMA. LET THOSE WHO KILL A SLAVER BE ABSOLVED OF THEIR CRIMES, LET THOSE WHO FREE A SLAVE BE HONORED, AND LET THOSE WHO SHELTER THE SLAVER BE AFRAID, FOR THE LEGION SEES ALL. I AM THE EMPIRE, AND I CLAIM YOU ALL. I DECLARE YOU TO BE FREE OF ALL TIES SAVE MY OWN, NOW AND FOREVERMORE."

I drew in a final deep breath, and I spoke the words Amon demanded of me.

"I AM JAX AMON. I AM AMON'S DESCENDANT, AND I CLAIM HIS OATHS AS MY OWN."

The power tore from me as I fell from the air, hundreds of feet up. My body plummeted toward the ground as the massive vortex of mana answered my summons and that of the Imperial Ability through me.

As I lost consciousness, and my notifications list exploded in frantic demands for attention. My eyes closed, the wind whistling as my fall built to a crescendo. Out of the blue, strong arms wrapped around me, a steady beat of huge wings slowing my fall.

"Dammit, Jax, it's supposed to be me before ye," I heard a voice whisper to me, filled with unshed tears. My lips quirked into the beginnings of a smile. Even my troubled soul accepted that now I was safe, that nothing could reach me, so long as my Valkyrie stood guard.

THOMAS

"**Y**ou did well, boy," the voice praised, and Thomas straightened up instinctively as Edvard stepped out of the small room, carefully closing the door behind him.

Thomas craned to look past his master and sponsor, gaining a brief glimpse of the small room filled with healers and priests surrounding the still, bone-white naked figure on the bed.

"P-paladin, I…"

Edvard held up one hand, shaking his head in negation.

"Lad, you ran over a hundred miles through recently claimed enemy land, carrying your sergeant on your back while sharing your own blood to keep her alive. Take a minute and recover."

"I am recovered!" Thomas snapped, a desperate fury filling him. "I am recovered, and I'm goddamn pissed off thrice over! Why haven't they healed her?"

"She has been healed," Edvard said. "Her body rejected it." The Dark Paladin watched Thomas carefully for a few seconds then nodded as though coming to a decision. Reaching out and putting one hand on Thomas's shoulder, he gently but firmly turned him aside.

"Come, Thomas, walk with me. We will discuss the apostate and the next steps to be taken."

Thomas reluctantly allowed himself to be drawn along.

The pair traversed down the long, onyx hallway, the clinking of the armored legionnaires' sabatons echoing as they crossed from the plush red carpet of the priestly areas into the more sparsely furnished warriors' areas. The pair moved down a short series of steps and slipped through the massive latched door of the battlements access.

As soon as the door was open, a tiny fraction of the weight Thomas was bearing fell away, carried free with the echoing of the seabirds and the crash of the waves from far beneath them.

The two men moved out, walking a dozen meters along the battlements, before Edvard turned and leaned against the crenellated stone, looking out across the small bay and over the city of Himnel.

"So, lad, tell me again what happened, from the beginning of the attack until you arrived here. She's truly being helped now, so banish her from your mind," Edvard ordered, not unkindly.

Thomas braced against the wall next to him, staring down at the waves flowing in and crashing against the rocks far below. "What happened?" He muttered. "It was a normal night. We'd covered a good distance, little less than we'd hoped for, but still. We'd hit a bog about an hour before, and the Trailmasters had to solidify the surface, bringing some of the surrounding rock inward. It'd tired them out, slowing us a little, so we camped, maybe a half mile from where we'd planned, I think?"

Thomas flicked a bit of loose rock off the battlement and watched it fall as he remembered that last night with his squad. The good-natured laughing, the abuse, the way Coran had screamed over the spider Turk had thrown at him.

The damn thing had been nearly a foot across, and Coran had smacked it hard enough with his mace that it had exploded, covering him in chitinous bits and thousands of tiny baby spiders.

They'd all laughed their asses off, until the little bastards started biting. Then it'd been a race to burn them all, while not setting fire to the forest.

"So, a normal day, nothing out of the ordinary?" Edvard probed carefully.

"No sir," Thomas said, biting back a sob at the vision of his friends fighting and laughing, the horseplay, the fun of it all. "We ate our meals, went to bed, stood our watch, and we'd just gotten back to sleep when it started."

"Describe it," Edvard said firmly.

"There was no warning." Thomas clenched his jaw. "No call for quarter or to surrender. The first we knew about it was the attack; arrows and crossbow bolts, dipped in poison, slamming into everyone, people screaming and throwing up everywhere. Something about the poison made it so they couldn't stand without being sick, then came the magic. Fireballs by the dozen, it felt like; but maybe ten really, I don't know? They were all targeted into the Trailmasters and the officer quarters; they took those out fast."

"Any survivors?"

"Only one, and he didn't last more than a few minutes," Thomas admitted, deliberately saying nothing more about that. "Then they pulled back, and it was, it…it was a clusterfuck."

"A cluster…fuck?" Edvard asked.

"Everyone just went berserk. How dare they attack us? I was getting my armor on, and people were streaming past us. The entire camp was up and screaming, chasing a few dozen of them.

"Belladonna was with them, trying to beat some sense into our soldiers, to spread them out. But they ignored her, desperate for blood. I'd been sleeping in most of my armor, anyway, too tired to change out of it. So I was dressed first, and I took off after them.

"By the time I made it to the chokepoint, most of the legion were gone, and some spell had gone off. Belladonna was down, injured, and a ritual circle was starting up. I dove in, got her out, and saw the one who'd cast it, standing proud as fucking punch on the ridge."

Thomas shook his head, looking back at that memory and silently cursing him.

"I fired off a spread of Magic Missiles, aimed at him, and he fired a fireball, before using an Ability to jump down to me."

"How far did he jump?"

"Uh, I don't know. A hundred feet?" Thomas mumbled, taken aback. "Sir, it was pitch black and heavily wooded; I honestly don't know."

"Fine, fine; go on," Edvard said, gesturing for Thomas to continue.

"He came for me, and we fought. He used some kind of fancy swordstaff, so I used Bella's to counter him. He was good, though, sir, damn good. He would have had me, if not for Turk. He took the asshole in the side, smashed him into a tree, and started battering him. Then the bastard slashed Turk's face off."

"Explain."

"The helm he wore; the others didn't have their fucking stupid plumes on, but he did. Damn thing was shiny, though. Turned out, it was a mess of tiny razor blades. He used it on Turk's face, shredded it to the bone. Then he just…flew up. Like really flew, up into the air. Fired off this spell that made everything fall into the center of it; some kind of gravity magic, I'd guess."

"I knew it," Edvard swore, shaking his head.

"Sir?" Thomas asked.

"Go on, lad, quickly now."

"Uh, well, Turk survived it, Shen didn't, and a lot of others got injured. I was helping Turk and Bella when the circle ran out, and it was like the floodgates opened. Everyone just took off roaring.

"There'd been a legionnaire in the path, and we'd caught him. He was…well, people were smearing bits of him on the trees as they chased the rest, made them wild.

"The next thing I knew, the entire forest lit up. Had to be some kind of trap. I'd barely managed to get Bella and Turk back awake. Turk was bad, like I'd never seen. His armor was twisted and cutting his bones, for fucks sake. There just wasn't a way to remove it. Even if we had a blacksmith and a fucking healer, he'd still be dying.

"Bella was furious, barely conscious, yet still pouring her healing potion on Turk's face when a piece of a tree hit her. It was like an airship had a hook in her at full speed, sir. One minute, she was there; the next, she was ten feet away, this chunk of wood sticking out of her." Thomas swallowed hard, shaking his head before forcing himself to go on, seeing the way Edvard was watching him.

"I picked her and Turk up, and I headed back to camp, sir. Three others made it back, and I rallied those who'd survived. We patched everyone up as best we could, and I got Bella sane enough to order a return. Turk took over from her and officially raised me to sergeant…then he…he…" Thomas stifled a sob as he struggled to get his voice under control.

"It's okay, lad. I know what has to be done sometimes. Move on."

"Thank you, sir," Thomas whispered. "We left the carts with the gear on them, and we started to run. I made an IV drip from me to Bella, then…"

"A what?" Edvard asked curiously.

"An…oh. An IV or intravenous drip, sir. I connected my veins to hers, figuring that I regenerate my health really fast, and with Nimon's gift, she might have a chance if I could give her blood faster than she was bleeding out. It worked; she lived, anyway, but she changed, sir. She got paler, weaker, then she started needing more of my blood, but no matter how much I gave her, she just…she never seemed to get enough. I'd left the column by then, had her strapped to my back. I knew she was bleeding internally, and her only chance was if I ran, so I did."

"There's still some of the advance team out there? Heading this way?" Edvard questioned. Thomas nodded, making him grunt. "Very well, lad. Well done. Go get some sleep, eat your own body weight in meat, and drink good ale in the high commissary, you hear me? Tell the commissar I told them to give you as much as you can handle, on my orders, then go sleep. We'll talk later."

"Sir, about Bella..."

"All that can be done is being done, Thomas. If you'd not done what you did, she'd be dead, but... Nimon only grants the Dark Gift the way He does with good reason. Without the excess in the chamber... well, she's getting the best care possible now. Go rest, and if it's decided to take her to the chamber, we'll come for you.

"If she dies, I'll make sure you know and get a chance to say goodbye. Now rest, and prepare. You need a new squad, and you'll be going back out soon, this time with the entire Dark Legion behind you. The road was made close enough that we can send a force along it, maybe even..."

Attention, Citizens of the Territory of Dravith!

Lord Jax, Imperial Scion, Master of the Great Tower, and High Lord of Dravith, today and effective immediately, revokes the title of Reeve of Cornut, Resheck Dumbarton, stripping him of lordship of the Village of Cornut, all additional titles, and possessions, and declares him outlaw.

Let no citizen offer the criminal Resheck succor, lest their titles be stripped from them and their lives declared forfeit.

All Hail Lord Jax of Dravith!

"Nimon!" Edvard swore, before starting to laugh.

"What is it, sir?" Thomas asked, confused.

"The fool! We know where he is!" Edvard pulled out a map and started working out distances and marking lines on it, running through quick calculations before rousing and looking up at Thomas. "Get to commissary. Eat and drink, but only water now, lad. Soon we march!"

"Lord Edvard!" a shout came from the Tower, and they both looked up.

"The Archpriest demands..."

"Yes, yes!" Edvard yelled up, cutting him off. "Tell him I'm on my way!"

Thomas saluted Edvard, who paused before leaving, taking the time to look Thomas over again.

"Thomas, you're a hell of a soldier, and I do not regret the morning that you turned up at the gates of the camp. Remember that. Now go, lad. As a soldier, you should have learned by now, never pass up a chance to eat your fill!"

With that, he was off, hurrying across the battlements and back inside the citadel. Thomas turned away again, reluctant to go and eat while Bella fought for her life and others from the column struggled through the jungle.

Thomas went back to overlook the sea, staring out across the crashing waves and watched as a body from washout bay was slowly torn apart, the various freaky as hell kinds of marine life making short work of whoever it had been.

Thomas winced, hoping that whoever had decided to take that way out of training had died quickly. With an internal shudder, he dismissed it from his mind and headed back inside the citadel.

He moved through the halls, descending from the nicer areas of the citadel into soldier territory. The massive building was spread out over nearly thirty floors, the uppermost levels given over exclusively to clerics and upper priests, then champions, paladins, and so on. Then came the regular and trainee priests, and finally, ceremonial areas, such as the chamber where Thomas had been sliced and diced in order to accept the black blood of Nimon into his body.

Fortunately, and most importantly to the soldiers of the Dark Legion, there were also three commissaries that were available to them inside the building, with two more out in the training grounds. Depending on your rank, you were allowed in different ones.

With Edvard's direct order, he was permitted in the one that the citadel reserved for officers, and he was going to damn well make the most out of it.

*

"He's laughing at you and your God just as much as he is Himnel and me, Archpriest Baruman," Barabarattas said, sitting forward and licking his lips nervously. Even now, more than a week after having his title stripped from him, the thought of his guard's reactions upon first seeing him after that upstart had stolen his title still rankled. "With all that he's done, I mean, he's been declared an apostate already by your God! Surely you can see the need to strike with your full force!"

"A hammer is not needed when a tap is sufficient, my child," Archpriest Baruman intoned, sitting back in the large, wing-backed chair and carefully regarding the sweating man seated across from him. He was almost ready, Baruman judged.

"A tap?!" Barabarattas screeched. "He's looted my city, slaughtered my forces, and stripped me of my title! He's bombarded your camp! He openly mocks you and all you stand for, your God included, and…"

"Our God," Baruman corrected coldly. "You say 'your God,' as though He is not your master as well. Perhaps you do not follow in His teachings as carefully as you claim? Perhaps this is why we rarely see you at the citadel and why you resist my reasonable requests?"

"Our God!" Barabarattas agreed quickly. "And no, my Lord Archpriest, I am a faithful follower of the one true God. I simply…"

"Because there are solutions available to the church in this situation. After all, your cousin Hern was once considered for the priesthood, before being pulled back into the noble path by his brother's death…perhaps we should speak to him. Raising him to city lord once the pretender is dealt with, and recognizing his claim, would be easier than all we must do to reinstate you."

"Hern is an idiot! He would have the city in flames inside a year; you know this! Less than half the nobility would follow him; none of the merchant class would support him."

"Yet with the full support of the church, he would need none of that."

"Because you'd be pulling his strings!" Barabarattas accused Baruman.

"Let us speak plainly, Barabarattas," Baruman said, smiling coldly. "You need us far more than we need you. In fact, it is only the remaining loyalty of a few key supporters that has permitted you to remain in this keep, let alone free, when many would happily seize you and hang you."

"I…" Barabarattas whispered, swallowing hard and sitting back, knowing he had only two cards left to play.

"I offer now what I've offered before: we will aid the City of Himnel, the Dark Church will assist in the governing of the territory, adding our officers and paladins to your guard, and our priests will spread throughout the city, bringing healing to those who deserve it. Our slaves will be put to work on the City of Himnel's projects, speeding production of the new ships and defenses, for example." Baruman smiled as he gestured around the room.

"You need no longer skulk in here, my dear *Lord Barabarattas.* The Scion of the Empire may have stripped you of your title, but upon his death, the Great God will return it to you. In the meantime, any who refuse to bend the knee will have it bent for them, forcibly if need be, by the church.

"All you need to do is accept that divine authority, that of the God himself, is higher than Imperial authority when you do regain control of the city. You will swear an Oath now, and when the time comes, you will swear to follow. If you cannot see the sense of this…well…Hern…"

"I know what you're asking for!" Barabarattas snapped. "You want to turn my city into a holy city! You'd be in charge here, not me!"

"Not so," Baruman soothed. "I'd simply rule over the ecclesiastical side of things. You'd still be the lord of the city; the master, under the God Nimon…"

"And the laws?" Barabarattas asked after pondering for a long moment, chewing on his knuckle.

"A few simple changes, nothing more. As always, you and your chosen would be above them, only the peasants and lesser nobility would be held to account. After all, who cares if a peasant kills another and is killed in turn or made a slave in the pursuit of justice?"

"Peasants? Not the nobles?" Barabarattas repeated, glaring at Baruman. "We'd be exempt?"

"Just as you are now. No laws would apply to you that didn't before, the punishments would simply be held for review, in some cases. Why execute someone who could be useful? Perhaps instead, a bounty could be paid to your personal coffers; a donation, if you will?"

"For any slaves you took?" Barabarattas asked quickly. "I'd receive a bounty for any of them? How much?"

"It depends on the skill. Shall we say a copper for a peasant, a silver for an apprentice, ten for a journeyman, and five gold for a master?" Baruman ruminated, rubbing his chin as though just picking the numbers at random.

"No!" Barabarattas snapped, before countering. "A gold for the apprentice, ten for the journeyman, and a hundred for a master."

"You drive a hard bargain, my friend," Baruman said slowly, making a show of reluctance, while inwardly he laughed and capered.

"And the guard!" Barabarattas snapped. "If you expect your Dark Legionnaires to help lead them, then you can pay for them! I want a force on the walls; I want the guard brought back up to full strength, and not the fodder! The Elites!"

"We can stretch to that," Baruman agreed with a sinister smile. "Provided, in turn, the army is folded into the Dark Legion. After all, they will need to be retrained to understand our ways."

"My personal guard will be exempt, as will I and those I choose, from any and all new laws and any additional ecclesiastical taxes. All my taxes remain in place, and I receive the full amount, with half of any new taxes you enforce!"

"A third, and the church is exempt from all taxation. Forever." Baruman countered.

"Half, and you pay tax for thirty years, then free of tax," Barabarattas countered, not caring in the slightest if he bankrupted the city once he was no longer lord of it. He'd not live another thirty years, he suspected. In truth, he'd be lucky to last a week without the church's aid as it was.

"Half, we pay taxes for five years, but it's to your personal coffers, not the city. Then the church is free of all taxes in perpetuity, and any territory we conquer along with the city is run in the same way." Baruman threw in that little addendum negligently at the end, making Barabarattas pause.

If they managed to kill this upstart scion, then wouldn't they effectively take over the Empire? If so, he'd no longer be a city lord. He'd be able to force the legion to obey, as that asshole had. He could take his gold and more; outfit ships and travel to the continent of Skelemon far to the south.

There were legion outposts there, he remembered. He could roll them up, compel them to accept him, and take over city after city. Who cared if the church took Himnel, if he could, in turn, take the Empire?

"If the Great Nimon names me Scion in place of the upstart at his death, then I accept…" Barabarattas whispered, holding his hand out and trying to ignore the sudden dryness in his mouth and the tremble in his fingers.

An answering rumble of thunder echoed through the air, making Barabarattas flinch, and the Archpriest smiled coldly.

"The God accepts your demands and welcomes you to the fold, my child." Baruman said, taking Barabarattas' hand and sinking the thin spine that rose from his ring into Barabarattas's palm, drawing a drop of ruby-red blood before beginning the Oaths the God required.

*

Four hours later, Thomas was sitting back, seriously contemplating ordering just one more goddamn bowl of the little meaty nut-coated things, even though his stomach whined and begged him not to, when Edvard sat down across from him, grinning widely.

"Well, lad, I know I told you to make the most of it, but by damn," Edvard said, shaking his head and letting out a low whistle of appreciation at the dozens of empty bowls, cups, dishes, and peculiar twisty things that had held all manner of good foods.

"Lord Edvard," Thomas said, straightening up to salute, and Edvard laughed, holding his hands out.

"No rank in the mess, lad, just calm down." Thomas froze at the familiar phrase, then sighed, wondering if this was where it had come from, making its way across the separating dimensions of the merging brain waves that accidentally synced from time to time, or if it was totally a coincidence.

"Lad?" Edvard asked again, and Thomas blushed.

"Sorry, Edvard, a stray thought," he said, then froze, waiting to see if he'd overstepped.

"Good man," Edvard chuckled. "Now, did you hear what I said?"

"Belladonna?" Thomas asked quickly.

"No word yet, hopefully soon though, no I meant the other bit?"

"Uh…"

"Ha! I asked if you had much gear to pack, or if you needed replacements? We're heading for the village. Chances are, he'll have left there already, but there's a slaver encampment set up on the river between here and there, so we'll inspect their wares as we pass, see if there's anything we can purchase to replace the losses we've suffered."

"Buying more slaves?" Thomas asked, shaking his head.

"Something wrong with that?" Edvard asked, raising one eyebrow. "That's how we ended up with you, after all, lad."

"It just sits poorly with me, that's all. They should be freed, and the slavers…don't get me started on the slavers," Thomas said grimly.

"I know, lad. Nobody likes their kind, but they provide a service, and simple souls like you and me cannot afford to step aside from that. We need people, well, we need meat, essentially, meat to soak up the crossbow bolts, the magic, and the traps, so that better men don't die," the paladin admitted. "If they volunteered like honorable men, then it wouldn't come to this, but it is as the God wills it."

Thomas considered Edvard for a moment and shook himself slightly, suddenly realizing the gulf of difference between their respective points of view.

Edvard didn't have an issue with the fact that the slavers existed, not really, and he viewed those who died as somehow less than valuable anyway, seeing their deaths as no loss to the church.

He simply saw those who were legionnaires and supporters of the church as a higher form of life than the rest, and he had no care for the others.

"So, we're heading for the village, Edvard, in force?" Thomas asked, wanting to be sure.

"Yes and no, lad; there'll be an iron core for the force, as we need to make sure if the Apostate is there, he doesn't get away, but, the Archpriest has made some sort of deal with Himnel, and the elites are being folded into the city, taking our rightful place in charge of the guard and the army, not to mention making sure people behave themselves and worship the one true God!"

"So how many?"

"Six hundred. A big enough force to slaughter anything that gets in our way, but it includes a lot of fodder, unfortunately. Then we either kill the apostate and mop up the legion, bringing peace back to the land. If he's gone, we turn around, check out the slave market, and come back here.

"By that time, the city should have been sorted, the gangs flattened under Nimon's rule, and we'll get a true assault team ready–the full thousand elites, the entire fodder core–and then we march! We'll flatten the 'Great Tower,' as they call it, and sow the earth with salt. It'll be glorious, boy, *glorious!*" Edvard whispered, his eyes shining with fervor.

Thomas ground out the only response he could make. "I'll slaughter the fucker, Edvard. I'll nail his balls to his ears and punt him off the Tower myself!" Thomas growled out, crushing the dish he held in one hand without intending to.

"Good man! Right; get yourself down to the quartermaster, get whatever gear you need drawn out, and have it marked to the sergeant's pool. I'm confirming your appointment as permanent; any man who can do what you did for their fellow legionnaire, well, you'll inspire more as a sergeant than you will as a simple soldier. Besides, as a sergeant, there'll be fewer eyebrows raised at you and Sergeant Belladonna."

Thomas flinched and looked at Edvard sheepishly, and the dark paladin laughed.

"Lad, you're not the first, and you'll certainly not be the last, to have your head turned by that one. But I will say you're the first I'll put coins on in the pool."

"The pool?" Thomas asked, dumbfounded.

"Ah, best to forget I mentioned that." Edvard said, winking. "We higher officers definitely don't pay attention to that sort of thing and certainly don't have a pool going on it, understand?"

"I...do, I think?" Thomas muttered.

"Excellent." Edvard said rubbing his hands together. "There's over three hundred gold in the pot these days, so, were you to be the man for the job, you'd pay me back for my faith nicely."

"Ah, I'll do my best?" Thomas offered.

Edvard laughed. "I bet you will, lad! Right, to the quartermaster, then to the Second Legion sergeant's quarters. You'll be getting assigned a squad, and we'll be moving out today. But nothing happens quickly, not even here, so you've got time to sleep some of your meal off before we leave.

"I've ordered one of the useless shits from the light God's healers to see to you before we leave. Should provide a decent base for those useless fuckers in the priesthood to heal from. Dark Mending never heals you right, I know; you always need a few hits extra, although it's practically blasphemy to admit that. Anyway, report for duty at third bell." With that, Edvard was up and moving away, ignoring the startled salute Thomas tried to give him.

"Well, shit," Thomas mumbled, slowly clambering to his feet and heading, woozily, down the corridor, down the stairs, and out into the rear courtyard.

He strode across the small punishment courtyard, passing the men locked in stocks or being flogged, and into the far side of the quadrangle's rooms, picking up speed as he hurried to the Quartermaster's office and his new gear.

CHAPTER FORTY-SIX

It was several hours later when I awoke again, and the first thing I did when I blinked my eyes open was to grit my teeth against the pain.

The world was broken, a confused welter of images, of twisted sounds that made no sense, and of scents and feelings that made me want to scream in protest.

I felt something rub against my skin, across almost my entire body, and it felt like I'd been flayed and dipped in salt. The sounds all around me were magnified to the point that my eardrums frantically vibrated on the edge of exploding.

The smells, my God, I smelled everything! An overpowering mélange of confusion; sweat, food, alcohol, harsh soaps, perfumes, shit, and more. It ransacked my brain, trying to find connections, and I shook as each one overpowered the next.

My madly rolling eyes must had gotten someone's attention, as there was a sudden burst of warbled sound, then fingers made of massive shovels, tipped with serrated daggers, were prying my eyes open and a face peered inside. My eyes refused to focus, sharpening up to perfect resolution of a tiny patch of skin and blurring back to being unable to recognize the image as human, Dwarf, or a fucking inflatable T-rex, for all I knew.

I felt the colossal pressure of divine presences, and I almost screamed in terror and pain as the air grew heavier. The only thing stopping me was the fact I'd bitten into my tongue and couldn't figure out how to force the muscles of my jaw to release rather than continuing to chew.

Blood and saliva frothed at the edges of my mouth, running down, then sudden blessed unconsciousness hit me again, and the world vanished.

I sagged back, muscles relaxing, and those who were carrying me through the driving wind and rain swore, demanding that the column pick up speed, even as the divine presences that had been with them continued to work, piecing together the broken being in their midst.

The next time I awoke, I was rocking gently, but there were screams in the distance. I coughed, retching and shaking, trying to make sense of what had happened to me.

"Hey, he's awake!" came a shout from next to me, making me flinch in shock before the blurry thing nearby resolved into Ronin. The discordant jangle of sounds washing all around me changed, suddenly becoming a melody that seemed almost familiar, right on the edge of recollection.

I relaxed instinctively at the sound, and Ronin grinned as he adjusted the song, making me feel so much better, calmer than I had a second before.

I started to sit up and froze, gritting my teeth as pain ripped through me, before sagging back.

"What the hell happened?!" I asked no one in particular.

"You did it again," Bane said from close by.

"I did what?" I asked, confused.

"Murderhobo." I felt the *thrum* of his laughter as I managed to weakly raise one finger to him.

"Jax, are you okay?" asked a voice from my feet. I looked down, the world starting to make sense as I realized that I was on a stretcher, being borne along by Grizz, and...I looked up, seeing the gleaming armor of Lydia above me, her wings hidden.

"I think so, I'm just..." I whispered, shifting as a whole new flood of pain rocketed through me.

"Yer be broken," Lydia said firmly. "Yer be broken, and it's all because yer went to help me and me ma."

"I'm not broken..." I winced as a new pain shot through me, and I let out a groan through gritted teeth. "Okay, maybe a little dented–cracked, even–but definitely *not* broken."

"Tha Goddess came to us," Lydia explained. "She gave us news, a lotta news. Said she an' her brethren be 'elpin' yer, said ye'd wake up, but tha' it'd be a while. We've got this under control, Jax; ye just sleep, okay? Trust in us; ye dinna have to worry." Lydia gave me a tight-lipped smile before raising her voice and shouting out a series of commands for people to move up and to pick up the pace.

I sagged back, the pain receding as I relaxed, and I pulled up my notifications, seeing them frantically flashing away.

Quest: Return the Rule of Law, Bring Freedom to the Enslaved and Peace to the Unquiet Dead III

Note: This Quest cannot be refused without losing your class as an Imperial Justicar.

Punish Breakers of Imperial Law: 842/250

Free Unjustly Imprisoned Citizens: 411/250

Grant Uneasy Revenants their Eternal Rest: 1,287/250

Reward: 1,250,000xp, Access to Fourth Tier of Evolving Quest

Note: Because you have gone above and beyond the base requirements, your achievements will be accepted toward the following tier, minus this tier's requirement.

*

Quest: Return the Rule of Law, Bring Freedom to the Enslaved, and Peace to the Unquiet Dead IV

Note: This Quest cannot be refused without losing your class as an Imperial Justicar.

Punish Breakers of Imperial Law: 592/500

Free Unjustly Imprisoned Citizens: 161/500

Grant Uneasy Revenants their Eternal Rest: 1,037/500

Reward: 2,500,000xp, Access to Fifth Tier of Evolving Quest

*

Congratulations!

Forces set free by your hand have slaughtered their former masters before demanding the right to follow where you lead!

Due to your lack of control over these forces, you receive no experience for the deaths they have inflicted.

*

Congratulations!

You have killed the following:

- 7x Slavers of various levels for a total of 36,410xp

- 11x Slaver Guards (Enslaved) of various levels for a total of 51,340xp

A party under your command killed the following:

- 31x Slavers of various levels for a total of 158,010xp

- 25x Slaver Guards (Enslaved) of various levels for a total of 98,430xp

Total party experience earned: 256,440xp

As party leader you gain 25% of all experience earned

Progress to level 26 stands at 1,570,952/640,000

*

Congratulations!

You have reached level 26 & 27

You have 21 unspent Attribute points and 1 Meridian point available

Progress to level 28 stands at 210,952/910,000

*

Warning!

You have activated an Imperial Ability without sufficient authority, and now you must pay the price!

All stats have been permanently reduced by five points, and your body has been damaged in ways both small and profound.

Think carefully before you overreach again.

*

You have resurrected the Oath of Imperial Allegiance!

Due to lack of mana and territorial control, Oath range is limited to a two hundred and seventy-nine mile radius. Three hundred and forty-seven

Citadel

Imperial Citizens have been found inside this territory, and their Oaths have become active, tied to yourself as Lord of Dravith and Scion of the Empire.

"I swear, upon pain of death, to faithfully execute all that the Emperor decrees. I swear upon my soul that I shall stand for the Empire when it calls. I shall be strong when the weak need me, generous when the poor are at hand, and merciless when my fellow citizens are threatened. I shall worship the Gods of my fathers, respect my elders, and raise up my children to stand tall.

I am an Imperial Citizen. I claim the right to call upon the Legion in my hour of need, to hold those that wrong me to justice, and to be avenged if I cannot be saved."

Those who swore the Oath in truth can now sense your location and are pulled to you by its power.

*

You have accepted three hundred and four legionnaires and supporters of the Narkolt Legion into the Empire.

I swore and swallowed hard, pulling my character screen up and lamenting over the lost points. I'd literally just lost fifty fucking points; that was like seven levels.

I perused the details, suddenly realizing exactly why I felt so rough. That many points had increased my capacity to nigh-on superhuman levels and losing them, well, it was the equivalent of entire sections of my nervous system dying off and shriveling, and my body had been totally unprepared for it.

I sighed, checking through the meridian placement options and quickly discounting the cores I had available as poor choices.

PRIMARY

Brain: 1/10 Spell Cost Reduction: -5% (Primary Bonus: 1 spell slot per point)
Head: Primary Node: Additional points invested will reduce mana cost by 5%.

SECONDARY

Eyes: 1/10 Vision Improvement (Secondary Bonus: +10% chance to notice important visual details)
Eyes: Important details will glow to your vision. This will level with the relevant skill.

Ears: 0/10 Hearing Improvement
Ears: Important sounds will become clearer with concentration. High levels will aid in translation.

Mouth: 0/10 Vocal Improvement
Mouth: Your voice will become 10% more likely to have a desired effect on a target, soothing, seducing, persuading as required.

Nose: 0/10 Tracking and Detection Improvement
Nose: Scents will be stronger, aiding in tracking.

Heart: 1/10 Health Increase
Heart: You will gain an additional ten points of health for each point invested in your Constitution.

Lungs: 1/10 Stamina Increase
Lungs: You will gain an additional ten points of stamina for each point invested in your Endurance.

Stomach: 0/10 Sustenance Improvement
Stomach: You will gain the abilities to resist poisons by 5% and to gain sustenance from more sources.

Legs: 0/10 Speed Increase
Legs: You will gain a boost of 10% to your speed, as well as better stability over various terrain.

Arms: 0/10 Strength Increase
Arms: You will receive a boost of 25% to your carrying capacity and your damage output with melee weapons.

Hands: 0/10 Dexterity Increase
Hands: You will develop crafting abilities at a 10% increased rate, along with a greater chance to succeed in crafting complicated items

I read through the options quickly, considering how to balance my current state. I'd invest a point in one of the more effective areas, I decided. Yeah, things like crafting increases would be great, and there was no real wrong choice, but as often as I was damn well injured?

I needed health, stamina, damage output, or mana. That meant Heart, Lungs, Arms, and Head, respectively.

I took a minute, comparing the details on the character sheet to the possible gains, and working out what I'd lost.

"Ladies and gentlemen, we have a winner," I whispered under my breath, selecting Lungs, and before I could think better of it, I slammed ten points into Charisma, as I was having to deal with leadership shit more and more. The five points lost there would come back to haunt me, I just knew it. Ten points went into Luck, and the single point left over into Intelligence, before I grunted out to my friends what I was doing and mentally hit accept, as I stared at the sheet before me, focusing on it to try and ignore the pain of the transformation.

Name: Jax Amon	

Titles: Strategos: 5% boost to damage resistance, Fortifier: 5% boost to defensive structure integrity, Champion of Jenae: One search for hidden knowledge every 24 hours, Kobold Ravager: +25% damage to Kobolds, Valspar's Bane: +25% damage to Valspar

Class: Spellsword > Justicar > Champion of Jenae > Imperial Magekiller > Imperial Justicar > Imperial Overlord	**Renown**: Imperial Scion, Lord of Dravith
Level: 27	**Progress:** 210,952/910,000
Patron: Jenae, Goddess of Fire and Exploration	**Points to Distribute**: 0 **Meridian Points to Invest**: 0

Stat	Current points	Description	Effect	Progress to next level
Agility	39	Governs dodge and movement.	+290% maximum movement speed and reflexes, (+10% movement in darkness, -20% movement in daylight)	27/100
Charisma	30 (25)	Governs likely success to charm, seduce, or threaten	+200% success in interactions with other beings	52/100
Constitution	52 (47)	Governs health and health regeneration	1040 health, regen 63 points per 600 seconds, (each point invested now worth 20 health)	89/100
Dexterity	58 (53)	Governs ability with weapons and crafting success	+480% to weapon proficiency, +48% to the chances of crafting success	85/100
Endurance	44 (41)	Governs stamina and stamina regeneration	1320 stamina, regen 34 points per 30 seconds, (each point invested now worth 30 stamina)	76/100
Intelligence	58	Governs base mana and number of spells able to be learned	580 mana, spell capacity: 32 (30 + 2 from items)	29/100
Luck	30	Governs overall chance of bonuses	+20% chance of a favorable outcome	82/100
Perception	43 (33)	Governs ranged damage and chance to spot traps or hidden items	+330% ranged damage, +33% chance to spot traps or hidden items	88/100
Strength	44 (41)	Governs damage with melee weapons and carrying capacity	+34 damage with melee weapons, +340% maximum carrying capacity	41/100
Wisdom	37 (27)	Governs mana regeneration and memory	+405% mana recovery, 5.5 points per minute, 270% more likely to remember things, (+50% increased mana regeneration from essence core)	13/100

Pain tore through me and I heard grunting as the others tried to keep me still. My muscles screamed as I thrashed and twitched, my mind howling in agony as it was almost overwhelmed and broken all over again.

Out of nowhere, soothing heat flooded through me, and a popup appeared, informing me that Hearthfire was in effect. The sensation calmed me and increased both health and stamina regeneration, as Her voice rang out in my mind.

"Jax, I turn my back for barely a second, and you try to break yourself all over again? Rest, little one. I will watch over you until you recover." Jenae's voice echoed in my skull, but as She finished speaking, I sagged, my body relaxing. The sounds of the others dopplered away into the distance just as Oracle made Her distant presence known to me.

"Sleep, my love. I'm nearly back to you, and I'll protect you." Reassured, I let it all go and slipped from consciousness again.

MAL

"O h, for the love of…" Mal swore, jerking back at the sudden appearance of the text across his vision, completely ruining the moment for him.

Attention, Citizens of the Territory of Dravith!

High Lord Jax, Imperial Scion, Master of the Great Tower, and High Lord of Dravith, today and effective immediately, revokes the title of Reeve of Cornut, Resheck Dumbarton, stripping him of lordship of the Village of Cornut, all additional titles, and possessions, and declares him outlaw.

Let no citizen offer the criminal Resheck succor, lest their titles be stripped from them and their lives declared forfeit.

All Hail High Lord Jax of Dravith!

"What…what does that mean?" Alyssa asked, sounding even more confused than normal, as Mal continued to swear to himself.

After a long minute, he pushed her away and rolled to the edge of the bed. As he staggered to his feet, he hunted around in the dimly lit room, trying to find his clothes.

"Wait, I thought you were stayin'…" Alyssa whispered.

He growled as he started pulling his pants on. "Well, that's us both disappointed, isn't it? That damn boy's gonna be the death of me, at this rate!" Mal snapped, quickly searching for his belt and hearing a subtle *click* from the wall next to the stand, where he suddenly remembered hanging it.

Mal snorted, taking three quick steps and kicking the seemingly solid wall just behind the stand as hard as he could.

It cracked down the middle, and he grabbed the sides of the revealed hidden door, yanking the panel free and grabbing the skinny girl who had been trying to back away in the tiny space, still holding the belt with the pouches attached. With barely any effort, he hauled her out into the room and threw her onto the bed.

"Shit!" Alyssa cried. Moving fast, she yanked the young girl across the bed. Then, as Mal stared in shock, she raced the three steps to her left, slamming her hand down on a table in the corner of the room.

The top of the table popped up, and she pulled out a whistle and a dagger. But before she could use either, Mal was there, slapping them out of her hands and shoving the pair roughly back toward the fire.

"Ah, ah!" He shook his head and picked up the dagger, noting both the unhealthy-looking smear across the blade and the seeming luck that Alyssa just happened to be close enough to this table to get the goods out…before both she and the girl started striking different pieces of furniture on that side of the room and retrieving additional daggers and whistles.

"Will ya just stop a goddamn minute!" Mal snarled, shaking his head in disgust. "A man comes for some relaxation and gets bad news; ain't no reason to goddamn poison him, is it?" He gestured with the knife before setting it back down on the table and inspecting the spring-loaded drawer.

"You were gonna hurt her," Alyssa countered defensively, pushing the young girl back with her left hand while holding up the dagger with her right. "Becca, honey, you just hold onto that whistle."

"But mama…"

"Hush, child," Alyssa snapped, still watching Mal with apprehension as he moved to gather his gear then stopped at the false wall to look inside.

Mal grunted and leaned into the narrow gap, snagging his belt and checking the pouches and pockets.

"Next time you're gonna snag somethin', girl, make it *from* the pouches, not the entire thing. I mighta missed that. Takin' it all, though? Sloppy," Mal advised, shaking his head.

"You moved too quick," she admitted. "I'd just got to tha pouch when tha words popped up. By tha time I'd read it, ye were movin'. I had to hide, an' quick. Dinna think about it."

"Still sloppy, girl," Mal admonished her.

"So, what happens now?" Alyssa asked after a long pause.

"Now I finish gettin' dressed, you send the girl to rob some other fool, and you say, 'thank you, Mal, I'm very sorry,' and you promise me a tumble for free next time to make up for it." Mal shrugged as he sat on the edge of the bed to pull his boots on. "But next time, maybe keep the girl out of the walls?"

"Thank you, Mal, I'm very sorry, and I'll actually put effort in the next time you come to visit, instead of workin' out what I'm gonna get from the market with your coin while I work," Alyssa promised with a sardonic smile as she slid the dagger back into the false back on the chair.

"Wait, what?!" Mal asked, looking stunned at her.

"Becca, honey, go on, get outta here, go tell Clara we'll need the door fixed." Alyssa sighed, taking the weapon and whistle from her daughter before pushing her gently, but firmly, toward the door. She continued to hold the items, watching Mal for a long minute.

He stared back at her before finally breaking eye contact and returning to getting dressed, cursing her the entire time under his breath.

"Seriously, Mal," Alyssa asked after he continued to ignore her, "what's happened?"

"You saw the message, same as me," Mal said shortly.

"That I did. That new lord kicked some other lord outta his village. Oh darn, what a shame. Means nothin', not to the likes of us…" She trailed off with narrowed eyes. "…unless you're somehow involved with it all: this new lord, the Empire, all of it. Tell me, Mal, how come you're an airship captain now, when I heard a few weeks back, you were master of the arena in Himnel?"

"Funny the way life changes, ain't it?" Mal smiled. "One day, it's all goin' smooth as silk, then boom. Real sudden-like, it's all gettin' complicated."

"I don't like complicated, Mal," Alyssa warned him, crossing her arms beneath her magnificent chest and setting her jaw. "Complicated's bad for business."

"What do you care?" Mal asked, watching her carefully. "You'll get your cut, as always."

"Mal, honey, you really ain't that stupid, are you?" She shook her head and moved to one of the seats by the unlit fire, putting her dressing gown back on and tying it shut properly, instead of artfully draping it as she had when he'd arrived to *visit* her. She sat down and gestured to the chair across from her. "Sit," she said simply.

"I got things I need to sort," Mal insisted, but he made no move toward the door.

"And you can go sort them, once you've made time for a little chat with an old friend. How long we been doin' this for? Five years? Seven? Whenever you're here, you visit me; surely you can spare a minute to talk?"

"Eleven years, I been visitin' you, Alyssa, and you damn well know it. Girl ain't mine, is she?" Mal asked, stomping across and sitting down hard, scowling at her.

"You don't need to worry about that, Mal," Alyssa said, her eyes hardening as she picked up one of the glasses they'd been sharing earlier. She took a drink and grimaced. "Always tastes like crap when it goes flat." She clicked her fingers at Mal and gestured for him to get on with it.

Mal watched her, before deciding that he could spare at least another minute. The damn boy must be a hundred or more miles away, and nothing happened instantly when it came to that kind of distance.

"All right, let's say, for the sake of old times, that I might know the noble in question. Maybe he's a friend...sort of."

"A noble for a friend, and the most powerful one in the land at that, eh, Mal?" She snorted softly. "I'd either be flutterin' my eyelashes at you and pretendin' to be all impressed, if I was playin' the game, or accusin' you of bullshit, if I hadn't seen your face when we both finished readin' that announcement. It meant a lot to you, and not in a good way. I want to know why."

"Fine. He's a friend...an ally...I mean...ah, fuck it. He's the lord of the continent, and I have a deal goin' with him, all right? He's a dumb-ass kid who fights things he should run away from and stands up for slaves. Maybe I like the kid, and if he's done what that announcement says, then he's painted a big sign on his ass and screamed at the Dark Dickhead to come and try to pound it.

"If I leave him there..." Mal cut off with a shake of his head. "I've got...friends...of his around the city. They'll be realizin' the same and tryin' to get to him. If they do it in their ship, it'll take longer than it will on mine. That's the truth."

Alyssa studied Mal in silence, finally nodding in satisfaction.

"And, for the first time in a long time, you've neither lied to me nor played with my tits, so I'll take that as progress." She chuckled lightly, winking at him.

"Bah. Anyway, I told you my secret; now it's your turn," Mal insisted, watching her just as carefully.

"Fine. I own the Kneeling Lady. Have done for the last five years, since Nicci's heart gave out," Alyssa admitted with an indifferent shrug.

"You, wait, you own the damn whorehouse, but you work it as well?" Mal asked, confused. "What, you tryin' to keep the staff costs down?"

"Oh Mal...I ain't been workin' the sheets for eight years. Three while I learned the trade with Nicci and five since I owned it." Alyssa smiled as she took another sip from her glass.

"But...then why?" Mal spluttered, gesturing to the bed and from Alyssa to himself.

"Just because I used to work don't mean I don't like a tumble as much as the next girl, Mal." She smiled wickedly. "You've been my little treat, somethin' to reward myself with, where I don't have to worry over you tryin' to take my business over. Shame, really."

"Why's it a shame?" Mal asked, his head spinning.

"Well, I assume you'll want to stop now?" She lifted one perfectly trimmed eyebrow.

"Alyssa, if I didn't have to save that little shit's ass, I'd be draggin' you back into bed right now for round three. But, as it is, ain't no time," Mal said as he stood up, grinning. "But next time I'm in Narkolt, dinner, and we talk, all right?"

"I'll think about it," she said with a small, if pleased, smile.

"Oh, and Alyssa? Keep that to yourself, okay?" Mal asked.

"Will do, so long as you do the same," she agreed, standing and finishing off the glass as Mal nodded, then left the room. She waited for a count of twenty before moving to the window and opening the slats slightly, allowing her to look down into the street below.

"Can he be trushted?" a voice asked from behind her. Alyssa shook her head, still watching as Mal hurried away into the night, passing under a flaming torch that spat and danced as the rain hit it, sending flickering shadows across the walls of the narrow street.

"No, but he'll keep my secret," Alyssa said absently, glancing back to look at the woman who'd stepped into the room in place of Mal, then returning to peering out into the darkness.

She was broad-shouldered, heavily muscled, and badly scarred. A long cut across one cheek and down to her mouth made even the happiest smile seem a leer on her face.

Between that and the missing teeth, she'd never have been able to work the way most of Alyssa's girls did, but behind the scenes of the whorehouse was a thriving business that ran a dozen others, from seamstresses to washer women, from apothecaries to surgeons.

Alyssa's girls needed them all, and her habit of hiring the destitute and freeing them from the indignity of the workhouses had resulted in a small empire that served the various needs of the other pleasure houses in the area.

"Panna, I want you to go to the airship docks, take Misha and Kern, and watch for Mal. Find out who boards his ship, who he talks to, and where they go from there. Then come back to me, and we'll see what happens."

"Yesh, mishtresh," Panna slurred, bowing her head and taking her leave, pausing at the door as Alyssa spoke up again.

"Oh, and Panna, get the door fixed, will you?" Alyssa said distractedly, gesturing towards the kicked-in panel as she continued to watch the falling rain, a thousand plans swirling and twisting in her mind.

THOMAS

"**G**et your arse in gear!" Thomas yelled at Sip, kicking the lad in the ass while internally wondering what in the seven hells he'd done to be stuck with this shower of shit, instead of a real squad like the one he'd been part of.

"Yessir!" Sip cried out desperately, grabbing the halberd he'd dropped and almost cutting his own damn hand off when Bertram in the second row stumbled, stepping on the haft of the weapon.

"Fuck's sake, man, are you trying to make me offer you as a sacrifice to Nimon?" Thomas bellowed, grabbing Sip by the scruff of the neck and yanking him upright again, slamming the halberd into the boy's hand. Thomas shoved the lad forward roughly, cursing internally.

Sip was a good enough lad; probably signed up to get away from life on the farm, if Thomas were any judge. But in the Dark Legion, he'd be lucky to last a week, at this rate. He had no grace, no presence, and crap, the boy was weak.

Thomas gritted his teeth and moved on, pushing himself to catch up to the rest of the squad. Sip falling over and tying up the entire line had been a blessing in disguise, as it allowed Thomas to rest for a second, but hauling Sip up had banished the slight relief he'd gained, and they had miles to go before they'd be able to rest, especially after the news they'd been given only a few hours ago.

The damn idiot, the God-damn fool who'd personally riled Nimon, slaughtered Thomas' friends, and declared war on practically the entire fucking world, not to mention probably killing Bella, was almost in reach!

They'd managed to track him to the remains of the slaver camp after he'd done some kind of insane magic then vanished again, but the options left to him were limited.

He had to be either with the airship that had taken off, headed back to the Tower in the north, or with the column that was headed south-west. Thomas was praying it was the column, as Himnel had sent its ships after the airship, and there was no way he'd be able to get his mace wet if the fool had gone that way…the column, though?

That, they could intercept.

The Dark Legion was in full flow. The reserves had been pulled out; from the slave-aspirants to full paladins, they were all pushing hard in pursuit now, and considering the report had counted a few hundred of them in the column?

Hell yes. Thomas was practically salivating at the thought of being able to level that fast. Hell, if he could figure out a way to kill a few dozen at once, a lucky spell or a rockfall or something, he could grow insanely powerful.

"Sergeant!" the cry from his right shook him from his thoughts, and he glanced over, seeing one of the sergeants from the next squad over glaring at him.

"Get your arse up to your squad and out of third's way!" he barked. Thomas gritted his teeth before nodding in acceptance of the order and picking up speed again, his entire body screaming in pain.

He'd not been healed, not properly. He'd been fed, and he'd had some kind of dark magic cast at him by a priest who'd just grunted when Thomas asked what the fuck he was doing. None of it touched the bone-deep damage that had been done over the last few days.

The run, carrying the woman he respected, after losing half his friends, most of those he knew in the Legion, and almost all those he considered his people, the worry, the strain on his already fucked-up body after a week or more of solid sprinting?

He was broken enough that the only things that would heal him were time and rest. As it was, it felt like ground glass between his bones. Each time his foot landed, he gritted his teeth to keep from slowing, from stopping, or from screaming.

Now some asshole sergeant who'd been in the mess all week, judging from his belly, was pissed because he'd strayed into another's place in the double column?

Fuck him. Fuck him and the horse he rode in on, Thomas thought, concentrating on putting his feet down one after the other and staring grimly ahead.

Ten more footsteps, and Thomas grabbed at Sip again, catching the boy's arm and yanking him upright before he could fall over.

"Dammit, Sip!" Thomas yelled at him, his mind growing foggy with pain as he yanked the halberd free of Sip's grasp and dumped it into his own bag. "Run, man! What the hell convinced you to choose such a fucking unwieldy weapon?!" Thomas snarled, half-carrying, half-dragging the exhausted boy along, the rest of the squad either unable or unwilling to help the kid.

Sip was mumbling some inane excuse as Thomas glared at the rest of the squad, only to find that more than half of them had dulled eyes, and they were on autopilot.

He hated that, absolutely hated it, and when Turk saw them, he'd...

Fuck.

Thomas bit back on the sudden flare of tears, missing the foul-tempered orc massively, somehow. They hadn't even been friends. At least once a day, he and Coran had fantasized about shanking the old bastard to death in his sleep.

Still, Turk had become, in a few short weeks, a symbol of the squad. The whole lot of them would do anything Belladonna said, charge a changing tide or a dragon with equal ferocity and lack of fear, but Turk had been the one who was always there, always watching over them all, and Thomas needed him badly.

He needed Turk, or someone to be him, to be the heart for the squad, so that he could be the brains. But the Squad Secondus—the Dark Legion version of a corporal—he had now was all kinds of shit for brains.

Thomas looked along the line of grunting and swearing soldiers, only to see Dashiki stumbling along, eyes just as glazed as the rest of them, staring forward impassively as his mouth worked frantically on something.

"Dashiki!" Thomas yelled, and the man flinched before staring fixedly ahead, as though he'd heard nothing.

"Motherfucker," Thomas snarled to himself. "All right, if that's how you want to play it..."

The next two hours were hard, terribly so, but eventually their destination for the evening halt was sighted, and Thomas almost wept with relief as the advance team came into sight, already working on the field fortifications Edvard and his fellows had ordered.

It was slowing their advance, true, but it also meant that there was no chance of an ambush like the one that had wiped out Thomas's last mission.

"Come on, men," Thomas called, coughing, then going on. "Last little push, up and over the hill and into camp. Hot meals, bedrolls, and a rest are calling my name!" A few other sergeants nearby took the hint and encouraged their people as well.

Thomas looked over and caught Dashiki glaring at him, until the man smoothed his face and looked away. Thomas spat on the ground, using the flare of anger to push himself that little bit harder as they climbed the last hill, then crossed the rough wooden bridge of freshly fallen timber that had been lashed together over the dry moat that surrounded the camp.

Thomas had no clue how the Legion engineers managed to make shit like this so quickly each day, but he was amazed and thankful they were on his side. As his foot left the end of the bridge and he turned into camp, the standard layout was being marked up, so he led his squad to their places.

"Second file, third row, north quadrant," Thomas mumbled to himself, counting along the line quickly, only to find another squad already starting to set up next to his, covering his spot in their gear.

"Oi!" Thomas barked, getting a glare from most of them that didn't lessen by much when they saw his gleaming sergeant's epaulettes.

"What?" answered one of the men, scowling at him.

"Your shit's in our space. Move it," Thomas ordered, in no mood to fuck about with the niceties.

"Fuck off," the man said, turning his back on Thomas, who stepped forward, reaching out for the man's shoulder and noting the scruffy epaulettes that marked him as Thomas's ostensible equal.

"No need for that, Sar..." Thomas started, prepared to duck his head if necessary to sort this out without causing issues, as injured and worn as he was.

The elbow took him in the side of the face, followed quickly by a kick, then a punch, and before Thomas could get himself in order, a dagger was headed for his throat.

He blocked it with an armored forearm, sweeping it aside, then grabbed the back of the man's head and yanked him in for a headbutt.

The man clearly knew how to brawl, ducking his head and making Thomas practically stun himself on the hardest part of his skull, rather than the softer face, before he punched Thomas again, catching him square on the jaw and sending him reeling.

A foot from behind caught his leg, and he fell backwards, landing on his back, before a shout rang out, and the fight was halted.

"What's this?!" a captain barked at them, moving through the camp and coming to a halt next to where Thomas laid in the mud, while his opponent and...Dashiki...stood nearby. "Well? I asked you a question!"

Thomas blinked, realizing the captain was focused on him alone. He twisted, forcing himself to his knees, then his feet as he answered.

"Nothing, sir!" Thomas bellowed, his training coming to the fore as he forced himself to stand to attention.

"Seems to me you've got an excess of energy, if you can afford horseplay when you arrive at camp…" The captain shot a look at Thomas then at the pair of squads gathered, with others watching on all around. "You just earned your squad an extra watch, Thomas. Well done. Congratulations on your first day as a sergeant being so memorable for the men!" The captain smirked before turning and wandering off, not bothering to listen for Thomas's response.

Thomas gaped after the man. He'd been blatantly attacked, then tripped, and as Thomas inspected where he'd been tripped, there was one set of boot prints, leading three steps to…Dashiki.

"Well, men, looks like we're already learning from Paladin Edvard's favorite," Dashiki grunted. A round of mutters rose from the rest of the squad, as Thomas remained frozen in shock.

Not only had he been blatantly attacked and tripped by his own fucking *Secondus*, he'd then been blamed for the fight they'd clearly damn orchestrated.

Thomas seethed at the squad, then at the sergeant of the other squad who was smirking at him, surrounded by his loyal people.

He had no chance, not here, not now, but Thomas silently vowed to get revenge for this. He wasn't sure what had caused this, not entirely. But clearly, Edvard's favor wasn't a good thing in this part of camp.

CHAPTER FORTY-SEVEN

"Jax?" her voice invaded my musings, and I turned my head, my attention shifting from the evening meal that Lydia had given me seconds before. I'd been blowing on a spoonful, waiting for it to cool, lost in my own thoughts as I watched the vegetables and meat bobbing in the clear broth. Then Oracle called to me.

She flew out of the early evening, the trees concealing her until she was close by, making a few guards jump as she blurred past them.

"Oracle!" I whispered, relieved beyond words that she was back at last. She landed, growing to full size and crouching by me, all in an instant. I slipped the bowl aside, feeling hands take it from me as I held her.

"Where the hell have you been?!" I asked, holding her tight as she let out a little moan of contentment at being back where she belonged. It was almost a full minute before she answered, and frankly, I didn't give a damn. I was enjoying having her back in my arms too much.

"I'm sorry, Jax. When you used your power, I had to move quickly..."

"I know; I know what you told Lydia, but what the hell?" I asked her.

"It was the effect of you using so much mana. You sparked off a storm in the area. If that wasn't enough, you literally filled the entire mouth of the river with light. I honestly think they could see it from the Tower!" Oracle said, forcing a laugh.

"Yeah, cost me fifty attribute points as well," I grumbled, getting a round of low whistles and shocked looks from those around me. "Sorry, guys. I haven't really spoken since it happened, I know."

"It be fine, Jax," Lydia said firmly.

"No, it wasn't," I replied, fixing her with a frown. "Thank you for leading them, Lydia. After what I did, my brain was totally scrambled. You stepped up, taking over as an Optio should, but I've been trying to get my head right for the last hour, and I should have been working instead of letting you keep going."

"We're a team," Giint said, surprising the entire group, and I regarded him cautiously, gesturing for him to go on.

"Look, Giint doesn't...*I* don't know things. A lot of things," Giint said, struggling with his words. "But Jian explained a team or squad to me. He said it's a group that works together, that cares, like family. A group that, when one is hurt, you help them get better, you make up for their mistakes and pretend they didn't happen. Like you do for Giint. Like we all keep doing for you."

"Uh, thank you, Giint," I replied, wondering at the "all keep doing" bit.

"S'okay," he muttered, going back to playing with the cube he always seemed to be holding if he wasn't holding a weapon.

"What is that?" I asked, curious.

"Gift from God," he said, tucking it away.

"Ooookay," I mumbled, noting the various grins and head shakes at that pronouncement. "So, Oracle, you tell me what you did, where, and why, then Lydia, then…then I guess we get this shit-show on the move again?"

"Definitely," Lydia said firmly. "We be leavin' a trail a blind man could follow. Only consolation is that at least we be headed right past where tha final quest was for my armor."

"We are?" I asked.

"Aye, we can scout it as we pass, an' then…"

"And then the Dark Wankers will scout it as well and steal it," Grizz grumbled from the other side of the fire, making me look at him.

"Right; Oracle, bring me up to speed, please," I said, shaking my head. "Actually, scratch that. Wait one second." I straightened, gingerly forcing myself upright and then back to one knee before taking a deep breath and weaving the spell together.

It built slowly, as though almost reluctant to form, before almost popping into place.

"Jenae?" I called out, getting a response in seconds.

"Jax, welcome back to the land of the living," She said, Her voice rolling around the clearing and making the flames of the firepit leap upward in joy at Her appearance. The rising firelight illuminated the outer edge of the clearing. As Her presence grew, other fires roared higher in celebration of Her, revealing the dozens of camps around us and the hundreds of people.

I blinked in shock, only then realizing that the low drone in the background was a rush of voices in dozens of accents and dialects all speaking quietly, made noticeable by their absence as they fell quiet at the presence of the Goddess.

"Thank you, Jenae," I said, shifting and involuntarily releasing a little groan of relief as I leaned my back against the mossy boulder that I'd been propped against earlier. "I have a few questions, if you don't mind?"

She let out a low chuckle. ***"When do you not? Ask, though, Jax. If I can answer, I will."***

"First off, what the hell happened? Why did using my Ability cost me so much?"

"There are many reasons. The simplest is that the people were broken. To be freed, they had to be healed as well, not only in body, but partially at least, in their minds. They were held by collars that eliminated their control over their bodies entirely. To heal such injuries takes tremendous mana, especially with your–I'm sorry–limited understanding.

"You essentially poured mana into every single person there like an ocean into a cup. They were healed and freed, their collars and controllers destroyed in an instant. The feedback caused the connected control devices to detonate, killing or injuring hundreds of slavers and traders."

"If they dealt in slaves, they deserved it," I said harshly.

"Yes, in the main, they did. However, Jax, you must be aware of the unintended consequences, as well as that which you aim to bring about. For every ten slavers and their ilk that you killed, a child died, simply for being too close to a beloved parent or playing with a shiny bauble. I urge you not to use this method without understanding the risks to the innocent, who were simply in the wrong place at the wrong time."

"Well, fuck." I groaned, suddenly feeling like I'd been punched in the gut. "How many…"

"Not as many were killed as you fear, but some innocents did lose their lives, and many were injured badly. I tell you this not to hurt you, Jax, but as you grow in power, you must grow in understanding."

"So, I killed a load of kids because I freed the slaves owned by their shitbag parents?" I asked, rubbing my temples.

"Not exactly; many were simply in the wrong place at the wrong time. This is, unfortunately, the reality of existence. Tomorrow, a tree will fall. It may crush a child, or an elder, or miss them all entirely. This is life. Do not let it break you."

"I'll try not to." I said, still feeling sick.

"This is part of Amon's curse as Emperor," Jenae clarified. *"To save a million people, he learned to accept the deaths of innocents. You have sworn to never do this, but in reality, these things sometimes happen. To conquer a city, you may have to destroy the walls. When they fall, they may crush an orphanage."*

"Oh fuck, Jenae, thank you for that wonderful example!" My anger sparked to life. "So, you're saying I should give it all up and go live in a cave?"

"No, I'm saying that you need to accept that good intentions matter, despite the consequences, but you must be aware of the possibilities. The reason it cost so much to use the ability is your lack of understanding, Jax. You are growing, in truth, at a tremendous rate, but it is still too slow.

"If you intend to use such abilities regularly–and be aware, the Imperial Throne comes with dozens of such abilities–then you must learn to use them wisely. If you have a greater understanding of your magic and the nature of control, this could have cost you nothing, at least in terms of your lost points."

"So, think before I act, learn what the hell is going on, and accept what cannot be avoided," I muttered sourly. "Thank you, oh wise seller of fucking platitudes."

"I understand your pain, and in that light, I'll overlook that," Jenae said, a warning in Her voice.

"Shit. I'm sorry, Goddess. I'm just a bit…"

"Broken, I know. Jax, it took Ashante, Tamat, Lagoush, and Sint and I working in concert to fix you, and still, you feel…"

"Like a bag of flesh and broken glass," I mumbled.

"Exactly. This is, in part, because we do not, or did not, interact with regular mortals frequently, only our champions and upper priests. Then there is the minor detail that you are far from regular, or even fully mortal."

"I seem to spend a fucking shit ton of my time unconscious, and it's getting annoying, I know that much," I grumbled.

She laughed. *"Well part of that is due to the nature of your body. You had immortal, mortal, and frankly monstrous elements all vying for different levels of growth."*

"Right?" I said, confused.

"Don't worry about the details, Jax. Just accept that there are differences in you, ones that have caused some issues and, unfortunately, will continue to do so for several more weeks. The more you use that interesting new spell, the more you'll find yourself growing in strength and capability."

517

"Uh, right. Will do!" I said, completely befuddled as I thought about my spells and glanced at Oracle, who nodded that she understood. "Okay, well last of all, I know we're running, and yeah, we're being chased, I'm assuming…I know I'm going to get all the details in a minute, but is there anything you can tell us? Like how far behind they are, or how many of them, or…"

"This is something I can tell you very little about, Jax, save only that those who pursue you do so under the banner of another God, and he clouds their movement but, Jax, there is something else you must know."

"Go on," I said hesitantly.

"Thomas is with them, and not as a prisoner."

There was a collective stunned silence as I digested this before I finally nodded, unable to speak.

"I will leave you to think, my champion, but please, do not rest too long. Call to me if you have need." With a final flare of the campfires, She was gone, and I slumped against the rock again, staring into the firelight.

Long minutes passed before Lydia passed me my meal again, by now cold, and I started to eat mechanically.

"Jax, you need to know what happened, so just listen, and we'll start moving in a few minutes," Oracle said softly, sitting next to me and reaching out to take my hand as soon as I set the empty bowl aside. "After you used your ability, you were broken. We fell from the sky, exhausted. Lydia caught you, and I became immaterial. Once we were on the ground, I recovered. I was stunned, but intact, and I could feel the Gods and their attention on us after what you'd done.

"It wasn't just Jenae and the rest of Her Pantheon, though, Jax. I could feel Him and his servants. When their eyes drew back, I gave the orders. There were hundreds of people, ex-slaves all of them, just milling around. They'd been told what to do for so long that, without direction, they just…wandered.

"They'd killed the few slavers and their people who survived the magic, then they just stopped. I could have left them, but that felt wrong, so I took a risk. I ordered Bane to lead the slaves and sent Tenandra to the sky. I went with her, giving off as much magic as I could raise with you as injured as you were, while sending you by foot with Lydia and the others."

"Why?"

Lydia spoke up. "Himnel and Narkolt were sendin' airships, Jax. We could see 'em leavin' the cities within minutes of tha magic, so Tenandra set off at a slow speed to draw their attention, while Bane led tha slaves and tha squad across tha hills an' through tha woods."

"I stayed with the ship until it was far enough away that I was certain the airships from Himnel at least were chasing her, firing a few Fireballs at them to make sure we got their attention, then I flew back towards you."

"Tenandra," I mumbled, trying to get my brain in gear.

"She'll be fine. She was heading at full power to the north when I left. The fleet will be able to see her coming, and they'll protect her. Himnel and Narkolt won't want to fight the fleet; they don't know its condition," Oracle confirmed. "Her orders are to get to the others, then come and get all of us with as many ships as possible."

"And us?" I asked Lydia. "Where are we?" I looked up, seeing only the towering trees overhead and the enveloping darkness, now that the firepits had dropped back into normal.

"We be in tha forest beyond Cornut, Jax…" Lydia said, sighing. "We were too close an' couldn't go in any other direction. North or east across tha river, an' we'd be closer for tha Dark Legion to reach us; south, an' it was tha same for tha Narkolt lot. That only left us northwest or west. Northwest be all open hills, and we'd be easily tracked. But due west was Cornut, then tha forest behind it. I took over, ordered the former slaves to carry everythin' they could, then we ran, leadin' 'em this way. I wanted to send yer on tha airship, but there was too much of a chance they'd catch Tenandra."

"So, instead, you ran, all of you taking turns to carry me?" I asked, getting a round of nods.

"Well, except Giint," Grizz said after a few seconds.

"Fuck you, asshole. I offered," Giint grunted.

"Yeah, but you know, he'd have fallen off the stretcher," Grizz said, making a forty-five-degree angle with one hand and mimicking something rolling down it as the angle was moved. He whistled. "Just like that."

"Giint, nobody expected yer to carry tha stretcher," Lydia said in an exasperated tone. "Just like nobody expected Grizz to be capable of thought, or Arrin to carry it."

"I carried it!" Arrin said, looking offended.

"For ten minutes," Grizz said to me in a stage whisper that carried across the fire, then gave Arrin a thumbs up and smiled, speaking louder. "You sure did, buddy, and it really helped!"

"Fuck you, Grizz," Arrin grumbled.

"Love you too, little buddy," the massive legionnaire said, winking at him.

"So, how long was I out?" I asked.

Lydia tilted her head in recollection. "A full day an' a half. We be about six hours into tha forest now, an' we've stopped for tha evenin' meal, figurin' it's better that we all have somethin' to keep us goin'. Then we're gonna start again. Tha former slaves are all in surprisingly good condition, to be honest, so I figured another hour of runnin' should be doable, an' we'll stop for tha night, 'ave a few hours' sleep, then start again."

"And we're being pursued by the Dark Legion of Dickbags, and Thomas is with them," I said woodenly.

"Ah, yeah." Lydia grimaced with a shrug, not knowing what else to say.

"Any idea how many of them there are?" I asked.

"About six hundred," Oracle said, and the silence spread with that pronouncement.

"Well, fuck," I eventually muttered, glaring at the fire.

"We can't fight that many," Grizz said firmly. "Look, boss, I'm sorry, but we have to be realistic. There's what, three hundred slaves with us?" he asked, getting a nod from Lydia.

"With three hundred fully trained legionnaires, we would stand a chance, provided we could pick the battleground, set up defenses, and, with luck, get an ambush going. We'd still take horrific losses, and it'd be touch and go if we'd win or not. With ten of us, you being broken, and three hundred slaves?" He shook his head.

"So what?" Lydia retorted grimly. "We just give up? Abandon tha people who gave up everythin' to follow us?"

"What?" My head shot up, and Lydia gestured to the people who were sitting around the clearing, many of them listening to the conversation with anxious expressions.

"The majority of Cornut came with us when we passed through; they believe in you, an' they want to come to the Tower," Lydia said, making me sit up.

"Well, fuck," I grunted again. "They left safety and basically declared for us, putting themselves at risk, now of all times?"

"They declared for *you*," Lydia said firmly. "Just like we all did. No backin' out just because things get a little hard."

"How many?" I asked carefully.

"Two hundred an' six."

"Holy shit, there's what…?" I asked.

"A total of five hundred an' seventy-three people; three hundred former slaves an' enslaved guards, two hundred an' six citizens of Cornut, tha ten of us, an' fifty-six people tha slavers had caught but 'adn't yet sold, so they're sort of free people, rather than former slaves, but yer know, they wanted to come, too."

"Nearly six hundred of us, and six hundred of them…" I whispered, shaking my head.

"They can't all fight," Lydia warned me. "The Dark Legionnaires would cut through 'em like butter."

"Not all of them," Grizz countered grimly. "I could take a hundred–the former guards, the strongest of the slave soldiers–and I could set up here, make an ambush. We'd take a load of the Dark fuckers down, maybe even…"

"You'd all die, and you'd slow them by, what? A few hours?" I asked him, shaking my head. "Not an option, Grizz, not by any chance."

"Boss, nobody wants to die, I grant you. But seriously, to go out tying up the Dark Legion so the Emperor can escape? That's my name going down in history. No legionnaire could ask for more."

"Rather than dying as an old man, in a whorehouse, by strenuous sex?" I offered, making him pause.

"Okay, yeah, that'd be fun, too, but you know…"

"No, Grizz. Thank you, but no," I said firmly. "Lydia, you said we're going to be passing the final area that your quest had marked out, right?"

"We'll be close; close enough that I was going to send Yen an' Tang to scout it," Lydia said.

"Not good enough." I paused, scratching at my beard. "If we're that close, then whoever thought about the risk is right. They'd likely find it and strip whatever's there. I'll stay with the main column. You go with Tang, Grizz, and Yen to search it, and I know it sounds weird, but if you do find a Valkyrie's body, bring her as well as the armor."

"The quest is to retrieve a trainer an' armor, Jax," Lydia objected.

"Yeah, but she was fighting a Demon, and she destroyed a village to try to kill the Valspar. No way she'd have just retired to sit there waiting for you to find her and happily become your trainer. She's almost certainly dead, as is the Demon, or we'd have heard about it. Recover what you can, hide it if not, then catch up to us. We'll be continuing the way we're going." I frowned and looked at Oracle.

"How long until Tenandra can get to us?" I asked.

"At least half a day, probably a full day or more. She should have reached the Tower about eight hours ago, but getting the fleet up and flying, and the legion ready and boarded will take time. If she made it back in that half a day, she'd most likely be alone, and I doubt the airships from Himnel and Narkolt will just see her outrun them and go back. More likely, they'd join the search for us."

"Great. How will she know where to find us?" I asked.

Oracle smiled. "Her vision as the ship is much better than a human's, and about fifteen miles away, I can still reach her. Failing that, I told her to look out for any fighting or a fireball fired into the sky."

"Fair enough; so we've got a few methods, I'm thinking we get to the far side of the forest, near the village of Wayland's Crossing. There, we make a break in a direct line for the mountains, get as far from both cities as we can, and just hope we can outdistance the Dark Legion."

"I don't think that's likely, Jax," Oracle said quietly, her voice low enough that the rest of the team could barely hear her.

"I know. That's all I've got, though; if anyone has a better plan, they're welcome to name it?" I offered in a similarly low voice.

I looked around, hearing no better strategies, and I nodded.

"In that case, Lydia, Grizz, Tang, and Yen, I love you guys, but get a move on. Go get the gear, then catch back up to us. We can't risk them getting it," I ordered, getting a round of nods and grimaces.

"I don't know…" Lydia hesitated.

I cut her off with an upraised hand. "I don't need to hear it, Lydia. All we're going to do is run. We'll be fine. You go, get the gear, and catch back up, that's an order."

"But…" she protested again, until she saw the look on my face and nodded, passing over a small bag full of potions. "Here. I got these from tha slave camp. They're good ones," she whispered, and I forced a smile as I accepted them.

"Thanks, Lydia. Now go on, get moving. I'll never forgive you if you miss this chance," I warned her.

"I'm glad you're back, Jax, but what about…" Lydia started, and I shook my head, cutting her off.

"I can't think about that right now. I need to get my people to safety, not worry about what might be." I swallowed hard, trying to match deed to word.

Lydia finally nodded in resignation, patting me on the shoulder before checking the map and gathering up her small group.

"You be careful, boss," Grizz said in a low voice as he passed me. "I didn't carry your heavy ass all this way for something to happen to you before we escape, alright?"

"Don't worry, man, I've got this," I lied, pushing myself up to my feet and stifling a groan as Oracle hit me with a Surgeon's Scalpel again, washing through my body. The heal spread quickly, excising small sections of damage, repairing them, yet I couldn't help frowning as I started to move.

"Jax," Oracle said, her voice clearly worried.

"Not now, tell me when we're moving," I sent to her though our bond, even as my body ached again.

"Okay, everybody!" Bane yelled, appearing next to me and grabbing my arm when I flinched back, helping me to catch my balance before releasing me. "Let's go. Only another few hours, then we can get some sleep!"

There were grumbles and mutters rising around us, but more and more people took up the cry. Ronin stepped up close, followed by Bob, who moved into view on the other side of the boulder, holding the stretcher.

"I don't need the stretcher; thank you, though, mate," I said to Bob, and I shook my head as Oracle started to say something in the bond.

"Lydia organized the groups into squads of ten, roughly," Ronin explained as we started to move, people shifting aside then falling in behind us. "Each squad has someone responsible for them; no titles, but essentially, each has their own Lydia kicking their arse and making them run."

"Good plan, that," I commented, checking the map and altering course slightly as I lifted my right hand into the air, conjuring a flame so that people could see me as I started to jog.

Each footfall, I gritted my teeth as the ache grew worse, going from a feeling like I was rubbing a blister to prodding a bruise, to getting a punch with each step.

"Jax, you're doing real damage," Oracle warned me. I grunted, glaring ahead determinedly. *"I mean it. Your regeneration is…there's something wrong with it. Whatever the Gods did is trying to change you, but it's doing so by breaking you down first, and the exercise is speeding that up."*

"Is this what Jenae meant about using a spell?" I asked.

Oracle shook her tiny, perfect head as she flitted alongside me. *"No, I think She meant the Genetic Drift Examination; using that to alter you at a genetic level to the most perfect version of yourself you could be."*

"Try it," I sent to her, wincing in pain. *"My legs; hell, the joints first. That's where it hurts the most,"* I almost begged her. I felt her going to work, grunting as I tried not to focus on the fact it was a damn expensive spell to use.

"Where's everyone else?" I asked aloud, and Bane appeared next to me. Ronin, staggering along behind us, played his lute with bleeding fingers and gritted teeth, and Oracle worked to heal me, occasionally hitting him with an extra healing and making him sigh in relief.

The faint music he played hung in the air, buffing all who heard it, and I'd judged it worth the risk to continue with it, especially as the entire damn column had torches, lanterns, and were generally grumbling and complaining as we went.

"Giint was here, probably kicking someone somewhere," Bane said, sounding totally fine. "Lydia, Grizz, Yen, and Tang, you sent off; Arrin is with Jian aboard the ship, since Lydia decided they could make the most effective use of magic from there, and Sehran is with them."

"Probably banging them both by now!" Ronin called before starting his next song.

"Fucking bards," I shook my head in disbelief. "Is that really all they think about?" I asked Bane under my breath.

"Apparently so. He actually tried it on with Lydia about three hours ago," Bane said nonchalantly.

"Really?"

"Yeah, one question whispered in her ear, one punch in response. He was out like a light." Bane grinned. "Oh, and Bob's behind us about a hundred meters, helping a woman. He's got two kids on his back and is carrying three more."

"Really?" I turned to look and staggered before Bane yanked me upright.

"Yes, really...are you okay? I mean it, Jax. Are you all right?" Bane asked carefully.

"Not really," I answered in an exceptionally low voice, knowing he'd still hear it. "Some kind of damage that either the Gods caused or couldn't fix. It needs to run its course; apparently, movement makes it worse." I abruptly realized how low my mana was and pulled out a potion.

I drank the mana potion, feeling it boost my regeneration as well as refilling the bar slightly, and pocketed the vial again, sighing as I focused on just putting one foot in front of the other.

"Keep track of the time for me, Bane," I asked him quietly. "Two hours from now, push us just that little bit more." I was genuinely afraid that, at any point, we could hear the first sounds of battle from behind as the Dark Legion scouts found us.

"I will. Just keep going, Jax; I'll do the rest," he said firmly. I nodded my thanks, letting go of everything else and focusing on just one more step, picking a tree and telling myself to get to that point, then just a little farther.

It felt like a solid month before Bane called a halt, and I staggered to a stop, collapsing to my knees then pitching forward and passing out, not even having the strength to pretend to be okay anymore.

CHAPTER FORTY-EIGHT

F our and a half hours later, Bane shook me, and I blinked up at him blearily. "They've found us." The fear and adrenaline those words triggered got me onto my feet despite the pain.

"How bad, and how far?" I asked.

"An hour, probably less." Bane coughed. "Any chance of a fountain?" he asked.

I cursed myself, summoning a clean fountain of water on the spot. The notification popped up alongside it. While he sank his head into it and breathed, I called out to Ronin and pulled the notification forward at the same time, allowing it to open in my vision.

"Ronin, get them moving. Ask for twenty volunteers to join me, people who will fight. Then you lead them and keep going as long as you can, man."

"Jax, I…" Ronin replied, but I was already reading.

"Just go Ronin, please," I ordered.

Congratulations!

You have raised your spell Summon Water to level 10.

You may now choose your first evolution of this spell.

*

Congratulations!

You have raised your spell Summon Water to its first evolution.

You must now pick a path to follow. Water flows where it will, but you have a chance to guide it, to improve upon it.

Which path will you choose?

Choose carefully, as this choice cannot be undone.

Healing Fountain:
You have a great store of healing knowledge, and having used the spell so many times, it has become second nature to summon. You now have the chance to add secondary effects to it. Drinking the water of the Healing Fountain will increase both health and stamina regeneration by 5 points per second for 60 seconds.

Burning Waters:
As the Champion of the Goddess of Fire, you may add a secondary effect to your fountain, raising the temperature of the waters to just below boiling, turning a simple spell into a weapon many will fear.

I immediately chose the first; it wasn't even a consideration, after all. Sure, I could boil someone in their armor, and it'd be good in a fight, but it was essentially just pain, and higher-leveled enemies could ignore that.

Removing the actual water that Bane needed to survive would be a completely dickish move, as would passing up the chance to help everyone. Besides, I needed that goddamn water as much as the next guy.

I cut off the spell, making Bane grunt in surprise. But before he could start to explain what he'd seen, I cast it again, and the added healing and stamina regeneration made him relax his shoulders and breathe deeply.

"Bob," I sent to the skeleton, seeing him appear to my right out of the gloom. *"You need to go as well, mate,"* I ordered, catching the flare of concern and disagreement in those bright blue eyes, before I overruled him. *"I'm sorry, man, but I'll need to be mobile to survive, and you're not; add to that, the kids. They need you. You can literally save their lives. Protect the children, Bob, that's my order, and my wish."*

He stared at me for a few seconds, then turned and stomped off, pausing at the edge of the firelight to look back at me.

"If you survive, you will aid me in my quest," he demanded. I nodded, getting a popup that I banished, not wanting to waste time on it now.

I gave Bane a few seconds as I summoned two more fountains at the far end of the clearing we rested in. Oracle summoned two more of them to the side of the ones I'd done, and I called out to the people who grumbled and cursed as Ronin started to rouse them.

"The Dark Legion is almost here!" I called, bringing silence then anxious mutters as people passed my words on at the outer edge. "I need twenty volunteers to stand with me. The rest of you, go; follow my bard, and run on, but—" I held up one hand. "—make sure you drink from the fountain on your way out; it has stamina boosting properties!" I popped a fresh mana potion and started to summon more of them.

I stopped once. With Oracle's help, there were ten fountains flowing, partially as I couldn't afford to waste any more mana, and partially because we had essentially created a bog.

I watched as people streamed past us. Harmon and his wife were close by, and I smiled to him and their son as they hurried on. Harmon reached out and clapped me on the shoulder, pausing until I gestured for him to move on, knowing that he'd been building up the courage to offer to stay and help.

"Your family needs you, man, go," I ordered, getting a nod of thanks as he hurried on with the others.

Bane stepped back from the fountain, shaking his head and letting his tendrils furl and unfurl before nodding his thanks.

"That feels a lot better. Thank you, Jax," he said quietly as people continued past us. "I was scouting back along our trail and saw their scouts heading back. I'd guess that the main body is less than a few hours behind the advance scouts, so it's time to make a decision…"

"We fight," I said simply. "We can only run so far, brother."

"Joy," Bane sighed before straightening his shoulders. "Do we at least have a plan?"

"I'm not wanting it to be too technical, so I think 'kill them all, let the Gods sort them out.' That work for you?" I asked, smiling around as a handful of people joined me by the wet ground that had been my fountain. Oracle summoned it again, and we waited, watching the passing people as they hurried on, while I did a quick headcount.

"Okay, people…" I said after a few minutes, noticing the vast majority were both armed and armored. "I asked for twenty volunteers, and I got seventy-three, so thank you all for that.

"Do you all have weapons?" I asked. The few who didn't were quickly passed some from storage bags, rings, and in one case, a codpiece.

The man who gingerly accepted a spear from the weirdly thrusting short, bald dude seemed to be considering stabbing him with it when I interrupted.

"Okay, then. Are any of you proficient in stealth?" Three people held up their hands. "You're all with Bane, and your job is to kill the scouts as they come for us. We'll be the bait, you be the consequence. Grab their gear whenever possible, as it's likely to have bonuses to stealth to help you further on."

"If you choose to wear the armor of the Dark Legion, leave one gauntlet off," Bane ordered loudly. "The left one; this way, we'll know who you are on sight, and you'll not have to worry about us stabbing you."

"Good point, thank you, Bane."

As he took the other three and started walking through the group, he passed me and put his hand on my shoulder, squeezing gently. "Take care of yourself, brother, and don't wait for me."

"The hell I won't," I retorted. "I came here looking for one brother. I'm sure as shit not leaving another to die. You get your arse back and join the group, Bane, or I'll drag you kicking and screaming out of the fucking grave and tell Cheena you professed undying love for her."

"Hah, then she'd kill me!" Bane called as he vanished.

"Probably!" I called after him looking around at the rest of my volunteers.

"Well, they'll be killing any scouts who find us while we get to be rabbits," I said tiredly to the group gathered around me.

"Explain." A blue skinned-giant of a man gazed down at me from the heights of his eight-foot-six frame.

"Essentially, we follow the rest, but at a slower pace, and we wait. If we get attacked, we fold in around them and kill them if we can. If not, we act like rabbits and run like fuck. Should we come across an area we can hold up, something to defend, then maybe that changes. If the main body catches up, then we turn and fight, because nothing dies easier than a running man."

The tall man grunted, and I waved to the trail left by the rest, jogging after the others.

It was twenty minutes before Oracle hissed a warning, and all hell opened up. *"Down!"*

I dove forward, repeating her shout aloud.

"Down!" I roared just as a pair of crossbow bolts slammed home in the chest of the man behind of me, taking him to the ground with a surprised grunt. All around us, screams started up, along with the twang of bolts.

I rolled to my feet and summoned the shield from my bag, grunting as the excess weight of the shield added a whole new layer of pain to my already screaming body. Focusing, I cast Explosive Compression, aiming at the point I'd last seen movement.

Even as I started casting, Oracle flew up from where she'd been riding on my shoulder.

"Jax, we're surrounded!" she sent. I cursed, even as I continued to build the spell.

"Weapons?" I sent.

"Light armor and crossbows; they expected the group to scatter, I think. They're trying to reload."

"Attack!" I roared, hurling the completed spell at a large fallen tree I'd just seen movement behind.

My spell blasted forth from my hand and covered the distance in seconds, arriving just as a triumphant-looking Elf stuck his head up again, swinging his crossbow into place.

The spell hit the wood about a foot to his left. He grinned at me, aiming down the crossbow carefully, until the second phase of the spell went active. He and three others, along with most of the mass of the tree, were dragged screaming inward, their armor crushed, weapons firing off randomly as they thrashed and died.

I grinned, summoning my naginata, and rushed around the right of the gap, leaping into the air and using a touch of Soaring Majesty to clear the wooden cover as it fell, cracking under the pressure at the other end.

I landed just behind a man who'd lifted his crossbow in the other direction. He heard something, twisted his head to look, and met the bladed tip of my naginata as it slammed home into the junction between helm and upper body.

I wrenched it left, then right, then down, popping his head loose like a cork from a bottle. Shifting my shield and taking a crossbow bolt in the middle of it, I sent it skittering off into the darkness, then ran at the tall elven woman who'd fired. I shield-bashed her in the face, twisting and using Lunge to cover the distance to the next in line. The Dwarf was frantically yanking on the thick cable of the crossbow, his foot lodged in a special stirrup by the business end of the weapon.

All around me, fighting and screams rang out, my mana dropping precipitously as lightning and Flames of Wrath rippled out.

I stabbed the bladed tip through the leather armor of the Dwarf, feeling something metallic crunch before the blade slid cleanly in. I fed fire mana into the weapon, feeling it flare to life, then I twisted the haft and yanked it free, letting the short figure sag and collapse to the ground.

I lifted the weapon into the air and called out, while spinning it in a circle.

"To me! Free men of the Empire, to me!" I flinched inwardly at the ostentatious shout but, considering I knew literally not a single one of their names, it was the best I could come up with.

The surviving former slaves turned and ran for me. Most of the scouting force that had somehow gotten ahead of us and laid the ambush were dead, and the few left alive, well, they were going to serve a greater purpose now.

"This way, to the ship!" I called, feeling my heart clench as I saw the hope on the faces of the former slaves.

I turned and started to run, feeling Oracle flitting ahead of me, high up in the forest canopy.

"Tell me the ships aren't far off," I sent to her, and I knew even before she responded that it had been a futile hope.

"I can't see anything, but the ships from the Tower are still hours away at best, and there are two ships approaching from Narkolt. They're going as fast as they can, but I…I think we need to run, Jax."

"We are!" I sent grimly.

"No, I mean <u>we</u> need to run, you and me," Oracle clarified in a small voice I could barely hear, even through the bond. **"The slaves don't have a chance, not without serious support. They'll all get caught soon, and I can't feel any of the squad nearby, I went up high enough to see the edge of the forest. It's three miles to the left. If the Dark Legion follows us, we might gain the slaves a few more hours, but those ships coming up from the south will see them, and it's only two hours 'til daybreak."**

"I won't abandon them," I sent to Oracle, shifting my grip and slamming my naginata, then my shield, into my bag and skidding to a halt at the top of a low rise.

I turned, seeing a dozen men running behind me, all slaves, the fights in the distance growing closer.

"What…what do we do, sir?" the tall, blue-skinned man panted. I reached out, catching his hand and pulling him up over the edge of the rise, glancing back down at the others coming.

"Go," I told him.

"Wha…?" he mumbled, confused.

"I said go, man!" I snapped at him. "I'll earn you some time, then I'll catch up. Take the others and run!"

With that, I started casting. I couldn't see much in the forest; the combination of the dark, the heavy underbrush, and the fact the bastards were most likely all scouts out there meant it was going to be a crap shoot, but I was fine with that.

I'd managed to collect and make a grand total of seventeen mana potions now, thanks to the ones that Lydia had given me before she left for the quest marker.

I downed two weak-ass ones that boosted my mana regeneration, then lifted my hands out to either side, palms up, and started to cast. I concentrated on speed of casting, nothing else, no extra effects, just standard Fireballs, and I prayed internally that I wouldn't accidentally catch Bane or anyone else from our side.

I finished them both at exactly the same time, hurling them forward, aimed a dozen meters apart, and immediately started casting again, then again, stopping only to chug a greater mana potion, which took me from a dozen mana left to nearly full in about two seconds.

Oracle hovered high above the area, concealed in the canopy, waiting as I laid down a barrage of flame. The Fireballs systematically cleared entire sections of the woods, setting trees ablaze and generally making absolutely sure nobody could miss me.

It wasn't long before the first skull floated up in my vision, apart from the various dozens of animals I'd accidentally gotten and wiped from the notifications without thought. When I saw that it was marked as a dark legionnaire, it was time for phase two.

Oracle started to launch off Fireballs in my place, as I began tying sections of spells together, figuring what the hell; might as well risk it for a biscuit.

After the Imperial Ability had sucked the mana right out of the air, I'd sensed something: a pattern. It felt similar to the way I'd been finding the patterns in alchemy, but instead of a plant, this was a section of reality.

Remembering it, and the way the power had flowed through it, the mana sparking off nodes and junctions that seemed to be highlighted in my mind for a split second had stayed with me, even when the rest of the world hadn't.

That meant one of three things.

I was batshit. Possible; probable, even, but not immensely helpful.

It was important, and I'd subconsciously recognized that. Also possible, but considering I occasionally lasted for an hour before realizing my sabatons were on the wrong feet, I wasn't going to give that argument much time.

Or the third option, and the one that was most likely to my mind: Amon had crammed a metric fuckton of magical knowledge into my mind, altering my brain in small ways, and now the Gods were fixing me. I was betting that this was a side effect from whatever the Gods or Amon had done, and as such, it was still running its course, but was important enough to have imprinted so deeply that, when I didn't know my own name, I still knew that.

I was risking it all on the final roll of the dice, and I could feel Oracle's determination as well, as she consciously altered slight sections of the weave. Not much, and never overriding, but the occasional tweak here and there made the pattern flow smoother.

Frantically, I searched the magical knowledge Amon had instilled, taking sections of this and that. I was seeing magic no longer as I kept being told it was, a series of incantations and formulas, but instead a living, breathing thing that needed to be set free.

I created a pattern that was a far, far smaller version of the one I'd seen before, but I added to it as well.

I didn't need this; no, I needed that, and this, and two of those.... and this! Yes, I needed a lot of this!

I occasionally had to chug more potions, Oracle guiding my hands practically by remote as she continued to rain down fire on our enemies, until I reached into the pouch and found nothing more.

I'd drank them all.

All seventeen potions over a matter of minutes as Oracle hammered out Magic Missiles, lightning bolts, and Fireballs, and I continually fed my creation.

I was on one knee, I realized, looking down the hill. Increasing numbers of Dark Legionnaires were coming out of the undergrowth, flattening the shrubs and small trees as more and more assholes appeared.

I saw them closing, saw the big bastard from the last fight at the far end of the huge charred clearing that Oracle and I had created. I grinned, suddenly feeling how sticky my face was, the mixture of blood running freely from my mouth, ears, and nose, and the sweat that plastered my clothes to me as I finished the last weave, feeling Oracle tuck it into place.

"Jax, what do we do?" Oracle asked as I lifted my right hand, holding a small black pearl that somehow glowed and rippled with light. "Jax, tell me what to do…I…" she whispered fearfully. I coughed, feeling the weakness ripping through me, and I shook myself.

"Go," I ordered her.

"What?!" she cried, shaking her head. "No, I'm not…"

"Go to the others. The Dark Legion want to capture me, if they can. They'll want to make a show of killing me. It's the only chance we have; if you can bring the Legion, you can save me. Stay here, and we both die."

"No, why would they…"

"Oracle!" I snapped, making her jump and stare at me, wide-eyed. "I love you. I've always loved you, and I will love you forever. Now go. Find Lydia, I ORDER YOU, WISP. GO TO LYDIA," I forced out, my heart feeling leaden as I sent her from me.

Oracle wailed in protest as, for the first time I could remember, I used the power of the bond in the way I'd always sworn not to, and I compelled her to obey.

She turned, unable to control herself, and flew up into the canopy, blurring as her speed increased by the second. I sighed, relief flowing through me as I looked down at the forces gathering at the bottom of my little knoll. I grinned at them, secure in knowing that Oracle had a chance.

The Legion had a chance. My people had a chance, thanks to me naming Augustus as my heir. Hell, I'd even given the slaves a chance, and when it all came down to it, what more could a man do?

I forced myself to my feet, watching the dozens surrounding me turn to hundreds as they took in my full Legion armor, my helm, and the quality of my gear.

I lifted my right hand up high and released the spell, feeling it tug itself upwards. The flow of mana I'd given it was enough to start the chain reaction that would scour this area of the forest clear.

I drew in a deep breath, feeling my shoulders relax of their own accord. The knowledge that running was no longer an option, and that I'd done all I could for my people was a balm to my soul, even as wondered if Tommy was truly here somewhere, I thought I could feel him, like before, but I shook off the thought.

I reached into my pouch; the one Lydia had given me had been dropped to the ground carelessly, now that it was empty. I pulled out a ruby-red healing potion, chugging it as the jackals moved in closer, the forest eerily quiet.

I could hear the creak of leather gauntlets as they squeezed the hafts of weapons, the slight shifting of their armor as they glanced at each other to see who would be first to attack.

I reached into my bag again and pulled out my naginata, the weapon I'd spent months training and learning to kill with.

The sight of it emerging into the air of the forest drew a low gasp from the Dark Legionnaires all around me, now literally in the hundreds, as they had my identity confirmed.

I slammed the butt of it down hard. The ringing as the metal-clad base hit a chunk of partially submerged granite hung in the air for long seconds before I spoke.

"I am Jax Amon," I called out. "I am the Scion of the Empire, lawful leader, and Champion of the Lady of Fire, Jenae. I call the Death God Nimon to account!"

My voice rang out in the silence until a priest called out from several ranks back.

"It is him!" he cried. "It's the apostate himself!"

"Aye!" I bellowed, feeding a little lightning magic into my naginata and making it burst into light, making dozens of them flinch back. "I am JAX, and I call for the Dark WANKER, Nimon!" My voice rolled through a suddenly supernaturally silent forest.

The air grew heavier, and I felt the presence of Nimon called forth, His attention upon the clearing as the shadows lengthened and even His chosen shook in fear.

"I HEAR YOU, MORTAL, HAVE YOU CALLED FOR ME SO THAT YOU MAY BEG FOR MERCY?" Nimon roared, His voice like thunderclaps of fury and pain ringing through the air.

"FUCK NO, YOU DICKBAG!" I bellowed up at the sky. "I SUMMONED YOU TO TELL YOU I'M COMING FOR YOU ONCE I'VE FUCKED UP YOUR SHITHEAD GUARDS! I'M GOING TO FUCK YOU SO HARD, YOU'RE GONNA THINK I USED A TELEGRAPH POLE AND A SANDPAPER CONDOM! FUCKING BRING IT, BITCH!"

With that, the spell detonated, set free of all constraint by my will, bringing death with it.

CHAPTER FORTY-NINE

The spell unraveled, pouring out and bringing daylight to the night. The crackle of flames was the first sound to break the shocked silence after I'd publicly made Nimon my bitch, and they went from a gentle sputter–a sound eerily reminiscent of the comfort of a hearth fire–to a roar and a blast of furnace-like heat that flattened the grass, blasted back the leaves on trees, and generally convinced the Dark Legionnaires that a portal to hell was opening.

I roared, lifting my naginata into the air as a ripple of flame rushed outward. A solid wave of fire, rushing across the sky, illuminated the clearing for several seconds before the fire began to rain from the sky.

"I'm the Champion of the Goddess of Fire, bitches!" I screamed at them and grinned inside my helm at how many took one or more steps backward.

"Destroy him!" Nimon roared at His faithful. I laughed, lifting my arms out to either side as I felt the attention of Jenae and Her brethren.

"Come and give it a go, if ya think yer hard enough!" I shouted, taunting the forces before me. Just as the first man stepped forward, I felt the tingle I'd been waiting for.

I knew the spell wouldn't last forever, but it'd last long enough. The FireStorm began to escalate, sending flaming spears of lightning into the great fields of metal below.

I was at equal risk of being hit; hell, I was higher up than the rest, so I needed to change that, but…

Metal was an attractor for lightning, and I'd made the storm repeat the same pattern over and over again: a simple lightning bolt with added flames, while the sky literally rained liquid fire and oil down on them.

I'd managed to load in what I thought would cause the storm to circle around me, a tether that would keep me in the eye of the storm, and therefore at the least risk. But it was also a spell that was horrifically complicated, and parts were written entirely without Oracle's help, so there was a good chance I was going to die at any second.

"Jax, you…you crazy bastard," Jenae said wonderingly into the air around me, Her divine presence making the Dark Legionnaires cower back even more.

"Hey, your Goddessness," I said, a manic grin on my face as I let it all go. All the fear, all the stress, all the having to be the head honcho. I let it all fade away as I stood there atop a small rise, looking down at the hundreds of dark legionnaires who were frantically trying to get their shields in place to protect them from the flaming oil that was dripping from the sky.

"Jax, we cannot help you, if we do, Nimon would be free to act as well, he…you…"

"I don't need your help," I said quietly, grinning down at the crowd below me. "I don't need it, and I don't want it."

"Jax," came a new voice, and I smiled, nodding to myself.

"Hey, Sint. Are you all there?" The overlapping rumble of assent almost hid the next crackle of the foot-thick lightning bolt that slammed down. It impacted forty feet to my right, blowing a hole a good six feet across into the ground and sending glowing fragments of at least a half dozen dark legionnaires' armor raining down on the others, cooked meat cooling inside the pieces.

"Well, do me a favor, all of you," I said, stepping up to the edge of the small rise to watch the milling crowd below as they tried to push back, to escape. Those at the back, outside the limited range of the spell, tried to push forward, to serve their God and master.

"Name it," Sint rumbled.

"Help get my people to safety, and, if it's not too much trouble, tell them I died a fucking hero," I said, before drawing a deep breath. "Even if it's not true."

"You are a hero, Jax. All the Gods agree on this beyond all else. Even Amon would be proud. You are a hero in truth, and I would have been proud to have named you my champion, had my sister not reached you first," Sint said firmly, pride in me filling His voice.

"Thank you, Sint," I said, and I felt the Gods back away, still bearing witness to the battle, serving the final vigil for me but no longer interfering.

I gathered myself and kicked off, flying off the edge of the short, rocky hillock and landing on the back of a man in fancy gold and black armor who was facing the other way, swatting at a flaming pauldron and trying to order the men farther back to do something.

I slammed my naginata down, spearing into the gap between helm and upper chest, left bare to allow movement. As I twisted the blade, yanked, and kicked off, jumping to land on an upraised shield and slashing at an exposed wrist of the next man along, I reflected for a second how important a gorget really was when you fought a man who could fly.

My body was screaming in agony, my mana dropping like a rock, despite the regenerative properties of the potions I'd chugged, and I leaped to the next shield, sliding off it as I slammed my naginata into an upraised face. The butt of the weapon filled the air with a nasty crunching of bone as I slid off the shield, falling into a space as the men below tumbled to the sides, not expecting the sudden extra weight.

I stabbed out, once, twice, each time driving the blade in deep, then twisting as I channeled a touch of mana, the sudden searing flare of heat enough to make it easy to yank the blade out. I spun my weapon around, and on instinct, I leaned back suddenly, sighting the gold-fletched arrow that flashed past me. The chisel-tipped head and power of the longbow it'd been fired from were definitely enough to have terminally ruined my day had it hit.

Instead, a shrill scream of dark legionnaire persuasion rang out, and I grinned at the look of horrified shock from the small group of archers to one side.

Before anyone could react, I slammed mana into Soaring Majesty and rocketed across the intervening space, twisting to avoid another two arrows, each of which were caught by their fellows. I landed, bladed-point-first, in the chest of the first to fire.

He screamed, the boiled leather of his scout armor blackening as my burning blade sliced deep. I yanked it to the right and up as I kicked off his chest, letting him fall backwards. As I twisted, I slashed the naginata around, crouching low and severing almost a dozen legs before leaping into the air again. The roar and blast of lightning slamming home almost close enough to touch, despite my protection, filled my mouth with the taste of pennies as I bit my tongue in shock.

I twisted, landing, skidding, and slashing out, severing two men's hamstrings then punching the blade deep into the back of another golden fool.

I shook my head, reflecting on how stupid it was to make the higher-up officers wear gold and the lower ranks blackened steel and boiled leather.

Still, it made them into great targets!

I yanked the blade free, spun, and…boom!

The next thing I knew, a hand was yanking my naginata free of my twitching, weakened grip.

"Damn fool!" someone snarled from above, kicking my helm and nearly breaking my neck. "What? You think we have no mages?" The man's black and gold armor reflected the firelight as he stared down at me, sneering.

I shook my head again and reached out, trying to snag my naginata, but his booted heel came down on my wrist too fast.

"Ah, I think not, boy. I shall personally break you and keep this as my souvenir!" the figure said, stamping on my helm, once, twice, and then punching the side of the helm as he dropped my naginata into a belt pouch.

The side of the helm smashed into my skull, and I saw stars for a second, then I felt him lifting me in one hand, hauling me into the air.

"I am Edvard, Paladin of Nimon, and I claim…" He never got any further with his speech, because I finally managed to find the new toggle that my gauntleted hands had been scrabbling for and flicked it over his forearm.

"Gotcha, motherfucker!" I snarled at him, yanking hard on one end then the other. The tiny, yet horrifically sharp points of the razor wire ripped out, slicing through the padded section that was all that covered the elbow joint, then through flesh and cartilage and out the other side in a welter of bloody chunks.

Edvard, high bellend of Nimon, screamed. I dropped to my feet, ripped the pouch from his waist, and launched myself into the air before jerking to the side, dipping low, then rocketing up and into the dark canopy of the trees.

I dumped the bag into my own bag of spatial folding, remembering at the last second Mal's advice about the quality of bags that held items of holding needing to be higher than any it held.

Once that was done, I looped my razor wire back into my belt and grinned, staying as close to the trunk as possible while I watched the frantically thrashing troops below me.

Someone had clearly lashed out, thinking I was there. Others had joined in, and from the angle I was at, it looked magnificent, as easily a dozen men I'd been nowhere near were hacking each other to death.

What made it even better was some kind of enchantment that struck a few seconds after they did, clearly aimed at punishing murder in the ranks. It was doing at least as much damage as I had, as more and more of the dark dickbags screamed and fell.

The confusion was epic in level, and I had a split second to wonder if I might actually survive this, when a bolt of black lightning rocketed from the heavens, slamming into the tree and blowing me over a hundred feet through the air to pile drive into the ground with a sound like a foundry collapsing.

Roaring rang out, somewhere in the distance, of furious Gods, and I guessed with the tiny surviving piece of my mind that Nimon had broken some kind of rule.

The vast majority of my mind, however, was consumed by terrible pain, and my armor actively glowing with heat.

I screamed, my armor cooking me. I tried to summon the fountain, one of my most-used and lowest-effort spells, actively costing me only nine mana to cast now…and I failed, as my fingers spasmed at exactly the wrong time, sending spell backlash ripping through me.

I screamed in agony, then had the scream cut off as a hammer slammed into my side, denting my armor and sending me sliding a few feet.

"Kill 'im slow!" someone yelled, and a boot slammed into my faceplate. It held, but it dented, and an axe thudded down next, bouncing off my cuirass, leaving a huge scratch down the side.

Had it been aimed better, or swung with slightly more force, it'd be embedded in me. Even as my brain felt the wonder of electric, red-hot needles rippling through it, I went balls to the wall and activated Soaring Majesty again.

I rammed through the legs of the man before me, sent the woman behind him flying, and got into the air before being slammed from it by a shield bash that altered my flight path straight into a tree.

The speed, the force, and the weakness of the tree, compared to the weight of a flying, fully armored legionnaire, meant I crashed through it. But the next second, I hit the ground, bounced, and slammed into someone else.

I shook my head, frantically trying to figure out which way was up, and fighting to focus enough to use the ability again, when a massive hand grabbed me by the helm, half-covering it in its entirety.

It lifted me by the head, the helm slowly crushing inwards, before the hand released me. My feet slammed into the ground, and I staggered, taking a hit in the side of the helm from a mace.

I was skidding across the forest floor when I regained consciousness, having blacked out for a brief second. When I stopped, the visor was half-filled with muck. I shook my head, managing to get my right hand flat against the ground. Clenching my teeth, I pushed hard, flipping myself over and to the side as the mace slammed down right where my head had been.

I yanked my left arm up, sending the mace flying, grabbed onto the wielder's forearm, and drove myself over, punching him in the face.

He rocked to the side then punched me back, sending me rolling over and over several times until I came to halt against a tree.

The world was full of screams and roars, countless demands for my blood. The last few lightning bolts fell, and the flaming rain stopped abruptly, as though water had been poured from a jug.

The world seemed to hold its breath as I made eye contact through his helm with the man who had just kicked the shit out of me, and I flinched, seeing the madness in his gaze as he booted me in the stomach.

The man was huge, if he was truly a man at all. His armor struggled to contain him, and he was snarling and screaming as he ripped sections free. His gauntlets were first, then the pauldrons and cuirass, his helm last of all, just as I struggled to sit upright.

The man spun, grabbing a fellow soldier by the face, pulling him in close, and ripping a spear from him, then half-threw the man back into the crowd that was gathering round.

He spun, stalking across the distance that separated us, and grabbed me by my throat, his massive sausage fingers barely fitting into the space between helm and cuirass. Effortlessly, he hauled me upright and slammed the point of his spear home, driving it straight through the weaker armor of my lower chest to impale me, pinning me to the tree.

THOMAS

Thomas grunted, running along with the rest of his squad, then shook his head as one of the legionnaires on the other side of the column, from the Secondus of the next group over, waited for an answer.

"You sure you don't know where the Sarge is?" the legionnaire repeated, and Thomas glared at him.

"I don't know where your useless, cock-sucking, piece of shit sergeant is right this very second, on my Oath to Nimon. Now fuck off back to your men before I throw you at them!" Thomas roared at the man. He'd told him twice already, and in complete honesty, he really didn't know where the man was. He'd nailed his hands and feet to a log and pushed him out to float down the river three hours ago, after all, so the fucker could be anywhere by now.

Thomas felt the Oath twist inside him, examining his words for falsehood but finding none.

"Gotta love shittily worded questions," Thomas muttered. Once they set up for the night, he just needed to find some time for a private chat with Dashiki, then then he could start to sort the squad out.

It was another forty minutes of steady running, trying to ignore the bullshit tales the legionnaires around him were telling, before the Trailmaster finally signaled that next camp was in sight.

Fifteen more minutes, and Thomas was leading his squad up to the designated space for them. Today, unlike yesterday, he'd had food, another healing from a Death Priest, and even a few hours of sleep.

As soon as Thomas arrived in the right area, and he saw the squad that arrived less than a minute ahead of his *dumping their gear on his allotted space deliberately,* he smiled.

"Dashiki!" Thomas bellowed, getting a grunt of disinterest from the Secondus. "You're with me. The rest of you, get ready to build the tent."

"Listen, you," the other squad's Secondus said as Thomas strode up. "I don't believe you don't know where…"

Thomas punched him in the face full-force, sending him flying backwards three steps and rolling in the dirt.

Before the stunned squad could react, Thomas was among them. He swept the first man's legs from under him with a low kick, stamped that foot into the ground right after impact, and used the momentum and a pop of his hips to twist his body around into a rising uppercut that fractured a jaw, then flipped into a spin kick that took the fourth man in the face.

All four, including their Secondus, were already out of the fight, and their sergeant was missing, mysteriously, since he'd had an argument with Thomas the night before as well, making the remaining five pause.

That proved to be a nigh-on fatal mistake, as by the time they'd realized what was going on, looked to each other to see who was going to step up, and then back to Thomas and the stunned-looking Dashiki, it was too late.

Thomas had rushed forward; the last five were arrayed in a semi-circle, and he charged the middle, jumping into the air to put his full body weight behind a punch that knocked out the centermost figure. The blow sent the soldier to the ground with a dented helm as Thomas landed and shoulder-charged the two to his left, bowling them over like pins before spinning to the right.

He twisted at the hip, bringing his right foot up at full extension and kicking the pommel of the sword that Asshole Eight was drawing, slamming it back into the sheath and staggering him. Twisting and ducking under a clumsy punch, he grabbed Asshole Nine then Eight, by the upper gap where their cuirasses ended for their necks.

Abruptly, Thomas slammed both men's heads together and dumped them on the floor.

All told, it'd taken less than thirty seconds for Thomas to take nine men down, and by the time the ever-watchful local captain had made it over to the site of the cries, the nine men were lying about with no sign of any attacker.

The captain turned to Thomas and observed the way the squad was regarding him in a mix of shock, terror, and adoration, and he grunted, kicking the men on the floor and assigning additional watches for being lazy and out of shape.

Thomas smiled at the captain, who marched away unconcernedly, and then he turned to face Dashiki and his own squad.

"Now, you little fucks," Thomas said. "All this shit you've been playing stops here. I was in Belladonna's squad, and I damn well know what you lot are compared to what we were. You're all lower than the shit on my fucking shoes, but we're going to change that. Oh, you can believe me, you're going from fodder straight to Elite, and fast, because if you don't, you don't get to last long enough to be fodder. *Understood?*"

"Yes, Sergeant!" they bellowed in unison, making Thomas grin.

"Glad to hear it. Now, sort out the tent, clear up this section, and get ready. We start exercises in twenty minutes, right after Dashiki and I have a little chat."

With that, Thomas grabbed Dashiki by the throat and hauled him in close, not even bothering to move aside to break the Secondus, deciding to make it very, very public, after the way he'd been undermining and betraying Thomas.

"Now listen here, you little bastard," Thomas growled, his face less than an inch from Dashiki's. "I don't know what's started this, or why you've been a fucking dickhead until now, but either it ends here, right now, or *you* do. Want to make a choice?"

"Uh…" Dashiki mumbled, and Thomas put his hand on the hilt of Dashiki's dagger, half drawing it. "I'm in! I'll be good!" Dashiki called out in a panicked voice, his hand frantically scrabbling on Thomas', trying to stop him from drawing the dagger.

"Glad to hear it, Dashiki…" Thomas said in a low growl. "Because if I'm going to have to retrain the entire fucking squad from scratch, I'm going to need a good Secondus, and if you're not…"

"I am! I can help!" Dashiki shouted out quickly.

"Thomas?" came a hesitant call from the left. Thomas turned, seeing a grey-haired priest-mendicant walking through the crowd of legionnaires setting up their tents. "Is there a Thomas in this section…?"

"Aye, Priest," Thomas said, straightening and lowering Dashiki to the ground with a bump. "I'm Thomas."

"Ah," the older priest said, hurrying forward. "I'm Priest-Mendicant Frencinate; this is Acolyte Jensen." The priest gestured to a smaller man, who followed him along. They both wore the sigils of the God of Light, a starburst in the center of their robes, but beneath a cloud of black, signifying that their God was, in fact, a lesser member of Nimon's pantheon. "I was ordered to examine you back at the citadel, but, well, everything was so hectic, you understand, legionnaire?

"Then it took simply forever to arrange a proper carriage to get caught up to you. Ghastly affair, it was…anyway…" The man blinked myopically at Thomas. "Are you sure you're Thomas? I'm looking for the man who survived an ambush in the forest? Ran to the citadel carrying his sergeant. You look, well, you look perfectly well, actually, a bit tired, could do with eating more greens perhaps, but…" The priest rambled on, stepping in close and peering up at Thomas, who grunted, shaking his head.

"That's me, Priest," he said flatly, working to contain his anger. Clearly, this was the priest that was supposed to have healed him two days ago, providing the base that the Dark Mending could be layered upon. Without that, he'd been seriously weakened, and all the old fart could do was ramble on about getting his five a day and how bad his fucking carriage ride to catch them had been.

"Oh! Oh, well, in that case, let's examine you. It's not every day we get to see someone in your situation, after all, come on, Jensen, don't be afraid. Honestly, you should have waited for us. I don't know what effect all this running about will have had on the Dark Gift that Nimon bestows on his chosen, but it won't be good, mark my words, not after what you did to that poor girl!" The priest rambled on as Thomas fumed silently at him, the acolyte stepping up and washing some kind of focus crystal over him, before casting a spell and making notes.

"What was that?" Thomas snarled suddenly. "About the girl, what girl?"

"What?" The priest started, jumping a little, before settling and shaking himself. "Oh…oh, the girl. Yes, you shared your blood with her, didn't you? A foolish thing to do for a man in your position; might as well have made her pregnant, considering all the issues that's going to cause for her now."

"Pregnant?!" Thomas repeated, confused and irritated. "I didn't…"

"You didn't, did you?" The priest asked quickly. "Because that'd make a serious change to the results…you didn't get her pregnant, did you?"

"No, I didn't get her fucking pregnant!" Thomas roared at the priest, causing the acolyte to scurry back to hide behind his master. "I didn't damn well touch her! I did what I had to do to keep her alive!"

"What you had to do, mark that down boy, it's his defense. Honestly, you need to pay attention, Jensen. Make a note," the priest said, gesturing to the trembling acolyte as Thomas looked on, bewildered.

"What the hell is going on here?!" boomed a voice that Thomas knew. He straightened instinctively, clapping fist to chest in salute, glaring at his squad, who sloppily mimicked him. "God dammit, Priest, what the hell are you doing here?

This a war camp!" Edvard boomed at the priest, who flinched back before straightening and coughing.

"Yes, well. I was ordered to see to the healing of this man..."

"Two days ago!" Edvard boomed, his face darkening noticeably. "You were ordered to heal him in readiness for this march, Priest. That was *two days ago*. You mean he's waited until *now* to be healed? We've run ninety miles! He'd already run over a hundred, carrying his sergeant to get to the citadel, wounded and bleeding out, and you mean to tell me you made him wait until NOW?!"

"I had rounds to make at the hospice, and once they were done, well, you'd already set off. It took time to get horses and a carriage; I barely made it to the camp last night in time for the evening meal, I'll have you know! I couldn't possibly have healed him after that. I needed rest, and then this morning, well, you all set off in such a rush..."

Edvard crossed the distance between himself and the blathering old priest in two quick strides and lifted him into the air by his collar, shaking him bodily.

"You mean to tell me that you made one of my men run for two days, injured, suffering from blood loss and who knows what else, because you had an appointment, then were tired?!" he snarled. "Your order exists at the mercy of Nimon, worm! Your power comes from Him, after your own pathetic God capitulated and knelt before the God of Gods! We *permit* you to heal those in your hospice *after* you heal the faithful! Examine him, now! I swear, if you've damaged a good soldier beyond service, I'll scour the whole lot of your order from the continent by flame and steel!"

"I...I..." the old man stammered, being shaken roughly by Edvard. "I'm sorry!" he wailed.

Edvard dropped him onto the ground, shaking his head in disgust. "I was unaware that you'd been assigned to this level of legionnaire, Thomas, or that you'd been denied the healing I ordered!" Edvard fumed, gesturing to his side, where Thomas saw the captain of his section standing white-faced.

"I gave clear orders that you were to be given command of a squad of a level appropriate to your heroism, and that, if you were unable to keep up on the march, you were to be healed and offered aid." Edvard glared at the captain. "Clearly *some idiots* took that to mean that I was trying to play favorites, not that a seriously wounded *dark berserker*, who'd performed acts of *heroism* and *injured himself in the process* should be granted allowances!"

Thomas forced a smile, inwardly groaning as he saw the way the legionnaires around him were watching now, a mixture of fear, of respect, and of weighing, trying to work out how they could change this to their advantage.

"Thank you, Sir, but I'm fine..." Thomas started to protest, grunting and staggering as the priest-mendicant hit him with a spell at exactly the wrong time.

"He's fine!" the old man said quickly. "He's fine, it's just a reaction to the...oh...oh dear..."

"Spit it out, you old fool!" Edvard snapped at the priest, who was on his feet and examining Thomas carefully.

"Jensen...look here, and...and there...do you see? His nodes...and there, where his mana channels should be...oh, this is very strange...perhaps..." At that point, the priest was cut off by Edvard's fist closing around his throat, and he was yanked backward to face the scowling dark paladin.

"Explain. Now," Edvard snarled.

"He had his…mana channels…damaged some time…ago…" the priest gasped, his fingers scrabbling on Edvard's iron grip. "It left…damage…the Dark God healed…it…with His…blood…but now….he's shared it…no…blood…left…"

"What?!" Thomas asked. "You mean?"

"Don't use…the dark gift…" the man gasped, before starting to choke properly as Edvard tightened his grip.

"You mean you not only sentenced one of my legionnaires to days of agony, leaving him only partially healed, but you've robbed him of his Gift from Nimon?!" Edvard hissed in fury as he shook the priest, who was turning purple.

"Sir…SIR…*Edvard*!" Thomas had to bellow to get the dark paladin's attention, and he flinched when the man glared at him. "I'm sorry, sir, but we need him!"

"He failed his duty!" Edvard snapped.

"Yes sir! But now he's with the Dark Legion, so he can damn well heal any injured we have. You know Dark Mending doesn't heal properly, not the way that his healing does, he fucked up, sir; give him a chance to fix it."

"You see that?" Edvard hissed at the priest, glaring at him, before dropping him to the dirt, where the acolyte frantically tried to help his master, and the old priest gasped for air and wept. "You see that, *priest?* You failed one of my legionnaires, and still he speaks for you! You owe him your *life,* worm! Serve him well, or by Nimon's name, I'll decorate every tree within ten miles of the Citadel with your kind!"

Edvard took a deep breath, huffing it out into the silence of the camp, dozens and dozens of legionnaires standing in awe and watching the little drama unfold.

"When I open my eyes, if I see a single goddamn one of you that's not busy…" Edvard said in a low, furious voice that carried, and the tableau shattered instantly as people darted away.

The dark paladin opened his eyes eventually, locking them on Thomas and shaking his head as he stepped in closer, so that they could speak without the others hearing as easily.

"Are you alright, lad?" Edvard asked, his voice clearly stressed and tired, but trying to maintain control. "Truthfully?"

"I am, sir…" Thomas said, before shrugging. "I'm still a bit weak, and yes, I feel…wrong…and there's some pain, but nothing I can't deal with."

"Good man. The feeling you're describing, I've heard of it before. From what the priests…" He glanced down at the man on the ground and scoffed, shaking his head in irritation. "Walk with me, Thomas," he ordered, setting off and leaving Thomas to gesture to Dashiki to tend to the camp as he hurried after the paladin.

"So, from what the real priests said, the effect you're suffering from is through the loss of the Blood. They guessed it might be a risk. That old fool was to heal you and examine you, then you were to be taken to the Chamber of Darkness and your veins opened, if need be, allowing you a second inversion of the Dark God's Blood. I argued for that to be given regardless, as you'd proven yourself capable of accepting His gift already, and it would have made you even stronger if you hadn't needed it. I was overruled."

Edvard sighed as they clanked along the narrow paths that were already being churned to mud by the countless passing feet. "Yet, what they feared happening has come to pass, it seems. Your own gift, with your unnaturally accelerated healing and regeneration, kept you going, your body producing more and more blood as you needed it, even as your blessed blood was watered down, sinking through that ingenious IV thing into Sergeant Belladonna."

"Is she alright, sir?" Thomas asked quickly.

"Last I heard, lad, she was. She's still unconscious, mind you, but she was being prepared to be taken to the Chamber, to be offered up to the Dark God in truth, considering His blood already flows in her veins."

"It is likely long since done, but considering I *knew* you'd been healed, and that clearly wasn't done...but I digress." Edvard shook his head, clasping his hands together behind his back as he walked, looking around the camp.

"What has happened, as I understand it, Thomas, is that your blood, and your ability, has been stripped, or at least weakened. That will be what you're feeling. As to the Dark Berserker Ability you've gained, I'd recommend you don't try to activate it, as it may end badly. Best to fight as you always managed until now. Then, when we return to the Citadel, we will go through the ceremony again."

"Thank you, sir," Thomas mumbled, staring into the distance, wondering who had stood with Belladonna, and who now would stand with him, considering most of his friends were dead, and...

"I'll stand with you," Edvard said, seeing the far-off look in his protégé's eyes. "I'll have another, the head of my order, perhaps, lead the ceremony, and I'll stand with you as you go before Nimon, lad."

"Sir!" Thomas gasped. "I couldn't, I mean..."

"Bah, you've earned it, and it's my trusting others to do their damn jobs that left us in this situation. Now, I'll hear no more of it. You'll join me and a few others for the evening meal, get some more good food into you, rather than the shit they serve to the fodder, maybe let the lord paladin get a look at you, as well. Can't hurt to let him know of your existence for when the time comes to increase our ranks, after all."

"Me?" Thomas gasped.

Edvard laughed at last. "Of course you, lad! You think I pick random legionnaires out of the mix and take them to dinner? I see things in you, Thomas. I see the potential, and I'll damn well see you dead or fulfilling it!"

Thomas couldn't help but grin at that, staring at Edvard in amazement. This man had literally given him more respect, more training, and more chances to prove himself than anyone had ever given him in his life.

He felt a sudden desire for Jack to be there, to introduce him, to lift his brother up to climb to the heights with him, before he shook that off. Jack was safe on Earth, and he'd be better off there. He was probably eating at Five Guys and chatting some girl up right now, knowing him.

Thomas pulled himself back to the present and went with Edvard, turning down the options of a reassignment, accepting instead a better equipment allocation. He also took the second squad under his wing for the time being, after he admitted to Edvard what he'd done to the other sergeant after the man had crossed him.

Edvard had laughed uproariously and made him tell the whole sorry tale again for the rest of his group over dinner.

Two hours later, as Thomas made his way back through the camp to his squad, he looked back at the meal and the conversations and wondered about it. The paladins, those who were supposed to be dedicated to upholding the rule of law and right in the land, yeah, they were paladins of the Death God, but still.

The memory of them laughing off what Thomas had done in a foul and evil mood, probably condemning a man to drown, nailed to a log and set off downriver…most had told similar and far more twisted tales after he'd told them his.

Thomas wasn't sure if he wanted to be a part of that…yes, he wanted the camaraderie and the freedom that came with the role. They seemed like good warriors, friendly enough, and certainly were soldiers at heart, the way they cared for their people and equipment, but the casual way they had with death. The little evils, as he'd have called the darkness in their souls, if he had to explain it.

Death was a common thing in this realm, and that hardened the heart, but…

"Up!" bellowed a voice ahead of him, and Thomas snapped out of his reverie, seeing his squad standing to attention, and the second squad quickly falling out of their tent as well, all of them unharmed and hale, with the priest standing by, waiting for his chance to speak to Thomas.

"Right, then." Thomas sighed, banishing the thoughts for now. "Looks like word filtered down already, so let's see what we have to work with, eh?"

The next day was long; hell, it was a slog, but as the sun set, and the legion staggered into its defenses, Thomas grinned to himself at the pathetically grateful priest who was healing his men's aches and pains.

Thomas had permitted the old man and his acolyte to ride in their carriage, rather than, as had been passed down, making them run with the men. That simple act of kindness, coupled with the fact that he'd literally saved the old man from being choked to death by Edvard, had gained him a loyal priest of his own.

Thomas had the men line up, and as soon as they'd been healed, they began the training regimen that had been instilled in him by Bella's squad.

It was common to the elite troops, but in this part of the camp, the fodder just generally collapsed, eating, sleeping, and rutting, rather than trying to improve on themselves. This was why, once they maintained this for a while, they ended up simply as arrow and bolt fodder.

Thomas, however, was determined to prove that they didn't have to be.

He was going to drag them up and out, make them into elites. Then, once he'd done it with these two squads, he'd adopt another, using these men as the examples.

"Uuuup!" came the call, and the horns were blown suddenly, interrupting the training Thomas was running through with the team, making everyone scramble for their armor and weapons, readying for the fight.

"Stay with the men, get them ready, and fall out in turn, if I'm not back," Thomas ordered Dashiki, quickly settling the removed sections of his armor back into place and hurrying through the camp to the gathering point.

He nodded to a few other squad sergeants as he slipped into the group, standing behind his new captain, who eyed him nervously before calling for quiet.

"Listen up!" the man snapped out. "The scouts have sent back word. Our quarry is two hours ahead; they're slipping around them and laying a trap to slow them now. They'll be the anvil; we're to be the hammer!"

"Do we know…" one of the men to Thomas's left asked quickly, and the captain grinned.

"It's them, all right, and we think the apostate is with them. Cooper from section five grabbed one of the weaker ones at the back and questioned him, so we know there's roughly five hundred of them. They're ex-slaves, and they were being led by the apostate. We don't know if he's still there, but he was yesterday. Then Cooper got the stat bump when he killed his prisoner, so it's all true, boys and girls. Easy boosts are right over that hill! Get your squads together and make me proud!"

Thomas and the others were dismissed, streaming back to their squads to spread the word, and the camp broke up in a frantic mess of running men, shouted orders, and abandoned gear, as everyone dumped what they didn't need, knowing they could return to the camp in a few hours.

The next hours were a frantic mess, the Dark Legion sprinting through the forest and their enemies running before them. The gradual running down of prey from the last few days was a thing of the past, as each squad was yelled at, kicked, and beaten by their furious sergeants, who in turn were shouted at by officers determined to get their share of the free boosts.

Thomas had started to wonder if it was all a lie, a clever trick that the apostate had come up with, before the night lit with hellfire and damnation.

Dozens died in the first salvos. Then the cry went up, searching for the scouts. Almost all of them were missing, they suddenly realized, picked off by other stealth fighters.

Fireballs and more slammed through the ranks, screams rising on all sides, before the pattern was figured out. The captains rolled out the squads, closing in on a small team, then on a single figure that stood atop a small hill in the middle of the woods.

Abuse was shouted, generally, and occasional spells flashed back and forth, but as Thomas waited for their mages to open up in return, he cursed, hearing the reports.

"…almost all dead, a couple of assassins got 'round the group, wearing our own damn armor. They slaughtered the Trailmasters and the warmages alike, yeah, we got some of them…"

Thomas gritted his teeth, preparing to cast some spells if he needed to, when the asshole apostate himself started to shout. Thomas almost blanked it out, viewing it as the third-rate ramblings of a madman. But then he heard the words and felt the presences that responded.

"Did…he just threaten to butt-fuck the God?" Dashiki asked Thomas in stunned amazement.

"Yeah, with a telegraph pole and a sandpaper condom." Thomas sniggered, unable to help himself, until he saw the look of confusion on Dashiki's face. "Look, a telegraph…wait…how…" Thomas faltered, confused as an edge of doubt entered his mind.

At that minute, the world went mad, the sky erupting in flames. Lightning lashed down, hammering into the massed forces around him.

"Shit!" Thomas cried out, partially blinded by the afterimage of that idiot Sip holding his halberd high in the air and literally guiding a lightning bolt down into his squad.

Thomas clinked furiously, shaking his head and trying to clear his vision, before bellowing as the rain that had begun falling suddenly ignited, and he realized it was oil, not water.

All around him, his people started to scream. The trees roared to life, ablaze, and the sudden howls and clashes of steel from somewhere to his right let Thomas know that the fight had started.

"Spread out!" Thomas roared into the air. "Lightning is attracted to metal, so spread out, for fuck's sake!" He ordered, barely able to see, shoving people outwards from him as he felt the tell-tale tingle in the air again and screwed his eyes shut.

The boom was to his left now. The clatter of blasted-apart armor thundered on shields, and the screams of the surviving and injured rose frantically.

"Shields overhead!" Thomas ordered, hearing the order come from his right and reflexively repeating it. Others nearby locked their shields against his own, trying to stop the boiling, flaming oil that was running into the cracks in people's armor.

Something hit the group to Thomas's rear, sending them staggering. Then an arrow flashed past, taking Dashiki in the side, as Thomas finally managed to make out what was happening.

The apostate, he was there!

He leapt into the air suddenly, like he was the man of fucking steel, before landing in the middle of the last group of scouts that Thomas could see, and started hacking them apart with...with that goddamn swordstaff thing!

It was *him*! It had been *him* who led them into the trap, who had tried to kill Bella, who had killed Turk and his friends! It was that *fucking asshole* who was the apostate!

Thomas screamed in fury, shoving people aside as he tried to get closer, only to see a blast of DarkLight, Nimon's gift to His mages, slam into the figure, hurling him from his feet. Then, of all people, Edvard was there, hauling the bastard upright!

Edvard shouted something, clearly about to kick the motherfucker's ass, when he suddenly screamed. The Apostate had torn his fucking arm off somehow, and as the limb fell, he snatched something from Edvard's belt and flew away.

Thomas raced through the crowd, his Dark Gift stuttering to life. His blood boiled and his inherent rage fed the power, activating his Dark Berserker Ability, despite the far weaker quantity of Nimon's Blood he had left.

As Thomas took raging step after step, he grew, his armor creaking and flexing. Rivets popped as the full musculature of an enraged berserker roared to life, his strength magnified. He skidded to a halt, crouching by Edvard, who looked up at him in shock, As Thomas fumbled a healing potion free of his pouch, he dropped it to the man, the fine motor skills needed to actually open the vial and get it into Edvard's mouth now beyond him.

Thomas screamed in fury, bellowing his hatred into the night. Face turned upwards into the flaming rain, he saw his God respond to his unspoken prayer. A strike of DarkLight flashed across the heavens, blasting the figure from his concealment in the treetops and into the ground a few dozen feet away.

A legionnaire reacted quickly, smashing his warhammer into the prone figure, his armor still glowing with radiant heat from the DarkLight before others closed in around him, kicking and swinging weapons.

Thomas grabbed people in his way, bodily throwing them aside as he raced at his enemy. His mace and shield felt puny in his grip…until the bastard tried to fly away again.

Thomas slammed his shield across the apostate's flight path, feeling the satisfying crunch of the impact, and sending him crashing through a tree.

Thomas raced forward, fury driving him as he discarded his bent and useless shield. He grabbed the figure and hauled him upright by his helm instead, then let go and smashed his mace into the side of the helm with stunning force.

The figure was sent hurtling to the side, sliding through the muck, and he jumped after it. Landing hard, he slammed the mace down, aiming for the back of his head with the intent to crush his skull like a grape against the solid earth.

The apostate managed to shove himself over a split second before Thomas buried the mace into the ground, and he lashed out, breaking Thomas's grip on the mace, then punching him in the face.

Thomas rocked back slightly, spat out half a broken tooth, and punched the little man in the face in return, sending him rolling over and over, the helm now dented and crushing one side of his face in.

Thomas roared in triumph, feeling his shoulders surge, his fingers struggling to move inside the constricting gauntlets. He snarled in fury, tearing the constraining metal free, throwing the gauntlets, then the pauldrons and cuirass free, finally reaching up and tearing his helm off, casting it aside and looking up at the heavens.

He roared again, the sound bestial and echoing around the clearing as the surviving dark legionnaires backed away from the monster in their midst.

He turned, searching, and took a few quick steps, grabbing a man, tearing his spear from him, then shoving him back towards his fellows as he stalked back towards the fallen apostate, just as the bastard fought to prop himself upright, clearly determined not to die on his knees.

Reaching down, Thomas wedged his fingers into the gap between the man's helm and cuirass, his swollen, sausage-like fist closing around his enemy's throat to yank him upright and slam him back against the tree.

Thomas was going to make this slow. He was going to make the man pay; pay for those he'd taken from Thomas, pay for the lives he'd destroyed. He was going to pay for Edvard's wound, for Bella's…

He rammed the spear forward, punching through the cheaper, thinner armor that covered the lower chest of the legionnaire, impaling his victim and nailing him to the tree before grinning down at him.

"I'm gonna make you pay, little man. I'm gonna fuck you up so hard, you're gonna wish your momma never met your papa!" Thomas snarled.

"I already do...and so do...you...Tommy...Gods, man...you always were...a twat...!" the figure grunted, his words forced out around Thomas's choking fingers.

Thomas froze, trying to make sense of the words, of the meaning behind them...then it started to come together: hints, phrases, the way he'd done things, the comments...the *name*...

Thomas reached out slowly, with a shaking right hand, and he took hold of the helm, crushed inwards on the left-hand side, and he gently, wincing inwardly, lifted the helm to expose the bloody, beaten face of Jack.

His brother.

CHAPTER FIFTY

I looked up at the confused face of Tommy, pain ripping through me. My left eye was crushed in, competing with the dull ache of my entire goddamn cheek, and my possibly fractured skull, not to mention the fact that I'd been fucking *run through* and nailed to a *goddamn tree by my own spear-wielding little brother*.

"What...how..." Tommy mumbled, his massive hulking frame seeming to sag inwards of its own volition, as he shrank a little. "Jack...?"

"Yeah, Tommy, you...dumb fuck...it's me. Surprise!" I gasped. "Fancy letting go...of my throat...dickbag?"

Tommy flinched, then steadied me, before looking down and grimacing.

"I'm gonna have to pull it out, bro."

"Please be gentle," I whispered, grinning at him and trying to lift my eyebrow suggestively, hoping to break the tension with an innuendo. Instead, I coughed, and blood ran out of my mouth.

"Ah, shit, man, how the hell...?" Tommy mumbled, pressing me back firmly. "Right, on three..."

"One..." I started us off.

"Two!" Tommy grunted and yanked the spear free, just like I'd known he would. He helped me to slither to the ground and slump there, feeling like my body was well and truly broken.

Thomas reached out again, steadying me, then grunted and reached for his belt pouch.

"I'm an idiot, I've got...fuck!" Tommy swore, remembering at the last second that he'd given the healing potion to Edvard.

"Belt...second bag, the green one," I muttered, and Tommy searched through the specified bag quickly, tugging out a ruby-red greater healing potion.

He bit the cork, yanking it out, and raised the potion to my lips, making me drink it, before a voice rang out in the silence behind him.

"Legionnaire Thomas!" the voice called. "What's the meaning of this?!"

"You rest, bro...I've got this," Tommy said, straightening up and turning around to face the hundreds of legionnaires who were left, forming a huge ring around the tree I was slumped against.

"I asked you a question, legionnaire!" barked out the voice. I lifted my head, trying to focus and not scream as my crushed-in face popped, the bones being forced back into the correct alignment, while my hand fumbled in the pouch for more potions.

"Captain..." Tommy started, then he shook his head, standing tall and proud between them and me. "Captain, he's my brother...He...I...neither of us knew."

"Legionnaire Thomas, you have your duty...but I understand. Step aside; I will bear this burden for you," the captain said, practically salivating as he took a step forward.

"Never! He's…"

"Step aside boy, or face your Oath! I will kill the apostate…"

"The fuck you will," Tommy growled, shaking his head. "You want him, you go through me." At that, he grunted, then fell to one knee, his body writhing as Nimon's Oath of fealty and the last remnants of His Blood began to punish him.

"You see, men? You give your Oath, and it stays given!" The captain shouted out. "Once given, an Oath must be honored!"

I gathered the dregs of mana I had and frantically injected them into the spell of communication I'd cobbled together, reaching out to Jenae.

"Please, help him," I begged.

"I cannot, Jax; he is the sworn servant of another God,"

"A God who nailed me with fucking lightning! Directly!" I snarled.

"Perhaps…" There was a long pause, before eventually, as Thomas started to scream, and great red lines began to streak across his skin, as the muscles began to tear themselves free, she spoke again. **"Listen carefully, Jax…I cannot help you; neither can the other Gods of the pantheon. We cannot help the chosen Champion of another God, but you have all you need to save him. His life hangs within your grasp."**

I looked down, following Her hint and seeing nothing. My badly battered self, the dirt and broken tree, the spear, my pouches…my pouches! I had to have something…

I grabbed at them, one after another, searching as Tommy screamed, before coming to the fancy-armor dickbag's pouch and yanking it open.

Inside were a dozen various minor items, camping equipment, a handful of potions…and a green-striated rock stored carefully…a rock that, when I touched it, I knew instantly was a fractured section that had once been an altar belonging to Lagoush.

I didn't question my good luck, yanking it free. I'd recognized it only through my awareness of the Gods, as it resembled nothing so much as a weathered stone with flowing symbols carved on it.

I threw myself forward, landing a few feet from Tommy and crawling to him, grabbing his hand and slamming the stone into it as I snapped at Tommy.

"Accept it!"

"Wha…?" Tommy half-moaned, half-screamed, and I grabbed him, staring into his eyes as his left cheek twitched and tore open.

"ACCEPT IT!" I roared into his face.

He shuddered as he nodded his head.

Suddenly, there was a boom of thunder and a scream of rage that echoed seemingly from one end of the land to the other, making the birds for miles around take flight.

Tommy collapsed forward, landing on his face in the muck and blood. I shook with fear and tension, until Jenae spoke to me, in the silence of my mind.

"Well done, Jax. Lagoush says you owe Her, and Thomas will take time to recover. Oracle and the others are coming, you must hold on!"

"Hold the line," I muttered to myself, standing straighter and stepping in front of my brother, fixating on that one thought. "I can hold the line," I declared, even if only to myself. I could feel the Gods watching still, but they weren't getting involved any further than they already had, so I started pulling potions out of the bag. Thankfully, Fancy-Pants had a pair of mana potions, and I chugged one of those, followed by a second healing and two stamina, grinning around at the gaping dark legionnaires.

"So…" I said, knowing they had no idea what Jenae had just said to me. "Who wants to step up and try their fucking luck, then?" I smiled fiercely, leaning my shield against Thomas's shaking form.

There was a long minute of silence before a huge figure pushed others out of his way, stomping up on twin cloven hooves and wielding a massive great axe in one hand.

He was nearly nine feet tall, enormously muscled, with the curved, sharp-tipped horns his mythical species had always been depicted with. I glared up at him as lesser legionnaires stepped aside.

"A Minotaur, really?" I grunted, looking up at the colossal figure and shaking my head in disgust.

"You are weak, human!" the figure snorted, brandishing his axe and starting to get the crowd worked up again. "I am Gronn, child of Sula and Ver'bash, Legionnaire of the Dark G…"

At that point, I interrupted him fatally. My naginata had been stashed in the same bag I'd stolen from that dark dick, and I whipped it out. I poured a tiny amount of air mana into it to make the blade even sharper, then darted forward, combining my Lunge and Soaring Majesty to return when I was done, a second later.

The result was that, as he looked proudly around at his fellow legionnaires and took his eyes off me, I was suddenly there, my arms blurring as I windmilled them around, guiding the naginata in a sparkling figure of eight cut. Then I flitted back, landing in the muck before Thomas and letting go of the power again.

Gronn paused, his mouth working, and everyone looked from him to me, and back again.

Seconds passed, then he shifted slightly, and the precariously balanced meat slid apart, his head falling backward as his arms fell to either side. His chest slid into sections, falling to the ground with a wet splat.

The silence was deafening until I leaned nonchalantly on the naginata and looked around at them all, playing for time.

"You know, I must have killed more than half of your entire force on my own by now, and if that was your *champion*…well…let's just say I'm not impressed." I shook my head sadly.

Internally, I was wishing for a beer and a cigar, as nothing would make me look more laid back…and that's when it all went wrong.

"Fire!" roared a voice from the back, and a dozen arrows flashed through the air, making me leap aside before being hit by a blast of dark lightning that sent me skidding on my side in the muck.

Thomas screamed as he tried to get up, arrows thudding into the shield as his muscles started to reknit. I rolled and jumped upright, then dodged to the right as three more arrows slammed past me.

Heart thundering, I raced forward, leaping into the air and flying, only to find the archers, around a dozen men with bows, all waiting for me.

I twisted in the air, fingers curling as I struggled to cast a spell. Then they released, and I dove, headed straight down, barely dodging the arrows and slamming the bladed tip into the upraised face of a particularly fugly legionnaire, pulling the spell back rather than letting it fail and cripple me.

I practically shish-kebabbed him, leaping back into the air and spinning the naginata around, still speared through his face and into his torso.

His corpse launched into the air as I frantically triggered Mana Overdrive, realizing it was that or abandon my weapon. I spun it around my head before slamming it downwards, igniting the naginata with flame mana to both free the corpse and make it look insanely cool.

The body rocketed free, slamming into a dozen legionnaires, all tightly packed together, and driving them to the ground in a wave. I darted in, landing atop one man's chest, and stabbed out.

I'd flipped the naginata over, holding it blade-down and gripping it loosely in my left hand, just below the blade, to aim, while holding tight with my right hand, enabling me to slam the blade up and down as quick as a power hammer in a factory. I stabbed it out, twisted, then yanked back, over and over again. Seven times, I managed, before lightning sent me crashing through another tree, and for seven of my strikes, there were seven of them I'd killed.

I rolled, feeling my mana dipping precipitously, my health taking a battering, and the Overdrive draining me at a hell of a rate, but I could feel him, now that I knew what to look for.

I reached out subconsciously to Tommy and *pulled* him into my team. He accepted, feeling that it was me, even while he fought his own battle to stay conscious as his body was being frantically repaired by Lagoush's gifts.

As he joined the squad, his symbol was added to the rest, and I felt all I needed to: his injuries, healing; his stamina, low; his mana, practically non-existent. He was getting stronger, though, and he was my brother!

All I needed to do was give him the time he needed, and by all the Gods above and below, I'd damn well give him that.

I roared in fury, dug my feet into the dirt, and kicked off. The feeling of my body, the ground glass that seemed to fill every joint, the constant grating as whatever the Gods had started continued, all of it was forgotten in the wash of adrenaline and determination as I raced forward. I saw them, the remaining Dark Legion, still easily numbering in the hundreds, despite the literal hundreds I'd already killed.

I leaped to the right, skidded slightly, then dove the left, rolling and jumping back to my feet as arrows and a thrown dagger slammed home where I'd been a second before. I cleared the last few feet and turned my naginata sideways, grinning as the dark legionnaire before me tugged his shield across his body, obviously expecting me to bounce off.

I dug my feet in and slammed my weight into him, shoving with all my magically enhanced strength, and sent him and the two men on either side of him staggering backwards. They fell heavily, tripping the men pushing forward, and I spun.

I faced my right; the sudden loss of the shield-bearing men between me and the next man in line meant his entire right side was exposed. I stabbed out, the bladed tip of the naginata dipping in between the upper vambrace and his pauldron, severing the muscles of his arm as he attempted to parry.

His arm fell numbly, the snapping of the final few ligaments like wires releasing under the skin. His face went white as the weapon fell from useless fingers to sail toward the floor.

I yanked my weapon back, brought the base up, and blocked a thrust from that side with the haft before yanking it downwards to trap the sword.

I twisted the weapon, keeping the sword away from my damaged armor and mostly mended flesh, suddenly releasing the naginata with my left hand and grabbing his forearm in a crushing grip.

I yanked him forward, slamming my other fist, still wrapped around the haft of my weapon, into his face, and sent him reeling backwards.

"Tommy!" I shouted, grabbing onto my naginata and slashing across the oncoming, slowly rising wave of enemies. I managed to give a few minor cuts, but ended up having to step back to get the room I needed to move more. I glanced over my shoulder when he didn't respond. He was still frozen in shock, shaking his head as he started to look about.

He straightened slowly, and the shield slid from being propped against him to clatter to the ground, the metal ringing out as it clanged off a stone. He looked up.

I spun, slashing the naginata again, this time putting enough force behind it that I cried out. I felt the difference, even as I started to hit the dregs of my recently refreshed mana.

The white-hot blade of the naginata slashed through mail shirts, wooden hafts, and crappy iron and low-grade steel swords alike, carving a line through five people before it slammed into something much, much harder.

I staggered, turning back to meet the gaze of a new fighter.

This man was clad in the same gold and black armor, like Fancy-Pants had been, all engraved and filigreed. But his upraised mace glowed with a malevolent dark light, like a nineties club UV light had been brought outdoors, instead of being used for its proper purpose of exposing how nastily stained your bedsheets were.

I staggered, the debuff from releasing Mana Overdrive hitting me hard as I faced the wrong damn man.

I twisted my naginata, blocking his first swing, and took a step back, then another, as he lashed out again.

"Tommy, now would be fucking good!" I shouted over my shoulder, glaring at the figure before me. He was slightly shorter than me, topping out at maybe six feet exactly. But damn, he was broad, and the armor was solid. His mace made me feel sick as I looked at it, and his huge, triangular tower shield had distinct hooks on the side.

I tried stabbing out at him, and he batted the blade aside, dragging the shield down the haft and trying to lock the hooks in. I took three quick steps back, twisting the weapon and lashing down, managing to score a glancing blow against the thick plates of his upper leg armor. But rather than cutting into it, as the magically enhanced blade had done with the others, it left a thin scar, instead, sliding off.

"Don't run, fool, you'll only die tired," the figure grated out.

"Really, is that the best you can do?" I mocked, circling to my right and trying to draw him away from Thomas. "I mean, seriously, that's such an old line!" I lunged, spearing the tip right at his throat, only to have it batted aside.

I pulled it back and struck again, holding the haft loosely in one hand and using the other to stab forward and yank back.

I grinned at him as he swung, and I pulled the haft back, making him miss and exposing the joint under his pauldron. I quickly stabbed out, scoring a glancing blow that sent a shower of sparks flashing to the left, making him grunt as I managed to slice into the muscle.

I pulled back just in time, avoiding the backswing, but I missed his shout until it was too late.

"Shield Bash!" he roared and covered the distance between us in under a second, slamming the shield into me and sending me flying.

I lost my grip on the naginata as I fell, my missing helm meaning I had all sense knocked out of me. With a grunt, I slammed back onto the churned ground and saw stars as I tried to make the world make sense again.

"Foolish child," a voice rumbled. I twisted my head, managing to focus one eye as a boot slammed down nearby.

It was a huge thing, wide as hell, and had an insane amount of gold worked into the boot. A hand roughly gripped me by the hair, fingers twisting to get a good grip.

I winced as the pain made the world fall back into place again, then squinted up at the figure above me, reading the contempt in the eyes behind the full-face helm as he drew the mace back.

"Say 'goodbye'," the glittery cocksucker growled, when a dagger slammed into the thin slit of his eyeslot. The point sank into his eye, then his brain, coming to a rest against the back of the helm with a solid *thunk*.

"Goodbye, motherfucker!" Tommy roared, grabbing the mace from the twitching hand and kicking the spasming man back from me. I fell back, my head smacking into the soil. Tommy slammed the mace down with blurring speed, making a high chime of crushed metal ring out across the clearing as he squashed the helm like a beer can.

"Right, you fucking dickbags," Tommy roared, shifting his back and rolling his shoulders. "He nearly slaughtered half the fucking Dark Legion on his own." He gestured down at me.

"And now…" I grunted, pushing myself back to my feet and spitting some blood onto the churned ground. "We're in the fight together!"

"Damn right, we are." Tommy leveled a hard look at the Dark Legion. They were slowly stepping forward again, clearly building up their courage and getting ready to charge us.

"Right, then, Jack!" Tommy shouted, clearly for their benefit. "I'm gonna kill these cheesedicks to the left…"

"I'll take the right," I called back, unable to help myself as I started to grin. "Bet I kill all of mine before you kill yours!"

"Bullshit; you're getting old!" Tommy laughed, the relief coming off him in waves. He wasn't alone anymore.

And neither was I.

"Surrender!" a voice commanded from the back of the Dark Legion.

"Get fucked!" Tommy shouted, and I heard the tell-tale hum, sputter, and pulse of engines closing in as an airship approached from above.

"That's your last avenue of escape cut off!" the voice continued from the back.

I started to laugh.

"Really? You think that?" I ached everywhere, but there was no way I was surrendering. I'd rather go down fighting with my brother beside me.

"For fuck's sake, Jax, shut up and let them surrender!" the voice called.

I paused, my mouth half open to shout some abuse back, before I felt it.

I reached out frantically, desperation banishing the wry acceptance of a few seconds before, and then I started to laugh in earnest.

The Dark Legionnaires looked at each other in confusion, when one of their remaining officers stepped forward and drew back his hand, a glowing ripple of black lightning starting to form, before a crossbow bolt rocketed out of the trees from behind me, punching through the gathering magic to take him in the chest. The force of the projectile sent him hurtling back, his armor dented in, and the bolt's fletching shuddering with the last spasms of the man's destroyed heart.

"LEGION!" I roared into the sudden silence, my hand yanking one of my ridiculous number of spare swords free of my bag to lift it into the air. "KILL THE DARK WANKERS!"

With that, I dug my feet in and raced forward, my half-destroyed armor clattering and banging. Tommy ran by my side, bearing my shield and the stolen mace.

I dipped my left hand into the bag and pulled forth an axe for my off-hand. It was a single-handed affair, a short, evilly curved hawksbill on the front and a spike on the back. I parried the first strike with my sword, hooked the bill of the axe around the shield, and yanked it aside, exposing the chest of the suddenly terrified man behind it.

I Sparta-kicked him, sending him staggering back, arms windmilling, then threw the axe, the blade taking him in the face with a sickening thump.

"He shoulda been wearing his fucking helm!" I shouted, slashing my sword to the right and catching a thrust with it as I pulled out a mace for my left hand.

"Fucking amateurs, man!" Tommy shouted. "Only place they're good for is porn!"

He beheaded someone to my left. I grinned, twisting and catching a blow aimed at his blind side with the mace, even as I heard the clang of a deflected strike behind me.

Tommy and I had fought back-to-back against insurgents in Afghanistan, against gangs in London, Leeds, and a dozen Newcastle neighborhood brawls over the years. While medieval fucking cutlery was a new one for us as a team, it was like we'd done it all our lives.

The weird bond that we'd always had as twins meant we instinctively knew where the other was moving. Now, we'd somehow allowed ourselves to sync again, and it was absolute poetry in motion as we spun, kicked, struck, and parried.

Screams came from beyond the group we fought, more flights of incoming arrows and magical explosions ricocheting nearby, and I grinned. Those I'd felt closing were here, and the battle had truly begun.

THOMAS

Thomas twisted and blocked a hammer strike from a dark paladin on his borrowed shield, grunting at the power of the blow, and wished for his ability back through gritted teeth.

He kicked out, smashing the heel of his right foot into the lower thigh of the man he fought and staggered him backward, freezing for a second as a voice spoke to him.

"You have gifts you don't understand yet, my Champion, but that ability was all your own, and it still sleeps within you."

Thomas frantically blocked the next strike, taking it on the shield and stabbing forward with the mace. He was trying to gain time to think more than to actually injure his opponent, as he frantically tried to make sense of the words.

It wasn't the mad old thing who occasionally spoke to him, not the voice that he and Jack had shared all their lives. Thomas knew he'd made some kind of pact when he was dying, something about that stone that Jack had made him take and the prompt he'd accepted when it wouldn't fuck off. But dammit, he didn't have time for this!

This was exactly the wrong fucking time to distract him with shittily-worded vague goddamn HINTS!

"This is stupid!" Thomas yelled, taking another blow on the shield and grunting in fury. This was too much; this was too fucking MUCH! He'd finally found his brother. His goddamn insane, batshit brother had come from another goddamn world and had fucking declared war on Thomas's God. Forcing Thomas to turn his back on him, on his life, on HER.

He'd lost her now. There was no way to fix that; she might as well have died. Died from his own brother's fucking goddamn stupid motherfucking trap!

Thomas' breath was coming in fast gasps, and he snarled as his mind raced, slamming out with the shield and staggering the paladin behind it before smashing the mace down hard. He wasn't even trying to avoid his opponent's shield, instead aiming right for the center.

He blasted down again as hard as he could, staggering the paladin again and sending him back several feet before lashing out to the left and right with his shield and mace. The blows killed one soldier outright and sent the other flying as he hissed in fury.

It was all fucked up.

Everything he'd had, all his life, was fucked up. He'd ended up here, in this goddamn *toilet* of a corner of reality. He'd lost his friends, his chance at a normal life, then he'd gotten captured, forced through the portal to here, and he'd made more friends. Then *they'd* been taken from him.

He'd finally been beaten down, broken in prison, abused and destroyed as a man, until the Dark Legion had freed him, buying him and giving him a new home, one that his own FUCKING BROTHER had taken from him.

All he had left though, was Jack. When all this was over, he was going to kick his goddamn ass for this shit, but these fucking pricks wouldn't STOP COMING!

Thomas let loose with a roar of fury as his rage passed the point of his control, and he started to change.

The muscles flexed, swelling as his damaged mana channels let loose their load. He screamed in absolute savagery, growing by the second.

Thomas threw his borrowed shield aside, smashing another dark legionnaire to the ground, stunned, and reached out, grabbing the haft of the dark paladin's hammer, ripping it free of the dazed man's grip before smashing the man's shield in half with a single blow.

He screamed again, the sound echoing off the surrounding trees as he started slamming the mace and hammer into the figure he had trapped below him, beating the life from it. Finally, he crushed the full-faced helm almost flat with a blow so powerful, it actually bent the haft of the hammer.

He roared in fury and threw the hammer aside, grabbing a dark legionnaire who stabbed his sword into Thomas's side, and yanked him in close. He saw the terrified look in the man's eyes and he opted to pile drive the man's face into the dirt, the force enough to break his neck on impact. Yet Thomas still booted the side of his head, half-tearing the head free, before yanking the sword out of his side and flipping it over to hold it by the hilt as he glared at the group slowly backing away before him.

He grinned wildly, his eyes glowing with a bright blue light as he picked targets to vent his fury on. Then a roar of challenge came from his right, making Thomas spin and glare through the gathered men.

From the other side of the group facing him, a huge man sprinted forward, his armor stripped from his upper body, helm alone still in place, bearing a hammer in either hand.

He was huge, bigger even than Thomas was, and he bellowed his defiance, sweeping a half dozen of his own fodder aside with a downwards swing of both hammers.

"FACE ME, LITTLE MAN!" the figure roared.

Thomas howled at him in contempt, sprinting forward.

CHAPTER FIFTY-ONE

I stabbed the Dark Legionnaire before me, driving the shortsword into the gap between forearm and elbow, then slammed my mace into her face, cutting her scream off. She fell sideways, unconscious or dead. I roared in pain as I staggered back, an enormous gold-fletched arrow sprouting from my left shoulder, having wedged into place between the pauldron and cuirass.

My left arm dropped, numb and twitching, and I snarled, grabbing at the arrow with my right hand, almost stabbing myself in the face with the sword I still held.

I tried to tug the bolt free and almost passed out from the pain.

The damn thing was huge and as thick as two fingers. I had a second of clarity, and I quickly dove to the side, just as two more streaked through the air where I'd stood.

I careened into the earth, the thick shaft of the arrow breaking halfway, and I struggled back to my feet, parrying a blow from an opportunist who'd seen me go down.

Another man, grinning through his open-faced helm, his blackened, rotting teeth and chubby cheeks filling the space, moved to my undefended side.

Tommy took off, screaming and seeming bigger somehow.

"Just when I needed you, bro," I growled, twisting and parrying a blow from my right, then running the few steps to get inside the slashing sword on my left.

I took the blow on the side of the cuirass, robbing it of force by intercepting it halfway through the swing. Then I stabbed the chisel point of my shortsword into the fugly bastard's throat, generally improving the quality of the gene pool for all concerned.

Yanking the blade free, I spun and parried the next strike, twisting to dodge a hit from a spear and backing up.

I checked my mana; I had enough for one healing spell, a flight to safety, or a Fireball or something equally fun.

I chose Fireball, backing up as my fingers writhed around the hilt of the shitty shortsword I held, and cursing as the sparking to life of the spell set fire to the sword.

I threw the blade end over end at the man with the spear. He batted it aside, and I chanted quickly, backing up and trying to get the entire spell out as the dark legionnaires tried to stop me, rushing forward.

I twisted sideways, then jumped back, ducked, and dove, the movements eerily reminiscent of dodgeball for the few seconds I needed before I thrust my right hand forward with a shout.

The spell covered the three feet between the man and me in about half a second. Instead of flashing past him and into the five behind him, who were equally hell-bent on catching me, he caught it with a wildly swinging blade, breaking its containment and detonating the spell early.

While I was generally protected from the effects of my spells as I cast them–after all, holding a fireball without that protection would be a once-in-a-lifetime event otherwise–once they were released, unless there were specific friend/foe sections tied into it, I was as much free game as anyone else.

The detonation picked me up and hurled me backwards, flames washing over me and burning my skin in a dozen places. The brief flare of heat turned sections of my armor, which had already partially melted and become welded to my skin, cherry red again, and I screamed, hitting the forest floor and rolling as I tried to avoid the flames.

The man who'd broken the spell was killed instantly, his armor flaring white-hot as temperatures over a thousand degrees cooked him alive. His various liquids erupted into steam, even as his rapidly charring remains fell to the forest floor.

The five behind and single man to the right of the detonation didn't fare much better. I, after all, was backing away, while they were rushing forward.

The flash of light and rising screams filled the forest for a handful of seconds. I came a halt, awkwardly propped against a tree, whimpering as my armor slowly dulled from glowing to merely smoking, my own fats popping and crisping.

"Oww…." I mumbled. "That…not…a good…idea…"

I blinked, finding that only one of my eyes was working, and that was blurry as all hell. I blinked furiously, feeling the ground shake under the heavy stomps as something massive came closer.

A hulking shape loomed over me suddenly and laughed, lifting something high into the air–I guessed an axe, judging from the shape. I gritted my teeth, trying to force myself upright, determined not to meet my end lying in a ditch.

As I fought internally, I heard a familiar sound, and I felt the pulsing of the airship engines come to a halt directly overhead, the bright blue flare of their mana lighting the forest and sending weird shadows dancing.

"Wha…" the figure above me grunted just before being slammed back as a blurry figure in silvery armor barreled into him, smashing him into the ground with a scream of utter rage.

"GET AWAY FROM 'IM!" Lydia screamed, her wings flaring out and reflecting the light, seemingly clad all in steel to my broken vision. She howled in abject fury and began slamming something into him. A single scream of pain escaped from him, then a wet squelch and a tearing sound. She bellowed in rage, lunging forward to smash another, much smaller figure into paste.

Other figures fell around me, their forms blotting out the light as they formed a solid perimeter around me. Then, she was there.

A gentle hand cradled my face, tilting it upright as her tears fell onto me, and her whisper reached my soul, even above the suddenly renewed sounds of battle.

"Oh, my love, what have they done to you?" Oracle said, her heart in her throat as she gazed down into my ruined face, the charred skin, the boiled away left eye, the melted lips.

I struggled to get a smile out for her before sighing as the first lick of healing magic sank into me. Another figure leaned in close, a sudden coolness settling over my skin and making me gasp.

"Hold on, Jax. We are here; the legion has come," Hellenica said, and I sank back, my part in all of this over.

Oracle and Hellenica worked together to lay me down, shifting my body as gently as possible, when Oracle sighed and stopped her.

"Jax, the armor is melted into you. Your skin, your clothes between it, all of it…it has to be removed. Do you understand?"

"You're…peel me…like…grape," I managed, my eyes still closed as I tried to control my heart rate, both from the fear of what was to come and from the damn pain I was feeling already.

"Yes, my love," Oracle said sadly. "We can't do this any other way. We need to separate you from it, and if we just heal you, we'll have buried matter inside of you that will fester. It's all going to have to come away."

"Options…" I wheezed.

"We can knock you out now; that's my preferred choice," Hellenica said firmly. "Your body is on the verge of catastrophic shock. From what I can tell, you've had most of your bones broken, you're bleeding internally, your skin is fused to your armor, and as for your organs…I've seen healthier-looking pâté."

She shook her head in amazement. "Jax, you should be *dead*. When we realized what was happening, we came as fast as we could. The few of my children who were with us exhausted themselves to make the winds blow enough to gain us mere minutes…I saved much of my power to be able to aid you when I arrived instead, and still…"

"We need to move quickly. The longer the remains of…well…everything are inside you, the harder this will be, and the longer it will take," Oracle said.

"No…the fight," I whispered. "Finish…the fight."

"You've finished your part in it, Jax," Oracle said firmly, even though I could hear screams and bellows all around us, the crash of metal, and the concussion of spells going off.

"I…Tommy…" I forced out, tears leaking from my one good eye. "Save…protect…"

"Jax," Lydia's voice soothed as she crouched next to me, resting one armored hand on my right shoulder. "I'm here. We'll get to him, an' we'll protect him."

"Save…" I mumbled, closing my eyes as the pain continued to build, the sheer exhaustion and frantic few days all building upon each other to bring me to the brink.

THOMAS

Thomas blocked a swing with his sword without thinking about it, his gaze locked like a laser on the new challenger. He twisted quickly at the waist and slammed the mace out, turning his opponent's chest into a mess of dented steel and broken bones before spinning back to the form that continued to stomp forward.

The figure was even bigger than he was, and here and there, others stalked out of the darkness, making him aware, distantly, that the lesser soldiers were all taken care of now, and only the *true* elites were left.

These numbered in their dozens, those blessed as he had been by Nimon. Some had already fallen, but those that were left were the equal of tens of lesser men and possibly hundreds of fodder.

Thomas dug in and leaped forward, pounding his feet into the soft, loamy soil of the forest. The pine needles and scattered branches barely gave him enough traction with the sheer power his push produced. But the giant figure only grinned as he raced towards it.

"Come, meat!" it screamed, pounding one hammer into the ground. "Come die!"

Thomas let out a bellow of rage and pushed even harder, digging his feet into the ground and leaping forward, ignoring the little voice that suddenly spoke to him…until it was too late.

Thomas landed, his arms whipped back, ready to slam his weapons forward, but before he could, the hammer came sailing around and slammed into his side, sending him reeling with an audible crunching of bones.

He staggered, then roared in pain as something too fast to see blurred past him, and knives sliced his flesh.

He slashed out, the sword held horizontal the ground, and swung with all the speed and frantic power he could master, only to see the tiny, blurring figure lean back and seemingly fucking *limbo* under the blade.

He had a split second to gape in amazement before a boot slammed into his opposite side, sending him staggering again and making him snarl as the blow stretched his pulverized ribs on the far side.

Thomas took two quick steps when the voice in his head spoke again. This time, he listened. It spoke of things he still understood, of prey, of power, and of motion.

Before he could think about it, he acted, listening to the voice and obeying its orders. His mace slammed down, aiming for the empty ground right behind his right leg.

Just before it could hit the earth, the speeding figure stepped into its path, and there was a split second in which Thomas could hear the scream rising before it was snuffed out in the savage crunch instead.

Thomas twisted, kicked the body off his mace, and blocked the next hammer strike from the big one. Sliding a handful of feet with the force of it, he slashed his sword around the head of the hammer and down at the hand that held it.

The hammer dropped free as the giant flinched back, raising his head to the heavens and screaming in fury over his digitless hand.

Thomas grinned, then threw the sword underhand to slam into the figure's belly and sink in over a foot, despite the thick-corded muscles that would have stopped a lesser man's blow.

Lunging, he swept up the hammer and spun in place like he was trying out for the shot-put back at school. The hammer whistled around, and the giant of a berserker opposing him snarled and tried to block using his own hammer. The weapon was smashed backwards, slamming into his face and turning it into meat paste as he dropped without a sound.

Thomas staggered to a halt, the spin having disoriented him, and snarled as three more men, each the size of the giant, stepped in closer. He growled, knowing that he had little chance, but was determined to take them with him.

Sweeping up the spare hammer from the dirt, Thomas had to step on the shoulder of the dead man to lever it out, before grinning at the new three. There was a second when he watched them for any move, then he was hit in the face with a weak lightning bolt from his right. All conscious thought evaporated again as he screamed in abject fury.

The voice screamed something, and Thomas ignored it, racing forward and leaping into the air, lifting both hammers high before being slammed from his trajectory by a trio of lightning bolts, two arrows, and three crossbow bolts.

He slammed into the ground, rolling, crisped, his skin blackened in patches. The arrows and bolts snapped off inside him, and before he could recover, a foot slammed down on his right wrist, followed by a second on his left. Two of the giant men he recognized as fellow berserkers stood on either side of him, as a third stepped up by his feet, looking down at him in disgust.

"Time to die, heretic!" the man rumbled, when his mouth went slack, his throat sprouting the hilt of a dagger that hadn't been there a second before, with a meaty smack.

"I agree," a grim voice stated as another set of boots slammed home into the dirt next to Thomas's head. He looked up, confused, and found a huge legionnaire standing there.

The man was dark-haired, handsome in a way that even Thomas, who didn't swing that way and was filled with a blood rage, still noticed, and had a chin that looked like it could be used as an anvil if needed. Where Hollywood would have fallen over itself trying to cast him as a hero, throwing starlets and mansions at him, the legionnaire was consumed only with duty, and it showed in his contempt for the dark legionnaires.

"You scum sully the name of the legion by simply *existing*," the man hissed, drawing his sword and slapping it against his shield once before lifting it into the air and roaring out a cry of *"legion, forward!"*

Satisfied his command was being followed, he turned back to the three men. "Now, let's remedy that," the figure declared grimly, even as Thomas saw dark legionnaires nearby turning and running in fear.

The dark haired man lunged forward, slid under a hammer blow, straightened, then stepped to one side casually as a second hammer blow slammed down an inch from his side, barely missing Thomas' foot. The legionnaire planted one foot on the hammer, preventing it from being lifted, and sliced the wielder's eyes out. Then he twisted and caught the next blow on his shield, angling it so that the massive hammer seemed to glide along the surface before slamming into the knee of the berserker next to him, his sword smoothly following its trajectory to sever the arm that controlled it.

The three massive men who had so easily pinned and stopped Thomas were now, respectively, blinded, missing an arm, and collapsing to the floor with a pulverized knee. The legionnaire simply stepped through them, slicing here and flicking his sword out there with an efficiency of motion that was both beautiful and terrible to behold.

The three men were dispatched in seconds, as were two of the bastards that seemed to move so fast, they blurred. The armored man didn't move as quickly as they did; he shifted easily and stuck his blade out, letting them do all the work, then shucked them off his sword.

Thomas felt his berserker fury slipping away, partially in horror and amazement, and partially through sheer exhaustion and injury. The legionnaire spun into a collection of nearby dark legionnaires who were attempting a counter charge, shrugging their attempts off like rain. In seconds, he was back, peering down at Thomas and grunting in recognition.

"I can see him in you, lad. I hope you're worth the efforts he's gone to," he said, as legionnaires streamed past him in the dozens, seemingly appearing out of nowhere to drive forwards. "Kill them until they surrender!" he bellowed. "Then fucking kill them twice!"

"Yes, Lord Augustus!" came the collective response. Thomas started to shake as his body returned to normal and the shock set in.

Augustus knelt close to him, popping the top off a healing potion and pouring it into Thomas's mouth, mumbling as he clumsily cast a healing spell on him as well.

"Sorry, lad, never had much skill with healing spells; always better with the old steel, but you know how it is…new day, new ways." Augustus smiled grimly. "I saw you fighting them, so I'm guessing you switched sides when you realized who Lord Jax is, right?"

"Yes…yes, sir!" Thomas ground out, forcing the words past shaking lips.

"Good man. Anything I need to know?"

"Blood…I had Nimon's blood in me…" Thomas attempted to explain, before faltering at the look on Augustus' face.

"No need to worry about that now, lad; your Goddess explained that."

"My…Goddess?" Thomas asked, confused.

"Perhaps a look at your notifications is in order, but for now, you'll understand that we'll be taking your weapons, and you'll be behaving yourself."

"Yes…sir…" Thomas sagged back into the mud. "Pouch on my hip," he said, and another legionnaire was there in an instant, freeing it and looking inside.

"Standard kit, sir; some camp gear, some weapons and spare armor, food, that kind of thing."

"Good man for volunteering it before being asked," Augustus said firmly. "We'll get along fine, I think. For now, sleep, recover, and we'll take care of the rest."

"Aye, sir…" Thomas cut off as he saw a bright flash of light and heard a scream of absolute fury in the distance.

"Sounds like someone pissed Lydia off again," Augustus said to one of the men nearby, chuckling as they all winced, although some sniggered as well.

They propped him up against a tree, and Augustus strode off, while two of the legionnaires stayed with him, watching him and the surrounding area with equal suspicion and intensity.

"Who's…Lydia?" he asked eventually. A second later, another blur of bright white light was followed by an explosion in the distance and the screams of men running.

"*That's* Lydia," one of the men said briskly. "Leader of Lord Jax's personal squad, Valkyrie, and generally not a woman to piss off."

"Heard she gelded her ex-husband the other day," the other man said in a low voice, and all three men winced in sympathy.

"Man, that's…" Thomas started to say, shaking his head, as a new figure appeared next to him, tapping him lightly on the shoulder with a dagger.

"That's deserved," the figure finished, and the pair of legionnaires who'd tensed, ready to attack, relaxed, one of them snorting and shaking his head.

"Wondered where you got to, Tang." the man said, and the newcomer pushed his hood back, revealing an Elf clad in the legion's version of high-quality scouting gear, Thomas guessed.

"Had to take a few of the Dark Wanker's rogues out…useless pissants. Anyway, friend, you hear about any stealth attacks on your forces when you were chasing the boss? Hmm?" Tang asked Thomas, who shook his head tiredly.

"I don't think so…but…it's kinda a blur," Thomas admitted, getting a snort from Tang. "Wait…yeah, someone…took out…the mages…"

"That's him alright, and a relief then. Ah well, no doubt he'll turn up when he gets bored."

"Bane still missing?" one of the men asked, concern clear in his voice.

"Yup; you know what that means, though," Tang said quietly.

"Someone else is going to have a very bad day?" the other legionnaire quipped. Tang laughed, nodding.

"Damn, yes. That bastard scares *me* at times. Right; good luck, guys. The boss is getting worked on now. He's okay, just needs a hell of a lot of healing. From what the Lady told me, he did most of this himself." Tang gestured around the several miles of charred forest and piled bodies.

"Fuck." The legionnaire closest to Thomas shook his head in amazement. "You hear what he said to the God of Death?" he asked, and the other nodded, as Tang moved off, jogging into the forest, clearly resuming hunting.

"The Lady passed word. Man, he's got balls the size of a kraken's."

There was a general nodding and agreement at this, and Thomas groaned as he settled back, wondering at the way these legionnaires spoke about Jack…for all he knew that he'd missed a lot of his brother's recent life, he was still just, well…Jack. Or Jax, even. These men spoke as though he was a step below the Gods, and the mad fucker was picking fights with the most powerful of them all.

"Any chance of going to my brother now?" Thomas asked wearily.

"I don't know who, or what, you're talking about lad, but you stay right where Lord Augustus put you until he says different. Healers will check you over, then you'll be loaded aboard ship, probably the brig, and you'll get your chance to sort it all out later."

"My brother's…"

"Enough!" I don't care if your brother is Lord Jax himself! You'll damn well stay quiet and small until Lord Jax or Lord Augustus say otherwise. Now, you want to keep your mouth shut, or do we need to gag you?"

"Fine," Thomas mumbled, closing his eyes. He could feel Jack…Jax…close by, and he figured that was enough…for now…

AUGUSTUS

A ugustus strode through the ranks of his men, occasionally nodding to a legionnaire as they paused to salute him, more often simply being seen, now that the Legion were fully engaged in mopping up.

"Brina!" Augustus called when he recognized a particularly fast-moving legionnaire as she caught a fleeing dark legionnaire, hamstringing him, lopping off a hand as it swung a mace at her, and then beheading the cheeky fucker that dared to imitate a real legionnaire.

"Yes, Lord Augustus?" she called, flicking her sword to free it of the blood and doubling back to jog over to him.

"Any word on Tribune Jon?" Augustus asked, and the pause before she answered made him sigh.

"He's still alive, Lord, but for how long?" She furrowed her brow, shaking her head sadly. "Honestly, if not for Lady Hellenica's efforts, he'd never have lasted this long. But frankly, I don't see him lasting much longer."

"You've not seen the shit I have, Brina," Augustus said with a grimace. "Believe me, if he can hold on just a little longer, he'll have a chance, and that's all any of us can ask."

"Still can't believe the Legion General…" She broke off, biting her lip and sighing heavily. "Anyway, my apologies, Lord, is there anything else?" she asked, glancing longingly after the fleeing dark legionnaires.

"No, no…you go have fun," Augustus said with a sigh, dismissing her. "Remember your orders. Secure the perimeter, scout for any survivors and stragglers, then pull the net in, and we continue on after our new citizens."

"Yes, Lord!" Brina confirmed, crashing fist to chest before sprinting off again, clearly determined to feed her blade one last time before they fell back.

Augustus clapped his fist to chest in return, then turned and started heading back, keeping a wary eye on the new legionnaires. After Narkolt, he felt the newly birthed suspicion warring with his inbuilt conviction that any legionnaire was a person to trust with his life.

He shook his head and hurried through the streaming men and women, catching glimpses of the flash and flutter of Alkyon and more flitting through the canopy of trees overhead. He paused for a moment, marveling at the devastation on all sides.

Three quarters of a damn mile, they'd estimated the destruction stretched, roughly in a circle, where practically everything was a mess of charred wood, dead bodies, and slaughter, and there Jax was, right in the damn center, armor glowing with heat and smoking, but still fighting when they arrived.

He covered the last hundred meters in a light jog, coming to a halt as he approached the ring of his own men, standing glaring outwards at any who came close.

They made room, two legionnaires stepping out of formation to permit him entry, then turning and guarding outward again, eyeing anyone and everyone with cold suspicion until the Scion was back on his feet.

Augustus stopped directly inside the ring and spoke quickly.

"It's me; password is 'Aurelius the Great'," he said quietly, and the legionnaire who'd moved behind him, silently, grunted and tapped him on the space between his neck and pauldron with the dagger he'd drawn.

"Good to have you back, sir," the man muttered before turning back to face outwards.

"Goddamn paranoia is killing me," another of the men complained, squinting out at the others who moved past. "I mean, I know they're legionnaires…but…"

"Better to be careful, after all we saw, lad," yet another murmured.

Augustus nodded to himself as he strode forward, covering the last few feet and sinking to one knee next to Oracle and Hellenica as they worked.

"How is he?" he asked, his heart clenching at the look Hellenica gave him and the slight shake of her head. "That bad?"

"No," Oracle said grimly. "He'll live, but his injuries…it'll take time, Augustus, that's all. I need time, I need mana, and I need to get him to the Tower. He needs its power and Nerin's aid…"

"Then we'll get him moving. Lydia?" he asked, pausing as she strode through the ring of guards, all stepping aside and bowing their heads for her in reverence.

If there was one person in the group he didn't have to worry about the goddamn Drow taking over and replacing, it was Lydia.

After her transformation, she was…magnificent. It was the only way he could describe her. Her hair had changed, brightening to a white blonde that was just on the verge of silver, her frame had filled out with muscle, and the armor…

Lydia had recovered the armor of her predecessor, the last Valkyrie. While he'd only gotten basic details from her and the others as to what had actually happened, she clearly had the Goddess of Air, Vanei's, grace now.

Her wings were no longer ephemeral, instead manifesting as huge things that made him think of an angel, or in this case, an angel of destruction.

Augustus snorted at the similarity of her wings to that of the Prometheans' and felt a rush of pride the way they would forever more be seen as pale imitations of Lydia's magnificence, not to mention the way the way her feathery pinions were encased in their own armor.

Her silvery scale-mail and heavy plate combination granted her tremendous mobility, but the reinforced sections across the upper bones of her wings, the sharpened edges, and bladed tips? The girl was lethal just standing still, and she practically glowed.

"If the Drow could imitate you, we'd all be fucked," Augustus muttered to himself. Lydia grinned at him, shaking her hair out. The short, chopped style she'd previously gone for no was longer needed with the helm she now wore, clearly adapted for a Valkyrie to have whatever hair she wanted.

"Yer had a question, Primus?" Lydia asked, her voice filled with a new level of determination and confidence.

"Ah, yes." Augustus couldn't help smiling at the change in the woman. "You were one of the first to Jax, and you cleared the area; do you sense anything else nearby?"

"I...there be somethin'...somethin' malevolent. I can sense it watchin' us, but...but I've literally just started to learn to use these class Abilities. I..."

"It's all right. The first days of the change to a new level and class are always disorienting, especially when they come with a barrage of new abilities." Augustus reassured her. "Is it close? The thing you sense?"

"Not...close. It be here, somewhere nearby. It be observin' us, an' it moved as soon as it heard me say I could sense it...it's still movin'..." She turned slowly, looking around at the streaming legionnaires moving in all directions.

"It's not within the ring, though?" Augustus asked carefully.

"No...no I think it be further back..."

"Then we worry about it later," Augustus said firmly. "Legionnaires, we need to prepare to move the Scion. I want a ring of steel between him and anything that means him ill. When we move, we go directly to the ship, six hundred yards to the north by northeast.

"That's where they said they'd land, and if Mal's anywhere else, I'll rip his damn stones off personally! We move, we get Lord Jax and his brother into the ship, below decks where he can't be seen, and we get the Legion aboard. I'll give more orders then. On three!"

"I'll take tha watch," Lydia said fiercely, as though daring any threat to come close. She beat her wings once, launching herself into the air and starting to fly, erratically, sometimes skimming the trees, but her gaze flicked around with a level of ferocity unmatched by most.

"One!" Augustus barked, and two of the legionnaires stepped in close, leaving their slots in the ring and laying down a stretcher that one slid from his bag, two simple poles with cloth bound to them.

"Two!" he bellowed, as the legionnaires, along with Augustus himself and both Hellenica and Oracle's help, slid Jax onto the stretcher and made sure he was secure.

"Three!" he snapped, and the men lifted Jax smoothly, pivoting to face the direction he indicated, as the two men watching over Thomas took an arm each and hoisted him upright at Augustus's gesture.

Thomas groaned, trying to stand, and two more legionnaires stepped in, covering the first two as they carried the big man.

They set off at a jingling trot, passing through the forest as Augustus called out orders.

"Legion! Break off pursuit and fall back to the ships; take only what you can carry easily, and no extended looting!"

There was a chorus of affirmations, with the legionnaires working in pairs. One stripped a corpse, the other kept watch, then they'd run, pause, and swap over, allowing each to gain a decent haul before retreating from the battlefield.

The ring around Jax never faltered, never slowed, and never requested their share of the loot; carrying their lord was all the reward they needed and more.

The run took just over two and a half minutes. They could have gone faster, even fully armored and carrying their burden, but Augustus was careful to lead them around obstructions and bodies that might, even now, be playing dead.

As soon as they cleared the rise and dipped down into the next gully, the clearing ahead revealed the side of Mal's ship, and Augustus let out a sigh of relief. His own cruiser was both larger and more powerful than Mal's *Falcon*, but the *Falcon* was faster, and Mal seemed to have an almost uncanny bond with the ship, sliding it in to land in the tightest of berths without so much as a scratch.

When the notifications had started to appear, and Augustus had realized that Jax would need him, he'd known which ship he needed to be aboard. It had damn well been the right decision to make, he reflected, considering that, by the time they arrived, right in the proverbial nick of time, his own cruiser was at least an hour behind, if not two.

They jogged down the side of the embankment, seeing Mal's crew watching them with weapons drawn, and boarded quickly, grateful for the way the crew moved to give them space before going back to tracking the forest.

"Legion, Halt!" Augustus bellowed, and they all drew to stop as he nodded to Mal, who grimaced at the state of Jax.

"Damn, boy…you don't do things by half, do you?" Mal muttered, shaking his head in amazement. "He even alive in there?" He gestured to the melted and corroded armor, the still-leaking blood that dripped onto his decks, and the burned smell that lifted from the stretcher's passenger.

"He is, but it's a close thing," Augustus stated. "We need to get him somewhere safe for now, get the Legion aboard, and catch up to the runners. Once there, I'll drop some of the Legion to assist, and we'll take him to the Tower."

"You not stayin' with the Legion?" Mal asked, looking up from his examination of Jax.

"I'll not be leaving Lord Jax's side until he's upright. Not after Narkolt," Augustus said, his expression hard.

"Yeah, that was a kick in the tits, wasn't it? Okay, get them aboard, and make sure those who left are the ones we get back. I don't want any of those fuckers aboard."

"You think I want any in the Legion? No, we do what we can, and once we get back to the Tower, we'll find a way to separate the sheep from the wolves."

"Fair enough. Get him downstairs, pick a cabin, and…" Mal paused before frowning in confusion. "Who's the dark wanker?" he asked Augustus.

"That's his brother, if you can believe it." Augustus gestured to the man the legionnaires were holding, making them look more closely at the Dark Legionnaire who dangled half-conscious between them in consternation.

They subtly adjusted their grip on his clothing and armor and lifted him into a more comfortable position as they heard the truth of his relation to Jax, exchanging looks.

"He looks like shit as well, so yeah, that I can believe. Want him in the same cabin, or in the brig?"

"The cabin, for now. When he proves he can't be trusted, we'll use the brig," Augustus said clearly, eyeing Thomas.

"Fine, now get the pair of them out of the way; you're clogging up my decks," Mal grumbled as he made his way back up to the upper deck and the controls for the ship. Legionnaires streamed out of the forest, boarding the ship after their small party.

"Let's get them below!" Augustus ordered, leading the way and glaring at anyone who got between him and his destination. Meanwhile, Lydia landed behind the small group and stalked along, watching their back.

CHAPTER FIFTY-TWO

I came to a few hours later, the pain waking me. I started to sit up, the sudden sharp agony over my heart enough to wake me from my rest with a hiss of pain and the beginnings of a Fireball forming in my hand, and she was there.

"Jax, no!" Oracle said quickly. "Stop, relax. It's okay."

I stared wild-eyed at her, my chest screaming with pain, before I finally recognized her. Forcing the spell weave to be reabsorbed, I laid back, looking down and gritting my teeth at what I saw.

The armor I'd been wearing, or more accurately, the remains of the armor, was in the process of being cut away. Literally.

Entire sections were scattered around me, complete with sections of flesh attached to the inside, and as I looked down, I could see a mixture of open, flensed chest and bloody bone, along with the pulse of barely hidden organs, and melted steel or shredded underpadding.

I swallowed hard as my brain caught up, and I sagged back slowly, laying my head back down and hearing a grunt from Tommy.

I took Oracle's hand as she offered it, squeezing in reassurance and simply being there for me, as Hellenica slowly excised sections of the armor with Augustus's aid.

"You look like shit," Tommy grunted as I glanced over at him.

"Look who's talking," I rasped out, stifling a laugh with a groan. "At least for me, it's temporary, unlike you, ya fugly bastard."

"Yeah, well, at least my nickname ain't 'pencil-dick'." Tommy winked at me.

"Only because it's so fucking small...they're never sure if it's there or not," I muttered back. "Mind you, I don't blame it, with some of the girls you used to bring home. That last one, what possessed you? I mean, seriously dude, she had her own zip-code."

"Seriously, five years since I saw you last, and you still throw her at me?"

"Throw? Nah, I'd never be able to lift her."

"She was better than the creature you were dating, I mean, she made Skeletor look like he needed to go on a diet."

"I used to hear you through the wall, bro." I snorted, rolling my eyes.

"Her screams of pleasure, you mean?" he shot over quickly.

I grunted, gritting my teeth as Augustus made a shallow incision and rooted around inside the pocket of flesh he'd just made, tugging free a section of padding that the regenerating flesh had grown around.

"No, man..." I whispered when I could speak again. "When you used to have to ask her to fart to give you a clue."

"Fuck, Jack!" Tommy laughed, beaming over at me. "How long you been planning that one?"

"Five years," I croaked, wincing again, before regarding my amused brother, sitting on a low stool and shaking his head in mock dismay.

"I expected better from you, mate…something like…"

"I think you can catch up on each other's sexual exploits later, maybe?" Hellenica asked coolly, gently smoothing the flesh down as Augustus cut another section free.

"Oh, I don't know…sounds like typical barracks shit-talking to me," Augustus countered with a quick grin.

"It doesn't get any better…" a voice agreed from by the door, and I lifted my head, finding Tang leaning there. "Personally, I'm only glad he's fucking decent. Usually, he's swinging his knob at Oracle by now."

"Yeah, well…I love you, too, mate," I whispered, letting my head thump back down on the thin pillow and trying to ignore the pain of what they were doing.

"Jax, if yer can talk me through a potion o' Somnolence," Lydia asked.

"Don't worry about it; I can take it," I said, wincing.

"Yes, but do you need to?" Oracle prodded me carefully. "My love, be realistic. You woke as soon as we started on your chest. There's at least a few hours' worth of work here, as we can't kill these nerves and simply regrow them the way we did your arms. What will take several hours if we work quickly will take days if we go slowly."

"Are we safe in the Tower?" I asked carefully, knowing the answer.

"No, we're aboard ship…"

"Are our people safe?" I continued.

"No," Oracle replied sadly.

"Then I need…to be conscious." I insisted, gasping as Augustus carefully sliced another section of skin free in order to excise the gnarled and twisted remnant of a metal plate from the mauled flesh that had grown over it.

"We can go slower," Hellenica said hesitantly.

"No." I bit down my fear and steeled myself. "Go faster." I ordered, looking at Augustus.

"That'll be more painful," he warned me.

"But it'll be over sooner," I countered, and Lydia passed me a slim chunk of wood. "What's this?"

"Bite down on it; it'll make it easier an' give yer somethin' to focus on," she said, her eyes tight with concern.

"Thank you," I took a proper look at her and smiling. She looked magnificent, even in a blood-smeared, overcrowded tiny cabin with her wings folded awkwardly and forcing her to hunch down. "Lydia…I'm so proud of you." I whispered, surprised at the bright red blush that filled her cheeks.

"Thank yer, my lord," she murmured softly.

"Told you not to bother with that shit," I muttered.

"We need a distraction," Oracle said firmly. "Let's get the reports in and get caught up. Then, once everything Jax can deal with is done, we can move out."

"Aye, Oracle," Lydia grunted, before turning to Tang. "Get Mal down here."

"Aye," Tang replied, slipping out the door, as Lydia turned back to me.

"Might as well give yer tha story while we wait, then." She shrugged, adjusting her wings before glancing at Tommy. "Do yer want him here while we talk?" she asked me bluntly.

"Yeah, he's my brother. He burned his bridges with the Dark Wankers when he realized who I was…you can trust him." I glanced over at my brother and *knew* in my bones it was true. One of the advantages of the bond between twins, and especially between us, was knowing when the other was hedging or trying to conceal something. In the past, it'd enabled us to cover for each other when we'd needed to. Here, it let me know what he was feeling, to a degree, with us being so close.

"I can leave if you want," Tommy offered.

"No; if you'd not been loyal to me, you could have killed me back there. Would have been a fuck-load easier for you."

"You're not wrong there; at least I'd sort of known what I was doing when I signed up to follow Ni…my last God," Tommy said thoughtfully. "Yeah, I had no fucking choice, but you know, I was actually conscious."

"Well, Lagoush is a better choice than that wanker, at least. We can talk about it all later; for now, I need to get the reports." I clenched my jaw with a grunt, eyeing the chunk of wood. "After that, you can give us your story, and, well, I guess you'll get mine. Think those tales are better told over beer, though."

"Yeah, kinda a fucked-up tale," Tommy muttered.

"You think mine ain't? Seriously, bro, we'll talk. For now, though, I need to make sure my people are okay. Lydia, you start," I ordered, closing my eyes again and sliding the wood into my mouth.

"Aye, Jax," Lydia said quickly, my word enough for her. "We ran fer tha marker; took a few hours, even at our fastest, but when we made it…it were a barrow we found. Looked like it'd been raised a long time back. We dug the capstone free, an' there were steps underneath. Led down into a pit, one filled with chains and lingerin' screams; don't know who built tha barrow. She said she dinna remember, but someone 'ad. Whole place was filled with warnin's. 'Don't go in, turn back now,' all that shit." Lydia scoffed, folding her arms. "I mean, really, who does that? Anyone sees signs like that, might as well be screamin', 'look, we've hidden treasure 'ere,' right?" An agreeing grunt lifted from the rest of the room.

"Anyway, we had to kill a few undead; somethin' about places like that just attracts 'em, like Grizz to tits," she quipped, getting a snort from a few of those in the room who knew him well.

"Once we'd cleared 'em out, an' made it to tha bottom o' the barrow, there were a big cavern. Remains of tha Demon were pinned to tha ground on tha far side, an' she were on this side. Pair of 'em were dead, but not, iffin yer know what I mean?

"They'd died killin' each other, but neither'd move on, not 'til they saw tha other go first, so they'd bound their souls to their forms. She'd animated her armor just enough to be able to smash his bones, and he'd managed to regrow his bones just enough to start to counter. Tha pair were locked in a stalemate, slowly recoverin' enough mana to move tha armor to smash 'is bones, and he'd drain her mana as she did it, lettin' 'im repair another bone…"

"So, they were endlessly repairing and smashing each other?" I asked, pulling out the wood and working my jaw as Augustus gave me a few seconds to catch my breath.

"Basically," Lydia confirmed. "Someone'd come along years later an' got freaked out, so they sealed 'em in, I guess, leavin' 'em to keep going. All we did was climb inside, kill a few low-level undead, an' then 'elp 'er.

"Just smashed tha shit outta tha rest of tha Demon's bones, then fed her enough mana to let her smash tha skull in properly 'erself. Once all that was done, she, well, she spoke to me, sort of. Told me to take her armor, an' 'er body. We stripped her gear away, she gave me her blessin', an' I put it on, then we came out, started runnin' to meet up with yer.

"Oracle arrived an' told us tha stupid shit ye were pullin', an' that she could sense Augustus an' Mal nearby. She got 'em to land, an' we got on, then we all came here, fucked up tha rest of tha Dark Legionnaires, an' boom. Yer all caught up. Fancy tellin' us why ye were tryin' to sacrifice yourself now? Rather than runnin' for it, an' lettin' us all come back later to save tha slaves, as that's what they'd have done; just capture 'em, I mean?"

Reluctantly, I spat the block of wood back into my hand. It really had been helping, as had listening to the story. "Because you don't know that," I said, just as the door opened and Tang and Mal slipped into the room, making it even more crowded.

"Don't know what?" Mal asked.

"We don't know that the Dark Wankers would have just captured the people we saved. They might have killed them all straight away, for all I knew, and I wasn't going to risk that."

"So instead, yer risked tha Empire?" Lydia asked me flatly.

"No, I risked a single man," I retorted, gritting my teeth. "I had already named Augustus my heir, so if I'd died, well, I could afford that."

"We couldn't!" Lydia argued, her eyes blazing.

"You'd have survived!" I snapped back at her. "I gave the orders I did to make sure you were all as safe as I could make you. Would I have preferred that you were all with me, instead of out there, doing your damn jobs? Of course, I would! You think I wanted to do what I did?"

"Yeah, I do!" Lydia cried suddenly, glaring fiercely at me. "I think yer be a little in love with tha idea of dying a martyr an' not having tha fuckin' stress anymore!"

"I…" I started, before pausing to consider, then sighed and leaned back. "I don't want to die. But I'll admit, when I thought I was going to, and I could finally go all out, just to try to buy you all some time? Yeah, I felt fucking relieved at that."

"Yer don't get to do that!" Lydia spat. Even Augustus nodded in agreement with her, before gesturing to the wood and starting to cut again. "Yer don't get to raise us up, then fuckin' die. Yer don't get to leave us to mourn, while you fuckin' sleep tha ages away! Yer try that shit again, an' I'll personally come get you an' tear your fuckin' soul back through the veil an' shove it into a body!"

"I love you too, Lydia," I whispered when I could speak again, after biting down hard and hissing my pain out. "I won't do it again, okay? Not unless I need to. I'd rather live a long and fucking awesome life than die, but if that's the only choice left to me, then I'll damn well take it." I bit back a moan, switching my attention from her to Mal.

"Mal, thank you, man," I said, sincerely grateful. "Seems like you're always there when I need you, even if you could be a little earlier to make my fucking life easier."

"Yeah, well, I had my own shit to take care of...you okay, kid?" he asked, after a little pause.

"I am," I whispered. "Give me good news, Mal; what's happening out there?"

"Not much right now; we're hoverin' about three hundred meters up from the makeshift camp. Grizz and the others are below, along with hundreds of people. They're sittin' about, really. We're just waitin' on the *Ragnarök*; she's about ten minutes out, should be here soon.

"Then we turn and set sail for the Tower. Three more ships incomin', but they're hopefully with us, rather than against. We'll have to see, though. They're about six hours out, with the *Sigmar's Fist* comin' up from the south now–she's about ten hours or so–and another six or eight for the flotilla from the Tower to reach us. All told, it's a bit of a shit show."

"That didn't make much sense," I admitted. "Run me through it again?"

"The *Ragnarök* is nearly here, behind her is another ship from Narkolt, probably holdin' my father and his men, and the last of the Legion are marchin' from the city, along with their dependents."

"Huh?" I asked intelligently.

"Your brains scrambled, boy?" Mal chided me, frowning. "There's the *Ragnarök*..."

"I heard that bit, you prick; I want to know where the legionnaires came from, and what the hell your father is doing with a ship and coming here?" I growled at Mal.

"Then clear the turds outta your ears and listen!" Mal snapped. "Augustus, you not told him?" He shot a glare at Augustus, who was up to his elbows in blood and slowly teasing a piece of cloth out from under a rib of mine.

"Do I look like I've had much time for idle chatting, smuggler?" Augustus snarled, pulling the fabric free and glaring back at Mal.

"You look like you've been here longer than I have, so why the hell is it on me to explain your fuckin' deeds in the city? I wasn't even there for most of 'em!"

"THAT'S BECAUSE YOU WERE DRUNK OR IN A WHOREHOUSE!" Augustus shouted, before stopping and visibly getting himself back under control. "I apologize, Jax; this kind of surgery is new to me, and doing it on the soon-to-be Emperor, while he watches, is slightly fraying my nerves."

"That's okay," I hissed as he plucked another section free. "It's a new one for...ah, for fuck's sake!" I broke off as he pulled on something, and a wash of blood poured out. The cloth that came free had been driven deep into my chest, and as it came loose, it sent my diaphragm spasming wildly, which tore more of the bloody flesh away.

"Jax, we need to not do this while you're conscious," Oracle insisted. "Augustus, stop. Give him a brief breakdown of what happened; then he can give orders, and you all leave him to Hellenica and me after this."

"No..." I started to object, and Oracle cut me off.

"Jax, do you trust me?" she asked.

"Of course, I do..."

"Then believe this: your chest is hanging open, and you're hemorrhaging blood. I keep having to cast healing spells every other minute to just keep your heart intact and going. You're literally operating on sheer adrenaline and lunacy right now, and you can't make clear command decisions on either. You have two minutes; then I'm going to knock you out and wake you up when you're actually sane enough to do anything."

"I…" I sputtered, scowling at Oracle, who glared back at me.

"Fuck me, Jack, when'd you get married?" Tommy muttered.

I shot him a glare, one that slid off him like water off a duck's back.

"Seriously, dude, I'm with her. I can literally see your lungs moving. It's kinda gross."

"Go suck…a bucket of…dicks." I snapped at him breathlessly.

"I would, but your breath smells like you beat me to it," Tommy retorted.

"One minute thirty and counting, Jax," Oracle said.

"Fuck's sake…fine, I'll let you put me under…BUT I need to…hear it all first, and I'll tell you…what I think, then…well, it's up to…Augustus, I guess." I grunted to Oracle and the room at large, panting with pain.

"Go, Mal, and make it quick, please," Oracle ordered.

"Fine," Mal snapped. "We got to Narkolt, found a bunch of Drow were impersonatin' people in the city, includin' the Legion General. Augustus killed a bunch of 'em, we saw you needed help, he ordered the Legion to mount up, and brought as many as he could fit on ships to the shipyards.

"I was uh…busy…then I headed straight for the ships, sent word to my father. While we talked, Rewn sent a message demandin' we attend him at the city lord's palace. We ignored them and ran while they were still waitin' for an answer, so yeah, they might be pissed about that later. *Sigmar's Fist* is incomin', as is what looks like, and should, be my father's new ship…"

"How new?" I asked, certain I'd never heard of Mal's father having a ship before.

"Depends on whether he bought the ship or stole it, really, but he was goin' shoppin' for the best one in the shipyards when we left. Now stop interruptin', I lost where I was…oh yeah. So, my father's on his way with a bunch of his people, as is *Sigmar's Fist*, with a bunch more legionnaires on those ships with men they trust, if they got out.

"Or, it might be full of Drow and Dark Legion dickheads. If it's our people, they can help protect the people below. If it's not, then it's two ships that are armed and manned by people with cannons they'll actually fire, so our two ships won't last long. The Tower ships will either arrive too late to do anything or just in time to load everyone up, and we all fuck off back to the Great Tower for cakes and fuckin' pastries. That sum it up alright for you?"

"Fuck me," I muttered. "Why the hell…"

"Jax," Augustus said calmly, and I looked at him, anxious and confused. "We will figure out who is who; leave that to me. For now, just tell me what you want, and I'll make it happen."

"Fine; protect the new…citizens, get them…aboard the ships, along…with the legionnaires, and…get everyone back…to the Tower."

"Of course. Now sleep, man, before you keel over and make this day harder."

"Is he in there?" the voice of Hannimish floated through the closed door. "Lord Jax? I must speak with you!"

"Fuck's...sake, you brought...him back?" I gasped as Mal yanked the door open and glared at Hannimish, who forced a smile to his face.

"Ah, Captain, I merely wished to discuss the situation regarding the Sunken City and Himnel with the...Lord...Jax?" He trailed off at the sight of me laid out in the middle of the room, chest shredded and blood dripping from the camp bed I was resting on. "Oh my God," he muttered, covering his mouth, clearly about to be sick.

"Yes, Hannimish?" I croaked. "Clearly there's...something of such...earth-shattering...importance that you had to interrupt...me?"

"No! No...my lord, I'm...I'm deeply sorry!" Hannimish called out as he rushed away, a gagging sound coming from him as he went.

"Pussy!" Tommy shouted after him. "Seriously, Jack, go to sleep, dude."

"Aye, Tommy, I will." I laid back and closed my eyes, feeling the screaming, leaden need to rest coming over me again as soon as I relaxed even slightly.

"I'll be here when you wake up, my love," Oracle whispered, leaning in close and kissing me on the forehead.

Then it was over as I sank into dreamless sleep.

CHAPTER FIFTY-THREE

I woke up two days later, cocooned in a bed, and for the first time, when I woke up here, I wasn't greeted with a vision of loveliness, as I'd come to expect. Instead of Oracle, Giint was leaning over me, peeling one of my eyelids back and staring in at point-blank range.

I screamed.

He screamed.

I twisted, shoved him to the side, and punted the little bastard off my bed, before sitting up to raucous laughter.

"Happy Birthday!" shouted dozens of voices all around the room. I rolled out of the bed, spinning and trying to make sense of the world.

I stood up straight, hands slapping to my chest and frantically feeling for injuries, then my arms, my thighs…I was healed! I was intact, and even my scars were gone! I was surrounded by my squad, my friends and…and half the Council of the Tower.

And I was stark goddamn naked. Just swinging in the wind.

"Ah, fuck you guys," I grunted, scowling around as the congratulatory shouts died away under a barrage of embarrassed silence, in which there came a muffled shout from Giint, who, it seemed, had landed in the laundry basket and was now lodged upside down, stumpy legs kicking wildly.

"Him awake!" came the cry.

I grumbled wordlessly, before shrugging in acceptance.

"Fuck it; you've all seen it by now, anyway." I sighed and wandered over to grab Giint and drag him out of the basket.

I set him back on his feet and looked over at Tommy.

"This was you, wasn't it?" I asked flatly, getting a wide grin in return. "I knew it. Considering it's at least a week until our actual birthday."

"How about we all go next door?" Lydia suggested, red-faced, and started hurrying people out of the bedroom.

"Nah, I keep track of shit like that. It's today," Tommy said, and I scoffed at him.

"You lying turd, you did this deliberately to see if you could embarrass me," I accused.

He grinned even wider.

"Damn right I did, but you know, it actually is today…"

"Bullshit," I snorted, raising a disbelieving eyebrow.

"Actually, Jax, you've been unconscious for two days, and when you add in the other days you've lost though injuries…" Oracle started to explain.

"Really?" I asked. "And what's the deal with letting Crazy McCrazyPants of the clan McCrazy wake me up like that?" I demanded, still fuming.

"Well, usually you try to fuck me first thing when I wake you up, so I went along with Thomas's suggestion of Giint, as it was less likely to result in you exposing yourself or me to everyone else."

"How'd that work out for you?" I grumbled, shaking my head.

"Well, I enjoyed the view, so not bad," she said with a twinkle in her eye, then laughed and flew out of the room, leaving Tommy and me alone.

"Seriously, bro, she is amazing; ten points for that one," Tommy said after a long, awkward pause.

"Mine!" I threw at him, then winked as he laughed.

"What about you then, bro?" I asked as I searched around, finding some clothes and starting to dress. "Any special ladies in your life?"

"Hah. Yeah, there was one," Tommy said, his mood dropping like a stone.

"What happened?" I asked.

"I…well…I think you might have killed her, man."

Silence lingered for a minute or two, before I swore.

"Shit. I'm…I'm sorry, man." I hesitated, no clue where to go from there.

"Don't," he said, shaking his head. "Just…don't. It's a war, and we were on opposite sides. Oracle filled me in on a lot of what happened."

"Fuck." I pulled my pants on, then a lightweight top, before walking over to him and standing awkwardly.

"Come here, you stupid bastard," Tommy said after a second, grabbing me in a bear hug and squeezing tight. I wrapped my arms around him as well, squeezing back, and we just stood there for a long moment before a cough came from the doorway.

We separated, and Oracle regarded us for a moment, smiling, then gestured us forward to join rest of the group waiting in Oracle and my sitting room.

"Thanks, man, for coming for me," Tommy said as we walked together. "Oracle told me about it."

"It's what brothers do," I responded. "Especially big brothers. I had to come, and not just because of that prick of a Baron."

"Ha, he is a fucking dickhead, that's for sure." Tommy chuckled, shaking his head. "Any way we can open a portal back to him and throw through a bunch of Feenals or something? Shut it real fast afterwards?"

"Tempting," I admitted. "You meet any of the other houses before you came through?"

"Falco," he said promptly. "Sent his hottie of a daughter to me, did me a deal for the Baron's stone. You?"

"Same; got a spellbook, access to the Tower, and put down close to you. What did you get?"

"Damn, you did better than me. I got a bow that broke after a week, a ring, and a few potions; sod-all else besides her."

"Her?" I repeated, looking at him in confusion.

"Oh, yeah, she was mental, man. Jumped my bones the minute she was in the room, offered the rest as a sweetener, then…wow."

"Lucky bastard!" I said, shaking my head in awe.

"What, you mean you didn't? I figured it was just what she did; I mean, for recruiting…you know?"

"Nope." I rubbed the back of my neck. "I tore her top, so the Baron thought I tried it on with her, and she went along with it."

"So, wait, the whole time, the Baron was watching you?" Tommy asked.

"Yeah, man; under guard the whole time, why?"

"Ha! That's my fault. He caught Sintara leaving the changing room after I'd won. She called in to congratulate me…rode me like a damn stallion, nearly broke it in half. Bet that's when he decided to watch over you."

"Motherfucker. You mean you got sexy time, and I paid the price?!" I snapped, taking my seat in the main room.

"Oh yeah," Tommy groaned happily, winking at me.

"You utter shitbag." I sighed, then looked around the room.

"Okay, now that I have pants on."

"Thank God," Tang interjected.

"Fuck you very much, Tang," I continued. "Now that I have pants on, though, let's try that one again!"

"Happy Birthday!" they chorused, and I laughed, especially as Lydia pulled the cover off a cake.

It was huge, at least a foot and a half across, and made up of flat sponges that, when she handed me her dagger, and I cut into it, could probably have been sharpened and used as offensive weapons, they were that overbaked.

That wasn't the point, though.

I sat there with nearly twenty people packed into a room that would hold five comfortably, cutting a cake with a dagger given to me by a Valkyrie that had probably slit someone's throat with it recently.

I handed out slices of cake to everyone, from Cai and Isabella, lithe and beautiful as the pair were, respectful and upright citizens of the Tower, and now the Empire. To Grizz and Giint, two utterly mad bastards, one a massive legionnaire who could maim you six ways from Sunday with his pinky, and yet was one of the most trustworthy untrustworthy bastards I'd ever met, and the other a crazed, drug-fueled Gnome who spent all his time trying to blow shit up or kill people.

God, I missed Bane. He'd not been amongst the dead nor the living when the rest of the Legion arrived and scoured the site. So I had to just hope and pray that he was alright. There was always goddamn something.

I let my gaze wander around the room, hearing people practically breaking their teeth on the cake, spotting the clumsily wrapped gifts people were trying to hide, and I knew my brother had arranged all of this and expected nothing for himself. He'd done it, despite everything I'd seemingly cost him, just because he was my brother, and he loved me.

And he was an asshole who wanted to see me squirm.

I loved him for it.

EPILOGUE 1

"So you're sure, the Dark Legion is in disarray?" I asked, sitting back in my seat in the command center, with my brother, Cai, Flux, Augustus and Romanus, Oren, and Lydia seated around the table, Oracle standing by my side, and Heph, Seneschal, and Tenandra gathered around the table itself in various forms.

"Tha's what I said, laddie," Oren confirmed, grinning. "I followed them halfway back ta Himnel. Ain't nobody in command, just a bunch o' wee groups, all sprintin' fer cover. Yer broke them, laddie!"

"Did I?" I frowned skeptically as I asked Tommy, or Thomas, as he went by now, it seemed.

"Nah, not really." Thomas shrugged. "They lost almost all the fodder to you and a fuck-load of the elites, I think. I know I saw over a dozen squads of elites mixed in with the shit when I was there. I didn't see any intact at the end of it, even if you only killed half.

"But the Dark Legion isn't what it seems from outside. I always thought they were this massive force of real hard bastards. They're not. There's maybe a third that are the elite forces; they're what people see killing monsters and slaughtering bandits and shit." He sat forward, taking a drink from his wine glass and sighing.

"I was one of them, you know? Sold as a slave to the Dark Church, then Edvard, the paladin whose arm you chopped off...you remember?"

"Fancy-Pants?" I mused, trying to think back. "All gold-embossed armor and shit?"

"Yeah." Thomas snorted.

"I stole that fragment of the altar to Lagoush from him," I said, remembering the pouch. "He literally saved your life, having that thing."

"Yeah, well, anyway," Thomas said, clearing his throat and not wanting to think about the incident that led to Edvard having that piece of the altar. "Edvard picked me up, gave me a chance, healed me; the works, you know?"

"Yeah, man, he was your sponsor, right?" I asked.

"Something like that," Thomas muttered dismissively. "He gave me the chance to advance through the ranks far faster than I should have. Because of that, I ended up in Bella...Belladonna's Squad." He corrected himself, blinking rapidly.

I watched him as he paused there, putting two and two together and getting a hint of the woman he'd loved.

"She trained us mercilessly, morning, day, and night; always, we were at it, you know? And not in the fun way, you prick," he shot at me, with a half-smile. "The thing is, the Slave-Aspirants, they get gear that looks like ours. So do the Soldier-Aspirants, but each level as you climb higher you get better gear, and more training.

"Someone figured out that they needed people just to catch arrows and shit, so that's the Aspirant classes. When you reach Legionnaire, then it all changes. We are the elite, and you might have killed maybe a hundred of us." He tapped his wine glass with restless fingers. "The rest were ordered to remain in the city, to 'bolster the guard and provide moral and ideological support'. Sounded like martial law to me; I was just glad to get out and go fight."

I watched him, noticing the black mood that had descended and the way he still referred to the elites as us, not them.

"So, you think that what we killed were the slaves and weaker members of the Dark Legion?" I asked to be sure. "And that while we got some of the elites, most of them were back at the city?"

"Yeah. You want to wipe out the Dark Legion, you need to take down the Citadel, kill the Archpriest, and clear out the holier-than-thou-pricks who call it home."

"I…" I opened my mouth when a new notification popped up, and I glared at it and the way it overrode my wishes, the rest of them were neatly corralled until I had time for them.

You have been offered a Divine Quest: My God is Better than your God (4)

Jenae and the Pantheon of the Flame have offered you a quest. Travel to the Fallen City of Himnel, storm its walls, and throw down its defenders. Conquer the Citadel of the Dark Church, and destroy Nimon's altar, as well as those of the Pantheon of the Dark.

Bonus: Free the City of Narkolt or bend it to your will: 0/1

Destroy the Dravith Dark Citadel: 0/1

Kill the Dravith Archpriest of Nimon: 0/1

Kill enemy Priests, Clerics, and Paladins: 0/100

Capture the City of Himnel: 0/1

Capture/Liberate the City of Narkolt: 0/1

Bonuses will be given for exceeding these numbers.

Reward: Territorial Claim increased, 100,000+ Citizens, Access to City treasuries and capabilities, 5,000,000xp

Accept: *Yes/No*

I sat for a long minute, reading and rereading the notification, noting the usual gold edging and glowing letters formed of smoke. This was the kind of notification that would signal a change in the entire continent.

"Fuck them if they can't take a joke," I muttered, reading it as I smiled. Bracing myself, I clicked the notification and accepted the quest, immediately receiving the next one that rolled out to everyone across the continent.

War!

War has been formally declared between the Great Tower of Dravith, Center of the Empire, Home of the Pantheon of the Flame and the upstart Cities of Himnel and Narkolt, with special emphasis on the Followers of the God of Death, Nimon!

"Citizens, step aside, and ye shall be permitted free passage. Linger, and be counted as an enemy of my Gods, my Empire, and myself."

– Jax Amon, Scion of the Empire

Choose your side well, as Religious Wars are never pleasant!

EPILOGUE 2

"Well, while unexpected, it does present us with an opportunity," one of the shadowy figures said laconically, and the others muttered agreement. A figure in the corner of the room flicked out his hand, shooting a spray of red fluid in the direction of a tiny patter of feet.

There was a squeak of protest, followed by an indrawn breath and the sound of a body collapsing to the floor, as the fluid retracted to the figure's wrist. The room was briefly lit by a flicker of life energy sliding along the web and back into the ganglion as it was withdrawn, eliciting a sigh of disgust from several members gathered for the impromptu meeting.

"Honestly, Cletus! If you can't at least train your protégé in common manners, then leave it outside the hall. It's disgusting to see it feed on lesser beings," one of the creatures snarled. The one she addressed let out a sharp laugh in return.

"Ah, Den'taan, were we truly that different when we were but a few weeks into our change? I seem to remember your feeding on an Elf maiden led to your expulsion from your clan?"

"A sentient!" Den'taan snapped as she gestured dismissively. "We all fed ravenously when the change first overcame us, but by the Dark Lady, at least we had the common sense to feed on that which would bring us the most enjoyment. Your...thing...feeds on anything!"

"Well, he'll learn, or he won't, and if he doesn't, we all know the sweetest meat comes from our own stocks," Cletus said, grinning evilly.

"Enough!" snapped an older voice, coming from the hooded figure at the head of the table. All conversation stopped as they leaned forward to hear the voice of their master. "The vagaries of a fledgling's feeding habits are of no interest to the wider situation. The Dark Church of Nimon moves to take control of the city. We have two choices: we permit this, or we do not..."

"The Dark..." Cletus's protégé started to say, suddenly springing to life and stepping out from the corner he had been seated in. Before he could take two steps, Cletus was there, backhanding him with shattering force and sending him sprawling to the floor in a spray of blood.

"Silence, fool!" Cletus snapped, all good humor and laid-back visage banished as he desperately moved to prevent the master's irritation from becoming deeper.

"Cletus..." the Master said slowly, his head lifting so that his mouth was visible under the cowl he wore, and the rest of the table drew back quickly, compelled not to be between the Master and the object of his ire. "You never did tell us the identity of your latest fledgling."

"Ah, I never sought to hide it, my master," Cletus said quickly, bowing low. "My pet was lord of the city above us. He came to me after his title was revoked, desperately seeking the power to balance the scales. He balked at the cost at first, but eventually, he came around to the Gift."

"Ah, this is *that* one," the master said with a sneer of amusement. "Fine, let it speak."

"Get up, you fool!" Cletus snarled, hauling Barabarattas to his feet, and glaring into his face. "You have a single chance to survive this; if not…" He held up his hand warningly, and the ganglion at the base of his wrist pulsed hungrily. Then he shoved his pet forward, retaking his own seat and watching him threateningly.

Barabarattas sniffed then spat blood on the floor before glaring around the room, and finally at the Master he'd been warned so many times about.

"I am Lord Barabarattas," he began loftily. "I have joined your little cabal, and sat there, exiled to the rear of the chamber, while you prattled on inanely long enough! You speak of permitting *MY* city to be taken by the Church of the Dark; well, I've already done that deal.

"I've already been forced into allowing the Church a say in almost everything! You think you can offer me a better deal? You think your…*our*…kind can hold the city any easier? With half the day lost to us through the accursed sun?"

"I see…your pet is very young indeed, Cletus," the Master rumbled, smiling widely.

At that sign, the others shifted in their seats, the sudden readiness to bolt hanging tangible in the air as the Master leaned forward and steepled his fingers on the table before him.

"I may be young in terms of…Aargh!" Barabarattas screamed as the Master moved, blurring through the middle of the table and sending it flying in a detonation of splinters and fractured wood. In a blink, he gripped the stunned Barabarattas in one claw-tipped hand, hauling him upwards. His shoes dangled a good two feet off the ground as he stared, terrified, into the shrouded face before him.

"Silence, worm!" the Master whispered, his eyes glowing like coals in the depths of his hood. "The only reason you are permitted to live is so that, should we decide to move on, you may be sacrificed to assure others of our doom. Remember this!"

"Ma…Master…" Barabarattas gasped, his face turning blue.

"Bah!" The Master spat in disgust, throwing the weakly struggling figure aside to smack off the wall with a sound like a steak dropped onto a paving slab as he returned to his seat.

"Cletus, you will have Persephone joining you. She will play the part of this one's new wife in public, and will work to limit the spread of the Dark Church and its paladins. You will be the knife, she the poisoned chalice.

"I expect the Church will run rampant in the short term; you may permit that. So long as they do not discover this cavern, nor interrupt our breeding efforts, I care not. Expand your efforts to seize control of the underside of the city through the gangs and slavers. Provided the bodies continue to come, and we are not interrupted, I leave the details to you."

The Master glared at the whimpering Barabarattas on the floor again before showing one gleaming canine in a snarl of contempt.

"If, however, this one fails to play his part, he can be removed, and Persephone will take his place. He, in turn, takes the place of the main course at our next little gathering." The Master gestured to a side table, where a stocky Dwarf lay on a platter, shaved, scented, and bound hand and foot, with a shiny red apple jammed in his mouth. He whimpered at the sudden attention of the creatures around the table.

EPILOGUE 3

"**I**s it true, sir?" Coran asked Edvard grimly, standing to attention. Edvard sat sweating and gritting his teeth as his arm was painfully regrown by the Dark Priest kneeling by his chair.

"It is! By the God, Coran, he betrayed us, he betrayed me…he betrayed us all." Edvard hissed out, fury mixed with the pain of regrowth.

"I…I don't know what to say, sir," Coran stammered, shaking his head in shocked dismay. "He never seemed the type, and I mean, he had the blood! Surely, he couldn't…is there no way…"

"There was no misunderstanding, lad," Edvard ground out harshly, his intact hand clutching the armrest so hard, the creaking of the oak could be clearly heard above the screams and moans of the survivors spread around the citadel's healing caverns.

"He drained his blood into Belladonna, then seized the opportunity, throwing his lot in with the apostate. How he managed to avoid his wrath, I've no idea, but he did. The last thing I saw, before loyal members of the Church bore me away, was the legion assaulting our people in a clearly planned ambush. He led us into a trap, lad. He is responsible for the deaths of hundreds of our brothers and sisters."

"Sir, I…I need to be part of the team that goes after him!" Coran demanded fiercely. "There must be more to this, but either way, he was my squad mate. I bound my life to his in the Chamber of Darkness, and I'll be sacrificed if I can't bring him back. So let me undergo the change, and I'll retrieve him, or I'll die trying!"

"You'll do more than that," Edvard promised with a dark scowl, before hissing in pain as the priest finished, the nerves in his new arm roaring to life. Edvard stood, backhanding the priest and sending him sprawling. "Damn your kind! Always with the pain!" He snarled, shaking his arm, as if to bring it to life after laying on it for too long.

The priest hissed at him before scurrying to the next injured man, determined to enjoy the pain he could draw from that one as he healed him.

"Tell me, sir!" Coran begged, falling to one knee. "Give me the chance to prove myself…I…"

"I've got a meeting with the Archpriest next, lad, and I'm going to ask, *beg* if I have to, for the right to create a squad of Dark Hunters."

"Truly?" Coran said, his gaze shooting up to gawk at Edvard. The Dark Hunters were legendary beings that gave their lives over to the Dark God entirely, having their bodies remade, altered, and massively over-powered. But they lived in terrible pain for the remainder of their lives, unable to take sustenance from any other source until their prey was taken down. Then they'd gorge themselves, feeding as much on their prey's soul as mere food before the God decided their fate.

If they had served well, they were transformed into the next state, becoming Evolved Warriors, leaping sometimes dozens of levels and gaining unique specialties, able to live their lives in luxury and respected as the ultimate pinnacle to aspire to. Even the Archpriest spoke of them reverently, but those who failed the Dark God?

They had their souls shredded, their remains nailed to the walls in the Wailing Hall, dead yet undying for all to see until they fell to dust, a process that took centuries.

"I volunteer!" Coran snapped after a heartbeat to consider. He had nothing now. He was the bonded brother of a traitor, and an apostate. He would be lucky if he were permitted to take his own life. More likely, he'd be forced to serve the army as a slave, banished from ever again holding a weapon. He'd barely dared to hope to be allowed to have the change administered, and to go after Thomas.

"Truly. I will be petitioning for all the survivors of your squad to be uplifted to the Dark Hunters, with me at your head," Edvard replied grimly.

"Sir! We'll get him," Coran said fervently. "We'll catch him, we'll bring him back, and force him into the Wailing Hall, nailing him up as an example for all to see…even if we starve!"

"Damn right we will, lad. Nobody betrays the God!"

JIAN

THE END OF BOOK FIVE

UnderVerse 7

6th December 2022

The War of the Gods has stalled while both sides recover, borders have been established, and a form of uneasy peace descends on the Imperial Territory of Dravith...

It should be a time of consolidation, of rest and giving the survivors the chance to rearm and train.

But life rarely goes as Jax expects.

New and old enemies are on the horizon, the land itself is disturbed, and worst of all, the Gods may not be all he believed they were...

The Dark Tide Rises...

REVIEWS

Hey! Well, I hope you enjoyed the book? If so, please, please remember to leave a review, its massively important, as not only does it let others know about the book, it also tells Amazon that the book is worth promoting, and makes it more likely that more people will see it.

That in turn will hopefully keep me able to keep writing full time, while listening to crazy German bands screaming in my ears, and frankly, I kinda really like that!

If you want to spread the good word, that'd be amazing, and if you know of anyone that might be interested in stocking my books, I'm happy to reach out and send them samples, but honestly, if you enjoy my madness, that's massive for me.
Thank you.

FACEBOOK AND SOCIAL MEDIA

If you want to reach out, chat or shoot the shit, you can always find me on either my author page here:

www.facebook.com/JezCajiaoAuthor

OR

We've recently set up a new Facebook group to spread the word about cool LitRPG books. It's dedicated to two very simple rules, 1; lets spread the word about new and old brilliant LitRPG books, and 2: Don't be a Dick!

They sound like really simple rules, but you'd be amazed...

Come join us!

https://www.facebook.com/groups/litrpglegion

I'm also on Discord here: **https://discord.gg/u5JYHscCEH**

Or I'm reaching out on other forms of social media atm, I'm just spread a little thin that's all!

You're most likely to find me on Discord, but please, don't be offended when I don't approve friend requests on my personal Facebook pages. I did originally, and several people abused that, sending messages to my family and being generally unpleasant, hence, the author page:

https://www.facebook.com/JezCajiaoAuthor

I hope you understand.

PATREON!

Okay then, now for those of you that don't know about Patreon, its essentially a way to support your favorite nutcases, you can sign up for a day or a month or a year, and you get various benefits for it, ranging from my heartfelt thanks, to advance access to the books, to signed books, naming characters and more.

At the time of me writing this, the advanced Patreon readers are getting a sneak peek at Age of Steel, and are voting on the next batch of Character Art as well, so yeah, you get plenty for the support!

There's three wonderful supporters out there that I have to thank personally as well; ASeaInStorm, Leighton, and Nicholas Kauffman, you utter legends you. Thank you all and as promised, the characters are in the works.

www.patreon.com/Jezcajiao

Note: All character details, maps and spell/ability details are on World Anvil:

https://www.worldanvil.com/

This requires an account to access, but a free one is fine, once logged in, search for 'UnderVerse' and the covers should show which is mine.

RECOMMENDATIONS

I'm often asked for personal recommendations, so if this book has whetted your appetite for more LitRPG, please have a look at the following, these are brilliant series by brilliant authors!

Ascend Online by Luke Chmilenko

The Land by Aleron Kong

Challengers Call by Nathan A Thompson

SoulShip also by Nathan

Endless Online by M H Johnson

Silver Fox and the Western Hero, also by M H Johnson

The Good Guys/Bad Guys by Eric Ugland

Condition: Evolution by Kevin Sinclair

Space Seasons by Dawn Chapman

The Wayward Bard by Lars M

LITRPG!

To learn more about LitRPG, talk to other authors including myself, and to just have an awesome time, please join the LitRPG Group

www.facebook.com/groups/LitRPGGroup

FACEBOOK

There's also a few really active Facebook groups I'd recommend you join, as you'll get to hear about great new books, new releases and interact with all your (new) favorite authors! (I may also be there, skulking at the back and enjoying the memes…)

www.facebook.com/groups/LitRPGsociety/

www.facebook.com/groups/LitRPG.books/

www.facebook.com/groups/LitRPGforum/

www.facebook.com/groups/gamelitsociety/

Printed in the USA
CPSIA information can be obtained
at www.ICGtesting.com
LVHW010203250324
775416LV00016B/231